Praise for these nationally bestselling authors:

Barbara Delinsky

"When you care to read the very best, the name of Barbara Delinsky should come immediately to mind."
—*Rave Reviews*

"One of this generation's most gifted writers of contemporary women's fiction."
—*Affaire de Coeur*

Stella Cameron

"Her narrative is rich, her style is distinct, and her characters wonderfully wicked."
—*Publishers Weekly*

"No one does suspense and sensuality like Stella Cameron."
—*New York Times* bestselling author Linda Lael Miller

Linda Howard

"Howard's writing is compelling…"
—*Publishers Weekly*

"Linda Howard makes our senses come alive… She knows what romance readers want."
—*Affaire de Coeur*

Author Bio

Barbara Delinsky was born and raised in suburban Boston. She worked as a researcher, photographer and reporter before turning to writing full-time in 1980. With more than fifty novels to her credit, she is truly one of the shining stars of contemporary romance fiction! This talented author has received numerous awards and honors, and her books have appeared on many bestseller lists. With over twelve million copies of her books in print worldwide, Barbara's appeal is definitely universal.

Stella Cameron is the bestselling author of forty books, and possesses the unique talent of being able to switch effortlessly from historical to contemporary fiction. In a one-year period, her titles appeared more than eight times on the *USA Today* bestseller list. This British-born author was working as an editor in London when she met her husband, an officer in the American air force, at a party. He asked her to dance, and they've been together ever since. They now make their home with their three children in Seattle.

Linda Howard claims that whether she's reading or writing them, books have long played a profound role in her life. She cut her teeth on Margaret Mitchell, and from then on continued to read widely and eagerly. In recent years her interest has settled on romance fiction, because she's "easily bored by murder, mayhem and politics." After twenty-one years of penning stories for her own enjoyment, Linda finally worked up the courage to submit a novel for publication— and has since met with great success. This Alabama author has been steadily publishing ever since.

Barbara DELINSKY

Stella CAMERON

Linda HOWARD

Heart and Soul

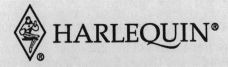

HARLEQUIN®

TORONTO • NEW YORK • LONDON
AMSTERDAM • PARIS • SYDNEY • HAMBURG
STOCKHOLM • ATHENS • TOKYO • MILAN • MADRID
PRAGUE • WARSAW • BUDAPEST • AUCKLAND

HARLEQUIN BOOKS
225 Duncan Mill Road, Don Mills,
Ontario, Canada M3B 3K9

ISBN 0-373-83401-2

HEART AND SOUL

The publisher acknowledges the copyright holders
of the individual works as follows:

THE DREAM
Copyright © 1990 by Barbara Delinsky

ALL THAT SPARKLES
Copyright © 1986 by Stella Cameron

AN INDEPENDENT WIFE
Copyright © 1982 by Linda Howington

This edition published by arrangement with Harlequin Books S.A.

® and TM are trademarks of the publisher. Trademarks indicated with
® are registered in the United States Patent and Trademark Office, the
Canadian Trade Marks Office and in other countries.

Printed in U.S.A.

The Dream
by Barbara Delinsky

1

Jessica Crosslyn lowered herself to the upholstered chair opposite the desk, smoothed the gracefully flowing challis skirt over her legs and straightened her round-rimmed spectacles. Slowly and reluctantly she met Gordon Hale's expectant gaze.

"I can't do it," she said softly. There was defeat in that softness and on her delicate features. "I've tried, Gordon. I've tried to juggle and balance. I've closed off everything but the few rooms I need. I keep the thermostat low to the point of freezing in winter. I've done only the most crucial of repairs, I've gone with the lowest bidders, and even then I've budgeted payments—" She caught in her breath. Her shoulders sagged slightly under the weight of disappointment. "But I can't do it. I just can't do it."

Gordon was quiet for a minute. He'd known Jessica from birth, had known her parents far longer than that. For better than forty years, he had been banker to the Crosslyns, which meant that he wasn't as emotionally removed as he should have been. He was deeply aware of the fight Jessica had been waging, and his heart went out to her.

"I warned Jed, you know," he said crossly. "I told him that he hadn't made adequate arrangements, but he just brushed my warnings aside. He was never the same after your mother died, never as clearheaded."

Jessica couldn't help but smile. It was an affectionate smile, a sad one as she remembered her father. "He was *never* clearheaded. Be honest, Gordon. My father wrote some brilliant scientific treatises in his day, but he was an eccentric old geezer. He never knew much about the workings of the everyday world. Mom was the one who took care of all that, and I tried to take over when she died, but things were pretty far gone by then."

"A fine woman, your mother."

"But no financial whiz, either, and so enamored with Dad that she was frightened of him. Even if she saw the financial problems, I doubt she'd have said a word to him about it. She wouldn't have wanted to upset him. She wouldn't have wanted to sully the creative mind with mention of something as mundane as money."

Gordon arched a bushy gray brow. "So now you're the one left to suffer the sullying."

"No," Jessica cautioned. She knew what he was thinking. "My mind isn't creative like Dad's was."

"I don't believe that for a minute. You have a Ph.D. in linguistics. You're fluent in Russian and German. You teach at Harvard. And you're published. You're as much of a scholar as Jed was any day."

"If I'm a scholar, it's simply because I love learning. But what I do isn't anything like what Dad did. My mind isn't like his. I can't look off into space and conjure up incredibly complex scientific theories. I can't dream up ideas. What I do is studied. It's orderly and pragmatic. I'm a foreign language teacher. I also read literature in the languages I teach, and since I've had access to certain Russian works that no one else has had, I was a cinch to write about them. So I'm published."

"You should be proud of that."

"I am, but if my book sells a thousand copies, I'll be lucky, which means that it won't save Crosslyn Rise. Nor will my salary." She gave a rueful chuckle. "Dad and I were alike in that, I'm afraid."

"But Crosslyn Rise was his responsibility," Gordon argued. "It's been in the family for five generations. Jed spent his entire life there. He owed it to all those who came before, as much as to you, to keep it up. If he'd done that, you wouldn't be in the bind you are now. But he let it deteriorate. I told him things would be bleak if he didn't keep on top of the repairs, but he wouldn't listen."

Jessica sighed. "That's water over the dam. The thing is that on top of everything else, I'm having plumbing and electrical problems. Up to now, I've settled for patches here and there, but that won't work any longer. I've been told—and I've had second and third opinions on it—that I need new systems for both. And given the size and nature of Crosslyn Rise..."

She didn't have to finish. Gordon knew the size and nature of Crosslyn Rise all too well. When one talked about installing new plumbing and electrical systems in a home that consisted of seventeen rooms and eight bathrooms spread over nearly eighty-five hundred square feet, the prospect was daunting. The prospect was even more daunting when one considered that a myriad of unexpected woes usually popped up when renovating a house that old.

Shifting several papers that lay neatly on his desk, Gordon said in a tentative voice, "I could loan you a little."

"A little more, you mean." She gave a tiny shake of her head and chided, "I'm having trouble meeting the payments I already have. You know that."

"Yes, but I'd do it, Jessica. I knew your family, and I know you. I'm the president of this bank, humble though it may be. If I can't pull a few strings, give a little extra for special people, who can I do it for?"

She was touched, and the smile she sent him told him so. But his generosity didn't change the facts. Again she shook her head, this time slowly and with resignation. "Thanks, Gordon. I do appreciate the offer, but if I was to accept it, I'd only be getting myself in deeper. Let's face it. I love my career, but it won't ever bring me big money. I could hurry out another book or two, maybe take on another course next semester, but I'd still come up way short of what I need."

"What you need," Gordon remarked, "is to marry a wealthy old codger who'd like nothing more than to live in a place like Crosslyn Rise."

Jessica didn't flinch, but her cheeks went paler than they'd been moments before. "I did that once."

"Chandler wasn't wealthy or old."

"But he wanted the Rise," she said with a look that went from wry to pained in the matter of a blink. "I wouldn't go through that again even if Crosslyn Rise were made of solid gold."

"If it were made of solid gold, you wouldn't have to go through anything," Gordon quipped, but he regretted mentioning Tom Chandler. Jessica's memories of the brief marriage weren't happy ones. Sitting forward, he folded his hands on his desk. "So what are your options?"

"There aren't many." And she'd been agonizing about those few for months.

"Is there someone who can help you—a relative who may have even a distant stake in the Rise?"

"Stake? No. The Rise was Dad's. He outlived a brother who stood to inherit if Dad had died first, but they were never on the best of terms. Dad wasn't a great communicator, if you know what I mean."

Gordon knew what she meant and nodded.

"And, anyway, now Dad's dead. Since I'm an only child, the Rise is mine, which means that no one else in the family has what you'd call a 'stake' in it."

"How about a fascination? Are there any aunts, uncles or cousins who've been intrigued by it over the years to the point where they'd pitch in to keep it alive?"

"No aunts or uncles, but there's a cousin. She's Dad's brother's oldest daughter, and if I called her she'd be out on the next plane from Chicago to give me advice."

Gordon studied her face. It told her thoughts with a surprising lack of guile, given that her early years had been spent, thanks to her mother, among the North Shore's well-to-do, who were anything but guileless. "I take it you know what that advice would be?"

"Oh, yes. Felicia would raze the house, divide the twenty-three acres into lots and sell each to the highest bidder. She told me that when she came for Dad's funeral, which was amusing in and of itself because she hadn't seen him since she was eighteen. Needless to say, she was here for the Rise."

"But the Rise is yours."

"And Felicia knew we were having trouble with the upkeep and that the trouble would only increase with Dad gone. She knew I'd never agree to raze the house, so her next plan was to pay me for the land around it. She figured that would give me enough money to renovate and support the house. In turn, she'd quadruple her investment by selling off small parcels of the land."

"That she would," Gordon agreed. "Crosslyn Rise stands on prime oceanfront land. Fifteen miles north of Boston, in a wealthy, well-run town with a good school system, fine municipal services, excellent public transportation... She'd quadruple her investment or better." His eyes narrowed. "Unless you were to charge her a hefty sum for the land."

"I wouldn't sell her the land for *any* sum," Jessica vowed. Rising from her seat, she moved toward the window. "I don't want to sell the land at all, but if I have to, the last person I'd sell to would be her. She's a witch."

Gordon cleared his throat. "Not quite the scholarly assessment I'd expected."

With a sheepish half smile, Jessica turned. "No. But it's hard to be scholarly when people evoke the kind of visceral response Felicia does." She slipped her hands into the pockets of her skirt, feeling more anchored that way. "Felicia and I are a year apart in age, so she used to visit when we were kids. She aspired to greatness. Being at the Rise made her feel she was on her way. She always joked that if I didn't want the Rise, she'd take it, but it was the kind of joking that wasn't really joking, if you know what I mean." When Gordon nodded, she went on. "By the time she graduated from high school, she realized that her greatness wasn't going to come from the Rise. So she went looking in other directions. I'm thirty-three now, so she's thirty-four.

She's been married three times, each time to someone rich enough to settle a large lump sum on her to get out of the marriage.''

"So she's a wealthy woman. But has she achieved that greatness?''

Wearing a slightly smug what-do-you-think look, Jessica gave a slow head shake. "She's got lots of money with nowhere to go.''

"I'm surprised she didn't offer to buy Crosslyn Rise from you outright.''

"Oh, she did. When Dad was barely in his grave." Her shoulders went straighter, giving a regal lift to her five-foot-six-inch frame. "I refused just as bluntly as she offered. There's no way I'd let her have the Rise. She'd have it sold or subdivided within a year." She paused, took a breath, turned back to the window and said in a quiet voice, "I can't let that happen.''

They were back to her options. Gordon knew as well as she did that some change in the Rise's status was necessary. "What are your thoughts, Jessica?'' he asked as gently as he could.

She was very still for a time, gnawing on her lower lip as she looked out over the harbor. Its charm, part of which was visible from Crosslyn Rise, not two miles away, made the thought of leaving the Rise all the harder. But it had to be faced.

"I could sell off some of the outer acreage," she began in a dubious tone, "but that would be a stopgap measure. It would be two lots this year, two lots next year and so on. Once I sold the lots, I wouldn't have any say about what was built on them. The zoning is residential, but you know as well as I do that there are dozens of styles of homes, one tackier than the next.''

"Is that snobbishness I detect?'' Gordon teased.

She looked him in the eye without a dash of remorse. "Uh-huh. The Rise is Georgian colonial and gorgeous. It would be a travesty if she were surrounded by less stately homes.''

"There are many stately homes that aren't Georgian colonial.''

"But the Rise is. And anything around it should blend in," she argued, then darted a helpless glance toward the ceiling. "This is the last thing I want to be discussing. It's the last thing I want to be *considering*.''

"You love the Rise.''

She pondered the thought. "It's not the mortar and brick that I love, not the kitchen or the parlor or the library. It's the whole thing. The old-world charm. The smell of polished wood and history. It's the beauty of it—the trees and ponds, birds and chipmunks—and the peace, the serenity." But there was more. "It's the idea of Crosslyn Rise. The idea that it's been in my family for so long. The idea that it's a little world unto itself.'' She faltered for an instant. "Yes, I love the Rise. But I have to do something. If I don't, you'll be forced to foreclose before long."

Gordon didn't deny it. He could give her more time than another person might have. He could indeed grant her another, smaller loan in the hope that, with a twist of fortune, she'd be able to recover from her present dire straits. In the end, business was business.

"What would you like to do?" he asked.

She started to turn back to the window but realized it wouldn't make things easier. It was time to face facts. So she folded her arms around her middle and said, "If I had my druthers, I'd sell the whole thing, house and acreage as a package, to a large, lovely, devoted family, but the chances of finding one that can afford it are next to nil. I've been talking with Nina Stone for the past eight months. If I was to sell, she'd be my broker. Without formally listing the house, she'd have an eye out for buyers like that, but there hasn't been a one. The real estate market is slow."

"That's true as far as private buyers go. Real estate developers would snap up property like Crosslyn Rise in a minute."

"And in the next minute they'd subdivide, sell off the smallest possible lots for the biggest possible money and do everything my cousin Felicia would do with just as little care for the integrity of the Rise." Jessica stood firm, levelly eyeing Gordon through her small, round lenses. "I can't do that, Gordon. It's bad enough that I have to break apart the Rise after all these years, but I can't just toss it in the air and let it fall where it may. I want a say as to what happens to it. I want whatever is done to be done with dignity. I want the charm of the place preserved."

She finished without quite finishing. Not even her glasses could hide the slight, anticipatory widening of her eyes.

Gordon prodded. "You have something in mind?"

"Yes. But I don't know if it's feasible."

"Tell me what it is, and I'll let you know."

She pressed her lips together, wishing she didn't have to say a word, knowing that she did. The Rise was in trouble. She was up against a wall, and this seemed the least evil of the options.

"What if we were to turn Crosslyn Rise into an exclusive condominium complex?" she asked, then hurried on before Gordon could answer. "What if there were small clusters of homes, built in styles compatible with the mansion and tucked into the woods at well-chosen spots throughout the property?" She spoke even more quickly, going with the momentum of her words. "What if the mansion itself was redone and converted into a combination health center, clubhouse, restaurant? What if we developed the harbor area into something small but classy, with boutiques and a marina?'' Running out of "what ifs," she stopped abruptly.

Unfolding his hands, Gordon sat back in his chair. "You'd be willing to do all that?"

"Willing, but not able. What I'm talking about would be a phenomenally expensive project—"

He stilled her with a wave of his hand. "You'd be *willing* to have the Rise turned into a condominium complex?"

"If it was done the right way," she said. She felt suddenly on the defensive and vaguely disloyal to Crosslyn Rise. "Given any choice, I'd leave the Rise as it is, but it's deteriorating more every year. I'm long past the point of being able to put a finger in the dike. So I have to do something. This idea beats the alternatives. If it was done with forethought and care and style, we could alter the nature of Crosslyn Rise without changing its character."

"We?"

"Yes." She came away from the window to make her plea. "I need help, Gordon. I don't have any money. There would have to be loans, but once the cluster homes were built and sold, the money could be repaid, so it's not like my asking you for a loan just to fix up the Rise. Can I get a loan of the size I'd need?"

"No."

She blinked. "No? Then you don't like the idea?"

"Of the condo complex? Yes, I do. It has definite merit."

"But you won't back me."

"I can't just hand over that kind of money."

She slid into her chair and sat forward on its edge. "Why not? You were offering me money just a little while ago. Yes, this would be more, but it would be an investment that would guarantee enough profit to pay back the loan and then some."

Gordon regarded her kindly. He had endless respect for her where her work at Harvard was concerned. But she wasn't a businesswoman by any stretch of the imagination. "No financial institution will loan you that kind of money, Jessica. If you were an accredited real estate developer, or a builder or an architect, you might have a chance. But from a banker's point of view, loaning a linguistics professor large amounts of money to build a condominium complex would be akin to loaning a librarian money to buy the Red Sox. You're not a developer. You may know what you want for the Rise, but you wouldn't know how to carry it out. Real estate development isn't your field. You don't have the kind of credibility necessary to secure the loan."

"But I need the money," she cried. The sharp rise in her voice was out of character, reflecting her frustration, which was growing by the minute.

"Then we'll have to find people who *do* have the necessary credibility for a project like this."

Her frustration eased. All she needed was a ray of hope. "Oh. Okay. How do we go about doing that and how does it work?"

Gordon relaxed in his chair. He enjoyed planning projects and was relieved that Jessica was open to suggestion. "We put together a consortium, a group of people, each of whom is willing to invest in the future of Crosslyn Rise. Each member has an interest in the project based on his financial contribution to it, and the amount he takes out at the end is commensurate with his input."

Jessica wasn't sure she liked the idea of a consortium, simply because it sounded so real. "A group of people? But they're strangers. They won't know the Rise. How can we be sure that they won't put their money and heads together and come up with something totally offensive?"

"We handpick them. We choose only people who would be as committed to maintaining the dignity and charm of Crosslyn Rise as you are."

"No one is as committed to that as I am."

"Perhaps not. Still, I've seen some beautiful projects, similar to what you have in mind, done in the past few years. Investors can be naturalists, too."

Jessica was only vaguely mollified, a fact to which the twisting of her stomach attested. "How many people?"

"As many as it would take to collect the necessary money. Three, six, twelve."

"Twelve people? Twelve strangers?"

"Strangers only at first. You'd get to know them, since you'd be part of the consortium. We'd have the estate appraised as to its fair market value, and that would determine your stake in the project. If you wanted, I could advance you more to broaden your stake. You'd have to decide how much profit you want."

Her eyes flashed. "I'm not in this for the profit."

"You certainly are," Gordon insisted in the tone of one who was older and wiser. "If the Rise is made into the kind of complex you mention, this is your inheritance. And it's significant, Jessica. Never forget that. You may think you have one foot in the poorhouse, but

Crosslyn Rise, for all its problems, is worth a pretty penny. It'll be worth even more once it's developed."

Developed. The word made her flinch. She felt guilty for even considering it—guilty, traitorous, mercenary. In one instant she was disappointed with herself, in the next she was furious with her father.

But neither disappointment nor fury would change the facts. "Why does this have to be?" she whispered sadly.

"Because," Gordon said quietly, "life goes on. Things change." He tipped his head and eyed her askance. "It may not be all that bad. You must be lonely living at the Rise all by yourself. It's a pretty big place. You could choose one of the smaller houses and have it custom-designed for you."

She held up a cautionary hand. He was moving a little too quickly. "I haven't decided to do this."

"It's a solid idea."

"But you're making it sound as if it can really happen, and that makes me feel like I'm losing control."

"You'd be a member of the consortium," he reminded her. "You'd have a voice as to what's done."

"I'd be one out of three or six or maybe even twelve."

"But you own the Rise. In the end, you'd have final approval of any plan that is devised."

"I would?"

"Yes."

That made her feel better, but only a little. She'd always been an introverted sort. She could just imagine herself sitting at the far end of a table, listening to a group of glib investors bicker over her future. She'd be outtalked, outplanned, outwitted.

"I want more than that," she said on impulse. It was survivalism at its best. "I want to head the consortium. I want my cut to be the largest. I want to be *guaranteed* control over the end result." She straightened in her chair. "Is that possible?"

Gordon's brows rose. "Anything's possible. But advisable? I don't know, Jessica. You're a scholar. You don't know anything about real estate development."

"So I'll listen and learn. I have common sense and an artistic eye. I know the kind of thing I want. And I love Crosslyn Rise." She was convincing herself as she talked. "It isn't enough for me to have the power to approve or disapprove. I want to be part of the project from start to finish. That's the only way I'll be able to sleep at night." She wasn't sure she liked the look on Gordon's face. "You don't think I can do it."

"It's not that." He hesitated. There were several problems that he could see, one of which was immediate. He searched for the words to tell her what he was thinking, without sounding offensive. "You have to understand, Jessica. Traditionally, men are the investors. They've been involved in other projects. They're used to working in certain ways. I'm...not sure how they'll feel about a novice telling them what to do."

"A woman, you mean," she said, and he didn't deny it. "But I'm a reasonable person. I'm not pigheaded or spiteful. I'll be open-minded about everything except compromising the dignity of Crosslyn Rise. What better a leader could they want?"

Gordon didn't want to touch that one. So he tried a different tack. "Changing the face of Crosslyn Rise is going to be painful for you. Are you sure you want to be intimately involved in the process?"

"Yes," she declared.

He pursed his lips, dropped his gaze to the desktop, tried to think of other evasive arguments, but failed. Finally he went with the truth, bluntly stating the crux of the problem. "The fact is, Jessica, that if you insist on being the active head of the consortium, I may have trouble getting investors." He held up a hand. "Nothing personal, mind you. Most of the people I have in mind don't know who or what you are, but the fact of a young, inexperienced woman having such control over the project may make them skittish. They'll fear that it will take forever to make decisions, or that once those decisions are made, you'll change your mind. It goes back to the issue of credibility."

"That's not fair!"

"Life isn't, sometimes," he murmured, but he had an idea. "There is one way we might be able to get around it."

"What?"

He was thoughtful for another minute. "A compromise, sort of. We get the entire idea down on paper first. You work with an architect, tell him what you want, let him come up with some sketches, work with him on revising them until you're completely satisfied. Then we approach potential investors with a fait accompli." He was warming to the idea as he talked. "It could work out well. With your ideas spelled out in an architect's plans, we can better calculate the costs. Being specific might help in wooing investors."

"You mean, counterbalance the handicap of working with me?" Jessica suggested dryly, but she wasn't angry. If sexism existed, it existed. She had worked around it before. She could do it again.

"Things would be simplified all around," Gordon went on without comment. "You would have total control over the design of the project.

Investors would know exactly what they were buying into. If they don't like your idea, they don't have to invest, and if we can't get enough people together, you'd only be out the architect's fee."

"How much will that be?" Jessica asked. She'd heard complaints from a colleague who had worked with an architect not long before.

"Not as much as it might be, given the man I have in mind."

Jessica wasn't sure whether to be impressed or nervous. The bravado she's felt moments before was beginning to falter with talk of specifics, like architects. "You've already thought of someone?"

"Yes," Gordon said, eyeing her directly. "He's the best, and Crosslyn Rise deserves the best."

She couldn't argue with that. "Who is he?"

"He's only been in the field for twelve years, but he's done some incredible things. He was affiliated with a New York firm for seven of those years, and during that time he worked on PUDs up and down the East Coast."

"PUDs?"

"Planned Urban Developments—in and around cities, out to suburbs. Five years ago, he established his own firm in Boston. He's done projects like the one you have in mind. I've seen them. They're breathtaking."

Her curiosity was piqued. "Who is he?"

"He's a down-to-earth guy who's had hands-on experience at the building end, which makes him an even better architect. He isn't so full of himself that he's hard to work with. And I think he'd be very interested in this project."

Jessica was trying to remember whether she'd ever read anything in the newspaper about an architect who might fit Gordon's description. But such an article would have been in the business section, and she didn't read that—which, unfortunately, underscored some of what Gordon had said earlier. Still, she had confidence in her ideas. And if she was to work with a man the likes of whom Gordon was describing, she couldn't miss.

"Who *is* he?" she asked.

"Carter Malloy."

Jessica stared at him dumbly. The name was very familiar. Carter Malloy. She frowned. Bits and snatches of memories began flitting through her mind.

"I knew a Carter Malloy once," she mused. "He was the son of the people who used to work for us at the Rise. His mom kept the house and his dad gardened." She felt a moment's wistfulness. "Boy, could I ever use Michael Malloy's green thumb now. On top of everything else, the Rise needs a landscaping overhaul. It's been nearly ten years since the Malloys retired and went south.'' Her wistfulness faded, giving way to a scowl. "It's been even longer since I've seen their son, thank goodness. He was obnoxious. He was older than me and never let me forget it. It used to drive him nuts that his parents were poor and mine weren't. He had a foul mouth, problems in school and a chip on his shoulder a mile wide. And he was ugly.''

Gordon's expression was guarded, his voice low. "He's not ugly now.''

"Excuse me?''

"I said,'' he repeated more clearly, "he's not ugly now. He's grown up in lots of ways, including that.''

Jessica was surprised. "You've been in touch with Carter Malloy?''

"He keeps an account here. God only knows he could easily give his business to one of the bigger banks in Boston, but he says he feels a connection with the place where he grew up.''

"No doubt he does. There's a little thing about a police record here. Petty theft, wasn't it?''

"He's reformed.''

Her expression said she doubted that was possible. "I was always mystified that wonderful people like Annie and Michael Malloy could spawn a son like that. The heartache he caused them.'' She shook her head at the shame of it. "He's not living around her, is he? Tell me, so I'll know to watch out. Carter Malloy isn't someone I'd want to bump into on the street.''

"He's living in Boston.''

"What is he—a used-car salesman?''

"He's an architect.''

Jessica was momentarily taken aback. "Not the Carter Malloy I knew.''

"Like I said, he's grown up.''

The thought that popped into her head at that moment was so horrendous that she quickly dashed it from mind. "The Carter Malloy I knew couldn't possibly have grown up to be a professional. He barely finished high school.''

"He spent time in the army and went to college when he got out.''

"But even if he had the gray matter for college,'' she argued, feeling distinctly uneasy, "he didn't have the patience or the dedication. He could never apply himself to anything for long. The only thing he succeeded at was making trouble.''

"People change, Jessica. Carter Malloy is now a well-respected and successful architect.''

Jessica had never known Gordon to lie to her, which was why she had to accept what he said. On a single lingering thread of hope, she gave a tight laugh. "Isn't it a coincidence? Two Carter Malloys, both architects? The one you have in mind for my project—does he live in Boston, too, or does he have a house in one of the suburbs?"

Gordon never answered. Jessica took one look at his expression, stood and began to pace the office. Her hands were tucked into the pockets of her skirt, and just as the challis fabric faithfully rendered the slenderness of her hips and legs as she paced, it showed those hands balled into fists. Her arms were straight, pressed to her sides.

"Do you know what Carter Malloy did to me when I was six? He dared me to climb to the third notch of the big elm out beyond the duck pond." She turned at the window and stared back. "Needless to say, once I got up there, I couldn't get back down. He looked up at me with that pimply face of his, gave an evil grin and walked off." She paused before a Currier and Ives print on the wall, seeing nothing of it. "I was terrified. I sat for a while thinking that he'd come back, but he didn't. I tried yelling, but I was too far from the house to be heard. One hour passed, then another, and each time I looked at the ground I got dizzy. I sat up there crying for three hours before Michael finally found me, and then he had to call the fire department to get me down." She moved on. "I had nightmares for weeks afterward. I've never climbed a tree since."

She stopped at the credenza, turned and faced Gordon, dropping her hands and hips back against the polished mahogany for support. "If the Carter Malloy I knew is the one you have in mind for this job, the answer is no. That's my very first decision as head of this consortium, and it's closed to discussion."

"Now that," Gordon said on a light note that wasn't light at all but was his best shot at an appeal, "is why I may have trouble finding backers for the project. If you're going to make major decisions without benefit of discussion with those who have more experience, there isn't much hope. I have to say that I wouldn't put my money into a venture like that. A bullheaded woman would be hell to work with."

"Gordon," she protested.

"I'm serious, Jessica. You said you'd listen and learn, but you don't seem willing to do that."

"I am. Just not where Carter Malloy is concerned. I couldn't work with him. It would be a disaster, and what would happen to the Rise, then?" Her voice grew pleading. "There must be other architects. He can't be the only one available."

"He's not, and there are others, but he's the best."

"In all of Boston?"

"Given the circumstances, yes."

"What circumstances?"

"He knows the Rise. He cares about it."

"Cares?" she echoed in dismay. "He'd as soon burn the Rise to the ground and leave it in ashes as transform it into something beautiful."

"How do you know? When was the last time you talked with him?"

"When I was sixteen." Pushing off from the credenza, she began to pace again. "It was the first I'd seen him in a while—"

"He'd been in the army," Gordon interrupted to remind her.

"Whatever. His parents didn't talk about him much, and I was the last person who'd want to ask. But he came over to get something for his dad one night. I was on the front porch waiting for a date to pick me up, and Carter said—" Her memories interrupted her this time. Their sting held her silent for a minute, finally allowing her to murmur, "He said some cruel things. Hurtful things." She stopped her pacing to look at Gordon. "Carter Malloy hates me as much as I hate him. There's no way he'd agree to do the work for me even if I wanted him to do it, which I don't."

But Gordon wasn't budging. "He'd do it. And he'd do it well. The Carter Malloy I've come to know over the past five years is a very different man from the one you remember. Didn't you ever wonder why his parents retired when they did? They were in their late fifties, not terribly old and in no way infirm. But they'd saved a little money over the years, and then Carter bought them a place in Florida with beautiful shrubbery that Michael could tend year-round. It was one of the first things Carter did when he began to earn good money. To this day he sees that they have everything they need. It's his way of making up for the trouble he caused them when he was younger. If he hurt you once, my guess is he'd welcome the chance to help out now."

"I doubt that," she scoffed, but more quietly. She was surprised by what Gordon had said. Carter Malloy had never struck her as a man with a thoughtful bone in his body. "What do you mean by help out?"

"I'd wager that he'd join the consortium."

"Out of pity for me?"

"Not at all. He's a shrewd businessman. He'd join it for the investment value. But he'd also want to be involved for old times' sake. I've heard him speak fondly of Crosslyn Rise." He paused, stroked a finger over his upper lip. "I'd go so far as to say we could get him to throw in his fee as part of his contribution. That way, he'd have a real stake in making the plans work, and if they didn't, it would be his problem. He'd swallow his own costs—which would be a far sight better than your having to come up with forty or fifty thousand if the project fizzled."

"Forty or fifty thousand?" She hadn't dreamed it would be so much. Swallowing, she sank into her chair once again, this time into the deepest corner, where the chair's back and arms could shield her. "I don't like this, Gordon."

"I know. But given that the Rise can't be saved as it is, this is an exciting option. Let me call Carter."

"No," she cried, then repeated it more quietly. "No."

"I'm talking about a simple introductory meeting. You can tell him your general thoughts about the project and listen to what he has to say in return. See how you get along. Decide for yourself whether he's the same as he used to be. There won't be an obligation. I'll be there with you if you like."

She tipped up her chin. "I was never afraid of Carter Malloy. I just disliked him."

"You won't now. He's a nice guy. Y'know, you said it yourself—it drove him nuts that he was poor and you were rich. He must have spent a lot of time wishing Crosslyn Rise was his. So let him take those wishes and your ideas and make you some sketches."

"They could be very good or very bad."

"Ah," Gordon drawled, "but remember two things. First off, Carter has a career and a reputation to protect. Second, you have final say. If you don't like what he does, you have the power of veto. In a sense that puts him under your thumb, now, doesn't it?"

Jessica thought back to the last time she'd seen Carter Malloy. In vivid detail, she recalled what he'd said to her, and though she'd blotted it from her mind over the years, the hurt and humiliation remained. Perhaps she would find a measure of satisfaction having him under her thumb.

And, yes, Crosslyn Rise was still hers. If Carter Malloy didn't come up with plans that pleased her, she'd turn her back on him and walk away. He'd see who had the last laugh then.

Jessica had never been a social butterfly. Her mother, well aware of the Crosslyn heritage, had put her through the motions when she'd been a child. Jessica had been dressed up and taken to birthday parties, given riding lessons, sent to summer camp, enrolled in ballet. She had learned the essentials of being a properly privileged young lady. But she had never quite fit in.

She wasn't a beautiful child, for one thing. Her hair was long and unruly, her body board-straight and her features plain—none of which was helped by the fact that she rarely smiled. She was quiet, serious, shy, not terribly unlike her father. One part of her was most comfortable staying home in her room at Crosslyn Rise reading a good book. The other part dreamed of being the belle of the ball.

Having a friend over to play was both an apprehensive and exciting experience for Jessica. She liked the company and, even more, the idea of being liked, but she was forever afraid of boring her guest. At least, that was what her mother warned her against ad infinitum. As an adult, Jessica understood that though her mother worshipped her father's intellect, deep inside she found him a boring person, hence the warnings to Jessica. At the time, Jessica took those warning to heart. When she had a friend at the Rise, she was on her guard to impress.

That was why she was crushed by what Carter Malloy did to her when she was ten. Laura Hamilton, who came as close to being a best friend as any Jessica had, was over to visit. She didn't come often; the Rise wasn't thought to be a "fun" place. But Laura had come this time because she and Jessica had a project to do together for school, and the library at the Rise had the encyclopedias and *National Geographic*s that the girls needed.

When they finished their work, Jessica suggested they go out to the porch. It was a warm fall day, and the porch was one of her favorite spots. Screened in and heavily shaded by towering maples and oaks, it was the kind of quiet, private place that made Jessica feel secure.

She started out feeling secure this day, because Laura liked the porch, too. They sat close beside each other on the flowered porch sofa, pads of paper in their laps, pencils in hand. They were writing poems, which seemed to Jessica to be an exciting enough thing to do.

Carter Malloy didn't think so. Pruning sheers in hand, he materialized from behind the rhododendrons just beyond the screen, where, to Jessica's chagrin, he had apparently been sitting.

"What are you two doing?" he asked in a voice that said he knew exactly what they were doing, since he'd been listening for quite some time, and he thought it was totally dumb.

"What are *you* doing?" Jessica shot right back. She wasn't intimidated by his size or his deep voice or the fact that he was seventeen. Maybe, just a little, she was intimidated by his streetwise air, but she pushed that tiny fear aside. Given who his parents were, he wouldn't dare touch her. "What are you doing out there?" she demanded.

"Clipping the hedges," Carter answered with an insolent look.

She was used to the look. It put her on the defensive every time she saw it. "No, you weren't. You were spying on us."

He had one hip cocked, one shoulder lower than the other but both back to emphasize a developing chest. "Why in the hell would I want to do that? You're writing sissy poems."

"Who is he?" Laura whispered nervously.

"He's no one," was Jessica's clearly spoken answer. Though she'd always talked back to Carter, this time it seemed more important than ever. She had Laura to impress. "You were supposed to be cutting the shrubs, but you weren't. You never do what your father tells you to do."

"I think for myself," Carter answered. His dark eyes bore into hers. "But you don't know what that means. You're either going to tea parties like your old lady or sticking your nose in a book like your old man. You couldn't think for yourself if you tried. So whose idea was it to write poems? Your prissy little friend's?"

Jessica didn't know which to be first, angry or embarrassed. "Go away, Carter."

Lazily he raised the pruning sheers and snipped off a single shoot. "I'm working."

"Go work somewhere else," she cried with a ten-year-old's frustration. "There are lots of other bushes."

"But this one needs trimming."

She was determined to hold her ground. "We want to be alone."

"Why? What's so important about writing poems? Afraid I'll steal your rhymes?" He looked closely at Laura. "You're a Hamilton, aren't you?"

"Don't answer," Jessica told Laura.

"She is," Carter decided. "I've seen her sitting in church with the rest of her family."

"That's a lie," Jessica said. "You don't go to church."

"I go sometimes. It's fun, all those sinners begging for forgiveness. Take old man Hamilton. He bought his way into the state legislature—"

Jessica was on her feet, her reed-slim body shaking. The only thing she knew for sure about what Carter was saying was that it was certain to offend Laura, and if that happened, Laura would never be back. "Shut up, Carter!"

"Bought his way there and does nothing but sit on his can and raise his hand once in a while. But I s'pose he doesn't have to do nothing. If I had that much money, I'd be sittin' on my can, too."

"You *don't* have that much money. You don't have *any* money."

"But I have friends. And you don't."

Jessica never knew how he'd found her Achilles' heel, but he'd hit her where it hurt. "You're a stupid jerk," she cried. "You're dumb and you have pimples. I wouldn't want to be you for anything in the world." Tears swimming in her eyes, she took Laura's hand and dragged her into the house.

Laura never did come back to Crosslyn Rise, and looking back on it so many years later, Jessica remembered the hurt she'd felt. It didn't matter that she hadn't seen Laura Hamilton for years, that by the time they'd reached high school Jessica had found her as boring as she'd feared she would be herself, that they had nothing in common now. The fact was that when she was ten, she had badly wanted to be Laura's best friend and Carter Malloy had made that harder than ever.

Such were her thoughts as the *T* carried her underground from one stop to the next on her way from Harvard Square to Boston. She had a two-o'clock meeting with Carter Malloy in his office. Gordon had set it up, and when he'd asked if Jessica wanted him along, she had said she'd be fine on her own.

She wasn't sure that had been the wisest decision. She was feeling nervous, feeling as though every one of the insecurities she'd suffered in childhood was back in force. She was the not-too-pretty, not-too-popular, not-too-social little girl once again. Gordon's support might have come in handy.

But she had a point to prove to him, too. She'd told him that she wanted to actively head the consortium altering Crosslyn Rise. Gordon was skeptical of her ability to do that. If he was to aggressively and enthusiastically seek out investors in Crosslyn Rise, she had to show him she was up to the job.

So she'd assured him that she could handle Carter Malloy on her own, and that, she decided in a moment's respite from doubt, was what she was going to do. But the doubts returned, and as she left the trolley, climbed the steep stairs to Park Street and headed for Winter, she hated Carter Malloy more than ever.

It wasn't the best frame of mind in which to be approaching a meeting of some importance, Jessica knew, which was why she took a slight detour on her way to Carter's office. She had extra time; punctual person that she was, she'd allowed plenty for the ride from Cambridge. So she swung over to West Street and stopped to browse at the Brattle Book Shop, and though she didn't buy anything, the sense of comfort she felt in the company of books, particularly the aged beauties George Gloss had collected, was worth the pause. It was with some reluctance that she finally dragged herself away from the shelves and set off.

Coming from school, she wore her usual teaching outfit—long skirt, soft blouse, slouchy blazer and low heels. The occasional glance in a store window as she passed told her that she looked perfectly presentable. Her hair was impossible, of course. Though not as unruly as it had once been, it was still thick and hard to handle, which was why she had it secured with a scarf at the back of her head. She wasn't trying to impress anyone, least of all Carter Malloy, but she wanted to look professional and in command of herself, if nothing else.

Carter's firm was on South Street in an area that had newly emerged as a mecca for artists and designers. The building itself was six stories tall and of an earthy brick that was a pleasantly warm in contrast to the larger, more modern office tower looming nearby. The street level of the building held a chic art gallery, an equally chic architectural supply store, a not-so-chic fortune cookie company, and a perfectly dumpy-looking diner that was mobbed, even at two, with a suit-and-tie crowd.

Turning in at the building's main entrance, she couldn't help but be impressed by the newly refurbished, granite-walled lobby. She guessed that the building's rents were high, attesting to Gordon's claim that Carter was doing quite well.

As she took the elevator to the top floor, Jessica struggled, as she'd done often in the five days since Gordon had first mentioned his name, to reconcile the Carter Malloy she'd known with the Carter Malloy who was a successful architect. Try as she might, she couldn't shake the image of what he'd been as a boy and what he'd done to her then. Not even the sleekly modern reception area, with its bright walls, indirect lighting and sparse, avante-garde furnishings could displace the image of the ill-tempered, sleezy-looking juvenile delinquent.

"My name is Jessica Crosslyn," she told the receptionist in a voice that was quiet and didn't betray the unease she felt. "I have a two-o'clock appointment with Mr. Malloy."

The receptionist was an attractive woman, sleek enough to complement her surroundings, though nowhere near as new. Jessica guessed her to be in her late forties. "Won't you have a seat? Mr. Malloy was delayed at a meeting. He shouldn't be more than five or ten minutes. He's on his way now."

Jessica should have figured he'd be late. Keeping her waiting was a petty play for power. She was sure he'd planned it.

Once again she wished Gordon was with her, if for no other reason than to show him that Carter hadn't changed so much. But Gordon was up on the North Shore, and she was too uncomfortable to sit. So, nodding at the receptionist, she moved away from the desk and slowly passed one, then another of the large, dry-mounted drawings that hung on the wall. Hingham Court, Pheasant Landing, Berkshire Run—pretty names for what she had to admit were attractive complexes, if the drawings were at all true to life. If she could blot out the firm's name, Malloy and Goodwin, from the corner of each, she might feel enthusiasm. But the Malloy, in particular, kept jumping right off the paper, hitting her mockingly in the face. In self-defense, she finally turned and slipped into one of the low armchairs.

Seconds later, the door opened and her heart began to thud. Four men entered, engaged in a conversation that kept them fully occupied while her gaze went from one face to the next. Gordon had said Carter Malloy had changed a lot, but even accounting for that, not one of the men remotely resembled the man she remembered.

Feeling awkward, she took a magazine from the glass coffee table beside her and began to leaf through. She figured that if Carter was in the group, he'd know of her presence soon enough. In the meanwhile, she concentrated on keeping her glasses straight on her nose and looking calm, cool, even a bit disinterested, which was hard when the discussion among the four men began to grow heated. The matter at hand seemed to be the linkage issue, a City of Boston mandate that was apparently costing builders hundreds of thousands of dollars per project. Against her will, she found herself looking up. One of the group seemed to be with the city, another with Carter's firm and the other two with a construction company. She was thinking that the architect was the most articulate of the bunch when the door opened again. Her heart barely had time to start pounding anew when Carter Malloy came through. He took in the group before him, shook hands with the three she'd pegged as outsiders, slid a questioning gaze to the receptionist, then, in response to the woman's pointed glance, looked at Jessica.

For the space of several seconds, her heart came to a total standstill. The man was unmistakably Carter Malloy, but, yes, he'd changed. He was taller, broader. In place of a sweaty T-shirt emblazoned with something obscene, tattered old jeans and crusty work boots, he wore a tweed blazer, an oxford-cloth shirt with the neck button open, gray slacks and loafers. The dark hair that had always fallen in ungroomed spikes on his forehead was shorter, well shaped, cleaner. His skin, too, was cleaner, his features etched by time. The surly expression that even now taunted her memory had mellowed to something still intense but controlled. He had tiny lines shadowing the corners of his eyes, a small scar on his right jaw and a light tan.

Gordon was right, she realized in dismay. Carter wasn't ugly anymore. He wasn't *at all* ugly, and that complicated things. She didn't do well with men in general, but attractive ones in particular made her edgy. She wasn't sure she was going to make it.

But she couldn't run out now. That would be the greatest indignity. And besides, if she did that, what would she tell Gordon? More aptly, what would Carter tell Gordon? Her project would be sunk, for sure.

Mustering every last bit of composure she had stashed away inside, she rose as Carter approached.

"Jessica?" he asked in a deep but tentative voice.

Heart thudding, she nodded. She deliberately kept her hands in her lap. To offer a handshake seemed reckless.

Fortunately he didn't force the issue, but stood looking down at her, not quite smiling, not quite frowning. "I'm sorry. Were you waiting long?"

She shook her head. A little voice inside told her to say something, but for the life of her she couldn't find any words. She was wondering why she felt so small, why Carter seemed so tall, how her memory could have been so inaccurate in its rendition of as simple a matter as relative size.

He gestured toward the inner door. "Shall we go inside?"

She nodded. When he opened the door and held it for her, she was surprised; the Carter she'd known would have let it slam in her face. When she felt the light pressure of his hand at her waist, guiding her down a corridor spattered with offices, she was doubly surprised; the Carter she'd known knew nothing of courtly gestures, much less gentleness. When he said, "Here we are," and showed her into the farthest and largest office, she couldn't help but be impressed.

That feeling lasted for only a minute, because no sooner had she taken a chair—gratefully, since the race of her pulse was making her legs shaky—than Carter backed himself against the stool that stood at the nearby drafting table, looked at her with a familiarly wicked gleam in his eye and said, "Cat got your tongue?"

Jessica was oddly relieved. The old Carter Malloy she could handle to some extent; sarcasm was less debilitating than charm. Taking in a full breath for the first time since she'd laid eyes on him, she said, "My tongue's where it's always been. I don't believe in using it unless I have something to say."

"Then you're missing out on some of the finer things in life," he informed her so innocently that it was a minute before Jessica connected his words with the gleam in his eye.

Ignoring both the innuendo and the faint flush that rose on her cheeks, she vowed to state her business as quickly as possible and leave. "Did Gordon explain why I've come?"

Carter gave a leisurely nod, showing none of the discomfort she felt. But instead of picking up on his conversation with Gordon, he said, "It's been a long time. How have you been?"

"Just fine."

"You're looking well."

She wasn't sure why he'd said that, but it annoyed her. "I haven't changed," she told him as though stating the obvious, then paused. "You have."

"I should hope so." While the words settled into the stillness of the room, he continued to stare at her. His eyes were dark, touched one minute by mockery, the next by genuine curiosity. Jessica half wished for the contempt she used to find there. It wouldn't have been as unsettling.

Tearing her gaze from his, she looked down at her hands, used one to shove the nose piece of her glasses higher and cleared her throat. "I've decided to make some changes at Crosslyn Rise." She looked back up, but before she could say a thing, Carter beat her to it.

"I'm sorry about your father's death."

Uh-huh, she thought, but she simply nodded in thanks for the words. "Anyway, there's only me now, so the Rise is really going to waste." That wasn't the issue at all, but she couldn't quite get herself to tell Carter Malloy the problem was money. "I'm hoping to make something newer and more practical out of it. Gordon suggested I speak with you.

Quite honestly, I wasn't wild about the idea." She watched him closely, waiting to see his reaction to her rebuff.

But he gave nothing away. In a maddeningly calm voice, he asked, "Why not?"

She didn't blink. "We never liked one another. Working together could be difficult."

"That's assuming we don't like one another now," he pointed out too reasonably.

"We don't *know* one another now."

"Which is why you're here today."

"Yes," she said, hesitated, then added, "I wasn't sure how much to believe of what Gordon told me." Her eyes roamed the room, taking in a large desk covered with rolls of blueprints, the drafting table and its tools, a corked wall that bore sketches in various stages of completion. "All this doesn't jibe with the man I remember."

"That man wasn't a man. He wasn't much more than a boy. How many years has it been since we last saw each other?"

"Seventeen," she said quickly, then wished she'd been slower or more vague when she caught a moment's satisfaction in his eye.

"You didn't know I was an architect?"

"How would I know?"

He shrugged and offered a bit too innocently, "Mutual friends?"

She did say, "Uh-huh," aloud this time, and with every bit of the sarcasm she'd put into it before. He was obviously enjoying her discomfort. *That* was more like what she'd expected. "We've never had any mutual friends."

"Spoken like the Jessica I remember, arrogant to the core. But times have changed, sweetheart. I've come up in the world. For starters, there's Gordon. He's a mutual friend."

"And he'd have had no more reason to keep me apprised of your comings and goings than I'd have had to ask. The last I knew of you," she said, her voice hard in anger that he'd dared call her 'sweetheart,' "you were stealing cars."

Carter's indulgent expression faded, replaced by something with a sharper edge. "I made some mistakes when I was younger, and I paid the price. I had to start from the bottom and work my way up. I didn't have any help, but I made it."

"And how many people did you hurt along the way?"

"None once I got going, too many before," he admitted. His face was somber, and though his body kept the same pose, the relaxation had left it. "I burned a whole lot of bridges that I've had to rebuild. That was one of the reasons I shifted my schedule to see you when

Gordon called. You were pretty bitchy when you were a kid, but I fed into it.''

She stiffened. "Bitchy? Thanks a lot!"

"I said I fed into it. I'm willing to take most of the blame, but you were bitchy. Admit it. Your hackles went up whenever you saw me.''

"Do you wonder why? You said and did the nastiest things to me. It got so I was conditioned to expect it. I did whatever I could to protect myself, and that meant being on my guard at the first sight of you."

Rather than argue further, he pushed off from the stool and went to the desk. He stood at its side, fingering a paper clip for a minute before meeting her gaze again. "My parents send their best."

Jessica was nearly as surprised by the gentling of his voice as she was by what he'd said. "You told them we were meeting?"

"I talked with them last night." At the look of disbelief that remained on her face, he said, "I do that sometimes."

"You never used to. You were horrible to them, too."

Carter returned his attention to the paper clip, which he twisted and turned with the fingers of one hand. "I know."

"But why? They were wonderful people. I used to wish my parents were half as easygoing and good-natured as yours. And you treated them so badly."

He shot her a look of warning. "It's easy to think someone else's parents are wonderful when you're the one who doesn't live with them. You don't know the facts, Jessica. My relationship with my parents was very complex." He paused for a deep breath, which seemed to restore his good temper. "Anyway, they want to know everything about you— how you look, whether you're working or married or mothering, how the Rise is."

The last thing Jessica wanted to do was to discuss her personal life with Carter. He would be sure to tear it apart and make her feel more inadequate than ever. So she blurted out, "I'll tell you how the Rise is. It's big and beautiful, but it's aging. Either I pour a huge amount of money into renovations, or I make alternate plans. That's why I'm here. I want to discuss the alternate plans."

Carter made several more turns of the paper clip between his fingers before he tossed it aside. Settling his tall frame into the executive chair behind the desk, he folded his hands over his lean middle and said quietly, "I'm listening."

Business, this is business, Jessica told herself and took strength from the thought. "I don't know how much Gordon has told you, but I'm thinking of turning Crosslyn Rise into a condominium complex, building

cluster housing in the woods, turning the mansion into a common fa-
cility for the owners, putting a marina along the shore.''

Gordon hadn't told Carter much of anything, judging from the look
of disbelief on his face. ''Why would you do that?''

''Because the Rise is too big for me.''

''So find someone it isn't too big for.''

''I've been trying to, but the market's terrible.''

''It takes a while sometimes to find the right buyer.''

I don't have a while, she thought. ''It could take years, and I'd really
like to do something before then.''

''Is there a rush? Crosslyn Rise has been in your family for generations. A few more years is nothing in the overall scheme of things.''

Jessica wished he wouldn't argue. She didn't like what she was saying
much more than he did. ''I think it's time to make a change.''

''But condominiums?'' he asked in dismay. ''Why condominiums?''

''Because the alternative is a full-fledged housing development, and
that would be worse. This way, at least, I'd have some control over the
outcome.''

''Why does that have to be the alternative?''

''Do you have any better ideas?'' she asked dryly.

''Sure. If you can't find an individual, sell to an institution—a school
or something like that.''

''No institution, or school or something like that will take care of the
Rise the right way. I can just picture large parking lots and litter all
over the place.''

''Then what about the town? Deed the Rise to the town for use as a
museum. Just imagine the whopping big tax deduction you'd get.''

''I'm not looking for tax deductions, and besides, the town may be
wealthy, but it isn't *that* wealthy. Do you have any idea what the costs
are of maintaining Crosslyn Rise for a year?'' Realizing she was close
to giving herself away, she paused and said more calmly, ''In the end,
the town would have to sell it, and I'd long since have lost my say.''

''But...condominiums?''

''Why not?'' she sparred, hating him for putting her on the spot when,
if he had any sensitivity at all, he'd know she was between a rock and
a very hard place.

Carter leaned forward in his seat and pinned her with a dark-eyed
stare. ''Because Crosslyn Rise is magnificent. It's one of the most beautiful, most private, most special pieces of property I've ever seen, and
believe me, I've seen a whole lot in the last few years. I don't even
know how you can think of selling it.''

"I have no choice!" she cried, and something in her eyes must have told him the truth.

"You can't keep it up?"

She dropped her gaze to the arm of her chair and rubbed her thumb back and forth against the chrome. "That's right." Her voice was quiet, imbued with the same defeat it had held in Gordon's office, and with an additional element of humiliation. Admitting the truth was bad enough; admitting it to Carter Malloy was even worse.

But she had to finish what she'd begun. "Like I said, the Rise is aging. Work that should have been done over the years wasn't, so what needs to be done now is extensive."

"Your dad let it go."

She had an easier time not looking at him. At least his voice was kind. "Not intentionally. But his mind was elsewhere, and my mother didn't want to upset him. Money was—" She stopped herself, realizing in one instant that she didn't want to make the confession, knowing in the next that she had to. "Money was tight."

"Are you kidding?"

Meeting his incredulous gaze, she said coldly, "No. I wouldn't kid about something like that."

"You don't kid about much of anything. You never did. Afraid a smile might crack your face?"

Jessica stared at him for a full second. "You haven't changed a bit," she muttered, and rose from her chair. "I shouldn't have come here. It was a mistake. I knew it would be."

She was just about at the door when it closed and Carter materialized before her. "Don't go," he said very quietly. "I'm sorry if I offended you. I sometimes say things without thinking them through. I've been working on improving that. I guess I still have a ways to go."

The thing that appalled Jessica most at that minute wasn't the embarrassment she felt regarding the Rise or her outburst or even Carter's apology. It was how handsome he was. Her eyes held his for a moment before, quite helplessly, lowering over the shadowed angle of his jaw to his chin, then his mouth. His lower lip was fuller than the top one. The two were slightly parted, touched only by the air he breathed.

Wrenching her gaze to the side, she swallowed hard and hung her head. "I do think this is a mistake," she murmured. "The whole thing is very difficult for me. Working with you won't help that."

"But I care about Crosslyn Rise."

"That was what Gordon said. But maybe you care most about getting it away from me. You always resented me for the Rise."

The denial she might have expected never came. After a short time, he said, "I resented lots of people for things that I didn't have. I was wrong. I'm not saying that I wouldn't buy the Rise from you if I had the money, because I meant what I said about it being special. But I don't have the money—any more, I guess, than you do. So that puts us in the same boat. On equal footing. Neither of us above or below the other."

He paused, giving her a chance to argue, but she didn't have anything to say. He had a right to be smug, she knew, but at that moment he wasn't. He was being completely reasonable.

"Do you have trouble with that, Jessica? Can you regard me as an equal?"

"We're not at all alike, you and I."

"I didn't say alike. I said equal. I meant financially equal."

Keeping her eyes downcast, she cocked her head toward the office behind her. "Looks to me like you're doing a sight better than I am at this point."

"But you have the Rise. That's worth a lot." When she simply shrugged, he said, "Sit down. Please. Let's talk."

Jessica wasn't quite sure why she listened to him. She figured it had something to do with the gentle way he'd asked, with the word "please," with the fact that he was blocking the door anyway, and he wasn't a movable presence. She suspected it might have even had something to do with her own curiosity. Though she caught definite reminders of the old Carter, the changes that had taken place since she'd seen him last intrigued her.

Without a word, she returned to her seat. This time, rather than going behind his desk, Carter lowered his long frame into the matching chair next to hers. Though there was a low slate cube between them, he was closer, more visible. That made her feel self-conscious. To counter the feeling, she directed her eyes to her hands and her thoughts to the plans she wanted to make for Crosslyn Rise.

"I don't like the sound of condominiums, either, but if the condominiums were in the form of cluster housing, if they were well placed and limited in number, if the renovations to the mansion were done with class and the waterfront likewise, the final product wouldn't be so bad. At least it would be kept up. The owners would be paying a lot for the privilege of living there. They'd have a stake in its future."

"Are you still teaching?"

At the abrupt change of subject, she cast him a quick look. "I, uh, yes."

"You haven't remarried?"

When her eyes flew to his this time, they stayed. "How did you know I'd married at all?"

"My parents. They were in touch with your mom. Once she died, they lost contact."

"Dad isn't—wasn't very social," Jessica said by way of explanation. But she hadn't kept in touch with the Malloys, either. "I'm not much better, I guess. How have your parents been?"

"Very well," he said on the lightest note he'd used yet. "They really like life under the sun. The warm weather is good for Mom's arthritis, and Dad is thrilled with the long growing season."

"Do you see them often?"

"Three or four times a year. I've been pretty busy."

She pressed her lips together and shook her head. "An architect. I'm still having trouble with that."

"What would you have me be?"

"A pool shark. A gambler. An ex-con."

He had the grace to look humble. "I suppose I deserved that."

"Yes." She was still looking at him, bound by something she couldn't quite fathom. She kept thinking that if she pushed a certain button, said a certain word, he'd change back into the shaggy-haired demon he'd been. But he wasn't changing into anything. He was just sitting with one leg crossed over the other, studying her intently. It was all she could do not to squirm. She averted her eyes, then, annoyed, returned them to his. "Why are you doing that?"

"Doing what?"

"Staring at me like that."

"Because you look different. I'm trying to decide how."

"I'm older. That's all."

"Maybe," he conceded, but said no more.

The silence chipped at Jessica's already-iffy composure nearly as much as his continued scrutiny did. She wasn't sure why she was the one on the hot seat, when by rights the hot seat should have been his. In an attempt to correct the situation, she said, "Since I have an appointment back in Cambridge at four—" which she'd deliberately planned, to give her an out "—I think we should concentrate on business. Gordon said you were good." She sent a look toward the corked wall. "Are these your sketches, or were they done by an assistant?"

"They're mine."

"And the ones in the reception area?"

"Some are mine, some aren't."

"Who is Goodwin?"

"My partner. We first met in New York. He specializes in commercial work. I specialize in residential, so we complement each other."

"Was he one of the men standing out front?"

"No. The man in the tan blazer was one of three associates who work here."

"What do they do—the associates?"

"They serve as project managers."

"Are they architects?" She could have sworn the man she'd heard talking was one.

Carter nodded. "Two are registered, the third is about to be. Beneath the associates, there are four draftspeople, beneath them a secretary, a bookkeeper and a receptionist."

"Are you the leading partner?"

"You mean, of the two of us, do I bring in more money?" When she nodded, he said, "I did last year. The year before I didn't. It varies."

"Would you want to work on Crosslyn Rise?"

"Not particularly," he stated, then held up a hand in appeasement when she looked angry. "I'd rather see the Rise kept as it is. If you want honesty, there it is. But if you don't have the money to support it, something has to be done." He came forward to brace his elbows on his thighs and dangle his hands between his knees. "And if you're determined to go ahead with the condo idea, I'd rather do the work myself than have a stranger do it."

"You're a stranger," she said stiffly. "You're not the same person who grew up around Crosslyn Rise."

"I remember what I felt for the Rise then. I can even better understand those feelings now."

"I'm not sure I trust your motives."

"Would I risk all this—" he shot a glance around the room "—for the sake of a vendetta? Look, Jessica," he said with a sigh, "I don't deny who I was then and what I did. I've already said that. I was a pain in the butt."

"You were worse than that."

"Okay, I was worse than that, but I'm a different person now. I've been through a whole lot that you can't begin to imagine. I've lived through hell and come out on the other side, and because of that, I appreciate some things other people don't. Crosslyn Rise is one of those things."

Jessica wished he wasn't sitting so close or regarding her so intently or talking so sanely. Either he was being utterly sincere, or he was doing one hell of an acting job. She wasn't sure which, but she did know that she couldn't summarily rule him off the project.

"Do you think," she asked in a tentative voice, "that my idea for Crosslyn Rise would work?"

"It could."

"Would you want to try working up some sketches?"

"We'd have to talk more about what you want. I'd need to see a plot plan. And I'd have to go out there. Even aside from the fact that I haven't been there in a while, I've never looked around with this kind of thing in mind."

Jessica nodded. What he said was fair enough. What wasn't fair was the smooth way he said it. He sounded very professional and very male. For the second time in as many minutes, she wished he wasn't sitting so close. She wished she wasn't so aware of him.

Clutching her purse, she stood. "I have to be going," she said, concentrating on the leather strap as she eased it over her shoulder.

"But we haven't settled anything."

She raised her eyes. He, too, had risen and was standing within an arm's length of her. She started toward the door. "We have. We've settled that we have to talk more, I have to get you a plot plan, you have to come out to see Crosslyn Rise." Her eyes were on the doorknob, but she felt Carter moving right along with her. "You may want to talk with Gordon, too. He'll explain the plan he has for raising the money for the project."

"Am I hired?" He reached around her to open the door.

"I don't know. We have to do all those other things first."

"When can we meet again?"

"I'll call you." She was in the corridor, moving steadily back the way she'd come, with Carter matching her step.

"Why don't we set a time now?"

"Because I don't have my schedule in front of me."

"Are you that busy?"

"Yes!" she said, and stopped in her tracks. She looked up at him, swallowed tightly, dropped her gaze again and moved on. "Yes," she echoed in a near-whisper. "It's nearly exam time. My schedule's erratic during exam time."

Her explanation seemed to appease Carter, which relieved her, as did the sight of the reception area. She was feeling overwhelmed by Carter's presence. He was a little too smooth, a little too agreeable, a little too male. Between those things and a memory that haunted her, she wanted out.

"Will you call me?" he asked as he opened the door to the reception area.

"I said I would."

"You have my number?"

"Yes."

Opening the outer door, he accompanied her right to the elevator and pushed the button. "Can I have yours?"

Grateful for something to do, she fumbled in her purse for a pen, jotted her number in a small notebook, tore out the page and handed it to him. She was restowing the pen when a bell rang announcing the elevator's arrival. Her attention was riveted to the panel on top of the doors when Carter said, "Jessica?"

She dared meet his gaze a final time. It was a mistake. A small frown touched his brow and was gone, leaving an expression that combined confusion and surprise with pleasure. When he spoke, his voice held the same three elements. "It was really good seeing you," he said as though he meant it and surprised himself in that. Then he smiled, and his smile held nothing but pleasure.

That was when Jessica knew she was in big trouble.

3

Carter *had* enjoyed seeing Jessica, though he wasn't sure why. As a kid, she'd been a snotty little thing looking down her nose at him. He had resented everything about her, which was why his greatest joy had been putting her down. In that, he had been cruel at times. He'd found her sore spots and rubbed them with salt.

Clearly she remembered. She wasn't any too happy to see him, though she'd agreed to the meeting, which said something about the bind she was in regarding Crosslyn Rise. Puzzled by that bind, Carter called Gordon shortly after Jessica left his office.

In setting up the meeting, Gordon had only told him that Jessica had wanted to discuss an architectural project relating to the Rise. Under Carter's questioning now, he admitted to the financial problems. He talked of putting together a group of investors. He touched on Jessica's insistence on being in command. He went so far as to outline the role Carter might play, as Gordon had broached it with Jessica.

Though Carter had meant what he'd said about preferring to leave Crosslyn Rise as it was, once he accepted the idea of its changing, he found satisfaction in the idea of taking part in that change. Some of his satisfaction was smug; there was an element of poetic justice in his having come far enough in the world to actively shape the Rise's future.

But the satisfaction went beyond that. Monetarily it was a sound proposal. His gut told him that, even before he worked out the figures. Given the dollar equivalent of his professional fees added to the hundred thousand he could afford to invest, he stood to take a sizable sum out of the project in two to three years' time.

That sum would go a long way toward broadening his base of operation. Malloy and Goodwin was doing well, bringing in greater profit each year, but there were certain projects—more artistically rewarding than lucrative—that Carter would bid on given the cushion of capital funds and a larger staff.

And then, working on the alteration of Crosslyn Rise both as architect and investor, he would see more of Jessica. That thought lingered with him long after he'd hung up the phone, long after he'd set aside the other issues.

He wanted to see more of her, incredible but true. She wasn't gorgeous. She wasn't sexy or witty. She wasn't anything like the women he dated, and it certainly wasn't that he was thinking of dating *her*. But at the end of their brief meeting, he had felt something warm flowing through him. He guessed it had to do with a shared past; he didn't have that with many people, and he wouldn't have thought he'd want it with *anyone*, given the sins of his past. Still, there was that warm feeling. It fascinated him, particularly since he had felt so many conflicting things during the meeting itself.

Emotions had come in flashes—anger and resentment in an almost automatic response to any hint of arrogance on her part, embarrassment and remorse as he recalled things he'd said and done years before. She was the same as he remembered her, but different—older, though time had been kind. Her skin was unflawed, her hair more tame, her movements more coordinated, even in spite of her nervousness. And she was nervous. He made her so, he guessed, though he had tried to be amenable.

What he wanted, he realized, was for her to eye him through those granny glasses of hers and see the decent person he was now. He wanted to close the last page on the book from the past. He wanted her acceptance. Though he hadn't given two thoughts to it before their meeting, that acceptance suddenly mattered a lot. Only when he had it would he feel that he'd truly conquered the past.

Jessica tried to think about their meeting as little as possible in the hours subsequent to it. To that end, she kept herself busy, which wasn't difficult with exams on the horizon and the resultant rash of impromptu meetings with students and teaching assistants. If Carter's phone number seemed to burn a hole in her date book, she ignored the smoke. She had to be in command, she told herself. Carter had to know she was in command.

She wasn't terribly proud of the show she'd put on in his office. She'd been skittish in his presence, and it had showed. The most merciful thing about the meeting was that he had waited until she had a foot out the door before smiling. His smile was potent. It had confused her, excited her, frightened her. It had warned her that working with him wasn't going to be easy in any way, shape or form, and it had nearly convinced her not to try it.

Still she called him. She waited two full days to do it, then chose Thursday afternoon, when she was fresh from a buoying department meeting. She enjoyed department meetings. She liked her colleagues and was liked in return. In the academic sphere, she was fully confident of her abilities. So she let the overflow of that confidence carry her into the phone call to Carter.

"Carter? This is Jessica Crosslyn."

"It's about time you called," he scolded, and she immediately bristled—until the teasing in his voice came through. "I was beginning to think you'd changed your mind."

She didn't know what to make of the teasing. She'd never heard teasing coming from Carter Malloy before. For the sake of their working together, she took it at face value and said evenly, "It's only been two days."

"That's two days too long."

"Is there a rush?"

"There's always a rush where enthusiasm and weather are concerned."

She found that to be a curious statement. "Enthusiasm?"

"I'm really up for this now, and I have the time to get started," he explained. "It's not often that the two coincide."

She could buy that, she supposed, though she wondered if he'd purposely injected the subtle reminder that he was in demand. "And the weather?" she came back a bit skeptically. "It's not yet May. The best of the construction season is still ahead."

"Not so, once time is spent on first-draft designs then multiple rounds of revisions." Carter kept his tone easygoing. "By the time the plans are done, the investors lined up and bidding taken on contractors, it could well be September or October, unless we step on it now." Having made his point, he paused. "Gordon explained the financial setup and the fact that you want sole approval of the final plans before they're shown to potential investors."

Jessica was immediately wary. "Do you have a problem with that?"

"It depends on whether you approve what I like," he said with a grin, then tacked on a quick, "Just kidding."

"I don't think you are."

"Sure I am," he cajoled. "A client pays me for my work, I give him what he wants."

"And if you think what he wants is hideous?"

"I know not to take the job."

"So in that sense," she persisted, not sure why she was being stubborn, but driven to it nonetheless, "you ensure that the client will approve what you like."

"Not ensure—" he dug in his own heels a little "—but I maximize the likelihood of it. And there's nothing wrong with that. It's the only sensible way to operate. Besides, the assumption is that the client comes to me because he likes my style."

"I don't know whether I like your style or not," she argued. "I haven't seen much of it."

She seemed to be taking a page from the past and deliberately picking a fight. As he'd done then, so now Carter fought back. "If you'd asked the other day, I'd have shown you pictures. I've got a portfolio full of them. You might have saved us both a whole lot of time and effort. But you were in such an all-fired rush to get back to your precious ivory tower—"

He caught himself only after he realized what he was doing. Jessica remained silent. He waited for her to rail at him the way she used to, but she didn't speak. In a far quieter voice he asked, "Are you still there?"

"Yes," she murmured, "but I don't know why. This isn't going to work. We're like fire and water."

"The past is getting in the way. Old habits die hard. But I'm sorry. What I said was unnecessary."

"Part of it was right," she conceded. "I was in a rush to get back. I had another appointment." He should know that he wasn't the only one in demand. "But as far as my ivory tower is concerned, that ivory tower has produced official interpreters for assorted summit meetings as well as for embassies in Moscow, Leningrad and Bonn. My work isn't all mind-in-the-clouds."

"I know," Carter said quietly. "I'm sorry." He didn't say anything more for a minute, hoping she'd tell him he was forgiven. But things weren't going to be so easy. "Anyway, I'd really like to talk again. Tell me when you have free time. If I have a conflict, I'll try to change it."

Short of being bitchy, which he'd accused her of being as a child, she couldn't turn her back on his willingness to accommodate her. She looked at the calendar tacked on the wall. It was filled with scrawled notations, more densely drawn for the upcoming few weeks. Given the choice, she would put off a meeting with Carter until after exams, when she'd be better able to take the disturbance in stride. But she remembered what he'd said about the weather. If she was going to do something with Crosslyn Rise, she wanted it done soon. The longer she diddled around with preliminary arrangements, the later in the season it would be and the greater the chance of winter closing in to delay the work even more. Instinctively she knew that the longer the process was drawn out, the more painful it would be.

"I'm free until noon next Tuesday morning," she said. "Do you want to come out and walk through Crosslyn Rise then?"

Carter felt a glimmer of excitement at the mention of walking through Crosslyn Rise. It had been years since he'd seen the place, and though he'd never lived there, since his parents had always rented a small house in town, returning to Crosslyn Rise would be something of a homecoming.

He had one meeting scheduled for that morning, but it was easily postponed. "Next Tuesday is fine. Time?"

"Is nine too early?"

"Nine is perfect. It might be a help if between now and then you wrote down your ideas so we can discuss them in as much detail as possible. If you've seen any pictures of things you like in newspapers or magazines you might cut them out. The more I know of what you want, the easier my job will be."

Efficient person that she was herself, she could go along with that. "You mentioned wanting to see a plot plan. I don't think I've ever seen one. Where would I get it?"

"The town should have one, but I'll take care of that. I can phone ahead and pick it up on my way. You just be there with your house and your thoughts." He paused. "Okay?"

"Okay."

"See you then."

"Uh-huh."

Jessica couldn't decide whether to put coffee on to brew or to assume that he'd already had a cup or two, and she spent an inordinate amount of time debating the issue. One minute she decided that the proper thing would indeed be to have it ready and offer him some; the next minute it seemed a foolish gesture. This was Carter Malloy, she told herself.

He didn't expect anything from her but a hard time, which was just about all they'd ever given each other.

But that had been years ago, and Carter Malloy had changed. He'd grown up. He was an architect. A man. And though one part of her didn't want to go out of her way to make the Carter Malloy of any age feel welcome in her home, another part felt that she owed cordiality to the architect who might well play a part in her future.

As for the man in him, she pushed all awareness of that to the farthest reaches of consciousness and chose to attribute the unsettled feeling in her stomach to the nature of the meeting itself.

Carter arrived at nine on the dot. He parked his car on the pebbled driveway that circled some twenty feet in front of the ivy-draped portico. The car was dark blue and low, but Jessica wouldn't have known the make even if she'd had the presence of mind to wonder—which she didn't, since she was too busy trying to calm her nerves.

She greeted him at the front door, bracing an unsteady hand on the doorknob. Pulse racing, she watched him step inside, watched him look slowly around the rotundalike foyer, watched him raise his eyes to the top of the broadly sweeping staircase, then say in a low and surprisingly humble voice, "This is...very...weird."

"Weird?"

"Coming in the front door. Seeing this after so many years. It's incredibly impressive."

"Until you look closely."

He shot her a questioning glance.

"Things are worn," she explained, wanting to say it before he did. "The grandeur of Crosslyn Rise has faded."

"Oh, but it hasn't." He moved toward the center of the foyer. "The grandeur is in its structure. Nothing can dim that. Maybe the accessories have suffered with age, but the place is still a wonder."

"Is that your professional assessment?"

He shook his head. "Personal." His gaze was drawn toward the living room. The entrance to it was broad, the room itself huge. Knee-to-ceiling windows brought in generous helpings of daylight, saving the room from the darkness that might otherwise have come with the heavy velvet decor. Sun was streaming obliquely past the oversized fireplace, casting the intricate carving of the pine mantel in bas-relief. "Personal assessment. I always loved this place."

"I'm sure," she remarked with unplanned tartness.

He shot her a sharper look this time. "Does it gall you seeing me here? Does it prick your Victorian sensibilities? Would you rather I stay out back near the gardener's shed?''

Jessica felt instant remorse. "Of course not. I'm sorry. I was just remembering—"

"Remembering the past is a mistake, because what you remember will be the way I acted, not the way I felt. You didn't know the way I really felt. *I* didn't know the way I really felt a lot of the time. But I knew I loved this place."

"And you hated me because I lived here and you didn't."

"That's neither here nor there. But I did love Crosslyn Rise, and I'd like to feel free to express what I'm thinking and feeling as we walk around. Can I do that, or would you rather I repress it all?''

"You?" she shot back, goaded on by the fact that he was being so reasonable. "Repress your feelings?"

"I can do it if I try. Granted, I'm not as good at it as you. But you've had years of practice. You're the expert. No doubt there's a Ph.D. in Denial mixed up with all the diplomas on your wall." His eyes narrowed, seeing far too much. "Don't you ever get tired of bottling everything up?"

Jessica's insides were beginning to shake. She wanted to think it was anger, but that was only half-true. Carter was coming close to repeating things he'd said once before. The same hurt she'd felt then was threatening to engulf her now. "I don't bottle everything up," she said, and gave a tight swallow.

"You do. You're as repressed as ever." The words were no sooner out than he regretted them. She looked fearful, and for a horrifying minute, he wondered if she was going to cry. "Don't," he whispered and approached her with his hands out to the side. "Please. I'm sorry. Damn, I'm apologizing again. I can't believe that. Why do you make me say mean things? What is it about you that brings out the bastard in me?''

Struggling against tears, she didn't speak. A small shrug was the best she could muster.

"Yell at me," Carter ordered, willing to do anything to keep those tears at bay. "Go ahead. Tell me what you think of me. Tell me that I'm a bastard and that I don't know what I'm talking about because I don't know you at all. Say it, Jessica. Tell me to keep my mouth shut. Tell me to mind my own business. Tell me to go to hell."

But she couldn't do that. Deep down inside, she knew she was the villain of the piece. She'd provoked him far more than he'd provoked her. And he was right. She was repressed. It just hurt to hear him say it. Hurt a lot. Hurt even more, at thirty-three, than it had at sixteen.

Moving to the base of the stairs, she pressed herself against the swirling newel post, keeping her back to him. "I've lived at Crosslyn Rise all my life," she began in a tremulous voice. "For as long as I can remember, it's been my haven. It's the place I come home to, the place that's quiet and peaceful, the place that accepts me as I am and doesn't make demands. I can't afford to keep it up, so I have to sell it." Her voice fell to a tormented whisper. "That hurts, Carter. It really hurts. And seeing you—" she ran out of one breath, took in another "—seeing you brings back memories. I guess I'm feeling a little raw."

The warmth Carter had experienced the last time he'd been with Jessica was back. It carried him over the short distance to where she stood, brought his hands to her shoulders and imbued his low, slow voice with something surprisingly caring. "I can understand what you're feeling about Crosslyn Rise, Jessica. Really, I can." With the smallest, most subtle of movements, his hands worked at the tightness in her shoulders. "I wish I could offer a miracle solution to keep the Rise intact, but if there was one, I'm sure either you or Gordon would have found it by now. I can promise you that I'll draw up spectacular plans for the complex you have in mind, but it doesn't matter how spectacular they are, they won't be the Crosslyn Rise you've known all your life. The thought of it hurts you now, and it'll get worse before it gets better." He kept kneading, lightly kneading, and he didn't mind it at all. Her blouse was silk and soft, her shoulders surprisingly supple beneath it. His fingers fought for and won successive bits of relaxation.

"But the hurt will only be aggravated if we keep sniping at each other," he went on to quietly make his point. "I've already said I was wrong when I was a kid. If I could turn back the clock and change things, I would." Without thinking, he gathered a stray wisp of hair from her shoulder and smoothed it toward the tortoiseshell clasp at her nape. "But I can't. I can only try to make the present better and the future better than that—and 'try' is the operative word. I'll make mistakes. I'm a spontaneous person—maybe 'impulsive' is the word—but you already know that." He turned her to face him, and at the sight of her openness, gentled his voice even more. "The point is that I can be reasoned with now. I couldn't be back then, but I can be now. So if I say something that bugs you, tell me. Let's get it out in the open and be done."

Jessica heard what he was saying, but only peripherally. Between the low vibrancy of his voice and the slow, hypnotic motion of his hands, she was being warmed all over. Not even the fact that she faced him now, that she couldn't deny his identity as she might have if her back was still to him, could put a chill to that warmth.

"I'd like this job, Jessica," he went on, his dark eyes barely moving from hers yet seeming to touch on each of her features. "I'd really like this job, but I think you ought to decide whether working with me will be too painful on top of everything else. If it will be," he finished, fascinated by the softness of her cheek beneath the sweeping pad of his thumb, "I'll bow out."

His thumb stopped at the corner of her mouth, and time seemed to stop right along with it. In a flash of awareness that hit them simultaneously came the realization that they were standing a breath apart, that Carter was holding her as he would a desirable woman and Jessica was looking up at him as she would a desirable man.

She couldn't move. Her blood seemed to be thrumming through her veins in mockery of the paralysis of her legs, but she couldn't drag herself away from Carter. He gave her comfort. He made her feel not quite so alone. And he made her aware that she was a woman.

That fact took Carter by surprise. He'd always regarded Jessica as an asexual being, but something had happened when he'd put his hands on her shoulders. No, something had happened even before that, when she'd been upset and he'd wanted to help ease her through it. He felt protective. He couldn't remember feeling that for a woman before, mainly because most of the women he'd known were strong, powerful types who didn't allow for upsets. But he rather liked being needed. Not that Jessica would admit to needing him, he knew. Still, it was something to consider.

But he'd consider it another time, because she looked frightened enough at that minute to bolt, and he didn't want her to. Slowly, almost reluctantly, he dropped his hands to his sides.

A second later, Jessica dropped her chin to her chest. She raised a shaky hand to the bridge of her nose, pressed a fingertip to the nosepiece of her glasses and held it there. "I'm sorry," she whispered, sure that she'd misinterpreted what she'd seen and felt, "I don't know what came over me. I'm usually in better control of myself."

"You have a right to be upset," he said just as quietly, but he didn't step away. "It's okay to lose control once in a while."

She didn't look up. Nor did she say anything for a minute, because there was a clean, male scent in the air that held her captive. Then, cursing herself for a fool, she cleared her throat. "I, uh, I made coffee. Do you want some?"

What Carter wanted first was a little breathing space. He needed to distance himself mentally from the vulnerable Jessica, for whom he'd just felt a glimmer of desire. "Maybe we ought to walk around outside first," he suggested. "That way I'll know what you're talking about when you go through your list. You made one, didn't you?"

She met his gaze briefly. "Yes."

"Good." He remembered the feel of silk beneath his fingers. She was wearing a skirt that hit at midcalf, opaque stockings and flat shoes that would keep her warm, but her silk blouse, as gently as it fell over her breasts, wouldn't protect her from the air. "Do you want a sweater or something? It's still cool outside."

She nodded and took a blazer from the closet, quickly slipping her arms into the sleeves. Carter would have helped her with it if she hadn't been so fast. He wondered whether she wanted breathing space, too— then he chided himself for the whimsy. If Jessica had been struck in that instant with an awareness of him as a man, it was an aberration. No way was she going to allow herself to lust after Carter Malloy—*if* she knew the meaning of the word *lust*, which he doubted she did. And he certainly wasn't lusting after her. It was just that with his acceptance that she was a woman, she became a character of greater depth in his mind, someone he might like to get to know better.

They left through the front door, went down the brick walk and crossed the pebbled driveway to the broad lawn, which leveled off for a while before slanting gracefully toward the sea. "This is the best time of year," he remarked, taking in a deep breath. "Everything is new and fresh in spring. In another week or two, the trees will have budded." He glanced at Jessica, who was looking forlornly toward the shore, and though he doubted his question would be welcome, he couldn't pass by her sadness. "What will you do—if you decide to go ahead and develop Crosslyn Rise?"

It was a minute before she answered. Her hands were tucked into the pockets of her blazer, but her head was up and her shoulders straight. The fresh air and the walking were helping her to recover the equilibrium she'd lost earlier when Carter had been so close. "I'm not sure."

"Will you stay here?"

"I don't know. That might be hard. Or it might be harder to leave. I just don't know. I haven't gotten that far yet." She came to a halt.

Carter did, too. He followed her gaze down the slope of the lawn. "Tell me what you see."

"Something small and pretty. A marina. Some shops. Do you see how the boulders go? They form a crescent. I can see boats over there—" she pointed toward the far right curve of the crescent "—with a small beach and shops along the straightaway."

Carter wasn't sure he'd arrange the elements quite as she had, but that was a small matter. He started walking again. "And this slope?"

She came along. "I'd leave it as is, maybe add a few paths to protect the grass and some shrubbery here and there."

They descended the slope that led to the shoreline. "You used to sled down this hill. Do you remember?"

"Uh-huh. I had a Flexible Flyer," she recalled.

"New and shiny. It was always new and shiny."

"Because it wasn't used much. It was no fun sledding alone."

"I'd have shared that Flexible Flyer with you."

"Shared?" she asked too innocently.

"Uh, maybe not." He paused. "Mmm, probably not. I'd probably have chased you into the woods, buried you under a pile of snow and kept the Flyer all to myself."

Wearing a small, slightly crooked smile, she looked up at him. "I think so."

He liked the smile, small though it was, and it hadn't cracked her face after all. Rather, it made her look younger. It made him feel younger. "I was a bully."

"Uh-huh."

"You must have written scathing things about me in your diary."

"I never kept a diary."

"No? Funny, I'd have pegged you for the diary type."

"Studious?"

"Literary."

"I wrote poems."

He squinted as the memory returned. "That's...right. You did write poems."

"Not about you, though," she added quickly. "I wrote poems about pretty things, and there was absolutely nothing pretty about you that I could see back then."

"Is there now?" he asked, because he couldn't help it.

Jessica didn't know whether it was the outdoors, the gentle breeze stirring her hair or the rhythmic roll of the surf that lulled her, but her nervousness seemed on hold. She was feeling more comfortable than she had before with Carter, which was why she dared answer his question.

"You have nice skin. The acne's gone."

Carter was oddly pleased by the compliment. "I finally outgrew that at twenty-five. I had a prolonged adolescence, in *lots* of ways."

The subject of why he'd been such a troubled kid was wide open, but Jessica felt safer keeping things light. "Where did you get the tan?"

"Anguilla. I was there for a week at the beginning of March."

They'd reached the beach and were slowly crossing the rocky sand. "Was it nice?"

"Very nice. Sunny and warm. Quiet. Restful."

She wondered whether he'd gone alone. "You've never married, have you?"

"No."

On impulse, and with a touch of the old sarcasm, she said, "I'd have thought you'd have been married three times by now."

He didn't deny it. "I probably would have, if I'd let myself marry at all. Either I knew what a bad risk I was, or the women I dated did. I'd have made a lousy husband."

"Then. What about now?"

Without quite answering the question, he said, "Now it's harder to meet good women. They're all very complex by the time they reach thirty, and somehow the idea of marrying a twenty-two-year-old when I'm nearly forty doesn't appeal to me. The young ones aren't mature enough, the older ones are too mature."

"Too mature—as in complex?"

He nodded and paused, slid his hands into the pockets of his dark slacks and stood looking out over the water. "They have careers. They have established life-styles. They're stuck in their ways and very picky about who they want and what they expect from that person. It puts a lot of pressure on a relationship."

"Aren't you picky?" she asked, feeling the need to defend members of her sex, though she'd talked to enough single friends to know that Carter was right.

"Sure I'm picky," he said with a bob of one shoulder. "I'm not getting any younger. I have a career and an established life-style, and I'm pretty set in my ways, too. So I'm not married." He looked around, feeling an urge to change the subject. "Were you thinking of keeping the oceanfront area restricted to people who live here?"

"I don't know. I haven't thought that out yet." She studied the crease on his brow. "Is there a problem?"

"Problem? Not if you're flexible about what you want. As I see it, either you have a simple waterfront with a beach and a pier and a boat house or you have a marina with a dock, slips, shops and the appropriate personnel to go with them. But if you want the marina and the shops, they can't be restricted—at least, not limited to the people who live here. You could establish a private yacht club that would be joined by people from all along the North Shore, and you can keep it as exclusive as you want by regulating the cost of membership, but there's no way something as restrictive as that is going to be able to support shops, as I think of shops." As he talked, he'd been looking around, assessing the beachfront layout. Now he faced her. "What kind of shops did you have in mind?"

"The kind that would provide for the basic needs of the residents— drugstore, convenience store, bookstore, gift or crafts shop." She saw him shaking his head. "No?"

"Not unless there's public access. Shops like that couldn't survive with such a limited clientele base."

Which went to show, Jessica realized in chagrin, how little she knew about business. "But I was thinking really *small* shops. Quaint shops."

"Even the smallest, most quaint shop has to do a certain amount of business to survive. You'd need public access."

"You mean, scads of people driving through?" But that wasn't at all what she wanted, and the look on her face made that clear.

"They wouldn't have to drive through. The waterfront area could be arranged so that cars never cross it."

"I don't know," she murmured, disturbed. Turning, she headed back up toward the house.

He joined her, walking for a time in silence before saying, "You don't have to make an immediate decision."

"But you said yourself that time was of the essence."

"Only if you want to get started this year."

"I don't *want* to get started at all," she said, and quickened her step.

Knowing the hard time she was having, he let her go. He stayed several paces behind until she reached the top of the rise, where she slowed. When he came alongside her, she raised her eyes to his and asked in a tentative voice, "Were you able to get the plot plan?"

He nodded. "It's in the car."

"Do you want to take it when we go through the woods?"

"No. I'll study it later. What I want is for you to show me the kinds of settings you had in mind for the housing. Even though ecological factors will come into play when a final decision is made, your ideas can be a starting point." He took a deep breath, hooked his hands on his hips and made a visual sweep of the front line of trees. "I used to go through these woods a lot, but that was too many years ago and never with an eye out for something like this."

She studied his expression, but it told her nothing of what he was feeling just then, and she wanted to know. She was feeling frighteningly upended and in need of support. "You said that you really wanted this project." She started off toward a well-worn path, confident that Carter would fall into step, which he did.

"I do."

"Why?"

"Because it's an exciting one. Crosslyn Rise is part of my past. It's a beautiful place, the challenge will be to maintain its beauty. If I can do that, it will be a feather in my cap. So I'll have the professional benefit, and the personal satisfaction. And if I invest in the project the way Gordon proposed, I'll make some money. I could use the money."

That surprised her. "I thought you were doing well."

"I am. But there's a luxury that comes with having spare change. I'd like to be able to reject a lucrative job that may be unexciting and accept an exciting job that may not be lucrative."

His argument was reasonable. *He* was reasonable—far more so than she'd have expected. Gordon had said he'd changed. *Carter* had said he'd changed. For the first time, as they walked along the path side by side, with the dried leaves of winter crackling beneath their shoes, she wondered what had caused the change. Simple aging? She doubted it. There were too many disgruntled adults in the world to buy that. It might have been true if Carter had simply mellowed. But given the wretch of a teenager he'd been, mellowing was far too benign a term to describe the change. She was thinking total personality overhaul— well, not total, since he still had the occasional impulsive, sharp-tongued moment, but close.

For a time, they walked on without talking. The crackle of the leaves became interspersed with small, vague sounds that consolidated into quacks when they approached the duck pond. Emerging from the path into the open, Jessica stopped. The surface of the pond and its shores were dotted with iridescent blue, green and purple heads. The ducks were in their glory, waiting for spring to burst forth.

"There would have to be some houses here, assuming care was taken to protect the ducks. It's too special a setting to waste."

Carter agreed. "You mentioned cluster housing the other day. Do you mean houses that are physically separate from one another but clustered by twos and threes here and in other spots? Or clusters of town houses that are physically connected to one another?"

"I'm not sure." She didn't look at him. It was easier that way, she found. The bobbing heads of the ducks on the pond were a more serene sight. But her voice held the curiosity her eyes might have. "What do you think?"

"Off the top of my head, I like the town house idea. I can picture town houses clustered together in a variation on the Georgian theme."

"Wouldn't that be easier to do with single homes?"

"Easier, but not as interesting." He flashed her a self-mocking smile, which, unwittingly looking his way, she caught. "And not as challenging for me. But I'd recommend the town house concept for economic reasons, as well. Take this duck pond. If you build single homes into the setting, you wouldn't want to do more than two or three, and they'd have to be in the million-plus range. On the other hand, you could build three town house clusters, each with two or three town houses, and scatter them around. Since they could be marketed for five or five-fifty, they'd be easier to sell and you'd still come out ahead."

She remembered when Gordon had spoken of profit. Her response was the same now as it was then, a sick kind of feeling at the pit of her stomach. "Money isn't the major issue."

"Maybe not to you—"

"Is it to you?" she cut in, eyeing him sharply.

He held his ground. "It's one of the issues, not necessarily the major one. But I can guarantee you that it *will* be the major issue for the people Gordon lines up to become part of his consortium. You and I have personal feelings for Crosslyn Rise. The others won't. They may be captivated by the place and committed to preserving as much of the natural contour as possible, but they won't have an emotional attachment. They'll enter into this as a financial venture. That's all."

"Must you be so blunt?" she asked, annoyed because she knew he was right, yet the words stung.

"I thought you'd want the truth."

"You don't have to be so *blunt*." She turned abruptly and, ignoring the quacks that seemed stirred by the movement, headed back toward the path.

"You want sugarcoating?" He took off after her. "Where are you going now?"

"The meadow," she called over her shoulder.

With a minimum of effort, he was by her side. "Y'know, Jessica, if you're going ahead with this project, you ought to face facts. Either you finance the whole thing yourself—"

"If I had that kind of money, there wouldn't *be* any project!"

"Okay, so you don't have the money." He paused, irked enough by the huffy manner in which she'd walked away from him to be reckless. "Why don't you have the money? I keep asking myself that. Where did it go? The Crosslyn family is loaded."

"Was loaded."

"Where did it go?"

"How do *I* know where it went?" She whirled around to face him. "I never needed it. It was something my father had that he was supposedly doing something brilliant with. I never asked about it. I never cared about it. So what do I know?" She threw up a hand. "I've got my head stuck in that ivory tower of mine. What do I know about the money that's supposed to be there but isn't?"

He caught her hand before it quite returned to her side. "I'm not blaming you. Take it easy."

"Take it easy?" she cried. "The single most stable thing in my life is on the verge of being bulldozed—by *my* decision, no less—and you tell me to take it easy? Let go of my hand."

But he didn't. His long fingers wound through hers. "Changing Crosslyn Rise may be upsetting, but it's not the end of the world. It's just a house, for heaven's sake."

"It's my family's history."

"So now it's time to write a new chapter. Crosslyn Rise will always be Crosslyn Rise. It's not going away. It's just getting a face-lift. Wouldn't you rather have it done now, when you can be there to supervise, than have it done when you die? It's not like you have a horde of children to leave the place to."

Of all the things he'd said, that hurt the most. The issue of having a family, of passing something of the Crosslyn genes to another generation had always been a sensitive issue for Jessica. Her friends didn't raise it with her. Not even Gordon had made reference to it during their discussion of Crosslyn Rise. The fact that Carter Malloy was the one to twist the knife was too much to bear.

"Let me go," she murmured, lowering both her head and her voice as she struggled to free her hand from his.

"No."

She twisted her hand, even used her other one to try to pry his fingers free. Her teeth were clenched. "I want you to let me go."

"I won't. You're too upset."

"And you're not helping." She lifted her eyes then, uncaring that he saw the tears there. "Why do you have to say things that hurt so much?" she said softly. "Why do you do it, Carter? You could always find the one thing that would hurt me most, and that was the thing you'd harp on. You say you've changed, but you're still hurting me. Why? Why can't you just do your job and leave me alone?"

Seconds after she'd said it, Carter asked himself the same question. It should have been an easy matter to approach this job as he would another. But he was emotionally involved—as much with Jessica as with Crosslyn Rise—which was why, without pausing to analyze the details of that emotional involvement, he reached out, drew Jessica close and wrapped her in his arms.

4

When Carter had been a kid, he'd imagined that Jessica Crosslyn was made of nails. He'd found a hint of give when he'd touched her earlier, but only when he held her fully against him, as he did now, did he realize that she was surprisingly soft. Just as surprising was the tenderness he felt. He guessed it had to do with the tears he'd seen in her eyes. She was fighting them still, he knew. He could feel it in her body.

Lowering his head so that his mouth wasn't far from her ear, he said in a voice only loud enough to surmount the whispering breeze, "Let it out, Jessica. It's all right. No one will think less of you, and you'll feel a whole lot better."

But she couldn't. She'd been too weak in front of Carter already. Crying would be the last straw. "I'm all right," she said, but she didn't pull away. It had been a long time since someone had held her. She wasn't yet ready to have it end, particularly since she was still in the grip of the empty feeling brought on by his words.

"I don't do it intentionally," he murmured in the same deeply male, low-to-the-ear voice. "Maybe I did when we were kids, but not now. I don't intentionally hurt you, but I blurt out things without thinking." Which totally avoided the issue of whether the things he blurted out were true, but that was for another time. For now there were more immediate explanations to be offered. "I'm sorry for that, Jessica. I'm sorry if I hurt you, and I know I ought to be able to do my job and leave you alone, but I can't. Maybe it's because I knew you back then, so there's a bond. Maybe it's because your parents are gone and you're alone. Maybe it's because I owe you for all I put you through."

"But you're putting me through more," came the meek voice from the area of his shirt collar.

"Unintentionally," he said. His hands flexed, lightly stroking her back. "I know you're going through a hard time, and I want to help. If I could loan you the money to keep Crosslyn Rise, I'd do it, but I don't have anywhere near enough. Gordon says you've got loans on top of loans."

"See?" The reminder was an unwelcome one. "You're doing it again."

"No, I'm explaining why I can't help out more. I've come a long way, but I'm not wealthy. I couldn't afford to own a place like Crosslyn Rise myself. I have a condo in the city, and it's in a luxury building, but it's small."

"I'm not asking—"

"I know that, but I want to do something. I want to help you through this, maybe make things easier. I guess what I'm saying is that I want us to be friends."

Friends? Carter Malloy, her childhood nemesis, a friend? It sounded bizarre. But then, the fact that she was leaning against him, taking comfort from his strength was no less bizarre. She hadn't imagined she'd ever want to touch him, much less feel the strength of his body. And he was strong, she realized—physically and, to her chagrin, emotionally. She could use some of that strength.

"I'm also thinking," he went on, "that I'd like to know more about you. When we were kids, I used to say awful things to you. I assumed you were too stuck-up to be bothered by them."

"I was bothered. They hurt."

"And if I'd known it then," he acknowledged honestly, "I'd probably have done it even more. But I don't want to do that now. So if I know what you're thinking, if I know what your sore spots are, I can avoid hitting them. Maybe I can even help them heal." He liked that idea. "Sounds lofty, but if you don't aim high, you don't get nowhere."

"Anywhere," she corrected, and raised her head. There was no sarcasm, only curiosity in her voice. "When did you become a philosopher?"

He looked down into her eyes, dove gray behind her glasses. "When I was in Vietnam. A good many of the things I am now I became then." At her startled look, he was bemused himself. "Didn't you guess? Didn't you wonder what it was that brought about the change?"

She gave a head shake so tiny it was almost imperceptible. "I was too busy trying to deny it."

"Deny it all you want, but it's true. I'll prove it to you if you let me, but I can't do it if you jump all over me every time I say something dumb." When she opened her mouth to argue, he put a finger to her lips. "I can learn, Jessica. Talk to me. Reason with me. Explain things to me. I'm not going to turn around and walk away. I'll listen."

Her fingers tightened on the crisp fabric of his shirt just above his belt, and her eyes went rounder behind her glasses. "And then what?" she asked, still without sarcasm. In place of her earlier curiosity, though, was fear. "Will you take what I've told you and turn it on me? If you wanted revenge, that would be one way to get it."

"Revenge?"

"You've always hated what I stood for."

He shook his head slowly, his eyes never once leaving hers. "I thought I hated it, but it was me I hated. That was one of the things I learned a while back. For lots of reasons, some of which became self-perpetuating, I was an unhappy kid. And I'm not saying that all changed overnight. I spent four years in the army. That gave me lots of time to think about lots of things. I was still thinking about them when I got back." His hands moved lightly just above her waist. "That last time when I saw you I was still pretty unsettled. You remember. You were sixteen."

The memory was a weight, bowing her head, and the next thing she knew she felt Carter's jaw against her crown, and he was saying very softly, "I treated you poorly then, too."

"That time was the worst. I was so unsure of myself anyway, and what you said—"

"Unsure of yourself?" His hands went still. "You weren't."

"I was."

"You didn't look it."

"I felt it. It was the second date I'd ever had." The words began to flow and wouldn't stop. "I didn't like the boy, and I didn't really want to go, but it was so important to me to be like my friends. They dated, so I wanted to date. We were going to a prom at his school, and I had to wear a formal dress. My mother had picked it out in the store, and it looked wonderful on her, but awful on me. I didn't have her face or her body or her coloring. But I put on the dress and the stockings and the matching shoes, and I let her do my hair and face. Then I stood on the front porch looking at my reflection in the window, trying to pull the dress higher and make it look better...and you came around the corner of the house. You told me that I could pull forever and it wouldn't do any good, because there was nothing there worth covering. You said—''

"Don't, Jessica—''

"You said that any man worth beans would be able to see that right off, but you told me that I probably didn't have anything to worry about, because you doubted anyone who would ask me out was worth beans. But that was no problem, either, you told me—''

"Please—''

"Because, you said, I was an uptight nobody, and the only thing I'd ever have to offer a man would be money. I could buy someone, you said. Money was power, you said, and then—''

"Jessica, don't—''

"And then you reached into your pocket, pulled out a dollar bill and stuffed it into my dress, and you said that I should try bribing my date and maybe he'd kiss me.''

She went quiet, slightly appalled that she'd spilled the whole thing and more than a little humiliated even seventeen years after the fact. But she couldn't have taken back the words if she'd wanted to, and she didn't have time to consider the damage she'd done before Carter took her face in his hands and turned it up.

"Did he kiss you?''

She shook her head as much as his hold would allow.

"Then I owe you for that, too,'' he whispered, and before she could begin to imagine what he had in mind, his mouth touched hers. She tired to pull back, but he held her, brushing his mouth back and forth over her lips until their stiffness eased, then taking them in a light kiss.

It didn't last long, but it left her stunned. Her breath came in shallow gasps, and for a minute she couldn't think. That was the minute when she might have identified what she felt as pleasure, but when her heart began to thud again and her mind started to clear, she felt only disbelief. "Why did you do that?'' she whispered, and lowered her eyes when disbelief gave way to embarrassment.

"I don't know.'' He certainly hadn't planned it. "I guess I wanted to. It felt right.''

"You shouldn't have,'' she said, and exerted pressure to lever herself away. He let her go. Immediately she felt the loss of his body heat and drew her blazer closer around her. Mustering shreds of dignity, she pushed her glasses up on her nose and raised her eyes to his. "I think we'd better get going. There's a lot to cover.''

She didn't wait for an answer, but moved off, walking steadily along the path that circled the rear of the house. She kept her head high and her shoulders straight, looking far more confident than she felt. Instinct told her that it was critical to pretend the kiss hadn't happened. She couldn't give it credence, couldn't let on she thought twice about it, or Carter would have a field day. She could just imagine the smug look on his face even now, which was why she didn't turn. She knew he was following, could hear the crunch of dried leaves under his shoes. No doubt he was thinking about what a lousy kisser she was.

Because he sure wasn't. He was an incredible kisser, if those few seconds were any indication of his skill. Not that she'd liked it. She couldn't possibly *like* Carter Malloy's kiss. But she'd been vulnerable at that moment. Her mind had been muddled. She was definitely going to have to get it together unless she wanted to make an utter fool of herself.

How to get it together, though, was a problem. She was walking through land that she loved and that, a year from then, wouldn't be hers, and she was being followed by a demon from her past who had materialized in the here and now as a gorgeous hunk of man. She had to think business, she decided. For all intents and purposes, in her dealings with Carter she was a businesswoman. That was all.

They walked silently on until the path opened into a clearing. Though the grass was just beginning to green up after the winter's freeze, the lushness of the spot as it would be in full spring or high summer was lost on neither of them. They had the memories to fill in where reality lay half-dormant.

Jessica stopped at the meadow's mouth. When Carter reached her side, she said, "Another grouping of homes should go here. It's so pretty, and it's already open. That means fewer trees destroyed. I want to disturb as little of the natural environment as possible."

"I understand," Carter said, and walked on past her into the meadow. He was glad he understood something. He sure didn't understand why he'd kissed her—or why he'd found it strangely sweet. Unable to analyze it just then, though, he strode along one side of the four-acre oval, stopping several times along the way to look around him from a particular spot. After standing for a time in deep concentration at the far end, he crossed back through the center.

And all the while, with nothing else to do and no excuse not to, Jessica studied him. Gorgeous hunk of man? Oh, yes. His clothes— heathery blazer, slate-colored slacks, crisp white shirt—were of fine quality and fitted to perfection, but the clothes didn't make him a gorgeous hunk. What made him that was the body beneath. He was broad shouldered, lean of hip and long limbed, but even then he wouldn't have been as spectacular if those features hadn't all worked together. His body flowed. His stride was smooth and confident, the proud set of his head perfectly comfortable on those broad shoulders, his expression male in a dark and mysterious way.

If he felt her scrutiny, it obviously didn't affect him at all. But then, she mused, he was probably used to the scrutiny of women. He was the type to turn heads.

With a sigh, she turned and started slowly back on the path. It was several minutes before Carter caught up with her. "What do you think?" she asked without looking at him.

"It would work."

"If you'd like more time there, feel free. You can meet me up at the house."

"Are you cold?" he asked, because she was still hugging the blazer around her.

"No. I'm fine."

He glanced back toward the meadow, "Well, so am I. This is just a preliminary walk-through. I've seen enough for now. What's next?"

"The pine grove."

That surprised him. "Over on the other side of the house?" When she nodded, he said, "Are you sure you want to build there?"

She looked up at him then. "I need a third spot. If you can think of someplace better, I'm open for suggestion."

Drudging up what he remembered of the south end of the property, he had to admit that the pine grove seemed the obvious choice. "But that will mean cutting. The entire area is populated with trees. There isn't any sizable clearing to speak of, not like at the duck pond or in the meadow." He shook his head. "I'd hate to have to take down a single one of those pines."

Jessica took in a deep breath and said sadly, "So now you know what I'm feeling about this project. It's a travesty, isn't it? But I have no choice." Determined to remain strong and in control, she turned her eyes forward and continued on.

For the first time, Carter did know what she felt. It was one thing when he was dealing with the idea—and his memory—of Crosslyn Rise, another when he was walking there, seeing, smelling and feeling the place, being surrounded by the natural majesty that was suddenly at the mercy of humans.

When they reached the pine grove, he was more acutely aware of that natural majesty than ever. Trees that had been growing for scores of years stretched toward the heavens as though they had an intimate connection with the place. Lower to the ground were younger versions, even lower than that shrubs that thrived in the shade. The carpeting underfoot was a tapestry of fine moss and pine needles. The pervasive scent was distinct and divine.

I have no choice, Jessica had said on a variation of the theme she'd repeated more than once, and he believed her. That made him all the more determined to design something special.

Jessica was almost sorry when they returned to the house. Yes, she was a little chilled, though she wouldn't have said a word to Carter lest, heaven forbid, he offer her his jacket, but the wide open spaces made his masculinity a little less commanding. Once indoors, there would be nothing to dilute it.

"You'll want to go through the house," she guessed, more nervous as they made their way across the back porch and entered the kitchen.

"I ought to," he said. "But that coffee smells good. Mind if I take a cup with me?"

She was grateful for something to do. "Cream or sugar?"

"Both."

As efficiently as possible, given the awkwardness stirring inside her, she poured him a mugful of the dark brew and prepared it as he liked it.

"You aren't having any?" he asked when she handed him the mug.

She didn't dare. Her hands were none too steady, and caffeine wouldn't help. "Maybe later," she said, and in as businesslike a manner as she could manage, led him off on a tour of the house.

The tour should have been fairly routine through the first floor, most of which Carter had seen at one time or another. But he'd never seen it before with a knowledge of architecture, and that made all the difference. High ceilings, chair rails and door moldings, antique mantelpieces on the three other first-floor fireplaces—he was duly impressed, and his comments to that extent came freely.

His observations were professional enough to lessen the discomfort Jessica felt when they climbed the grand stairway to the second floor. Still she felt discomfort aplenty, and she couldn't blame it on the past. Something had happened when Carter had kissed her. He'd awoken her to the man he was. Her awareness of him now wasn't of the boy she'd hated but of the man she wished she could. Because that man was calm, confident and commanding, all the things she wanted to be just then, but wasn't. In comparison to him, she felt inadequate, and, feeling inadequate, she did what she could to blend into the woodwork.

It worked just fine as they made their way from one end of the long hall down and around a bend to the other end. Carter saw the once-glorious master bedroom that hadn't been used in years; he saw a handful of other bedrooms, some with fireplaces, and more bathrooms than he'd ever dreamed his mother had cleaned. He took everything in, sipping his coffee as he silently made notes in his mind. Only when he reached the last bedroom, the one by the back stairs, did his interest turn personal.

"This is yours," he said. He didn't have to catch her nod to know that it was, but not even the uncomfortable look on her face could have kept him from stepping inside. The room was smaller than most of the others and decorated more simply, with floral wallpaper and white furniture.

Helpless to stop himself, he scanned the paired bookshelves to find foreign volumes and literary works fully integrated with works of popular fiction. He ran a finger along the dresser, passed a mirrored tray bearing a collection of antique perfume bottles and paused at a single framed photograph. It was a portrait of Jessica with her parents when she was no more than five years old; she looked exactly as he remembered her. It was a minute before he moved on to an old trunk, painted white and covered with journals, and an easy chair upholstered in the same faded pastel pattern as the walls. Then his gaze came to rest on the bed. It was a double bed, dressed in a nubby white spread with an array of lacy white pillows of various shapes and sizes lying beneath the scrolled headboard.

The room was very much like her, Carter mused. It was clean and pure, a little welcoming, a little off-putting, a little curious. It was the kind of room that hinted at exciting things in the nooks and crannies, just beyond the pristine front.

Quietly, for quiet was what the room called for, he asked, "Was this where you grew up?"

"No," she said quickly, eager to answer and return downstairs. "I moved here to save heating the rest of the house."

The rationale was sound. "This is above the kitchen, so it stays warm."

"Yes." She took a step backward in a none-too-subtle hint, but he didn't budge. In any other area of the house, she'd have gone anyway and left him to follow. But this was her room. She couldn't leave him alone here; that would have been too much a violation of her private space.

"I like the picture," he said, tossing his head toward the dresser. A small smile played at the corner of his mouth. "It brings back memories."

She focused on the photograph so that she wouldn't have to see his smile. "It's supposed to. That was a rare family occasion."

"What occasion?"

"Thanksgiving."

He didn't understand. "What's so rare about Thanksgiving?"

"My father joined us for dinner."

Carter studied her face, trying to decide if she was being facetious. He didn't think so. "You mean, he didn't usually do it?"

"It was hit or miss. If he was in the middle of something intense, he wouldn't take a break."

"Not even for Thanksgiving dinner?"

"No," she said evenly, and met his gaze. "Are you done here? Can we go down?"

He showed no sign of having heard her. "That's really incredible. I always pictured holidays at Crosslyn Rise as being spectacular—you know, steeped in tradition, everything warm and pretty and lavish."

"It was all that. But it was also lonely."

"Was that why you married so young?" When her eyes flew to his, he added, "My mother said you were twenty."

She wanted to know whether he'd specifically asked for the details and felt a glimmer of annoyance that he might be prying behind her back. Somehow, though, she couldn't get herself to be sharp with him. She was tired of sounding like a harpy when his interest seemed so innocent.

"Maybe I was lonely. I'm not sure. At the time I thought I was in love."

Obviously she'd changed her mind at some point, he mused. "How long did it last?"

"Didn't your mother tell you that?"

"She said it was none of my business, and it's not. If you don't want to talk about it, you don't have to.

Jessica rested against the doorjamb. She touched the wood, rubbed a bruised spot. "It's no great secret." It was, after all, a matter of public record. "We were divorced two years after we married."

"What happened?"

She frowned at the paint. "We were different people with different goals."

"Who was he?"

She paused. "Tom Chandler." Her arm stole around her middle. "You wouldn't have known him."

"Not from around here?"

She shook her head. "Saint Louis. I was a sophomore in college, he was a senior. He wanted to be a writer and figured that I'd support him. He thought we were rich." The irony of it was so strong that she was beyond embarrassment. Looking Carter in the eye, she said, "You were right. Bribery was about the only way I'd get a man. But it took me two years to realize that was what had done it."

Carter came forward, drawn by the pallor of her face and the haunted look in her eyes, either of which was preferable to the unemotional way she was telling him something that had to be horribly painful for her. "I don't understand."

"Tom fell in love with Crosslyn Rise. He liked the idea of living on an estate. He liked the idea of my father being a genius. He liked the idea of my mother devoting herself to taking care of my father, because Tom figured that was what I'd do for him. Mostly, he liked the idea of turning the attic into a garret and spending his days there reading and thinking and staring out into space."

"Then you tired of the marriage before he did?"

"I...suppose you could say that. He tired of me pretty quickly, but he was perfectly satisfied with the marriage. That was when I realized my mistake."

There was a world of hurt that she wasn't expressing, but Carter saw it in her eyes. It was all he could do not to reach out to help, but he wasn't sure his help would be welcome. So he said simply, "I'm sorry."

"Nothing to be sorry about." She forced a brittle smile. "Two years. That was all. I was finishing my undergraduate degree, so I went right on for my Ph.D., which was what I'd been planning to do all along."

"I'm sorry it didn't work out. Maybe if you'd had someone to help with the situation here—"

"Not Tom. Forget Tom. He was about as adept with finances as my mother and twice as disinterested."

"Still, it might not have been so difficult if you hadn't been alone."

She tore her eyes from his. "Yes, well, life is never perfect." She looked at the bright side, which was what she'd tried hard to do over the years. "I have a lot to be grateful for. I have my work. I love that, and I do it well. I've made good friends. And I have Crosslyn—" she caught herself and finished in a near whisper "—Crosslyn Rise." Uncaring whether he stayed in her room or not, she turned and went quickly down the back stairs.

When Carter joined her, Jessica was standing stiffly at the counter, taking a sip of the coffee she'd poured herself. Setting the mug down, she raised her chin and asked, "So, where do we go from here as far as this project is concerned?"

Carter would have liked to talk more about the legacy of her marriage, if only to exorcise that haunted look from her eyes. His good sense told him, though, that such a discussion was better saved for another time. He was surprised that she'd confided in him as much as she had. Friends did that. It was a good sign.

"Now you talk to me some more about what you want," he said. "But first I have to get my briefcase from the car. I'll be right back."

Left alone in the kitchen for those few short moments, Jessica took several long, deep breaths. She didn't seem able to do that when Carter was around. He was a physical presence, dominating whatever room he was in. But she couldn't say that the domination was deliberate—or offensive, for that matter. He was doing his best to be agreeable. It wasn't his fault that he was so tall, or that his voice had such resonance, or that he exuded an aura of power.

"Do you have the list?" he asked, striding back into the kitchen. When she nodded and pointed to a pad of paper waiting on the round oak table nearby, he set his briefcase beside it. Then he retrieved his coffee mug. "Mind if I take a refill?"

"Of course not." She reached for the glass carafe and proceeded to fix his coffee with cream and sugar, just as he'd had it before. When he protested that he could do it, she waved him away. She was grateful to be active and efficient.

Carrying both mugs, she led him to the table, which filled a semicircular alcove off the kitchen. The walls of the alcove were windowed, offering a view of the woods that had enchanted Jessica on many a morning. On this morning, she was too aware of Carter to pay much heed to the pair of cardinals decorating the Douglas fir with twin spots of red.

"Want to start from the top?" Carter asked, eyeing her list.

She did that. Point by point, she ran through her ideas. Most were ones she'd touched on before, but there were others, smaller thoughts—

ranging from facilities at the clubhouse to paint colors—that had come to her and seemed worth mentioning. She began tentatively and gained courage as she went.

Carter listened closely. He asked questions and made notes. Though he pointed out the downside of some of her ideas, not once did he make her feel as though something she said was foolish. Often he illustrated one point or another by giving examples from his own experience, and she was fascinated by those. Clearly he enjoyed his work and knew what he was talking about. By the time he rose to leave, she was feeling surprisingly comfortable with the idea of Carter designing the new Crosslyn Rise.

That comfort was from the professional standpoint.

From a personal standpoint, she was feeling no comfort at all. For no sooner had that low blue car of his purred down the driveway than she thought about his kiss. Her pulse tripped, her cheeks went pink, her lips tingled—all well after the fact. On the one hand, she was gratified that she'd had such control over herself while Carter had been there. On the other hand, she was appalled at the extent of her reaction now that he was gone.

Particularly since she hadn't liked his kiss.

But she had. She had. It had been warm, smooth, wet. And it had been short. Maybe that was why she'd liked it. It hadn't lasted long enough for her to be nervous or frightened or embarrassed. Nor had it lasted long enough to provide much more than a tempting sample of something new and different. She'd never been given a kiss like that before—not from a date, of which there hadn't been many of the kissing type, and certainly not from Tom. Tom had been as self-centered in lovemaking as he'd been in everything else. A kiss from Tom had been a boring experience.

Carter's kiss, short though it was, hadn't been boring at all. In fact, Jessica realized, she wouldn't mind experiencing it again—which was a *truly* dismaying thought. She'd never been the physical type, and to find herself entertaining physical thoughts about Carter Malloy was too much.

Chalking those thoughts up to a momentary mental quirk, she gathered her things together and headed for Cambridge.

The diversionary tactic worked. Not once while she was at work did she think of Carter, and it wasn't simply that she kept busy. She took time out late in the afternoon for a relaxed sandwich break with two male colleagues, then did some errands in the Square and even stopped at the supermarket on her way home—none of which were intellectually demanding activities. Her mind might have easily wandered, but it didn't.

No, she didn't think about Carter until she got home, and then, as though to make up for the hours before, she couldn't escape him. Every room in the house held a memory of his presence, some more so than others. Most intensely haunted were the kitchen and her bedroom, the two rooms in which she spent the majority of her at-home hours. Standing at the bedroom door as she had done when he'd been inside, sitting once again at the kitchen table, she saw him as he'd been, remembered every word he'd said, felt his presence as though he were there still.

It was the recency of his visit, she told herself, but the rationalization did nothing to dismiss the memories. By walking through her home, by looking at all the little things that were intimate to her, he had touched her private self.

She wanted to be angry. She tried and tried to muster it, but something was missing. There was no offense. She didn't feel violated, simply touched.

And that gave her even more to consider. The Carter she'd known as a kid had been a violater from the start; the Carter who had reentered her life wasn't like that at all. When the old Carter had come near, she'd trembled in anger, indignation and, finally, humiliation; when the new Carter came near, the trembling was from something else.

She didn't want to think about it, but there seemed no escape. No sooner would she immerse herself in a diversion than the diversionary shell cracked. Such was the case when she launched into her nightly workout in front of the VCR; rather than concentrate on the routine or the aerobic benefits of the exercise, she found herself thinking about body tone and wondering whether she looked better at thirty-three for the exercise she did, than she'd looked at twenty-five. And when she wondered why she cared, she thought of Carter.

When, sweaty and tired, she sank into a hot bath, she found her body tingling long after she should have felt pleasantly drowsy, and when she stopped to analyze those tingles, she thought of Carter.

When, wearing a long white nightgown with ruffles at the bodice, she settled into the bedroom easy chair, with a lapful of reading matter that should have captured her attention, her attention wandered to those things that Carter had seen and touched. She pictured him as he had stood that morning, looking tall and dark, uncompromisingly male, and curious about her. She spent a long time thinking about that curiosity, trying to focus in on its cause.

She was without conclusions when the phone rang by her bed. Startled, she picked it up after the first ring, but the sudden stretch sent the books on her lap sliding down the silky fabric of her gown to the floor. She made a feeble attempt to catch them at the same time that she offered a slightly breathless, "Hello?"

Carter heard that breathlessness and for an awful minute wondered if he'd woken her. A glance at his watch told him it was after ten. He hadn't realized it was so late. "Jessica? This is Carter." He paused. "Am I catching you at a bad time?"

Letting the books go where they would, she put a hand to her chest to still her thudding heart. "No. No. This is fine."

"I didn't wake you?"

"No. I was reading." Or trying to, she mused, but her mind didn't wander farther. It was waiting for Carter's next words. She couldn't imagine why he'd called, particularly at ten o'clock at night.

Carter wasn't sure, either. Nothing he had to say couldn't wait for another day or two, certainly for a more reasonable hour. But he'd been thinking about Jessica for most of the day. They had parted on good terms. He wanted to know whether those good terms still stood, or whether she'd been chastising herself for this, that and the other all day. And beyond that, he wanted to hear her voice.

Relieved now that he hadn't woken her, he leaned back against the strip of kitchen wall where the phone hung. "Did you get to school okay today?"

"Uh-huh."

"Everything go all right? I mean, I didn't get you going off on the wrong foot or anything, did I?"

She gave a shy smile that he couldn't possibly see, but it came though in her voice. "No. I was fine. How about you?"

"Great. It was a really good day. I think you bring me good luck."

She didn't believe that for a minute, but her smile lingered. "What happened?"

Carter was still trying to figure it out. "Nothing momentous. I spent the afternoon in the office working on other projects, and a whole bunch of little things clicked. It was one of those days when I felt really in tune with my work."

"Inspired?"

"Yeah." He paused, worried that she'd think he was simply trying to impress her. "Does that sound pretentious?"

"Of course not. It sounds very nice. We should all have days like that."

"Yours wasn't?"

She thought back on what she'd done since she'd seen him that morning. "It was," she said, but cautiously. "It's an odd time. I gave the final lecture to my German lit class, and I was really pleased with the way it went, but the meetings I had after that were frustrating."

Carter was just getting past the point of picturing her with her nose stuck in a book all day. He wanted to know more about what she did. "In what way?"

"At the end of the term, students get nervous. They're realizing that a good part of their grade is going to depend on a final exam, a term paper or both. If they go into these last two weeks with a solid average, they're worried about keeping it up. If they go in with a low average, they're desperate to raise it. Even the most laid-back of them get a little uptight."

"Didn't you when you were in school?"

"Sure. So I try to be understanding. It's mostly a question of listening to them and giving them encouragement. That's easy to do if I know the student. I can concentrate on his strengths and relate the class material to it. If I don't know the student, it's harder, sort of like stabbing in the dark at the right button to help the student make the connection."

Carter was quiet for a minute. Then he said, "I'm impressed. You're a dedicated professor, to put that kind of thought into interactions with students. The professors I studied under weren't like that. They were guarded, almost like they saw us as future competition, so they wanted us to learn, but not too much."

She knew some colleagues who were like that, and though she couldn't condone the behavior, she tried to explain it by saying, "You were older when you started college."

"Not that much. I was twenty-three."

"But you were wise in a worldly way that was probably intimidating."

A day or a week before, Carter might have taken the observation as an offense. That he didn't take it that way now was a comment on how far he'd come in terms of self-confidence where Jessica was concerned. It was also an indication of how far she'd come, her tone was gentle, conversational, which was how he kept his. "How did you know I was world wise at twenty-three?" She'd seen so little of him then.

"You were that way at seventeen, and you were very definitely intimidating."

He thought back to those years with an odd blend of nostalgia and self-reproach. "I tried to be. Lord, I tried. Intimidating people was about the only thing I was good at."

"You could have been good at other things. Look where you are now. That talent didn't suddenly come into being when you hit your twenties. But you let everyone think you had no brains."

"I thought it, too. I was messed up in so many other ways that no brains seemed part of the package."

Jessica wanted to ask him about being messed up. She wanted to know the why and how of it. She wanted to be able to make some sense of the person he'd been and relate it to the person he was now. Because this person was interesting. She could warm to this Carter as she would never have dreamed of doing to the one who had once been malicious.

The irony of it was that in some ways the new Carter was more dangerous.

"Are you still there?" he asked.

"Uh-huh," she answered as lightly as she could given the irregular skip of her pulse.

He figured he was either making her uncomfortable by talking about the past or boring her, and he didn't want to do either, not tonight, not when they finally seemed to be getting along. So he cleared his throat. "You're probably wondering why I called."

She was, now that he mentioned it. A man like Carter Malloy wouldn't call her just to talk. "I figured you'd get around to it in good time," she said lightly. She wanted him to know that she was taking the call in stride, just as she'd taken his kiss in stride. It wouldn't do for him to know that she was vulnerable where he was concerned.

"Well, now's the time. When I was driving back to town from Crosslyn Rise this morning, it occurred to me that it might help both of us if you were to see some of the other things I've done."

"I saw those sketches—"

"Not sketches. The real thing. I've done other projects similar in concept to the one you want done. If you were to see them in person, you might get a feeling for whether I'm the right man for this job."

Jessica felt something heavy settle around her middle. "You're having second thoughts about working here."

"It's not—"

"You can be honest," she said, tipping up her chin. "I'm not desperate. There are plenty of other architects."

"Jessica—"

"The only reason Gordon suggested you was because you were familiar with the Rise. He figured you'd be interested."

"I *am*," Carter said loudly. "Will you please be quiet and let me speak?" When he didn't hear anything coming from the other end of the line, he breathed, "Thank you. My Lord, Jessica, when you get going, you're like a steamroller."

"I don't want to play games. That's all. If you don't want this job, I'd appreciate your coming right out and saying so, rather than beating around the bush."

"I *want* this job. I *want* this job. How many times do I have to say it?"

More quietly she said, "If you want it, why were you looking to give me an out?"

"Because I want you to *choose* me," he blurted. Standing well away from the wall now, he ran his fingers through his hair. "I'd like to feel," he said slowly, "that you honestly want me to do the work. That you're *enthusiastic* about my doing it. That it isn't just a case of Gordon foisting me on you, or your not having the time or energy to interview others."

She was thinking that he wasn't such a good businessman after all. "You're an awful salesman. You should be tooting your own horn, not warning me off. Are you this way with all your clients?"

"No. This case is different. You're special."

His words worked wonders on the heaviness inside her. She felt instantly lighter, and it didn't matter that he'd meant the words in the most superficial of ways. What he'd said made her feel good.

"Okay," she breathed. "I'm sorry I interrupted."

Stunned by the speed and grace of her capitulation, Carter drew a blank. For the life of him, he couldn't remember what had prompted the set-to. "Uh..."

"You were saying that maybe I ought to see some of the things you've done."

Gratefully he picked up the thread. "The best ones—the ones I like best—are north of you, up along the coast of Maine. The farthest is three hours away. They could all be seen in a single day." He hesitated for a second. "I was thinking that if you'd like, we could drive up together."

It was Jessica's turn to be stunned. The last thing she'd expected was that Carter would want to spend a day with her, even on business. Her words come slowly and skeptically. "Isn't that above and beyond the call of duty?"

"What do you mean?"

"You don't have to go to such extremes. I can drive north myself."

"Why should you have to go alone if I'm willing to take you?"

"Because that would be a whole day out of your time."

"So what else is my time for?"

"Working."

"I get plenty of work done during the week. So do you, and you said you were coming up on exams. I was thinking of taking a Sunday when both of us can relax."

That was even *more* incredible. "I can't ask you to take a whole Sunday to chauffeur me around!"

"Why not?"

"Because Sundays are personal, and this would be business."

"It could be fun, too. There are some good restaurants. We could stop and get something to eat along the way."

Jessica returned her hand to her chest in an attempt to slow the rapid beat of her heart.

"Or you could shop," he went on. "There are some terrific boutique areas. I wouldn't mind waiting."

She was utterly confused. "I couldn't ask you to do that."

"You don't have to ask. I'm offering." He was struck by an afterthought that hardened his voice. "Unless you'd rather not be with me for that length of time."

"That's not it."

"Then what is?"

"*Me*. Wouldn't you rather not be with *me* for that length of time? You'll be bored to tears. I'm not the most dynamic person in the world."

"Who told you that?"

"You. When I was ten, you caught me sitting on the rocks, looking out to sea. You asked what I saw, and when I wouldn't answer, you said I was dull and pathetic."

He felt like a heel. "You were only ten, and I was full of it."

"But Tom agreed. He thought I was boring, too. I've never been known as the life of the party."

"Sweetheart, a man can only take being with the life of the party for so long. Let me tell you, *that* can get boring. You, on the other hand, have a hell of a lot going for you." He let the flow of his thoughts carry him quickly on. "You read, you think, you work. Okay, so you don't open up easily. That doesn't mean you're boring. All it means is that a man has to work a little harder to find out what's going on in that pretty head of yours. I'm willing to work a little harder. I think the reward will be worth it. So you'd be doing me a favor by agreeing to spend a Sunday with me driving up the coast." He took a quick breath, not allowing himself the time to think about all he'd said. "What'll it be— yes or no?"

"Yes," Jessica said just as quickly and for the very same reason.

5

Jessica had a dream that night. It brought her awake gradually, almost reluctantly, to a dark room and a clock that read 2:24 a.m. Her skin was warm and slightly damp. Her breath was coming in short whispers. The faint quivering deep inside her was almost a memory, but not quite.

She stretched. When the quivering lingered, she curled into a ball to cradle it, because there was something very nice about the feeling. It was satisfying, soft and feminine.

Slowly, even more slowly than she'd awoken, she homed in on the subject of her dream. Her reluctance this time had nothing to do with preserving a precious feeling. As Carter Malloy's image grew clearer in her mind, the languorous smile slipped from her face. In its place came a look of dismay.

Jessica had never had an erotic dream before. Never. Not when she'd been a teenager first becoming aware of her developing body, not when she'd been dating Tom, not in the long years following the divorce. She wasn't blind to a good-looking man; she could look at male beauty, recognize it, admire it for what it was. But it had never excited her in a physical sense. It had never buried itself in her subconscious and come forward to bring her intense pleasure in the middle of the night.

Flipping to her other side, she shielded her face with her arm, as if to hide her embarrassment from a horde of grinning voyeurs masked by the dark.

Carter Malloy. Carter Malloy, beautifully naked and splendidly built. Carter Malloy, coming to her, kissing her, stroking her. He'd been exquisitely gentle, removing her clothes piece by piece, loving her with his hands and his mouth, driving her to a fever pitch that she'd never experienced before.

With a moan, she flipped back to the other side and huddled under the covers, but the sheet that half covered her face couldn't blot out the persistent images in her mind. Carter Malloy, kissing her everywhere, *everywhere,* while he offered his own body for her eager hands and lips. In her dream, he was large and leanly muscled, textured at some spots, smooth and vulnerable at others, very, very hard and needy at still others.

Sitting bolt upright in bed, she turned on the lamp, hugged her knees to her chest and worked to ground herself among the trappings of the old and familiar. To some extent she was successful. At least the quivering inside her eased. What she was left with, though, was an undertone of frustration that was nearly as unwelcome.

She couldn't understand it. She just wasn't a passionate person. Lovemaking with Tom had been a part of marriage that she'd simply accepted. Occasionally she'd enjoyed it. Occasionally she'd even had an orgasm, though she could count the number of times that had happened on the fingers of one hand. And she hadn't minded that it was so infrequent. Sex was a highly overrated activity, she had long since decided.

That didn't explain why she'd dreamed what she did, or why the dream had brought her to a sweet, silent climax.

Mortified anew, she pressed her eyes to her knees. What if someone had seen her? What if someone had been watching her sleep? Not that anyone would have or could have seen her, still she wondered if she had made noise, or writhed about.

It was something she'd eaten, she decided. Certain foods were known to stir up the senses. Surely that was what had brought on the erotic interlude.

But she went over every morsel of food that had entered her mouth that day—easy to do, since she was neither a big eater nor an adventurous one—and she couldn't single out anything that might have inspired eroticism.

Maybe, she mused, it had to do with her own body. Maybe she was experiencing a hormonal shift, maybe even related to menopause. But she was only thirty-three! She wasn't ready for menopause!

The hormonal theory, though, had another twist. They said that women reached their peak of sexual interest at a later age than men. Women in their thirties and forties were supposed to be hot—at least, that was what the magazines said, though she'd always before wondered whether the magazines said it simply because it was what their thirty- and forty-year-old readers wanted to hear.

Maybe there was some truth to it, though. Maybe she was developing needs she'd never had before. She had been a long time without a man, better than eleven years. Maybe the dream she'd had was her body's way of saying that it was in need. Maybe that need even had to do with the biological clock. Maybe her body was telling her that it was time to have a baby.

Throwing the covers back, she scrambled from the bed, grabbed her glasses and, barefoot, half walked, half ran down the back steps to the kitchen. Soon after, she was sitting cross-legged on one of the chairs with an open tin of Poppycock nestled in her lap.

Poppycock was her panacea. When she'd been little, she had hidden it in her room, because her mother had been convinced that the caramel coating on the popcorn would rot her teeth. Now that her mother wasn't around to worry, Jessica kept the can within easy reach. It wasn't that she pigged out on a regular basis, and since she didn't have a weight problem, it probably wouldn't have mattered if she had, but Poppycock was a treat. It was light and fun, just the thing she went for when she was feeling a little down.

She wasn't feeling down now, but frustrated and confused. She was also feeling angry, angry at Carter, because no matter how long she made her list of possible excuses for what had happened, she knew it wasn't coincidence that had set Carter Malloy's face and body at the center of her dream. She cursed him for being handsome and sexy, cursed herself for being vulnerable, cursed Crosslyn Rise for aging and putting her into a precarious position.

One piece of popcorn followed another into her mouth. In time, she helped herself to a glass of milk, and by the time that was gone, it was well after three. Having set her mind to thinking about the material she had to cover in her Russian seminar that afternoon, she'd calmed down some. With a deep, steady breath, she rose from the chair, put the empty glass into the sink and the tin of Poppycock into the pantry, and went back to bed.

When Jessica had agreed to drive north with Carter, he had wanted to do it that Sunday for the sake of getting her feedback as soon as possible. She had put him off for a week, knowing that she had far too much work to do in preparation for exams, to take off for the whole day. In point of fact, the following Sunday wouldn't be much better; though she had teaching assistants to grade exams, she always did her share, and she liked it that way.

But Carter was eager, and she knew that she could plan around the time. So they had settled on the day, and he had promised to call her the Saturday before to tell her when he would be picking her up. She wasn't scheduled to hear from him until then, and in the aftermath of that embarrassingly carnal dream, she was grateful for the break. Given twelve days' time, she figured she could put her relationship with him into its proper perspective.

That perspective, she decided had to be business, which was what she thought about during those days when she had the free time to let her mind wander. She concentrated on the business of converting Crosslyn Rise into something practical and productive—and acclimating herself to that conversion.

To that end, she called Nina Stone and arranged to meet her for dinner at a local seafood restaurant, a chic establishment overlooking the water on the Crosslyn Rise end of town. The two had met the year before, browsing in a local bookstore, and several months after that, Jessica had approached her about selling Crosslyn Rise. Though Nina hadn't grown up locally, she'd been working on the North Shore for five years, and during that time she had established herself as an aggressive broker with both smarts and style. She was exactly the kind of woman Jessica had always found intimidating, but strangely, they'd hit it off. Jessica could see Nina's tough side, but there was a gentler, more approachable side as well. That side came out when they were together and Nina let down her defenses.

Despite her reputation, despite the aggressiveness Jessica knew was there, Nina had never pressured her. She was like Carter in the sense that, having come from nothing, she was slightly in awe of Crosslyn Rise—which meant that she was in no rush to destroy it.

For that reason among others, Jessica felt comfortable sharing the latest on the Rise with her.

"A condominium community?" Nina asked warily. She was a small woman, slender and pixieish, which made her assertiveness in business somewhat unexpected and therefore all the more effective. "I don't know, Jessica. It would be a shame to do that to such a beautiful place."

"Condominium communities can be beautiful."

"But Crosslyn Rise is that much more so."

Jessica sighed. "I can't afford it, Nina. You've known that for a while. I can't afford to keep it as it is, and you haven't had any luck finding a buyer."

"The market stinks," Nina said, sounding defensive, looking apologetic. "I'm selling plenty on the low and middle end of the scale, but precious little at the top." She grew more thoughtful. "Condos are going, though, I do have to admit. Particularly in this area. There's something about the ocean. Young professionals find it romantic, older ones find it restful." She paused to sip her wine. Her fingers were slender, her nails polished red to match her suit. "Tell me more. If this was Gordon Hale's idea, I would guess that it's financially sound. The man is a rock. You say he's putting together a consortium?"

"Not yet, but he will when it's time. Right now, I'm working with someone to define exactly what it is that I want."

"Someone?"

After the slightest hesitation, she specified, "An architect."

Nina studied her for a minute. "You look uncomfortable."

Jessica pushed her glasses up on her nose. "No."

"Is this architect a toughie?"

"No. He's very nice. His name is Carter Malloy." She watched for a reaction. "Ever heard of him?"

"Sure," Nina said without blinking an eye. "He's with Malloy and Goodwin. He's good."

Jessica felt a distant pride. "You're familiar with his work, then?"

"I saw something he did in Portsmouth not long ago. Portsmouth isn't my favorite place, but this was beautiful. He had converted a textile mill into condos. Did an incredible job combining old and new." She frowned, then grinned at the same time. "If I recall correctly, the man himself is beautiful."

"I don't know as I'd call him beautiful," Jessica answered, but a little too fast, and that roused Nina's interest.

"What would you call him?"

She thought for a minute. "Pleasant looking."

"Not the man I remember. Pleasant looking is someone you'd pass by and smile at kindly. A beautiful man stirs stronger emotions. Carter Malloy was ruggedly masculine—at least, in the picture I saw."

"He is masculine looking, I suppose."

Nina came forward, voice lowered but emphatically chiding. "You suppose, my foot! I can't believe you're as immune to men as you let on. One lousy husband can't have neutered you, and you're not exactly over the hill. You have years of good fun still ahead, if you want to make something of them." She raised her chin. "Who was the last man you dated?"

Jessica shrugged.

"Who?" Nina prodded, but good-naturedly as she settled back in her seat. "You must remember."

"It's a difficult question. How do you define a date? If it's going somewhere with a man, I do that all the time with colleagues."

"That's not what I mean, and you know it. I'm talking about the kind of date who picks you up at your house, takes you out for the evening, kisses you when he brings you home, maybe even stays the night."

"Uh, I'm not into that."

"Sleeping with men?"

"Are you?" Jessica shot back, in part because she was uncomfortable doing the answering and in part because she wanted to know. She and Nina had become friends in the past year, but the only thing Jessica knew about her social life was that she rarely spent a Saturday night at home.

Nina was more amused than anything. "I'm not into sleeping around, but I do enjoy men. There are some nice ones around who are good for an evening's entertainment. Since I'm not looking to get married, I don't threaten them."

"You don't want to get married?"

"Honey, do I have the time?"

"Sure. If you want."

"What I want," Nina said, sitting back in her chair, looking determined but vulnerable, "is to make good money for myself. I want my own business."

"I thought you were making good money now."

"Not enough."

"Are you in need?"

"I've been in need since the day I learned that my mother prostituted herself to put milk on our table."

Jessica caught in a breath. "I'm sorry, Nina. I didn't know."

"It's not something I put on the multiple-listings chart," she quipped, but her voice was low and sober. "That was in Omaha. I have a fine life for myself here, but I won't ever sell myself like my mother did. So I need money of my own. I refuse to ever ask a man for a cent, and I won't have to, if I play my cards right."

"You're doing so well."

"I could be doing even better if I went out on my own. But I'll have to hustle."

Jessica was getting a glimpse of the driven Nina, the one who was restless, whose mind was always working, whose heart was prepared to sacrifice satisfaction for the sake of security. Jessica found it sad. "But you're only thirty."

"And next year I'll be thirty-one, and thirty-two the year after that. The way I figure it, if I work my tail off now and go independent within a year, by the time I'm thirty-five, I can be the leading broker in the area, with a fully trained staff, to boot. Maybe then I'll be able to ease up a little, even think of settling down." She gave a crooked smile. "Assuming there are any worthwhile men out there then."

"If there are, you'll find them," Jessica said, and felt a shaft of the same kind of envy she'd known as a child, when all the other girls were prettier and more socially adept than she. Nina had short, shiny hair, flawless skin and delicate bones. She dressed on the cutting edge between funky and sophisticated and had a personality to match. "You draw people like honey draws bees."

"Lucky for me, or I'd be a loss at what I do." She paused to give Jessica a look that was more cautious than clever. "So I've made the ultimate confession. And you? Do you ever think of settling down?"

Jessica smiled and shook her head. "I don't attract men the way you do."

"Why not?" Nina asked, perfectly serious. "You're smart and pretty and gainfully employed. Aren't those the things men look for nowadays?

Pretty. Carter had used that word. *A man has to work a little harder to find out what's going on in that pretty head of yours.* It was an expression, of course, not to be taken seriously. "Men look for eye-catching women like you."

"And once they've done the eye-catching, they take a closer look and see the flaws. No man would want me right now. I'm too hard. But you're softer. You're established. You're confident in ways I'm not."

"What ways?" Jessica shot back in disbelief.

"Financial. You have Crosslyn Rise."

"Not for long," came the sad reminder.

While the waiter served their lobsters, Nina considered that. As soon as he left, she began to speak again. "You're still a wealthy woman, Jessica. The problem is fluidity of funds. You don't have enough to support the Rise because your assets are tied up *in* the Rise. If you go through with the project you've mentioned, you'll emerge with a comfortable nest egg. Besides, you don't have the fear—" she paused to tie the lobster bib around her neck "—of being broke that I have. You're financially sound, and you're independent. That gives you a head start in the peace-of-mind department. So all you have to do—" she tore a bright red feeler from the steaming lobster "—is to find a terrific guy, settle down somewhere within commuting distance of Harvard and have babies."

"I don't know," Jessica murmured. She was looking at her lobster as though she weren't sure which part to tackle first. "Things are never that simple."

"You watch. Things will get easier when this business with the Rise is settled." That said, she began to suck on the feeler.

Jessica, too, paused to eat, but she kept thinking about Nina's statement. After several minutes, she asked, "Are we talking about the same 'things'?"

"Men. We're talking about men."

"But what does my settling the Rise have to do with men?"

"You'll be freer. More open to the idea of a relationship." When Jessica's expression said she still didn't make the connection, Nina said, "In some respects, you've been wedded to the Rise. No—" she held up a hand "—don't take this the wrong way. I'm not being critical. But in the time I've known you, I've formed certain impressions. Crosslyn Rise is your haven. You've lived there all your life. Even when you married, you lived there."

"Tom wanted it."

"I'm sure he did. Still, you lived there, and when the marriage fell apart, he left and you were alone there again."

"I wasn't alone. My parents were there."

"But you're alone now, and you're still there. Crosslyn Rise is like a companion."

"It's a house," Jessica protested.

But Nina had a point to make. "A house with a presence of its own. When you're there, do you feel alone?"

"No."

"But you should—not that I'm wishing loneliness on you, but man wasn't put on earth to live in solitude."

"I'm with people all day. I like being alone at night."

"Do you?" she asked, arching a delicately shaped brow. "I don't. But then, my place isn't steeped in the kind of memories that Crosslyn Rise is. If I were to come home and be enveloped by a world of memories, I probably wouldn't feel alone, either." She stopped talking, poked at the lobster with her fork for a distracted minute, then looked up at Jessica. "Once Crosslyn Rise is no longer yours in the way that it's always been, you may need something more."

Jessica shot her a despairing look. "Nothing like the encouragement of a friend."

"But it *is* encouragement. The change will be good for you. More so than any other person I know, you've had a sameness to your life. Coming out from the shadow of Crosslyn Rise will be exciting."

The image of the shadow stuck in Jessica's mind. The more she mulled it over, the more she realized that it wasn't totally bizarre. "Do you think I hide behind the Rise?" It was a timid question, offered to a friend with the demand for an honest answer.

Nina gave it as she saw it. "To some extent. Where your work is concerned, you've been as outgoing as anyone else. Where your personal life is concerned, you've fallen back on the Rise, just because it's always been there. But you can stand on your own in any context, Jessica. If you don't know that now, you will soon enough."

Soon enough wasn't as soon as Jessica wanted. At least, that was what she was thinking the following Sunday morning as she dressed to spend the day driving north with Carter. He'd called her the morning before to ask if eight was too early to come. It wasn't; she was an early riser. Her mind was freshest during those first postdawn hours. She did some of her most productive work then.

She didn't feel particularly productive on Sunday morning, though. Nor, after mixing, matching and discarding four different outfits did she feel particularly fresh. She couldn't decide what to wear, because the occasion was strange. She and Carter certainly weren't going on a date. This was business. Still, he'd mentioned stopping for something to eat, maybe even shopping, and those weren't strictly business ventures. A business suit was too formal, jeans too casual, and she didn't want to wear a teaching ensemble, because she was *tired* of wearing teaching ensembles.

At length, she decided on a pair of gabardine slacks and a sweater she'd bought in the Square that winter. The sweater was the height of style, the saleswoman had told her, but Jessica had bought it because it was slouchy and comfortable. For the first time, she was glad it was stylish, too. She was also glad it was a pale gray tweed, not so much because it went with her eyes but because it went with the slacks, which, being black, were more sophisticated than some of her other things.

For a time, she distracted herself wondering why she wanted to look sophisticated. She should look like herself, she decided, which was more down-to-earth than sophisticated. But that didn't stop her from matching the outfit up with shiny black flats, from dusting the creases of her eyelids with mocha shadow, from brushing her hair until it shone and then coiling it into a neat twist at the nape of her neck.

She was a bundle of nerves by the time Carter arrived, and the situation wasn't helped by his appearance. He looked wonderful—newly showered and shaved, dressed in a burgundy sweater and light gray corduroy pants.

Taking her heavy jacket from her, he stowed it in the trunk of the car with his own. He held the door while she slipped into the passenger's seat, then circled the car and slid behind the wheel.

"I should warn you," Jessica said when he started the car, "that I'm a terrible passenger. If you have any intention of speeding, you'll have a basket case on your hands."

"Me? Speed?"

Without looking at him, she sensed his grin. "I can remember a certain squealing of tires."

"Years and years ago, and if it'll put your mind at ease, the last accident I had was when I was nineteen," Carter answered with good humor, and promptly stepped on the gas. He didn't step on it far, only enough to maintain the speed limit once they'd reached the highway, and not once did he feel he was holding back. Sure, there were times when he was alone in the car and got carried away by the power of the engine, but he wasn't a reckless driver. He certainly didn't vent his anger on the road as he used to do.

But then, he didn't feel the kind of anger at the world that he used to feel. He rarely felt anger at all—frustration, perhaps, when a project that he wanted didn't come through, or when one that did wasn't going right, or when one of the people under him messed up, or when a client was being difficult—but not anger. And he wasn't feeling any of those things at the moment. He'd been looking forward to this day. He was feeling lighthearted and refreshed, almost as though the whole world was open to him just then.

He took his eyes from the road long enough to glance at Jessica. Her image was already imprinted on his mind, put there the instant she'd opened her front door, but he wanted a moment of renewed pleasure.

She looked incredibly good, he thought, and it wasn't simply a matter of having improved with age. He'd noted that improvement on the two other occasions when he'd seen her, but seeing her today took it one step further. She was really pretty—adorable, he wanted to say, because the small, round glasses sitting on her nose had that effect on her straight features, but her outfit was a little too serious to be called adorable. He liked the outfit. It was subtle but stylish, and seemed perfectly suited to who she was. He was pleased to have her in the car with him. She added the class that he never quite believed he'd acquired.

"Comfortable?" he asked.

She darted him a quick glance. "Uh-huh."

He let that go for several minutes, then asked, "How are exams going?"

"Pretty well," she said on an up note.

"You sound surprised."

"I never know what to expect. There have been years when it's been one administrative foul-up after another—exams aren't printed on time, or they're delivered to the wrong place, that kind of thing."

"At Harvard?" he teased.

She took his teasing with a lopsided smile. "At Harvard. This year, the Crimson has done itself proud."

"I'm glad of that for your sake."

"So am I," she said with a light laugh, then sobered. "Of course, now the rush begins to get things graded and recorded. Graduation isn't far off. The paperwork has to be completed well before then."

"Do you go to graduation?"

"Uh-huh."

"Must be...uplifting."

Her laugh was more of a chuckle this time, and a facetious one at that. Carter took pleasure in the sound. It said that she didn't take herself or her position too seriously, which was something he needed to know, given all the years he'd assumed she was stuck-up. She didn't seem that way, now. More, she didn't seem conscious of any social difference between them. He was convinced that the more he was with her, architect to client, the less she'd think back on the past, and that was what he wanted.

He wanted even more, though. Try as he might, he couldn't forget the time he'd kissed her. It had been an impulsive moment, but it had stuck in his mind, popping up to taunt him when he least expected it.

Jessica was, he decided during one of those times, the rosebud that hadn't quite bloomed. Having been married, she'd certainly been touched, but Carter would put money on the fact that her husband hadn't lit any fires in her. Her mouth was virginal. So was her body, the way she held it, not frightened so much as unsure, almost naive.

Carter had never been a despoiler of virgins. Even in his wildest days, he'd preferred women who knew the score. Tears over blood-stained sheets or unwanted pregnancies or imagined promises weren't his style. So he'd gone with an increasingly savvy woman—exactly the kind who now left him cold.

Kissing Jessica, albeit briefly, hadn't left him cold. He'd felt warm all over, then later, when he'd had time to remember the details of that kiss, tight all over. It amazed him still, it really did. That Jessica Crosslyn, snotty little prude that she'd been, should turn him on was mind-boggling.

But she did turn him on. Even now, with his attention on driving and the gearshift and a console between them, he was deeply aware of her— of the demure way she crossed her legs and the way that caused her slacks to outline shapely thighs, of the neat way her hands lay in her lap, fingers slender and feminine, of the loose way her sweater fell, leaving an alarmingly seductive hint of her breasts beneath. Even her hair, knotted with such polish, seemed a parody of restraint. So many things about her spoke of a promise beneath the facade. And she seemed totally unaware of it.

Maybe it was his imagination. Maybe the sexy things he was seeing were simply things that had changed in her, and it was his lecherous mind that was defining them as sexy. He saw women often, but it had been a while since he'd slept with one. Maybe he was just horny.

If that was true, of course, he could have remedied the situation through tried and true outlets. But he wasn't interested in those outlets. He wasn't running for any outlet at all. There was a sweetness to the arousal Jessica caused; there was something different and special about the tightness in his groin. He wasn't exactly sure where it would take him, but he wasn't willing it away just yet.

"You got a vote of confidence from a friend of mine," Jessica told him as they safely sped north. "She said she'd seen a project you did in Portsmouth."

"Harborside? I was thinking we'd hit that last, on the way home."

"She was impressed with it."

He shrugged. "It's okay, but it's not my favorite."

"What is?"

"Cadillac Cove. I hate the name, but the complex is special."

"Who decides on the name?"

"The developer. I just do the designs."

Jessica had been wondering about that. "Just the designs? Is your job done when the blueprints are complete?"

"Sometimes yes, sometimes no. It depends on the client. Some pay for the blueprints and do everything else on their own. Others pay me to serve as an advisor, in which case I'm involved during the actual building. I like it that way—" he speared her with a cautioning look "—and it has nothing to do with money. Moneywise, my time's better spent working at a drafting table. But there's satisfaction in being at the site. There's satisfaction seeing a concept take form. And there's peace of mind knowing that I'm available if something goes wrong."

"Do things go wrong often? I've heard some nightmarish stories. Are they true?"

"Sometimes." He curved his long fingers more comfortably around the wheel. "Y'see, there's a basic problem with architectural degrees. They fail to require internships in construction. Most architects and would-be architects see themselves as a step above. They're the brains behind the construction job, so they think, but they're wrong. They may be the inspiration, and the brains behind the overall plan, but the workmen themselves, the guys with the hammers and nails, are the ones with the know-how. The average architect doesn't have any idea how to build a house. So, sometimes the average architect draws things into a blueprint that can't possibly be built. Forget things that don't look good. I'm talking about sheer physical impossibilities."

A bell was ringing in Jessica's mind. "Didn't Gordon say you had hands-on building experience?"

"I spent my summers during college working on construction."

"You knew all along you wanted to be an architect?"

"No." He smirked. "I knew I needed money to live on, and construction jobs paid well." The smirk faded. "But that was how I first became interested in architecture. Blueprints intrigued me. The overall designs intrigued me. The guys who stood there in their spiffy suits, wearing hardhats, intrigued me." He chuckled. "So did the luxury cars they drove. And they all drive them. Porsches, Mercedes sportsters, BMWs—this Supra is modest compared to my colleagues' cars."

"So why don't you have a Porsche?"

"I was asking myself that same question the other day when my partner showed me his new one."

"What's the answer?"

"Money. They're damned expensive."

"You're doing as well as your partner."

He shrugged. "Maybe I don't trust myself not to scratch it up. Or it could be stolen. I don't have a secured garage space. I park in a narrow alley behind my building." He pursed his lips and thought for a minute before finally saying in a quieter voice, "I think I'm afraid that if I buy a Porsche, I'll believe that I've made it, and that's not true. I still have a ways to go."

Jessica was reminded of Nina, who defined happiness as a healthy bank account. Instinctively she knew that wasn't the case with Carter. He wasn't talking about making it economically, but professionally.

Maybe even personally. But that was a guess. She didn't know anything of his hopes and dreams.

On that thought, she lapsed into silence. Though she was curious, she didn't have the courage to suddenly start asking him about hopes and dreams, so she gave herself up to the smooth motion of the car and the blur of the passing landscape. The silence was comfortable, and surprising in that Jessica had always associated silence with solitude. Usually when she was with a man in a nonacademic setting, she felt impelled to talk, and since she wasn't the best conversationalist in the world, she wound up feeling awkward and inadequate.

She didn't feel that way now. The miles that passed beneath the wheels of the car seemed purpose enough. Moreover, if Carter wanted to talk, she knew he would. He wasn't the shy type—which was really funny, the more she thought of it. She'd always gravitated toward the shy type, because with the shy type she felt less shy herself. But in some ways it was easier being with Carter, because at any given time she knew where she stood.

At that moment in time, she knew that he was as comfortable with the silence as she was. His large hands were relaxed on the wheel, his legs sprawled as much as the car would allow. His jaw—square, she noted, like his chin—was set easily, as were his shoulders. He made no effort to speak, other than to point out something about a sign or a building they passed that had a story behind it, but when the tale was told, he was content to grow quiet again.

They drove straight for nearly four hours—with Carter's occasional apology for the lengthy drive, and a single rest stop—to arrive shortly before noon at Bar Harbor.

The drive was worth it. "I'm impressed," Jessica said sincerely when Carter had finished showing her around Cadillac Cove. Contrary to Crosslyn Rise, the housing was all oceanfront condominiums, grouped in comfortable clusters that simultaneously managed to hug the shore and echo the grace of nearby Cadillac Mountain. "Is it fully sold?"

He nodded. "Not all of the units are occupied year-round. This far north, they wouldn't necessarily be. A lot of them are owned on a time-sharing plan, and I think one or two are up for resale, but it's been a profitable venture for the developer."

"And for you."

"I was paid for my services as an architect, and I've cashed in on the praise that the complex has received, but I didn't have a financial stake in the project the way I might with Crosslyn Rise."

"Has Gordon talked with you more about that?"

"No. How about you?"

She shook her head. "I think he's starting to put feelers out, but he doesn't want to line up investors until we give him something concrete to work with."

Carter liked the "we" sound. "Does he work with a list of regular investors?"

"I don't really know." Something on his face made her say, "Why?"

"Because I know of a fellow who may be interested. His name's Gideon Lowe. I worked with him two years ago on a project in the Berkshires, and we've kept in touch. He's an honest guy, one of the best builders around, and whether or not he serves as the contractor for Crosslyn Rise, he may want to invest in it. He's been looking for something sound. Crosslyn Rise is sound."

"So you say."

"So I *know*. Hey, I wouldn't be investing my own money in it if it weren't." Without skipping a beat, he said, "I'm starved. Want to get something to eat?"

It was a minute before she made the transition from business to pleasure, and it was just as lucky she didn't have time to think about it. The less she thought, the less nervous she was. "Uh...sure."

He took her hand. "Come on. There's a place not far from here that has the best chowder on the coast."

Chowder sounded fine to Jessica, who couldn't deny the slight chill of the ocean air. Her jacket helped, as did his hand. It encircled hers in a grip that was firm and wonderfully warm.

The chowder was as good as he'd boasted it would be, though Jessica knew that some of its appeal, at least, came from the pier-front setting and the company. Along with the chowder, they polished off spinach salads and a small loaf of homemade wheat bread. Then they headed back to the car and made for the next stop on Carter's list.

Five stops—three for business, two for pleasure—and four hours later, they reached Harborside. As he'd done at each of the other projects they'd seen, Carter showed her around, giving her a brief history of the setting and how it had come to be developed, plus mention of his feelings about the experience. And as he'd done at each of the other projects, he stopped at the end to await her judgment.

"It's interesting," she said this time. "The concept—converting a mill into condominiums—limits things a little, but you've stretched those limits with the atrium. I love the atrium."

Carter felt as though he were coming to know her through her facial expressions alone, and her facial expression now, serious and somewhat analytical, told him that while she might admire the atrium, she certainly didn't love it. "It's okay, Jessica," he teased. He felt confident enough, based on her earlier reactions, to say, "You can be blunt."

She kept her eyes on the building, which was across the street from where they were standing. "I am being blunt. Given what you had to start with, this is really quite remarkable."

"Remarkable as in wildly exciting and dramatic?"

"Uh, not dramatic. Impressive."

"But you wouldn't want to live here."

"I didn't say that."

"Would you?"

Looking up, she caught the mischievous sparkle in his eye. It sparkled right through her in a way that something mischievous shouldn't have sparkled, but she didn't look away. She didn't want him to know how wonderfully warm he was making her feel by standing so close. "I think," she conceded a bit wryly, "that I'd rather live at Cadillac Cove."

"Or Riverside," he added, starting to grin in his own pleasure at the delightfully feminine flush on her cheeks. "Or the Sands."

"Or Walker Place," she tacked on, finishing the list of the places they'd visited. "Okay, this is my least favorite. But it's still good."

"Does that mean I have the job?"

Her brows flexed in an indulgent frown that came and went. "Of course, you have the job. Why do you ask?"

"Wasn't that the point of this trip—to see if you like my work?"

In truth, Jessica had forgotten that point, which surprised her, and in the midst of that surprise, she realized two things. First, she had already come to think of Carter as the architect of record. And second, she was enjoying herself and had been doing so from the time she'd first sat back in his car and decided to trust his driving. Somewhere, there, she'd forgotten to remember what a hell-raiser he'd been once. She was thinking of him in terms of the present, and liking him. Did she like his work? "I like your work just fine."

His handsome mouth twitched in gentle amusement. "You could say it with a little enthusiasm."

Bewitched by that mouth and its small, subtle movements, she did as he asked. "I like your work just fine!"

"Really?"

"Really!"

The twitch at the corner of his mouth became a tentative grin. "Do you think I could do something good for Crosslyn Rise?"

"I think you could do something great for Crosslyn Rise!"

"You're not just saying that for old times' sake?"

Gazing up at him, she let out a laugh that was as easy as it was spontaneous. "If it were a matter of old times' sake, I'd have fired you long ago."

Behind the look in her eye, the sound of her laugh and the softness of her voice, Carter could have sworn he detected something akin to affection. Deeply touched by that thought, he took her chin in his hand. His fingers lightly caressed her skin, while his eyes searched hers for further sign of emotion. And he saw it. It was there. Yes, she liked him, and that made him feel even more victorious than when she'd said she liked his work. Unable to help himself, he moved his thumb over her mouth. When her lips parted, he ducked his head and replaced his thumb with his mouth.

His kiss was whisper light, one touch, then another, and Jessica couldn't have possibly stopped it. It felt too good, too real and far sweeter even than those heady kisses she'd dreamed about. But her body began to tremble—she didn't know whether in memory of the dream or in response to his kiss—and she was frightened.

"No," she whispered against his mouth. Her hands came up to grasp his jacket. "Please, Carter, no."

Lifting his head, Carter saw her fear. His body was telling him to kiss her again and deeper; his mind told him that he could do it and she'd capitulate. But his heart wasn't ready to push.

"I won't hurt you," he said softly.

"I know." Though her hands clutched his jacket, her eyes avoided his. "But I...don't want this."

I could make you want it, Carter thought, but he didn't say it, because it was typical of something the old Carter would say, and the last thing he wanted to do was to remind her of that. "Okay," he said softly, and took a step back, but only after he'd brushed his thumb over her cheek. Half turning from her, he took a deep breath, dug his fists into the pockets of his jacket and pursed his lips toward the mill that he'd re-designed. After a minute, when he'd regained control over his baser instincts, he sent her a sidelong glance.

"You like my work, and I like that. So a celebration's in order. What say we head back and have dinner at the Pagoda. Do you like Chinese food?"

Not trusting her voice, Jessica nodded.

"Want to try it?" he asked.

She nodded again.

Not daring to touch her, he chucked his chin in the direction of the car. "Shall we?"

To nod again would have seemed foolish even to her. So, tucking her hands into her pockets, she turned and headed for the car. By rights, she told herself, she ought to have pleaded the need to work and asked Carter to drive her home. She didn't for three reasons.

First, work could wait.

Second, she was hungry.

And third, she wasn't ready to have the day end.

6

There was a fourth reason why Jessica agreed to have dinner with Carter. She wanted to show him that she could recover from his kiss, or was it herself that she wanted to show? It didn't matter, she supposed, because the end result was the same. She couldn't figure out why Carter had kissed her again, unless he'd seen in her eyes that she'd wanted him to, which she had. Since it wasn't wise for her to reinforce that impression, she had to carry on as though the kiss didn't matter.

It was easier said than done. Not only did the Pagoda have superb Chinese food, but it was elegantly served in a setting where the chairs were high backed and romantic, the drinks were fruity and potent, and the lights were low. None of that was conducive to remembering that she was there on business, that Carter's kisses most surely stemmed from either professional elation or personal arrogance, and that she didn't want or need anything from him but spectacular designs for Crosslyn Rise.

The atmosphere had *date* written all over it, and nothing Carter did dispelled that notion. He was a relaxed conversationalist, willing to talk about anything, from work to a television documentary they'd both seen, to the upcoming gubernatorial election. He drew her out in ways that she hadn't expected, got her thinking and talking about things she'd normally have felt beyond her ken. If she had stopped to remember where he'd come from, she'd have been amazed at the breadth and depth of his knowledge. But she didn't stop, because the man that he was obliterated images of the past. The man that he was held dominance over most everything, including, increasingly, her wariness of him as a man.

So her defenses were down by the time they returned to Crosslyn

Rise. Darkness had fallen, lending an unreality to the scene, and while the drink had made her mellow, Carter had her intoxicated. That, added to her enjoyment of the evening, of the entire day, was why she gave no resistance when he slipped an arm around her as he walked her to the door. There, under the glow of the antique lamps, he took her chin again and tipped up her face.

"It's been a nice day," he told her in a voice that was low and male. "I'm glad you agreed to come with me, and not only to see the real estate. I've enjoyed the company."

She wanted to believe him enough to indulge in the fantasy for a few last minutes. "It has been nice," she agreed with a shy smile, feeling as though she could easily drown in the depths of his charcoal-brown eyes and be happy.

"The real estate? Or the company?"

"Both," was her soft answer.

He lowered his head and kissed her, touching her lips, caressing them for an instant before lifting his head again. "Was that as nice?"

It was a minute before she opened her eyes. "Mmm."

"I'd like to do it again."

"You thought it was nice, too?"

"If I didn't, I wouldn't want to do it again," he said with the kind of logic that no mind could resist, particularly one that was floating as lightly as Jessica's. "Okay?"

She nodded, and when he lowered his head this time, her lips were softer, more pliant than before. He explored their curves, opening them by small degrees until he could run his tongue along the inside. When she gasped, he drew back.

"It's all right," he whispered. He slid his arms around her, fitting her body to his. "I won't hurt you," he said when he felt the fine tremors that shook her. "Flow with it, Jessica. Let me try again."

That was just what he did, caressing innocently at first, deepening the kiss by stages until his tongue was playing at will along the inside of her mouth. She tasted fruity sweet, reminiscent of the drinks they'd had, and twice as heady. When his arms contracted to draw her even closer, he wasn't thinking as much about her trembling body as his own. He needed to feel the pressure of her breasts, of her belly and thighs, needed to feel all those feminine things against his hard, male body.

Jessica clung to his shoulders, overwhelmed by the fire he'd started within her. It was like her dream, but so much more real, with heat rushing through her veins, licking at nerve ends, settling in ultrasensitive spots. When Carter crushed her closer, then moved her body against his, she didn't protest, because she needed the friction, too. His hardness was a foil for her softness, a salve for the ache inside her.

But the salve was only good for a minute, and when the ache increased, she remembered her dream again. She'd had a similar ache in the dream—until her mind had sparked what was necessary to bring her release.

For a horrid split second, she feared that would happen again. Then the split second passed, and she struggled to regain control of herself. "Carter," she protested, dragging her mouth from his. Her palms went flat against his shoulders and pushed.

"It's okay," he said unevenly. "I won't hurt you."

"We have to stop."

It was another minute before his dark eyes focused. "Why? I don't understand."

Freeing herself completely, Jessica moved to the front door. She grasped the doorknob and leaned against the wood, taking the support from Crosslyn Rise that she'd taken from Carter moments before. "I'm not like that."

"Like what?"

"Easy."

Carter was having trouble thinking clearly. Either the throbbing of his body was interfering with his brain, or she was talking nonsense. "No one said you were easy. I was just kissing you."

"But it's not the first time. And you wanted more."

"Didn't you?" he blurted out before he could stop himself. And then he wasn't sorry, because the ache in his groin persisted, making him want to lash out at its cause.

Her eyes shot to his. "No. I don't sleep around."

"You wanted more. You were trembling for it. Be honest, Jessica. It won't kill you to admit it."

"It's not true."

"In a pig's eye," he muttered, and took a step back. Tipping his head the slightest bit, he studied her through narrowed lids. "What is it about me that you find so frightening? The fact that I'm the guy who made fun of you when we were kids, or the fact that I'm a guy, period."

"You don't frighten me."

"I can see it. I can see it in your eyes."

"Then you see wrong. I just don't want to go to bed with you. That's all."

"Why not?"

"Because."

"Because why? Come on, Jessica. You owe me an explanation. You've been leading me a merry chase all day, being just that little bit distant but closer than ever before. You've spent the better part of the day being a consummate tease—"

"I have not! I've just been me! I thought we were having a nice time. If I'd known there was a price to pay for that—" she fumbled in her purse for her keys "—I'd have been careful not to have enjoyed myself as much. Is sex part of your professional fee?"

Carter ran a hand through his hair, then dropped it to the tight muscles at the back of his neck. With the fading of desire came greater control, and with greater control, clearer thought. They were on the old, familiar road to name-calling, he knew, and that wouldn't accomplish a thing.

He held up a hand to signal a truce, then set about explaining it. In a very quiet voice, he said, "Let's get one thing straight. I want you because you turn me on."

"That's—"

"Shh. Let me finish." When she remained silent, he said even more slowly, "You turn me on. No strings attached. No price I expect you to pay for lunch or dinner. You...just...turn me on. I didn't expect it, and I don't want it, because you *are* a client and I don't get involved with clients. It's not the way I work. Sex has nothing to do with payments of any kind. It has to do with two people liking each other, then respecting each other, then being attracted to each other. It has to do with two people being close, but needing to be even closer. It has to do with two people wanting to know each other in ways that other people don't." He paused to take a breath. "That was what I wanted just now. It was what I've been wanting all day."

Jessica didn't know what to answer. If she'd been madly in love with a man, she couldn't have hoped for a sweeter explanation. But she wasn't madly in love with Carter, which had to be why she was having trouble believing in the sincerity of his desire.

"As for sleeping around," Carter went on in that same quiet voice, "it means having indiscriminate sex with lots of different people. I'm not involved with anyone else right now. I haven't been intimately involved with anyone for a while. And I feel like I know you better than I've known any woman in years. So if I took you to bed, I wouldn't be sleeping around. And neither would you, unless you've been with others—"

She shook her head so vigorously that he dropped that particular line of inquiry. He'd known it wasn't true anyway. "Have you been with anyone since your husband?"

She shook her head more slowly this time.

"Before him?"

She shook her head a third time.

"Was it unpleasant with him?" Carter asked, but he knew that he'd made a mistake the minute the words were out. Jessica bowed her head and concentrated on fitting the key to the lock. "Don't go," he said quickly, but she opened the door and stepped inside.

"I can't talk about this," she murmured.

He took a step forward. "Then we'll talk about something else."

"No. I have to go."

"Talk of sex doesn't have to make you uncomfortable."

"It does. It's not something two strangers discuss."

"We're not strangers."

She looked up at him. "We are in some ways. You're more experienced than me. You won't be able to understand what I feel."

"Try me, and we'll see."

She shook her head, said softly, "I have to go," and slowly closed the door.

For a second before the latch clicked in place, Carter was tempted to resist. But the second passed, and the opportunity was gone. Short of banging the knocker or ringing the bell, he was cut off from her.

It was just as well. She needed time to get used to the idea of wanting him. He could give her that, he supposed.

He gave her nearly an hour, which was how long it took him to drive back to Boston, change clothes and make a pot of coffee. Then he picked up the phone and called her.

Her voice sounded calm and professional. "Hello?"

"Hi, Jessica. It's me. I just wanted to make sure you're okay."

She was silent for a minute. Then she said in the same composed voice, "I'm fine."

"You're not angry, are you?"

"No."

"Good." He paused. "I didn't mean any harm by asking what I did." He tapped a finger on the lip of his coffee cup. "I'm just curious." He looked up at the ceiling. "You're afraid of me. I keep trying to figure out why."

"I'm not afraid of you," came her quiet voice, sounding less confident than before.

"Then why won't you let yourself go when I kiss you?"

"Because I'm not the letting-go type."

"I think you could be. I think you want to be."

"I want to be exactly what I am right now. I'm not unhappy with my life, Carter. I'm doing what I like with people I like. If that wasn't so, I'd have changed things. But I like my life. I really like my life. You seem to think that I'm yearning for something else, but I'm not. I'm perfectly content."

Carter thought she was being a little too emphatic and a little too repetitive. He had the distinct feeling she was making the point to herself as much as to him, which meant that she wasn't as sure of her needs as she claimed, and that suited him just fine.

"You're not content about Crosslyn Rise," he reminded her, then hurried on, "which is another reason I'm calling. I'm going to start making some preliminary sketches, but I'll probably want to come to walk around again. I'd like to take some pictures—of the house, the land, possible building sites, the oceanfront. They're all outside pictures, so you don't have to be there, but I didn't want to go wandering around without your permission."

"You have my permission."

"Great. Why don't I give you a call when I have something to show you?"

"That sounds good." She paused. "Carter?"

He held his breath. "Yes?"

After a brief hesitation, her voice came. This time it sounded neither professional nor insecure, but sincere. "Thanks again for today. It really was nice."

He let out the breath and smiled. "My pleasure. Talk with you soon."

"Uh-huh."

What time Jessica spent at home that week, she spent looking out the window. Or it seemed that way. She made excuses for herself—she was restless reading term papers, she needed exercise, she could use the time to think—but she managed to wander from room to room, window to window, glancing nonchalantly out each one. Her eyes were anything but nonchalant, searching the landscape for Carter on the chance that either she'd missed his car on the driveway or he'd parked out of sight.

She saw no sign of him, which mean that either he'd come while she was in Cambridge or he hadn't come at all.

Nor did he call. She imagined that he might have tried her once or twice while she was out, and for the first time in her life she actually considered buying an answering machine. But that was in a moment of weakness. She didn't like answering machines. And besides, it would be worse to have an answering machine and not receive a message, than to not have one and wonder. Where one could wonder, one had hope.

And that thought confused her, because she wasn't sure why she wanted hope. Carter Malloy was...Carter Malloy. They were involved with each other on a professional basis, but that was all. Yes, she'd enjoyed spending Sunday with him. She'd begun to realize just how far he'd come as a person in the years she'd known him. And she did hope, she supposed, that there might be another Sunday or two like that.

But nothing sexual was ever going to happen between them. He wasn't her type—a perfect example being his failure to call. In Jessica's book, when a man was romantically interested in a woman, he didn't leave her alone for days. He called her, stopped in to see her, left messages at the office. Carter certainly could have done that, but there had been no message from him among the pink slips the department secretary had handed her that week.

He was showing his true colors, she decided. Despite all his sweet talk—sex talk—he wasn't really interested in her, which didn't surprise her in the least. He was a compelling man. Sex appeal oozed from him. She, on the other hand, had no sex appeal at all. Her genes had been generous in certain fields, but sex appeal wasn't one.

So what did Carter want with her? She didn't understand the motive behind his kisses, and the more she tried to, the more frustrated she became. The only thing she could think was that he was having a kind of perverse fun with her, and that hurt. It hurt, because one part of her liked him, respected him personally and professionally and found him sexy as all get out. It would be far easier, she realized, to admire him from a distance, than to let him come close and show her just how unsatisfying she was to a man.

Knowing that the more she brooded, the worse it would be, Jessica kept herself as busy as possible. Rather than wander from window to window at home, by midweek she was spending as much time as possible at school. Work, like Poppycock, had a soothing effect on her, and there was work aplenty to do. When she wasn't grading exams, she was reading term papers or working with one of the two students for whom she was a dissertation advisor. And the work was uplifting—which didn't explain why, when she returned to Crosslyn Rise Friday evening, she felt distinctly let down. She'd never had that experience before. Work had always been a bellwether for her mood. She decided that she was simply tired.

So she slept late on Saturday morning, staying in bed until nine, dallying over breakfast, taking a leisurely shower, though she had nothing but laundry and local errands and more grading to do. She didn't pay any heed to the windows, knowing that Carter wouldn't come on a Saturday. Work was work. He'd be there during the week, preferably when she wasn't around. Which was just as well, as far as she was concerned.

It was therefore purely by accident that, with her arms loaded high with sheets to be laundered, she came down the back steps and caught a glimpse of something shiny and blue out the landing window. Heart thundering, she came to an abrupt halt, stared out at the driveway and swallowed hard.

He'd come. On a Saturday. When she was wearing jeans and a sweatshirt pushed up to the elbows, looking like one of her students playing laundress. But someone had to do the laundry, she thought a bit frantically; the days of having Annie Malloy to help with it were long gone.

Ah, the irony of it, she mused. Then the back bell rang, and she ceased all musings. Panicked, she glanced at her sweatshirt, then at the linens in her arms, then down the stairs toward the door. If she didn't answer it, he'd think she wasn't home.

That would be the best thing.

But she couldn't do it. Tucking the sheets into a haphazard ball, she ran down the stairs, crossed through the back vestibule and opened the door to Carter.

His appearance did nothing to ease her breathlessness. Wearing jeans and a plaid flannel shirt, he looked large and masculine. His clothes were comfortably worn—a far cry from the last time she'd seen him in jeans, when they'd been dirty and torn—and fit his leanly muscled legs like a glove. The shirt was rolled to the elbow, much as her sweatshirt was, only his forearms were sinewy, spattered with dark hair, striped on the inside with the occasional vein. His collar was open, showing off the strength of his neck and shoulders, and from one of those shoulders hung a camera.

"Hi," she said. In an attempt to curb her breathlessness, she put a hand to her chest. "How are you?"

He was just fine, now that he was here. All week he'd debated about when to stop by; he couldn't remember when he'd given as much thought to anything. Except her. She'd been on his mind a lot. Now he knew why. Looking at her, taking in the casual way she was dressed, the oversized pink sweatshirt and the faded blue jeans that clung to slender legs, he felt relieved. Her features, too, did that to him. She was perfectly unadorned—long hair shiny clean and drawn into a high ponytail, skin free of makeup and healthy looking, smile small but bright, glasses sliding down the bridge of her nose—but she looked wonderful. She was a breath of fresh air, he decided, finally putting his finger on one of the things he most liked about her. She was different from the women he'd known. She was natural and unpretentious. She was refreshing.

"I'm real fine," he drawled with a lazy smile. "Just stoppin' in to disturb your Saturday morning." His gaze touched on the bundle she held.

Wrapping both arms around the linens, she hugged them to her. "I, uh, always use Saturdays for this. Usually I'm up earlier. I should have had two washes done by now. I slept late."

"You must have been tired." He searched for shadows under her eyes, but either her glasses hid them, or they just weren't there. Her skin was clear, unmottled by fatigue, a smooth blend of ivory and pink. "It's been a busy week?"

"Very," she said with a sigh and a smile.

"Will you be able to relax this weekend?"

"A little. I still have more work to do, but then there are things like this—" she nodded toward the linens "—and the market and the drugstore, none of which are heavily intellectual tasks. I relax when I do those."

"No time to sit back, put your feet up and vegetate?"

She shook her head. "I'm not good at vegetating."

"I used to be good at it, back in the days when I was raising hell." His mouth took on a self-effacing twist. "Used to drive my mother wild. Whenever the police showed up at the door, she knew she'd find me sprawled out in the back room watching TV." The twist gentled. "I don't have much time for vegetating now, either—" he jabbed his chin toward the camera "—which is why I'm here. I thought I'd do that exploring. I have nothing to think about but Crosslyn Rise, and it's a gorgeous day." He made a quick decision, based on the open look on her face. "Want to come?"

Nothing seemed to be helping Jessica's breathlessness or the incessant fluttering of her insides. Suddenly she didn't seem to be able to make a decision, either. "I don't know...there's this laundry to do...and vacuuming." She could feel the warm air coming in past him, and it beckoned. "I ought to dust...and you'll probably be able to think more creatively if I'm not around."

"I'd like the company. And I won't talk if the creative mode hits. Come on. Just for a little while. It's too special a day to miss."

His eyes weren't as much charcoal brown today, she decided, as milk chocolatey, and their lashes seemed absurdly thick. Had she never noticed that before?

"Uh, I have so much to do," she argued, but meekly.

"Tell you what," Carter said. "I'll start out and follow the same route we took last time. You take care of what you have to, then join me."

That sounded like a fair compromise to Jessica. If he was willing to be flexible, she couldn't exactly remain rigid. Besides, Saturday or not, he was working on her project. Maybe he wanted to bounce ideas off her. "I may be a little while," she cautioned.

"No sweat. I'll be here longer than that. Take your time." With a wink, he set off.

The wink set her back a good ten minutes. Several of those were spent with her back against the wall by the door, trying to catch up with her racing pulse. Several more were spent wandering through the kitchen into the den, before she realized that she was supposed to be headed for the laundry, which was in the basement. The rest were spent getting the washer settings right, normally a simple task, now complicated by a sorely distracted mind.

Never in her life had she done the vacuuming as quickly as she did then. It was nervous energy, she told herself, and that reasoning held on through a dusting job that probably stirred more than it gathered. Fortunately, the rooms in question were only those few she used on a regular basis, which meant that she was done in no time. The bed linens were in the dryer and her personal things in the wash when she laced on a pair of sneakers, grabbed a half-filled bag of bread and slipped out the door.

Carter was sitting cross-legged on the warm grass by the duck pond. Though for all intents and purposes he was concentrating on the antics of the ducks, he'd kept a lookout for her arrival. The sight of her brought the warm feeling it always did, plus something akin to excitement—

which was amusing, since in the old days he'd have labeled her the least exciting person in the world. But that was in the old days, at a time in his life when he'd appreciated precious little, certainly nothing subtle and mature, which were the ways in which he found Jessica exciting. He could never have appreciated her intellect, the way she thought through issues, the natural curiosity that had her listening to things he said and asking questions. She was a thoroughly stimulating companion, even in silence—unless she felt threatened. When that happened, she was as dogmatic and closed minded as he'd once thought her to be.

The key, of course, was to keep her from feeling threatened. Most of the time, that was easy, particularly since he felt increasingly protective of her. The times when it was difficult almost always had to do with sex, which was when he was at his least controlled both physically and emotionally.

But he'd try. He'd try, because the prize was worth it.

"Watch out for the muck!" he called, and watched her give wide berth to a spot of ground that hadn't quite dried out from the spring thaw. His eyes followed her as she approached, one hand tucked into the pocket of her jeans, her ponytail swaying gently with her step. "That was fast."

"Don't you know it," she said in a way that stunned him, then pleased him in the next breath. She'd drawled the words. Yes, there was self-mockery in them, but there was playfulness, too. Opening the bag of bread, she began breaking off chunks and tossing them toward the ducks, who quacked their appreciation. "I hate cleaning. I do it dutifully. But I hate it."

"You should hire someone—and don't tell me you can't afford it. That kind of help is cheap."

But she nixed the idea with the scrunch of her nose, which served the double purpose of hitching her glasses up. "There's really not enough to do." She tossed out another handful of bread and watched the ducks try to outwaddle each other to where it landed. "I hire a crew twice a year to do the parts of the house that I don't use, but there's no good reason why I can't do the rest myself." She turned to stare at him hard, but her voice was too gentle to be accusing. "Unless someone stands at my door tempting me with the best spring weather that's come along so far." She looked around, took a deep breath, didn't pause to wonder whether the exhilaration she felt was from the air or not. She was tired of wondering about things like that. She was too analytical.

For once, she wanted to—what was it he'd said—go with the flow. "So," she said, reaching for more bread, "are you being inspired?"

"Here? Always. It's a beautiful spot." Tossing several feathers out of the way, he patted the grass by his side.

She sat down and shot a look at the camera that lay in his lap. It wasn't one of the instant models, but the real thing. "Have you used it?"

He nodded. "I've taken pictures of the house, the front lawn and the beach. Not here, yet. I'm just sitting."

She aimed a handful of bread crumbs toward the ducks. "Are you a good photographer?"

"I'm competent. I get the shots I need, but they're practical, rather than artistic." He took the camera up, made several shifts in the settings, raised it to his eye and aimed it at her.

She held up a hand to block the shot and turned her head away. "I hate having my picture taken even more than I hate cleaning!"

"Why?"

"I don't like being focused on." She dared a glance at him, relaxing once she saw that he'd put the camera back down.

"Focused on" could be interpreted both broadly and narrowly. Carter had the feeling that both applied in Jessica's case. "Why not?" he asked, bemused.

"Because it's embarrassing. I'm not photogenic."

"I don't believe that."

"It's true. The camera exaggerates every flaw. I have plenty without the exaggeration."

Looking at her, with the sun glancing off her hair and a blush of self-consciousness on her cheeks, Carter could only think of how pretty she was. "What flaws do you have?"

"Come on, Carter—"

"Tell me." The quacking of the ducks seemed to second his command.

Sure that he was ridiculing her, she studied his eyes. She saw no teasing there, though, only challenge, and where Carter challenged her, she was conditioned to respond. "I'm plain. Totally and utterly plain. My face is too thin, my nose is too small, and my eyes are boring."

He stared at her. "Boring? Are you kidding? And there's nothing wrong with the shape of your face or your nose. Do you have any idea what a pleasure it is for me to look at you after having to look at other women all week?" At her blank look, he said, "You've grown up well,

Jessica. You may have felt plain as a child, but you're not a child anymore, and what you think of as plainness is straightforward, refreshing good looks.''

Her blankness had yielded to incredulity. "Why do you say things like that?''

"Because they're true!''

"I don't believe it for a minute," she said. It seemed the only way to cope with the awkwardness she felt. Rising to her feet, she tossed the last of the bread from the bag and set off. "You're just trying to butter me up so I'll like your designs.'' Wadding up the bag, she stuffed it into a pocket.

Carter was after her in a minute, gently catching her ponytail to draw her up short as he overtook her. His body was a solid wall before her, his hand in her hair a smaller but no less impenetrable wall behind. Against her temple, his breath was a warm sough of emotion. "If I wanted to butter you up, I'd just do my work and mind my own business about the rest. But I can't do it—any more than I can sit back and listen to you denigrate yourself. I'm highly attracted to you. Why can't you believe that?''

Struck as always by his closeness, Jessica's breathing had quickened. Her eyes were lowered, focusing on his shirt, and though there was nothing particularly sensual about the plaid, there was something decidedly so about the faintly musky scent of his skin.

"I'm not the kind of women men find highly attractive,'' she explained in a small voice.

"Is that another gem of wisdom from your ex-husband?''

"No. It's something I've deduced after thirty-three years of observation. I don't turn heads. I never have and never will.''

"The women who turn heads—the sharp lookers, the fashion plates— aren't the women men want. Call it macho, but they want softer women. You're a softer woman. And I want you.''

"But you have your choice of the best women in the city.''

"And I choose you. Doesn't that tell you anything?''

"It tells me that you're going through a phase. Let's call it—'' she raised her eyes to his to make her point ''—the give-the-little-lady-a-thrill-for-old-times'-sake phase.''

Dangerously close to anger, Carter drew her closer until she was flush against him. "That's insulting, Jessica.'' His dark eyes blazed into hers. "Can't you give me a little credit for honesty? Have I ever lied to you?'' When she didn't answer, he did it for her. "No. I may have said cruel things, or downright wrong things, but they were the things I was honestly feeling at the time. We've already established that I was a bastard. But at least give me credit for honesty.''

His blood was pulsing more thickly as her curves imprinted themselves on his body. ''I've been honest with words. And I've been honest with this.'' He captured her mouth before she could open hers to protest, and he kissed her with an ardor that could have been from hunger or anger.

Jessica didn't know which. All she knew was that her defenses fell in less time than ever before, that she couldn't have kept her mouth stiff if she'd tried, that she should have been shocked when his tongue surged into her mouth, but the only source of shock was her own enjoyment.

That thought, though, came a moment too soon, because she was in for another small shock. Well before she was ready, he ended the kiss. She hadn't even begun to gather her wits when he took her hand from its stranglehold of his shirt and lowered it to the straining fly of his jeans.

''No way,'' he said hoarsely, ''no way could I fake that.'' Keeping his hand over hers, he molded her fingers to his shape, pressing her palm flat, manipulating it in a rubbing motion. A low sound slipped from his throat as he pressed his lips to her neck.

Jessica was stunned by the extent of his arousal, then stunned again when the heat of it seemed to increase. Her breathing was short and scattered, but Carter's was worse, and a fine quaking simmered in the muscles of his arms and legs.

No, he couldn't fake what she felt, and the knowledge was heady. It made her feel soft and feminine and eager to know more of the strength beneath her hand. Without conscious thought, she began to stroke him. Her eyes closed. Her head tipped to give his mouth access to her throat. Her free arm stole to the bunched muscles of his back. And when she became aware of a restlessness between her legs, she arched toward him.

Carter made a low, guttural sound. Wrenching her hand from him, he wrapped her in his arms and crushed her close, then closer still. ''Don't move,'' he warned in a voice that was more sand than substance. ''Don't move. Give me a minute. A minute.''

The trembling went on as he held her tight, but Jessica wasn't sure how much of it was her own. Weak-kneed and shaky, she was grateful that his convulsive hold was keeping her upright. Without it, she'd surely have slid down to the grass and begged him to take her there, which was precisely what the tight knot at the pit of her stomach demanded.

That was probably the biggest shock of all. The dream she could reason away. She could attribute it to any number of vague things. But when she was being held in Carter's arms, when she felt every hard line of his body and not only took pleasure in the hardness but hungered to have it deeper inside her, she couldn't lie to herself any longer.

The issue, of course, was what to make of the intense desire she felt for him. The moment would pass now, she knew. Once Carter regained control of his libido, he would set her back, perhaps take her hand and lead her on through the woods. He might talk, ask her what she feared, try to get her to admit to his desire and to her own, but he wouldn't force her into anything she didn't want.

It wasn't that she didn't want sex with Carter, rather that she wasn't ready for it. She'd never been a creature of impulse. It was one thing to "go with the flow" and spurn housekeeping chores in favor of a walk on the woods, quite another to "go with the flow" and expose herself, body and soul, to a man. She'd done that once and been hurt, and though she'd never made vows of chastity, the memory of that hurt kept her shy of sex.

If she was ever to make love with Carter, she had to understand exactly what she was doing and why. She also had to decide whether the risk was worth it.

Carter didn't leave right away. Nor did he allow Jessica to leave. He insisted she stay while he took the pictures he needed at the duck pond, then walked her back to the house. She had feared he'd want to talk about what had happened, but either he was as surprised by its power as she, or he sensed she wasn't ready. He said nothing about the kiss, about the way she'd touched him, or about the fact that he'd nearly lost it there and then in front of the ducks.

Instead, he sent her inside to finish her chores while he completed his own outside. Then he drove her to the supermarket and walked up and down the aisles with her, tossing the occasional unusual item into her cart. When they returned to Crosslyn Rise, he made his special tuna salad, replete with diced water chestnuts and red pepper relish.

After lunch, he left.

He called on Monday evening to say that the photos he'd taken had come out well and that he was getting down to some serious sketching.

He called on Thursday evening to say that he was pleased with the progress he was making and would she be free on Sunday afternoon to take a look at what he'd drawn.

She was free, of course. The semester's work was over, exams and papers graded, grades duly recorded—which was wonderful in the sense of freeing her up, lousy in the sense of giving her more time to think. The thinker in her decided that she definitely wanted to see what he'd drawn, but she didn't trust him—or herself—to have a show-and-tell meeting at Crosslyn Rise.

So they arranged to meet at Carter's office, which satisfied Jessica's need on several scores. First, she was curious to see more of him in his professional milieu. Second, even if he kissed her, and even if she responded, the setting was such that nothing could come of it.

She guessed she was curious to see him, period. It had been a long week since the Saturday before, a long week of replaying what had happened, of feeling the excitement again, of imagining an even deeper involvement. Though it still boggled her mind, she had to accept that he did want her. The evidence had been conclusive. She still didn't know *why* he wanted her, and the possibilities were diverse, running from the wildly exciting to the devastating. But that was another reason why the setting suited her purpose. It was safe. She could see him, get to know him better, but she wouldn't have to take a stand on the physical side of the issue.

And then, there was Crosslyn Rise. The part of her that had acclimated itself to the conversion of the Rise was anxious to see what he'd drawn. That part wanted to get going, to decide on an architectural plan, have it formally drawn up and give it to Gordon so that he could enlist his investors. That part of Jessica wanted to act before its counterpart backed out.

Jessica wasn't sure what she'd expected when she took a first look at Carter's drawings, but it certainly wasn't the multicolored spread before her. Yes, there were pencil sketches on various odd pieces of paper, but he'd taken the best of those ideas and converted them into something that could well have been a polished promotion for the place.

"Who drew these?" she asked, slightly awed.

"I did." There were times when he left such drawings to project managers, but he'd wanted to do this himself. When it came to Crosslyn Rise, he was the project manager, and he didn't give a damn whether his partner accused him of ill-using the resources at hand. Crosslyn Rise was his baby from start to finish, even if it meant late nights such as the ones he'd put in this week. They were worth it. Concentrating on his work was better than concentrating on his need.

"But this is art. I never pictured anything like this."

"It's called a presentation," he said dryly. "The idea is to snow the client right off the bat."

"Well, I'm snowed."

"By the presentation, maybe, but do you like what's in it?"

At first glance, she did. At his caveat, she took a closer look, moving one large sheet aside to look at the next.

"I've drawn the main house in cross sections, as I envision it looking once all the work is done," he explained, "and a head-on view of the condo cluster at the duck pond. Since the clusters will all be based on the same concept, a variation on the Georgian theme, I wanted to try out one cluster on you first."

Her eyes were glued to the drawing. "It's incredible."

"Is it what you imagined?"

"No. It looks more Cape-ish than Georgian. But it's real. More modern. Interesting."

He wasn't sure if "interesting" was good or bad, but when he asked, she held up a hand and studied the drawing in silence for several minutes. "Interesting," she repeated, but there was a warmth in the word. Then she smiled. "Nice."

Carter basked in her smile, which was some consolation for the fact that he wanted to hug her but didn't dare. Not only did he sense that she wasn't ready for more hugs, but he feared that if he touched her, office or no, he wouldn't be able to stop this time. As it was, her smile, which was so rare, did dangerous things to him.

He cleared his throat. "Obviously this is rough. But I wanted to convey the general idea." He touched a lean finger to one area, then another. "The roof angle here is what reminds you of a Cape. It can be modified, but it allows for skylights. Today's market loves skylights." His finger shifted. "I've deliberately scaled down the pillars and balconies so that they don't compete with the main house. The main house should set the tone for stateliness. The clusters can echo it, but they ought to be more subtle. I want them to nestle into their surroundings. In some ways the focus of the clusters *is* those surroundings."

Jessica cast a sideways glance at him. He had a long arm propped straight on the drafting table and was close enough to touch, close enough to smell, close enough to want. Ignoring the last and the buzzing that played havoc with her insides, she said, "I think you're hung up on those surroundings."

"Me?" His dark eyes shone with indulgence one moment, vehemence the next. "No way. At least, not enough that it would color my better judgment. And my better judgment tells me that people will buy at Crosslyn Rise for the setting, nearly as much as for the nuts and bolts of what they're getting. Which isn't to say that we can skimp on those nuts and bolts." Again he referred to the drawing, tracing sweeping lines with his finger. "I've angled each of the units differently, partly for interest, partly for privacy. Either you and Gordon—or if you want to wait, the consortium—will have to decide on the size of the units.

Personally, I'd hate to do anything less than a three bedroom setup. People usually want more space rather than less.''

Jessica hadn't thought that far. "The person to speak with about that might be Nina Stone. She's a broker. She'd have a feel for what people in this area want.''

"Do I know Nina Stone?'' Carter asked, trying to place the name.

"She knew you,'' Jessica replied, wondering whether the two of them would hit it off and not sure she liked that idea. "Or rather, she knew *of* you. Your reputation precedes you.''

Once he'd left New York, Carter had worked long and hard to establish himself and his name. "That's gratifying.''

"Uh-huh. She already has you pegged as a ruggedly masculine individual.''

Which wasn't the most professional of assessments, he mused. "You discussed me with her?''

"I mentioned we were working together.''

He nodded his understanding, but, to Jessica's selfish delight, had no particular interest in knowing more about Nina. His finger was back on the drawing, this time tapping his rendition of the duck pond. "We may run into a problem with water. The land in this area is wetter than in the others. When we reach the point of having the backers lined up, I'll have a geological specialist take a look.''

"Could the problem be serious?''

"Nah. It shouldn't be more than a matter of shifting the clusters to the right or the left, and I want them set back anyway so the ducks won't be disturbed. The main house draws water from its own wells. I'm assuming the condos would do the same, but an expert could tell us more on that, too.''

Up to that point, Jessica had been aware of only two problems—coming to terms with the sale of Crosslyn Rise, and dealing with Carter Malloy. Now, mention of a possible water problem brought another to mind. "What if we can't get enough backers?''

Surprised by the question, he shot her a look. Her eyes were wide with concern. "To invest in the project? We'll get enough.''

"Will we? You've had more experience in this kind of thing than I have. Is there a chance we'll come up with plans that no one will support?''

"It's not probable.''

"But is it possible?''

"Anything's possible. It's possible that the economy will crash at ten past ten tomorrow morning, but it's no more probable that it will happen than that Gordon won't be able to find the backers we need." He paused, sliding his gaze over her face. "You're really worried?"

"I haven't been. I haven't thought about it much at all, but suddenly here you are with exciting drawings, and the project seems very real. I'd hate to go through all this and then have the whole thing fizzle."

Throwing caution to the winds, he did put his arm around her then. "It won't. Trust me. It won't."

The confidence in his voice, even more so than the words, was what did it. That, and the support his body offered. For the first time, she truly felt as though Carter shared the responsibility of Crosslyn Rise with her, and while a week or two before, that thought would have driven her wild, she was comfortable with it now. She'd come a long way.

"I have theater tickets for Thursday night," came Carter's low voice. "Come with me."

Taken totally off guard, she didn't know what to say.

His breath was warm on her hair. "Do you have other plans?"

"No."

"They're for *Cat on a Hot Tin Roof.*"

Tipping her head, she looked up at him. "You got tickets," she breathed in awe, because she'd been trying to get them for weeks without success. But going to the theater with Carter was a *date*.

"Will you come?"

"I don't know," she said a bit helplessly. Everything physical about him lured her, as did, increasingly, everything else about him. He was so good to be with. The problem, as always, lay with her.

"If you won't, I'm giving the tickets back. There's no one else I want to take, and I don't want to go alone."

"That's blackmail," she argued.

"Not blackmail. Just a chance to see the hottest revival of the decade."

"I know, I know," she murmured, weakening. It was easy to do that when someone as strong as Carter was offering support.

"The semester's over. What better way to celebrate?"

"I have to be at school all day Thursday planning for the summer term."

"But the pressure's off. So before it's on again, have a little fun. You deserve it."

She wasn't as concerned with what she deserved as with what going on a date with Carter would mean. It would mean a shift in their relationship, a broadening of it. Going on a date with Carter would mean being with him at night in a crowded theater, perhaps alone before or after. All kinds of things could happen. She wasn't sure she was ready.

Then again, she wasn't sure she could resist.

"Come on, Jessica. I really want to go."

So do I, Jessica thought. Her eyes fell to his mouth. She liked looking at his mouth. "I'd have to meet you there."

"Why can't I pick you up?" he asked, and the corners of that mouth turned down.

"Because I don't know exactly where I'll be."

"You could call me at the office and let me know. It's only a ten-minute drive to Cambridge."

Her eyes met his. "More in traffic. And it's silly for you to go back and forth like that."

"I want to go back and forth." If he was taking her out for the evening, he wanted to do it right. Besides, he didn't like the idea of her traveling alone.

Jessica, though, was used to traveling alone. More than that, she was determined to keep things light and casual. It was the only way she could handle the thought of a date with Carter. "Tell me where to meet you and when. I'll be there."

"Why are you being so stubborn?" he asked. In the next breath, he relented. "Sorry. Six-thirty at the Sweetwater Café."

"I thought *Cat on a Hot Tin Roof* was at the Colonial." She knew very well it was—and what he was trying to do.

His naughty eyes didn't deny it. "The Sweetwater Café is close by. We can get something to eat there before the show." When she looked momentarily skeptical, he said, "You have to eat, Jessica." When still she hesitated, he added, "Indulge me. I'm letting you meet me there, which I don't like. So at least let me feed you first."

Looking up into his dark eyes, she came to an abrupt realization. It was no longer a matter of not being sure. She *couldn't* resist—not when he had an arm draped so protectively across her shoulders, not when he was looking at her so intently, not when she wanted both to go on forever and ever. He made her feel special. Cared for. Feminine. She doubted, at that minute, that she'd have been able to refuse him a thing.

So she agreed. Naturally she had second thoughts, but after a day of suffering through those, she lost patience with herself. Since she'd agreed to go out with Carter, she told herself, she was going, and since she was going, she intended to make the most of it. She had her share of pride, and that pride dictated that she do everything in her power to make sure Carter didn't regret having asked her out.

He didn't regret it so far, at least; he called her each night just to say hello. But talking on the phone or having a business meeting or even driving north on a Sunday was different from going out at night to something that had nothing to do with work. She wanted to look good.

To that end, she arranged to finish up with work by two on Thursday. The first stop she made then was to the boutique where she'd bought the sweater she'd worn to Maine; if stylish had worked once, she figured it would work again. But stylish in that shop was funky, which wasn't her style at all. She was about to give up hope when the owner brought a dress from the back that was perfect. A lime-green sheath of silk that was self-sashed and fell to just above the knee, it was sleeveless and had a high turtleneck that draped her neck in the same graceful way that the rest of the fabric draped her body. The dress was feminine without being frilly. She felt special enough in it not to look at the price tag, and by the time she had to write out a check, she was committed enough to it not to mind the higher-than-normal cost.

Her second stop was at a shoe store, where she picked up a pair of black patent leather heels and a small bag to match.

Her third stop was at Mario's. Mario had been doing her hair—a blunt cut to keep the ends under control—bimonthly for several years, and for the first time she allowed him more freedom. Enhancing her own natural wave with rollers and a heat lamp, he gave her a look that was softer and more stylish than anything she'd ever worn. As the icing on the cake, he caught one side high over her ear with a pearl clip. The look pleased Jessica so much that she left the salon, went to the jewelry store next door and splurged on a pair of pearl earrings to match the clip. Then she returned to her office, where she'd left cosmetics and stockings.

The day had been warm and humid, as late spring days often were, and when Jessica left Harvard, retrieved her car and set off for Boston, dull gray clouds were dotting the sky. She barely noticed. Her thoughts were on the way she looked and the comments she'd drawn from the few of her colleagues she'd happened to pass as she left. They had done double takes, which either said she looked really good, or so different from how she usually looked that they couldn't believe it was her.

She couldn't quite believe it was her. For one thing, the fact that she liked the way she looked was a first. For another, the fact that she was heading for a date with a man like Carter Malloy was incredible. Unable to reconcile either, given that her nerves were jangling with excitement, she half decided that it wasn't her in the car at all, but another woman. That thought brought a silly grin to her face.

The grin faded, but the excitement didn't. It was overshadowing her nervousness by the time she parked in the garage under the Boston Common, and by the time she emerged onto the Common itself and realized that she was at the corner farthest from where she as going, she was feeling too high to mind. Her step was quick, in no way slowed by the unfamiliarity of the new heels.

What gave her pause, though, were the drops of rain that, one by one, in slow succession, began to hit her. They were large and warm. She looked worriedly at the sky, not at all reassured by the ominous cloud overhead or the blue that surrounded it in too distant a way. Furious at herself for not having brought an umbrella, she walked faster. She could beat the rain, she decided, but she wished she'd parked closer.

To her dismay, the drops grew larger, came harder and more often. She broke into a half run, holding her handbag over her head, looking around for shelter. But there was none. Trees were scattered on either side of the paved walks, but they were of the variety whose branches were too high to provide any shelter at all.

For a split second she stopped and looked frantically back at the entrance to the parking garage, but it seemed suddenly distant, separated from her by a million thick raindrops. If she returned there, she'd be farther than ever from the Sweetwater Café—and drenched anyway.

So she ran faster, but within minutes, the rain reached downpour proportions. She was engulfed as much by it as by disbelief. Other people rushed along, trying to protect themselves as she was, but she paid them no heed. All she could think of was the beautiful green silk dress that was growing wetter by the minute, the painstakingly styled hair that was growing wilder by the minute, the shiny black shoes that were growing more speckled by the minute.

Panicked, she drew up under a large-trunked tree in the hope that something, *anything* would be better than nothing. But as though to mock her, the rain began to come sideways. When she shifted around the tree, it shifted, too. Horrified at what was happening but helpless to stop it, she looked from side to side for help but there was none. She was caught in the worst kind of nightmare.

Unable to contain it, she cried out in frustration, then cried out again when the first one didn't help. The second didn't, either, and she felt nearly as much a fool for making it as for standing there in the rain. So she started off again, running as fast as she could given that her glasses were streaked with rain, her shoes were soaked and her heart felt like lead.

It was still pouring when she finally turned down the alley that led to the Sweetwater Café. As the brick walkway widened into a courtyard, she slowed her step. Rushing was pointless. There was nothing the rain could do to her that it already hadn't. She couldn't possibly go to the theater with Carter. The evening was ruined. All that was left was to tell him, return to her car and drive home.

Shortly before she reached the café's entrance, her legs betrayed her. Stumbling to the nearby brick wall, she leaned her shoulder against it, covered her face with her hands and began to cry.

That was how Carter found her, as he came from the opposite end of the courtyard. He wasn't sure it was her at first; he hadn't expected such a deep green dress, such a wild array of hair or nearly so much leg. But as he slowed his own step, he sensed the familiar in the defeated way she stood. His insides went from hot to cold in the few seconds it took him to reach her side.

"Jessica?" he asked, his heart pounding in dread. He reached out, touched the back of her hand. "Are you all right?"

With a mournful moan, she shrank into herself.

Heedless of the rain that continued to fall, he put a hand to the wall and used his body to shield her from the curious eyes of those who passed. "Jessica?" He speared his fingers into her hair to lift it away from her face. "What happened?" When she continued to cry, he grasped her wrist. "Are you all right? Tell me what happened. Are you hurt?"

"I'm wet!" she cried from behind her hands.

He could see that, but there was still an icy cold image of something violent hovering in his mind. "Is that all? You weren't mugged or...anything?"

"I'm just wet! I got caught in the downpour, and there wasn't anywhere to go, and I wanted to look so nice. *I'm a mess,* Carter."

Carter was so relieved that she hadn't been bodily harmed in some other, darker, narrower alley, that he gave her a tight hug. "You're not a mess—"

"I'll get you wet," she protested, struggling to free herself from his hold.

He ignored her struggles. "You're looking goddamned sexy with that dress clinging to every blessed curve." When she gave a soft wail and went limp, he said, "Come on. Let's get you dry."

The next few minutes were a blur in Jessica's mind, principally because she didn't raise her eyes once. For the first time in her life, she was grateful that her hair was wild, because it fell by her cheeks like a veil. She didn't want Carter to see her, didn't want *anyone* to see her. She felt like a drowned rat, all the more pathetic in her own mind by contrast to the way she looked when she left Cambridge.

With a strong arm around her shoulder, Carter guided her out of the alley and into a cab. He didn't let her go even then, but spoke soft words to her during the short ride to his apartment. Wallowing in misery, she heard precious few of them. She kept her head down and her shoulders hunched. If she'd been able to slide under the seat, she'd have done just that.

He lived on Commonwealth Avenue, on the third floor of a time-honored six-story building. Naturally the rain had stopped by the time they reached it. He knew not to point that out to Jessica, and ushered her into the lobby before she could figure it out for herself. Though she'd stopped crying, she was distraught. The tension in her body wasn't to be believed.

"Here we go," he said as he quickly unlocked the door to his place. He led her directly into the bathroom, pulled a huge gray bath sheet from a shelf and began to wipe her arms. When he'd done what he could, he draped it around her, took a smaller towel, removed her glasses and dried them, too. "Better?"

Jessica refused to look at him. "I'm hopeless," she whispered.

"You're only wet," he said, setting the glasses by the sink. "When I saw you crying, leaning against the wall that way in the alley, I thought you'd been attacked. I honestly thought you'd been mugged. But you're only wet."

She was beyond being grateful for small favors. Turning her face away from him, she said in a woefully small voice, "I tried so hard. I wanted to look nice for you. I can't remember the last time anything meant so much to me, and I almost did it. I was looking good, and I was looking forward to tonight, and then it started to rain. I didn't know whether to go back or go on, and the rain came down harder, and then it didn't matter either way because I was soaked." Her eyes were filled with tears when they met Carter's. "It wasn't meant to be. I'm a disaster when it comes to nice things like dinner and the theater. There was a message in what happened."

"Like hell," Carter said, blotting her face with the smaller towel. "It rained. I would have been caught in it, too, if I'd walked, but I was running late, so I took a cab." He began to gently dry her hair. "Sudden storms come on like that. If it had come fifteen minutes earlier or later, you'd have been fine."

"But it didn't, and I'm not. And now everything is ruined. My dress, my shoes, my hair—"

"Your hair is gorgeous," he said, and it was. Moving the towel through it was like trying to tame a living thing. Waving naturally, it was wild and exotic. "You should wear it down like this more often. Then again, maybe you shouldn't. It's an incredible turn-on. Let everyone else see it tied up. Wear it down for me."

"There was a clip in it. It looked so pretty."

Carter found the clip buried in the maple-hued mass. "Here. Put it back in."

"I can't. I don't know how to do it. Mario did it."

"Mario?"

"My hairdresser."

She'd gone to the hairdresser. For a dinner and theater date with him. That fact, more than anything else she'd said, touched him deeply. He doubted she went to the hairdresser often, certainly not to have something as frivolous as a clip put in. But she'd wanted to look nice for him.

"Ah, Jessica." Towels and all, he took her in his arms. "I'm sorry you got rained on. You must have looked beautiful."

"Not beautiful. But nice."

"Beautiful."

"But I'm a mess. I can't go anywhere like this, not to dinner, not to the theater. Call someone else, Carter. Get someone else to go with you."

He held her back and stared down onto her face. "Are you kidding?"

"No. Call someone."

He was about to argue with her when he caught himself. "You're right," he said. "Stay put." He left the bathroom.

Sinking down onto the lip of the tub, Jessica hugged the towel around her. But it was no substitute for his arms. It had neither living warmth nor strength—either of which might have helped soothe the soul-deep ache of disappointment she felt.

She knew it shouldn't matter so much. What was one date? Or one dress? Or one hairdo? But she'd so wanted things to be right. She hadn't realized how *much* she'd wanted that. But it was all ruined. The dress, the hairdo, her evening with Carter.

"All set," he said, returning to the bathroom. He'd taken off his jacket and tie and was rolling up his sleeves.

"What are you doing?" she asked, staring at the finely corded forearms that were emerging.

"Getting you dry."

"But I thought you phoned—"

"The ticket agent. I did. He's calling the tickets in to the box office. They'll be resold in a minute. We've got new ones for next week. Friday night this time. Okay?"

"But I thought—"

Hunkering down before her, he said softly, "You thought I was calling someone else to go with me, when I've been telling you all along that I don't want to go with anyone else." Leaning forward, he gave her a light kiss. "You don't listen to me, Jessica."

"But I've ruined your evening."

"Not my evening. Our evening. And it's not ruined. Just changed."

"What can we possibly do?" she cried. Absurdly her eyes were tearing again. He was being so kind and good and understanding, and she hadn't been able to come through at all on her end. "I'm a mess!"

Carter grinned. It was a dangerously attractive grin. "Any more of a mess and I'd lay you right down on the floor and take you here. You really don't know how sexy you are, do you?"

"I'm not."

"You are." His grin faded as his eyes roamed her face. "You are, and I want you."

"Carter—"

"But that's not what we're going to do," he vowed as he rose to his full height. "We're going to dry you off and then go out for dinner."

She wanted that more than anything. "But I can't go anywhere! My dress is ruined!"

"Then we'll order in dinner and wait for your dress to dry. First, you'll have to take it off."

Her cheeks went pink. "I can't. I haven't anything to put on."

Raising a promising finger, he left her alone for as long as it took him to fetch a clean shirt from his closet. Back in the bathroom, he dropped it over the towel bar, stood her up, turned her and unwound the towel enough so that he could get at the back fastening of her dress.

"I can do that," she murmured, embarrassed.

"Indulge me." Gathering her hair to one side, he carefully released the hooks holding the turtleneck together. Her hair had protected that part of her dress from the rain, so the lime color there was more vivid. Carter wished he'd seen her before the storm, wished it with all his heart. He knew how sensitive Jessica was about her looks, but she'd felt good about herself then. He would have given anything to be able to share that good feeling with her.

Not that he didn't think she looked good now. He meant it when he said she looked sexy. He was aroused, and being so close to her, gently lowering her zipper, working it more slowly as the silk grew wetter wasn't doing anything to diminish that arousal. Nor was watching as each successive inch of ivory skin was exposed. He told himself to leave the bathroom, but the heat in his body was making his limbs lethargic. He knew he'd die if he couldn't touch that smooth soft skin just once.

His fingertips were light, tentative on her spine between the spot where her zipper ended and her bra began. He heard her catch her breath, but the sound was as feminine as the rest of her and couldn't possibly have stopped him. Leaving his thumb on her spine, he flattened his fingers, moved them back and forth over butter-softness, spread them until they disappeared under the drape of her dress.

"Carter?" she whispered.

He answered by bending forward and putting his mouth where his fingers had been. Eyes closed, he reveled in the sweet smell of her skin and the velvet smoothness beneath his lips. He kissed her at one spot, slid to the next and kissed her again.

Each kiss sent a charge of sexual energy flowing through her. She clutched the towel to her front, but it was a mindless kind of thing, a need to hold tight to something. Carter's touch sent her soaring. Her embarrassment at his helping her undress was taking a back seat to the pleasure of his caress, which went on and on. His mouth moved over her skin with slow allure, his breath warming what his tongue moistened, his hand following to soothe it all.

Her knees began to feel weak, but she wasn't the only one with the problem. Carter lowered himself to the edge of the laundry hamper. Drawing her between his thighs, he slid both hands inside her dress. His fingers spanned her waist, caressing her while his mouth moved higher.

His hands followed, skipping over the slim band of her bra to her shoulders, gently nudging the silk folds of her dress forward.

Jessica tried again, though she was unable to produce more than a whisper. "Maybe this isn't such a good idea."

His breath came against the back of her neck, his voice as gritty as hers was soft. "It's the best one I've had. Tell me it doesn't feel good."

The days when she might have told him that, in pride and self-defense, were gone. "It feels good."

"Then let me do it. Just a little longer."

A small sigh slipped from her lips as she tipped her head to the side to make room for his mouth below her ear. What he was doing did feel good. His thighs flanked hers, offering support, and the whispering kisses he was pressing to her skin were seeping deep, soothing away the horror of the rain. The warmth of his hands, his mouth, his breath made her feel soft and cherished. Eyes closed, she savored the feeling as, minute by minute, she floated higher.

With the slightest pressure, Carter turned her to face him. Her eyes opened slowly to focus on his. She didn't need her glasses to see the heat that simmered amid the darkness there.

He touched her cheek with the side of his thumb, then slid his fingers to the back of her neck and brought her head forward. His mouth was waiting for hers, hot and hungry, and it wasn't alone in that. Jessica's met it with an eagerness that might have shocked her once, but seemed the most natural thing now. Because something had happened to her. She would never know whether it was the words of praise and reassurance he'd spoken, or the gentle, adoring way he touched and kissed her. But she was tired of fighting. She was tired of doubting, of taking everything he said and trying to analyze his motives. If she was being shortsighted, she didn't care. She wanted to feel and enjoy, and if there would be hell to pay in humiliation later, so be it. The risk was worth it. She wanted the pleasure now.

So she followed his lead, opening her mouth wider when he did, varying its pressure from heavy to feather light. There were times when their lips barely touched, when a kiss was little more than the exchange of breath or the touch of tongues, other times when the exchange was a more avid mating. She found one as exciting as the next, as stimulating in a breath-stopping, knee-shaking kind of way. When the knee-shaking worsened, she braced her forearms on his shoulders and anchored her fingers in his hair. She held him closer that way, wanted him closer still. And while the old Jessica was too much with her to say the words, the new Jessica spoke with the inviting arch of her body.

Carter heard her. His hands, which had been playing havoc over the gentle curves of her hips, came forward to frame her face. After giving her a final fierce kiss, he held her back.

For a time, he said nothing, just let himself drown with pleasure in the desire he saw in her eyes. If there'd ever been a different Jessica, he couldn't remember her. The only reality for him was the exquisitely sensual creature he now held between his legs.

Something else was between his legs, though, and it wasn't putting up with prolonged silence. Its heat and hardness were sending messages through the rest of his body that couldn't be ignored. His need to possess Jessica was greater than any need he'd ever known before.

His hands dropped from her face to her shoulders, then lower, to her breasts. He touched them gently, shaping his hand to their curve, brushing their hardened tips. Jessica gave a tiny sound of need and closed her eyes for a minute. When she opened them, Carter was smiling at her. "You're so beautiful," he murmured, and rewarded her for that with another kiss. This one was slower and more gentle, and by the time their lips parted, her breathing had quickened even more.

With her forearms on his shoulders and her forehead against his, she whispered, "I didn't know a kiss could do that."

"It's more than the kiss," Carter said in a low, slightly uneven voice. "It's my looking at you and touching you. And it's everything else that we haven't dared do. We've been thinking about it. At least, I have. I want to make love to you so badly, Jessica. Do you want that?"

It was a minute before she whispered, "Yes."

"Will you let me?"

"I'm frightened."

"You weren't frightened when I kissed you or when I touched your breasts."

"I was carried away."

His eyes met hers. "I'll carry you even further, if you let me. I want to do that. Will you let me?"

"I'm not good at lovemaking."

"Could've fooled me just now. I've never been kissed like that."

"You haven't?"

"You're a bombshell of innocence and raw desire. Do you have any idea how that combination turns a man on?"

She didn't, because she wasn't a man. But she knew that she was turned on herself. She could feel the pulsing deep inside her. "Will you tell me when I do things wrong?"

"You won't—"

"Will you tell me? I don't think I could bear it if we go through the whole thing and I think it's great, and then you tell me it wasn't so hot after all."

She'd spoken with neither accusation nor sarcasm, which was why Carter was so struck by what she said. After a moment of intense self-reproach, he murmured, "I wouldn't do that to you. I know you still don't trust me, but I swear, I wouldn't do that."

"Just tell me. If it's no good, we can stop."

He put a finger to her mouth. "I'll tell you. I promise. But that goes two ways. If I'm doing something you don't like, or something that hurts, I want you to tell me, too. Will you?" His finger brushed her lips, moving lightly, back and forth. "Will you?" he whispered.

She gave a small nod.

"Then come give me a kiss. One more kiss before we hang this dress up to dry."

8

Jessica kissed him with every bit of the love that had been building inside her for days. She hadn't put the correct name to it then, nor did she now, but that didn't matter. Under desire's banner, she gave her mouth to him in an offering that was as selfless as the deepest form of love. And when his kiss took her places she'd never been, she gave in to the luxury of it. And the newness. She'd never known such pleasure in a man's arms. She'd dreamed it, but to live the fantasy was something else.

Her headiness was such at the end of the kiss that she didn't demur when he drew her dress down. Leaving the damp silk gathered around her waist, he put his mouth to the soft skin that swelled above the cup of her bra. She held tight to his neck as he shifted his attention from one breast to the other, and what his mouth abandoned, his hand discovered. In no time, he had released the catch of her bra and was feasting on her bare flesh.

Jessica tried to swallow the small sounds of satisfaction that surged from inside.

"Say it," Carter urged against her heated flesh. "How does it feel?"

"Good," she gasped. She bent her head over his. "So good."

"I'm not doing it too hard?"

"Oh, no. Not too hard."

"Do you want it harder?"

"A little."

Her nipple disappeared into his mouth, drawn in by the force of his sucking, and she couldn't have swallowed her satisfaction this time if she'd tried. She choked out his name and buried her face in his hair.

He was a beautiful man, making her feel beautiful. She was on top of the world.

The feeling stayed with her for a time. Gently, between long, deep kisses that set her heart to reeling, Carter eased the dress over her hips and legs. Then, keeping her mouth occupied without a break, he lifted her in his arms and carried her into the bedroom. His body followed hers down to the spread, hands gliding over her, learning the shape of her belly, her hips, her thighs. He couldn't quite believe she was there, couldn't seem to touch enough of her at once. And everywhere he touched, she responded with a sigh or a cry or the arch of her body, which excited him all the more. His breathing was ragged when he finally pulled away and began to tug at the buttons of his shirt.

Jessica missed the warmth of his touch at once. Opening her eyes to see where he'd gone, she watched him toss the shirt aside and undo his belt. Her insides were at fever pitch, needing him back with her, but her mind, in the short minute that he was gone, started to clear. She couldn't tear her eyes from him. With his hair ruffled and falling over his forehead, his chest bare and massive, and his clothes following one another to the carpet, he was more man than she had ever seen in her life.

She couldn't help but be frightened. She was too inexperienced, for one thing, to take watching him in stride. For another, she'd lived too long thinking of herself as a sexless creature to completely escape self-doubt. Inching up against the headboard, she drew in her legs and folded her arms over her breasts.

"Oh, no, you don't," Carter said, lunging after her. "No, you don't." The mattress bounced beneath his weight, but his fierceness gave way to a gentle grin as he took her wrists and flattened them on the pillow. "Please don't get cold feet on me now, honey. Not when we're so close, when I want you so badly."

"I—"

"No." His mouth covered hers, kissing her hungrily, but if he meant to drug her, he was the one who got high. His kiss gentled, grew lazier, and, in that, more seductive. With a low groan, he pulled her away from the headboard, up to her knees and against his body. She cried out when her breasts first touched his chest, but he held her there, stroking her back in such a way that not only her breasts, but her belly moved against him.

He groaned again. "That feels...so...nice."

She thought so, too. The hair on his chest was an abrasive against her sensitive breasts, chafing them in the most stimulating of ways. His stomach was lean, firm against her, and his arousal was marked, a little frightening but very exciting. Coiling her arms around his neck, she held on for dear life as the force of desire spiraled inside her.

"You were made for me," he whispered brokenly. "I swear you were made for me, Jessica. We fit together so well."

The words were nearly as pleasurable as the feel of his hard body against hers. His approval meant so much to her. She desperately wanted to please him.

"I'm not too thin?"

He ran a large hand over her bottom and hips. "Oh, no. You've got curves in all the right places."

"You didn't think so once."

"I was a jackass then. Besides, I didn't see you like this then." He dipped his fingers under the waistband of her panty hose, then withdrew them in the next breath and gently lay her back on the bed. His eyes were dark and avid as they studied her breasts, his hand worshiping as it cupped a rounded curve. Then he met her gaze. "I'm going to take off the rest. I want to see all of you."

She didn't speak over the thudding of her heart, but she gave a short nod. Though she'd never have believed it possible, she wanted him to see her. She wanted him to touch her. She wanted him to make love to her. She was living the fantasy, and in the fantasy, she was a beautiful, desirable woman. Her insides were a dark, aching vacuum needing to be filled in the way that only he could.

She lifted her hips to help him. Her panties slipped down her legs along with the nylons, and all the while she watched his eyes. They followed the stockings off, then retraced the route over her calves and thighs to the dark triangle at the notch of her thighs. There they lingered, growing darker and more smoky.

Lifting his gaze to hers, he whispered in awe, "You are so very, very lovely."

At that moment, she believed him, because that was part of the fantasy. She was trembling. Her bare breasts rose and fell with each shallow breath she took, and the knot of desire grew tighter between her legs. She wanted him to touch her, to ease the ache, but she couldn't get herself to say the words.

Carter didn't need them. He had never seen such raw desire in a woman's eyes, had never known how potent such a look could be. It was pushing him higher by the minute, making him shake beneath its force. His body clamored for release. He wasn't sure how much longer he could hold back. But he wanted it to be good, so good for her.

"So very lovely," he repeated in a throaty whisper. Tearing his eyes from hers, he lowered his gaze to her body. With an exquisitely light touch, he brushed the dark curls at the base of her belly. When she made a small sound, he looked back up in time to catch her closing her eyes, rolling her head to the side, pressing a fist to her mouth. He touched her again, more daringly this time. She made another small sound and, twisting her body in a subtly seductive way, arched up off the bed.

It was his turn to moan. He was stunned by the untutored sensuality he saw, couldn't quite believe that a woman with Jessica's potential for loving had lived such a chaste life. But she had. He had no doubts about it, particularly when she opened her eyes and seemed as stunned as he.

"How do you feel?" he whispered. He stroked her gently, delved more deeply into her folds with each stroke.

Raising her hands to the pillow, she curled them into fists and swallowed hard. "I need you," she whispered frantically. "Please."

Between the look in her eyes, the sound of her whisper and the intense arousal to which her straining body attested, Carter was pushed to the wall. His blood was rushing hotly through his veins. He knew he couldn't wait much longer to take the possession his throbbing body demanded.

He paused only to shuck his briefs, before coming over her. "Jessica?" Unfurling her fists, he wove his fingers through hers.

She tightened the grip. Her body rose to meet his. "Please, Carter."

Rational thought was becoming harder by the second. He fought to preserve those last threads. "Are you protected, honey? Are you using something?" When she gave a frustrated cry and lifted her head to open her mouth against his jaw, he whispered, "Help me. Tell me. Should I use something?"

"No," she cried, a tight, high-pitched wail. "I want a baby."

Swearing softly—and not trusting himself to stay where he was a minute longer, because the idea of her having his baby sent a shock wave of pleasure through him—he rolled off her and crossed the room to the dresser.

"Carter," she wailed.

"It's okay, honey. Hold on a second."

"I need you."

"I know. I'll be right there." A minute later, he was back, sitting on the edge of the bed to apply a condom. A minute after that, he was back over her, his hands covering hers, his mouth capturing hers. While he took her lips with a rabid hunger, he found his place between her thighs. Slowly and gently in contrast to his ravishment of her mouth, he entered her.

Her name was a low, growling sound surging from his throat, a sound of pleasure and relief when her tightness surrounded him. He squeezed his eyes shut in a battle against coming right then, but she wasn't helping his cause. She lifted her thighs higher around his in an instinctive move to deepen his penetration.

He looked down at her. Her face was flushed, lips moist and parted, eyes half-lidded and languorous. Her hair was wild, the dark waves fanning out over the slate-gray spread.

In an attempt to slow things down, he anchored her hips to the bed with the weight of his own and held himself still inside her. "Am I hurting you?" he whispered.

"Oh, no," she whispered back. "Does it feel okay?"

"More okay than it's ever felt," he answered. His words were hoarse, his breathing ragged. "You're so small and tight. Soft. Feminine. You have an incredible body. Incredible body. Are you sure I'm not hurting you?"

She managed a nod, then closed her eyes because even without his moving, the pressure inside her was building. "Please," she breathed.

"Please what?"

"Do something. I want...I need..."

He withdrew nearly all the way, returned to bury himself to the hilt. In reward for the movement, she cried out, then caught in the same breath and strained upward. "Carter!"

"That's it, honey," he said, and began to move in earnest. "Do you feel me?"

"Yes."

"That what I want." Catching her mouth, he kissed her while the motion of his hips quickened. He pulled out and thrust in, filling her more and more, seeming to defy the laws of space. A fine sheen of sweat covered his body, blending with hers where their skin touched.

He had never known such pleasure, had never dreamed that such a physical act could touch his heart so deeply. But that was what was happening, and the heart touching was an aphrodisiac he couldn't fight. Long before he was ready to have the pleasure end, his body betrayed him by erupting into a long, powerful climax. Only when he was on the downside of that did he feel the spasms that were quaking inside Jessica.

Forcing his eyes open, he watched her face while the last of her orgasm shook her. With her head thrown back on the pillow, her eyes closed, her lips lightly parted, she was the most erotic being he'd ever seen in his life.

Her breathing was barely beginning to calm when his arms gave out. Collapsing over her, he lay with his head by hers for several minutes before rolling to the side and gathering her close. Then he watched her until she opened her eyes and looked up at him.

He smiled. "Hi."

"Hi," she said, shyly and still a bit breathlessly.

"You okay?"

She nodded, but when he expected her to look away, she didn't. Her eyes were increasingly large, expectant, trepidant.

"Having second thoughts?"

"One or two."

"Don't. Do you have any idea how good that was?" When she hesitated, then gave a short shake of her head against his arm, he brushed her eyebrow with a fingertip. "It was spectacular."

Still she hesitated. "Was it?"

"Yes." His smile faded. "You don't believe me."

She didn't say a thing for a minute, then spoke in a small voice, "I want to."

"But?"

She didn't answer at all this time, simply closed her eyes and lay her cheek on his chest. Carter would have prodded if he wasn't so enjoying lying quietly with her. But her body was warm, delicate, kittenish by his. Gently he drew her closer.

Her voice was flat, sudden in the silence. "Tom used to say things after it was over. He'd tell me how lacking I was."

Carter felt a chill, part anger, part disbelief, in the pit of his stomach. "Didn't he come?"

"Yes, but that didn't matter. He told me I wasn't much better than a sack of potatoes. I suppose I wasn't. I used to just lie there. I didn't want to touch him."

Carter remembered the way her hands had tightened around his, the way she'd arched to touch him with her body when he had restrained her hands, the way she brought her knees up to deepen his surge. She had been electric.

"That was Tom's fault," he said in a harsh voice. "It was his fault that he couldn't turn you on."

"I always felt inadequate."

"You shouldn't have. You're exquisite." Cupping her face in his hand, he kissed her lightly. "I have no complaints about what we did, except that I wanted it to last longer. But that was my fault. I couldn't hold back. I've been wanting you for days. I've been imagining incredible things, and to find out that the imagining wasn't half as incredible as the real thing—" He kissed her again, more deeply this time. His tongue lingered inside her mouth, withdrawing more slowly, reluctantly leaving her lips. "Jessica," he said in a shaky whisper and clutched her convulsively. But the feel of her body did nothing to dampen his reawakening desire.

Moaning, he released her and lay back on the bed.

Jessica came up on an elbow to eye him cautiously. "What's wrong?" she whispered.

He covered his eyes with his arm. "I want you again."

She looked at that arm, looked at the silky tufts of dark hair beneath it, looked at his chest, which was hairy in thatches, then his lean middle. By the time her eyes had lowered over his belly to the root of his passion, she was feeling tingly enough herself not to be as shocked by his erection as she might have been.

Without forethought, she touched his chest. He jumped, but when she started to snatch her hand away, he caught it, placed it back on his chest and laughed. "It's like lightning when you touch me. I wasn't prepared. That's all." Her hand was lying flat. "Go on. Touch. I like it."

Very slowly she inched her hand over the broad expanse of hair-spattered flesh and muscle. She felt those muscles tighten, felt his heartbeat accelerate, knew that her own was doing the same, but she wasn't about to stop. "I never dreamed..." Her fingertips lightly skimmed the dark, flat nipples that were already pebble hard.

"Never dreamed what?" he asked in a strained voice.

"That I'd...that we'd...you know."

"That we'd make love?"

"Mmm." Her thumb made a slow turn around his belly button.

Clapping a hand over hers, he pinned it to his stomach. When she looked up at him in surprise, his dark eyes smoldered. "Once before you touched me. Remember? By the duck pond?" She nodded. "I was wearing jeans then, and more than anything I wanted to unzip them and put your hand inside." He swallowed, then released her hand. "Touch me, Jessica?"

She looked from his eyes to his hardness and back.

"Touch me," he repeated in a beseechful whisper. The same beseechfulness was reflected in his eyes. More than anything else, that was what gave her courage.

Slowly her hand crept the short distance down a narrow line of hair to its flaring, finally to the part of him that stood, waiting straight and tall. She touched a tentative finger to him, surprised by the heat and the silkiness she found. Gradually her other fingers followed suit.

Taking in a ragged breath, Carter pushed himself into her hand. He wanted to watch her, wanted to see the expression on her face while she stroked him, but the agony of her touch was too much. She seemed to know just what to do and how fast. Closing his eyes, he savored her ministrations as long as he could before reaching down and tugging her back up. Then, when his mouth seized hers, his hands went to work.

He touched her everywhere, taking the time to explore that which he hadn't been able to do before. Where his hands left, his mouth took over. It wasn't long before Jessica was out of her mind with need, before he was, too.

Incredibly they soared higher this time. When it was done, their bodies were slick with sweat, their hearts were hammering mercilessly, their limbs were drained of energy.

They dozed off, awakening a short time later to find the sun down and the room dark. Carter left her side only long enough to light a low lamp on the dresser and draw the bedspread back. Then he took her with him between the sheets, settled her against him and faced the fact that he wanted her there forever.

"I love you," he whispered against her forehead.

Her eyes shot to his, held them for a minute before lowering. "No." She couldn't take the fantasy that far. "You're not thinking straight."

"I am. I've never said those words to a woman. I've never felt this way, felt this need to hold and protect and be with all the time. I've never wanted to wake up next to a woman, but I want it now. I don't like the idea of your going back home."

"I have to. It's where I belong."

His arm tightened. "You belong with me." When she remained silent, he said, "Do you believe in fate?"

"Predestination?"

"Mmm."

She didn't have to think about it long. "No. I believe that we get what we do. God helps those who help themselves."

But Carter disagreed. "If that were true, I'd never have returned home from Vietnam."

His words hovered in the air while Jessica's heart skipped a beat. Sliding her head back on his arm, she looked up at him. He was regarding her warily. "What do you mean?"

"I deserved to die. I hadn't done a decent thing in my life. I deserved to die."

"No one deserves to die in war."

"But someone always does." He looked away. "Good men died there. I saw them, Jessica. I saw them take hits. Some died fast, some slow, and with each one who went, I felt more like a snake."

"But you were fighting right alongside them," she argued.

"Yes, but they were good men. They were intelligent guys, guys with degrees and families and futures. A lot of them were rich—maybe not rich, but comfortable, and here I was walking around with a chip on my shoulder because I didn't have what they did. So they died, and I lived." He made a harsh sound, half laugh, half grunt. "Which says something, I guess, about the important things in life."

Jessica was beginning to understand. "That was what turned you around."

"Yes." His eyes held the fire of vehemence when they met hers. "Someone was watching over me there. Someone didn't let me die. Someone was telling me that I had things to do in life. I knew other guys who survived, but me, I never got the smallest scratch. That was fate. So was your asking me to work on Crosslyn Rise."

"Not fate. Gordon."

"But the setting was ripe for it." He turned on his side to look her in the eye. "Don't you see? You weren't married. You had been, but you were divorced. I never married. Never even had the inclination until I met you. Never wanted to think of having babies until I met you." Hearing the catch of her breath, he lowered his voice. "You do want them."

Her cheeks went red at the memory of what she'd cried out in the heat of passion.

He stroked that flush with his thumb. "I'll give you babies, Jessica. I couldn't take the chance before, because I wasn't sure you meant it. But you do, don't you?"

Silently she nodded.

"And until now the chances of it seemed remote, so you pushed it to the back of your mind. Then I said something about having children to leave the Rise to—"

"I won't be able to do that anyway. The Rise as I knew it will be gone."

"As you knew it. But all that's good about the Rise—its beauty and dignity, strength and stability—is inside you. You'll give that to your children. You'll make a wonderful mother."

Tears came to her eyes. What he was saying was too good to be true. *He* was too good to be true.

It was the aftermath of lovemaking, she decided. She didn't believe for a minute that he'd really want to marry her. Give him a day or two and he'd realize how foolish his talk was.

"I love you," he whispered, and she didn't argue. He kissed her once, then a second time, but the stirring he felt wasn't so much in his groin as in the region of his heart. He wanted to take care of her, to give her things, to do for her. She was a gentle woman, a woman to be loved and protected. He would do that if she let him.

Rubbing her love-swollen lips with the tip of his finger, he said, "You must be hungry."

"A little."

"If I order up pizza, will you have some?"

"Sure."

He kissed her a final time, then rolled away from her and out of bed. She watched him cross the room to the closet. His hips were narrow, his buttocks tight, the backs of his thighs lean and muscled, and if she'd thought that his walk was seductive when he was dressed, naked it was something else. When he put on a short terry-cloth robe, the memory of his nudity remained. When he returned to her, carrying the shirt from the bathroom, she felt shy.

"Uh-uh," he chided when she averted her eyes. "None of that." He helped her on with the shirt. "I've seen everything. I *love* everything."

"I'm not used to this, I guess," she murmured, fumbling with the buttons.

He could buy that, and in truth, he liked her shyness. It made the emergence of her innate sensuality that much more of a gift. "I'll give you time," he said softly, and led her out of the bedroom.

He was going to have to give her plenty of that, she mused a short time later. They sat on stools at the kitchen counter, eating the pizza that had just been delivered. Though it was a mundane act, she'd never done anything so cataclysmic. She couldn't believe that she was sitting there with Carter Malloy, that she was wearing nothing under his shirt, that she'd worn even less not long before.

Carter Malloy. It boggled her mind. *Carter Malloy.*

"What is it?" he asked with a perplexed half smile.

She blushed. "Nothing."

"Tell me."

Tipping her head to the side, she studied a piece of pizza crust. "I'm very...surprised that I'm here."

"You shouldn't be. We've been building toward this for a while."

He was right, but she wasn't thinking of the recent past. "I'm thinking farther back. I really hated you when I was little." She dared him a look and was struck at once by his handsomeness. "You're so different. You look so different. You *act* so different. It's hard to believe that a person can change so much."

"We all have to grow up."

"Some people don't. Some people just get bigger. You've really changed." Studying him, she was lured on by the openness of his features. "What about before Vietnam? I can understand how your experience there could shape your future, but what about your past? Why were you the way you were? It couldn't have been the money factor alone. What was it all about?"

Thoughtfully pursing his lips, Carter looked down at his hands. His mouth relaxed, but he didn't look up. "The money thing was a scapegoat. It was a convenient one, maybe even a valid one on some levels. Since my parents worked at Crosslyn Rise, we lived in town, and that town happens to be one of the wealthiest in the state. So I went to school with kids who had ten times more than me. From the very start, I was different. They all knew each other from kindergarten. I was a social outcast from the beginning, and it was a self-perpetuating thing. I was never easy to get along with."

"But why? If you were still that way, I'd say that it was a genetic thing that you couldn't control. But you're easy enough to get along with now, and you don't seem to be suffering doing it. So if it wasn't genetic, it had to come from outside you. Some of it may have come from antagonism in school, but if you were that way when you first enrolled, it had to come from your family. That's what I don't understand. Annie and Michael were always wonderful, easygoing people."

"You weren't their son," Carter said with a sharpness reminiscent of a similar comment he'd made once before.

Not for a minute did Jessica feel that the sharpness was directed at her. He was thinking back to his childhood. She could see the discomfort in his eyes. "What was it like?" she asked, needing to understand him as intimately as possible.

"Stifling."

"With Annie and Michael?" she asked in disbelief.

"They loved me to bits," he explained. "I was their pride and joy, their hope for the future. I was going to be everything they weren't, and from the earliest they told me so. I'm not sure that I understood what it all meant at the time, but when I was slow doing things, they pushed me. I didn't like being pushed—I still don't, so maybe that's a biological trait after all. I stayed in the terrible-two stage for lots of years, and by that time, a pattern had been set. My parents were always on top of me, so I did whatever I could to thwart them. I think I was hoping that at some point they'd just give up on me."

"But they never did."

"No," he said quietly. "They never did. They were always loyal and supportive." He looked at her then. "Do you know how much pressure that can put on a person?"

Jessica was beginning to see it. "They kept hoping for the best and you kept disappointing them."

"By the time I was a teenager, I had a reputation of being tough. That hurt my parents, too. People would look at them with pity, wondering how they ever managed to have a son like me."

She remembered thinking the same thing herself, and not too long before. "They are such quiet, gentle people."

Again Carter looked away, pursing his lips. He felt guilty criticizing his parents, yet he wanted Jessica to know the truth, at least as he saw it. "Too quiet and gentle. Especially my dad."

"You would have liked him to be stronger with you?"

"With me, with *anyone*. He wasn't strong, period."

It occurred to Jessica that she'd never thought one way or another about Michael Malloy's strength. "In what sense?"

"As a man. My mother ran the house. She did everything. I can't remember a time when Dad doted on her, when he stood up for her, when he bought her a gift. The only thing he ever did was the gardening."

"Do you think she resented that?"

"Not really. I think it suited her purposes. She liked being the one in control." He took a minute to consider what he'd said. "So maybe when I use the word 'stifling' I should be using the word 'controlling.' In her own quiet way, my mother was the most controlling woman I've ever met. That was what I spent my childhood rebelling against—that, and the fact that my father never once opened his mouth to complain when, in her own gentle way, she ran roughshod over him.''

He grew quiet, then looked down. ''Lousy of me to be bad-mouthing them, when I treated them so poorly, huh?''

''You're not bad-mouthing them. You're just explaining what you felt when you were growing up.''

He met her gaze. ''Does it make any sense?''

''I think so. I always thought of Annie as, yes, gentle and quiet, but also efficient. Very efficient. She definitely took control of things in our house. I can understand how 'taking control' could become 'controlling' in her own house. And Michael was always gentle and quiet... just...gentle and quiet. That was what I liked about him. He was always pleasant, always smiled. For me, that was a treat.''

''It used to drive me wild. I'd do anything just to rile him.''

''Did you manage?''

Carter smirked. ''Not often. And he's still like that. Still quiet and gentle. I doubt he'll ever change.''

Jessica was relieved to hear the fondness in his voice. ''You've accepted him, then?''

''Of course. He's my father.''

''And you're close to him now?''

''Close? I don't know, close. We talk regularly on the phone, but for every five minutes Dad's on, Mom's on for ten. I suppose it's just as well. They like to hear what I'm doing, but I'm not sure they appreciate the details.'' He gave an ironic smile. ''I've finally made it, just like they wanted me to, but that means my world is very different from theirs.''

''Are they happy?''

''In Florida? Yes.''

''For you?''

''Very.'' His smile was sheepish this time. ''Of course, they don't know why I have a partner, since I can do so much better by myself. And they don't know why I'm not married.''

Jessica knew they'd be pleased if Carter ever told them he loved her, but she prayed he wouldn't do that. To tie their hopes to something that would never go anywhere was a waste. Even if Carter did believe that he loved her, he'd see the truth once he got back to his normal, everyday life. The fewer people who knew of the night he'd spent playing at being in love, the better.

Jessica returned to Crosslyn Rise on Friday, soon after Carter left for work. She wanted to immerse herself in her own world, to push the events of Thursday night to the back of her mind.

That was easier said than done, because after dinner, they'd gone back to bed. Time and again during the night, they'd made love, and while Jessica never once initiated the passion, she took an increasingly aggressive part in it. That gave her more to think about than ever.

She seemed to bloom in Carter's arms. Looking back on some of the things she'd done, she shocked herself. She, who had never hungered for another man, had lusted for his body, and she couldn't even say that he taught her what to do. Impulses had just...come. She had wanted to touch him, so she had. She had wanted to taste him, so she had.

And he hadn't complained. Every so often, when she'd caught herself doing something daring, she'd paused, but in each case he had urged her on. In each case his pleasure had been obvious, which made her feel all the freer.

Freer. Free. Yes, she had felt that, and it was the strangest thing of all. Making love to Carter, even well after that first pent-up desire had been slaked, was a relief. With each successive peak she reached, she felt more relaxed. It was almost as if she'd done just what he had once accused her of doing—spent years and years denying her instincts, so that now she felt the sheer joy of letting them out.

She fought the idea of that. Once discovered, the passion in her wouldn't be as easily tucked away again—which was just fine, as long as Carter stayed with her. But she couldn't count on that happening. In the broad light of a Crosslyn Rise day, she had too many strikes against her.

She was plain. She was boring. She was broke.

Carter was just the opposite. He was on his way up in the world, and he would make it. She knew that now. She also knew that he didn't need someone like her weighing him down.

That was one of the reasons why, when he called at four to say that he was leaving the office and would be at Crosslyn Rise within the hour, she told him not to come.

9

"Why not?" Carter asked, concerned. "Is something wrong?"

"I just think that I ought to get some work done."

"You've had all day to do that."

"Well, I slept for some of the day, and I didn't concentrate well for the rest."

He didn't have to ask why on either score. "So give it up for today. You won't get much done anyway."

"I'd like to try."

"Try tomorrow. We agreed on dinner tonight."

"I know, but I'm not very hungry."

"Not now. But it'll be an hour before I get there, another hour before we get to a restaurant and get served." He paused, then scolded, "You're avoiding the issue. Come on, Jessica. Spit it out."

"There's nothing to spit out. I'd just rather stay home tonight."

"Okay. We'll stay home."

He was being difficult, she knew, and that frustrated her. "I'd rather be alone."

"You would not. You're just scared because everything that happened last night was sudden and strong."

"I'm not scared," she protested. "But I need time, Carter."

"Like hell you do," he replied, and slammed down the phone.

Forty minutes later, he careened up the driveway and slammed on his brakes. He was out of the car in a flash, taking the steps two at a time, and he might well have pounded the door down had not Jessica been right there to haul it open after his first fierce knock.

"You have no right to race out here this way," she cried, taking the offensive before he could. She was wearing a shirt and jeans, looking as plain as she could, and as angry. "This is my house, my life. If I say that I want to spend my evening alone, that's what I want to do!"

Hands cocked low on his hips, Carter held his ground. "Why? Give me one good reason why you want to be alone."

"I don't have to give you a reason. All I have to say is yes or no."

"This morning you said yes. What happened between now and then to make you change your mind?"

"Nothing."

"What happened, Jessica?"

"Nothing!"

His brown eyes narrowed. "You started thinking, didn't you? You started thinking about all the reasons why I can't possibly feel the way I say I do about you. You came back to this place, and suddenly last night was an aberration. A fluke. A lie. Well, it wasn't, Jessica. It isn't. I loved you then, and I love you now, and you can say whatever stupid things you want, but you can't change my mind."

"Then you're the fool, because I don't want to get involved."

"Baloney." His eyes bore into hers, alive with a fire that was only barely tempered in his voice. "You want a husband, and you want kids. You can pretend that you don't, and maybe it used to work, but it won't work now. Because, whether you like it or not, you *are* involved. You can't forget what happened last night."

"What an arrogant thing to say!"

"Not arrogant. Realistic, and mutual. I can't forget it, either. I want to do it again."

"You're a sex fiend."

His voice grew tighter, reflecting the strain on his patience. "Sex had nothing to do with what we did. That was lovemaking, Jessica. We *made* love, because we *are* in love. If you don't want to admit it, fine. I can wait. But I'm going to say it whenever I want. I love you."

"You do not," she scoffed, and pushed up her glasses.

"I love you."

"You may think you do, but give yourself a little time, and you'll come to your senses. You don't love me. You can't possibly love me."

"Why not?" He took a step toward her, and his voice was as ominous as his look. "Because you're not pretty? Because you lie like a sack of potatoes in my bed? Because you're a bookworm?"

"It's Crosslyn Rise that you love."

He eyed her as though she were crazy. "Crosslyn Rise is some land and a house. It's not warm flesh and blood like me."

"But you love it, you associate me with it, hence you think you love me."

"Brilliant deduction, Professor, but wrong. You're losing Crosslyn Rise. There's no reason why I would align myself with you if the Rise is what I want."

She took a different tack. "Then it's the money. If this project goes through, you'll be making some money. So you're confusing the issues. You feel good about the money, so you feel good about me."

"I don't want the money that bad," he said with a curt laugh. "If you were a loser, no amount of money would lure me into your bed."

"What a crass thing to say!"

"It's the truth. And it should say something about my feelings for you. We did it last night more times than I've ever done it in a single night before. My muscles are killing me. Still I want more. Every time I think of you I get hard."

She pressed her hands to her ears, because his words alone could excite her. Only when his mouth remained still did she lower her hands and say very slowly, "Revenge is a potent aphrodisiac."

"*Revenge.* What in the hell are you talking about?"

She tipped up her chin. "This is the ultimate revenge, isn't it? For all those years when I had everything you wanted?"

"Are you kidding?" he asked, and for the first time there was an element of pain in his voice. "Didn't you hear a word I said last night? Didn't any of it sink in—any of the stuff about Vietnam or my parents? I've never told anyone else about those things. Was it wasted on you?"

"Of course not."

"But I didn't get through. You wanted to know what caused me to change over the years, and I told you, but I didn't get through." He paused, and the pain was replaced by a sudden dawning. "Or was that what frightened you most, because for the first time you could believe that the change was for real?" He took a step closer. "Is that it? For the first time you had to admit that I might, just might be the kind of guy you'd want to spend the rest of your life with, and that scares you." He took another step forward. Jessica matched it with one back. "Huh?" he goaded. "Is that it?"

"No. I don't want to spend the rest of my life with *any* man."

"Because of your ex-husband? Because of what he did?"

She took another step back as he advanced. "Tom and I are divorced. What he did is over and done."

"It still haunts you."

"Not enough to shape my future." She kept moving back.

"But you don't trust me. That's the crux of the problem. You don't trust that I'm on the level and that I won't hurt you the way that selfish bastard did. Damn it, Jessica, how can I prove to you that I mean what I say if you won't see me?"

"I don't want you to prove anything," she said, but her heels had reached the first riser of the stairs. When he kept coming, she sat down on the steps.

"Okay." He put one hand flat on the tread by her hip. "I'll admit things have happened quickly. If you want time, I'll give you time. I won't rush you into anything, especially something as important as marriage." He put his other hand by her other hip. His voice lowered. His eyes dropped to her mouth. "But I won't stand off in the distance or out of sight, either. I can't do that. I need to see you. I need to be with you."

Jessica wanted to argue, but she was having trouble thinking with him so close. She could see the details of the five-o'clock shadow that he hadn't had time to shave, could feel the heat of his large body, could smell the musky scent that was his alone. He looked sincere. He sounded sincere. She wanted to believe him...so...badly.

His mouth touched hers, and she was lost. Memory of the night before returned in a storm of sensation so strong that she was swept up in it and whirled around. She had to wrap her arms around his waist to keep herself anchored to something real, and then it wasn't memory that entranced her, but the sensual devouring of his mouth.

Over and over he kissed her, dueling with her lips for supremacy in much the same way they'd argued, though neither seemed to care who won, and, in fact, both did. When her glasses fogged up, he took them off and set them aside. Pressing her back on the stairs, he touched her breasts, then slid his fingers between the buttons of her shirt to reach bareness. When that failed to satisfy his craving, he unbuttoned the shirt and unhooked her bra, but no sooner had he exposed her flesh than she brushed the back of her hand over the rigid display on the front of his slacks.

"Oh, baby," he said, "come here." Slipping a large hand under her bottom, he lowered himself and pressed her close. In the next breath, he was kissing her again, and in the next, tugging at the fastening of her jeans.

"Carter," she whispered, breathless. "What—"

"I need you," he gasped, pushing at her zipper.

"Now?"

"Oh, yeah."

"Here?"

"Anywhere. Help me, Jess." He'd turned his attention to his belt, which was giving him trouble. Jessica did what she could, but her hands were shaky and kept tangling with his, and when it came to his zipper, his erection made things even more difficult. After a futile pass or two, the most important thing seemed to be freeing her own legs from their bonds.

She didn't quite make it. Her jeans were barely below her knees when Carter pressed her back to the steps. With a single strong stroke, he was inside her, welcomed there hotly and moistly. Then the movement of his hips drove her wild, and she didn't care that they were in the front hall, that they were half-dressed, that the ghosts of Crosslyn Rise were watching, turning pink through their pallor. All she cared about was sharing a precious oneness with Carter.

That weekend was the happiest Jessica had ever spent, because Carter didn't leave her for long. He made love to her freely, wherever and whenever the mood hit. And wherever or whenever that was, she was ready. Hard as it was to believe, the more they made love, the more she wanted him.

As long as he was with her, she was fine. As long as he was with her, she believed his words of love, believed that his ardor could be sustained over the years and years he claimed, believed that his head would never be turned by another woman.

When he left her on Monday morning to go to work, though, she thought of him at the office, in restaurants, with clients, and she worried. She went to work, herself, and she was the quiet, studious woman she'd always been.

Maybe if people had looked at her strangely she would have felt somehow different. But she received the same smiles and nods from colleagues she passed. No one looked twice, as had happened when she'd dressed up the Thursday before. No one seemed remotely aware of the kind of weekend she'd spent.

She didn't know what she expected. Aside from a bundle of tender muscles, she was no different physically than she'd always been. But no one knew about the muscles. No one knew about Carter Malloy. No one knew about the library sofa, the parlor rug or the attic cot.

So she saw herself as the others saw her, and everything that was risky and frightening about her affair with Carter was magnified.

Until she saw him that night. Then the doubts seemed to waft into the background and pop like nothing more weighty than a soap bubble, and she came to life in his arms.

The pattern repeated itself over the next few weeks. Her days were filled with doubts, her nights with delight. Graduation came and went, and the summer session began, but for the first time in her life, there was a finite end to a day's work. That end came when Carter arrived. He teased her about it, even urged her to do some reading or class preparation on those occasions when he had brought work of his own with him to do, but she couldn't concentrate when he was with her. She would sit with a book while he worked, but her eyes barely touched the page, and her mind took in nothing at all but how he looked, what he was doing, what they'd done together minutes, hours or days before.

She was in love. She admitted it, though not to him. Somehow, saying the words was the most intense form of self-exposure, and though one part of her wished she had the courage because she knew how much he wanted to hear it, she wasn't that brave. She felt as though she were driving on a narrow mountain path where one moment's inattention could tip her over the edge. She wanted to be prepared when Carter's interest waned. She wanted to have a remnant of pride left to salvage.

His interest waned neither in her nor in Crosslyn Rise. Sketch after sketch he made, some differing from the others in only the most minor of features, but he wanted them to be right. He and Jessica had dinner one night with Nina Stone to get her opinion on the needs of the local real estate market; as a result of that meeting, they decided to offer six different floor plans, two each in two-bedroom, three-bedroom and four-bedroom configurations.

Also as a result of that meeting, Jessica learned that Carter wasn't interested in Nina Stone. Nina was interested in him; her eyes rarely left his handsome face, and when she accompanied Jessica to the ladies' room, she made her feelings clear.

"He's quite a piece of man. If things cool between you two, will you tell me?"

Jessica was surprised that Nina had guessed there was something beyond a working relationship between her and Carter. "How did you know?" she asked, not quite daring to look Nina in the eye.

"The vibes between you. They're hot. Besides, I've been sending him every come-hither look I know, and he hasn't caught a one. Honey, he's smitten."

"Nah," Jessica said, pleased in spite of herself. "We're just getting to know each other again." Far better, she knew, to minimize things, so that it wouldn't be as humiliating if the relationship ended.

Still there was no sign of that happening. On the few occasions that Carter mentioned Nina after their meeting, it was with regard to the project and with no more than a professional interest.

"Didn't you think she was pretty?" Jessica finally asked.

"Nina?" He shrugged. "She's pretty. Not soft and gentle like you, though, or half as interesting."

As though to prove his point, he spent hours talking with her. They discussed the economy, the politics in Jessica's department, the merits of a book that he'd read and had her read. He was genuinely curious about what she was thinking, was often relieved to find that she wasn't lost on some esoteric wavelength where he couldn't possibly join her.

When it came to Crosslyn Rise, he took few steps without having her by his side, considered few ideas without trying them out on her first. Though her feedback wasn't professional from an architectural standpoint, it was down-to-earth. When she didn't like something, she usually had good reason. He listened to her, and while he didn't always agree, he yielded as many times as not. Their personal, vested interests balanced each other out; when he was too involved in the design to think of practicality, she reminded him of it, and when she was too involved in the spirit of Crosslyn Rise to see the necessity of a particular architectural feature, he pointed it out.

By the middle of July, there was a set of plans to show Gordon. As enthusiastic about them as Carter was, Jessica set up the meeting. Then the two of them stood side by side, closely watching for Gordon's reaction as he looked over the drawings.

He liked them, though after he'd said, "You two make a good team," for the third time in ten minutes, Jessica was wondering what particular message he was trying to get across. She had tried not to look at Carter, and when he caught her hand behind her skirt and drew it to the small of his back, she was sure Gordon couldn't see.

Possibly he had sensed the same vibes Nina had, though she hadn't thought Gordon the type to sense vibes, at least not of that kind. She finally decided that it was the little things that gave them away—the light lingering of Carter's hand on her back when they first arrived, the way he attributed her ideas to her rather than taking credit for them himself, the mere fact that they weren't fighting.

The last made the most sense of all. Jessica remembered her reaction when Gordon had first mentioned Carter's name. She thought back to that day, to her horror and the hurt in those memories. At some point along the way, the hurt had faded, she realized. She had superimposed fondness and understanding on the Carter Malloy who had been so angry with the world and himself, and doing that took the sting off the things he'd once said. Not that she dwelt on those memories. He had given her new ones, ones that were lovely from start to finish.

"Jess?" Carter's low, gentle voice came through her reverie. She looked up in surprise, smiled a little shamefacedly when she realized her distraction. He motioned to the nearby chair. Blushing, she sank into it.

"Everything all right, Jessica?" Gordon asked.

"Fine. Just fine."

"You know these highbrow types," Carter teased, smiling indulgently. "Always dreaming about one thing or another."

Her cheeks went even redder, but she latched onto the excuse as a convenient out. "Did I miss anything?"

"Only Gordon's approval. I have to polish up the drawings some, but he agrees that we're ready to move ahead."

Jessica's eyes flew to Gordon. "Getting the investors together?"

Gordon nodded and opened a folder that had been lying on the corner of his desk. He removed two stapled parcels, handed one to each of them, then took up his own. "I've jumped the gun, I guess, but I figured that I'd be doing this work anyway, so it wouldn't matter. These are the names and profiles of possible investors, along with a list of their general assets and the approximate contribution they might be counted on to make. You can skip through page one—that's you, Jessica—and page two—that's you, Carter. The next three are William Nolan, Benjamin Heavey and Zachary Gould. You know Ben, don't you, Carter?"

"Sure do. I worked with him two years ago on a development in North Andover." To Jessica, he said, "He's been involved in real estate development for fifteen years. A conservative guy, but straight. He's selective with his investments, but once he's in, he's in." He looked at Gordon. "Is he interested?"

"When I mentioned your name, he was. I didn't want to tell him much else until the plans were finalized, but he just cashed in on a small shopping mall in Lynn, so he has funds available. Same with Nolan and Gould.''

Jessica was trying to read as quickly as possible, but she'd barely made it halfway down the first sheet on Benjamin Heavey when Gordon mentioned the others. "Nolan and Gould?" She had to flip back a page to reach Nolan, ahead two to reach Gould.

"Are you familiar with either name?" Gordon asked.

"Not particularly." Guardedly she looked up. "Should I be?"

Carter shot her a dry grin. "Only if you're into reading the business section of the paper," which he knew, for a fact, she was not, since they'd joked about it just the Sunday before, when she'd foisted that particular section on him in exchange for the editorials.

"Bill Nolan is from the Nolan Paper Mill family," Gordon explained. "He started in northern Maine, but has been working his way steadily southward. Even with the mills up north, he has a genuine respect for the land. A project like this would be right up his alley."

Carter agreed. "From what I hear, he's not out for a killing, which is good, since he won't get one here. What he'll get is a solid return on his investment. He'll be happy." Turning several pages in his lap, he said to Gordon, "Tell me about Gould. The name rings a bell, but I can't place it."

"Zach Gould is a competitor of mine."

"A banker?" Jessica asked.

"Retired, actually, though he's not yet sixty. He was the founder and president of Pilgrim Trust and its subsidiaries. Two years ago he had a heart attack, and since he was financially set, he took his doctor's advice and removed himself from the fray. So he dabbles in this and that. He's the type who would drop in at the site every morning to keep tabs on the progress. Nice guy. Lonely. His wife left him a few years back, and his children are grown. He'd like something like this."

Jessica nodded. Determined to read the fine print when she had time alone later, she turned to the next page. "John Sawyer?"

Gordon cleared his throat. "Now we start on what I like to call the adventurers. There are three of them. None can contribute as much money as any of these other three men, or you or Carter, but each has good reason not only to want to be involved but to be sure that the project is a success." He paused for only as long as it took Carter to flip to the right page. "John Sawyer lives here in town. He owns the small bookstore on Shore Drive. I'm sure you've been there, Jessica. It's called The Leaf Turner?''

She smiled. "Uh-huh. It's a charming place, small but quaint." Her smile wavered. "I don't remember seeing a man there, though. Whenever I've been in, Minna Larken has helped me."

Gordon nodded. "You've probably been in during the morning or early afternoon hours. That's when John is home taking care of his son. By the time two-thirty rolls around, he has high school girls come in to play with the boy while he goes to work."

"How old is the kid?" Carter asked.

"Three. He'll be entering school next year. Hopefully."

At the cautious way he'd added the last, Jessica grew cautious herself. "Something's wrong with him?"

"He has problems with his hearing and his eyesight. John had tried him in a preschool program, but he needs special attention. He'll have a tough time in the public kindergarten class. There is a school that would be perfect for him, but it's very expensive."

"So he could use a good money-making venture," Carter concluded. "But does he have funds for an initial investment?"

Gordon nodded. "His wife died soon after the boy was born. There was some money in life insurance. John was planning to leave it in the bank for the child's college education, but from the looks of things he won't get to college unless he gets special help sooner."

"How awful," Jessica whispered, looking helplessly from Gordon to Carter and back. "She must have been very young. How did she die?"

"I don't know. John doesn't talk about it. They were living in the Midwest when it happened. He moved here soon after. He's a quiet fellow, very bright but private. In many respects, the stakes are higher for John than for some of these others. But he's been asking me about investments, and this is the most promising to come along in months."

"But will the money come through in time for him?" Carter asked. "If all goes well, we could break ground this fall and do a fair amount of framing before winter sets in. We may be lucky enough to make some preconstruction sales, but most of the units won't be ready for aggressive marketing until next spring or summer, and then the bank loans will have to be paid off first. I can't imagine that any of us will see any raw cash for eighteen months to two years. So if he's going to need the money sooner—"

"I think he's covered for the first year or two. But when he realized that the child's education was going to be a long-time drain, he knew he had to do something else."

"By all means," Jessica said, "ask him to join us." She focused her attention on the next sheet. "Gideon Lowe." She glanced at Carter. "Didn't you mention him to me once?"

"To you and to Gordon. You did call him then?" he asked the banker.

"By way of a general inquiry, yes. I named you as the contact. He thinks you're a very talented fellow."

"I think he's even more so. He takes pride in his work, which is more than I can say for some builders I know. Now that they're getting ridiculous fees for the simplest jobs, they've become arrogant. And lazy. Cold weather? Forget it—they can't work in cold weather. Rain? Same thing. And if the sun is out, they want to quit at twelve to play golf."

"I take it Gideon Lowe doesn't play golf?" Jessica asked.

"Not quite," Carter confirmed with a knowing grin. "Gideon would die strolling around a golf course. He's an energetic man. He needs something fast."

"Like squash?" she asked, because squash was Carter's game, precisely for its speed, as he'd pointed out to her in no uncertain terms.

"Like basketball. He was All-American in high school and would have gone to college on a basketball scholarship if he hadn't had to work to support his family."

Jessica's eyes widened. "Wife and kids?"

"Mother and sisters. His mother is gone now, and his sisters are pretty well-set, but he's too old to play college basketball. So he plays on a weekend league. Summers, he plays evenings." Recalling the few games he'd watched, Carter gave a slow head shake. "He's got incredible moves, for a big guy."

"And incredible enthusiasm," Gordon interjected. "He made me promise to call him as soon as I had something more to say about Crosslyn Rise."

"Then you should call him tomorrow," Jessica said, because Carter's recommendation was enough for her. She turned to the final page on her lap and her eyes widened. "Nina Stone?" She looked questioning at Gordon.

"Miss Stone called me," Gordon explained with a slight emphasis on the me. "She knows something of what you're doing since you've talked with her. She knows that I'm putting a group together. She wants to be included in that group and she has the money to do it."

Jessica sent him an apologetic look. "She was insistent?"

"You could say that."

"It's her way, Gordon. Some people see it as confidence, and it sells lots of houses. I can imagine, though, that it would be a little off-putting with someone like you, particularly on the phone. Wait until you meet her, though. She's a bundle of energy." As she said it, she had an idea. Turning to Carter, she said, "I'll bet she and Gideon would get along. You didn't say if he was married."

"He's not, but forget it. They are two very forceful personalities. They'd be at each other's throats in no time. Besides," he added, and a naughty gleam came into his eye, "they're all wrong physically. She's too little and he's too big. They'd have trouble making...it, uh, you know what I mean."

She knew exactly what he meant, but she wasn't about to elaborate in front of Gordon any more than he was. The only solace for her flaming cheeks was the rush of color to Carter's.

Fortunately, that color didn't hinder his thinking process. Recovering smoothly, he said, "If Nina has the money, I see no reason why she shouldn't invest." More serious, he turned to Jessica. "What's her motive?"

"She wants to go into business for herself. She wants the security of knowing she's her own boss. How about Gideon?"

"He wants the world to know he's his own boss. Respect is what he's after."

"Doesn't he have it now?"

"As a builder, yes. As a man who works with his hands, yes. As a man with brains as well as brawn, no. He's definitely got the brains—that's what makes him so successful as a builder. But people don't always see it that way. So he wants to be involved with the tie-and-jacket crowd this time."

Jessica could understand how Carter might understand Gideon better than some. He'd seen both sides. "If Gideon wants to invest, would that rule out his doing the building?"

"I hope not," Carter said, and looked questioningly at Gordon.

"I don't see why it would," Gordon answered. "The body of investors will be bound together by a legal agreement. If Gideon should decide to bid on the job and then lose out to another builder, his position in the consortium will remain exactly the same."

"There wouldn't be a conflict of interest?"

"Not at all. This is a private enterprise." He arched a brow toward

Jessica. "Theoretically, you could pick your builder now, and make it part of the package."

"I wouldn't know who to pick," she said on impulse, then realized that she was supposed to be in charge. Recomposing herself, she said to Gordon, "You pointed out that I have to be willing to listen to people, especially when they know more about things than I do. I think that Carter will help me decide on the builder. Do you have any problem with that?"

"Me? None. None at all."

Something about the way he said it gave Jessica pause. "Are you sure?"

Gordon frowned at the papers before him for a minute before meeting her gaze. "I may be out of line saying this—" his gaze broke off from hers for a minute to touch on Carter before returning "—but I didn't expect that you two would be so close."

"We're very close," Carter said, straightening slightly in his seat. "With a little luck we'll be married before long."

"Carter!" Jessica cried, then turned to Gordon, "Forget he said that. He gets carried away sometimes. You know how it is with men in the spring."

"It's summer," Carter reminded her, "and the only thing that's relevant about that is that you'll have a few weeks off between semesters at the end of August when we could take a honeymoon."

"Carter!" She was embarrassed. "Please, Gordon. Ignore this man."

To her chagrin, Gordon looked to be enjoying the banter. "I may be able to, but the reason I raise the issue is that other people won't." He grew more sober. "It was clear from the minute you two walked in here that something was going on. I think you ought to know just what that something is before you face the rest of this group. The last thing you want them to feel is that they're at the end of a rope, swinging forward and back as your relationship does."

"They won't," Jessica said firmly.

"Are you sure?"

"Very. This is a business matter. Whatever my relationship is or isn't with Carter, I'll be very professional. After all, the crux of the matter is Crosslyn Rise." She shot Carter a warning look. "And Crosslyn Rise is mine."

"You're being unreasonable," Carter suggested, lengthening his stride to keep up with her brisk pace as they walked along the street after leaving the bank. Jessica hadn't said more than two words to him since the exchange with Gordon. "What was so terrible about my saying I want to marry you?"

"Whether we marry is between you and me. It's none of Gordon's business."

"He had a point, though. People see us together, and they wonder. Some things you can't hide. We are close. And there was nothing wrong with your deferring to me on the matter of a builder. As your husband, I'd want you to do that."

"You're my architect," she argued crossly. "You're more experienced than I am on things like choosing a builder. My deferring to you was a business move."

"Maybe in hindsight. At the time, it was pure instinct. You deferred to me because you trust me, and it's not the first time that's happened. You've done it a lot lately. Crosslyn Rise may be yours, but you're glad to have someone to share the responsibility for it." He half turned to her as they walked. "That's what I want to do, Jess. I want to help you, and it's got nothing to do with Crosslyn Rise and everything to do with loving you. Giving and sharing are things I haven't done much of in my life, but I want to do them now."

She had trouble sustaining crossness when he said things like that. "You do. You are."

"So marriage is the next step. Why are you so dead set against it?"

"I'm not dead set against it. I'm just not ready for it."

"Do you love me?"

She swung around the corner with him a half step behind. "I've been married," she said without answering his question. "Things change once the vows are made. It's as if there's no more need to put on a show."

That stopped Carter short, but only for a minute. He trotted a pace to catch up. "You actually think I've been putting on a show? That's absurd! No man—especially not one who spent years feeling second-rate, being ashamed of who he was—is going to keep after a woman the way I have after you if he doesn't love her for sure. In case you haven't realized it, I do have my pride."

She shot him a glance and said more quietly, "I know that."

"But I'll keep asking you to marry me, because it's what I want more than anything else in my life."

"It's what you *think* you want."

"It's what I *want*." Grasping her arm, he drew her to a stop. "Why won't you believe that I love you?"

She looked up at him, swallowed hard and admitted, "I do believe it. But I don't think it will last. Maybe we should just live together. That way it won't be so painful if it ends."

"It won't end. And we're practically living together now, but that's not what I want. I want you driving my car, living under my roof, using my charge cards. And my name. I want you using my name."

She eyed him warily. "That's not a very modern wish."

"I don't give a damn. It's what I want. I want to take care of you. I want to be strong for you. I resented my father because he rode through life on my mother's coattails. I refuse to do that."

Jessica was astonished. "You couldn't do that with me. I don't *have* any coattails. My life is totally unassuming. You're more dynamic than I could ever be. You're more active, more aggressive, more success-ful—"

He put a finger to her lips to stem the flow of words. "Not successful enough, if I can't convince you to marry me."

With a soft moan, she kissed the tip of his finger, then took it in her hand and wagged it, in an attempt at lightness. "Oh, Carter. The problem is with me. Not you. Me. I want to satisfy you, but I don't know if I can."

"You do."

"For now. But for how much longer? A few weeks? A month? A year?"

"Forever, if you'll give yourself the chance. Can't you try, Jessica?"

* * *

She could, she supposed, and each time she thought of marrying Carter, her heart took wing. Still, in the back of her mind, there was always an inkling of doubt. More so than either dating or living together, marriage made a public statement about a man and a woman. If that marriage fell apart, the statement was no less public and far more humiliating—especially when the male partner was Carter Malloy. Because Carter Malloy was liked and respected by most everyone he met. That fact became clear to Jessica over the next few weeks as they met with Gordon, with lawyers, with various investors. Despite Jessica's role as the owner of Crosslyn Rise, Carter emerged as the project's leader. He didn't ask for the position, in fact he sat back quietly during many of the discussions, but he had a straight head on his shoulders and seemed to be the one, more than any other, who had a pulse on the various elements involved—architectural plans, building prospects, environmental and marketing considerations, and Jessica.

Especially Jessica. She found that she was leaning on him more and more, relying on him for the cool, calm confidence that she too often lacked. Gone were the days when her life maintained a steady emotional keel. She seemed to be living with highs and lows. Some had to do with Crosslyn Rise—highs when she was confident it would become something worthy of its past, and lows when the commercial aspects of the project stood out. Some had to do with Carter—highs when she was in his arms and there was no doubt whatsoever about the strength of his love, and lows when she was apart from him, when she eyed him objectively, saw a vibrant and dynamic man and wondered what he ever saw in her.

As the weeks passed, she felt as though she were heading toward a pair of deadlines. One had to do with Crosslyn Rise, with the progress of the project, with the approach of the trucks and bulldozers and the knowledge that once they broke ground, there was no going back.

The other had to do with Carter. He would only wait so long. He'd been so good about not mentioning marriage, but she knew he was frustrated. When August came and it was apparent there would be no honeymoon, he planned a vacation anyway, spiriting her away for a week in the Florida Keys.

"See?" he teased when they returned. "We made it through a whole week in each other's company nonstop, and I still love you."

By late September, he was pointing out that they'd made it for five months and were going strong. Jessica didn't need that pointed out. Her life revolved around Carter. He was her first thought in the morning and her last thought at night, and though there were times when she scolded herself for being so close to him, so dependent on him, she couldn't do differently—particularly with the ground-breaking at Crosslyn Rise approaching fast. It was an emotional time for her, and Carter was her rock.

Even the most solid of rocks had its weak spot, though, and Jessica was Carter's. He adored her, couldn't imagine a life without her, but the fact that she wouldn't marry him, that she didn't even say that she loved him was eroding his self-confidence and hence, his patience. When he was with her, he was fine; he loved her, she loved him, he wasn't about to ruin their time together. Alone though, he brooded. He felt thwarted. He was tired of waiting. Enough was enough.

Such were the thoughts that he was trying unsuccessfully to bury when, late in the afternoon on the last Wednesday in September, he drove to Crosslyn Rise. Before Jessica had left him in Boston that morning, she had promised to cook him dinner. He hadn't spoken with her during the day, which annoyed him, since he wanted *her* to call *him* once in a while, rather than the other way around. He needed the reassurance. She wouldn't say she loved him, so he needed her to show she cared in other ways. A phone call would have been nice.

But there'd been no call. And when he opened the back door and came into the kitchen, there didn't look to be anything by way of pots and pans on the stove. Nothing smelled as though it were cooking. Jessica was nowhere in sight.

"Jessica?" he called, then did it again more loudly. *"Jessica?"*

He was through the kitchen and into the hall when he heard her call, "I'll be right there." He guessed she was upstairs in the bedroom—the master bedroom with its king-size bed, which she'd started using when he'd begun to sleep over regularly—and that thought did bring a small smile to his face. He was early. She always freshened up, changed clothes, combed out her hair when she knew he was coming. So she wasn't quite done. That was okay. He'd help her. He'd even help her with dinner.

Which went to show how lovesick he was. The thought of being with her, of maybe getting in a little hanky-panky before dinner was enough to wipe all the frustrating thoughts from his mind. And it wasn't just that the lovemaking could do it, but when they made love, he knew that she loved him. She came alive in his arms, showed him a side of her that the rest of the world never saw. No woman could respond to him—or give—in that way if she wasn't in love.

He took the stairs two at a time, but he hadn't reached the top when she came down the hall. One look at her face and he knew there would be no hanky-panky. Indeed, she looked as though she'd newly brushed her hair and changed her clothes, even put on a little makeup, but the dab of blusher didn't hide her pallor.

"What's wrong?" he asked, coming to an abrupt halt where he was, then taking the rest of the stairs more cautiously.

"We have a problem," she said in a tight voice.

"What kind of problem?"

"With Crosslyn Rise. With the construction."

He let out a relieved breath. "A problem with the project I can handle. A problem with us I can't." He reached for her. "Come here, baby. I need a hug." Enveloping her in his arms, he held her tightly for a minute, then relaxed his hold and kissed her lightly. She was the one who clung then, her face pressed to his neck, her arms trembling. There was something almost desperate about it, which made him a little nervous. "He-ey." He laughed softly and held her back. "It can't be all that bad."

"It is," she said. "The town zoning commission won't give us a permit. They say our plans don't conform with their regulations."

Putting both hands on her shoulders, Carter ducked his head and stared at her. "What?"

"No permit."

"But why? There's nothing unusual about what we're doing. We're following all the standard rules, and we did go through the town for the subdivision allowances. So what are they picking on?"

"The number of units. The spacing of the units." She tossed up a hand, and her voice was a little wild. "I don't know. I couldn't follow it. When I got the call, all I could think of was that here we are, ready to break ground, and now the whole thing's in danger."

"No." Slipping an arm around her shoulder, he brought her down beside him on the top step. "Not in danger. It only means a little more work. Who did you speak with?"

Jessica looked at her hands, which were knotted in her lap. "Elizabeth Abbott. She's the chairman of the zoning commission."

"I know Elizabeth Abbott. She's a reasonable woman."

"She wasn't particularly reasonable with me. She informed me that the decision was made this morning at a meeting, and that we could apply for a waiver, but she suggested I call back the trucks. She didn't see how we could break ground until next spring or summer at the earliest.'' Jessica raised agonized eyes to Carter's. ''Do you know what a delay will mean? Carter, I can't afford a delay. I barely have the money to keep Crosslyn Rise going through another winter. I'm already up to my ears in loans to the bank. The longer we're held up, the longer it will be until we see money on the other end. That may be just fine for men like Nolan and Heavey and Gould, and it may be okay for you, but for me and the rest of us—it's too late!''

''Shh, honey. It's not too late.'' But he was frowning. ''We'll work something out.''

''She was vehement.''

Releasing her, Carter propped his elbows on his thighs and let his hands hang between his knees. ''Small towns aren't usually this rigid with one of their leading citizens.''

''I'm no leading citizen.''

''Crosslyn Rise is. It's the leading parcel of land here.''

''That's probably why they're being so picky. They want to know exactly who's coming in and when.''

Carter shook his head. ''Even the snobbiest of towns don't do things like this. Something stinks.''

Jessica held her breath for a minute. She looked at Carter, but his frown gave away nothing of his deeper thoughts. Finally, unable to wait any longer, she said, ''It's Elizabeth Abbott. I could tell from her voice. She's the force behind this.''

He eyed her cautiously. ''How well do you know her?''

''Only enough to say hello on the street. We never had anything in common. I'm not saying that she's deliberately sabotaging our progress, but she's clearly against what we're doing. She seemed pleased to be making the call, and she wasn't at all willing to even *consider* accommodating us.'' Jessica's composure began to slip. ''They could hold a special meeting, Carter. How difficult would it be for three people to meet for an hour? When I asked, she said that wasn't done. She said that they'd be more than happy to consider our waiver at their next scheduled meeting in February.'' Her voice went higher. ''But we can't wait that long, Carter. We can't wait that long.''

Carter continued to frown, but the curve of his mouth suggested disgust.

''Talk to her,'' Jessica said softly. ''She'll listen to you.''

His eyes shot to hers. ''What makes you say that?''

"Because you had something going with her once. She told me."

His expression grew grim. "Did she tell you that it happened seven years ago, when I was still living in New York, and that it lasted for one night?"

"Go to her. You could soften her up."

"One night, Jessica, and do you want to know why?" His eyes held hers relentlessly. "Because she was something I had to do, something I had to get out of my system. That's all. Nothing more. We were classmates here in town way back when. She was a witness to some of my most stupid stunts. Far more than you in some ways, she was synonymous in my mind with the establishment around here. So when she came up to me that night—it was at a reception in one of the big hotels, I don't even remember which—I had this sudden need to prove to myself that I'd really made it. So I took her to bed. And it was the most unsatisfying thing I've ever done. I didn't see her again in New York, and I haven't seen her since I moved back here."

Jessica's heart was alternately clenching tightly and pounding against her ribs. She believed every word Carter said—and the truth was echoed in his eyes—still she pushed on. "But she'd like to see you again. I could tell. Maybe if you gave her a call—"

"I'll call one of the other members of the commission."

"She's the chairman. She's the one who can make things happen, but only if she wants. Talk to her, Carter. Make her want to help us."

Carter was beginning to feel uneasy. Sitting back against the banister to put a little more space between them, he asked cautiously, "How would you suggest I do that?"

Jessica had been tossing possibilities around for the better part of the afternoon, which was why she hadn't called him earlier to tell him about the problem. The solution she'd found was as abhorrent as it was necessary, but she was feeling desperate on several counts. "Smile a little. Sweet-talk her. Maybe even take her to dinner."

"I don't want to take her to dinner."

"You take prospective clients to dinner."

"Prospective clients take *me* to dinner."

"Then make an exception this time. Take her to dinner. Wine and dine her. She'll listen to you, Carter."

"Okay. You and I will take her to dinner."

"You're missing the point!" Jessica cried.

"No," Carter said slowly. His eyes were chilly, reflecting the cold he felt inside. "I don't think I am. I think that the point—correct me if

I'm wrong—is that I should do whatever needs to be done to get a waiver from the commission, and if that means screwing Elizabeth Abbott, so be it.'' While he didn't miss the way Jessica flinched at his choice of words, he was too wrapped up in his own emotions to care. The coldness inside him was fast turning to anger. "Am I right?"

The harsh look in his eyes held Jessica silent for a minute.

"Am I right?" he repeated more loudly.

"Yes," she whispered.

"I don't believe it," he murmured, and though his voice was lower, the look in his eyes didn't soften. "I don't believe it. How can you ask me to do something like that?"

"It may be the only way we can go ahead with this thing."

"Is that all that matters to you? This *thing*? Crosslyn Rise?"

"Of course not."

"Could've fooled me. But then, it's no wonder. You won't say you love me, you won't say you'll marry me, and now you come up with this idiotic scheme."

"It's not idiotic. It would work. Elizabeth Abbott has a reputation for things like this."

"Well, I don't. I wouldn't demean myself by doing something like this. I'm no goddamned gigolo!" Rising from the stairs, he stormed down three steps before turning to glare at her. "I love you, Jessica. If I've told you once, I've told you dozens of times, and I'm not just blowing off hot air. I love you. That means *you're* the woman I want. Not Elizabeth Abbott."

Jessica swallowed hard. "But you were with her once—"

"And it was a mistake. I knew it at the time, and I know it even more now. I won't go so far as to say that she's holding up things for Crosslyn Rise because of me, because even when she used to call me and I wouldn't see her, she was gracious. I never thought of her as being vindictive, and I'm not about to now, but I won't sleep with her." Agitated, he thrust a hand through his hair. "How can you ask me to do that?" he demanded, and through the anger came an incredible hurt. "Don't I mean anything to you?"

Jessica was so stunned by the emotions ranging over his face that it was a minute before she could whisper, "You know you do."

But he was shaking his head. "Maybe I was fooling myself. Part of love is respect, and if you respected me for who and what I am, you wouldn't be asking this of me." Again he thrust a hand into his hair; this time it stopped midway, as though he were so embroiled in his thoughts that he couldn't keep track of his gestures. "Did you honestly think I'd go along? Did you think I'd seduce her? Did you think I'd really be able to get it *up*?" He swore softly, and his hand fell to his side. "I blew it somewhere, Jessica. I blew it."

In all the time she'd known him, Jessica had never seen him look defeated, but he did now. It was there in the bow of his shoulders and the laxness of his features, either of which put him a galaxy apart from the angry and vengeful boy he'd been so long ago. She knew he'd changed, but the extent of the change only then hit her. She was still reeling from it when she caught the sheen of moisture in his eyes. Her knuckles came hard to her mouth.

"I'd do most anything for you, Jessica," he said in a gut-wrenching tone. "So help me, if you asked me to lie spread-eagle on the railroad track until the train blew its whistle, I'd probably do it, but not this." Swallowing once, he tore his eyes from hers, turned and started down the stairs.

"Carter?" she whispered against her knuckles. When he didn't stop, she took her hand away. "Carter?" Still he didn't stop, but reached the bottom of the stairs and headed for the door. She rose to her feet and called him again, more loudly this time, then started down. When he opened the door and went through, she quickened her step, repeating his name softly now and with a frantic edge. By the time she reached the door, he was halfway to his car.

"Carter?" Her eyes were filled with tears. "Carter!" She was losing him. "Carter, wait!" But he was at the driver's side, reaching for the door. "Carter, stop!" He was the light of her life, leaving her. Panicked, she opened her mouth and screamed, *"Carter!"*

The heartrending sound, so unusual coming from her, stopped him. He raised his head wearing such a broken look that she couldn't move for another minute. But she had to keep him there, had to touch him, had to tell him all he meant to her. Forcing her legs into action, she ran toward the car.

Stopping directly before him, she raised a hand halfway to his face, wavered, mustered enough courage to graze his cheek with a finger before pulling back, then went with her own need and slipped her hand to the back of his neck. "I'm sorry," she tried to say, but the words were more mouthed than anything. "I'm sorry." She put her other hand flat on his chest, moved it up, finally slid it around his neck, went in close to him and managed a small sound against his throat. "I'm sorry, Carter, I'm sorry. I love you so much."

Carter stood very still for a long minute before slowly lifting his hands to her hips. "What?" he whispered hoarsely.

"I love you. Love you."

It was another long minute before he let out a breath, slid his arms around her and gathered her in.

Unable to help herself, Jessica began to cry. She could no more stop the tears than the words. "That was s-such a stupid thing for me to think of—and an insult t-to you. But something happened to me wh-when she said she'd known you before. Maybe I wanted to know what w-would happen—she's very attractive—but I l-love you so much—I don't know what I'd d-do if you ever left me."

He buried his face in her hair. Even muffled, his voice sounded rough. "You were pushing me away."

"I didn't know what else t-to do."

"You should have called me right away." He tightened his hold in a punishing way, and his voice remained gruff. "There's a solution, Jessica. There's always a solution. But you've got to keep your priorities straight. Top priority is us."

She knew that now. For as long as she lived, she'd never forget the sight of big, bad Carter Malloy with tears in his eyes. They had been tears of pain, and she'd put them there. They were humbling and horrifying. She never wanted to see them again.

Going up on tiptoe, she coiled her arms more tightly around his neck. "I love you," she whispered over and over again until finally he took her face in his hands and held her back.

"What do you want?" he whispered. His face was inches from hers, his thumbs brushing tears from under her glasses while his palms held her still. "Tell me."

"You. Just you."

"But what do you want?"

She knew that he needed to hear the words, and though they represented the ultimate exposure, she was ready for that, too. "I want to marry you. I want to take your name and use your credit cards and drive your car. I want to have your babies."

Carter didn't react, simply looked at her as though he weren't quite sure whether to believe her. So, clutching his wrists, she added, "I mean it. All of it. I think it's what I've wanted since the first time we made love, but I've been so afraid. You're so much more than me—"

"I'm not."

"You are. You've done so much more, come so much further in life, and that makes you so much more interesting. I want to marry you. I do, Carter. But if we got married and then you wanted out, I think I'd *die*, I love you so much."

"I won't want out," he said.

"But I didn't know that for sure until just now."

"I've been telling it to you for weeks."

"But I didn't know." She closed her eyes and whispered, "Oh, Carter, I don't ever want to lose you. Not ever."

"Then marry me. That's the first way to tie a man down."

Her eyes came open. "I'll marry you."

"And give me kids. That's the second way to tie a man down."

"Okay."

"And keep on teaching, because I'm so *proud* of what you do."

"You are?" she asked with a hesitant half smile.

"Damn it, yes," he said and crushed her to him. "I've always been proud of you. I'll always *be* proud of you—whether you're a scholar, mother of my kids, my wife or my woman."

Jessica smiled against his neck, feeling lighter and happier than she'd ever felt before. "I do love you," she whispered.

"Then trust me, too," he said. Taking her by the shoulders, he put her back a step and eyed her sternly. "Trust that I mean what I say when I tell you I love you. I don't want other women. I never *have* wanted other women the way I want you. I've never asked another woman to marry me, but I've asked you a dozen times. I *choose* you. I don't *have* to marry you. I *choose* you. I *want* to marry you."

"I get the point," she murmured, feeling a little shamefaced but delighted in spite of it.

"Do you also get the point about priorities?" he went on, and though a sternness remained in his voice, there was also an exciting vibrancy. "Crosslyn Rise is beautiful. It is venerable and stately and historic. I've got a whole lot of time invested in it, and money now, too, but if I had to choose between the Rise and you, there'd be no contest. I'd turn my back on the time, the money and the Rise just to have you. And I'd do it without a single regret." His eyes grew softer. "So I don't want you worrying about the zoning commission. We'll call Gordon and Gideon and the others. We'll work something out. But all that is secondary. Do you understand?"

"I do," she whispered, and it was true. In those few horrible minutes when she had seen his tears, when he had walked away from her and she'd had the briefest glimpse of the emptiness of life without him, Crosslyn Rise had been the last thing on her mind. Yes, the Rise was in trouble, but she could handle it. With Carter by her side, she could handle anything.

All That Sparkles
by Stella Cameron

Chapter One

"Why did you lie to us?"

"Lie? What do you mean, lie? Did your father send you to Holland to call me a liar? I knew you when you were a boy, Christophe St-Giles, a boy in short pants."

Christophe swore under his breath and turned back to the window. "The past has no part in our business now. Nor does emotion. This is a fine old diamond house with a great reputation. Or it was—"

Benno Kohl's fist slammed into his desk. "Enough!" His vehemence jarred Christophe. "When you were a boy you also had some respect for your elders. I won't tolerate this insult. Kohl's is still great, the best. We've had some problems. The diamond industry always has problems from time to time. Natural recessions—or deliberately engineered ones—are a part of life with us. We need a loan to get us through a bad time. Is that so much to ask of the bank my family has done business with for generations?"

"Normally, no." Christophe narrowed his eyes to peer morosely from the third-floor window onto Rokin, the street that housed the cream of Amsterdam's diamond dealerships. "And I hold you in the deepest respect, sir. But we aren't talking about a normal situation here, are we?" He heard Benno's chair creak, and the sound of the older man breathing heavily. The ball was in Benno's court now. Christophe rubbed a knuckle over cool, rain-splattered glass and waited. The weather, and the row of stone buildings facing him, matched his mood—gray.

Benno came to stand beside Christophe. "Why did your father send you? Couldn't any questions you had have been cleared up on the phone?"

"This can't go on," Christophe said, suddenly weary. He turned to face Benno. Odd how the years changed men. Not so long ago, Benno had towered over him; now he, Christophe, was the taller.

"What can't go on?" Benno prompted.

"I've already spent a week digging through mountains of confusing records," Christophe said as tonelessly as possible. Anger wouldn't help. "You could have saved me the effort—by being honest. I'm sorry dealing with me is proving uncomfortable for you. My father believed it would be otherwise. We could have sent someone else to look into this. I came as head of our bank's special loan investigations department because you and your family mean so much to us. We at St-Giles wanted to give you special consideration."

"Oh, thank you." Benno's mouth turned down at the corners. His thin features were set inscrutably as his pale blue eyes shifted from Christophe's face to the scene outside. "Such kindness. And now, have you finished your digging, as you put it? If so, I'd appreciate receiving the money I've asked for as soon as it can be released. I hope your return flight to Zurich will be uneventful." Benno straightened his tall, reedy frame. The man had lost weight in the four years since Christophe had last seen him, and his once iron-gray hair had turned totally white.

Christophe clamped his hands on his hips. As soon as he'd arrived in Amsterdam, he'd figured out this would be a tough assignment, and he'd been right. "There will be no loan, Benno."

Benno grasped Christophe's elbow, the expressionless mask slipping from his face. "Yes," he rasped. "Yes, there will be a loan. There has to be a loan. Without that money, we will fail. Kohl's House of Diamonds will die. Do you understand? Your father has worked to keep St-Giles a successful banking institution—for you, just as his father did for him. You're being groomed to take his place one day. It's the same with Lukas and me. You and your family cannot watch another old family business fail and do nothing because...because..."

"Because someone is stealing from you?"

Seconds of silence slipped away. Christophe stared hard into the other man's eyes, eyes so much older than his own, paler and strangely defeated. He felt the strength and vitality of his own thirty-five years, the advantage of his prime over the other's failing vigor. The sensation gave him little pleasure.

Finally Benno shook his head and dropped his hand. "That's madness. You don't know what you're talking about."

"I know exactly what I'm talking about." Fumbling for a cigarette, Christophe was adamant. He felt vaguely sick. "I know because everything I've learned so far makes theft the only possible reason for your difficulties. Cigarette?'' He offered the pack of Gitanes to Benno who waved dismissively.

"Suppose you tell me what you've learned.'' He ran a hand over his thinning hair and returned to slump in his chair.

"I'd be glad to,'' Christophe said simply, rounding the desk to sit opposite Benno. He lit up and inhaled deeply, hunching his powerful body forward. "At first everything seemed to coincide with your report to the bank. But—''

Benno interrupted quickly, "Why didn't St-Giles simply give me the advance? Why did your people question me?''

"Because,'' Christophe said patiently, "Kohl's has been through a dozen of the recessions you just talked about and never needed a loan of any kind. This time, you not only need a loan, you need a very large sum. You've also poured other personal sources of capital into the business in a brief period of time. Yet you're still in trouble. We have to know why—what's so different on this occasion. No bank can risk the kind of money you ask for simply in the name of friendship.'' What he said was fact, but he hated every cold statement he'd had to make.

"Go on.'' The bone in Benno's hawklike nose whitened when he pinched his bridge. He was fighting for composure. "My young friend,'' he said softly, "will you please say what you have to say—quickly.''

Christophe shoved his own straight brown hair back from his brow. Hurting this distinguished old merchant wasn't what he wanted. "It didn't take long to sniff something out of line, something sinister. Benno, two months ago, a few weeks before you asked for the loan, you made refunds on a number of valuable stones—thirteen, I believe the number was.''

Benno's head came up. "Our policy has always been total satisfaction to the customer. Any buyer may change his mind if not completely happy with a purchase.''

Christophe caught and held the other man's eyes. "I understand that. But where are the stones you took back? Why weren't they reentered in your inventory lists to be sold again?''

"I—I—'' Benno made a steeple with his fingers. His hands trembled. "I can explain.''

"Yes,'' Christophe said softly. "I'm sure you can, if you want to. Someone stole those stones before they could be replaced in stock, didn't they? And our job is to find out who, how, and to stop it from happening again. You think an infusion of money will buy the time you need to recover. It won't if we don't stop the thefts. And your reputation in the industry is already sinking. We heard rumors as far away as Zurich—another reason I'm here. Rumors are a luxury you can't afford in your business. Distrust is death to the diamond merchant."

Silence settled in around them, broken by the tick of an antique clock on one wall and the muted whirring of grinding wheels in the workroom outside the office.

"You have it almost right," Benno said at last, shaking his head slowly. He leaned heavily into his chair. "Only we know the diamonds disappear before they ever get to the buyer's hands."

Christophe rested his elbows on the desk and sent another plume of pungent smoke into the air. "I don't understand. You mean they never arrive?"

"Yes and no. Stones arrive. They are of almost duplicate weight and cut to those purchased. And they are diamonds. But they are of vastly inferior quality." He tilted his chin, stretching hollows and rigid tendons in his neck. "Somewhere between this building and the point of delivery our flawless gems disappear. Clever, so very clever."

"My God," Christophe muttered. "You know what this means, don't you? Since no one on staff has reported the switch, the answer has to be here, right here in your own operation."

"No!" Benno made fists on the desk. "That cannot be. The switches must have occurred when the stones were being...when they were..."

"Being delivered?" Christophe raised one brow. "In which case your people would still be implicated. Our first step must be to start taking Kohl's employees apart."

Benno leaped to his feet, drawing up to his full height. "Over my dead body. I know how it looks. It was meant to look like this. Sabotage, Christophe. We are being sabotaged. And I suggest you look at Metter Brothers, not here. Philip Metter hates me, just as his father hated my father. For four generations that firm has competed with Kohl's, tried to find ways to overtake us in the trade and never managed it. This time they're close, but they won't make it by tearing apart the trust I've built, both with my customers and with my employees. Nothing, you hear me, Christophe, nothing will be done or said to undermine my people. They are above reproach. If you have to play detective, do it with Philip Metter's staff."

"Sit down," Christophe begged quietly. Benno's face was mottled, and a faint blue tinge darkened his lips. "You look ill. Please, Benno. I'm here to help you. Believe that. We'll work together and I won't do anything to undermine Kohl's."

Benno sank to his chair once more, his chest rising and falling rapidly. "The thefts have stopped. There's been nothing for three weeks, and I don't believe it will happen anymore."

"I do." Christophe stubbed out the half-smoked Gitane and immediately reached for another. "I don't know for certain why they're laying off for a while, but I have a pretty good idea, and unless we find out who's behind the scam, it'll start again. Remember, Benno, my arrival has been anticipated for about three weeks, which fits in with the possibility that I may be what's holding them up, and as soon as I leave, they'll hit again." He flipped his lighter, changed his mind and stuffed it back into the pocket of his suit jacket. "I talked to Lukas—"

"That's another thing," Benno broke in, agitated. "One of Metter's boys, Herbert, I think, smiled at Lukas the other day. He *smiled* at my son. Enemies who haven't spoken for a hundred and fifty years don't suddenly smile at each other. They are involved. I know it. And they've done what they intended to do—tainted our reputation. Now we must recoup as quickly as possible. The way to do that is to make no more fuss. Carry on as usual and rebuild our reputation."

"You don't think an official investigation—"

"No!" Benno shook his head vigorously. "No, no. That would finish us for sure."

"Very well." Christophe squared his broad shoulders. "You need me to okay the loan and you won't consider an official investigation, therefore you must play by my rules and trust me to do the best, for everyone."

"Which is?" Benno asked flatly.

"An investigation of my own—my way. Anyone who had anything to do with those missing diamonds, or could have, no matter how insignificantly, is a suspect. Why didn't you tell me about this Renfrew woman?"

"Paula?" Benno's throat moved convulsively. "Why should I tell you about Paula? What would I say? She's only been with us nine months."

"Exactly." Christophe settled against his chair and propped an ankle on the other knee. "She's the newest Kohl employee. And she also has an interesting history. You might have considered telling me about that, too."

Benno massaged his temples. "This is too much. Who has been talking to you? And you—" he glared at Christophe "—what made you think you had the right to ask questions behind my back? If you wanted to know something, *I* was the one to ask." He collected himself, averting his face. "Anyway, there's nothing to know about Paula. She is the daughter of an old American friend who is now dead and she's studying to become a polisher. She will make an excellent craftswoman."

"And?"

"And?" Benno flexed his fingers. "And her parents apparently divorced some years ago. Her mother remarried. There is a brother in the American Air Force. Paula is, of course, single—twenty-six years old. A delightful young woman. What more can I say? That's all there is."

"Not quite all," Christophe said. He twisted the ring on the small finger of his left hand, weighing what he would say next. "My old friend, Lukas, is cool to say the least, but he does understand the necessity to supply the information I need if we are to get you out of this mess. Your son resents me as much as you do; however, he answered my questions about your personnel. Too bad he didn't also explain the stones were switched. That gives another interesting dimension to our little puzzle. Perhaps now you will both work with me, rather than against me."

Benno bristled. "Lukas should have cleared anything he intended to say to you with me first. But I understand his reasoning. What did he tell you?"

"That Paula Renfrew's father worked for your father many years ago. Michael Renfrew was also an apprentice diamond finisher, just as his daughter is now."

"That's correct." Benno relaxed visibly. "Michael and I were the same age. We became friends and I was sorry when he decided to return to America. He died a year ago and his daughter asked to come here and work. Naturally, I was delighted. Anna is delighted. Since Lukas married, our home has become empty. Now we have Paula living in our guest house and she is like the daughter we never had."

"But Michael Renfrew didn't simply *decide* to return to America, did he?"

"Lukas..." Benno closed his eyes for an instant. "Lukas has obviously said too much. I'm tired, Christophe. I'm getting old. Stop this game of hide-and-seek and tell me exactly what you know—or think you know."

Christophe leaned to grip one of Benno's thin wrists. "There was another theft—a long time ago. That, too, was hushed up, and Kohl's was lucky because only one stone disappeared. But a man disappeared, too, didn't he Benno? Michael Renfrew skipped Holland and returned to the States. There was never absolute proof he was the thief, but why else would he run away at just that time? And now, after his death, his daughter shows up, pretending to be nothing more than an aspiring craftswoman. Can you believe she knows nothing of the other crime? Can you honestly convince yourself she's oblivious to this one—that her presence is purely coincidence? What about vengeance, Benno? Don't you think Renfrew probably told his daughter what happened here, insisted on his own innocence—suggested he was framed, perhaps? And now she's collecting on the debt you owe her father."

"That will do." Finality colored Benno's words. "That is all I will listen to about Paula. Her father was innocent. I've always known it. Lukas should never have told you about the incident. If you insist on checking the records of my employees, so be it. Do so with discretion. But I never want to hear another suggestion like this about Paula."

He would back off for a while, Christophe decided. At least, Benno knew where they stood. "Trust me, Benno. I'll do nothing you wouldn't approve of." *Please, God, let that be possible.* "I admit I'm puzzled by Lukas's hostility. He has his reason, of course, but is that enough to totally withdraw from me? We've been friends a long time. I didn't think anything could completely destroy that."

Benno looked away. "That year you spent with us when you were— how old?"

"Twenty-two," Christophe supplied promptly.

"A special time. For all of us. For Lukas you became a brother. Give him time to understand that you must put your own business interests first."

A rush of gratitude warmed Christophe. "Thank you for that. For understanding. This is hard on all of us."

"We would have liked you to stay with us." Benno made circles on the desk with a forefinger. "Anna wanted that."

"It wouldn't have done. Not this time. When I come to dinner next week, I'll talk to her about it myself."

Benno nodded. "Your hotel is comfortable?"

"Ah!" Christophe exclaimed. "I forgot to tell you. Peter insisted I use his houseboat. Now he lives in that apartment in Lukas and Sandi's house; he rents the barge, but it was vacant and he thought I'd be more comfortable—and private there."

"Good, good," Benno said with a laugh. "That old barge should be enough to bring you and Lukas back together. Peter Van Wersch is a good man. The most faithful friend Lukas ever had. I remember the three of you working to convert the houseboat. The Three Musketeers, you called yourselves.'' He smiled broadly. ''Anna and I spent many nights wondering what you did when you weren't hammering loose decking.''

Christophe joined the laughter. ''Nothing you wouldn't have done, sir, I assure you.''

Tension had evaporated from the comfortable office. ''Perhaps that's what worried us, eh?'' Benno asked wryly.

''I wonder,'' Christophe began tentatively. ''Do you think this would be a good time for you to introduce me to some of your people?''

''Now?'' The strain returned to Benno's features. ''Why? How—I wouldn't know how to explain what you're doing here?''

''You mustn't explain,'' Christophe said quickly. ''Not exactly. But you needn't lie. Just say I'm an old friend and a business associate, and that I'm interested in what goes on. I am interested. I haven't been through your workrooms since I was a boy visiting with my parents.''

Benno seemed to consider, then pushed heavily to his feet. ''No questions?''

''You have my word.'' Christophe raised both hands. ''Only polite interest.''

Benno crossed quickly to the door with the air of a man anxious to dispose of an unpleasant task.

No head lifted as they entered the long, narrow room. Perhaps a dozen men and one woman sat at benches behind curved glass screens. Each worker concentrated intently on a rapidly rotating wheel surrounded by piles of grimy steel equipment. Deft hands repeatedly turned, pressed, turned crystalline lumps against grinding surfaces. These shapeless chunks would emerge as beautiful pieces of cold fire, many of them worth small fortunes. Now they resembled oily clots in their tight metal clamps.

''Come.'' Benno took Christophe's elbow and resolutely approached an elderly, balding man wearing half glasses. ''This is Victor Hodez, my senior polisher. He worked for my father before I took over the firm.''

The man looked up, pushing his glasses to the top of his nose. He made no attempt to speak but watched Benno politely, clearly waiting for some sign of what he was supposed to do.

''Victor,'' Benno said. ''This is Christophe St-Giles, a...business associate and friend.'' He smiled nervously at Christophe. ''More Lukas's friend than mine, I suppose. He hasn't been through the workrooms since he was a boy.''

Victor seemed to consider this before wiping his right hand on his blue overall and half rising to shake Christophe's hand. "Little changes here," he allowed, indicating the bare room with its single window and powerful angle lamps.

"Certainly looks much the same," Christophe responded pleasantly, trying to keep his eyes on the man while he wanted to look at the woman seated to Victor's right. "Don't let me interrupt you. I'll just watch, if you don't mind.''

Benno exerted gentle pressure to move him toward the man on Victor Hodez's left. Christophe stood fast. "A woman," he said a little loudly to make himself heard above the equipment. "This, I think, is certainly quite a big change.''

Paula Renfrew looked directly into his eyes. "I'm sorry," she said. "What did you say?''

He smiled and felt his mouth go dry. She was lovely in that wholesome, American way. Gorgeous teeth and skin. Like an ad for health food. Masses of shining dark hair. And those eyes—the bluest damned eyes. Dammit all. "I said you're the first woman I've seen working in this room. I didn't think diamond polishing was considered woman's work.''

He'd started to cringe until she laughed, dulling his embarrassment at his stupid comment. "I'm Paula Renfrew, Mr.—?''

"Christophe," he said, "Christophe St-Giles. And I'm not a chauvinist. Honest—how do you say it? Honest to Betsy?''

"I don't know if I believe that," she teased, laughing again, "but I'm certainly glad to hear some good old American slang again. I'm not sure I'll ever master your language. Dutch is so complicated.''

"I'm not Dutch." Christophe plunged his hands into his pockets. Time to close off the male-female reaction. And with this lady that might not be easy to do. She was looking at him quizzically. "Oh," he muttered, feeling a total fool. "I'm not Dutch, I'm Swiss—from Zurich. Benno and I—" he risked a glance at the older man's face and quickly turned back "—Benno and I joke that we speak four languages between us and can only communicate in one—English.''

"There's Lukas," Benno broke in, a trace of desperation in his voice. "I'll show you around some more later.''

Christophe backed away, still studying Paula Renfrew. She returned his gaze with equal frankness and no sign of nervousness. But why should she be nervous? She had no idea who he was, or why he was here.

"See you again," he said, uncertain if she could hear him now. "Maybe you'll explain more of what goes on here?"

She smiled and as he turned to follow Benno, his last impression was of a full, soft mouth devoid of lipstick. Lucky St-Giles, they'd called him in school, partly because of his reputation with women students. Lucky was the last thing he hoped to feel in the near future, particularly if Paula Renfrew turned out to be a thief.

Lukas Kohl waited at the open door to his father's office. Christophe was struck once more by his austere good looks. An inch or so shorter than Christophe, about six feet, with blond hair and gray eyes, Lukas had the face and body of a film star. Christophe remembered well the bevy of adoring admirers Lukas had attracted at twenty-one. Then he'd been an attractive boy; now thirty-four, he was a handsome man who wore power and maturity as only men of privilege wore them—naturally. Little wonder he'd married one of Amsterdam's most successful models.

Christophe lengthened his stride, only to feel the smile freeze on his face when Lukas turned his back. With Benno, Christophe went into the office and closed the door.

"Let's get this over with," Lukas said harshly. He swung to face Christophe, his eyes pure slate. "My father and I have suffered enough. We want to get on with our business—and our lives."

Christophe opened his mouth to speak, but Benno cut him off, "Lukas, Lukas, my son. Christophe is our friend, not our enemy. This is hard on him, too. We must work together."

Lukas studied the back of his right hand, then the palm, before fingering his wedding band. "I must do what I must do, Father. And I must also be true to myself and what I believe to be right. Victimizing one's friends isn't right."

"Dammit," Christophe exploded, finally unable to control his temper. "Can't you be man enough to understand this is business?"

"How much of a man I am isn't the question here," Lukas replied coolly. "But perhaps you should think about it yourself."

Christophe exhaled sharply and automatically reached for a cigarette. "This isn't your style, Lukas. And none of us needs a sniping match. Please, both of you, it's time to get started on cleaning up this chaos. Tell me, step by step, what happens to a stone after it's ready for sale."

"Oh, hell—" Lukas began.

Benno cut in sharply. "Do it. Now, Lukas. The sooner we stop fighting each other, the sooner this will all be over."

Lukas shrugged eloquently. "There isn't that much to know, actually. But if you insist...the stones are graded, cataloged, placed in paper packets—a blue sheet inside a white sheet—the packet is marked, then filed in a small box with other packets." He stood and paced between the desk and the window. "Always the same, always the same. Satisfied?"

"Lukas," Benno said quietly. "Christophe knows exactly what happened—the thirteen stones, everything. He's only trying to figure out how."

"He knows?" Lukas's eyes widened incredulously. "You told him?"

"I didn't have to tell him. The books did that. All I supplied was the fact that the stones disappeared after they left Kohl's and before they reached our customers." A curtain of defeat lowered over Benno's features. "Now he needs to know how, and make sure there can be no repeat performance, or..."

"Or?" Lukas's mouth turned up in a bitter, questioning grimace.

"Or there will be no loan," Benno finished.

Christophe rubbed a hand over his eyes. "After the diamonds are filed, what then?"

"They're put in the strong room," Benno said.

"I'll tell him," Lukas interjected. "The strong room is in the basement. It's the same room the customer enters when he intends to select stones for purchase. My father or I, or sometimes both, conduct the sale, then close the packets and deal with formalities, date for payment and so on. We pass the stones to the page who gives them to the messenger for delivery. It is our policy to secure the packages ourselves. A guard travels with the messenger. Once these things were handled directly, stones of immense value carried in a man's breast pocket. Today that is not possible. Amsterdam is a different city now."

"Do you understand the bottom line here, Christophe?" Benno asked, his eyes strangely bright.

"I think so." He wasn't certain.

"No, no you don't. I'll help you, but sit down. Your job, however you decide to pursue it, will not be simple."

Christophe hesitated, then did as Benno asked, dropping to the edge of a straight-backed chair. "Go on."

"The counterfeit goods arrived in packages that did not appear to have been tampered with. You have not only to find the thief, but to discover where he got his so excellent copies and how he made his switches.''

Lukas stopped pacing and stood beside his father.

"Here," Benno said clearly, "here at Kohl's, Lukas and I were the last to see the real merchandise. So you see, my dear Christophe, you had better look elsewhere than Kohl's for your criminals. Unless you want to report to your father that I've been stealing from myself.''

"Or that I have," Lukas added softly.

Chapter Two

Monday of the Second Week:

An elbow in the middle of Paula's back sent her grabbing for Peter Van Wersch's arm. Ice cream went up her nose and she sneezed violently. "Yuck," she groaned, wiping her chin with the back of one hand. "Anyone got an extra napkin?"

Peter hitched his camera strap higher and dug in his pockets until he produced a kleenex. "Strawberry suits you, darling. Wipe it off if you must, but please, let me get a shot of your face first. Hey, Lukas, Sandi, hold up a minute, we're having a significant experience here."

"Clown," Paula sputtered, taking the tissue to finish her mopping job. "If everyone didn't keep telling me how nice you are, Peter Van Wersch, I'd say you were a sadist."

Lukas and Sandi Kohl pushed a path back through the crowd, Lukas's arm protectively around his tall wife's shoulders. "So, Paula, what happened? You don't like our Queen's Day celebrations? They are too wild for you, perhaps?" Lukas took her crushed ice cream cone and tossed it in a trash can.

"Not if I don't get mangled by the crowd." Paula grimaced at her sticky hand. "Every April 30th the city goes wild like this, right?"

"April 30th and any other day we can make an excuse for a bash," Sandi said, lifting a heavy, auburn braid behind her shoulders. "We Amsterdammers love our festivals."

Paula smiled into Sandi's green eyes and wondered, not for the first time that day, why the beautiful woman's expression lacked her usual animation.

Peter put a long arm around Paula's waist and smiled his sunny smile at all of them. "She's loving every minute, too, aren't you Paula?" He bent to search her face briefly, then moved her forward without waiting for a reply. Lukas and Sandi fell in behind.

At least she'd become familiar with Amsterdam's warren of narrow streets and canals, Paula thought with satisfaction. After nine months she was beginning to feel like a native. She took a deep breath of warm late afternoon air and sighed.

"A happy sigh," Peter remarked sagely. "Good. We like our inhabitants to be happy."

Peter was a delight. A big, rangy, blond man with laughing blue eyes, he made Paula feel a comradeship with him, a safety. He was a man a woman could have as a friend—she hoped. There was nothing in Peter that seemed to touch her romantically, but his humor and strength were irresistible. Sandi had explained how Peter and Lukas were the same age, thirty-four, and had met in school. Somehow Peter seemed much younger than the frequently somber Lukas, or even twenty-nine-year-old Sandi.

The closeness Lukas and Sandi shared with Peter was easy to understand. He lived in an apartment on the top floor of their house, yet it was clear he knew how not to intrude in their life at the wrong times. And his schedule as a successful commercial photographer with a big, new studio kept him busy.

Today was a national holiday, and Peter had insisted he would take the day off like everyone else: "To teach Paula to be a true Dutchwoman," he'd announced while lunching with Paula and Sandi the previous week, "and to make sure Lukas takes some time to relax. That man is growing old before his time. He's too serious these days."

Paula had agreed to go without hesitation. Sandi had seemed less enthusiastic, but soon gave in to Peter's persuasive charm.

"Come on, you lot," Peter said, forging ahead, pulling Paula with him. "Leidse Plein and the American Hotel in sight." He hopped to see over the boisterous crowd's massed heads, pointing toward the square at the end of the street, Leidse Straat. "You promised us all drinks, Lukas," he called. "And I'm dying of thirst."

Lukas and Sandi caught up. Sandi was tall, almost as tall as her handsome husband. They made an impressive couple, and heads turned as they passed.

Paula trotted to keep stride with the other three. Even at five foot seven, she felt short between these long, lean people. "You don't make allowances for pygmies," she complained, dodging weaving cyclists every few seconds. "Have pity, please." Her pleading went unheeded, possibly unheard, in the din, and she leaped from the path of yet another bicycle. She'd already learned cyclists ruled the streets here—and the sidewalks. They were a fearless, ferocious bunch. "I'm going to get one of those!" she shouted breathlessly.

Peter stopped, Sandi and Lukas with him. "One of what?" Sandi demanded.

The remark had only been for effect really. "A bicycle," Paula explained. "I'm going to buy a bicycle and finally get some respect around here."

Lukas gave one of his rare and quite delightful smiles. "Can you ride one, Paula?"

She shook her head. "Never learned. But I will. I'm going to pick one out."

The peals of laughter that met her announcement made it impossible to remain serious. "Okay, okay. Glad I'm so entertaining. Why shouldn't I have a bicycle? Everyone else does. Average of three a year per city dweller, I read. I only want one."

"Didn't you wonder why anyone would need to buy three bicycles in a year?" Peter draped an arm over her shoulders and made owl eyes. "You didn't sniff a little foul play in that statement?"

"No—I—"

"Knock it off, Peter." Lukas punched his friend's shoulder. "Give the girl a break. This has been a long day. We'll tell her all about bicycles and anything else you think her education needs—at the American. I want that drink, too, now."

Peter pretended to be insulted for an instant before whipping his camera from its case and insisting on a candid photo in front of a garishly painted barrel organ. When the shutter clicked, Paula was flinching and covering her ears against a hurdy-gurdy tune, punctuated by the rattle of coins in the organ grinder's brass cup.

Within seconds, they passed from the narrow, cobbled street with its skinny old buildings and colored awnings over shop doors, into the broad expanse of Leidse Plein. The American Hotel dominated the north side of the square, and Sandi, holding Lukas's hand, moved quickly ahead. Paula watched the woman's fawnlike grace, the way she stayed almost shyly close to her husband. How could such a reserved creature become the pouting temptress featured in so many glossy fashion magazines? The stab of envy Paula felt came and went quickly. Even if she had what it took to be a model, her temperament was all wrong. She smiled at the thought of the photo Peter had just taken. There was unlikely to be much market for shots like that.

At that moment, Sandi swung back, smiling. The Kohls had seemed tense all day, and Paula was relieved to sense a lightening of their moods. Her relief was short-lived.

"Lukas!" Sandi stopped, almost tripping Peter who was close behind.

Lukas grabbed her arm. "What is it, my love?" He shook her gently. "What's wrong?"

Sandi looked beyond Paula, frowning, some indefinable emotion darkening her eyes. Paula checked over her shoulder, searching the shifting crowd for a sign of what had troubled Sandi. Only a mass of shouting, singing strangers confronted her.

"Sandi, listen to me." It was Peter, speaking low and earnestly. "I don't know what it is with Lukas and Christophe—and you. But Christophe has a right to be here, too. Couldn't we let it go for now?"

Paula stared at Peter who leaned close to Sandi, reaching behind her to grip Lukas's shoulder. What the hell was wrong here? She made another sweep of the crowd...and saw him—*Christophe St-Giles*. Why would that upset them all?

"Stay out of it, Peter," Lukas muttered. "This is something that doesn't affect you. Let's move."

"Damned if I will," Peter said, suddenly very serious. "And anything that makes my two oldest friends behave like deadly enemies *does* affect me. Anyway, it's too late, unless you want to make a complete ass of yourself by running away. He's seen us."

Paula watched, fascinated, as Christophe St-Giles approached. Her attention was divided between the striking, powerfully built man who swung his shoulders purposefully through the crowd toward them and Sandi and Lukas Kohl. Sandi appeared to shrink and grow paler by the second. Lukas's patrician features were cast, stonelike, his eyes hard. The jumpiness in Paula's stomach reminded her of the feeling she always got in the dentist's waiting room. Painful confrontation seemed inevitable.

"Small world," Christophe called, waving and swiveling his narrow hips to sidestep a group of children sporting bright paper crowns. "Hoped I might run into someone I knew. Queen's Day in Amsterdam shouldn't be spent alone."

"Hey up, Christophe," Peter whooped, going to meet the newcomer and slapping him on his broad back. "Good to see you. Forgive me, friend, I should have thought to invite you today. Guess I'm not used to having you with us again yet."

Paula glanced at Lukas and read a clear message in his expression: *I don't want to get used to you, buddy. I hate your guts.* She pressed her lips together and her chin quivered. Nausea pooled in the pit of her stomach. Conflict was an element she couldn't handle. She'd run from it, even as a small child.

When she looked at Christophe again, he was studying her, a friendly smile on his wide mouth. His lips had a natural upward tilt.... She forced a weak grin. "Are they treating you well, Paula?" he asked, laughter in his deep voice. "Let me know if they don't and I'll take over. I love to play tour guide, and this city is my second home."

The odd noise Lukas made startled her, and she glanced at him. He immediately bent to tie his tennis shoelace.

"Would we neglect anyone so gorgeous," Peter put in, a trifle too hurriedly. "As you know, Christophe, I'm kind to children, dogs, the aged—how much kinder would I be to such an angel?"

"My God," Christophe moaned. "Your lines haven't changed, Peter. Still sickening. Paula, watch this roué. Three times engaged, three times an escapee—significant, I think."

She couldn't stand much more of this banter, this circling. "Yes" was as brilliant an answer as she could manage.

An awkward silence followed before music burst from a nearby bandstand. A single horn blared a deep note that rose to a piercing height. Paula drew in a sharp breath of protest before she recognized a raucous rendition of "Wish I Could Shimmy Like My Sister Kate." Dixieland, well played or otherwise, was her favorite kind of music.

The group turned together toward the noise, but Paula was most acutely aware of Christophe St-Giles standing behind her shoulder. He was as intriguing as his name. On Friday, in dark suit and tie, he'd exuded elegant professionalism; today jeans and a soft cotton shirt made even better use of a very tall, very athletic body. She glanced from his chest to his face and found him watching her, too—with candid interest. They didn't smile, nor did she blush. No man or woman objected to being admired. Why pretend?

"You're very quiet," he said, too low for anyone else to hear.

Paula tilted her head, openly taking in his straight, well-cut brown hair, graying at the temples and determined to fall over his broad forehead. "I'm always quiet when I concentrate," she replied. Daylight was seeping out of the afternoon, and low sun formed a shadow beneath his cheekbones, emphasizing the creases beside his mouth. Every visible inch of his skin was olive, right down to the open V at his neck where she glimpsed the start of dark hair that must cover his chest. "I'm also quiet when I feel an emotional bomb about to explode and I can't do a thing about it.'' She met his eyes squarely then—deep, deep brown eyes. Oh, Christophe St-Giles was one sexy man, and she enjoyed the pleasure looking at him brought her.

"There'll be no explosion," he whispered. "Trust me. We are all old friends who just need time to get to know one another again." He put a finger in each ear and shouted, "Peter, where are you off to?"

"We've about had it," Lukas began in a rush. "We thought we'd head—"

"To the America," Peter inserted, cutting him off. "Drinkies time for the Three Musketeers and their ladies." He frowned, first at Sandi, then at Paula. "We're missing a lady, which never happened in the old days. Ah, me. We'll just have to make do. I'll share Paula with you, Christophe."

Christophe met her gaze steadily. "Maybe the lady won't like that."

"The lady will manage, Mr. St-Giles," Paula parried. "The lady is very capable."

For a fleeting moment, Paula thought a hard light entered Christophe's gentle eyes. Immediately she decided she was mistaken. He slid a cool hand beneath her arm. "I'm absolutely sure you are capable. But if you call me Mr. St-Giles, you'll have to be Miss Renfrew, and I like Paula so much better."

Sandi, who had been silent almost since Christophe arrived, whirled away and bent to examine a pile of treasures spread for sale on a blanket. "Look at this, Lukas." She held up a crimson beaded purse. "I used to play with one like this when I was a child. Hans bought it for—" She stopped abruptly and stood, dropping the purse. Tears brimmed in her eyes, and she walked into Lukas's outstretched arm.

Paula leaned toward Peter, "Who's Hans?"

"I don't know. Old boyfriend maybe... Look out!"

His warning was too late. Bodies pushed in on Paula. Somehow, a foot tangled with hers and she started to fall sideways. Christophe tried to grab her and so did Peter, but the throng swept her down until her shin met something hard and she cried out. Sandi's reaching hands only succeeded in landing them both in a crumpled heap on filthy cobblestones.

Facedown on the ground, Paula covered her head instinctively and waited to be crushed. "Get back!" It was Lukas's voice she heard as a small space opened around her. Sandi was pulled up.

Large hands closed about her waist and lifted her with swift ease. "Okay, *chérie*?" Christophe turned her to face him. He wrapped one arm firmly around her and pushed the tousled hair out of her eyes. "Okay?" He peered at her closely.

Paula looked around. "I guess," she said shakily, bending to rub her leg. Lukas was already dusting Sandi off. "I don't know what happened except I hit one of those damned Amsterdammagers."

"Thank God she hasn't lost her sense of humor," Peter said. "That means she's okay. You have to watch out for our little red posts or they'll get you—particularly if you really do decide to become a cyclist."

Ruefully, Paula checked her grit-embedded palms. "They're useless." She glared at the knee-high posts lining the sidewalk that were designed to keep cyclists—and sometimes motorists—from plowing down pedestrians. With sidewalks as crowded as Amsterdam's, she was convinced they were more of a hazard than help.

Paula became aware of Christophe once more. He held one of her hands and carefully flicked away tiny rocks. He took a handkerchief from his pocket and wiped her palm before starting on the other hand. Paula watched the top of his bent head, the movement of muscle in his wide shoulders, and suppressed a smile. One wasn't supposed to be glad when knocked on one's face, but if the consolation prize was the undivided attention of a man like Christophe, she might have to fall more often.

"I hate to break up this touching Florence Nightingale scene," Peter said, shattering the moment all too effectively. "But you're standing on your purse, Paula, dear, and half your possessions are probably smashed."

"Good Lord," Paula exclaimed. "I didn't even notice."

Christophe stopped her in the act of bending. "Allow me," he said, holding her wrist a fraction longer than necessary before dropping to his knees to gather her bag and its spilled contents.

Lukas helped by retrieving a pen and a tiny perfume atomizer, miraculously untouched, and handing them to her. "You women and your bits and pieces." He shook his head, but a smile hovered about his lips. "When will you learn a few guilders in your pocket is all you need?"

"Lukas," Sandi said warningly. "Don't be mean."

"Here you are." Christophe stood, dropping a comb and wallet inside Paula's purse. "I think that's everything and all intact."

Peter swooped to pick something up. "Except this." He held a folded piece of paper aloft. "A secret love note, no doubt."

Paula glanced at the sheet. "Not mine, I'm afraid, Peter. No one writes love letters to me." Immediately she closed her mouth, avoiding Christophe's eyes.

"Then you won't mind if I read it?" Peter flapped the yellow paper in front of her eyes.

Unaccountably, Paula felt irritated. Sometimes Peter went too far. "Be my guest, Peter. This is a day for sharing, right?"

If he felt her asperity, Peter showed no sign. He shook the paper open and read quickly. Silence made Paula turn her full attention to him. The smile had disappeared from his face. Lukas, Sandi and Christophe were staring expectantly at him.

Peter glanced at Paula, his brilliant smile once more in place. "Nothing to do with us, after all." He started to crumple the paper.

"No," Christophe said. "We all get to see this, Peter. You love to make mysteries, my friend."

With a wordless shrug, Peter handed over the note. "I want my drink, darlings. Come on."

No one moved. Christophe scanned the lined sheet and gave it to Lukas, who read it with Sandi looking over his shoulder.

Paula grew edgy. What was the big deal? She hooked a hand through Peter's elbow and leaned against him. Her shin and hands still stung.

"Yes," Lukas said slowly, starting to push the paper into his pocket, "Sustenence for the weary. Onward."

Christophe stayed him with a firm hand. "Soon, Lukas. Soon. But don't you think Paula should read that, too? After all, if she hadn't dropped—fallen, we wouldn't have had this little diversion. Surely she shouldn't be the only one to miss the fun."

She sighed. These people did love their jokes. Lukas gave her the rumpled sheet and she scanned a single printed line before she began to laugh. Peter immediately joined in.

Paula read aloud, "'They're getting closer. Watch for slips.'" She looked up to find Lukas, Sandi and Christophe watching her expectantly while Peter wiped his eyes. "Well." She shoved the paper in her purse. "I don't know where this came from, but it was certainly meant for me. It would have been even better if it read, 'Watch for Amsterdammagers.'" Paula thought her joke was funny. She was surprised when no one laughed.

Chapter Three

"Mata Hari, Peter?" Paula said with patent disbelief. "The spy?"

Christophe settled deep into his tufted velvet chair, every nerve alert, while Peter nodded seriously and said, "I swear. She was married in this Jugenstil restaurant in 1894. That's what keeps the American Hotel so famous. Must have been your mysterious note that reminded me."

Paula ignored the comment and looked around the packed room with its brilliant blue and yellow stained glass windows and odd contrast of exposed brick and squared dark paneling. Christophe kept a bland smile on his face but didn't take his eyes off Paula. She was becoming more of a disturbing enigma by the minute.

Finally, she folded her arms and frowned. "An architectural monument, you said, Lukas? Because of Mata Hari, I assume. This looks more like a shrine to me."

Everyone laughed. "I take it you don't go for Greek frescos and potted palms," Peter suggested. "Or maybe the Japanese parasol lamps with lighted handles are what throw you?"

She raised her brows as a waiter approached to take orders for Black Forest cake and jenever all around. It hadn't taken her long to learn that everyone drank the strong Dutch national drink with everything—including cake.

As soon as the waiter left, squeezing through a sea of crowded little tables, Paula leaned toward Sandi. "What do they keep announcing?"

The noise level was as Christophe remembered—deafening and punctuated by constant loudspeaker messages.

"Nothing, really." Sandi's cheeks turned slightly pink. "It's all a game. The Jugenstil has always been known as an artists' haunt. A lot of theatrical people hang out here, too—everyone trying to make an impression. Someone wants to look important, so they get someone else to page them. With the right arrangements, a telephone can be brought to your table. It goes on all the time."

"Ridiculous," Christophe put in. "Juvenile."

"And you did it yourself, Christophe," Peter said, pretending to trace stains on the gold tablecloth with a fingernail. "I know because I placed some of the calls."

He had to laugh. That seemed so very long ago. "Only to keep up with you arty types. Even a young man doomed to the life of a banker can dream of fame and recognition." Not quite true, not in a glitzy way. But at twenty-two he had played the games here. "Remember, Lukas?" He met those familiar gray eyes, hoping for some softening, but found none. Muscles tightened in his jaw. Forget old friendships, he instructed himself grimly. Forget the past. This was today and this was business. He might not be an artist in the conventional sense but he was a creator, constantly arranging and testing the intricate patterns spawned in the financial world. He thrived on what others might term his own games.

He turned sideways toward Paula. Her hair fell softly forward to hide her face, and he looked at the pale skin at the back of her neck above a striped T-shirt. Her figure was enticing, slender, gently feminine in the way that had always turned him on. What were her legs like, he wondered? She wore jeans today, and on Friday she'd been sitting. He squinted into the distance. Her legs were about the last thing he should be wasting thought on.

"And you, Paula," he said quietly. "What do you think of silly games—ploys to achieve effect—results even?" Some sign. He needed signs. A subtle change in her expression. Telltale tension in those capable, well-shaped hands.

Blue eyes turned on him slowly. "I've never had time for ploys, Mr.—Christophe. I've always been too busy doing what had to be done."

Had her voice risen—just slightly? "And what always had to be done?" His nerves jumped. He was reading too much into every comment. She wouldn't give direct hints. It was that damned note that had got him going.

She seemed to consider, winding a strand of hair around a forefinger. "Getting through school. Helping my father. Just living, I guess. Nothing important."

He bit back the urge to say he thought she was very important. "Your father. What did he do?" She mustn't find out how much he knew about her.

"Here's the waiter," Lukas interrupted.

Christophe looked at Lukas and quelled a surge of irritation when he saw the satisfaction on his face. The irrational bastard intended to hamper any attempt to question Paula, dammit. Benno had probably given him hell for talking about the woman's past, told him to protect her. Christophe locked his hands behind his neck and inhaled deeply. If the Kohls hoped to sidetrack him from finding out what was going on here, they'd chosen the wrong tactics. Nothing would divert him now.

Huge wedges of cake and shot glasses of jenever, the Dutch gin that seemed a part of every meal, arrived. Paula had ordered the citron, or lemon flavor, rather than the stronger clear variety the rest of them had chosen.

Paula sipped her drink and immediately reached for a water glass.

"Too strong for you, Paula?" Peter asked solicitously. "You'd prefer something else."

She patted his hand on the tabletop. "It's fine, thank you, Peter. Not what I'm used to before dinner, that's all." She laughed and stuck her fork into the cake. "This isn't what I'm used to for dinner, either."

"Queen's Day madness," Peter said, gazing intently at her face. "We'll eat properly later, maybe Indonesian, if you like." He held her fingers and turned her hand to check the palm. "You really went down with a bang. This looks bruised. I hope your fingers don't stiffen up."

"As long as she can work that wheel tomorrow, she'll be too engrossed to notice," Lukas said lightly. "Victor says he never saw anyone more eager than Paula, or with more natural talent."

Christophe watched and listened. Was Paula already talented enough to copy gems? Benno had said the counterfeit efforts were good, but not perfect. Tomorrow he'd make more inquiries, find out just how advanced Paula Renfrew was in the execution of her work.

He switched his attention to Peter. "Three times engaged, three times escaped" had been his own quip. He might have said three times disappointed, had he not known how important pride was to Peter. Now he was giving Paula the kind of attention an infatuated man gave a woman. Christophe drained his own jenever, scarcely noticing its sting in his throat. He couldn't be put off by anything. If she turned out to be a criminal, Peter would be better off saved from her.

The note had been Paula's. Christophe was sure of it. And she'd tried to pretend ignorance. Lukas had been disturbed by the incident—Sandi, too, yet Lukas was still determined to run interference for Paula. So what, Christophe thought, pushing cake crumbs around his plate. The note had served a purpose for him. He'd been almost certain one person couldn't have pulled off the thefts. Now he knew he was right—Paula had an accomplice, or more than one.

Watch for slips. He stopped eating, his fork halfway to his mouth. Could the note have been meant for him? Had someone meant to tip him off to Paula? "They," could be anyone. But who would warn him, and why? Unless the Kohls weren't the only potential losers in this scam.

"You're very thoughtful, Christophe."

At the sound of Paula's voice, he started. "I was thinking about work," he said, smiling, feeling the effort might crack his face. "I have difficulty thinking of anything else for very long."

She regarded him seriously. "You're a banker. Is that really dull?"

"Not so dull," he said, setting down his fork. She was cool—he'd give her that. "I probably get as much of a charge out of solving money puzzles as you do when you make a perfect facet in a diamond."

She looked doubtful. "I can't imagine finding money very interesting—as a job," she finished faintly.

"This is a vacation for you, isn't it, Christophe?" Peter asked. "You said you needed a rest. Take it. That's why I thought the houseboat would be more relaxing than a hotel."

"It is," Christophe said quickly. "But I do have to combine a little business with pleasure. Benno and Lukas and I have a few matters to deal with, don't we, Lukas?"

"Yes." Lukas finished his drink and signaled the waiter. "Another round?" He didn't look at Christophe.

Only Paula declined Lukas's offer, and he placed the order.

"Paula Renfrew. Call in the lobby for Paula Renfrew."

The paging system announced a call for Paula. Christophe gripped his empty glass tightly. His Dutch was rusty, but he had no difficulty understanding the message.

"That was my name?" She looked blank. "What did it say?"

"A call, darling," Peter said, frowning. "In the lobby. I'll come with you."

"Who would call me?"

If she wasn't completely surprised, the woman was quite an actress. "Better find out," Christophe said evenly. "Stay put, Peter. I'll go with her. It'll remind me of old times."

He started to get up. Paula pressed his forearm. "I can manage. Please, all of you, carry on. I'm sure it's a mistake. I'll be right back."

Christophe let out a slow breath. He'd bet she could manage. And she wouldn't want an audience if she was receiving another message from an accomplice. While he watched Paula's retreating figure, he felt Lukas's eyes upon him.

"You're a joker, Peter," Lukas said. "How did you manage to arrange that?"

"What?" Peter looked startled. "Arrange what?"

"You can't pull the wool over my eyes, friend. I remember your tricks from years ago. Who did you get to make the call?"

Christophe studied Lukas. He was smiling for the first time since they'd met in the square. Maybe he'd hit the truth. Unwillingly, Christophe acknowledged how strongly he hoped Lukas was right and that Peter had engineered a ruse.

"I didn't fix anything, Lukas. When would I have been able to? I thought you had," Peter said and leaned back to allow the waiter to put their fresh drinks on the table.

Christophe stopped Lukas from paying by throwing a handful of guilders on the waiter's tray and telling him to keep the change.

"Must have been you then, Sandi," Peter said, sighing deeply. "And I always thought you were such a sensible woman."

"Could there be some emergency?" She spoke directly to Lukas. "Perhaps there's been a call from America to your parents and they're trying to track her down. Did you mention we'd be coming here?"

"Ah—yes, yes. Now I think of it, I did."

Christophe lowered his gaze and took out a pack of cigarettes. Lukas was a liar, but this wasn't the time to say so.

The four of them sat in uncomfortable silence, the room around them a noisy blur. Even Peter said nothing. He made little circles with his glass and checked the door every few seconds until Paula wove her way back.

"Weird." She sounded breathless. Christophe noted the heightened color in her cheeks. "There was no one on the line."

"Really?" He propped his chin on one fist and drew on a cigarette. "Was it a man or a woman?"

She sat beside him. "No one. I said no one was on the line."

"I mean, was it a man or a woman who placed the call and hung up?" He turned to face her. "Would you like a cigarette?"

"I—no, thank you. I don't smoke."

"Do you mind if I do?"

"No."

"Was it a man or a woman?"

Her lips parted. He'd pushed her off balance. "Oh, I see." She threaded her fingers through her hair. "I didn't ask the desk clerk."

"Maybe we only thought it was your name," Lukas said.

Christophe made sure their eyes met and he didn't hide his disgust. "Yes," he said clearly. "We all made a mistake. We must really be in a mood to invent mysteries today. A bad habit we'll have to watch."

"I'm just glad it wasn't an emergency," Sandi said, scooting her chair away from the table. "Excuse me. I see some people from my agency. If I don't go over there, they'll come here and bore all of us instead of just me." She squeezed Lukas's shoulder and walked to another table where an animated group quickly made room for her to sit. Seconds later she was back, urging Peter to his feet. "They want to meet you. Your reputation as a hot photographer precedes you these days, Peter. Lukas, could you bear to come, too, just for a few minutes? Christophe and Paula don't need to suffer."

Peter immediately got to his feet. Lukas hesitated fractionally before standing. "Of course. We'll be right back, you two." No one would have missed the warning in the look he gave Christophe. Christophe raised a brow and his glass in mock salute. He'd use whatever opportunities presented to get what he wanted.

He waited just long enough to be sure Lukas couldn't hear before saying, "What did you say your father did?"

A vaguely disoriented light flickered in Paula's eyes. Tossing her back and forth, forcing her into a mental balancing act, could produce a slip. *Slip.* Not if she was heeding all the warnings she appeared to be getting.

"Your father?" he prompted.

"My father was a jeweler."

He didn't know what he expected. Certainly not that. After his early experiences, Michael Renfrew might have been expected to stay away from anything to do with jewels. Christophe cleared his throat and stubbed out the Gitane. "He had his own business?" That took a lot of capital, didn't it?"

"Yes. In New Jersey. He was a gifted designer. We did quite well." Her voice was markedly tighter.

"You said 'was.' Has he retired?" He saw her swallow and instantly disliked what he was doing. Regardless of present circumstances, he hated hurting another human being.

"My father died a little over a year ago. Fourteen months now."

Dammit, she had tears in her eyes. He steeled himself. Deep love and deep loyalty went hand in hand. Blind faith and a willingness to do anything to preserve a memory belonged to the same group of emotions. "I'm sorry," he said after a while. She'd averted her face. "Is your mother running the shop now?"

"I don't know where my mother is." Paula turned her head and riveted him with a sharp glare. "And I don't care. My brother and I sold the shop. Grant's in the Air Force. We're both doing what we wanted most in life. Dad would like to know that."

"Good."

"How about you?" She took a good swallow of her jenever and flinched. "Are you doing what you want to do?"

He'd touched some raw nerves. "Yes. I already told you I like my work."

"The other day, on Friday, you said you and Benno spoke four languages but only communicated in English. I thought most people in Zurich spoke German, but you speak French, don't you—your name's French, isn't it?"

Laughing, he held up a hand. "Slowly, slowly So many questions."

"I thought you liked questions. Asking them, anyway." Her eyes were dry now, and appraising.

She had him. "Okay. Yes, I'm an inquisitive devil. And to be fair, you're right, I'm French-Swiss. You're also right in thinking there are far more German-Swiss in Zurich. I also speak fluent German. I have to in my business. And, let me see. I have a father and two uncles and one cousin all actively involved in the bank. My mother is dead. I have no brothers or sisters."

"A wife, perhaps? Children?"

He took in a breath and stared at her. She could give lessons in shock tactics. "No wife. No children. Should have at thirty-five, right?"

She shrugged.

"Well—" Without thinking, he touched her hair. Soft. Good Lord, he must stay on track. "Well, I had a very long and very meaningful relationship with someone I probably loved. Unfortunately things didn't work out. Now she's married and seems happy. And I'm glad for her. Life goes on." He wasn't supposed to be telling his life history to the only feasible suspect in the Kohl case.

"Yours will." The softness in her voice unnerved him. He'd best back away from the personal stuff for a while until he gained some perspective. She was reaching him in a way that he didn't want to be reached—not in this situation.

"What made you do something as...as—"

"As off-the-wall as coming halfway around the world from my home to take up a man's profession?" Her eyes challenged him.

"I asked for that when we spoke last Friday, didn't I?" he said wryly. "But yes, that's what I meant. I don't imagine many little American girls grow up wanting to become diamond polishers in Amsterdam."

She was so lovely when she smiled. "This one did. My father made me fall in love with diamonds." The smile was broad now, ingenuous. "Many years ago he worked for Benno's father. That's what made me decide to see if I could get a job here. When Benno agreed to hire me I could hardly believe my luck."

Christophe's heart missed a beat. Just like that. She'd told him the truth, at least the truth that her father had worked at Kohl's before her. "I see," he said lamely. "Following in father's footsteps like so many of us."

"Oh, yes. And he would have been thrilled. You have a couple more questions coming, you know." She had a single dimple—beneath her right cheekbone.

"I seem to have forgotten what they were." And he had, too, dammit.

"I'll just give you the answers, then. I'm twenty-six and I'm not married, either."

"Ah. Congratulations." He'd almost said he was glad. Could a woman who looked like this be crooked? The note could have been a fluke. Lukas or Peter, probably Peter, could have arranged the call as a joke. Her father could have been... He raked his hair back. "You're living in Benno and Anna's guest house?"

"Benno must have told you that. Yes, I'm in the backhouse, as they all those places. I love it there. Have you seen what they're like—the backhouses?"

"I stayed where you are once myself. And yes, I've seen a lot of backhouses. Clever how the Dutch built high and deep to save taxes on their front footage. I always liked the little courtyard between the backhouse and the main house at Anna and Benno's. Lukas and I used to..." He trailed off, unable to allow the memories to become important again.

Paula appeared not to notice his change of mood. "I like the courtyard, too," she said. "I've planted tubs of bulbs out there. I have my own tulip patches. Appropriate, don't you think?"

"Yes," he said, watching as her enthusiasm animated her features. "Will you be at dinner with Benno and Anna when I come on Saturday?"

She hesitated, glancing up as Peter returned with Lukas and Sandi.

They sat, and Paula turned to Christophe once more. "Anna invited me this morning. I'll be there. I can't imagine turning down anything Anna cooks."

"You'll be where?" Lukas interrupted. Without asking, he took a cigarette from the pack Christophe had left on the table and offered one to Peter, who accepted. "What's all this about an invitation for my mother's cooking?"

"Dinner," Christophe said, flipping his lighter, first for Peter, then for Lukas. Sharing used to be so natural between them. "I'm having dinner with your parents on Saturday, and now I discover I'll also have the pleasure of Paula's company."

"How nice," Lukas said, sounding anything but pleased. "Too bad Sandi and I can't join all of you. We've accepted another invitation."

The heavy silence sifted in around them once more, and Christophe remembered the other question he should have asked Paula. The one that might have made a real dent in her composure: why had Michael Renfrew decided to leave Amsterdam so suddenly? He'd have to wait now—maybe for Saturday evening.

Paula found herself unable to keep her gaze from Christophe's face for more than moments at a time. She liked him, truly liked him. And something more, much more. The staggering relief she'd felt when he'd said he wasn't married didn't come from any need for a simple friend. Paula had friends. What she didn't have was a lover. She shivered, almost pressed her thighs where the muscles ached. This was a first. Just as she'd told him, she'd been too busy coping with day-to-day life to play games. He hadn't asked her if she included romance and sex in those games she's had no time for. But the answer would have been yes—most of the time. She had never experienced an attraction this strong or instant.

"Perhaps we should start for the home front," Peter said. "It'll take a while to make our way back. The crowd will only be getting rowdier."

"True," Lukas agreed.

What was it with Lukas, Paula mused? She hadn't forgotten Peter's comments when Christophe approached them outside. Lukas and Christophe were supposed to be old friends. Nothing in Lukas's manner backed up that idea.

She scraped her chair away from the table at the same time as she noticed a familiar face at a table half-hidden by a screen. Frank Lammaker glanced up and saw her, too. Paula waved and smiled.

Lukas looked over his shoulder, then back at Paula. "What the devil's he doing here?"

The reaction puzzled Paula. "It's a holiday for everyone, isn't it, Lukas? Frank included?" Frank also worked for Kohls.

"Of course," Lukas replied formally. "I'm surprised to see him here, that's all." He raised his hands, indicating their surroundings. "Sandi, you know some of that group he's with, don't you? Aren't they a little rich for the average man's blood?"

Sandi followed Lukas's stare and nodded at Frank. "Yes," she muttered. "Mostly writers. Saul Otis paints. They're all fairly well-heeled and on the inside track, if that's what you mean."

"That's what I mean." Lukas's voice dropped. "I didn't think we paid our messenger enough to allow him to move in that kind of company." He glanced around again. "Or to dress like a visiting prince and evidently pay his share of the money and they're probably expecting to drop in a place like this. They look settled in for a long night."

Christophe became restless at Paula's side. She noticed that he stared at Frank and his friends with interest. "Your messenger, Lukas? Is he Kohl's only messenger?" he asked.

"We only need one," Lukas said shortly.

Now Paula was more angry than puzzled. This wasn't fair. Why shouldn't Frank have a life outside work? He was a nice man, open, a breath of fresh air around Kohl's. He was twenty-two and full of energy. She'd found him friendly and helpful since she'd arrived. His mother did Anna Kohl's cleaning. Perhaps that was it. Lukas didn't think Frank should be frequenting the same places he considered suitable for himself. She pushed the idea aside. Lukas was no snob.

Peter tapped the table. "I remember him. His mother used to work for yours, didn't she, Lukas?"

"Yes," Lukas said distantly. "Madeleine. She still does. She's my mother's housekeeper."

"Ah, yes, of course." Peter tipped up his chin. "Frank was the one you thought Benno shouldn't hire for some reason. Unstable as a kid, or something."

"That's history," Lukas said.

"Shall we go," Sandi suggested, obviously edgy. "I'm tired, and we could all use a decent meal."

"In a minute," Lukas snapped. He moved his chair closer to Paula's where he could see Frank without turning around. "The man to Lammaker's right, Paula. Do you know him?"

"Yes." By now everyone at the other table must know they were under scrutiny. Paula shifted uncomfortably. "Lukas, what's wrong. Is there any reason why Frank shouldn't be here? We are."

"Who is that man?" Lukas pressed as if he hadn't heard her. "I'm sure I recognize him."

"You should," she said impatiently. "Willem Bill. He works for Metter Brothers as a page."

Chapter Four

Tuesday of the Second Week:

"How many times must I tell you to spit in it?"

Paula's face bobbed up. "Oh, Victor—" she looked into the pestle and mortar where she was mixing diamond paste to coat her wheel, then back at Victor Hodez's wizened face "—why on earth do you insist I have to spit in it? Why can't I use just olive oil like others do?"

A Gallic shrug lifted permanently hunched shoulders. "I am the expert, Paula—correct?"

"Correct, Victor, but..."

"I am also said to be somewhat superior to most other polishers, yes?"

"Absolutely. I just..."

"The others use only olive oil in their paste. I spit, as well." He bent over his wheel again, and Paula spat into the mixture of diamond dust, abrasive powder and olive oil. The paste created the cutting action between stone and wheel. Only diamond could cut diamond, so no part of the rough material was wasted. Minute chips became the dust that fashioned other gems.

"You are a good girl, Paula."

At first she thought she'd misheard. She stopped pounding and stared at Victor. His head remained bent over the spinning wheel.

Paula cleared her throat. "Thank you, Victor." He'd never shown any real sign of accepting her until now.

"You have the instinct," he muttered, stopping to examine the piece he worked on, "but any child of Michael Renfrew was bound to have the touch. He was good."

Without her prompting, Victor had actually broached the subject of her father. Paula slid from her stool, clenching her fists on the bench. Her father had known this man. Benno told her so, but before this morning Victor had evaded any attempt she'd made at finding out more about Michael Renfrew's time in Amsterdam.

She'd moved a step closer to Victor, deciding what might be safe to ask, what would be unlikely to make the old polisher close up again, when the outer door swept open. Benno entered, closely followed by Lukas and Christophe St-Giles.

Excitement shot into Paula's nerve endings. All her senses were sharpened. She stood very still, scarcely breathing, knowing any moment Christophe would turn her way and smile.

His hands were characteristically sunk into his pockets as he walked into Benno's office and closed the door. He hadn't even glanced in her direction.

Paula flipped her hair behind her ears. Her skin felt clammy. Quickly she checked around the workroom to see if anyone had noticed her reaction. All heads were down. She was a fool. Yesterday, she'd misinterpreted Christophe St-Giles polite attention for the same type of interest she'd felt—darn it, still felt—toward him.

Heat crawled uncomfortably up her neck to her cheeks, and she sat on her stool once more. At least he hadn't seen her staring at him like a smitten sophomore. Dammit all, she'd allowed a dumb emotional reaction, based on a brief interlude, to ruin a perfect opening to talk to Victor about her father.

Paula was deeply sunk in thought when she realized Victor was talking again, this time to Kersten Gouda, Kohl's senior page. Kersten spent time working in the showroom on the ground floor, dealing with retail clients. She also escorted the more important wholesale buyers in and out of the strong room. Kersten, Paula had soon discovered, wore many hats and was very knowledgeable.

Kersten stayed in front of Victor's glass shield. They spoke in Dutch, and Paula could only wait until she caught the older woman's eye and smiled.

"How are you?" Kersten asked politely. "Victor tells us you are a prize student."

Two compliments in one morning, Paula thought. The unexpected praise was almost sufficient to make up for her chagrin over Christophe's cold-shoulder treatment. "Victor is a prize teacher," she said honestly.

"Hmm" was Victor's offhand response. He stopped working and reached for an oily rag to wipe his hands.

"This arrived from Antwerp." Kersten gave Victor a small package. "Mr. Kohl said you'd know what to do with the delivery."

Victor set the parcel beside his scaife. "Yes." He nodded, unsmiling, at Kersten. "I was expecting it, Mrs. Gouda. Thank you."

The formality caught Paula's interest. She'd been at Kohl's only nine months, and although Kersten Gouda was reserved, they'd immediately used each other's first name. Victor must have known the woman for the fourteen years she'd been employed in the same building, yet he behaved like a rusty courtier around her. He even bowed slightly when Kersten turned to leave. Could Victor...? No, Victor couldn't be interested in Kersten Gouda. He'd mentioned his wife and children and grandchildren, with undisguised pride. And slight, blue-eyed, blond Kersten could be no more than forty-five, at least twenty years Victor's junior. And she was married. Still...

Curiosity got the best of Paula. "Kersten is a pretty woman." She moved closer as Victor unwrapped the brown-paper package. "She makes me feel dowdy when she arrives in the morning. Her clothes are so beautiful."

He took a padded plastic bag from a small box. "Mrs. Gouda doesn't like to wear her uniform outside the building."

The response surprised Paula. It was true that Kersten waited until she arrived for work to change into the navy blue suit Kohl's provided for her. That had never seemed unusual to Paula. "The junior salesgirls downstairs wear pretty much the same outfit for work. Don't they all change into uniform when they get here?"

"No." Victor slit the bubble plastic. "Only Mrs. Gouda."

Paula's attention was divided between their conversation and the already cut stone Victor slid from its protective cocoon. "Her own suits must cost a bundle," she commented abstractedly. "Maybe I'll buy something like that when I can afford it."

Victor grunted, peering at the gem through his high-powered loupe. "I wouldn't know about such things. You will look at this, Paula. I want you to tell me what you see."

Before she could pick up her own magnifying glass, Benno's office door opened again and he emerged with Christophe. The two men laughed, exchanged several low-spoken comments while they shook hands, then Christophe turned away. He paused to find a cigarette and cupped his hands to draw against the flame of his lighter. Paula held her breath. He was going to ignore her again, walk out as if she didn't exist. She couldn't look away.

Christophe lifted his chin. The tip of his cigarette glowed briefly and he exhaled. Paula gripped the edge of her bench with both hands. The blood in her body seemed to stop circulating. Dark eyes, narrowed to slits found her face through a thin veil of smoke. She smiled tentatively before the muscles around her mouth quivered and cold slid up her spine. Christophe didn't smile. He stared at her as he might a stranger, or perhaps a dull anatomical specimen in its glass case. She sat with a thump and pushed tools from one side of the wheel to the other. He didn't even remember she was there.

"Goodbye, then." Benno's voice had a penetrating quality.

Cautiously she glanced up. Lukas's animosity toward Christophe hadn't been imagined. But Benno's warm smile suggested he didn't share his son's dislike of this man.

Christophe's parting remark was inaudible over the machinery. He held his lighter between finger and thumb, twisting it in circles before he strode away. Paula returned her gaze to Benno. She mustn't think of that empty stare.

Benno hesitated, one hand braced against the door to his office. Paula watched thoughtfully. Again she'd misread signals. He'd made a tight fist of the hand by his side while he stared into space his smile gone, deep lines of worry etched in its place. The complete transformation turned her stomach. So Lukas wasn't the only Kohl who reacted violently to M. St-Giles, after all. He simply wasn't as adept as Benno at hiding his feelings.

"Paula!"

She swiveled toward a man, another worker, who called her name. "Yes, Jacob?"

"For you." He waved the receiver of the wall telephone. She hadn't even heard its ring.

Hesitantly she took the instrument from him, waiting until he turned curious eyes back to his work. She remembered yesterday's call at the American Hotel. If this was another dead line she'd start looking over her shoulder from now on.

"Hello," she said uncertainly. "This is Paula Renfrew."

"Hello, Paula Renfrew. This is Christophe St-Giles."

Confused, she glanced toward Benno's office. Benno had gone inside again. "I..." What did this mean? A few minutes ago he'd been in the same room and ignored her. "Where are you calling from?"

"Downstairs."

"In the showroom?" The showroom where at least a couple of curious employees could listen. Evidently Christophe hadn't forgotten how to play games. "You were just here, Christophe. In this room, where you know I work. Didn't you see me?"

"Of course." There was laughter in his voice.

"I'm afraid I don't understand. Did you think you shouldn't say hi in front of anyone else or something?"

There was a noticeable pause. "Or something, I guess. Forgive me. But I didn't want to leave without reminding you how much I'm looking forward to seeing you at dinner on Saturday evening."

"Good." What else could she say? She didn't know the man well enough to tell him she thought he was rude.

"I've offended you." His voice became deep velvet. "That's the last thing I want to do. But sometimes we have to put our own wants aside. We'll have more time to talk on Saturday."

The receiver slipped in her hand and she held it tighter. "Yes," she mumbled and listened to his warm goodbye before realizing she'd allowed him to get away with giving her the brush off, while leading him to believe she was looking forward to being with him again. Slowly she hung up the phone and rubbed her damp palms together. She *did* want to be with him again—desperately.

"Are we ready, Paula?" Victor asked sharply. "Or do you have better things to do?"

The diamond. She'd forgotten the diamond he'd told her to look at. "Sorry," she mumbled. "I'm ready. Why are they sending you already finished stones?"

"Look at it," he said abruptly.

Paula pressed her glass to her eye and bent over the stone Victor had set in the adhesive wax used during polishing. "An excellent brilliant cut," she murmured, tipping her head to peer through the facets from one side. "Eight carats?"

"Slightly more. But you have a good eye."

"I can't..." She twisted her wrist slightly. "I can't find any flaw. It's perfect—no, almost perfect. There's a small minor natural flaw. That should have been taken care of when the rough stone was cleaved. But by the time you finish and this is mounted it *will* be perfect."

Victor chuckled. "Good, Paula. Very good. You learn fast. Mr. Kohl obtained this stone specially for a client. It's already sold. I will attend to that little imperfection you so accurately noted, and this will be on its way."

Paula remained at his side, soaking up every move he made. One day, she'd be as good as Victor Hodez. The prospect exhilarated her.

Victor checked through his loupe once more and began to lower the arm that held the gem against the wheel. His curse, even in Dutch, wasn't wasted on Paula. She jumped. For the first time, she'd seen Victor make a mistake. His hand had jerked, twisting too far left and bringing the stone down in the groove between the wheel and its surrounding rigid plate. He corrected the error quickly, but Paula saw that his hands trembled slightly.

A masculine voice snapped the tension, "Is everything all right, Victor?"

Startled, Paula looked up into Lukas's intent gray eyes. An inexplicable anger overtook her. He'd obviously seen Victor's slip and chosen to comment. She'd never heard him offer encouragement to Victor or thanks for his excellent work. In fact, she'd never seen him taking any interest in the artists who created the product that kept him rich.

Victor had made no attempt to give Lukas a reply. He continued to work, and Paula noted with satisfaction that his fingers were as steady as usual.

"Good morning, Paula," Lukas said. "Have you recovered from yesterday's revels?"

Why, she wondered, must he always be so formal? "Yes. Thank you for taking me. I'll call Sandi and Peter later. I had a wonderful time." Lukas, she knew, had had a miserable time, not that his smooth expression betrayed other than calm today.

He checked his watch and remarked offhandedly, "Almost twelve." His suit jacket was slung over his left shoulder. "How about lunch?"

Paula almost gaped. Mr. Iceberg wanted to have lunch? With her? This was a first. She set down her loupe. "Sounds marvelous. I think I saw a little sun somewhere outside. Fresh air and food are just what I need." She glanced at Victor who was ignoring the exchange. "I'll finish up here and meet you downstairs in a few minutes, if that's okay."

"Fine. I'll be in the showroom." Shrugging on his jacket, Lukas headed for the door.

Paula began to untie her coverall. "Lunch with the boss. I must be doing something right."

Victor wasn't listening. Paula stood very still, her coverall trailing from one arm. This was turning into a strange day. There was no mistaking the expression on Victor's face: hatred. He stared at Lukas's back until the younger man left the room, then continued to watch the closed door blindly. Slowly Paula finished taking off the coverall. She straightened her tools, giving Victor time to recover. The reason for his obvious loathing for Lukas was something she couldn't begin to guess at. And personality conflicts here were none of her business.

"Right," she said finally. "Guess I'm as ready as I'm going to be. You don't mind if I leave for a while, do you Victor?" Usually, all the finishers brought sandwiches for lunch and ate in the workroom.

Victor looked at her blankly for an instant, then he said, "Why should I mind?" and bent immediately over his wheel.

A few minutes later, walking along Rokin beside Lukas, Paula lifted her face to a warm wind and tried to forget her shabby, oil-stained workclothes. Lukas, as elegant as ever, drew the admiring glances his good looks and panache would always command. They must make an odd pair, Paula decided.

Lukas walked her to a comfortable but nondescript sandwich bar on Spuistraat, half a mile away. They sat at a window table and placed their orders before Lukas fell silent and stared outside, apparently lost in thought.

Paula watched the people in the street, too, then the other patrons inside the café, and the waiters. She might as well be alone. Self-consciousness built until she fidgeted with her silverware. Lukas Kohl was a complex, disturbing man, and Paula wished she were back in the workroom, eating pickled herring on soft rolls and laughing with the others.

"Your work is going well?" Lukas said suddenly at the same moment their food arrived.

"Very well, thank you." Paula sipped water and waited. Lukas returned his attention to the passersby. He crossed his arms tightly.

Now what?

"This was nice of you, Lukas. Unexpected. I always eat at my bench." She would have to prompt him to disclose whatever was apparently tying him in knots. She took a bite of her open-faced liverwurst sandwich. Lukas made no attempt to eat. Paula tried again. "Did Sandi enjoy yesterday? I wish you could both be at dinner with your parents and Christophe on..." *Nice going, Renfrew.*

"St-Giles," Lukas almost shouted, then, dropping his voice to an urgent whisper he said, "Has he spoken to you since yesterday?"

His desperation bemused Paula. "We did speak—briefly. Why?"

"When? Did he call you last night? What did he ask you?"

She ignored the first two questions. "Christophe asked me nothing.

He merely said he looked forward to seeing me on Saturday. It was an unimportant conversation. He was being polite. Please, Lukas. What is it? What's going on?''

Lukas leaned back in his chair, gripped the arms so tightly that his knuckles turned white. "I knew it." He moistened his lips. "Look— listen, Paula. You shouldn't be involved in any of this. No one should. St-Giles is mixing up a bloody mess purely for his own gratification.''

"Lukas. I know something about the man is eating you. But you aren't making much sense. If there's something I should know, tell me. As it is, I can't imagine how I figure in your differences with Christophe, or the way you feel about him. He's nothing to me. Why should I be a factor?''

"Damn." Lukas motioned a waiter and ordered a shot of jenever. Paula said she'd rather stick to coffee. "As I've already said," he went on, "you shouldn't be involved at all. But Christophe's obviously ze- roing in on you and he must have a reason." He met her eyes squarely. "You're a beautiful woman, Paula. But Christophe has no shortage of beautiful women. I'm confused. For him to pursue you suggests he has some motive other than the obvious, yet...I don't know. I just don't know.''

Paula blushed and sipped her coffee. Even when she did get a com- pliment, it was double-edged.

"I'm going to tell you some things you must promise never to re- peat," Lukas said, leaning across the table. "Most particularly, you must not let Christophe know I've spoken to you. Can you agree to that?''

For an instant she considered refusing. But how could she? Her loy- alty belonged to the Kohls. They'd given her so much when they owed her nothing. "I can do it," she agreed slowly.

"First... Thanks." His drink was delivered, and he swallowed it in one gulp. He immediately signaled for a refill.

Paula looked away. Lukas hadn't eaten, and the middle of the day wasn't the time to start tipping back glasses of neat liquor—not if he valued a clear head.

"Anyway," Lukas continued. "As I was saying. First, I want to warn you that Christophe may hope to find an ally in you—an inside track to tidbits of information on the business.''

"That's ridiculous," Paula said before she could stop herself. "I mean, I'm an apprentice who works for you and your father—a nothing, at this stage. I don't know anything about the business.''

"But if he starts seeing more of you, he might try to coach you into noticing—or I suppose reporting would be a better word—reporting other people's movements, chance comments, anything he could use against us.''

"Lukas," Paula snapped, exasperated. "Why does Christophe want to find out things to use against you? He's your banker, right?"

"That's correct." The jenever refill arrived and promptly disappeared, as rapidly as the first drink.

"Don't bankers want their clients to be successful?" While Lukas seemed to be gaining some relief from his tension, Paula's own nerves had begun a slow burn. "Well, don't they?"

"Usually." Lukas ran a fingertip around the rim of his glass. His sandwich remained untouched. "Unless you've already hit bad times and they're looking for a way out of their obligations."

Paula stiffened. "Kohl's has hit bad times?"

"No...no, not really." He didn't meet her eyes. "The diamond market fluctuates. It's just been a bit worse for us lately. We need a small loan. Nothing unusual—an interim measure to help us through a rough spot. Within a few months we'll be as strong as we ever were. Kohl's has always been a success."

"So what's the problem? Are you suggesting Christophe's resisting the loan or something? I don't know a thing about any of this. I ran a small store by the seat of my pants for a few months after my father died. And I did it with the help of a very good accountant."

"Waiter!" Lukas shouted and Paula cringed. He jiggled his glass back and forth. "Christophe St-Giles isn't a banker in the ordinary sense. Oh, it's his family's bank and he's slated to slide into the president's chair eventually, but he isn't a banker. The man knows the business and he's smart, too damned smart for his own good, but he doesn't care to settle down and work at it. He prefers to flit around the Continent playing sleuth. He's what he terms a financial investigator. That's a polite title for insatiable snoop. He doesn't give a damn about what happens to our firm. Tradition, an old establishment with a great reputation...means nothing to him." He paused while the waiter brought a bottle, poured, then left.

Paula caught curious glances from nearby tables. "Lukas," she said persuasively. "I know you're upset, but don't you think you should eat something."

"Sure." He laughed shortly and took a bite of bread and cheese. "There. Satisfied? Good. Christophe St-Giles is a crusader for truth, justice, and above all, for Christophe St-Giles. He's determined to make his mark by ensuring his precious bank only deals with clear winners. He's going to prove we aren't a good risk. Throw us away if he can. The guy's a shark out to gobble up extraneous flotsam on his family's beautiful, swelling ocean of money. Their fortune is so large you wouldn't even be able to imagine it.''

Paula shifted restlessly in her seat. Lukas was downing more liquor, yet he still seemed in control. She prayed he wouldn't drink any more.

"Do you believe any of this?" His abrupt question startled her.

"I...I believe you think this is what he intends," Paula replied quietly. "But, Lukas, isn't he perhaps doing what's always done—making sure everything's okay before they hand over the money you need? Is that kind of approach routine, do you think?" She was speaking too slowly, too much like a patient adult to an obtuse child.

"No, I don't." Lukas's own thoughts absorbed him. He didn't appear to notice how she'd spoken. "I think he's out to make himself into even more of a golden boy with daddy and his uncles by showing them how astute he is. And the process is killing my father."

Paula turned icy. "Benno? Lukas, is Benno ill?"

"Yes, he's ill," Lukas replied bleakly. "Sick of fighting for what's rightfully ours. Every day I watch him get thinner. It was bad enough for him to have to ask for money in the first place. Since then he's been drawing into himself. If St-Giles had agreed without any fuss, he'd have gotten over it. It's only going to take a matter of time before we're firmly in the black. As it is, Christophe's poking around in every corner he can find—some we never knew we had. He's taken over the books and asks Father a hundred questions a day." His disgusted shove sent his plate clattering against Paula's. "That man is ruining my father's and my mother's lives. I want him out of here as quickly as possible...after he okays the loan.

"You shouldn't have to listen to all this, but the way he came on to you was transparent. I could be wrong, I suppose, but I had to warn you to be on the watch."

Paula made a doughy ball out of crumbs from her sandwich. Without knowing why, she believed Lukas. A stunning man like Christophe could have his pick of gorgeous women. Why bother to cultivate her, unless he thought she might prove useful?

"I'll be careful," she said simply.

"You must be more than careful." Lukas grasped her wrist painfully. "This Saturday you must watch every word that's said. Take note of questions he asks my father, and the way he responds to answers. And above all, Paula, don't let him get you alone where he can find a way to catch you off guard. Do you understand?''

She wanted no part of this. "I understand. But I don't think you have anything to worry about."

"Paula." The grip on her wrist made her wince. "Christophe was once my friend. We were closer than brothers. I look at him today and I see an executioner, the potential killer of my father. Will you take what I tell you with absolute seriousness?"

Her flesh crawled. "Yes, Lukas," she whispered. "I'll take you absolutely seriously."

"Good girl." He motioned the waiter for more jenever. "You may never meet a more dangerous man than Christophe St-Giles."

Chapter Five

Thursday of the Second Week:

Christophe zipped his windbreaker up to the neck and pushed damp hair away from his brow. He couldn't have chosen a more miserable evening for what he must do. But there really wasn't a choice, was there? Timing was everything in this dangerous game he was playing. Time was running out. In the end there would be winners and losers. He intended to be on the right team.

He spotted his quarry now, on the other side of Rokin, moving quickly. Christophe crossed and fell in behind, shielded from the man by the hurrying mass of workers on their way home.

Dodging, pressing close to the buildings, he kept the other's dark blue blazer in sight. The man carried a briefcase in one hand, a plastic sack in the other, and his step was purposeful. Christophe smiled grimly and risked drawing nearer. The chase sent adrenaline pumping through his veins. He'd spent too many hours behind a desk lately, and in boardrooms and his father's office with its smell of cigar smoke and old leather. This new challenge was what he'd needed...as long as he could guide the course of what would surely follow.

The man in the blazer slipped right, down a narrow street, and Christophe lengthened his stride. They were heading west, but where, where and to meet whom, to do what? He had his own ideas, but little proof as yet.

Awnings almost touched over gray cobbles. Signs swung above Christophe's head as he passed—Heineken, Cinzano, Coca-Cola, and the ever-present Sex Shop. This seething, open city didn't change. But he'd lost some of his familiarity with the labyrinthine streets and canals, and he could not let his man out of sight with any hope of heading him off farther on.

A surge of movement made him pause. Running children, their sport bags flying, careened around him, shouting, urging each other on. They would miss their bus. They'd be late for their game, maybe even have to forfeit.

Christophe hesitated, making room for the children's charge. When he looked ahead again, he was just in time to see the man in the blazer squeezing between vegetable stalls to enter a tiny bar.

Damn, damn. Christophe cast around until he saw a boy selling newspapers. He bought an issue and took up position outside a delicatessen. What if there was a back way out of the bar? He gritted his teeth and immediately reached for a cigarette. He could do nothing but wait, and hope. The bar was too small to allow him to go in without being noticed.

Words passed unread beneath his eyes. Every few seconds, he checked the doorway of the bar. Finally two men emerged. He shifted impatiently and glanced back at the paper. More movement in the doorway brought his attention up once more, but this patron was again the wrong one.

Christophe started. He wasn't the wrong man. Frank Lammaker had changed clothes and now wore casual tan pants and suede jacket. That accounted for the contents of the briefcase or the sack—probably the sack. Christophe ground his cigarette underfoot, feeling the flood of energy once more. Frank's briefcase was what really interested him, that and where the messenger was going. On Tuesday and Wednesday Christophe had watched Frank leave Kohl's after work, each time with the unexpected briefcase, each time alone and hurrying, and had decided to follow today if the pattern was repeated.

Frank left the bar, setting a stiff pace, threading an artful path through the tide of people, still heading west and farther from the city center. He cut along alleys and over narrow canal bridges with the skill of a man who knew his territory unerringly. Christophe was surprised when a turn brought them into Leidse Plein. In the next couple of days he must spend some time walking, and studying a map to reacquaint himself with Amsterdam's lesser-known streets.

Without looking to right or left and, Christophe hoped fervently, oblivious of his pied piper role, Frank passed the American Hotel, reached the next major street and hopped between horn-blasting cars and cursing cyclists. Christophe followed, ducking his head against loud comments and waving fists offered through open vehicle windows.

The chase became trickier now. Once away from dense crowds, Christophe heard his own footsteps like whip-cracks on the concrete. He fell back slightly, but dared not stroll for fear Frank would make an unexpected move.

They walked on, past a ruined church, an unlikely sight between rows of already deserted offices. Frank's next turn was sharp. He broke into a trot, rounding the end of the church and heading into a park. Vondel Park, Christophe remembered suddenly. Years ago he'd come here on Sunday afternoons to lie on the grass with crowds of students. He also remembered the place as a maze of serpentine paths, bandstands, little bridges leading nowhere in particular...and dense trees. A perfect place to meet someone privately...or to lose an unwelcome follower.

Christophe was almost certain Frank didn't realize he was being tailed. At the bottom of a short flight of steps, after checking his watch, he set off more slowly, tucking the plastic bag beneath his arm, swinging his briefcase. Christophe thought he heard a whistled tune, but couldn't be sure. The mist thickened by the second, blanketing the air with dense moisture, deadening sound. The thud of his own feet on sodden turf echoed back at him.

Frank's sudden halt brought Christophe's heart into his mouth. Swiftly he slipped from the path, walked without looking back for a hundred yards, then veered into a grove of trees parallel to the trail. When he dared look sideways he saw no movement. He tipped up his head and exhaled sharply then crisscrossed between the trees, drawing closer to the path again.

With the trunk of a huge tree as a shield, he looked ahead and saw a gate leading out of the park. Frank must have been heading for this. Spreading his hands on the tree trunk, bracing his weight, Christophe calculated rapidly. If the other man had run, he could be outside by now, gone, and this charade had been for nothing. He slumped against rough bark and drove his fists into his pockets.

A piercing noise reached him. This time he definitely heard whistling. He leaned back and saw Frank come into view, heading for the gate. For the moment there was no alternative but to stay put and watch. Frank moved slowly, strolled, twirling the bag now, nonchalant.

Christophe narrowed his eyes. Maybe this young man was too convenient a suspect, but he certainly was a suspect. Managing a few glances at the Kohl employees personal files was taking ingenuity on Christophe's part. What he'd read in Frank's records so far was definitely interesting. Benno was either extremely generous, with a deep understanding of the hidden strengths in human nature, or he was a fool. Frank Lammaker had spent more of his teenage years in correctional institutions than anywhere else. His crimes had been petty: shoplifting, stolen bicycles and hubcaps, stolen... Christophe crossed his arms.

Frank had been a small-time thief, but most big-time thiefs started out that way. And Benno knew the man's history, had written his intention to give Frank more and more responsibility to "give him a chance to prove himself. Responsibility," Benno's notation had gone on, "brings out the best in men."

Christophe wasn't so sure Benno was right in this case. The steady drone of an engine punctured the mist and he moved to the other side of the tree. *Dammit!* He started to run.

Too late.

Why hadn't he noticed the small white car at the curb?

Frank broke into a loping stride and slid into the passenger seat. Immediately the car sped away.

Christophe kicked up a muddy divot. He'd been careless. With his eyes closed, he stood, arms outstretched, a hand on each gatepost, breathing deeply of the scent of damp earth and leaf mold. There would be no way out but to repeat this procedure tomorrow. Tomorrow he'd be ready. He only hoped Frank hadn't noticed him, and that the scenario would be reenacted.

The distinctive squeal of tires snapped him to attention and he flattened against one gatepost, edged out as far as he dared. The white car had only gone to a wide spot in the street to make a U-turn. Now it sped back, and as it passed, Christophe had a clear view of the two men inside.

For an instant, he frowned, groping for the name that went with the other face. Then it came. *Willem Bill.* Once more Kohl's messenger and Metters' page were together, this time deep in conversation...and alone.

"DON'T TURN ON THE LIGHTS."

The man stared briefly at the woman, then nodded and moved past her into the gloomy bedroom. "I'm worried," he said quietly. "One piece of bad luck, even a tiny one, and they'll find out."

"There will be no bad luck," the woman replied. She shut the door. "We've done everything exactly as we planned, and our plans were perfect. As long as we keep our nerve, we'll get what we want. Everything we want."

"It's almost dark." The man peered through a slit between the drapes. "We drop one more tonight, then wait. Did he say anything when you spoke to him last?"

"Only that he's getting closer and we should not worry. As long as the supply of stones can be kept up, we are assured of achieving our goal.''

"The supply cannot be kept up indefinitely. We all knew that from the beginning.''

The woman sighed. "We'll have four diamonds left after tonight?''

"Yes. The best four.'' The response was curt. "He will have received nine exceptional stones, but none like these. Look. Turn on the light. No one will see.''

She did as he asked then crossed the room to stand beside him at a small desk. He reached beneath a ledge, feeling, until a slender drawer clicked open. Five diamonds glittered on a bed of black velvet.

"Sparklers,'' the woman said, her voice silken. "No wonder men die for them. Which one goes tonight?'' She touched a long fingernail to the closest stone.

"That one.'' He picked it up and folded it carefully inside a sheet of paper. "These—'' and he covered the rest "—are flawless. We may need them.''

"You know so much about these things.''

"I've learned my lessons well. I had to.''

She smiled tightly. "Soon this will be over and we'll be in the clear. No one knows and no one ever will know.... We'll have it all.''

"Right.'' The man's voice was less sure. "You did remember to tell him we had only nine gems?'' He watched her nod, anxiety clouding his eyes. "Good, good. Then these shouldn't have to go anywhere we don't want them to go.''

"Yes,'' she said softly, prying his hand away from the stones. "But we do have these for insurance if we need them, although—'' the fingernail outlined a huge, pearshaped diamond. "—I hope we never have to let this one go.''

Without replying, he brushed her hand aside and snapped the drawer shut. "Paula Renfrew should be watched.''

"Why?''

"I'm not sure. The company she keeps could mean trouble. I can't figure out exactly where she fits in—if she does—but she might just be behind our secretive friend. If she is...''

Rain began a steady tapping at the window. The woman laughed nervously. "Another wet walk,'' she said. "I hope this will be the last.'' In the pause that followed, they stared at each other and listened to the rain. "What made you bring up Paula Renfrew?'' she asked cautiously.

"I read some things. The lady definitely has her skeletons. If she's trying to bury them, and I think she could be, she may have to be left holding the whole bundle.''

"Oh, God." The woman huddled on the edge of the bed. "We've come too far to turn back now. We're winning. I know we are."

"Yes. And one way or another we'll make it all the way without anything touching us."

She drew in a deep breath. "No death, though, my dear friend. Please tell me there won't be need for that."

He looked at the folded paper in his hand. "I hope not. But, as you said, no wonder men have died for these...and women...."

Saturday of the Second Week:

Paula flopped on the bed and spread her arms wide. "I don't want to go to the damned dinner party," she said loudly to the beamed ceiling. "I don't want to worry about every word Benno says, and Anna says, and *I* say. *Damn, damn, damn.*"

She was crushing her dress, too. Hell, she wouldn't go. If she slipped over to the main house quickly, she could plead a headache and escape before Christophe arrived.

Christophe, Christophe. He fascinated her. Even this bed in the little guest house that had become so dear to her reminded her of Christophe St-Giles. He'd said he once stayed there. Now she never climbed into bed without instantly remembering he must have lain in the same spot, looking at the same ceiling. Had he always slept here alone...? She even imagined him descending the spiral stairs leading from the loft bedroom to the living room and kitchen below. Paula saw him everywhere. *Good God.* She was suffering from a sophomoric crush.

Mumbling irritably, she got up and smoothed her skirt. That was another aggravating element about this evening—she hated dressing up. Already she longed to slip back into a comfortable pair of jeans.

The clock on her bedside table read six-thirty. She'd promised to help Anna with last-minute preparations, though Paula wasn't fooled by the request. Anna would have everything under control. The older woman had simply sensed Paula's reticence over attending the dinner and had contrived a reason for her not to back out. At Paula's protest that her presence wouldn't be appropriate, Anna had cajoled, "Christophe's like family—and so are you. Of course you'll come. And it would be so nice to have a little help in the kitchen for a change."

Paula clattered down the metal stairs and let herself out into a central courtyard. The houses along the canals mostly adjoined each other.

Benno and Anna's property butted with another house on one side, a wall screening an alley barely wide enough for a man, on the other. Paula's backhouse formed the fourth side of the courtyard, and she came and went through the Kohls' home.

She shivered. The last pallid wisps of gold showed above the high rooftops. The day's timid sun was slinking away, sucking with it any hint of warmth. A jacket would have been a good idea, but if she turned back she might completely lose her nerve.

Delicious smells met her when she entered the main house. Paula went first to the kitchen. The room was empty and, true to her guess, everything appeared perfectly organized for the meal.

She dithered, gathering courage.

"There you are, Paula. Good, good. We're all waiting for you." Anna Kohl breezed into the kitchen and slid a hand through Paula's arm.

"I...you said I could do something to help. Give me a job," Paula said hurriedly, too hurriedly. "Can I peel something...or..."

Anna's blue eyes looked unwaveringly into Paula's. "Why are you so nervous?" She tilted her head and light shone on her still-blond hair drawn back into an elegantly loose chignon. "You've already met Christophe, I understand."

"Yes," Paula said, hoping she'd hit a firm note. "We've met." What, she wondered, would Anna think if she knew how Lukas felt about Christophe?

"So why do you back away this evening? Is he so difficult to be with?"

Paula instantly blushed. "No, Anna. He's, he's... he's..." He's what, should she say? Charming, intriguing, and Lukas says he could be dangerous and could ruin your life and his? Should she tell Anna that Lukas had accused Christophe of slowly killing Benno and destroying his business, that tonight she, Paula, was supposed to listen to every word spoken and then make a report?

She felt sick.

"Ah, I see." Anna smiled gently. "I understand. Please forgive me, Paula. It must be too long since I was your age. Christophe is very attractive, isn't he, and delightful? Yes, of course. Come on, my dear, I think perhaps the appeal is mutual. He's already asked about you twice."

Smiling wanly, at a loss for words, Paula allowed Anna to lead her into the passageway and up a short flight of stairs to the living room.

On the threshold she took several breaths through her mouth. The air seemed thin and this wasn't the time to hyperventilate.

She saw Benno first. He turned from a rosewood trolly where he was mixing drinks. "Paula." His haggard face showed genuine pleasure. "I was afraid you'd forgotten."

A wave of protectiveness freshened her determination and she lifted her chin. "Sorry I'm late." She wasn't, but it didn't matter. "I got too relaxed in my little nest and didn't watch the time closely enough."

"Hello, Paula. How are you?"

At the sound of Christophe's voice, she turned, concentrating on moving naturally. "Hi, Christophe. Nice to see you again. I'm fine—you?" She sounded cool, just right.

"Better now you're here."

Paula felt rather than saw Anna and Benno look at each other. She *would not* blush. "I was warned about Frenchmen," she said lightly. "Silver-tongued devils, I think the description went."

Christophe sketched an airy gesture. "We are blessed with a certain skill when it comes to words. Can I help it if charm comes naturally?"

Benno and Anna laughed. Paula kept her eyes on Christophe and saw little humor in his expression. He might be charming, but there was something else about him, something...? Dangerous would do. That's the word Lukas had used, and it fitted the aura surrounding this almost too-handsome man as well as the dark suit he wore.

Benno coughed, interrupting the heavy silence. "All right, you two. You can discuss each other's charms later. Christophe's having a martini, Paula. What would you like?"

"Nothing for now," she replied, deliberately giving Benno her full attention. "I'm sure Anna has planned wine with dinner, so I'll wait."

"Wise," Anna said. "In fact, why don't you men bring your drinks into the dining room. Dinner's ready and I shall be insufferable if my soufflé collapses."

Christophe came to Paula's side as they crossed the marble entry hall behind the Kohls. He settled a hand at her waist—a firm hand that radiated heat through the thin fabric of her dress. By the time they'd covered the short distance to the dining room table, her nerves felt filleted.

Anna presided over the meal with practiced efficiency, whisking away plates, replacing each dish with the next delicious course. Paula wasn't hungry, but she made herself eat.

"Everything is perfect, Anna," Christophe commented as chocolate mousse was served in delicate stemmed dishes. "But why isn't Madeleine helping you?"

Glass clattered on china. Anna barely missed tipping the dessert she set in front of Christophe. "Madeleine?"

He looked up at her. "Madeleine's still with you, isn't she?"

"I...yes, yes. She's in Haarlem for the weekend."

Paula glanced at Benno and found him staring back. She looked at her hands in her lap. It was beginning. The questioning she'd been told to expect. Christophe knew Madeleine still worked here. Lukas had told him. But why would Anna lie about her housekeeper? Surely there could be no harm in Christophe's showing interest in the woman.

"Yes." Benno's voice was too loud. "Madeleine's visiting her sister's son, I think. She left yesterday."

Madeleine had been in the courtyard at three that afternoon. She'd admired Paula's tulips and talked about the new television Frank had bought her and that she looked forward to watching this evening.

"She's been with you a long time," Christophe said between mouthfuls of mousse. "Her son works for you now I see, Benno." He half rose from his chair while Anna sat again.

Paula lifted her own spoon at the same time as she noticed Benno's expression change and an unnatural pallor replace the color in his cheeks. He swallowed uncomfortably. It suddenly occurred to Paula that Benno and Anna had lied about Madeleine to spare her the questions that Christophe was probably about to subject them to.

"Frank, isn't it?" Christophe persisted.

"Frank, yes," Anna put in. "A good boy. He's been the man of the family since he was fourteen. Very responsible, isn't he, Benno?"

"I trust him implicitly," Benno said tonelessly. "He is our messenger."

"Yes." Christophe turned his fine brown eyes on Paula. "Paula and I saw him at the American Hotel on Monday. Lukas seemed surprised."

"Surprised?"

Benno's question hung in the air for several seconds.

"Mmm. He seemed to think Frank's friends outclassed him. And one of the men he was with disturbed Lukas." Christophe frowned quizzically at Paula. "What was that man's name—the one who's a page with, ah, with the other firm?"

She blinked, shifting her spoon back and forth. Kohl's employees weren't supposed to fraternize with Metter's people. She was certain Christophe knew as much, yet he was deliberately headed in that direction, steadily closing a net around Frank Lammaker. Why? Indecision thickened her tongue. Lying was out of the question, yet if she mentioned Willem Bill, Benno could become angry with Frank.

"Paula," Christophe prompted. "You remember. You told Lukas who that was."

"No," she said at last, inspired. "Sandi did. Someone called Otis, I think—a painter."

Christophe's lips came together, drawn down at the corners. She felt he could see inside her head. He definitely knew she was skirting the issue.

"You're right," he said smoothly. "Sandi did say that. But I meant the other man, from Metter's, is it? Yes, Metter's. You said he was a page named...?"

Give up, she thought miserably. "Willem Bill."

"That's it," Christophe responded heartily, slapping the table.

Anna jumped, spilling the remnants of her wine and Benno instantly went to her aid, mopping with his napkin. Paula noted that as he leaned across his wife, he squeezed her arm quickly.

Slowly, inexplicably, irritation gnawed at Paula. She didn't know what line she'd expected Christophe to take. Certainly not a blatant attempt to put Frank Lammaker in a bad light with Benno. The effort seemed small-minded and pointless, unworthy of a man of Christophe's standing.

Benno finished tending the linen tablecloth and subsided into his chair once more. His dessert remained untouched while he faced Christophe, a fixed smile on his lips. "I don't know why Lukas should be surprised to see Frank at the American. Young people have always gathered there. Even in my time we did. Paula—" he turned to her and his smile softened "—I remember Anna and I and your—" He stopped abruptly, his mouth working slightly, before he pushed away from the table and stood. "Anna and I used to go there," he finished lamely. "Stay where you are, my love. I'll pour coffee.

He'd been going to say something about her father. Paula was certain "father" was the word Benno had choked on. She couldn't take any more of this. For what it was worth, she'd tell Lukas about Christophe's reference to Frank. If more information was needed, Lukas must find a way to get it himself. Let him sit through a tense meal like this. She had to get out.

"Anna," she said, trying to sound calm. "I'm sure you and Benno have things you'd like to talk with Christophe about alone. I think I'll take a walk before it gets too dark."

"No," Benno said quickly. "Absolutely not, Paula. Amsterdam is no place for a lovely young woman to walk alone at night."

She got up. "I'll be careful, I promise. I won't be long and I won't stray from the main streets."

Anna started to protest, but Paula was already backing away. In the hall she hesitated, wondering if she should take time to go for her coat. She did have to get out, to walk and think. Her long-sleeved dress and a brisk enough pace would keep her warm, she decided, opening the heavy front door. She closed it behind her and ran down the worn stone steps to the sidewalk.

A light wind snatched at her full skirt, swirling it around her knees. Paula crossed to the canalside. Herengracht was one of the only major canals where there were still privately owned homes. In the dusk, shadows of the narrow, tippy buildings wavered across rippling gray water.

Paula was glad to be in the fresh air. She loved this old city. Walking faster, she swung her arms and wished she wore pants and tennis shoes. Tonight she'd like to run, to forget all the barely restrained anxiety she'd left behind in that dining room.

Footsteps sounded behind her, rapid footsteps that soon become the even clip of someone running. She quelled the urge to look back, concentrating instead on keeping her own pace steady.

When a hand clamped her shoulder and spun her around she gasped, disoriented, and opened her mouth to shout.

Christophe smiled down at her, his eyes black and glinting in the coming night's light. "Why the hurry, Paula?"

Chapter Six

Paula's heart did nasty things. Deep breathing only increased her light-headedness.

"I'm sorry." Christophe bent closer. "I frightened you. Dammit, I'm sorry."

"You didn't frighten me," Paula managed, then laughed and pressed her chest. "You only made me feel I was going to die right here and now."

Christophe put a hand behind her neck. "I should have shouted instead of leaping at you like that. I was afraid I'd lose sight of you, so I just ran. Forgive me?" He had to feel her tremble. She hoped he wouldn't guess fright wasn't the main cause.

"Consider yourself forgiven," she said, inching away. "I suppose Anna and Benno sent you after me. They worry too much."

"Nobody sent me. I wanted to come." He rubbed her nape lightly. "But Anna was tired. She's probably glad to get rid of me early. I said I'd keep an eye on you and make sure you got home safely."

Paula wished his voice, the flawless English spoken with an incredibly sexy French accent, had no effect on her. She wished she didn't like the idea of Christophe wanting to join her, that she could summon a retort about how capable she was of getting herself home safely. "You're very kind, but I don't think I'm in mortal danger on a busy street like this" was the best she could muster. She wanted to see the look in his eyes—clearly.

"Young women should not walk city streets alone at night. Any city. Particularly streets as notoriously, ah, shall we say, colorful, as Amsterdam's?"

"But—"

"But," he broke in. "But this is a 'busy' street, Paula? Let's look around, shall we? You and I are the only humans in sight. One cannot know if there are others we do not see."

She shivered convulsively. *"Don't give him a chance to get you on your own,"* Lukas had warned. "I'll be fine." Her voice sounded as unsure as she felt.

"I think not." Christophe turned her around, guiding her south along the canal. "And you're cold. Here." He began to take off his jacket.

"No!" She held his forearm. "I'm fine, really."

Christophe rubbed her fingers, then gently pried them loose. "You're not fine, woman. Not fine at all." He finished taking off the jacket and draped it around her. "You shot out of that dining room as if you couldn't bear to be there a moment longer. If you'd been thinking rationally, and simply wanted what you said you wanted, a walk, you'd have taken the time to get a coat. Want to let me in on the problem? Was something said to upset you? Did I say or do something?"

She was out of her depth. "Nothing was said. I thought I might be in the way," she lied. There was no alternative but to lie.

Christophe appeared to consider. Paula waited, listened to water lapping concrete, concentrated on walking over the cobbles in her high heels. Caution was everything. She'd promised Lukas that Christophe would never know of their lunchtime conversation earlier in the week.

Finally Christophe said, "You weren't in the way, but good, I'm glad you aren't upset," and put an arm across her back to hold her upper arm. A long sigh moved his chest against her shoulder. "So we'll enjoy our walk. It's a beautiful evening and I haven't done this in too long."

Done what in too long? Paula wondered. Walked through the night with his arm around a woman? She doubted that was what he meant. "I love all the little lights on the bridges," she murmured and thought how much more romantic they seemed when she was held against the muscular side of an attractive man.

Christophe didn't reply. They walked on. Occasionally he gave her arm a gentle squeeze, but she sensed his preoccupation. Was he formulating his next line of questioning?

"We don't have to go on." Paula glanced up at him. "You'll be the one who's cold soon." His white shirt showed luminous, the top button undone, his tie loosened. "Let's get back," she insisted. Forgetting discretion in this setting, with this man, would be too easy.

"I'm a hot-blooded animal," he responded easily.

For an instant, Paula contemplated how hot-blooded Christophe might be under his cool Continental exterior. The pictures she formed, a complicated mix of how he would react when angry...what he might be like as a lover...made her glad he couldn't see her face. Hiding emotion had never been her strong suit.

"Paula," he said when the silence had lasted too long. "*Is* there anything you'd like to tell me...or ask me?"

Someone had sucked the oxygen out of the night breeze. She laughed and hated the sound. Why couldn't she just forget Christophe's real reason for being in Amsterdam? For tonight, why couldn't she pretend they'd met under different circumstances, lose herself in the power that emanated from him, in the snap his energy lent to the air? He turned her on emotionally and physically. What she felt now was unique in her experience and she wanted it—all of it.

His hand moved downward to her elbow. "Is there something, Paula?"

Illusion had almost pulled her in. "No." Paula lifted her chin, expanding her lungs deliberately. "Nothing at all, Christophe." She glanced at his hazy profile, hesitating a moment, catching a hint of the subtle scent of his after-shave. *Be careful,* the inner voice reminded her too distantly. "What could I possibly want to say, or ask?"

She'd hoped to turn the tables on him. Christophe's relaxed laugh let her know he'd never be readily caught off guard. "I can't know what's in your mind, Paula, can I? But I can feel when a woman—or man— is uncomfortable. You became disturbed at the dinner table and I wondered why, if I could help. Forget it, please. A flight of fancy on my part perhaps. Have you been on the canals yet?"

His rapid change of topic surprised Paula. "Yes...no. You mean *on*, in a barge?"

"Uh-huh. I haven't taken a cruise here since I first visited with my parents. Let's do it. We're almost at a terminal." He was already steering her toward a brightly lit booth at the end of a dock. On one side swayed a glass-enclosed barge.

"Wait." Paula hung back, pulling Christophe to a halt. "It would take too long. Anna and Benno are bound to wonder where I am."

"You're with me." He smiled down at her. "I told them I'd look after you—" She could see his eyes clearly now and the smile didn't reach them. "And I will look after you, I promise."

Mesmerized, carried along by a potent blend of foreboding and fascination, Paula let him take her hand. What could happen to her on a little barge trip? They'd look at the sights, she'd field whatever course of interrogation he might be planning, then he'd take her home and say good-night. The end. Or would it be?

She was uptight, Christophe decided, too uptight for a woman who insisted nothing was wrong. Her hand was stiff and icy in his. He had to go slowly with her or she'd shy away and clam up completely. He bought two tickets for the cruise, tucking her hand into his elbow while he fished for money. Somehow he was going to lull her, coach her into letting go. Then, if he was lucky, he might get at the truth about Paula Renfrew.

They walked wordlessly down the shifting wooden dock, and he helped her board the craft. "Go all the way to the back," he instructed automatically. "The view's better." She passed him and he smelled her perfume—light, gardenia or something. He looked down on the top of her head. The black hair, whipped into curls by the breeze, had a burnished sheen. God, he didn't want her to be involved in cheating the Kohls.

"This is something." She slid into a bench seat and he sat close beside her. "The skyline looks almost on fire from here."

"Yes," he said. He must keep her talking. "Good Lord, I just had a thought." Turning sideways, he hitched up a knee and held it with both hands.

Paula raised her brows expectantly. "What? You look... What's so funny?"

"Don't you ever tell Lukas or Peter we did this."

Her mouth tightened. "I hadn't planned to." She sounded frosty, Christophe noted, and immediately wondered why. "What makes you think Lukas or Peter would be interested in our taking a trip on the canals?" she added.

Could Lukas have warned her to be careful? Or Benno? Damn their asinine hides if they had. Christophe made himself smile. "Paula," he began. "I worked hard to become a transplanted Amsterdammer. Natives don't behave like tourists. If those two found out about this they'd never let me live it down."

She stared for an instant before her features softened and she grinned. "I have you in my power." She shook a finger at him. "Never give the opposition a weapon they can use against you."

Keeping the smile on his lips became harder. "And I thought you were a friend, Paula Renfrew. Or at least a friend in the making." Her comment could have been a meaningless figure of speech. But he didn't imagine the sensation that they were feinting around each other. He was sure she knew more than she should about him and his reason for being here.

Her mumbled "Mmm" gave no hint of what she was thinking. She stared through the barge's curved rear window. A swinging overhead lantern played shadows across her face. Her expression had become distant.

With a grinding shudder, the barge pulled away from its moorings and swung to the center of the canal. Paula peered upward. He looked at her face, then at the smattering of stars in a dark sky turned golden around the illuminated roofs of buildings, the spires and domes of churches and towers. Too bad they weren't like the other couples aboard, out to enjoy the night—and each other.

He spread an arm along the seat back behind her. She shifted slightly, but he pretended not to notice.

"Christophe." Her eyes, when she faced him, were deeply shadowed. "You said you stayed in Benno and Anna's backhouse before. I'm sorry to put you out of a bed. Peter mentioned a houseboat. Is that where you're staying?"

"Yes, it is."

"Really. Where?" Her interest was genuine.

"Oh, not far from here. On Singel. I can see the Mint Tower from my bunk and walk to the flower market in a few minutes. It's a great spot. The barge belongs to Peter. Lukas and I helped him renovate it years ago."

"Peter's?" She tilted her head. "Peter has an apartment in Lukas and Sandi's house. What would he do with a houseboat?"

"He used to live there and have his photographic studio there, too. Now he rents out the boat. Fortunately for me, it was available when I decided to visit this time. Would you like to see it? We could get off at the flower market and walk back."

Not subtle enough, he thought wryly. Her reaction had shown instant disapproval. "Not tonight, Christophe," she said without inflection. "I'd like to get off at Bloemenmarket, anyway, and head home. But I'd better not be too much later."

"Don't you trust me?" *Damn.* He shouldn't have tried that tack until he was more sure of his subject.

Paula met his eyes squarely. "Is there some reason why I shouldn't trust you, Christophe?"

"Of course not. I was being flippant." He'd have to give her that one...and be more subtle in future. "You lived in New Jersey. I don't think you told me the name of the town."

"Bayonne."

"And you gave up New Jersey and...Bayonne...for Amsterdam and strangers. An unusual choice."

"Why?" she asked sharply. "You chose your course in life, didn't you?"

He was taken aback by her vehemence. "Yes," he agreed, studiously keeping his voice level. "To a certain extent. But I always knew what I wanted to do."

"So did I." She laughed shortly. "I just wasn't born as directly into it as you were."

A chink had appeared in her armor and he lunged for it. "You were, in a way. You said your father was here before you and left. You followed in his footsteps. Why did he decide to give up?"

Her knuckles whitened where she clutched the lapels of his jacket across her breasts. "I never knew," she said tonelessly. "And once I realized he'd rather not discuss the subject, I stopped asking."

She sounded so convincing. He wanted to be convinced, but he couldn't be, not so easily. "Perhaps you'll find out one day, by accident. And perhaps when you do you'll tire of all this and decide to go home like he did."

"Never!" Was that fervor in her eyes, or anger? "This is my home now," she went on. "Everything that matters to me is here. There's no one to go back to in the States anymore."

His breath quickened. Instinctively he knew her passion could be her undoing. Making her angry might be the key. "Everything that matters?" He pulled the corners of his mouth down. "Why would a lovely woman, who could undoubtedly find something exciting to do with her life—something lucrative—choose such a dull career?" He ran his eyes over her slowly, knowing she'd see him assessing her.

"Diamonds aren't dull." Her cheeks were flushed now. "Why would such an attractive man choose a career in a dusty field like banking?"

Breaking her down wouldn't be easy. She was too mature, too sure of herself. "What can I say?" He waved his free hand. "You're right, of course. We all find adventure and stimulation in different ways."

"I grew up watching my father work. He designed one-of-a-kind pieces and then threw away the setting molds. And all the time he talked about the diamonds he'd worked on here while I learned and waited for my chance—this chance." Her fingers dug deep into the fabric of his jacket. "Dad's favorite piece was a marquis, six flawless carats for the sixth birthday of a European count's daughter..." She'd averted her face.

Every muscle in Christophe's body tensed. *A marquis cut, six carats, flawless.* The exact description of the gem stolen shortly before Michael Renfrew's rapid departure from Amsterdam. Had he loved the stone so much because it had become his ticket to independence...and because he'd done the impossible: stolen it successfully?

"One day," Paula continued very softly, "people will come thousands of miles, to have *me* turn their *dull* diamonds, as you seem to regard them, into perfect treasures. My name will be known in those quiet rooms around the world where people discuss who's the best finisher for their diamond."

Her intensity threw him off for a moment. She sounded honestly involved in her craft for its own sake. But that wouldn't fit with his suspicions. He collected his wits. "Aha." His voice betrayed nothing of what he felt. He smoothed away strands of hair from her cheek. "I begin to see, I think. Paula Renfrew isn't a simple woman, at all. She covets fame in her own way—obscure fame, but fame nevertheless. I like that."

"You like ambition. You relate to what you perceive as your own kind," she retorted, then quickly lowered her lashes. "I'm sorry. That was snippy and uncalled for. How long do you expect to be in Amsterdam?"

Was she asking because she cared, Christophe wondered, or because someone else had fed her questions to which they'd like answers? Benno had been keen for him to come after her tonight. "No idea yet," he said. "How about you?" Had this outing been a trap he'd fallen into?

"We've already covered that. I'm a resident now. What do you hope to accomplish while you're here?"

He knew he must appear impassive. Someone *had* primed Paula. "This is a routine visit."

"Do you spend most of your time in Zurich, or making...routine visits?"

"My duties vary." At any other time he might have enjoyed the verbal fencing match. Tonight it made him edgy. He must stay with the subject of her father. "You ran the store after your father died. You didn't enjoy that?"

She opened her mouth, then turned away, but not before he saw the sheen in her eyes. "Not alone," she muttered. He had to strain to hear the words.

"You still miss your father?"

"More than ever, sometimes."

Enough to want vengeance against people he may have said perse-cuted him? "Aren't you afraid being here may dredge up information that could prove painful?" He held his breath.

"Like what?" She swung to face him, staring hard. "He loved being here. Why should anything about that be painful?"

"Simple association can sometimes be overwhelming. That's all I meant." This time he looked away. He was hitting a nerve, repeatedly, but not getting any positive information.

Across the aisle, a couple kissed. Christophe could see the white arch of the woman's neck beneath the man's tanned hand, their lips moving leisurely back and forth, their flickering lashes. He pulled his arm from behind Paula and leaned forward to rest both elbows on his knees. Good God, he was shielding the couple from her view. Why? What was the matter with him?

His thigh touched hers and he felt her muscle tense, but she didn't move away. He glanced at her. Her features were set, her expression remote. A guide's voice droned on about the sights they passed. Chris-tophe barely heard and knew Paula was also removed from her sur-roundings, except from him. They were acutely aware of each other.

"We aren't exactly burning verbal trails, are we?" he said when silence seemed to gape between them. "I make you uncomfortable. I knew it from the minute you walked into Benno and Anna's dining room."

"You were—are—wrong. I haven't had a lot of experience with so-cial gatherings, that's all. I never know exactly what to say."

He cupped his chin and studied the shadows her eyelashes made on her rounded cheeks, the soft lines of her mouth. What he wanted to believe couldn't be allowed to matter now. His first priority must be to do what must be done with the Kohls' business, anything else was a distant second.

"We can get off at the next stop if you still want to see the flower market."

She sat straighter. "I'd love to. I went there in the daytime, but never at night with all the lights on."

"You're in love with beautiful things, aren't you?" He hadn't known he was going to say that.

A faint blush touched her cheeks and she said, "Yes," quietly. Her intensely blue eyes were on his mouth while her own lips parted slightly. His gut contracted, and he didn't know if he was glad or sad to feel the thump of the barge against the dock.

They climbed ashore on the other side of a bridge from the market. The street was crowded and noisy, the air pungent with a heady concoction of scents: spicy Indonesian food, the canal's mixture of oil and fumes, and, faintly, flowers.

"Stay close," Christophe instructed, wrapping an arm around her once more. She felt so good, so right. Duty could be a difficult son of a bitch. "Tell me more things you like. Paintings, theater, music? Keep talking to me. You make me nervous when you're silent."

She stood still. "You? Nervous? Come on, Christophe."

His jacket had fallen open. It took willpower to do no more than glance at the rise and fall of her breasts beneath her silk dress. In future he'd steer clear of cases involving beautiful women. "Well, maybe not nervous." He almost choked on the words. "But tell me what you like, anyway."

They walked slowly while she considered. "I like music, Dixieland jazz mostly. And I love to dance. Satisfied? I expect you hate both."

Christophe laughed heartily and it felt good. She was undeniably charming when she made one of her definite stands and then waited for an argument.

"What's so funny?" She kept a straight face.

He led her across the bridge to the first of the barges housing the flower market. "You." He matched her serious expression, then started to laugh again. "For a generally reserved lady, you can be pretty feisty. I don't hate jazz—or dancing. And I'd *love* dancing, as you put it, with you." He couldn't believe he'd said it, not Christophe St-Giles, not the man who never spoke without thinking first.

Paula's quick appraisal was wary. His open admission of more than a mild interest in her had broken through her guard.

"Smell the flowers?" he asked lamely.

"I smell garbage in the canal," she replied flatly.

He suppressed a smile. He liked her, truly liked her, and he wished he didn't. "Okay, keep those feet of yours firmly on the ground if you like. *I* smell flowers." Ahead, strings of lights sent shards of glittering color from the Bloemenmarket barges, across oil-coated water. For the rest of this evening he was going to let go and enjoy himself.

A passerby bumped Paula closer to him, and she made no attempt to draw away again. "Don't Amsterdammers ever go to bed?" she said breathlessly.

"Not if they can help it." He squeezed her arm. "That dress of yours deserves a flower—something to show off the color. What do you call that?''

She shrugged, suddenly relaxed and smiling, young. "I'm not sure. Aquamarine, maybe?''

"Trust you to come with a gemstone color. What kind of flower would you like?''

The lightness of the moment was infectious. She smiled, and he knew she'd fallen under the evening's charm. "I—you choose. I wouldn't know what to have. No one ever bought me flowers."

Her guilelessness made his heart tighten. "Right." He wanted to say many men should have bought her flowers, that men were fools, and that, nevertheless, he was glad they were.

He led her between stalls and across gently sloping boards to a tented barge. "Orchids...? I don't think so. Too severe. I've never been big on roses. A gardenia?'' He raised a waxen, ivory bloom to his face, then held it while she bent to smell. "Your perfume. Perfect."

She met his eyes, a little crease between her brows. He'd started out this evening giving her mixed messages. For the past half hour the message had been pretty straightforward—intense interest and close awareness of everything about her. She was trying to decide what to think. But maybe that wasn't all bad. So was he.

The bloom paid for, they returned to the sidewalk and he grasped her shoulders firmly. "Stand still while I pin this on." He lowered his head, blessing fortune for a chance to hide his face, and slid two fingers beneath the neck of her dress. Her skin was warm, smooth. Her breast rose and fell harder than it should. His own body's reaction was unmistakable.

He finished with the pin. "There." Now he had to meet her eyes. "Lovely." And he knew he wasn't talking purely about the flower. This evening hadn't gone the way he intended.

"Thank you."

Christophe barely heard what she said. A row of shops ran parallel to the flower barges, a narrow strip of rough concrete dividing the two. He felt more than saw a movement in a shop doorway.

He pulled Paula against him so hard that she gasped. "Put your arms around me," he ordered. "Pretend. Pretend anything you like but keep your head down and don't move."

"What is it?" she whispered into his shirt. "You're hurting me."

"Do this my way or one of us may end up really hurt. But perhaps that's what you want." Dimly, he cursed himself for the remark, but he had seen a figure, and the glint of something shiny. Whether or not she'd set him up, his first instinct was survival. Paula was rigid against him, trembling violently. "We're going to start walking. Keep your face turned to me. And if you shout you'll wish you hadn't."

She did as he instructed, moving with him, clinging like an absorbed lover. Only he could feel how weak she'd become, the way her body sagged slightly as if she might fall. He gripped her tightly. The shadow in the doorway moved, too, out and along the sidewalk. He was dressed in dark, probably black, clothing, a hat pulled low over his eyes—a tall, slender man who was almost invisible, except for the glint by his right thigh.

"Christophe, please." Paula's voice was muffled. "Let me go. Say something."

Let her go to leave a clear field for her friend with the knife, Christophe thought bitterly. Never. "Keep quiet," he ordered. "You're loving every minute of this, remember?" Why hadn't he seen it coming? He'd walked right into her trap. Why did this have to be the moment the crowds chose to thin? The only living souls he saw were a couple strolling ahead, two stall owners deep in conversation...and the dark shape slipping past shop windows.

If he could just make it back to the corner. Buses rumbled past there, and he could see clusters of people.

The figure darted from cover and Christophe tensed, ready for action. He started pushing Paula out of the way at the same moment as a crowd of teenagers barreled from a tavern onto the sidewalk, cutting the man off from Christophe. He broke into a run, dragging Paula with him until they reached the corner and a bus just pulling out. He leaped, half carrying her, and made it aboard a second before the doors closed.

His breath came in gasps as he stared through the window at a man who pulled his cap farther over his eyes.

"Christophe." Paula held on to his arm and his shirtfront, no trace of color in her face. "Christophe, what's the matter? What happened out there?"

Either she didn't know a thing about what had happened, or she was an incredible performer. "I'm not sure. Probably nothing." He pushed her into a seat and sat beside her. Silence and a chance to think were all he wanted.

"You said something about what *I* wanted. I—"

"Let it go. I think we were being followed, that's all. I overreacted." He watched her face closely. Again she showed only the fear she had a right to show. He sank back and tried to relax. "It was just one of those things, I'm sure. Probably a potential pickpocket sizing up a couple who looked like good targets. Forget it."

But pickpockets didn't wait for crowds to disperse before they struck. Pickpockets loved crowds. And they rarely used knives.

Chapter Seven

Tuesday of the Third Week:

She was fed up. Absolutely, totally sick of the pointless circles her wits had scurried around since Saturday night.

Paula let herself out of the backhouse into the walled courtyard and took several gulps of early morning air. The day promised to be cool, like yesterday. Her tulips were still tightly closed, hiding, the way she was beginning to wish she could hide, at least from her own thoughts and feelings.

Damn Christophe St-Giles and his on-again, off-again attitude, his constant innuendos. And damn the way she couldn't forget him for more than a few minutes at a time.

She pressed her fingers to her face. More than two days had passed since she'd laid eyes on the man, and she still felt the cool firm lips he'd used—yes, used was the right word—on each of her cheeks a few seconds before he left her, utterly confused, at the Kohls' front door. *"Good night, Paula,"* he'd said, bowing faintly as he took back his jacket. *"Thank you for an interesting evening."* There had been no emphasis on the word "interesting," but Paula didn't miss his choice of an adjective, or the formality in his manner. What the hell did he mean by "interesting," anyway? And what had all his running and pushing and oblique accusations meant? On the way home she'd repeatedly begged him to tell her what had spooked him. He'd said, *"Forget it,"* so many times that she'd felt like wringing his self-possessed neck. Boy, she was sick of everything.

She let herself into the main house. Sunday had been a misery of waiting and worrying, trying to sort out the events of the previous evening, hoping in vain that Christophe would call or show up. Yesterday was worse. First she'd suffered Lukas's interrogation about Saturday, then Victor's explosion when she'd made a tiny mistake, and, finally, an emotion-charged episode with Kersten Gouda whom Paula had found crying in the staff room. The only bright spot had been her lunchtime expedition to buy the bicycle she'd coveted for days.

The bicycle, sleek and black, waited for Paula now in the basement stairwell of the Kohls' house. The need to gain confidence on her new steed was Paula's main reason for setting out for work at seven, an hour before she normally left. The streets shouldn't be too crowded yet. She also intended to arrive early to try talking with Kersten alone once more. The woman was troubled, but Paula hadn't been able to find out why, and she wanted to help.

Struggling, grunting, she hauled the machine to the kitchen level of the house. The Dutch penchant for saving ground footage by building upward, floor upon floor, might be charming to look at, quaint to the foreign eye; it was a pain when the fear of theft forced one to keep a heavy bicycle in the basement.

Halfway up the flight to the hall, Paula stalled, leaning against the wall. Good Lord, she thought, she was scared to death of riding this thing. "Onward," she ordered herself firmly. "If Amsterdammers can risk their limbs every day and manage to live, so can you, Renfrew."

She was puffing by the time she reached the entry hall. She needed this bike for more reasons than one. If she didn't get more exercise, her body would fall apart, anyway.

Paula had a hand on the front door when she heard a muffled sound from the living room. A clink, then shuffling...and something else. Soft crying? With one toe, she gently flipped out the bicycle stand, leaned the machine to one side and tiptoed closer to the living room. Madeleine didn't arrive this early. The Kohls rarely came downstairs before eight.

But someone was crying.

The clink came again, the sound of china on china, and Paula smelled fresh coffee. She approached the door and heard another sob. Anna was crying and drinking coffee when she should still be in bed. Paula's palms sweated. She couldn't leave not knowing what was wrong, yet she couldn't barge in on a woman who might resent the intrusion.

"Anna." Benno's voice, firm and consoling, startled Paula, and she took a step backward. For an instant she hesitated, then turned away. The couple's problems were their own affair. They would only be embarrassed if they knew she'd overheard. Not that she understood the stream of Dutch Benno used.

"Speak in English, Benno," Anna said clearly.

The effect of the request was to electrify Paula. She glanced quickly over her shoulder, expecting to find Benno and Anna staring at her. But the living room door still rested slightly open against its catch, a rim of light outlining the edge.

Paula stood motionless, scarcely breathing, waiting for them to call her and wondering what she would say when they did.

Benno spoke in Dutch once more.

"Madeleine may get here early," Anna replied in a shaky voice. "Use English, please, Benno. Just in case she hears us talking. She mustn't know any of this."

"Yes, yes, of course." Benno's reply was fainter. He must have moved to the other side of the room. "I don't know how much longer this will go on, my love, you have to try to be strong...for my sake."

Paula relaxed slightly. They didn't know she was there. But she was afraid to move. She wished she could materialize, bicycle beside her, on the sidewalk. Maybe creating lots of noise as if she'd just entered the hall would be best. She opened her mouth to call good morning, then couldn't bring herself to make a sound.

"Everything will work out, Anna. You'll see." Benno's voice became louder, and his footsteps. He was pacing. "Christophe is a good man. He wants what's best for us."

"Are you so sure?" Anna's sharpness surprised Paula.

"I have to be," Benno said. "If I could only convince him I'm right. Philip Metter is tied up in all of this—I know it. But Christophe keeps hounding me for more and more information about our people. He doesn't say if he's found out anything, or if he suspects someone specific, but I know he thinks the criminal is inside Kohl's."

Anna began to cry again, very softly. "Can't we send Christophe home? Please, Benno, tell him we don't want the loan anymore. Tell him we'll manage without it."

"Even if Christophe were the kind of man who could be sent anywhere, and he's not, I can't tell him I don't want the loan anymore because we can't manage without it." Benno sounded desperate. "And before you suggest it, no other bank will look at us now."

"So what will happen? Oh, Benno, I can't bear what may happen."

"Shh. The thefts have stopped. We've had no complaints in five weeks. Whoever did this thing got what they wanted, whether it was simply the thirteen priceless gems they took or a chance to ruin our reputation. If the plan was to finish us, they won't succeed. Christophe wants full access to the personnel files and all our records. I'm going to give him everything—put our future totally in his hands. Any questions he asks, I'll answer honestly. Lukas must do the same. If we want to survive, we can't go on protecting our people from Christophe's scrutiny. We can trust him to be fair. I believe that. He'll rule out our employees as suspects because they aren't guilty. Then he'll have to look elsewhere. I don't expect him to prove anything except the innocence of Kohl's staff. When he's done that, I believe he'll approve the loan and our enemies will give up.''

Anna sniffed. "How can you be sure there won't be more thefts?"

"From now on, Lukas or I will watch the stones packed and go with Frank to make deliveries personally, as it was done in my father's time."

"Then it will be as I feared," Anna sobbed. "Christophe will read the files. Then he will see you policing Frank. He'll know...think he knows..."

"Anna," Benno said patiently. "There is no alternative. And there is just the possibility that Frank did have something to do with our trouble. Not deliberately, but he's young, he talks. You heard that he's friendly with someone from Metter's. He could have given information without realizing—"

"No!" Anna shouted. "Not Frank. I know Frank had nothing to do with this, but Christophe will think otherwise. He'll read all those... those things from long ago and start to question Frank. And then...and then...Madeleine's Frank will run just like—" The rest of the sentence was lost in strangled noise.

Paula felt frozen; her hands had never been so cold. There had been thefts, and the resulting loss was great enough to threaten Kohl's survival. And Frank was suspected of being involved, and Metter's. Lukas's interest in Frank at the American Hotel made sense now, deadly clear sense. And the way Christophe made sure Benno knew Frank and Willem Bill were friends. She needed air, desperately.

"I won't let anything happen to Frank," Benno was saying. "I trust him, too, remember. I just wanted you to know the way Christophe's mind could work. We have to worry far more about our finishers. Someone made those copies of the stolen gems and they were good copies, Anna, so very good. If I know Christophe, finding that craftsman is on the top of his list. In the same way, keeping our invaluable artists happy is on the top of *my* list. I must try to make sure he doesn't offend their sense of honor."

Copies? Paula struggled to piece together what she was hearing. Copies were made of diamonds that disappeared. For what purpose?

"Benno," Anna began querulously. "Does Christophe think Paula's involved? Is that why he wanted to know so much about her before she arrived on Saturday? He did make sure we realized she was familiar with Metter's page.''

In the silence that followed, Paula reached to brace herself against the banister. *''...or one of us may end up really hurt. But maybe that's what you want.''* Christophe's strange remarks the other night became significant. He *did* think she was guilty of something. And he also thought she was a part of whatever had sent him running through the night.

''Paula is talented,'' Benno said distinctly. ''She also arrived in Amsterdam a few months before the low-grade copies rather than the real thing started showing up with our customers. I know what he thinks. He believes she could have something to do with planning the thefts. We spoke yesterday, and in that way he has of saying without saying, he suggested as much. He even explored whether she could have been the one who'd made the substitute pieces. Ridiculous. I told him she's good, but only nine, almost ten months good, four years away from completing her apprenticeship—''

Paula covered her ears. She must get out of here. Blindly she grabbed the bike and slid open the front door. Once outside, she closed it again, slowly, carefully, and stood on the wide top step trying desperately to collect herself. She would find Christophe St-Giles, confront him with his mad theories, make him agree to grant the loan and go away.

City noises had already begun. Trucks on their way to early deliveries made the street tremble. Through open basement traps, Paula heard the familiar sound of the water that sloshed between the pillared foundations of many canal-side buildings. A street-cleaner whistled while he pushed his broom, and a woman knelt on the steps of the house next to Benno and Anna's, scrubbing vigorously.

Fueled by resolution, Paula set off, wobbling wildly at first. When she'd said she hadn't learned to ride a bike she'd been almost honest. Her father had been too busy to take time to teach her, but her brother had occasionally held the saddle of his big racing model while Paula pedaled furiously, undaunted by numerous falls. Today, fury tinged with undercurrents of indecision took her mind off her inexperience. She pumped her legs as enthusiastically as she had with Grant all those years ago, though with less concentration, and the result was gratifying. She'd be a pro at this in no time.

Soon the exercise and the air rushing past her face felt good, calming. She must proceed cautiously, after all. An impulsive reaction to what she'd accidentally learned could be disastrous. If she wasn't very careful—and wily—Christophe would somehow deflect her before she could do anything to help Benno.

Paula rode on, heading first south along Herengracht, then east toward Dam Square. Christophe had picked her out as a criminal. *Criminal.* Paula stopped at an intersection, momentarily distracted. Lukas had been right in thinking Christophe St-Giles wouldn't bother with her unless there was something he thought she could do for him. But she was sure Lukas hadn't known the direction his old friend's suspicions were taking. Christophe *had* made a point of linking her to Frank Lammaker and Willem Bill in front of Benno. And he was forever asking questions.

Two women passed carrying baskets and talking volubly. Brought back to the moment, Paula checked for oncoming traffic and set off again. As she went, she tried to reconstruct the conversation during the canal cruise. A lot of stuff had been said about her choice of career being strange, or dull, for a woman. How long would she stay? Christophe had asked more than once—as if he thought she might trip and tell a different story eventually. Did he think that if she were a thief she'd be stupid enough to allude to plans for clearing out—presumedly with her loot?

Her front tire hit a groove between cobbles, and Paula turned the handlebars sharply to retain balance. Just for today, she'd make her way along a less-traveled route. She didn't need to worry about any cyclist but herself yet. The series of alleys she began to follow would take her around Dam Square and onto Rokin.

She was calmer now. Offense, as her father had so often said, was not necessarily the best defense. Her most sensible bet was to go about her day's work as planned and let Christophe make the next move.

The roar of an engine startled her. The noise rumbled along the walls each side of Paula. She glanced over her shoulder, then quickly back as one of her wheels slewed sideways. The approaching white car was small enough to pass her with ease.

Paula slowed and pulled close to the wall on the one-way street. The engine sound dropped back to a muted, regular clack. She looked back again and risked letting go of one handlebar to wave the old vehicle past. It continued to putter steadily, keeping the same distance between them. Shadow in the alley obscured the driver.

Uncomfortably aware of her own unsure progress and the measured pace of whoever was behind her, Paula riveted her eyes ahead on a point where the alley curved sharply to the left. Apprehension mounted, gripping her belly, gnawing at the muscles in her thighs. *Relax,* she told herself silently. Her experiences of the past few weeks, added to what she'd heard this morning, were making her jumpy. The car's driver was being careful. When they reached the next main road, he would go on his way.

Paula wasn't prepared for the screech of tires that blasted her ears a second later. Disoriented, she backpedaled, slowing down.

There was only another second, the second when she started to check behind again, then the car was there. A flash of white and a glare on windows, a dim impression of chrome. The rusted door handle was clear.

Paula screamed, turned sharply, scraping her body along sandblasted brick. "Don't!" she yelled. "Don't hit me!"

While she shouted, the car's side mirror slammed into her hip, caught beneath the handlebar and Paula shot forward, sideways, and down.

Then it was over. Stunned, she lay very still, the bicycle a painful heap on her legs. She was too shocked to move. The car stopped, backed up and idled beside her, its engine a steady drone. The sound of glass scraping through rubber told her the driver had rolled down his window, but he didn't speak, made no attempt to come to her aid. Without being sure why, Paula kept her eyes closed, her body inert until she heard tires rolling, picking up speed, squealing, first loudly, then fading, fading, until the alley was silent again.

Paula struggled to a sitting position, pushing the bike away. Her hair fell in a tangled mass over her face. She raked at it with shaking hands and felt blood and grit at her temple. The shaking became violent. Blood seeped through the knees of her jeans and oozed from grazes on her palms. Her throat burned and she retched, feeling as if her insides were tearing. She didn't vomit.

Breathing through her mouth, Paula waited for the nausea to pass and willed her mind to clear. No one came. No one had seen what happened. If she'd been killed, she might have lain on her concrete deathbed for hours. She'd chosen a passage between the windowless sides of houses and offices. A murderer's dream...no witnesses. Her attempt to stand failed, and she slid to the ground once more. That car had followed her this morning, she was sure of it, and the driver had blessed his luck when she took an unexpected turn. He, if it had been a he, had made his hit and gone on his way. She was supposed to be dead.

Within minutes Paula managed to get up. Shock had affected her more than injury. Gradually her heart slowed and she tested her legs, rotated her wrists. Bruises were going to be her distinguishing feature for a while, and, after a day or two, scabs, but no joints were swelling, everything moved that should move. *Thank God.* She automatically glanced skyward. Bruises and scabs she could take. She was alive, apparently with no broken bones, and that was a miracle.

Pushing her mangled bike with its bent wheels, Paula made slow, painful progress into Dam Square. Usually she sent admiring glances in the direction of the Royal Palace with its great green dome. Today she knew it was there, took some solace from being in the open among a smattering of people, and limped on, affecting nonchalance whenever a curious glance came her way.

Outside Kohl's she almost lost her nerve. She had no intention of discussing what had happened to her. Talk must be kept to a minimum. A dagger of fear pierced her. From now on she had to be vigilant, to watch and wait. Friends were no longer clearly discernible from enemies—enemies she hadn't known existed until today.

She shoved the bike among the collection piled inside the work entrance doors. Several employees rode in each day. The next trick was to get to the staff room, tidy herself and cover her tattered jeans with her long coverall.

Paula almost made it out of the changing rooms without encountering anyone. Kersten Gouda stopped her at the door and motioned her back inside. Paula groaned inwardly. She had troubles of her own and she hurt all over.

"Paula," Kersten said urgently. "Yesterday. You were kind and I was a fool crying like that. I don't want you to misunderstand. There is nothing wrong. Nothing."

Self-consciously Paula made sure her hair covered the wound at her temple. "It's all right," she assured Kersten, registering at the same time that self-contained women rarely cried for no reason. "I would never say anything, if that's what you're worried about."

Kersten smiled faintly. "I believe you. It was a weak moment, Paula. Do you understand that? There are those times when we cannot hide our feelings as we should."

A dim thought that this was one more puzzle, and she didn't want to deal with it now, added impatience to Paula's discomfort. "I hope you feel better now," she said, certain this was not the case.

"I..." Kersten's beautifully manicured nails twisted buttons on her suit jacket. "A long time ago I lost someone I cared about deeply. I never believed what the police said. They thought he wanted to go away, or that he'd been killed. But there was no trace of where he went and no body was ever found.''

Paula no longer felt like escaping. She stared, fascinated, at Kersten. ''Who was this?''

''I must not say.'' Kersten sat on a bench with a thump, presenting the top of her shining blond hair. ''I must just wait and hope. Things have happened... I've said too much, but I wanted you to understand that I don't normally bring personal troubles to work. Yesterday was hard because it was the anniversary of our... It was a day that reminded me so strongly of what happened.''

Impulsively Paula sat, trying not to wince at the pain in her knees, and put an arm around the woman's shoulders. ''Don't tell me more than you want to. I understand you're unhappy. I won't mention this conversation, but if you ever want to talk to me, I'm a good listener.''

''Thank you,'' Kersten said simply. ''I knew you were kind.''

Kersten got up and smoothed her skirt. She smiled before she left, and the sadness in her eyes tugged at Paula's heart.

After checking her appearance once more, Paula took the elevator to the workshop floor. Climbing stairs would be low on her list of favored occupations for a while.

She was late, but it didn't seem to matter. The steady hum of machinery comforted her and she stepped into the room, hoping to slide into her place without having to talk to anyone.

Christophe St-Giles lounged on her stool, a cigarette burning unattended between his fingers while he talked to Jacob and another polisher. Victor bent over his scaife, fierce concentration furrowing his brow.

Paula took in the scene and quashed an instant desire to flee. The desire drained away rapidly, to be replaced by slowly rising fury. This man, occupying her place as if he owned it, suspected her of dishonesty. He was steadily disrupting the lives of people she had come to love. And while he played Remington Steele to the diamond industry, she confronted the possibility that someone was trying to kill her and she didn't even know why, or whom to turn to for help.

''So the stones aren't marked to indicate who the craftsman was?'' Christophe was asking. He showed no sign of having noticed her. ''Doesn't that bother you? An artist signs his paintings, a writer has his name on his work.''

Jacob, clearly expansive and enjoying the attention, gestured magnanimously. ''In the trade we can recognize each other's work. Isn't that so, Victor?''

Victor grunted, but didn't look up.

"And a log is kept," Jacob carried on, undaunted. "Descriptions are carefully noted, together with the polisher's name. It is enough."

Paula walked behind the bench and stood between Christophe and Victor. Jacob nodded at her over Christophe's shoulder. Victor stopped working long enough to glare up at her. His glance held a venom that turned Paula's stomach. "You are late," he said, his eyes shifting to Christophe's back. Immediately Paula gained the impression that it was the Swiss, not her who had provoked the old man's ire.

"I'm sorry, Victor," she said, but looked at Christophe. He didn't turn around. "I had a little trouble on the way." Still Christophe kept his back turned. For a crazy instant she was tempted to thump him.

"Your troubles are no concern of mine," Victor said harshly, swiveling from his stool. "You are to be here on time, like everyone else. There cannot be favoritism because of…connections. The others will not like it." He stalked from the room, leaving Paula with her mouth open.

Another wave of nausea overcame her and she hurriedly sat on Victor's vacated seat. Unconsciously her hand went to her temple where an ache had started.

"Good morning, Paula." Christophe's voice was soft.

She raised her eyes to his face. He stood close beside her. Coming in after the accident had been a mistake. She should have returned to Herengracht.

While she watched, his pupils dilated. "What has happened to you?" he whispered urgently, bending closer, moving aside her hair. "What the hell has happened?"

"Shh." She glanced around, desperate not to arouse curiosity. Weakness turned her skin clammy. "A little fall, that's all."

His hand on her elbow almost produced a cry. She moved instantly, propelled on shaky legs toward Benno's office. Once inside, Christophe let her go and she faced him.

"Getting any *interesting* information?" she said through her teeth. This wasn't the way she'd planned their next meeting.

"Very interesting," Christophe said distractedly. He was looking at his fingers. Paula looked, too. Blood. She crossed her arms and felt dampness on her right sleeve.

"All right," Christophe said tightly. "What's going on? You're bleeding from your face and your elbow, at least. What sort of 'little' accident did you have?"

"I fell," she said evasively. Tension mounted steadily inside her. "I fell." This time she repeated the words more loudly. She was frightened—frightened. "A car hit me and I fell, I tell you. It meant to hit me. He wanted me to die. I know he did." Tears began to stream down her cheeks, and she couldn't check them. Christophe's face was a blur. He was pushing her backward into a chair, kneeling at her feet. "Did you know someone would do that to me?" The words wouldn't stop coming. "Did you ask for it to be done? You think I'm something awful. Did you get someone to hurt me?"

"Paula, hush. You're not making any sense."

"You want to prove I'm guilty of stealing. Then you won't give Benno the loan and you'll go back to Switzerland and be a hero with your family and their important bank because you'll have saved them money. You don't care about an old business failing. You'll say Kohl's can't protect their only asset, diamonds, and then make sure they go out of business. You'll make me have to go home—or get the police—or—"

His mouth, gently pressed to hers, brought her eyes wide open, cleared her vision instantly. She tried to pull back. He leaned closer, slid his hands beneath her arms to circle her body.

The kiss went on and on, soothing the pain from her head, numbing her aching bones. Slowly she lifted her fingers to his face, framed his high cheekbones, pushed deeply into his hair and held on tightly.

Christophe broke away momentarily. "Are you quiet, now, Paula?" He kissed her again as she stared back at him, dazed. "I would never hurt you." Soft brushing, skin on skin, smoothness, the touch of tongue to teeth, mingling scents, one clean, hint of leather, male, the other gentle flower. Paula succumbed rapidly to her own arousal. A dozen small kisses outlined her jaw, the tender corners of her mouth, her brow. He held her as he might a troubled, fragile child, stroking, reassuring. He kissed her as only a passionate man kisses a woman he wants.

"Now," he said against her cheek. "Let me hold you. I want to hold you, *chérie*. Perhaps I shouldn't, but I do."

She turned her lips to his ear. "This isn't right, Christophe. I don't understand anything anymore."

"Tell me what happened to you." He kissed her mouth once more. "Forget what we should or shouldn't do. Trust me."

Of course, she thought, she would do as he said—trust. She had to trust someone. The words tumbled out, the overheard conversation at Benno and Anna's, the discovery that he, Christophe, thought she had uone something dishonest, and the ride through the streets. When she told him about the hit-and-run accident a shudder shook him.

"Paula," he said softly. "Think. If I believed you were guilty of something and I was going to need you as a suspect, would I try to have you killed, or even seriously hurt? I would want to keep you in one piece. You agree?"

Yes, she nodded.

He eased off her coverall. Confronted by her torn jeans, he recoiled. "You will go home, Paula. I will take you and then you will rest."

"Anna and Benno mustn't know—or Lukas. They have enough worries. I'm only cut and bruised. I can say I fell from the new bicycle. They knew I was still learning to ride. Please, Christophe, don't tell them what happened."

"I won't." He was looking at her temple. His fingers were so gentle. "I won't as long as you do what I say from now on."

"Anything," she whispered and closed her eyes.

She felt his mouth brush her lids and wanted only to sleep—and know his arms were around her.

"The side mirror hit your hip." A broad hand covered her side. "The bone only, or soft tissue, as well? Do you think you might be hurt inside?" He unsnapped her waistband and she made no attempt to stop him.

"I'm sure it was just the bone."

He eased down the zipper and carefully peeled aside her jeans to expose a purple welt on pale skin above bikini panties. *"Mon Dieu,"* he muttered and let out a low whistle. "Perhaps we should take you to a doctor."

"No!" Paula grabbed his arm. "I'm going to be fine."

"You must be fine." His intensity silenced her clamoring nerves. He ran the tips of his fingers around the edges of the injury, and on, across her stomach. Paula watched, mesmerized, pain forgotten. "You must be fine," he repeated and bent slowly to touch warm lips to her belly.

"Christophe." Paula rallied, remembering their surroundings and the unanswered issues between them. "Thank you for being kind." She coughed on the words and cleared her throat. Hurriedly she fastened her jeans and pulled the coverall back on. "I feel better now. And I'm sorry for all the wild accusations."

His dark eyes never left her face. "But we've reached another level, haven't we, Paula? You now know things you must not reveal. I trust you to be careful. And you *will* trust me, correct?"

"Correct." She was emphatic. At least she hadn't blurted anything out about her agreement with Lukas. Immediately she remembered Lukas had also exhorted her to be careful. Working on appearing calm, she stood, and Christophe immediately stood with her. "I'm going home," she announced matter-of-factly. "A few hours sleep and I'll be fine. The car probably hit me accidentally and then the driver panicked." She paused, laughed. "And then *I* panicked. Stupid of me." What had happened to her resolve of earlier in the morning? Christophe was supposed to have made the next, she'd hoped, revealing move. She'd blown that.

"You're right, I'm sure. Will you have dinner with me on Friday evening?"

"Dinner?" she repeated and knew she sounded surprised. She was surprised.

"A peace offering." That wonderful smile could do magic. "You've had some bad moments because of me."

"Oh...yes, dinner." There would be a chance to talk about all their differences. "Yes. I'd like that. Thank you."

An hour later Christophe had helped her from the gunmetal Saab she hadn't known he owned and ushered her into the Kohls' house. Only Anna was at home. She listened to Christophe's edited explanation of the cycling accident and sympathetically echoed that Paula should go to bed. Within minutes, she'd done just that and lay with shades drawn, ice packs on the strategic sore spots on her body.

She'd agreed to go to dinner with Christophe on Friday. Her frown was directed at fuzzy lines of light on the wall. And he'd asked—no, instructed—her to trust him. *"Think,"* he'd said, *"if I believed you were guilty of something...would I try to have you killed?"* No, he wouldn't. But the truth held small comfort. No questions had been answered, and no statement made that he thought her innocent.

Paula pushed a pillow behind her spine to ease the hip. They had "passed to another level." She felt vaguely sick again. Unfortunately, Christophe's "other level" had nothing to do with the kisses she was never going to forget.

THE WOMAN WOUND AND UNWOUND the paper, pleating it, crushing it between her fingers, then flattening the sheet again.

"My God," the man said tightly. "My God."

"No." She tossed the paper aside. "Please. Sit down." With one hand she smoothed the padded top of a chest in a corner of the elegant living room. "We're getting close. I can feel it now. I wish it was all over, just as you do, but it will be soon."

He remained standing. "You dream. Oh, you dream. It's all starting again. I told you this would never work."

Slender fingers curled into a tight fist. "We have to do what the man says." She slammed the fist into her other palm. "I believe him. He knows every detail exactly as it happened. The last sighting before the disappearance, where the police looked, what the reports said, everything. He couldn't know these things unless he has direct sources."

"We should stop." The man finally sat on the chest. "If we stop now, we may still salvage something."

"Salvage something?" Her voice rose. "What about a man's life? Isn't that worth saving more than a few lumps of crystal?"

A deep sigh hissed past the man's lips. "I cannot argue about that. But how many diamonds will this 'friend' of ours need to complete the *rescue* he talks about? When will he have enough for his *cause*?"

"I don't know." She paced distractedly. "We need more stones, just in case. And a transfer has to be made exactly as he instructs. We've come too far to risk holding out now."

The man sprang to his feet. "More stones. Can't you understand we're being taken for a ride? This... this...whoever he is will take everything we've worked for and keep squeezing us for more."

"We can get more." All inflection had left the woman's voice. "I will continue to make the deliveries."

LATER, THE WOMAN stood on the gently swaying flower barge, surveying rows of plants in wooden trays. Each time she heard footsteps, she looked up expectantly. The man who called them had never said when the exchange might take place. It could be anytime. She could hardly believe after all this time the moment was so near. She could be looking into those dark blue eyes she'd never forgotten, returning the dear smile with its wry turned-down corners. Tears of longing welled in her own eyes, and she looked at the plants once more.

In one corner she spotted it—a dormant miniature rose bush in a clay pot. The packet she carried was small but distinctive, and the bare branches of the bush would provide little cover. She experienced a moment of fear. If someone else found the stone first... *"Do as you're told. Never question me."* The only time she'd argued with her contact, he'd shut her up with chilling authority. Her instructions were to lay the packet flat on the soil at the back of the plant and walk away.

Soon, too soon, she was stepping over frayed boards to the sidewalk and blending quickly with other shoppers. Again she found herself staring into faces. She saw no one she knew.

HE DUCKED to clear the awning in front of the barge and stepped swiftly aboard. Looking neither to left nor right, he made for the corner and slid his left hand behind the rose bush.

"You like the plant, sir. It's a little sad, but with love it'll do well. I'll give you a good price."

Damn. Constant irritations. His plans weren't going smoothly anymore. Slowly he withdrew his hand, the packet in his palm. "Perhaps it would take too much love." He smiled benignly. "More than I have to give. I'll look around and think about it." Something sharp had snagged beneath his ring; a thorn? He stiffened his features against a wince and whistled as he edged away.

Once on the sidewalk he made himself pause to light a cigarette. He thought he felt the stall owner watching him. Or was he simply getting jumpy? He'd started sauntering away before he felt stickiness in the palm still shielding the small packet. Nonchalantly he put his lighter back in his pocket, the diamond packet with it, and examined his hand.

Damn. Blood trickled from a puncture wound beneath his ring. The rose thorn was still embedded. He'd never liked roses.

Chapter Eight

Thursday of the Third Week:

"Finally," Christophe muttered, pulling farther into the shadows. Blessing good fortune and his own patience, he waited several more seconds in a doorway opposite the bar Frank Lammaker had just left. Finally the man was going through the steps Christophe had waited a week to see repeated.

Every afternoon for the past seven days, he'd positioned himself where he could watch Frank leave Kohl's. Every afternoon, Frank had emerged, no briefcase or bag in sight, and immediately boarded a bus. Until today.

Christophe gave Frank a short head start before falling in behind him. The weather was beginning to feel like spring and the messenger had changed into lighter clothes this time: sleeveless V-necked sweater over a long-sleeved shirt and gray pants. One more well-dressed young man blending into the late afternoon crush of homeward-bound workers.

At the next corner, Christophe hung back, watching Frank set off in the same direction he'd taken the previous Thursday.

Christophe broke into a run. He'd studied a detailed map of the city, planning his own strategy for this moment. Instead of getting into Vondel Park by the north entrance Frank had used before, he planned to enter the most easterly gate, skirt along a southern path and arrive on the far side before Frank. The only hitch would be if Frank and Willem had decided on a different meeting point.

By the time Christophe sprinted into the park he was breathing heavily. He'd seen how fast Frank was capable of moving. Every second counted. *God,* he prayed silently, *don't let them make any fresh moves.*

As on all the other afternoons since the first chase, Christophe's new Saab was parked in a side street angling off the cul-de-sac where Willem Bill had made his U-turn. Christophe hesitated at an exit a few hundred yards from the one Frank had taken. Once he left the cover of trees and shrubs, he'd be clearly visible to anyone waiting in the remote street.

He heard the high, tuneless whistle an instant before the sound of rapidly thudding footsteps. Frank and Willem were pulling a repeat performance to the letter. Cautiously Christophe peered through the gate. The car was there, its engine idling. He counted to ten and made a run for the Saab. As he went, he caught the glint of low sun on Frank's fair hair. The man was already bending to climb into Willem's car.

Christophe was inside his own vehicle, gunning the powerful engine to life, when Willem and Frank cruised past the side street. They returned, and Christophe counted to ten once more before slipping into gear and following.

They sped south, then west, gradually leaving behind the areas Christophe knew. Willem didn't hesitate once. He knew his course well.

A sudden left turn almost undid Christophe. He overshot, unable to stop in time, and missed the street the white car took. Cursing aloud, he turned in the middle of traffic, drawing loud horn comments from irate motorists.

Damn. All this and he was probably going to lose them.

He negotiated the corner, unconsciously leaning into the curve, and swore again. Willem Bill's car was parked half a block ahead, and the two men were on the sidewalk pulling possessions from the back seat.

Christophe drove past, staring ahead. From the corner of his eye, he saw Willem lead the way up a flight of steps.

When he'd allowed an interval to pass, Christophe drove back and slowed opposite a white stone house sandwiched between almost identical pink facades in a terrace of clearly expensive homes.

He locked his elbows, gripping the steering wheel tight and let out the breath he'd been holding. Seventy-nine. No need to write down the number of the house, or the street name: 79 Overstraat. He'd remember.

Smiling faintly, he depressed the accelerator, changed gears and pointed the Saab toward the city center.

Friday of the Third Week:

"We want to know all about it, don't we, Sandi?" Peter Van Wersch held out a chair for Paula. "Are you sure you're comfortable, Paula?" He fussed while a waiter seated Sandi.

Sandi leaned forward and touched Paula's hand. "Are you all right, Paula? I couldn't believe it when Anna said you'd gone back to work today. You mustn't overdo. That's why Peter and I hatched a plot to spring you for lunch.''

"And it was a lovely plot," Paula said, appreciatively checking the plant-strewn decor of a sumptuous restaurant overlooking Amsterdam's Central Station. "Almost worth getting knocked off a bicycle..." She bowed her head and reached for her napkin, furious with herself for making a stupid slip.

"I thought Anna said you fell," Sandi commented quietly.

"That's right," Paula agreed quickly—too quickly. She breathed deeply and met Sandi's gaze squarely. "I fell."

An awkward silence followed, broken by the waiter taking their order and returning with cocktails. Peter and Sandi were watching Paula intently. This was why she'd made such a lousy poker player. Every emotion showed on her face.

"Something's wrong," Peter said at last, his blue eyes unwavering. "You're not telling us everything about this *accident* of yours."

Paula thought fast. "My beautiful bike is ruined," she said, a laugh catching in her throat. "All that money down the drain. It would cost as much to fix it as to buy a new one."

Sandi made a clucking sound. "You're safe, Paula. That's what matters. If you try again, get more practice first."

"You must have had some fall," Peter said as if no one else had spoken.

Paula stared at him, a sinking sensation in the pit of her stomach. "It wasn't pleasant."

"But you totaled your bike? Paula, a simple fall shouldn't do that much damage to the machine, unless you went off a bridge or something."

He wasn't going to be deflected. Paula laced her fingers tightly together. Confiding in someone would feel so good. These were her friends. Why shouldn't she tell them what was happening? Even if they couldn't help, they'd support her and she wouldn't feel so alone. For all Christophe's show of concern—and passion—other than calling once to ask how she was, he'd ignored her since Tuesday.

"A car hit me."

She'd spoken so softly that she wondered if they'd heard. Immediately she hoped they hadn't. Christophe had warned her to keep her own counsel.

"Why didn't you say that before?" Peter frowned at her. "How did it happen?"

"I don't know." She felt sick yet again. If the questioning went on, she'd be forced to relive the horror she'd been through.

Sandi had covered her mouth. Her eyes were huge.

"A car just hit you?" Peter shook his head. "It ruined your bicycle and caused you to cut your arms and legs and your head? Just like that? And you don't know how it happened? Come on, Paula. We warned you not to try riding in Amsterdam when you have no experience. For God's sake, don't try it again, practice or no practice. Your nerves are bound to be shot now."

What did it matter if Christophe had warned her to say nothing—to "be careful." He didn't own her. If she didn't get help from someone she trusted, she'd never get to the bottom of what was happening here.

Peter sat beside her, his elegant body inclined in her direction. Paula slid shaky fingers into his, and he immediately covered them with his other hand. "Peter," she said. "It happened in an alley on the other side of Dam Square. I'm probably paranoid, but I almost thought he meant to do it. There was plenty of room for him to pass, but he hung back, then speeded up and hit me. I was lucky—he only winged my hip and caught the handlebar. My wheels went sideways when I started to fall and his rear tire must have gone over them."

"Paula," Sandi whispered. "What are you saying? You believe someone *tried* to hurt you...?" The green eyes filled with tears, and Sandi started to cry. She fumbled with the neck of her blouse.

Peter rubbed Sandi's back. The concerned expression on his slender face was new to Paula, who always thought of him as an irrepressible clown. She'd been right to speak up. She was certain of it now.

"Is there anything else, Paula?" Peter asked, his hand still on Sandi's shoulder. He massaged the base of her neck. "Why would anyone want to hurt you? It doesn't make sense."

"Sandi," said Paula gently. "You and Peter are my friends. There are some other things I'd like to tell you. Maybe we could help each other sort them out. But you can't tell Lukas, you know—that I've mentioned them, rather. You don't need me to explain how upset he is. If he finds out what happened to me...after...well, after some other things...he's likely to go on overload."

She had their full attention. Sandi sat very straight, mascara smudged beneath her eyes. Peter took a slow swallow from his drink and lit a cigarette, never looking away from Paula. His blond hair had slipped over his brow, but he didn't seem to notice.

"What other things, Paula?" He squinted through smoke.

Her nerve faded. Impulsiveness was a luxury she couldn't afford. "Maybe they'd be better not mentioned," she said and sipped from her own glass. "Forget it." Now she sounded like Christophe.

"No," Sandi interjected sharply. "Tell us, now. I want to know. Lukas would want to know. We aren't children who can be shielded." She glanced at Peter, her pale skin flushing. "Peter, please, whatever you learn here must go no further."

He pushed the small finger of the hand holding his cigarette back and forth across his brow. "You've got my full attention, friend—and my loyalty—as always."

"Go on, Paula," Sandi said. Their meals arrived but they ignored them.

Paula launched into a full description of her accident and worked backward, explaining some of the conversation she'd overheard at the Kohls'. At that point, Sandi became deathly pale again and Paula noticed she plucked nervously at a button on her jacket. Perhaps Lukas didn't tell his wife everything. Paula almost wished she'd never begun her story, but there could be no stopping now.

"You mean Kohl's is in trouble?" Peter commented thoughtfully. He raised his brows in Sandi's direction. "There've been thefts? Why didn't you and Lukas tell me?" Paula didn't miss the hurt in his eyes, and instantly her heart went out to him. She'd never considered he might know nothing of his friends' business trials.

Sandi stroked his forearm. "We couldn't talk about it, Peter. We shouldn't be talking about it now. This thing with Paula brings us into a new dimension, but nothing else can be allowed to change. There must be no talk, no gossip. You understand how important reputation is in the diamond market."

"You thought *I* might share your problems with others?" Peter's tone was aggrieved. "You really believed I would take pleasure in my two best friends' pain and use it as a casual conversation-maker?"

Paula hated the turn this conversation was taking. "I'm sure Lukas and Sandi didn't think that," she put in hastily. "Benno and Lukas hoped to get their loan and put everything right without anyone finding out about the thefts."

"And how do you know that?" Peter watched her intently. "Did you learn that outside Benno and Anna's door, too?"

She blushed. "No. It was mentioned, but I already knew. Lukas told me about the loan. And I didn't plan to listen, Peter."

A small sound escaped Sandi's throat. Peter touched her hand, then turned her face toward him. "Are you all right?"

Sandi wordlessly nodded her head.

Paula rushed on, filling any possibility of an awkward silence. She explained Lukas's concern over Christophe's sudden interest in her. The words tumbled over one another. Soon she'd retold Lukas's theory that Christophe intended to deny the loan Kohl's needed and that he was determined to find concrete reasons to do so. Christophe's deliberate tying of Frank Lammaker to Metter's and then the dinner at the Kohls' when Christophe raised her own connection to Frank and to Willem Bill were soon added to the information she unloaded, with an increasing sense of relief.

"Is there more?" Sandi had pushed her full plate aside.

"Only that Christophe took me on a barge trip and then behaved very strangely. He ran and hauled me aboard a bus as if someone were following. Then he wouldn't tell me why."

"I wonder what the point of that was." Peter speared a forkful of omelet and ate slowly. He swallowed. "Sounds wild. Anything else?"

"No. I don't think so." Had she done the right thing in telling all this?

"This is a nightmare," Sandi muttered. "I never thought we'd go through something so awful."

"I shall speak to Christophe," Peter announced, smacking down his fork with enough noise to attract attention from nearby diners. "I shall talk to him and find out what's happening."

Paula and Sandi clutched his arms simultaneously. "You won't." Sandi's order shocked Paula. "You will say nothing, you understand? Nothing, Peter."

"But, I—"

"Nothing," Sandi spat out. "This is why Lukas and I have been alone in this—with Benno and Anna, of course. We cannot afford to risk any upheaval now. Support us, Peter. Love us and understand our difficulty. Please, do not interfere."

He bowed his head and said, "I cannot understand Christophe. This is the man Lukas and I shared everything with. We shared our best and worst times. Are you sure I can't talk to him? You know he's on my houseboat and I see him some evenings. I could stop by and just chat—steer the conversation and see what happens."

"If you do—" Sandi's voice was urgent "—you could bring about our end. Lukas doesn't understand him anymore, either. That's why he's so hostile. But Christophe holds all the cards. We must play his game his way.''

Paula watched Peter, her stomach tight with apprehension.

He stubbed out the cigarette he'd left burning in the ashtray and patted Sandi's hand. ''I understand, darling. Of course I do. Whatever you say is the way it'll be. As long as you promise to tell me if I can help.''

Sandi relaxed visibly. ''I will, Peter. You're a dear. I've wanted to tell you, but Lukas and Benno are so determined to keep our trouble within the family and I have to respect their decision. Paula—'' she dropped her voice even lower ''—do you really think that car driver intended to hurt you, because if you do—''

Paula broke in quickly, ''No, no I don't. I think too much has been going on, and after overhearing Anna and Benno I was upset and my imagination ran away with me. Why would anyone want to hurt me?''

''You're right.'' Sandi found a kleenex and blew her nose. ''I feel better. Thanks for agreeing to do things my way, Peter.''

He shoved back his hair. ''Not a word from me, I promise.''

''I won't say anything, either,'' Paula said fervently. ''I'm just glad we all know what's going on.'' And she was. A few more days of solitary struggling with her thoughts and fears and she might have gone mad.

''Listen, both of you.'' Sandi made fists on the table. ''Benno and Lukas have decided on how they want to handle things. I think it's best they don't know we've had this talk. At least for now. We will be here and ready if and when they need us—agreed?''

''Agreed,'' Paula said.

''Agreed,'' Peter echoed.

''FRANK WILL COME to pick me up.'' Madeleine Lammaker spoke happily while she flicked a duster over polished surfaces in the Kohls' living room. ''I have a—a—date,'' she laughed, ''as you, Paula. Frank is taking me to the fancy restaurant in Rembrandts Square. He is a good boy.'' Her English was sketchy, spoken slowly and with a heavy accent.

Paula sat on a carved oak chair, watching the plump woman's happy, expressive face. ''I like Frank,'' she said simply. ''You're lucky to have him.'' *And if you knew what he's suspected of now, you'd be destroyed,* she thought miserably.

Pale eyes met hers and shone. A heavy network of wrinkles on Madeleine's face belied her serene air. Her life could not have been an easy one. Uncomfortable with the knowledge she couldn't share, Paula got up and went to peer through the windows. The less she concentrated on Frank, on anything to do with the cloud of distrust steadily gathering on the horizon of her world, the better. She felt sad about what might be lurking in Madeleine's future.

The canal was crisscrossed with ripples running against one another. Like deep green crumpled satin, it reflected the last remnants of day in the darkening sky. The Kohls had gone out for the evening and Paula had opted to wait for Christophe in the main house, rather than have him come to the backhouse. She knew her reason. The thought of his being there, among the few possessions she valued, seemed too personal, made her feel vulnerable. She shrugged. Maybe he wouldn't even show up. He hadn't made any attempt to confirm their date.

"When do you leave?" Madeleine asked behind her.

"Eight, I think," Paula said absently. The afternoon had dragged by, her thoughts turning into a festering mass of indecision as her appointment with Christophe got closer. This invitation was one more part of his strategy. The indelible memory of his blistering kisses aside, Paula had no illusions about the depth of his interest in her. It went no further than the limit of his calculated use of her. As Lukas had so kindly pointed out, Christophe St-Giles was a man unlikely to be short of feminine company.

Madeleine had spoken again.

"I'm sorry, Madeleine," Paula apologized. "I didn't hear that. And why are you still here, anyway?" She checked her watch. "It's almost eight."

"It is easier for Frank to pick me up here than go all the way home. He was busy after work, but he should be here soon. I might as well work until he arrives."

Paula opened her mouth to comment when Christophe's Saab slid into angle parking beside the canal. He got out, tossed down a cigarette and ground it underfoot. Paula stepped back but not before he'd glanced at the window. She smiled and waved.

"Bye, Madeleine," she called, rushing from the room. "Enjoy your evening."

"Bye," she heard Madeleine echo.

Paula was already yanking open the front door. She barreled into Christophe and he laughed, catching her against him to keep their balance. "What's the hurry? Missed me, huh?"

The rush of hot blood to her face only added to her chagrin. "I've got a thing about not keeping people waiting," she responded lamely.

She could hardly admit her stomach was one big knot at the thought of spending an evening with him. Or that she wasn't sure what percentage of the knot was made up of anticipation, what of apprehension. She also couldn't tell him that if she'd allowed one more second for reflection before running from the house, she might have chickened out of going with him at all.

Christophe had chosen an Indonesian restaurant in the trendy Jordaan district. Jaya's owner hovered over his staff and clients with the concentration of a man whose mission in life would fail if a single unsatisfied stomach left his simply decorated premises.

For two hours Paula bravely sampled dish after dish, all delicious, all filling. Christophe's absorption in the food, and his capacity, made her determined to keep eating enthusiastically.

"You're slowing down. Had it?"

Paula heard amusement in Christophe's voice and realized she'd been staring for a long time at the skewer of spicy chicken she held. "Whew!" she sighed. "I guess so. But it was a beautiful dinner. Thank you."

"I like it here," Christophe replied, taking the skewer from her fingers and deftly chewing off a grilled pepper. "The place is unpretentious, but the food's great."

He finished eating and paid the bill.

Outside, he placed a hand loosely at Paula's nape and asked, "How about some dancing?"

Paula hesitated, deciding what to say. Throughout their meal, the conversation had been innocuous—Christophe had seen to that. Nothing heavier than the spring's influx of tourists had been discussed. There was no guarantee that he would be more forthcoming while dancing, but he might.

"Big decision, Paula?" He opened the car door and lifted her skirt clear of the door. "I thought you told me you liked dancing—to Dixieland." He shut her in and walked around the hood, bouncing keys in one palm.

He was right, she had said she liked to dance. And she did. And she'd like to dance with him. "Let's go dancing," she said as he climbed in. "You may have to make allowances for my battered knees."

"How are the bruises coming?" He maneuvered from a parking area in the center of the street and started back the way they'd come.

"Fine," Paula replied. "Just call me scabby. My elbows haven't looked this way since I was the neighborhood's ten-year-old tomboy."

He glanced sideways at her. "I can't imagine you as a tomboy, Paula."

The way he had of looking at her, his simple comments, wielded a power he couldn't possibly guess. She clasped her hands together in her lap.

"You were frightened that day." He stopped for a light, then leaned forward to check in each direction before turning left. "I meant to ask you. You didn't happen to notice the license, did you?"

"License?"

"The plate on the car."

She grimaced. "No, dammit. I was so rattled that all I remembered afterward was a rusty door handle and scratched white paint. And it was a small car. I don't know much about European cars, so I can't even tell you what make it was."

He didn't answer immediately. "A white car?" he said at last. "Small?"

"Yes." Paula shifted, tired of the subject. She wanted to forget the incident. "And I'm sure the driver was as scared as I was. He probably thought he *had* killed me and made a run for it out of instinct."

"Brave of him," Christophe muttered.

And something you would never have done, Paula thought instantly. "We can only operate within the range of our physical and emotional capabilities."

"You're philosophical tonight."

He became silent again, and Paula was grateful he'd dropped the subject.

"Where are we going?" she asked abruptly, recognizing the Singel Canal. "I didn't know there were any good jazz places along here—not where you can dance, anyway."

"Ah." In the light from the dash, she saw the shadow deepen beneath his cheekbone. He was smiling. "The very best place to dance to jazz is right here." They drew up between two trees planted in tiny squares of earth beside the canal.

Paula sat still until Christophe opened her door. He took her hand and helped her out. "Watch your step," he said. "The gangplank's a bit mossy. Don't slip."

"Christophe, stop." She planted her feet. "I thought you said we were going dancing. This is Peter's houseboat, isn't it?" Even in the darkness, fresh paint gleamed on the deckhousing of the converted barge.

"Yes. It's also my home—for now. And I have an excellent selection of jazz records and more than enough space for one couple to dance."

Every instinct in Paula's body went on alert.

"Do I frighten you, Paula?" Christophe asked softly. "Are you afraid to be alone with me?"

Egotistical bastard. "Hardly. Surprised, that's all. Lead on."

His muffled chuckle filtered to her as he led the way across the shifting plank. Paula narrowed her eyes at his broad back. M. St-Giles was a fascinating, powerful man. He was accustomed to getting his own way. If he thought his charm, physical as well as verbal, would lull her into pouring out facts he wanted to know, he was about to be disappointed. She didn't know anything that might be of use to him; he, on the other hand, could help her considerably—by agreeing to get out of her friends' lives. And she wouldn't be resorting to seduction to reach her goal.

Half an hour later, nestled against plump cushions on a low corduroy couch, a glass of brandy in her hand, Paula felt less secure. Christophe was sorting through piles of records reading titles aloud to himself in French, discarding some, removing others from their jackets. "I must confess," he said without turning, "these are Peter's. I borrowed them."

Paula tensed. "For this evening?"

"We-e-ll—yes. Honesty's the best course, right?" Smiling brown eyes quickly met hers.

"You assumed I'd agree to come here with you?"

He put on a record and watched until the needle met the first groove. "Let's say I didn't intend to give you a chance to refuse." His grin was just short of wolfish. "Do you mind?"

She should mind, but she didn't. Paula wasn't about to tell him so.

Christophe took her glass and set it aside. "Shall we try some of that dancing?"

He pulled her into his arms and moved effortlessly to the slow beat of an old blues piece Paula didn't recognize. It was beautiful, the horn work heart-wrenching in its clarity. Christophe was beautiful, tall, straight, his muscles flexing beneath her hands, against her breasts, her thighs. A heavy ache started deep inside her. The rhythm was insistent. Christophe moved with it, became a fluid part of the music, wrapped her tighter, his chin on top of her head.

"Peter knows I was taking you out this evening."

His breath moved her hair. "Yes." She looked up and immediately wished she hadn't. Christophe's face was inches above hers.

"Does he mind, do you think?" Firm lips spoke against her temple before moving down to the side of her neck.

Half Paula's attention responded to Christophe's roving mouth, half to his question. Would Peter wonder at her motive for seeing Christophe? Sandi had begged both Paula and Peter not to intervene with Christophe. The warm breath was at her throat now; strong hands but gentle came to rest under her arms, thumbs slowly stroking the sides of her breasts. She had to keep a clear head, to remember she was with a sophisticated man, a practiced lover doing what came so very naturally.

"Paula." He brought his face close to hers. "Are you and Peter... Have you and Peter been more than just friends?"

"No." Her own husky whisper brought a deeper flush to her cheeks. Sometimes the body didn't heed the brain. "Peter is a good, good friend—nothing more." Why couldn't she just want to have *this* man as a good, good friend? Why did she want much more with Christophe?

He stared down into her eyes. "I'm glad. I like Peter, too, but some things come ahead of that kind of friendship." His hips and thighs guided their dance, an old dance, the oldest—the movement of their bodies, molded as one, surrounded them in a sexual force field. Paula's breathing speeded. Christophe's hands moved from her sides, to her bottom, pressed her urgently against his thrusting arousal.

"I want to make love to you," he murmured the instant before their mouths met. He held her against him with one hand, with the other he unbuttoned the front of her dress and pushed it aside. His tongue slipped past her teeth, reached and Paula reached back. Her womb pulsed, the muscles in her thighs, her buttocks. Unable not to, she slid a hand from his chest, down, over his belt to touch the hardened part of him. His groan made her smile against his mouth and their kisses became more frenzied.

"Paula, Paula." He nuzzled her head back. "Come to bed." He'd pushed her dress from her shoulders, slid down her bra straps. "Sleep with me tonight." He smoothed lace from her breasts and bent to kiss her throbbing flesh.

Paula moaned softly, far back in her throat. He pushed her gently onto the couch and half covered her with his big body. "Say something, Paula." One large hand slid beneath her dress and up her thigh. "I want you."

"I want you too, but—" Her words were cut off by his next kiss, deeper and deeper, more and more demanding.

When they came up for air he said, "But what?" and his hand moved higher, pressing between her legs.

"No!" Paula wriggled. Christophe mumbled incoherently into the cushion beside her neck and gripped her hip.

Paula cried out, jackknifing to sit, shoving him away. His fingers, digging into the bruise, had brought a sharp pain…and the harsh return of reason.

Christophe sat upright on the couch, staring. "What? What is it, for God's sake?"

She started hauling her bra back into place and buttoning her dress. "We don't even trust each other," she said dazedly. "I won't be used, or use you that way. Maybe in time being together will be right, but not now." This was awful. She'd allowed the unthinkable to happen, let him get close enough to her to switch off coherent thought and action.

"God." He leaned against the couch, eyes closed, his chest rising and falling rapidly. "You've got fantastic timing, lady."

Once her clothes were straightened, she smoothed her hair awkwardly. Her mouth felt swollen. With trembling fingers, she reached for her brandy and swallowed enough to make her cough. "I'm sorry," she said when Christophe had been silent a long time.

He didn't reply.

"I didn't expect that to happen. I…"

"Didn't you?" He looked at her, the softness erased from his eyes. "You aren't a child, Paula. You knew what could happen…but maybe you're right—you didn't have to expect it." He lifted his own glass and reached a cigarette from a box on a glass end table.

For the first time, Paula was aware of the slight motion of the houseboat. This one was sumptuously furnished, its overhead decking raised to a height even a tall man would find comfortable. She hadn't seen the rest of the boat and wondered exactly where the sleeping quarters were. Immediately she decided they were bound to be too close. The sooner she extricated herself from this mess, the better.

Christophe was smoking, watching the tip of his cigarette turn red when he drew on it. He appeared composed again.

"We allowed ourselves to get carried away," she began tentatively. "What happened had nothing to do with people—just mood, a man and a woman—"

"You're right," he cut her off impatiently, leaning to rest his elbows on his knees. "I tried to push you too far, too fast. Forget it."

A small light came on in Paula's brain. "Forget it. *Forget it?* Is that how you cope with any conflict? *Forget it?* I won't, not this, or a lot of other things you could easily explain to me."

He squinted sideways at her. Every feature held a wariness. "Such as?"

"Why did you haul me aboard that bus the night we went on the canal?"

"I told you. I thought I saw someone following us. Forget—"

"It!" she finished for him. She was tired, bone aching tired. "Okay. You aren't about to tell me anything about your investigations here in Amsterdam. Why should you—you don't even tell Benno."

He stood with enough force to splash Paula's drink over her hand. "I told you to back off and leave things alone. I told you to trust me. There's nothing you can do about Benno's problems, so stay out of them."

Paula swallowed painfully, rubbing at drops of brandy on her fingers. She thought a moment and said, "I'm not trying to interfere in anything that doesn't concern me. What I say to you I say because I think you're a good man, a caring man. Benno is becoming ill over this difficulty with the firm. He needs the loan your bank can give him to make good the losses he's sustained. Please, Christophe, will you let him have the money and give him credit for being able to make sure there are no more thefts?"

Christophe sat again, bringing his fist down against the table in the same motion. The pistol-shot sound of his ring on the glass echoed in her brain. "It's not enough that Benno and Lukas won't give me full backing," he fumed. "I have to have a foreign do-gooder poking her nose into my business. I'm doing what has to be done. I don't have to explain any of this to you, but I will say one thing—think about it. If I don't get to the bottom of those thefts, two things will happen. One, there will be no loan, and two, the thefts will start again. Do you understand?"

A stinging sensation crawled up her back, and heat into her face. She felt horribly foolish and embarrassed. "You think I'm a meddling airhead."

"I think you don't know what you're getting into. Remember your *accident*, Paula. It was probably just that, but do you know for sure? Could it be that you've trodden on other toes with your probing and someone's trying to frighten you off?"

Other toes. "I take it I've totally alienated you simply by being worried about Benno? I'm not going to say I'm sorry, because I'm not. These people have been good to me and I care about them." She stood. "It's late. I'd better get home."

Christophe rose and stood in front of her. He wound a curl behind her ear. "I came on too strong, as usual. I *am* sorry. Will you forgive me?"

"Yes." But not completely. "I'm sorry, too. I don't often lose my temper, and when I do it's never effective."

"I'll drive you home." He picked up his jacket and found his keys. "But you are going to have to promise me to stay out of what I'm doing here."

"I..." Paula closed her eyes and made herself wait before replying. She would do what she had to do. "Thank you for a lovely evening. I'd rather get a taxi home, if you don't mind."

"I do mind. That's out of the question." He was determined to call all the shots.

"Christophe," she said clearly. "I'm going to take a taxi. They pass along here all the time."

"You'll let me drive you." He took her elbow.

Paula shrugged free. Not shouting or showing her true feelings was taking superhuman effort. "Good night, Christophe. Thank you for everything. Please—don't push this any further."

She left him, closing the door without looking back, and walked ashore. All she needed to rattle her nerves to shreds again was another drive in the close confines of a small car—with Christophe.

Paula set a brisk pace. People still strolled the canalside, and she saw a taxi weaving a path among them. Her waving arm was ignored and she realized the cabbie already had a fare. She walked on, looking back several times to make sure Christophe wasn't following. He was nowhere in sight, and she didn't try to fool herself that there was no disappointment mixed with her emotions.

She headed in the general direction of home, constantly checking for a cab. None had shown by the time she had to turn away from Singel onto a street that would take her to a point on Herengracht, a dozen blocks from the Kohls'.

Once away from busy Singel Canal, Paula found herself alone in the dark streets. Her heels clipped a staccato tattoo on the sidewalk.

Slowly at first, then increasingly rapidly, her heart began to pulse in her throat, sound in her ears. At a scurrying noise she cried out, then shook her head in self-derision when two cats scampered across her path. She was a scared ninny.

Paula began to hum, then stopped, irritated to realize the tune was the one she and Christophe had danced to. She should have let him drive her home. Refusing had been pigheaded. Her high heels were a nuisance, but she broke into a trot.

Halfway along the next block she stopped. The echo she heard seemed a beat slower than it should be for her own feet. Maybe Christophe had followed her, after all. She turned, a smile on her face, and saw no one. She *was* jumpy. Amsterdam was an active city, all right, but everything she read suggested there was nothing to fear if you stayed out of the wrong areas.

Slowly, deliberately keeping her pace steady, she crossed the silent street.

The prickling sensation that began at the base of her spine, crept upward, vertebra by vertebra. Her own footsteps tapped, slender heel tips nick-nicking cobbles. The other feet that had started moving behind her made the unmistakable sound of a man's leather-soled shoes.

Chapter Nine

Paula ran. So did the other. Horrified, she slowed to look back, still sidestepping. The shadow was a distance behind her, but it loomed tall—a man—and he was chasing her.

Panic ripped at her throat. She was a fool, a fool. Her own pride had brought her this terror.

The middle of the street. If she ran down the center of the pavement she'd feel safer. Damn her flimsy shoes. There was no time to take them off. *Yell!* she ordered her pounding brain. *Scream!* She opened her mouth but no sound came out. Rape victims, black shapes facing away from television cameras, said they couldn't scream. *Rape.* Paula choked on jarring sobs. Where was he? Why didn't he just grab her and get it over with? She'd never outrun him.

If a car would come, she'd be picked up in its headlights. No car would come.

She darted to the other sidewalk, her chest one racking pain. Shadows from narrow alleys between buildings sliced across her path. Each black wedge lived, had substance. Again and again she flinched, waiting for impact with each dark barrier, only to run on and face another.

The strap of her purse slipped from her shoulder. Paula grabbed it and caught her heel at the same time. Stumbling, flailing, she lunged into a wall and dropped the purse. She rushed on without it. The footsteps were closer, right behind her. He had to be there now, inches from reaching out to grab her.

Ahead yet another alley shadow loomed. Burning sweat ran into her eyes. She made as if to run on, then veered abruptly into the tiny passage, fled, elbows bent, fists clenched, into its waiting nothingness. If she could make it to another street, maybe a busier street, she might lose him.

She saw the wall seconds before she would have smashed into it.

"Help!" Even she barely heard her cry. She'd run into a blind alley.

The only way out was the way she'd come. The way the man was coming. Chest heaving, she turned. The shadow wasn't running anymore. He walked on feet that seemed quieter, not hurrying, closing in.

There was nowhere to go.

Paula flattened against the wall, pressed her palms into its brick surface and waited. The man's silhouette loomed against the fuzzy shaft of light from the street.

She wouldn't just stand there and do nothing. Awkwardly, keeping her eyes on the advancing form, she dragged off one shoe, then the other. She threw one aside and spread her feet, bracing, holding a shoe aloft, its heel poised for a sweeping jab.

He stopped.

Paula rubbed the sweat from her eyes with the back of a forearm. "Okay," she whispered, "come on." She heard his breathing and the tiny flicker of resolve died.

He dropped abruptly, catching Paula off guard. For seconds she couldn't see him. Then he leaped up before her, grabbing her wrists, wrenching away the shoe. It hardly made a sound as it ricocheted off the wall and disappeared.

She had never known such fear. She opened her mouth but again no sound would come.

"Be still," the man hissed. His head was close and she saw his pale eyes glint through slits in a ski mask.

"No!" she shouted, surprised at the noise. "No!" And she kicked at him with her bare feet.

"You will be still and quiet." The voice, heavy with a Dutch accent, was accompanied by cold sharp pressure on the front of her neck.

A knife. This man was going to kill her. Paula struggled with the fuzz creeping into her brain. She mustn't faint.

More footsteps sounded, more running. Paula moved, trying to see over her captor's shoulder.

"I said, be quiet," he ordered. "Or you're dead. Believe me, lady, you will feel, but where I cut you will make no sound."

Paula closed her eyes.

"Listen carefully," the deep voice ground on insistently. His breath fanned her face. "If you want to live, Paula Renfrew, get out of Amsterdam."

For an instant she didn't notice. Then her eyes were wide open and staring. He'd used her name. This wasn't an accidental encounter arising out of being in the wrong place at the wrong time. He *knew* her.

"Do you understand what I say?" he persisted, pressing the knife harder.

"Who are you?" Paula asked. "Why are you doing this?"

"That isn't important. Let the past die. What happened years ago is finished. We want it to stay finished. It's all over and done with. *Do you understand?*"

She understood she wanted out of this alley. Paula nodded, then stifled a cry when she felt the knife break her skin.

"Good," he said, backing away. "That is very good. Make your excuses for leaving. What you say to your friends means nothing to us. But make it convincing, then start to withdraw. Go home to your safe place in America and forget what took place here."

When he'd put several yards between them, he turned and slipped swiftly from the alley and out of sight.

She was going to faint, Paula thought, groping against the wall, lowering herself to sit in a doubled-over heap. Violent trembling shook every muscle, and her sobs, when they came, hurt her chest. Cautiously she touched her neck and felt a drizzle of blood. Her teeth chattered uncontrollably.

"Is there someone in there?"

A man's voice boomed hollowly to her. She shrank farther back, trying to stem the croaking noises she made.

"Answer me." This time the voice was closer. "Where are you?

"Paula? Oh, my God, Paula."

Strong arms that made no attempt at care, gathered her up and hauled her to the sidewalk. Christophe, minus his jacket, his hair a disheveled mess, stared into her face. "What's happened to you?" He looked down. "Where are your shoes? Speak to me, dammit."

All she could do was cry.

Christophe pulled her farther out until they were beneath a streetlight. He pushed back her tangled hair and lifted her chin, searching her eyes, touching her cheeks. His hand stopped in midmotion. "Your neck," he whispered. "Your neck's cut. How...?"

"Hold me," she moaned at last. "A man followed me. He had a knife."

He gripped her upper arms, shaking her slightly. "Don't fold up on me, Paula. You can't let go yet. Did he...did he..."

She shook her head slowly. "Rape me? No. He just said a lot of things I didn't understand and cut my neck. I want to go home."

Christophe took a handkerchief from his pocket and bent to examine the wound. "It's small," he said. "Antiseptic and a dressing will fix it. Are your shoes in the alley?"

At her murmured "Yes" he retrieved them and helped her put them on. He jogged down the block to find her purse.

"Thank you," she said brokenly when he returned, grateful for the arm he put around her.

"Come back to my place," he said. "It's closer and I can fix that nick for you."

"No," Paula said. "Thank you, but I want to go home."

Christophe didn't argue except against her intention to continue walking. He lifted her easily, carried her back to where the Saab was parked and settled her inside.

The drive to Herengracht and the Kohls took less than ten minutes. Outside the house, Christophe switched off the engine and turned to Paula. "I started to follow you as soon as you left, then lost you. First I thought you'd taken that one taxi—it slowed, but then I realized he must have had a fare. I caught sight of your dress, but you were a long way ahead. I should have made you let me take you home, used force, if necessary."

She edged closer to the door. Bits and pieces of something nebulous began to take shape in her mind. "I must get into the house," she said.

"Okay " Christophe was out of the car and opening her door before she could say anything more. "Benno and Anna will be in bed by now. I'll play Florence Nightingale to that neck and make you a hot drink. Then you can give me a blow-by-blow description of tonight's fiasco." While he spoke he helped her to the sidewalk.

"Thanks, Christophe," Paula said evenly. "For everything. But you've done your bit. Now I just want to stick on that dressing you talked about and collapse for the night."

"But I thought you'd want to talk..."

"I don't" she said more shortly than she intended. She tapped his shoulder lightly to soften her manner. "Not now, anyway. We'll talk when I've stopped quaking like a scared kid. I'll call you, okay?" She started up the steps.

"Wouldn't you like me to stay with you until you're calmer?"

She'd like what was best for her, Paula thought, keeping her face averted. "Don't worry. I'm fine. We'll be in touch."

She did give him a quick glance as she closed the door. His face was upturned but she couldn't see his expression. That might have told her a lot, she decided.

Inside the door she kept the light off and waited until the Saab roared away.

Someone had told that crazy man where to find her this evening. He'd been waiting for her, assured she would eventually come from the houseboat.

Only one person knew she was going out with Christophe tonight: Christophe.

Chapter Ten

Sunday of the Fourth Week:

"Good grief." Peter yawned, peering at Paula with bleary eyes. "What time is it?"

"Almost three in the afternoon," she said dryly. "And it's Sunday, in case you've forgotten that, too. Should I come back when you're more rested?" Two sleepless nights had left her incapable of diplomacy.

Peter straightened with evident effort and opened his door wider. "Come in, smartass. You're certainly in fighting form." His eyes narrowed as she passed him. "You look like hell," he said slowly.

"Thanks." Paula flopped full length on his leather couch, shoving several cushions beneath her head. "You don't look so hot yourself."

"Hard night," he said, smiling as he made his way to the abbreviated kitchen in the corner of his big living room. "I'll make us both coffee. We could obviously use it."

Paula sat up and glanced apprehensively in the direction of Peter's bedroom. He caught her look and shook his head. "I don't have company, love, so relax."

She was too tired to blush. "I've got to talk to you, Peter."

"Talk away, darling. I'm all ears."

"Peter, this isn't a joke."

"Oh, I know—believe me, three o'clock on a Sunday afternoon tells me this is going to be serious stuff."

"Dammit," Paula muttered, exasperated. She got up and went to lean on the counter separating the kitchen from the rest of the room. "See this, Peter?" She tilted up her chin. "There's a cut under this dressing."

He poured boiling water over coffee in its filter before glancing up. "Let me guess," he said. "You got so upset you decided to end it all?"

Paula rounded the counter and stood next to him. "Close, Peter, close. Except someone else decided to end it all for me."

He stared, his lips slowly parting.

She touched the dressing. "A man in a ski mask followed me into an alley on Friday night and held a knife to my throat."

The kettle clattered to the stove. Peter grabbed it before it could tip off a burner and fall to the floor. "Good God, Paula. You aren't serious."

"Oh, Peter, Peter." She rubbed her eyes wearily. "I haven't slept in two nights. Coming here this afternoon is the first trip I've made out of the house since Friday and all the way I was looking over my shoulder."

"Sit down now," Peter said, taking her hand and leading her back to the couch. "Sit there and tell me everything. And unwind, would you. I'm here. Nothing's going to happen to you."

Unfamiliar tears burned her eyes and she lowered her head. "It's all going to sound pretty mad." She sat close beside him, her fingers entwined in his. "I went to dinner with Christophe. I thought it might give me a chance to talk him into giving Benno and Lukas their loan. Afterward we went back to his houseboat—your houseboat. My mediation efforts didn't go well and I left."

"Alone?"

"Stupid, right? I wouldn't let Christophe drive me home. Anyway, I couldn't get a taxi and some creep followed me."

"And held a knife on you." Peter's grip on her hand tightened. "Did he do anything else to hurt you?"

"No." She looked up into his bright blue eyes. "I was afraid that's what he wanted, too. It wasn't. Peter, he knew who I was. He'd been waiting for me. He must have known exactly where I was and that I was going to leave alone."

Peter bit into his bottom lip. He got up and began to pace. "What are you suggesting? Are you saying Christophe had something to do with this guy frightening you? Why would he do a thing like that?"

"To make me back off. He knows I'm aware of the thefts and his own plan to make life impossible for Benno and Lukas. He came rushing up immediately after that joker with the knife left. He poured on the concern, said he'd followed me as soon as I left the boat but lost me. I don't believe him."

"No, Paula, no." Peter shook his head slowly. "Christophe wouldn't do a thing like this. There's got to be another explanation. Did the guy say anything? You said he knew who you were."

Paula buried her face in her hands. She needed sleep. "He told me to leave things alone, or something like that," she said between her splayed fingers. "Get out. It's all over. That kind of stuff. He told me to go back to the States. And he threatened to kill me, Peter." She dropped her hands between her knees and Peter stopped in front of her. "He said he'd cut me where he'd stop me making any noise," Paula finished.

Peter looked pale. "The bastard. He's got to have something to do with whoever stole those stones. Maybe because you've been seen with Christophe and he's effectively put a stop to their scam—at least for now—they hope to get at him through you. Who knows?" He rubbed his forehead in frustration. "They've singled you out for some reason. It begins to look as if the car thing was deliberate, too. We all agree Christophe's motive for being so hardheaded is his need to make his reputation even bigger with daddy and the uncles. But he wouldn't sink so low as to do these things to you, Paula, believe me."

What Peter said made sense. Relief warmed every aching part of Paula. Whatever Christophe might do to gain his own ends, he wouldn't hurt her. Of course he wouldn't. How could she have been so foolish? But being seen with him might be the cause of her problems.

"Peter," she said, "you're right. Someone thinks I'm a threat. I'm going straight to Lukas. He has to know about this. Or maybe I should speak to Sandi first—"

Peter hauled her to her feet. "Neither," he said flatly. "I know you're concerned about Kohl's. I'm more worried about you. Maybe it wouldn't be such a bad idea for you to take a vacation until the dust settles."

"Leave Amsterdam?" Paula said disbelievingly. "Allow these... these whoever they are to frighten me away from what I've wanted all my life?"

"Only for a little while." Peter went to rattle around in a cupboard. He produced two mugs and poured coffee.

Paula took the mug he offered her. "I'm not going," she announced. "And Lukas and Benno need to know what's happened. I think you've hit the nail on the head. I'm probably being victimized as a way of trying to get at Christophe. He needs to realize that and so do Benno and Lukas. They all have to be on guard for more trouble. As for me, I've already received their ultimate threat. I don't know what else could happen to me."

Peter pressed his lips together and absently tapped his fingers against his mug. "Okay," he said quietly. "You came to me because you say you trust me, right?"

"I do." She nodded emphatically.

"Do you trust me enough to do what I ask? I've known all these people a lot longer than you, and I think I'm in a better position to figure out the best course to follow."

"What are you thinking of doing?" Paula asked. She waited while he considered. The seconds seemed like minutes.

"Lukas has too much on his mind," he said at last. "And Sandi. And I don't know how much more pressure Benno can take. Christophe's the one I have to talk to. Me, Paula, not you. *I'll* talk to Christophe as soon as the time seems right. Meanwhile, you're to stay away from him. Don't call him. Don't accept calls *from* him if you can avoid it. If you see him when you're at work, make an excuse to duck out. Sit tight, you understand? You've gone through enough as it is, and you certainly don't need to take any more chances."

"You're sure I shouldn't at least speak to Lukas?" Paula persisted uncertainly.

"I'm sure. It could be enough to send him after Christophe in a way that would make sure Kohl's doesn't get a guilder from St-Giles. *That* will be the end for our friends, Paula. Don't do it. Leave everything to me, please."

Several hours later, Paula let herself into the backhouse. The phone was ringing. She walked around it, willing the noise to stop. The caller was likely to be Christophe. She'd agreed to follow Peter's instructions to the letter, and the last person she could risk talking to so soon was Christophe. The ringing stopped. Paula sighed with relief and headed for her loft bedroom. She wasn't alone anymore. Now she had Peter to help her.

Her foot was on the bottom step when the phone jangled again. She backed to the wall and waited. Each blast of sound made her wince and the ringing went on and on.

She couldn't live in fear. In a rush, Paula covered the few feet to the phone and snatched up the receiver. "Yes?" she said sharply.

"Paula, is that you?" A man's voice whispered.

The all too familiar fear made her clutch the receiver hard. "Yes."

"This is Lukas. Don't talk—listen. Meet me in the workroom as fast as you can get there. Don't tell anyone where you're going. I need your help."

"Lukas…" she began, but a steady buzzing told her he'd hung up.

Paula hovered over the phone, trying to decide if she should alert Peter. Lukas had instructed her to tell no one. And he'd sounded desperate. She grabbed her purse and fled, not stopping to think until she'd got off the bus at the corner of Rokin and arrived at the work entrance to Kohl's in already gathering dusk.

The door was ajar.

Lukas must have been so distracted that he'd forgotten to lock it. Normally during nonbusiness hours she would have expected to ring, then wait for the alarm system to be turned off before she could enter.

She must get to Lukas. Inside, she took the steps two at a time and almost fell over a barricade across the second flight. Two boards, crossed, held her back. A paint can and brush stood behind them. Paula raced down again and wrenched aside the elevator's grill door.

The old car clanked slowly upward. Paula pressed her hands against the side walls in the tiny cubicle, tapping her toe with impatience. She passed the second floor and looked upward as the third began coming into view. One more to go.

The elevator stopped.

"Come on, come on," Paula groaned. "Don't foul up now, you old beast." She punched the button for the fourth floor. Nothing happened.

Paula flexed her fingers, trying to remain calm. She pressed the button for the fourth floor again, then every other button. There was no response, only the gentle creaking of the ropes and wires above and below her.

"Lukas!" she yelled, craning, trying to see upward. "Lukas! Down here. In the elevator. Lukas!" He must hear her. "Lukas!"

The lights went out.

Paula screamed and immediately covered her mouth. The power had failed. What was the matter with her? A simple power failure had stopped the elevator— No, the elevator stopped before the lights went out. She would not panic. She *would not.* Common sense, not panic, would get her out of here.

Opening the door would be tricky, but not impossible. Reaching the third floor from her position was out of the question, but she could open the inner grill and reach down to work the latch on the second floor's guard door.

She worked the stiff grill open and dropped flat on her stomach, stretching to feel for the handle she needed. Her fingers found only metal bars, each one the same as the next. Her arm wasn't long enough, and even if she dared risk trying to climb down, there wasn't enough room. Unless someone came along, she was trapped. Where was Lukas? If he'd come and gone already, no one was likely to show before morning.

Paula sat up and scooted into a corner. Lukas wasn't here. If he were, he'd already be on the stairs, making noise, something. She thought of his call. *His* call. The hoarse whisper on the phone could have belonged to any man. What a fool. She'd walked straight into another trap.

The sound of the third floor safety door opening brought Paula to her feet. "Lukas, it that you?" She laughed and cried at the same time. "Thank God. I thought I was stuck in here till morning."

There was no reply.

"Can you get the lights on?" she yelled. "Or find a flashlight? There's one in the staff changing rooms. In the first cupboard inside the door."

A crash reverberated through the car and it began to rock. Paula was thrown against a wall. More thunderous blows to the roof of the elevator followed. She slid down to sit, her skin crawling while she strained to make out some shape, any shape in the darkness above. "Lukas," she whispered, knowing whoever was doing this to her wasn't Lukas.

The hammering increased, punishing her eardrums until she hunched on all fours, shielding her head, pressing the insides of her wrists to her ears. Why hadn't she called Peter? He'd have come with her, or more likely, stopped her from coming at all.

Paula curled into a tighter ball. She heard her own sobs, a harsh, croaking noise. Where was Christophe now? What was he doing this very moment? Her thoughts made a quiet place in the middle of her anguish. She wanted him. With Christophe she'd always feel safe. The admission shocked her. Several seconds of silence passed before she realized she was no longer rocking. The banging had stopped.

Slowly, Paula sat up again, pushing her damp hair away from wet cheeks. She settled back into the corner, hugging her knees. What would they do to her now?

The next sound was of footsteps clipping carefully downstairs, then the front door latch clicked.

Paula rested her head back. So this was her lot tonight, to be scared into close hysteria and then left alone in the dark.

"Christophe," she said brokenly and closed her eyes, seeing his face in her mind. She felt again his powerful arms, gentle hands, the soft touch of his mouth. Whether she liked it or not, love could come without bidding and regardless of what Christophe thought of her, she was falling in love with him. And Peter was right, for her own safety she must stay away from the man. *Dammit.*

The seconds crawled by, and the minutes, blending into great endless hours. Paula heard the clock on a nearby tower strike twelve. She shouldn't sleep in case someone came back, in case...

CHRISTOPHE POURED A STIFF SCOTCH and returned to the couch. He closed the file he'd been reading and tossed it to the growing pile on the deck. Beside him lay a much shorter stack.

He crossed his arms and drank, staring blindly at one of Peter's blown-up black-and-white shots. Again he thought of Paula Renfrew, as he'd thought of her a thousand times before in the last two days. She'd insisted she'd contact him. The message had been implicit: don't call me, I'll call you. He sniffed and picked up one of the files beside him.

Benno and Lukas had finally shaken loose on all records. He'd spent the afternoon with personnel data and hadn't exactly found earthshattering material. Still, there were some possible leads here, some titillating bits and pieces.

"I'll call you," Paula had said. He glanced at the phone. So why didn't she? Hell, he was getting a case on the woman, and he couldn't allow himself the luxury. The hit-and-run deal, the attack on Friday night—what did they mean? What conclusion was he supposed to draw from them? Paula had come right out and asked him to back off from his investigations here. Could she be part of a larger network of criminals who had started out using her as a decoy with him, then turned on her when she failed to make progress? Was her life in danger? His insides contracted and the reaction sent off a warning flare in his mind. He was beginning—scratch beginning—he already cared about Paula and he must stop. Persecution and protection made unlikely bedfellows. There was only one thing that could make it worse... No. He didn't love Paula, he was attracted to her. Christophe drank again. Balancing protecting her with finding out what she might be guilty of should be enough to keep his mind and body away from other possibilities with her.

The file in his hand was Frank Lammaker's. Nothing here he didn't already know. Christophe set it down and picked up Kersten Gouda's. He'd almost discarded it, but something kept drawing him back to the scribbled notes, most in Benno's handwriting, about the woman. She took her vacation time all at once, usually in midwinter, and headed for the south of France. Her vacation address was noted. Christophe stared at the hotel name again. He knew the place and it was expensive, a little rich for most diamond pages, he would have thought. But she could have resources outside the obvious.

He glanced to the top of the page, to Benno's entries from his initial interview with Mrs. Gouda. Evidently she'd been very forthcoming with information about her personal status. The wife of a policeman missing for some years, she believed at that time he'd been abducted. She refused to accept the opinion of his chief that he had simply decided to disappear, that people didn't stay abducted for long without someone hearing something. Kersten, then thirty—Christophe checked the date and noted that she must now be forty-four—had stated confidently that she was sure her husband would eventually contact her and need her help.

Christophe began to close the file. Kersten Gouda was certainly an interesting woman, but not remarkable for his purposes. He slapped the folder wide open and stared at the address beneath Kersten's name: *79 Overstraat.* He'd missed it! After days of searching telephone books, a dozen trips past the house to see if he could observe someone coming or going, and one risky direct approach when there'd been no reply to his ring at the door of 79 Overstraat, he'd almost allowed the occupant to slip through his fingers.

Kersten Gouda lived at 79 Overstraat. He whooped and flapped the file back and forth. Pieces were sliding together.

Grinning to himself, he put Kersten's records with Frank's and picked up Victor Hodez's. The diligent Victor had been a contemporary of Paula's father, Michael. He, too, had been a suspect in the theft of a large gem, then cleared by Michael Renfrew's rapid defection. Christophe flipped through the stack of papers on Victor. He'd started with Kohl's as an apprentice and come through the rough period of the theft to rise to his present position as head polisher. Apart from that one incident, his history was squeaky clean.

Christophe sifted through several record books to a scuffed volume from thirty-five years previously. All employees from that time were listed. He found Victor's name under the apprentice classification, and Michael Renfrew, together with a notation that he left without notice. A Lars Hugo was another contemporary of Hodez and Renfrew. Hugo had left after his apprenticeship to take a job in Antwerp. A fourth young man, Leo Erkel, rounded out the number. Erkel's entry had elicited an exclamation point after "Has decided to finish out apprenticeship with Metter's." Christophe shook his head faintly. That must have pleased whichever Kohl had been in charge at the time.

Another book held descriptions of stones and the names of craftsmen who worked on them. Another column stated buyers' names and date of sale. He easily located entries for the thirteen stolen stones Benno had tried so hard to cover. Christophe checked the finisher's initials for each one, hoping his latest hunch would check out. It didn't. Four different men had worked on the stones. Damn. He lit a cigarette and stretched his limbs. Where was the common thread?

The last file on the couch was thin. *Paula Renfrew.* He flipped open the top cover without lifting the folder. Paula's picture, clipped to a letter, lay on top. Slowly he raised the photo to eye level, studied the lovely, uncomplicated face. In black and white the gentle curves of her features were accented, and the thickness of her lashes, the way they shadowed her eyes. He read the letter quickly. It was the first she'd written Benno, asking for a job.

Christophe stood and walked to a window on the canal. Paula Renfrew did have a connection with the diamond thefts. No way could he persuade himself out of the obvious. He looked back at the pile of personnel records. How did these people fit together? With a long sigh, he leaned against the window. This operation could probably use the expertise of the entire Interpol, Scotland Yard and FBI organizations; there were certainly enough trails to follow and loose ends dangling to keep more than a platoon of trained men busy.

He looked at Paula's picture again. This beautiful woman—for him, this increasingly desirable woman—had been at the center of every overt act since he'd arrived. If only he could stop himself from wishing they'd met when neither had more to gain or more to lose.

Chapter Eleven

The man threw himself on the bed. "How do you know this?"

"He told me," the woman replied.

"You've had another contact?"

She sighed. "We'll keep having to deal with this man until we get what we want."

"But he cut her neck? My God."

"He said her neck had been cut accidentally, not that *he* cut it."

"My God," the man repeated and gripped a bedpost above his head with one hand. "We've got to get out of this. She might have been killed. Murder would only accomplish one thing—we'd almost certainly be caught."

"She wasn't killed and we aren't going to be caught." The woman sat on the edge of the bed. "And maybe the scares she's had will keep her out of our hair."

"The car was stupid, too." He scooted around her and stood. "That was stupid and unnecessary. A sure way to point in certain directions if she decides to go to the police."

"Evidently she's too concerned about her benefactors for that." The feminine laugh was unnaturally high. "Anyway, I can't worry about her now. We've got other problems."

"What problems?"

"We've gone through all but three stones. He wants another tonight, which will leave one and the pear-shape. We need more diamonds just in case."

"Let him have the pear." The man's voice dropped.

"No," his companion stated flatly. "We keep that as our trump card, if we need it. That gem is enough for any man's ransom, if it comes to that."

"Ransom," he snorted. "I think you finally used the right term for what we've been paying, only we've gone beyond that, haven't we?"

Pale skin became paler. "Meaning?"

"Meaning why not be honest with ourselves. We're being black-mailed now. We can't go back and there's no end in sight. He'll squeeze us forever."

She started to cry soundlessly.

"Don't." He put a hand on her shoulder. "Don't cry. I'll do what has to be done, but slower from here on. One stone at a time."

Monday of the Fourth Week:

Paula listened to footsteps on the stairs. Dawn had long ago sent meager dustings of pale gray light into the elevator. She could read her watch, and it was time for the first Kohl employees to arrive. Still she was afraid to shout.

She stood up, straightening her sweater and brushing her jeans. She found a comb in her purse and dragged it through her hair. What happened to her from now on could hang on how well she calculated each move.

Whoever was climbing the stairs started to whistle, and Paula almost collapsed with relief. Frank Lammaker. Only one man around here had that tuneless whistle and insisted upon using it endlessly.

She cleared her throat. "Frank." Her first call was tentative, then she shouted, "Frank! The elevator's stuck. Can you get me out of here?"

Several seconds passed before the car jerked and moved upward. Paula shook back her hair and hitched her purse strap over her shoulder. *Look normal,* she instructed herself, preparing to smile. Frank mustn't know she'd spent the night there. No one else should be involved in what was happening—not if she hoped to extricate herself from danger, *and* help Benno. She had to appear nonchalant to Frank, then make it to the bathroom—quickly. Next on the agenda would be a call to Peter.

"How long have you been in there?" Frank asked, peering down as she came into view. "Why didn't you yell before?" He swept open the fourth floor doors, laughing, his blond curls still tousled from walking in the wind.

Paula liked Frank. Without any proof, she was certain he was innocent of any wrongdoing against his employers. "I was only in here a few minutes," she lied, stepping out, trying not to let her stiffness show. He would assume she'd entered through the retail showrooms as most manufacturing employees did early in the morning.

"You should have hailed old Victor. He's always up there at the crack of dawn." Frank looked at her closely. "You okay? You look pretty ragged around the edges."

"I'm fine. Stayed up too late last night." Of course Victor would be in by now, but he also used the stairs and she hadn't heard him. Maybe he'd come early while she'd dozed without knowing it. "I tried calling Victor, but you know he's going deaf, don't you?" Deception upon deception, but what choice did she have anymore?

"I wonder who switched off the power to the elevator?" Frank said almost to himself.

Paula wiped her palms on her jeans, thinking madly. "The power panel's in the hall outside the showrooms, next to the one for the lights. Anyone could have done it by mistake." She was going to have to watch every word. "I'd better get moving, Frank. Victor gets on my case if I'm late."

Frank rolled his eyes. "Victor gets on everyone's case for something. Hey, how about lunch? You do look a bit like a wilted hothouse flower at the moment. Come out with a bunch of us to the Pilsener Club. Great place. Great beer and food."

"I don't know." Paula could think of nothing but the bathroom now. "Maybe."

"Great," Frank said, starting up the stairs again. "I'll come and find you when I've finished my morning deliveries."

Paula hung around long enough to check the lower flights. As she'd suspected, the crossed boards and paint can were gone.

Half an hour later she was feeling better. She blessed her resourcefulness in always carrying a travel toothbrush and small quantities of the basic makeup she used. Given the ghastly night she'd spent, sleeping in snatches, only to awaken with violent starts, she looked fairly human. Bustling, making much of gathering odds and ends from her bench and announcing she had to speak to someone downstairs, Paula made it through the workroom and out from Victor's eagle eye without his comment.

Calling Peter from Kohl's was out of the question. Dressed in her blue coverall, she ran along Rokin toward Dam Square and found a booth.

There was no reply at Peter's home. Paula searched the phone book and found the number of his studio. He answered at the first ring.

"Peter," she said urgently. "I want to bring you up to date so you'll know what's happened if something...if anything...Peter, I want to make sure I'm missed if I disappear."

Dead silence met her comment.

"Are you there?" she asked sharply.

"Yes," Peter said and she heard him swallow. "Did something else happen?"

Paula expelled a shaky breath. "When I got home from your place I received what I thought was a call from Lukas. He asked me to meet him in the workroom of Kohl's. Then I was trapped in the elevator all night. I just got out."

"Good God," Peter said explosively. "Lukas wouldn't trap you in an elevator, Paula, or anywhere else. Why should he? This is getting crazy. We're going to the police."

"No," Paula insisted. "If we blow this wide open, where will Benno and Lukas be, then? They'll be lucky to see Christophe's dust as he leaves town, sans the loan. St-Giles wouldn't touch them for sure, then. And afterward the whole of Amsterdam would know what's been going on. They'd be finished."

"Okay, okay," Peter said testily. "But we don't need a second Joan of Arc. Martyrs are out of fashion. Let's talk this through and decide what to do. First, why would anyone do this to you?"

"To remind me I'm supposed to get out of town? To frighten me enough to make me hurry?" Paula suggested.

Peter clucked his tongue thoughtfully. "Shouldn't have thought it necessary so soon after the little knife number. Oh, hell... I've got it."

"What?"

"They're watching every move you make. You must have been seen coming to my place yesterday. Only when you rang the intercom outside the front door there would be no way for a watcher who wasn't close to know it was my bell and not Lukas's you pressed. Of course they'd think of Lukas first."

Paula thought an instant. "But even if I *was* going to Lukas, so what?"

"If they decided you might be spilling the beans about the threats against you—getting Lukas on your side—they might want to change your opinion of him. Make you think he was responsible for the threats in the first place. They might even hope to plant the idea Lukas is involved in the thefts. Or, if they know Christophe is hot on their trail, and we're both pretty sure they do, these turkeys could have it in their heads to use you to set Christophe and Lukas against each other. But I'm sure of one thing, Paula, they desperately want you out of Amsterdam as soon as possible."

"I think so, too," Paula sighed. "And I'm not going."

"Are you sure it wouldn't be best."

"I've never been more sure of anything, Peter. Just the fact that something about me keeps them stirred up is valuable. They're going to make a mistake and reveal themselves. Wait and see. I'm right."

Peter didn't answer for a while. "I hope you are right," he said finally. "I'll get to Christophe as soon as the time seems right. I don't want to deal with him unless I'm sure we can both be rational. Paula, anything happens, *anything*, and you tell me, promise?"

"Promise," she agreed fervently.

"What are your favorite flowers?" he asked.

Paula blinked. "Flowers? Oh...all kinds. Gardenia..." she hesitated, feeling Christophe's presence all around her. "Roses, I guess." Another reminder of Christophe was the last thing she needed.

"Typical woman." Peter laughed. "I'm going to send you some. You deserve a treat. Just make sure you don't stick yourself on a thorn. With your track record—"

"Thanks, Peter," Paula broke in dryly. "Talk to you soon."

By eleven-thirty, Paula was longing for her lunch date with Frank and his friends. A chance to be with young, uncomplicated people sounded heavenly. She needed an opportunity not to think of anything heavier than what beer to order.

"Still eleven-thirty I believe, Paula."

Victor's voice had an ice-water quality. She looked up guiltily from her watch. "Eleven thirty-one," she corrected, smiling.

His expression remained deadpan. "Hmm. The young find it hard to concentrate these days." He bent to his work once more. "What happened to your neck? Cut yourself shaving?"

Paula had to laugh. Victor had just made his closest attempt at humor in her experience.

"You should watch out," he added. "You might cut your whole throat."

The smile slipped from Paula's face. *If you only knew,* she thought. "I'll be more careful next time, Victor." What should she say when someone asked what she'd done. "I caught the skin in the zipper of my windbreaker," she said. Victor grunted, accepting the explanation. Lying was becoming easier, and she hated it.

Promptly at twelve, Frank stuck his head through the door. "Ready to go, Paula?" He kept a wary eye on Victor, who didn't appear to hear.

"You bet," she said with alacrity, stopping her wheel.

"Great. Meet you out front when you're ready."

Paula hurried into the empty staff room and opened her locker. She'd give almost anything for a change of clothes.

The door opened and closed behind her. Paula slipped off her coverall before turning around.

"I'm still waiting for that call." Christophe stood with his hands sunk in his pants' pockets. "Remember the call you said you'd make to me?"

She hung the coverall inside her locker and fished out her purse. *"Duck out if you see him at work,"* Peter had warned. With Christophe looming between her and the door, ducking out would take swift maneuvers. "How are things going, Christophe?" she asked with as much lightness as she could muster. "Figured out which of us is the arch criminal?"

"Dammit, woman." He reached to grab her wrist and pull her close. "We're past the game-playing stage here. The last time I saw you, some madman had made a pretty good attempt at sticking a knife in your throat. You weren't so flip then. What happened to calm you down?"

"The guy was a mugger." She tried to jerk free. "He lost his nerve. I got lucky, I guess."

"A mugger who told you to get out of Amsterdam and didn't try to steal from you?"

Paula thought fast. "He must have seen I didn't have a purse and he just said a lot of stuff because he was mad."

Christophe's face was a rigid mask, his eyes brown steel. "Why are you avoiding me? I've had plenty to worry about since Friday night, without you adding to the pot."

He worried about her. Paula closed her eyes a fraction, gathering her composure. Whether she wanted to or not, she cared about his man, but she'd be a fool to imagine he felt the same, or to forget the enormous barriers separating them.

He tightened his hold on her.

"You're hurting my wrist, Christophe," Paula said, speaking as evenly as she could manage. "Let me go, please. I've got a date."

"No." He released her wrist and immediately clasped her in his arms, holding her hard against him. "I'm not letting you go without a lot more conversation, Paula."

She only struggled once. He was too strong for her. "Get this over with." Her hands came to rest on his shirtfront between the lapels of his jacket. She fastened her gaze on his striped tie and tried, uselessly, not to feel the hard lines of his body against hers.

"We felt something special together the other evening, Paula."

He was a master of understatement, she decided. Her flesh had already begun to ache. "Brandy and music are a heady combination," she said, not daring to look into his eyes.

"Not good enough," he said softly, backing against the door, pulling her with him. No one would be able to open it until he moved. "You aren't the type of woman to... I don't think just any man with a bottle of brandy and a few jazz records could turn you on."

Her head snapped up. She made fists against his chest. "You don't know what type of woman I am. If you did, you'd know—" She clamped her mouth shut. He'd know she was in love with him? Had she really almost said that?

"I know you're in trouble," he said promptly.

No beat in the conversation had been missed. She'd done nothing to give away her feelings. "My trouble is you," she said. "You're a lot of people's trouble around here. Go home, Christophe St-Giles. And give the good people who thought you were a friend the chance they need."

He regarded her levelly. "You are certainly convincing. And I want to believe you're for real. God, how I want to believe it."

Her heart sank. He still suspected her of involvement in those thefts. But there was another element. His voice had a real note of regret when he said he wanted to believe her.

"Nothing to say?" he persisted. "Are you sure there isn't something you'd like to tell me—something you'd like help with? I would help you, Paula, and I know it would be worth it—to both of us."

"Stop it!" she blurted, her heart breaking into rapid thuds. He was staring at her, his eyes narrowed. "We've got nothing else to talk about." She had spooked without being sure why.

Christophe saw her eyes widen and glanced at her neck. A hard pulse beat there. He'd frightened her. He didn't want that. He couldn't bear... Why did she have to be mixed up in something illegal?

Her body leaned into his, slumping. He supported her weight. The poor little devil had got into more than she'd bargained for and now she was caving in. Absurdly he wanted to keep holding her up—forever, if possible. She'd buried her face in his shirt. "Look at me," he said firmly, intending to try again to draw her out. She did as he asked, and he stared into depthless blue eyes fringed with lashes spiky from tears. "Oh, Paula, damn you," he groaned and pressed his lips to hers.

He heard a sob catch in her throat and drew back. Her eyes were closed and he kissed her lids, the salty, wet lashes. "You know what you do to me, don't you?" Again he checked her expression. This time it held pain, pain he instantly shared and felt strike deep at his insides.

"Let me go, Christophe," she whispered.

He kissed her again, sliding his hands beneath her sweater to span her supple waist. Her lips parted and she stood on tiptoe, clung to his neck, ran her fingers through his hair. The force of their coming together exploded the last fragments of his reason. He wanted her. He wanted her desperately. And she wanted him. Raw heat burned him, driving, thrusting him against her firm belly. Her tongue was in his mouth. He met it, then withdrew, took her bottom lip gently in his teeth.

"Paula. We need to be together."

"I know," she said softly. "I know."

Together, he thought, they needed to be together, alone and far from here, from the distrust threatening to rob him of a woman he was never going to forget. He'd like to take her away, forget the whole shooting match in this miserable city he was coming to hate. They'd make wild love all day, all night; come out of their nest only when weakness threatened to kill them both. His attempt at lightening the train of his thoughts only made his muscles more rigid. He couldn't take much more.

"*Merde.*" The pressure of the door handle cracked into his spine. He released Paula and she shot away, turning her back. "Paula." He lifted a hand toward her, then dropped it to his side, resigned, and rubbed a thumb across his mouth a second before pulling open the door.

"Geez." Frank Lammaker squeezed through the narrow space Christophe allowed him. "First stalled elevators, then doors that won't open." He fiddled with the lock and glanced at Christophe. "Did you have trouble with this thing?"

"No," Christophe said shortly. What did elevators have to do with it, he wondered. He didn't miss the knowing look in Frank's eyes. The other man knew there was nothing wrong with the door, or its lock.

Frank leaned to see around Christophe's shoulder. "Paula," he said. "You ready?"

Desperation threatened to undo Christophe. He flexed his fingers helplessly at his sides. He didn't want her to go, but he couldn't stop her.

"Coming," Paula said. Her voice was unmistakably husky.

Christophe turned in time to see her finish running a comb through shining hair. He shoved his hands into his pockets, willing his nerves to quit jumping.

Paula walked past him without meeting his eyes. Frank led the way from the room, but not before he'd cast a curious glance from Christophe to Paula's bowed face.

"Paula," Christophe said quietly. She stopped halfway through the doorway and faced him. He looked at his shoes and took a deep breath before saying, "Please think before you do anything."

Their eyes met. She didn't reply, didn't have to. Her mirrored emotions sent him all the messages he feared and hoped for: indecision, suspicion, pain...and so clearly—desire.

Chapter Twelve

"How many kinds of beer are there?" Paula asked, keeping her smile in place with difficulty.

Frank's friend Willem Bill waved his hands expansively and said, "Dozens, a dozen—who knows? Pick your poison. Light or dark, from a bottle or a barrel."

Paula liked the dark-haired young man with his animated brown eyes. "From a barrel," she announced, determined to enter the spirit of the occasion, "and light." She couldn't forget the look in Christophe's eyes as she'd left him.

A flaxen-haired young woman to her right touched Paula's arm. "Aren't you going to ask?" she said.

"Ask what?" Paula replied, puzzled.

"Why we call these pubs brown pubs? Tourists always want to know." This was Willem's girlfriend, Ghislaine, a fledgling actress.

"Ghislaine," Willem turned back from placing their order. "Paula lives here. She isn't a tourist, my love."

"I know what she means," Paula interrupted. "Newcomers. And I don't know why they're brown pubs."

The torrent of Dutch that followed made Paula laugh. Frank's "bunch" of friends, with the exception of Willem and an apprentice finisher from Metter's, were writers, painters and theatricals, twelve highly strung men and women in all. Evidently each had something to add to the explanation of why De Pilsener Club and hundreds of similar establishments in Amsterdam were labeled brown pubs.

Finally, Frank stood up and demanded silence. Shouts gradually subsided into snickers and he announced, "They are brown either because the floors and tables and most other parts of them are brown wood, or because the wallpaper is never changed and cigarette smoke turns it brown. Take you choice, okay?"

A disgruntled chorus went up and the dispute continued, occasionally translated into English when someone remembered Paula didn't speak Dutch.

She drank her beer in preoccupied silence and ate little sausages and lumps of cheese on toothpicks, dipping each one into hot mustard. As her thoughts deepened, she mentally drew apart from her boisterous companions. When would Peter talk to Christophe? Peter believed in her innocence; maybe he could convince his old friend.

A glint caught her eye, a bright flash from the other side of the smoke-filled, dimly lit room. Paula screwed up her eyes. The smoke stung and she was tired. The flash came again and this time she located its source, a stone in a man's ring reflecting the flame of a candle on his table. He sat alone, turning a glass of jenever around and around. Paula stared at the ring, and the hand, large and knotted, gripping the glass.

Even before she glanced up, she knew he would be watching her. Pale eyes bored into hers and Paula recoiled instinctively. The man wasn't old, or was he? A tall, wiry body, close-cropped, iron-gray hair and impassive features made his age difficult to estimate. With an effort, she turned her attention to Frank. "We mustn't be late getting back," she said tightly.

Frank patted her hand. "We just arrived," he said, a note of concern in his voice. "Are we too loud for you?" He indicated the rest of the group. "We're always like this."

"I love listening to you," she assured him honestly. "It's just..." She glanced past him. The man still watched her unflinchingly. Hair raised on the back of Paula's neck. "There's a man over there who gives me the creeps. He's staring and I keep getting the sensation I know him."

Frank started to swivel in his chair.

Paula gripped his forearm, shaking her head faintly. "Don't look, please. I'm being silly. I never saw him before in my life."

He ignored her and turned around. "Willem," he said over his shoulder, then swung back and dropped his voice. "Isn't that some head honcho from Metter's over there?"

Willem dragged his attention away from Ghislaine and checked in the direction of Frank's jabbing thumb. A sour twist turned his pleasant mouth down. "You could say so. Our polisher extraordinaire. The charming Leo Erkel himself. If the rest of the employees held a least-liked, most admired contest, old Leo would win hands down. The guy's a genius with the nature of a rattlesnake. He lies in wait, then strikes when you least expect it."

"Ignore him, Paula," Frank muttered when Willem was once more engrossed in Ghislaine. "I've noticed him in here before, and he always looks that way."

There was no ignoring Leo Erkel, Paula soon decided. No matter how hard she worked at becoming part of the table talk and pretending the man wasn't there, she felt his eyes on her. When he got up she was instantly relieved...until he returned within minutes.

She clock-watched and tried to appear involved, willing the hands of her watch to move.

The heavy curtain covering the door billowed, and a wedge of smokey light appeared briefly while a hunched man entered. Paula stared, slowly reached to squeeze Frank's wrist. "It's Victor," she hissed. "Frank, you didn't tell me Victor came here for lunch." She hesitated before answering her own remark. "He doesn't. He never leaves Kohl's in the middle of the day."

Frank groaned. "Of all the lousy luck."

Victor peered around the room, allowing his eyes to adjust to the gloom. The next instant he was at Paula's side, bending over to whisper, "Come with me now. What do you think you are doing here?" He threw Frank a venomous glare, then pointedly ignored him.

Quelling embarrassment and indignation, Paula made an excuse to Frank and the others and followed Victor outside, where he immediately faced her. "How could you be such a fool?" he demanded. "To come here, with those people?"

Paula could only stare askance.

"This is where Metter's employees come every day. There is a feud between their house and ours. Mr. Kohl, old Mr. Kohl and young Mr. Kohl do not like—no—do not allow their employees to be with these people."

Paula barely contained the urge to tell Victor the Kohls couldn't control their staff outside work. "I didn't know, Victor." She managed to keep her voice level. "No mention of our work or the business was made. Most of the people I was with aren't even in the diamond trade. If it's such a sin, why does Frank feel comfortable?" She instantly regretted the last question.

"Frank isn't my concern," Victor said coldly. "*You* are. You are my apprentice and I will not have the work I've put in with you wasted because you choose the wrong company."

"Why should going out to lunch with a few friendly people waste the work you've done with me?" She was becoming exasperated.

"If you are... If Mr. Kohl decides not to allow you to continue with us... Paula, listen to me carefully. There are things I do not think you know. It's time you did."

Paula pushed her hair back. A cool wind flattened her cotton sweater to her back. "What things don't I know?" A curious, tentative excitement snagged her stomach. Victor had a trusted position with Kohl's. Perhaps he could tell her facts that would help her present impossible circumstances.

He took her elbow and backed her against the dark windows of De Pilsener. "First, it is important you not draw undesirable notice to yourself, Paula. Coming here was a great mistake. You are being watched."

Her scalp tightened. "Go on."

"Next, the reason for your being in Amsterdam is known, although not, I think, exactly what you intend to do."

He'd lost her. "I'm sorry, Victor." She shook her head. "I don't understand what you mean."

"You don't deny that you know your father left Amsterdam accused of theft? That he stole a single perfect diamond and got away with it?"

She opened and closed her mouth, aghast.

"No. Of course you don't deny it," Victor went on, apparently taking her silence for agreement. "I knew what happened at the time. Nothing was proved for sure, of course, but when Michael left without warning, we all knew—it was assumed—that he was indeed the guilty one. When you were hired I was surprised. But I know the older Mr. Kohl's kindness. He would want to give you a chance. But I don't think he realizes you know what happened to your father, does he?"

Paula found her voice. "I don't know what you're talking about," she began slowly. "My father never stole anything. He was the most honest man I ever knew."

"Paula." Victor touched her arm awkwardly. "I understand how you feel. Michael told you what happened, didn't he, and he insisted he was innocent? You came here to...to what? To clear his name? To seek revenge? Whatever you had in mind, give it up. This is a tight industry, and as soon as people in it find out what you're doing they'll close ranks on you. I'm just grateful someone mentioned where you were coming today. You must stay away from any element that could draw undue attention to you and concentrate on your craft. One day you will be a credit to Kohl's, my girl."

The blood in her body seemed to have drained to her feet. Her head was light. "This is bizarre."

Victor ignored her. "I only hope I'm not too late. Our diligent hunter from Zurich also followed you here. He's across the street now, waiting to see what you do next."

Christophe had followed her. Paula struggled not to search him out.

"I knew something was wrong as soon as he showed up in Amsterdam and then stayed, looking at books, poking around. Whatever is making Benno Kohl and his son so changed these days has to be St-Giles's fault, and I've noticed his interest in you. I believe there must have been enough trouble for the firm to need financial help..." He paused as if making a decision. "There could have been more thefts, and this Swiss is trying to find out more about it before he will agree to a loan. I can only guess at these things. But if I am right, and if he has also discovered your history, Paula, he could suspect you of being involved."

She laughed bitterly. Victor had fitted the pieces together with deadly accuracy. But he'd also given her the missing piece in her own study—the real reason Christophe suspected her. "I tell you this, Victor." For Paula, spring's caress had deserted the wind. She crossed her arms tightly. "I've never heard the story you tell about my father. Why would I? He didn't do what he was accused of. And now I *will* find a way to make sure everyone else knows it."

Victor clamped a hand on her shoulder. "Do nothing until this man Christophe is gone from Amsterdam. If you insist on probing, and I think you should not, at least wait. But that period of all our lives we shared with Michael is closed. I do not believe he would wish you to involve yourself. And now—we must hope it isn't too late to deflect this Christophe. In a few moments, we will walk past him and pretend to be surprised. I will deal with things."

"I can't." She was suddenly desperate.

"You can," he insisted. "I will tell you one more thing and then we will go quickly, before our time here appears too long to explain. Robbery at Kohl's is more than a figment of my imagination. Word has it that a number of stones have been taken. Big stuff. You must not talk of this—to anyone. Benno and Lukas know about your father and I'm absolutely sure now that M. St-Giles does, too. The coincidence of your presence is too great. You are bound to be suspect. *I* know you have nothing to do with these thefts and that's why I'm here, to help you. I saw St-Giles ahead of me as I arrived on the street. I'm sure he's watching you."

Victor paused, scrubbing at his jaw. "What is best?" he muttered.

"What is best? Perhaps you should go to your home in America where you will be safe. Amsterdam could become too dangerous for you. A foreigner in trouble with Dutch law is really in trouble." He considered, frowning deeply. "For now, we will *accidentally*, bump into our friend."

They started walking and Paula sighted Christophe. He was buying flowers from a woman with a basket of bouquets and appeared absorbed. She tried to breathe slowly, counting, inhaling, exhaling.

Within yards of Christophe, Paula halted, transfixed by a car at the curb. It was small and white, its paint scratched. A Volvo, she noted. Her anxiety deepened. She glanced at the handle on the driver's side and knew she had seen its rusty surface before. Paranoia had taken over. Paula caught up with Victor who had stopped to wait for her. She made herself smile. There must be thousands of little white cars with rusty handles in Amsterdam. This one didn't have to be the one that had hit her.

"Well, well." Christophe looked up as they approached. "What a surprise, Paula. And you, Victor. I hardly recognize you away from your wheel."

"M. St-Giles." Victor bowed slightly. "I, too, am surprised. I didn't know so many people knew this little street. Are you, er, are you going to De Pilsener Club?"

Paula couldn't believe his approach, to actually bring up the place she wasn't supposed to have visited. Perhaps Christophe hadn't seen her go in or come out. Oh, she was fooling herself, she decided angrily.

Christophe finished paying for the flowers. "For a friend." He showed the brilliant assortment of blooms. "I often walk around here. I know the area from when I spent a year in the city."

"You would do well not to frequent De Pilsener," Victor advised in a low voice.

"Why?" Christophe raised his brows. "It's one of the best brown pubs in town."

"Ah, yes," Victor agreed. "But as I just told Paula, Philip Metter's people gather there almost every day and Mr. Kohl doesn't like us to be close to them. Paula didn't know. Fortunately I discovered she'd been invited there and I came to take her back. She understands now—don't you, Paula?"

She nodded, feeling stupid. "Victor is very good to me."

"I'm sure he is," Christophe said before adding to Victor, "Thank you for warning me. Why don't you leave Paula with me? We have a few things to discuss. I promise I'll get her back safely."

Victor's eyes found Paula's. He opened his mouth as if he would say something, then only shrugged. "If you insist. Will you be all right, Paula?" he said with emphasis.

She felt a warm rush of gratitude and sympathy toward the old man. "I'll be fine," she reassured him. "I'll see you soon."

Standing at Christophe's side, she watched Victor's retreating back with a sense of panic. What "things" did Christophe want to discuss with her?

"You okay?" Christophe asked, his voice oddly lacking its usual authority.

Paula avoided looking at him. "Fine, thanks."

A burst of noise from the door of De Pilsener Club preceded the eruption of Frank and his friends onto the sidewalk. Waving and shouting, Willem and Frank, with Ghislaine between them, crossed directly to the white car. Paula's lungs felt compressed. She glanced at Christophe, but he was gazing across the street.

Paula looked, too, and saw the tall form of Leo Erkel lope from the pub. He collided with Victor and sent up a loud oath.

"Aha, Leo." Willem, poised beside the driver's door of the little car, laughed, hands on hips. "Swearing at Victor? Your friend must have been beating you at your beloved cards again. How many times must we tell you not to bet with a friend if you want to keep him?"

Frank and Ghislaine ran to shove Willem into the car, Frank with a worried expression on his face. Paula heard him tell Willem he'd regret his meddling, that they might both regret it.

Again she became engrossed in the Volvo. She didn't want to believe Willem or Frank would hurt her, yet...

"What is that man's name?" Christophe asked suddenly.

Paula snapped her attention to his face, then to the direction in which he stared. "You mean the tall one putting on a cap? Leo Erkel, I think Willem said. He's the head polisher for Metters'." Erkel had turned in the same direction as Victor but walked several yards behind. If, as Willem suggested, these two were friends, they weren't pleased with each other today.

"Too complex," Christophe murmured. "In English they say something about tangled webs and deceit. I think I begin to understand."

"What do you understand?" Paula asked. Willem's car sped away, and she was left alone with Christophe.

"Let's start back," he said, automatically putting an arm around her shoulder.

Paula lifted his hand and put a few feet between them. She wasn't playing games anymore. Now Christophe would learn that she knew exactly what he thought about her and why. Let him try grappling with surprise, she thought, too angry and confused to enjoy the prospect. She half ran and he strode beside her.

Christophe reached for her arm but she shook loose and hurried on. "You knew what was said about my father, all the lies about his being a thief, and you started your tidy case against me. You needed a scapegoat for the recent robberies from Kohl's, an excuse to say the firm is losing its touch and shouldn't be trusted with a loan from your precious bank. An outfit that employs the daughter of a man they're sure once stole from them cannot be taken seriously. And the fact that I must be the one responsible for the second batch of thefts seals your opinion." Tears sprang into her eyes, and she wiped them furiously away. "You were only too willing to think I was my father's daughter." She rounded on him, breathing heavily. "You never knew my father. He was beautiful and honest. A quiet man everyone respected. Now I know what he carried around with him all those years, and I hate the people who did that to him. You should be helping me find them, not trying to persecute me."

Christophe moved a step closer. With the fingertips of one hand he smoothed tears from her cheeks. He still held the riotous bouquet.

"Paula," he sighed. "I'm almost as convinced as you that your father wasn't guilty. And I'm sure I can prove it. But doing so and making sure we both end up alive may not be easy."

He thrust the flowers into her trembling hands.

Chapter Thirteen

Christophe didn't speak again until they were within yards of Kohl's. He'd held Paula's elbow firmly as he rushed her along. "Now." He stepped into a doorway, taking her with him. "I have to meet with Benno and Lukas. I may or may not be able to get back to you today. But I *will* make a chance to talk soon, okay? Can you live with that?"

"Tell me what you'll be doing," Paula demanded. He'd spoken of fear for their lives, and now he wanted her to wait quietly like a good little girl.

"You'll just have to trust—"

"Don't," Paula broke in. "Please don't ask me for any more blind trust. I'm fresh out."

He held her hand and brought it to his lips, keeping his eyes on hers. "It's safer for you to know as little as possible for a while," he said urgently. "That way you're less likely to give off vibes the wrong people can pick up."

"I'm not a kid," Paula insisted. "Please don't treat me like one. Who *are* these 'wrong' people? Will you tell me what you know, what you think? I'm going slowly—no, rapidly—mad. You don't think Frank did have anything to do with it, do you? I don't see how." She thought of the white car but said nothing.

"I'm not ruling anyone out yet," he said, glancing anxiously over her shoulder. "Look, I'm working on a lot of conjecture. A few hard facts mixed in, but not enough. This afternoon may tell me a lot—I expect it to. I promise I'll at least touch bases with you before the day's over. Beyond that you'll have to—"

"Trust you," she finished for him. "All right, Christophe. I don't have much choice. But if I don't hear from you today, I'll be looking for you by tomorrow. And I can't wait forever for some answers. I've got this weird feeling time's closing in on me." She gave an involuntary shiver.

Christophe hugged her quickly. "Not weird, *chérie*, accurate. It's closing in on both of us."

BENNO AND LUKAS STOOD side by side at the window in Benno's office. The air felt funereal as Christophe closed the door behind him and waited for one of them to acknowledge him.

After several seconds, he cleared his throat. "We had an appointment, I believe," he announced.

Lukas turned first, and Christophe took an involuntary step toward him before checking an urge to throw his arms around the other man. Lukas Kohl was beaten. Defeat had erased the light from his eyes, the confidence from his handsome features. His shoulders sagged in a way no suit would be expensive enough to conceal.

"Lukas, I—" Christophe searched for the words he wanted. "You don't look well, my friend." He flinched as he said it. They had been friends, but the time seemed so very long ago.

"You'd better sit down," Benno said, approaching his own chair and gripping the arms while he lowered his bony frame. "We'd all better sit. There's much to talk about, Christophe. I don't think you'll want to continue with your plan for this afternoon."

Christophe sat slowly in a chair opposite Benno and looked inquiringly from Lukas to Benno.

Lukas sank to the edge of his father's desk and crossed his wrists on his thigh. "There's *no* point in doing what you suggested."

"Why not?" Christophe asked. "Somewhere between that room—" he indicated the workroom "—and the buyer, those stones were switched. I haven't been through the procedure. You have. So many times you could easily be missing something that will seem obvious to me. So we act out the process, step by step, and see if we can find the link, the second when this...this sleight of hand...was possible on each occasion. And it was done in a second—I'm certain of that."

"Too late." Lukas found a cigarette and Christophe half rose to light it for him. "It may be too late for everything, Christophe. There's a possibility, if you could arrange a lot of money for us fast, that we could..." He shook his head. Smoke seeped through his almost closed lips.

Christophe inhaled the strong scent of the Gitane and something else—fear? If fear had an odor, it was in this room. He kept the lighter in his hand until he'd lit one of his own cigarettes. Emotion must be kept in check, he reminded himself. *Let them do the talking.* The Kohls must give all the information in this exchange, while he listened and analyzed.

"Lukas, tell him." Benno shrank back in his chair and closed his eyes. "Tell him exactly what's happened. What he does then is up to him."

"Yes," Lukas said softly, "it will all be up to you Christophe, *my friend.*"

Christophe rested his elbows on his knees, made a steeple out of his fingers and positioned it against his lips. Smoke from his own cigarette made him squint, but he watched Lukas closely.

At last Lukas said, "They changed the rules on us," and laughed bitterly. "Another flawed stone has turned up in the hands of one of our oldest and most respected customers."

"I see." Christophe flicked ash into a brass ashtray. "I wondered how long it would be before this happened." He sought Benno's eyes. "All the more reason to do what I had in mind. We must move quickly."

"You don't understand," Lukas snapped. He slid from the desk and walked to the door and back. He stopped in front of Christophe and spread his arms wide. "I told you they changed the rules on us. This stone didn't go through the usual channels. I bought it myself in Antwerp. It was sold before it arrived in Amsterdam. The buyer had specified his needs, and I merely had to find the right product."

Christophe narrowed his eyes. "What difference does...? Oh, I see. You mean this stone required no work here. Kohl's simply bought it on behalf of someone else and delivered it."

"Yes," Lukas said shortly.

Benno drummed his fingers on his knees. "Lukas, Christophe doesn't understand these things. The diamond was already essentially finished, yes, but it required some work before delivery, otherwise there would have been little need for us in the transaction—except for the buyer needing our access to trading circles in Antwerp. We were both go between and final finisher in this sale."

"Then I don't see what was different," Christophe said.

Lukas exhaled slowly. "Everything else was different," he said. "The stone was with us for a much shorter time than most. It wasn't cleaved here, or offered for sale here. It never entered the strong room after it was finished. Christophe—" He rubbed his eyes. "I bought the thing in Antwerp. I arranged for it to be shipped here. It arrived. When it arrived, it was the same stone I'd bought. I saw it wrapped for delivery *and I took it myself,* for God's sake. The pattern has been broken, and everything that has gone before means nothing in your investigations anymore." He turned to Benno. "Father, tell him what it has come to if we are to survive."

Benno rubbed his chest absently. "We have only one chance, Christophe. Cut our losses and try to rebuild."

"Benno—" Christophe begun.

The old man broke in quickly, "No. Let me finish. I know what you're going to say. Call in the authorities. No. In our business we take care of our own problems—when and as best we can. Then you will say you cannot help us because this will keep happening and St-Giles is not a charitable organization.

"I do not ask for charity. From now on, we will change our procedure. The buyer will be expected to pick up his purchases here. All we need is the capital to build back our stock."

Christophe stood and ground out his cigarette. He'd been right, dammit. The rotten little hunch he'd hoped would prove wrong was dancing into the light. "I hear everything you say," he said evenly. "And I get the picture. I still want to watch the way you've dealt with gems until now. It's getting late. Let's go."

Without waiting for replies—or arguments—he opened the office door and stood back until Lukas, Benno following slowly, led the way into the workroom.

For the next hour they traced and retraced the progress of a stone from workroom to delivery pouch. A gray tinge hovered around Benno's mouth when they finally climbed into the firm's small van and wound through the streets to the Kohls' house. There, Benno played the part of a jeweler's employee likely to accept the small package from Frank, whose place Lukas took. Christophe stood by in what would have been the guard's position. He no longer concentrated on the charade. *Damn, damn.* He *had* to be wrong. He *had* to have missed something.

"Well?" Lukas touched his arm, and Christophe jumped. This was the first voluntary contact Lukas had made with him since his return to Amsterdam. *"Well?"* Lukas repeated.

Christophe stared at him for a moment. "Yes," he said, rousing himself. "I think I've seen just about all I need to see. But I'd like to run through the stuff at the building one more time."

Lukas said in a steely voice, "My father can't take much more. This is killing him."

Christophe nodded faintly. "It'll soon be over."

Lukas's eyes held his a fraction too long for comfort before he waved Benno back into the van.

Another hour later, Lukas looked up from a glass-topped case in the strong room and removed his loupe from his eye. "What are we accomplishing here?" he asked wearily.

Benno sat behind the case, an array of diamonds displayed on their opened tissue packets in front of him. "Have you seen enough, Christophe?" He remained stoic, letting Christophe know he was prepared to keep this up as long as necessary if it would help Kohl's.

Christophe made up his mind, and a heaviness formed in his heart. "Yes, thank you. You would now pack away the stones not purchased, correct, Benno?" He waited for the affirmative flicker in Benno's eyes. "These—" he indicated several packets, already closed and stacked to one side "—would be sent by messenger to their new owner, when?"

"Immediately," Benno replied, beginning to slip the folded white sheets with their sparkling treasures inside back into small wooden file boxes. The boxes he put into a safe behind him.

"The stolen diamonds were always among the ones selected?" Christophe indicated the three packages still on the case.

"Of course." With evident asperity, Lukas pushed aside the velvet mat he'd been using under the stones and handed his father the three packets. "They were sold before they were switched, remember?"

"I remember," Christophe said levelly.

Benno finished locking the safe and they exited the two doors, parallel, which were the only way into and out of, the basement room. A space of approximately an inch separated the massive sheets of metal. Before closing the second door, Benno used a key to engage an alarm. Another alarm protected the outer door.

Christophe stood a while, looking at the fortification. *Foolproof?* he pondered—yes, absolutely foolproof.

PAULA PULLED HER FEET beneath her on the couch. Christophe had arrived half an hour earlier, and apart from giving her an absentminded greeting—in French—and accepting the drink she'd offered him, he'd been silent. He sat, or rather stretched, his head tilted back, his legs straight, at the other end of the couch. He balanced his untouched drink on one thigh and stared vacantly at the beams high above.

She plucked at a loose thread in her sweater, gathering courage to prompt him. After she'd arrived home from work, Peter had called and she'd told him everything was under control, that Christophe would make sure nothing else went wrong. Peter had sounded unsure. He'd warned her to be cautious. Dear Peter. Paula smiled to herself. She was grateful he worried about her, but she must follow her own instincts and they told her Christophe would take care of any problems.

Enough waiting, she told herself, reaching to rub his shoulder. The distance between them must be closed. From now on, whatever was to be faced would be faced by them—together. "Tell me about it," she said, still rubbing.

Christophe lifted his head and drank some Scotch before looking at her. Paula's heart constricted. In his eyes she saw pain.

"There's been another robbery," he said at last, and drank some more. "This time the thief used a different method."

"Another...?" Paula withdrew her hand and covered her mouth. "Oh, no."

He offered her the glass and she sipped. "It's all going to be such a bloody mess," he muttered.

"You won't be able to give them the money, will you?" Paula asked in a small voice. "Kohl's will be finished."

Christophe shrugged. "Possibly. A lot depends on... The next couple of days will decide everything."

Paula blinked back tears of frustration. "I wish I could help."

"You probably already have."

"I don't see how. What was different about this theft?"

"It doesn't concern you, Paula." Christophe sighed deeply.

"It does," she insisted. "And I want to know."

"The stone was sold before it arrived at Kohl's. Does that mean anything?"

"No—no, I guess not," Paula said slowly. "Wait! You mean it was bought for someone sight-unseen?"

He sat up and faced her. "Yes. Do you know anything about that kind of transaction?"

"Not really. Only I remember when we worked on a stone that had been bought in Antwerp expressly for a jeweler in Amsterdam."

Christophe moved closer. "Do you remember anything about it—the stone, I mean. That what's his name—Jacob—told me each diamond is different and finishers remember them."

Paula closed her eyes to concentrate. "Slightly more than eight carats, brilliant cut, minor natural—that's a tiny flaw—that Victor took care of. Flaws like that are often eliminated during cleavage, but some...."

Christophe shoved the glass into her hands. "I've got to go," he said, grabbing his coat on the way to the door. In the act of reaching for the handle, he turned back. "I...I care what happens to you. Wait for my call, please."

She felt the rush of the night air, smelled flowers in the courtyard. "Christophe, wait!" The door slammed, and she heard his running footsteps before Benno and Anna's basement door opened and closed.

"Wait," she said disgustedly. "Wait and trust, wait and trust."

The rest of the Scotch went down her throat before she realized she'd upended the glass. Paula coughed. The stuff burned.

At midnight she trailed to the loft, carrying the phone, its long cord snaking behind her. She lay down fully dressed. If Christophe needed her, Paula would be ready to go.

The city's bells tolled one in the morning, and she watched the lighted panel on her clock blink away the seconds.

When the phone did ring, her brain went into shock and she lifted the received in slow motion. "Yes," she whispered.

"How about a provisional date?" Christophe asked.

"What?" Paula struggled to sit up. "What did you say?"

"A provisional date for Wednesday night. If everything goes as I expect, I'll take you dancing for real this time, and we'll celebrate."

Paula's nerves jumped. His flat voice sent ice into her veins. "You've found out something else, Christophe," she said, breathing hard. "And you don't like it. Tell me what you know now. What are we going to celebrate?"

"If I find what I expect to find in the next couple of days, we'll celebrate the uncloaking of our thief. The only problem is—what will we all decide to do about it?"

Chapter Fourteen

Thursday of the Fourth Week:

"Thursday," Paula said. "Amsterdam never sleeps." Laughter spattered in bursts through the club Christophe had chosen for their date. Couples alternately slunk or gyrated around an eight-sided dance floor.

Christophe shifted his morose gaze from the champagne he swirled in his glass to his watch. "So it is," he remarked without interest. "Thursday for two hours now."

Paula slumped in her chair, mentally and physically exhausted. As Christophe had promised, they'd spent the evening dancing. That's all they'd done. Between numbers, executed by Christophe with as much enthusiasm he might have been expected to show had his partner been a blown-up dummy, they'd sat in a darkened alcove while she valiantly attempted conversation. Christophe had grunted, ordered more champagne from time to time, presumedly for their "celebration," and eyed her speculatively whenever he thought she wasn't watching him.

"Christophe," Paula begun hesitantly. She rocked her head from side to side, her eyes closed, gathering strength and courage. "Christophe, are you going to tell me *anything*?"

"How's the champagne?"

She shoved the glass aside. "I've had it. I don't know how the champagne is. I don't remember what I ate for dinner. I'm not even sure what kind of music is playing. All I know is you've been giving me the cold shoulder all night and I don't understand why. You invited me out, remember?"

"I'm sorry you've had a rotten time."

"Dammit all!" she exploded. "What is it with you? You're as uptight as hell. Just answer my one simple question, will you? What gives? Did you find out what you expected? *Do* you know who's behind the thefts from Kohl's?"

"Maybe." Christophe set down his own glass and stared at her yet again. His eyes had a penetrating quality Paula found magnetic and infuriating at the same time.

"Maybe?"

"Okay, yes. I know who stole those diamonds."

Paula wiped damp palms on her skirt and leaned closer to him. "Tell me."

"I'm not sure I'm ready." He took his time lighting one of his wretched cigarettes, drawing deeply, checking the tip.

"That's it, Christophe." Paula's head began to ache. "I can't take any more of this. You've been sending me mixed messages for days. I thought we'd decided to trust each other. So why don't you share what you found out?"

"Perhaps I'm still waiting for something—like the reason for the robberies."

This time Paula stared. "Money," she blurted. "Why else would someone steal priceless gems except for money?"

He shrugged. "Let's go back to your place. The noise here is getting to me."

They left the club and drove home to Herengracht in Christophe's Saab. He dogged her through the Kohls' basement and across the court-yard to her backhouse as if there were no question of his not going with her. Paula's tension grew second by second. He wasn't enjoying this any more than she, yet he trudged on like a man following a script he had to perform. What was in his mind, she agonized. What did he intend to do next?

"Don't you ever wish for privacy?" he asked when they were inside with the door closed.

Paula faced him, hands on hips. "I've got privacy," she said, confused. "This is my place. I pay rent for it."

"But you always have to come through Benno and Anna's house. That would drive me nuts."

"I seem to remember you telling me you stayed here for several weeks once. Did it drive you nuts then?" She hated the way she sounded. He was deliberately baiting her.

"We always used the gate from the alley. Lukas lived out here, too, and Peter when he didn't have another place and while the barge was in pieces."

"Benno prefers to keep the gate permanently locked for security reasons," Paula said. All she wanted at this moment was for Christophe to go away. "And I'm perfectly comfortable going in and out through their house. They don't keep tabs on me."

"No," Christophe remarked offhandedly. "Do you have any coffee?"

"I don't—" She bit off the blunt refusal forming in her head. Patience would be her ally now. "I'll brew some. Take off your jacket and relax. I don't like seeing you so uptight."

From the kitchenette, Paula watched him, helplessly fascinated by every move he made. He took off his jacket and rolled up his sleeves. Light reflected along the moving muscles in his powerful forearms. He loosened his tie and caught her eye. She looked away and clattered the coffeepot over the tiled counter, found a filter and some mugs.

"Where'd you get the roses?" he asked suddenly.

For an instant she couldn't think what he was talking about. Then she remembered and said, "Those—Peter sent them to me. He's a nice man." Since Christophe hadn't mentioned talking to Peter about her problems, she must assume he hadn't. Best continue to leave the timing of that to Peter—if there was going to be a time now.

Christophe gathered fallen pink petals. "Roses," he murmured. "Lovely and dangerous. Look, but don't touch or they may hurt you. Like some people."

Paula busied herself with the kettle. "Peter said something like that. You must think alike," she said and wondered what Christophe's comment really meant.

"Peter's always going to be special to me," Christophe said. "He seemed glad I was seeing you tonight. He stopped by today. If it wasn't for him, I'd think I didn't have a friend left in this city."

What about me? Paula longed to ask. "Lukas is bound to be cool— and the rest of his family," she said instead. "They'll get over it when they accept you only want what's best for them."

He was staring at her again. Paula closed her mouth firmly and finished making coffee.

When they sat side by side on the couch, she tried again. "Christophe, you said you'd let me know what you found out."

His striking face could be so hard, Paula thought. Christophe's fist, firmly placed beneath his chin, let her know he didn't intend to include her in anything he might have discovered. Awkwardness sent its sting across her skin before she saw something else in the way he had arranged his features. Hurt? Uncertainty? He glanced sideways at her, and she had to stop an impulse to reach for his hand. Had the corner of his mouth quivered—jerked almost imperceptibly?

The next idea to hit Paula brought tears to her eyes. She blinked them away and went to the kitchen for more coffee. Christophe was close to the end of this assignment. How could she have been such a fool? He would finish here, then leave, and he was nice enough not to want to hurt her. Her attraction to him was pretty obvious and not reciprocated. He was suffering the pangs of a kind man uncertain how to let a woman down gently.

Instantly Paula made up her mind what to do. "Boy, am I tired," she said, yawning and returning to sit on a chair opposite the couch rather then beside him. "It's after three." She slid back the sleeve of the loose sweater she'd put on over her dress and looked pointedly at her watch.

The clatter of Christophe's mug on the table startled her. She met his eyes and recoiled. So dark, they appeared black, all expression erased. "Christophe…" she began and paused to swallow. "Christophe…"

"You want me to leave, Paula? Is that what you're saying?"

Two days ago he'd said he cared what happened to her. They'd touched. She'd been sure some deep attachment had started growing between them. She even thought she…she'd thought love might be what they felt for each other.

"I guess so," Paula heard herself say. "Tomorrow's a workday." Emptiness threatened to bring the tears she could not allow in front of this man.

"You're sure?"

Paula bowed her head. Christophe was a mystery. What did *he* want? For her to invite him to sleep with her? She felt blood rush to her cheeks. He'd have let her know if that's what he wanted. "I'm sure," she murmured without raising her face.

His jacket rustled as he put it on. When she smelled his after-shave, she knew he stood only inches from her.

"Good night, Paula," he said quietly.

Now she looked at him. She *did* love him. She could tell him and let him decide with to do about it. Paula opened her mouth, then averted her face. "Good night," she echoed. Christophe was too mature to laugh at her declaration, but neither of them deserved the discomfort it would bring.

His kisses were swift, finding the corner of her mouth, moving over her cheek to the dip beneath her ear, lingering gently against her neck. He held her briefly, tightly, and when he let go, she stumbled slightly, and he grasped her elbow. "I'm sorry," he said, meeting her eyes one last time before he strode outside.

"I'm sorry." "I'm the one who's sorry," Paula said aloud. That final glance had been easy to read. He regretted he couldn't be more, feel more for her. Whatever he'd wanted in a woman, she didn't fill the bill. He'd decided to work his way through the rest of this assignment alone and retreat. No doubt the future of Kohl's would be settled in a few days, and either she'd have a job or she wouldn't. She could probably find another position easily now, but she cared desperately what happened to Benno and Lukas—and all the people who'd become a part of her life.

For a long time she stood inside the door, her arms crossed. She cared about Christophe and always would.

Ignoring the dirty coffee cups, she climbed to the loft and pulled off her sweater. Christophe St-Giles came from a different world. Someone of ordinary means with aspirations to be a craftswoman for the rest of her life was unlikely to do more than arouse mild interest in him. Wealth and power were his past, present and future. He'd been alone with her tonight and hadn't even attempted to make love. She touched her neck. If she'd responded to him when he held her he'd have stayed. He couldn't offer her anything more than this night, but she could have chosen to take it rather than nothing.

Someone knocked the door sharply. Paula held her breath. Christophe. He'd come back. She ran her hands over her hair, deciding. If she let him in, he was bound to stay the night. Then would she be able to let him go in the morning and not break apart?

She couldn't leave him standing there. Paula ran downstairs, turning on the living room light as she reached the bottom.

A square of paper, one corner still underneath, lay close to the door. She picked it up and opened the door at the same time. The night was still. Paula stepped outside, searching the short path to the main house. The courtyard was empty. He'd come with his note and left rapidly, not wanting to face her again.

Misery overwhelmed her. Whatever happened, this episode must be forgotten, and in future she'd be more wary. Paula unfolded the paper, expecting to see his apology repeated. "If you want to help me save Benno, come to Brouwersgracht. Now. The barge at Palm Straat bridge. For Sale sign."

Christophe needed her. All the silence, the waiting and watching throughout the evening had been because he was trying to decide whether to ask for help. Now something awful had happened—she couldn't guess what—and he'd run back with the note. He'd given her the choice. She could go to him and share whatever risks he faced, or stay safely where she was.

Paula rushed upstairs for her sweater and headed to the street.

She knew the route. Lukas and Sandi lived on Brouwersgracht. Palm Straat was some blocks northwest of their house. Paula ran, grateful for her low-heeled shoes. Dawn couldn't be far away, but the moonless night still closed in around her like a black, oppressive bowl. Shapes of parked cars loomed, and trees. A cat spat as Paula sped into its path. She felt no fear. Christophe would be waiting.

On Brouwersgracht, the distance between the canal and houses was narrower than on Herengracht. Brouwersgracht, home to many young professionals, had once been lined with warehouses. Now the rickety structures were transformed into apartments and the occasional single house. The buildings seemed to shift slightly, blacker than the black sky, their roofs murky outlines. Paula felt safer close to the canal. Barges creaked and scraped at their moorings, and she smelled oil on the sucking water, and tar, and, subtly, the scent of air cooled and cleaned by night.

Yards short of the intersection with Palm Straat, Paula slowed and began checking each barge she passed. She peered closely at swaying vessels, searching for a sign. Christophe had meant a For Sale sign would be visible. Boat after boat, closed curtains at the windows of raised deckhousing failed to display the message she needed. Her heart began a slow, hard thump. Ahead the curved railings of a bridge crossed the canal at Palm Straat. Paula hurried on and saw the sign. An old barge, its bow obscured beneath the bridge, sported a luminous white board on a frame atop the long cabin. The lettering she needed to see stood out boldly.

Cautiously she stepped along the edge of the street until she located a warped board sloping to the vessel's deck. For the first time since he had read the note, Paula hesitated. No light showed in the cabin's old-fashioned round portholes. Where was Christophe? She took in her surroundings. No other houseboats were moored nearby. The closest buildings felt derelict.

At her first step on to the plank, boards gave. Paula jumped swiftly to the deck. A door, closed by a bar dropped into a hook on each side, led to the cabin. Christophe had to be here. She couldn't have arrived first.

A flicker caught her eye, and she stared hard at the closest porthole. The glass was an obsidian mirror. Then she saw it again, a rising glow that quickly faded. Candlelight. Christophe was already inside. Thank God he'd asked her to come. The bar on the door must have slid back into place without his knowing. He'd have been trapped.

Paula struggled to raise the heavy bar and hook it aside with a length of chain. Apart from this hardware, the rest of the barge appeared about to disintegrate.

The door opened outward and Paula's throat instantly seized. A sickening stench came from the cabin. She put a hand over her nose and mouth and held the doorjamb with the other. "Christophe?" she whispered, edging inside. "Christophe, are you here?"

Only a faint sloshing noise greeted her. The candlelight came from a nub waxed to an old saucer and placed on a low shelf near the door. Paula took two more steps inside and stopped, horrified. Her feet and ankles were submerged in water. "Hello," she said more loudly, then pressed the hand tighter over her mouth.

The eddying wash around her feet felt thick. Paula took the candle and looked down. She made herself breathe through her mouth. Sludge, littered with rotting garbage, slithered back and forth almost to her calves.

Paula turned back to the door, lured by the open air and meager light the street offered. Why hadn't she brought a flashlight?

As if her thought were heard, a blinding beam hit her squarely in the face. Paula dropped the candle, vaguely heard it hiss and die while she held parted fingers in front of her eyes. "Turn it off," she said. "Move the thing."

Abruptly the beam swung upward, painting the cabin an eerie, shifting gunmetal and yellow, and showing Christophe's solid body framed in the doorway. He walked toward her.

Paula smiled at him, held out her hands. Relief hit her like a warm cushion.

Christophe didn't smile. "You had me fooled," he said.

Paula dropped her hands slowly.

"It was my own fault," he said. "I believed what I wanted to believe. There was never any absolute proof you weren't involved." He motioned her across the narrow cabin.

"Stop it," she cried, backing away. "Stop it. You're frightening me." She caught a heel and fetid water wetted the hem of her skirt.

"Christophe!" Paula screamed as her elbow struck the opposite bulkhead.

He waded toward her, oblivious to the wash soaking his pant legs. "I believed your whole act. And what I found out on Monday night seemed to back it up. Or it didn't disprove it, anyway. I had everything worked out and you weren't a part of it. But I was wrong, wasn't I?"

Paula couldn't speak.

"Where is it?" Christophe said. "Give it to me."

When Paula uttered a word it came out as a croak, "What...?" She tried again. "What are you talking about?"

"Surprised, huh? Didn't you think your friends might double-cross you. You should have. They already threatened you, didn't they? You were supposed to put me off, persuade me to leave town, but you failed." He was very close now. "One big black mark against you. Then you were warned to leave Amsterdam yourself and you didn't. Another black mark. Why didn't you go? Too greedy? You had to force one more theft, didn't you? And you came here to make the drop. Only your partners set you up."

Tears clogged her throat, but her eyes were strained wide open and dry. "Who set me up—how?"

"I was warned."

"How?"

"I had a call before I left to pick you up last night. The gentleman didn't identify himself. He said you'd leave for an appointment as soon as I was out of the way and he told me you'd come here. He also said I'd understand what he meant by an *appointment*. I watched to see if you'd leave your place once I'd gone. Paula, I hoped you wouldn't, but you did and I followed. No wonder you could hardly wait to get rid of me."

"No." Paula looked him directly in the eyes. "You're wrong, Christophe."

He placed a hand each side of her shoulders. "You asked me to leave. You couldn't wait for me to go."

She flinched. "You're mad. After the way you treated me all evening, I'd had it. I thought you couldn't stand being with me, so I put you out of your misery." Damn her shaking legs. She *would not* let him see how scared she was. "And after you'd been gone a while I got this— see?" Her fingers closed on the note in her pocket. She withdrew it and flapped the paper at Christophe.

He waved her hand aside. "Forget it." His voice was barely above a whisper. "No more stalling tactics, Paula. Neither of us is leaving until I get what you intended to deliver here."

"I don't—Christophe!"

A muffled boom shook the boards beneath their feet. With a sickening roll, the barge listed to starboard and the door smashed shut.

Christophe spun away, then fell against her. "My God!" he yelled. "This thing's going to sink! We've got to get out of here!"

Paula knew what the next sound was before its dull clang faded.

"The bar," she groaned. "The bar's dropped over the door. We *can't* get out."

Chapter Fifteen

Water swirled around his thighs. "Son of a bitch," Christophe swore. "He found out what I knew and did this to me."

"Christophe!" Paula was clinging to his jacket. His body trapped her against the bulkhead.

He swore again, silently this time, and staggered away. "Keep calm," he ordered when he leaned beside her—feeling anything but calm. "I think that was an explosion in the bilges, and if it was, we could go down fast."

Paula grabbed his hand. "Look," she said, nodding to her right. "The water's coming in here."

He leaned around her, slid the flashlight beam along the side until he saw a swell forcing masses of bubbles immediately below the surface. "That's what I was afraid of," he said, fighting down panic. "The bastard knew what he was doing. He made sure this tub was well vented, then blew the bottom out. No chance of any air pockets slowing down the process with a good hole in the hull up here."

"The other side," Paula gasped. "We have to make it out of this slime. Come on, but be careful. It's slippery."

He glanced at her face. Her skin gleamed white, but her expression was determined. Whatever she might be guilty of, she had guts. "Yes," he agreed. "Keep holding my hand and forget everything but a handhold over there."

They waded up the sloping deck. The barge listed slowly, but not slowly enough. Christophe shone his beam ahead and clasped Paula's hand tighter. Second by second the port side of the vessel rose. At almost the same speed, the water gushed through the half-submerged starboard gash.

"Hold— Oh, no!" Paula shouted. Muscles in his arm stiffened against her weight as she fell to her knees, slithering, until her skirt ballooned on the wallowing surface.

Christophe felt his own feet slide. "It's okay," he said. "We'll make it." He bent his knees, finding better purchase, and hauled Paula out of the sucking murk.

The flashlight picked out a hook on the port bulkhead. He struggled on to grab it with two fingers, half expecting the thing to break loose. The hook held. "We're there, Paula," he said and thought, *where, where are we? We can't get out.*

"My God," she whispered. "This is hell. Look at the water. It's coming in so fast. We can't have long to make it out of this thing."

Her control gave him courage. "At least we're not tipping much now. This thing's sliding toward the middle of the canal."

"Sure," she said quietly. "Probably the way it was planned. Deeper water out there."

He looked at her, his stomach tightening. She was a bright lady. "Keep an arm around my waist," he said. "I'm going to work my way to the door just in case the bar missed."

The door was only feet away. Within seconds, he turned to Paula and shook his head. They were locked in.

"The portholes," she said and immediately grimaced. No man, or woman, could get through those small apertures.

He edged back to the hook, guiding Paula with him. "You'd think a good punch would make a hole in this worm-eaten stuff." The wood he touched flaked beneath his fingers.

She was quiet, staring at him. Slowly her lips parted. "Hit it with the flashlight. Make a hole and we'll rip out enough boards."

"It would take too long," Christophe replied. Regardless of what she might have done, he wished he could save her from this. He rubbed her arm and tried to calculate how much time they had left.

"Give me the flashlight," Paula demanded, and he handed it over without comment.

The light swept back and forth through the interior. "There's got to be something," she muttered. "Something we could use—Christophe—" Her voice rose. "Keep a tight grip on me."

He did as she asked while she stretched and groped. "Got it!" she exclaimed, holding a container above her head while she struggled beside him once more. "Where's your lighter."

"Lighter?"

"To blow this up with."

"Blow what up, Paula? Explain." The boat lurched and his heart matched the motion.

"Damn," she muttered. "We need something to tie this to the port-hole. My dress is wet. This sweater would only melt or something."

"Paula, what are you trying—"

"We're going to blow the port out with this aerosol can. Then we should be able to make a big enough space to crawl through. Quick. Help me."

For an instant he didn't understand. When her thought became clear, he whistled. "Smart woman." He yanked off his jacket, transferring his wallet to a back pocket. One fear-powered tug tore his shirt-sleeve from the shoulder. Thank God it was cotton, not silk, he thought. "Give me the can." He knotted the fabric swiftly about the cylinder and tied the bundle to the porthole bolts.

"The lighter, the lighter," Paula begged. "Quickly. The water's coming in faster."

The flame of his lighter caught brightly at the cotton, then smoldered and died. Christophe cursed and tried again. "Come on, come on," he muttered through clenched teeth. This was their last—their only—chance.

"It's not going to work," Paula moaned. "There won't be enough heat to set it off."

He'd almost forgotten the gun. "Dammit," he said. "I *must* be mad. Get behind me. Move back carefully and cover your head." Carrying a weapon wasn't his habit. The last-minute decision to keep one in the Saab, and to bring it with him to the barge tonight, could save their lives. "Cover up!" he ordered.

The small gun he pulled from his pocket felt foreign. Christophe braced an elbow on the bulkhead, steadied his right wrist on his left forearm and took aim. He ducked his head as he squeezed the trigger.

The bullet missed.

His own expletive shocked him. He gritted his teeth. "Keep your head down," he ordered. And the second shot found its mark. A sharp crack sounded and a brief red glow penetrated his closed eyelids. Slivers of glass pricked his arms and he smelled the acrid scent of burned powder.

"You did it. Oh, thank God," Paula cried. She clawed past him and started pounding and pulling.

The port rim had blown out with the glass. Christophe threw himself at the jagged hole, dragging at boards that ripped away in strips. Frenzy fueled their strength. The gap grew, widened, and he stopped Paula's frantic tearing.

"Out!" he yelled. The barge shifted abruptly. They were both cling-ing to the opening, their legs submerged. "Hold my belt and I'll go first, then pull you."

He made it to sit on the hull with Paula, clutching his thighs now, still dangling into the cabin. More of the barge than he expected still showed above the canal, but it would soon disappear.

Paula let go of him with one hand and fumbled at her waist.

"What's the matter?" he yelled. "Come on!" He leaned to grasp her beneath the arms.

"No," she gasped, looking up. "Not until you read this. It'll be gone by the time we're all the way in that water."

"Come on, Paula. Not now."

She clung to the side, refusing to budge. "You've still got the flash-light. Read it." Something white showed between her fingers and the boat's dark wood.

"You're going to kill us both." He wound his legs around her body and took the paper she offered. The flashlight must be tossed when they swam.

"Read it," she implored.

Blood thundered in his ears, but he did as she asked and immediately threw the flashlight away to drag her bodily into his arms.

She muttered, "Christophe," as he balanced on the camber of the hull, holding her against him. They hit the water flat and he kept one arm around her, pulling hard with the other, terrified the suction of the sinking barge would drag them down.

Lagging pressure tugged from below, but he fought against it, made headway, first slowly, than with increasing speed. "I can swim by my-self," he heard Paula gasp. He ignored her. She stroked with her free arm and kicked hard, helping their progress.

Christophe's hand scraped the slime-coated wall of the canal and he bobbed up, paddling, his breath raking past his throat. "We made it, Paula."

A shudder convulsed her body. He couldn't see her face clearly. "Yes." Her voice was barely audible.

With Paula beside him, Christophe swam along the wall, searching for a way up. He found a trailing rope, probably one of the barge's snapped mooring lines, hanging limply from a post above. "Don't let go of this," he told Paula and shinnied up the wall. Lying flat, he stretched down until he could hold her wrists and help her climb. She scrambled to the street, bumping a knee or elbow with every move.

Paula stood a little apart from him, watching the glimmering hull roll gently. Dawn's gray had begun its stealthy creeping into the sky. In the pale light he saw the droop of Paula's shoulders, the way her skirt clung in sodden folds about her legs. She swayed slightly and he reached to pull her against him.

"You don't believe me, do you?" she said. Her shivers coursed into him. She was crying.

"Yes," he said. "I do believe you. We were both set up. And if we'd died out there, it would have been my fault."

"I don't see why," Paula murmured, trembling violently now. Tentatively she pushed her hands under his arms and gradually tightened her grip until she dug her nails into his back. Her gentle crying became wrenching sobs, and he knew she'd used up all of a very big reserve of courage.

"It's going." With one finger, he turned her chin toward the canal. The last inches of the old hull slipped from sight. Ripples arched outward, huge bubbles flew to the surface, then nothing. The surface closed silkily over their robbed tomb as if it had never existed.

Paula pressed her face into his soaked shirt. "It *was* deliberate, wasn't it?"

"Deliberate and clever," Christophe replied. "You have to know what you're doing to sink something on cue like that. He vented the hull, then placed his bomb or dynamite, or whatever he used, in the right spot to make sure the barge would go down in the direction he wanted. Like you said—into the deeper water in the middle where it wouldn't be found for a long, long time. Only we got out."

"Why did you say it was your fault—or would have been your fault if we'd drowned?" Her fingers found his mouth. She stroked it slowly while she looked into his eyes.

The ache in his limbs had nothing to do with cold or fear. Some reactions were beyond control. "Because I should have trusted my instincts...about what I'd found out and needed to do about it, at once...and about you. My heart told me you were innocent and I knew as much in my head, only I've always got to be so damned sure. I never know when to give in and be human. I wait and see, and this time my waiting nearly killed us both." Concentration was tough. Exhaustion battled with his desire. Christophe knew exhaustion would have to be allowed to win.

"Why *did* you wait?"

He'd tell her everything in the next few hours, he thought, everything.

Including the reason for his hesitation. "We'll talk," he said. "I'll explain what I know—and I don't know. The next couple of days won't be easy. We're going to need each other."

An ocher cast behind the warehouses promised sun. He must get her home and go back to his own place.

"Christophe," Paula said. "Why did they try to murder us?"

"I think, because of what I *don't* know yet," he said, pushing back her streaming hair. "And that's what scares the hell out of me."

Chapter Sixteen

Seven hours later, Paula entered the Kohls' basement. In one hand she carried the small, severed head of a tulip. The front doorbell rang while she climbed to the main level of the house.

She heard Benno say, "Come in," and knew she would see Christophe enter the hall.

"Paula?" Benno turned at the sound of her shoes on the marble. "Are you ill, my dear?"

He would wonder why she wasn't at work, she realized. She looked past Benno to Christophe. His dark eyes stared back and he smiled, a small, strained smile intended to reassure her. "Paula isn't ill, Benno," he said. "Just tired. But we'll talk about that."

Benno lifted his palms, shaking his head. "Is Paula to be with us also this afternoon? What can you have to say to us all, Christophe?"

Christophe offered a hand to Paula and waited until she took it. "Is everyone here?" He sounded weary and Paula wished they could leave, now, be somewhere together and be quiet.

"They're here, Christophe," Benno said, indicating the living room. "Although I can't imagine what you hope to accomplish."

He fell silent and Paula began to feel sick. No sound came from the big room. The others must be sitting there, thinking, worrying. She shoved her fist into her pocket and kept it there, mashing the tulip petals.

"Let's get this over with." Christophe stood back for Benno to pass and moved his hand to Paula's waist.

She took in the still tableau awaiting them: Lukas standing, hands behind his back, before the brass-encrusted fireplace, Sandi sitting very upright at one end of the damask couch. Anna leaned forward slightly in a small chair, her fingers curled around its carved arms. Paula yearned to tell the older woman everything would be all right. But she couldn't. Nothing would ever be the same for any of them.

"Christophe's here," Benno announced superfluously and with false heartiness. He slapped Christophe's shoulder and frowned at Paula as if he hadn't remembered she was there. "And Paula," he added faintly before going to the rosewood trolly with its array of silver and crystal. "Paula's going to be with us, too. What would each of you like to drink?"

Paula looked up at Christophe. "Is this the only way?" she implored. "Please, are you sure we should do this?"

He rubbed her nape absently. "You know the answer to your questions, Paula. I don't think we'll be wanting any drinks, Benno. Sit down, please."

"I expect magic tricks next, Christophe," Lukas said cynically while his father sat down near Anna. "I didn't know you had such a flair for the dramatic, and much as I like a good show, I do have work to do. Could we get on with whatever you have in mind?"

"Lukas," Anna said in a small, reproachful voice. "Don't insult our guest. Christophe wouldn't ask us all here if he didn't have something important to say." Dark blotches beneath her eyes accentuated her colorless cheeks.

Sandi hadn't spoken and Paula noticed the way she clenched and unclenched her laced fingers in her lap.

"We should get to the point quickly," Christophe said. He made no attempt to move from the middle of the room, and his hand remained at Paula's neck. "When I finish, I hope someone will help me fill in what I've missed. You will, won't you, Lukas?"

Paula's heart began to palpitate uncomfortably. She looked not at Lukas but at Benno. In the past few weeks she'd watched him grow markedly older. He had to be strong now.

"Lukas—" Christophe went on when the younger man failed to reply. "I didn't want this to happen. I still don't. Perhaps it will all turn out to be a mistake, but I don't think so. Do you remember that first interview we had in your father's office?"

"Which one?"

"I think you know which one, friend. The one when you said the facts would make it appear you were stealing from yourself." Christophe's fingers tightened on the back of Paula's neck.

Lukas shrugged and lit a cigarette.

"That was clever of you," Christophe continued. "At the time it was enough to push me in the direction you wanted—away from Lukas Kohl. But you weren't kidding, were you? You were the one who stole those stones. Who else could possibly have done it?"

"Christophe!" Benno broke in. "What are you saying? How dare you?" He half rose, then collapsed into his chair, his face ashen.

"Why not make this easier," Christophe suggested. "Explain how it happened, Lukas. All of it."

Paula put an arm around his waist and prayed. If only Lukas *would* explain it all, including the mysterious missing element that could still creep up to finish them.

Lukas drew leisurely on his cigarette, eyeing Christophe narrowly. "You have all the answers, Christophe. I wouldn't dream of upstaging you."

He sensed there was something Christophe still groped for, Paula thought desperately. Lukas intended to hold out as long as possible, to play for time and a break.

"As you prefer." Christophe bowed slightly. "Sit, Paula. We may be here longer than I expected."

Automatically she sat on the rug beside his legs, loath to be out of his reach.

"*You* switched the stones, Lukas," Christophe said. "Exactly as you suggested. I thought it was so days ago. After our little run-through on Monday I was sure. There was no other way. Each theft went the same. You were in the strong room with the customer. You waited until he selected a stone you'd had copied and while he examined another one, you made the switch from your pocket with the packets set to one side on the counter. I remember saying the act was a sleight of hand—a magic trick—something that happened in a second. That's the way it was, correct?"

Lukas's cigarette burned down between his fingers. Ash dropped to the rug, but he didn't appear to notice.

Christophe shifted his weight. "The little ploy with the so-called change in system—the stone stolen a few days ago—didn't fool me. Again you insisted you must be the most obvious suspect because you'd dealt with the transaction. And this time you said you delivered the thing yourself. That threw me for a few seconds because it didn't tie in with your effort to implicate Frank Lammaker. I hoped for a while I'd been wrong about everything."

"My God," Lukas breathed. "You *are* wrong. You have no proof of anything. You're bluffing and trying to climb out of a hole by pinning something on me. What are you afraid of? Going back to Switzerland a failure?"

"I'm not planning to go back to Switzerland," Christophe said. "But that's not the point here."

Paula's stomach contracted. Did he mean he was staying in Holland?

"I don't have to pin anything on you, Lukas," Christophe continued. "You've done the job for me. You and Sandi." He directed the last comment to the silent woman on the couch.

"Leave her out of this!" Lukas shouted, his composure visibly shattering. "She has no part in it."

"Christophe," Anna broke in. "Do we have to go on? Just tell us what's happened and we'll try to forget it."

Benno patted her hand. "Hush, my love. Don't get upset."

"I thought that last stone would be unloaded quickly," Christophe said. "On Monday night, late, I started watching for you to get rid of it, Lukas. At first I was afraid I might be too late—that it was already gone. I followed you all Tuesday and waited near your house in the evening. When Sandi left around ten, I followed. I saw her put a packet between the pages of a telephone directory in a booth in Dam Square. What I didn't allow for was the group of people who poured off a bus between you and me, Sandi. When they'd gone, so had you and so had the package. I never saw who picked it up. But you'll tell me, I'm sure."

"Sandi," Lukas said, crossing to sit beside his wife. "He knows nothing. He's fishing in the dark, darling. We should leave."

"You will not leave, my son." For an instant, Benno's sharp command froze the room's occupants. "What's begun must now be finished. Go on, Christophe."

Christophe took Lukas's place by the fireplace. "For a while Frank Lammaker seemed to be our man."

"No," Anna cried.

"No," Christophe agreed. "Frank is clean. He's quite a special young man. He wants to write—did you know that?"

Anna shook her head, brushing tears from her cheeks.

"He does," Christophe went on. "And he wants to be a part of the art scene in Amsterdam. Not so hard to understand in one his age. He really has outgrown the stunts he pulled as a kid. His clothes and entertainment are what he spends his extra money on. He augments his salary from Kohl's by working as a night janitor in a department store. His employee discount there also helps buy his clothes. He and his mother live simply. Much of what he earns pays for private tutoring to bring his academics up to scratch."

"And his attachment to Willem Bill?" Lukas rejoined. "What of that? Our people have never mixed with Metter's employees."

"What of his *attachment*, Lukas?" Christophe crossed his arms. "Convenient for you, but it means nothing as far as Kohl's troubles go. Willem also writes—and goes to classes after work. They led me to another suspect—Kersten Gouda." He laughed hollowly. "That possibility had me excited for a while. Willem and Frank went to Kersten's apartment regularly, and I thought I had a neat little conspiracy worked out."

Lukas pushed an arm through Sandi's. "You're quite the sleuth, Christophe," he said.

Christophe pinched the bridge of his nose. "A lot of things about Kersten puzzled me. Her standard of living, the wardrobe she wore to and from work."

"Oh," Paula stared at him, remembering. "I wondered about that, too."

"Means nothing," Christophe said. "It's Kersten who tutors Frank and Willem, and a lot of others, in her home. She's proud and doesn't want anyone to know the way she makes additional money, or why. Her fault is pride, if that's such a fault—nothing more and certainly not vicious. Not a crime that could bring the world down around the heads of people who have loved her since she was born." He eyed Lukas significantly.

"What does all this have to do with us?" Lukas said. He'd slumped against the couch back. Paula didn't remember the lines around his eyes and mouth being so deep, or the silvery glint at his temples.

"I gave you a chance to save us all this, Lukas," Christophe said, pacing to lean against the door. "You insisted I tell the sordid little tale, so hear me out. Kersten's husband left her years ago. That shamed her and she missed him—still does in a way. She even continues to hope he'll come back. And in the meantime, she buys pretty clothes and takes exotic vacations to snatch back a little of the romance she had for so short a time. And she pays for these pleasures with what she earns, honestly, at Kohl's and through tutoring many young men and women in her spare time."

"Fascinating," Lukas said sarcastically. "Everyone loves a martyr."

"Lukas, be quiet." Sandi's voice, its brittle cadence, electrified the atmosphere.

"So you see," Christophe continued, pointedly ignoring Sandi, "I'd run through the most convenient suspects and Paula became more and more the candidate of choice—as Lukas intended she should, if I didn't bite on Frank. Frank was to appear the obvious first choice, since the stones were substituted after sale and he was responsible for delivery. Without Frank, I had to look again at Paula and wonder if she was truly like her father. Was she both a thief as he was supposed to have been, and bent on avenging him? Someone copied those gems, and I tried to figure out if she was capable of that yet.

"You didn't waste any time telling me about her father, Lukas. But I still can't believe the man you once were, the man I knew, would deliberately endanger an innocent woman's life to steal from his own family. And where is the money, Lukas? *Where* is it? I have the necessary resources to find out if you've made any big deposits. There are no records of any."

Benno raised his hand, silently demanding recognition. "Michael Renfrew wasn't a criminal," he said. "I always knew that."

"So did I," Anna whispered. "He was our friend. We were sure he was framed, then frightened away to make him seem guilty."

"Just the way they tried to frighten me," Paula said slowly. She looked at Lukas, appealed to him with her eyes. "Was I supposed to go away like my father so you could say I must have been guilty of those thefts? You planted that note near me on Queen's Day to make Christophe suspicious. Then you had me paged. Lukas, you sent that man after me. He—"

Sandi left the couch swiftly and came to stand over Paula. "Lukas had nothing to do with that," she said. "*I* slipped the note when we fell. I knew we'd meet Christophe because Peter told me. Peter wanted us all to be friends again, so he told Christophe where to find us. And I arranged the telephone call when I went to the bathroom on the way into the hotel. It was also to please me that Lukas told Christophe about your father. It seemed like a good smoke screen."

"I should never had told Lukas what happened to Michael," Benno said quietly.

Sandi didn't seem to hear. "Those threats to you were nothing Lukas or I could do anything about," she said. "They—"

"We'll come back to that," Christophe interrupted. "As soon as I knew enough about diamond finishing to be certain Paula couldn't have made those copies, I stopped considering her, although—" he glanced at Paula, his expression softening "—you people didn't give up trying to convince me. But at that point, I knew she couldn't reproduce the missing gems. Victor, on the other hand—"

"Okay, okay. You know how we did it." Lukas was on his feet. "We'll sort our our own problems from here on. We want you out of our business."

"I don't know how you did it," Benno interjected softly. "Go on, please, Christophe."

"Father—"

"Quiet," Benno snapped, and Lukas retreated to stare out the window.

"Benno," Christophe said. "There's something I don't know yet, something I hope Lukas will explain. I'm sure he didn't intend to hurt anyone. He hoped to get through this mess before needing to implicate anyone. You went along with the idea of keeping the thefts to yourselves and applied for a loan from us. I'm sure neither of you expected that loan to be questioned, and if we hadn't, perhaps Lukas's plan would have worked. Unfortunately we didn't think all was well with you, and we were right. My concern now is that we get at the final truth—the *why* in all this. Until we find that out, I believe there's still danger somewhere in this situation."

A rustle preceded Benno's passage to the drinks cart where he poured a hefty brandy. "What were you going to say about Victor?" he asked.

"Paula led me to the answer," Christophe replied. "Each entry in the log where the inventory is kept is initialed by the finisher. I was excited about that until I discovered the thirteen missing stones had been worked on by different people—according to the book. Then Paula remembered that last stone, the presale, and told me Victor had dealt with it. Jacob's initials, not Victor's, were entered for the job. When I compared the other entries closely, I decided the initials were probably forged in several places. Victor worked on all those stones."

"You can't know that for sure," Lukas murmured dispiritedly.

"He admits it," Christophe retorted. "I confronted him. All I had to do was tell him I knew his history and start praying. It worked. He spilled everything. How he was part of the theft Michael Renfrew was supposed to have committed. You suspected he was and blackmailed him into making the copies. The only payment he got for doing what you wanted was your silence.

"It was Victor who told Michael the police were on to him and he'd better get out of the country even if he was innocent. *You* led Victor to believe Paula was here to find out the truth about her father. That added to Victor's stress and led to the efforts to make her go home. Victor's old fellow-apprentice, Leo Erkel, was an accomplice in the original theft and he felt equally threatened by Lukas's blackmail. Erkel helped Victor get the inferior gems to make the duplicates with. Thanks to you, Lukas, Erkel set out to get rid of Paula any way he could. By the way, Paula, Erkel borrowed Willem's car that morning you were hurt.''

"Stop!" Sandi breathed heavily. "Lukas had nothing to do with the threats to Paula. Neither did I. It was all that man Erkel's idea. I found out afterward…'' She hesitated. "We heard from…from Victor…about the car and the thing with the knife in the alley and how Paula was locked in the elevator—''

"What elevator?" Lukas asked, turning around.

Sandi stared at him, her lips parted. "I probably forgot to tell you. They locked you in the elevator at Kohl's didn't they, Paula?'' She knelt, her fingers working together once more. "I'm sorry, Paula. We never expected them to try to hurt you.''

Exhaustion overwhelmed Paula, and intense sadness. "I remember his eyes now," she said, tracing patterns on the Oriental rug. "At De Pilsener Club he watched me, and I felt strange. I saw his eyes before, through a ski mask.''

"And I knew him when he came out of the club," Christophe added. He moved without Paula hearing him and gently helped her up. "He followed the night we went on the canal cruise after having dinner here. He had a knife then, too, and expected to use it.

"Victor made sure I knew you'd been at the club with Frank and the people from Metter's. What he didn't expect was to run into Leo Erkel outside and have the man's name linked to his. That must have killed him. As soon as I heard it, I remembered the personnel records from all those years ago when your father and Victor and Leo worked for Benno's father.''

"I want to leave," Paula said.

Christophe put an arm around her shoulders. "We aren't finished here.''

"It's up to them now." She looked from Lukas to Sandi, who still sat on the floor. "They must decide what happens next.''

"The way they tried to decide last night? We were supposed to be dead now, Paula, don't forget that.''

"Dead? What do you mean, *dead*?" Anna rose and walked around to grasp the back of her chair. "Tell me what you mean.''

Paula rested her cheek against Christophe's shoulder. "I don't want to do this," she murmured.

"I can't believe you would try to kill us, Lukas, but there doesn't seem to be any other explanation.'' Christophe put Paula gently from him. "Wasn't it you who tried to drown us on a barge in Brouwersgracht last night?''

Benno's glass bounced when it hit the rug.

"Oh, my God," Lukas said. "What are you saying?" He helped his father to the couch.

"Brouwersgracht?" Sandi said incredulously. "Isn't that where you're buying a barge, Christophe?"

Paula swung toward Christophe and caught his blank expression. "I'm not buying a barge. A house. Not a barge and not on Brouwersgracht," he said distractedly.

"You never mentioned buying a house here," Paula murmured.

"Someone tried to kill you," Benno said quietly, almost to himself. His eyes were unfocused. "I don't understand."

Christophe went to the old man's side. "Last night someone tricked Paula and me aboard an old barge on Brouwersgracht. We were trapped inside and the thing was deliberately sunk. Thanks to Paula's quick thinking, we didn't go down with it." His words came rapidly. He was trying to soften this for Benno, Paula thought, feeling afresh her love for Christophe St-Giles.

"But you think my son did this?" The veined hand Benno held up trembled.

Christophe took the man's fingers between his own hands. "I *don't* think that. But I believe whoever did could tell us why Lukas stole what would eventually be his when I know he's never wanted for anything."

"You speak as if I weren't here," Lukas said. "We will attend to our own problems. Everything will work out—you'll see. We'll start with the pear-shaped—"

"Don't!" Sandi interrupted harshly. "Don't let this man bully you into anything. Make him go away."

"Allow me this," Benno said, removing his hand from Christophe's. "I know there may be charges to be brought for what this man Erkel did. Victor I will deal with. But please, allow me time with my son to find out why he did such a terrible thing to us—and to decide what the future must hold. We'll make everything right with you, I promise."

"I'm not worried about that," Christophe said softly. "Take the time you need, Benno. I pray to God we can save Kohl's."

Paula and Christophe didn't speak until they were in his Saab. "You didn't want to go back to your place, did you?" Christophe asked. "I need you with me."

"I couldn't be anywhere without you today, Christophe. I don't want to think about what's happened."

"We can't wait long to sort out what it is Lukas isn't telling us. But I think we need time to catch our breath first."

They drove in silence for several minutes.

Christophe maneuvered the car through streets teeming with late-afternoon traffic to another canal and turned south. "They let my secret out," he said finally. "I did something impulsive, which is not supposed to be my style."

Paula immediately knew what he meant. "Buying a house? Surprising, but not so out of character." She rolled down the window and closed her eyes against the strong breeze. "Perhaps you're more impulsive than you like to admit. Some people would have said you were out of character when you did as Benno asked and left them alone. *I* know you would never have done anything else."

"Thank you for that." He touched her cheek and she turned her head toward him. Christophe glanced at her mouth, then concentrated on the road. "Buying a house after seeing it once is different, though, don't you think? Would you like to see it?"

"I'd love to." And, Paula thought, she'd love to know why he'd bought it, and if he intended to live there permanently. Some questions couldn't be asked because the asking gave away too much.

"Do you like this canal?" Christophe asked, parking close to the water. "This area?"

"Prinsengracht? It's lovely."

She got out while he was switching off the engine. All the narrow adjoining buildings were seventeenth century, but each was unique.

"Okay," Christophe said with a sigh. "This is it."

"The sandstone one?"

"Yes."

The hesitancy in his voice caught her attention. "What's wrong? You sound funny. It's a beautiful house. Must have cost a for—" She clapped a hand over her mouth and felt herself blush.

Christophe laughed. "A fortune, yes. It did. But if I'm going to open a branch here for St-Giles, I have to live somewhere and if a barge didn't seem quite right before, after last night I *know* it's out of the question."

Her heart did strange things. "You're going to live and work here?"

"Yes," he said easily and guided her up a flight of worn steps. "The decorators have already started work, but I don't feel too secure about what they're doing. Someone Peter recommended is arranging everything, but...well, I want you to tell me what you think. There's still some beautiful old furniture in the place. It's in bad shape but I think it should be refinished. I'll show you the living room first." He let them in and shut the door. "The place was divided into apartments before it came up for sale. There's a lot to be done, but..." His face flushed slightly. "Tell me what you think of the color in here."

Double doors led into a long room. Exposed oak beams, old and slightly crooked, spanned the width of a high ceiling. A few shrouded pieces of furniture stood in a central clump: a table, two straight-backed chairs and a desk. The wooden floors were bare. A ladder, paint supplies and tools littered the space by a far wall.

Paula managed not to gasp when she looked at a partly painted area.

"You don't like the color," Christophe said flatly.

Paula glanced from his disappointed face back to the peacock-blue walls. "It's fine." She hated to hurt him.

"It's not fine." He frowned. "You hate it. *I* hate it." He threw his windbreaker on the covered table. "I should have waited for your opinion before they started."

"The house is wonderful," she hedged, moving to the window. "You'll be able to look out on one of your beloved canals whenever you feel like it." And he would be here, in the same city as Paula, indefinitely. Her heart soared.

"I wanted you to like it."

"What?" She stared at him blankly.

"The—my house." His tone exuded dejection, and she quelled the urge to run and hold him.

"I do like it, Christophe," she said hastily. "I already said so. It's marvelous."

He grimaced, forming deep grooves in his cheeks. "All of it?"

"Oh, you!" Paula stuck her right forefinger into a painter's tray. "This is a lovely color, one of my favorites. It's too dark in a small space, that's all." She dabbed playfully at the end of his nose, leaving a smear. "So what? If you don't like it, either, have it redone with something pale. White, even. To make the room feel larger."

"I knew it." He paced, hands behind his back. "When the decorator suggested this I almost said I wanted your opinion. But I didn't have the right, did I?"

"I'd have been glad to help." Was he simply overreacting, or suffering from the same intense sensual awareness as she? "Why does it matter what I think?'' She knew what she wanted him to say—and that he'd know she was fishing.

Christophe stopped in front of Paula. He rubbed at his nose, then studied his paint-stained fingers. Apparently deeply absorbed, he made a careful line from the point of her chin, down to the low V at the neck of her blouse, between her breasts. ''Now we match,'' he said.

Paula tried to hide a shudder. ''You didn't say why you care if I like this room—the house.'' His rapt attention on her mouth made it hard to think. ''The paint looks silly. On your nose, I mean. Here, let me wipe it off.'' She wetted a decorator's rag with water from a jar containing a lonely lilac bloom.

Christophe stood patiently still during her ministrations. Finally he caught his bottom lip with his teeth and Paula realized his eyes were closed. She paused to watch his quiet face and felt his hands come to rest on her shoulders, lightly, yet burning her flesh.

He turned his head abruptly, clasped her hand and kissed the palm. ''Finished?'' he asked. His stillness had been plainly forced, a supreme effort.

''Christophe,'' Paula whispered, touching his sharp jaw, feeling the slight roughness of his beard. ''We aren't finished. I think we just began.'' She trailed the backs of her fingers down his neck.

''Meaning?'' His voice was equally soft. He wouldn't push, yet they both knew he'd planned this time alone. ''Paula,'' he persisted when she didn't immediately respond. ''What are you telling me? What do you...we want?''

She turned away, walked slowly to the lone table, then faced him, edging backward until she sat, feet swinging. ''You want to make love to me, Christophe—and I want it. We've waited long enough—far too long.''

''Ah, *chérie*, my lady. Always direct. You destroy any control I have—and I'm glad. I can't see anything but you anymore and I don't want to. But...'' He made a sweeping gesture. ''Not here.''

''Aren't you going to do something about this?'' She lowered her head and undid the top button of her blouse to reveal the faint trail of paint between the shaded cleavage. ''Fair exchange—do you know that saying?'' Her smile was softly questioning and deliberately provocative.

Christophe stared at her, light from the bowed window casting a burnished glow about his windblown hair. With evident preoccupation, he began to take off his shirt. ''Fair exchange—yes. I think I remember that.'' The shirt was pulled free of his pants, slid from broad shoulders, until his torso was naked—beautifully, muscularly naked, dark hair spreading wide across his tanned chest and narrowing to a slender line at his navel before it disappeared beneath his belt. He dipped a shirttail in the same water Paula had used.

Paula couldn't breathe. He was so incredibly sexy, so dear—familiar, yet mysterious—intoxicating.

"Come close to me, Christophe." The little, distant voice didn't sound like her own. "Touch me."

He came, trailing the shirt. At her knees he stopped, resting fingertips lightly beneath the hem of her skirt. He slid his palms upward over smooth skin until he grasped both thighs. "As you say, sweet, I want to make love to you." He leaned to place a fleeting kiss at the corner of her mouth. "But I want to sleep with you afterward—to feel you in my arms when I wake up and then make love to you all over again. I want...." He faltered, then seemed startled to remember the shirt he still held. In a single sweep, he wiped her tingling skin, stopping at the shadowy dip beneath her blouse. He rested two tentative fingers on the spot, then replaced them with his lips.

As he raised his head, Paula kissed him, holding his face between her hands and leaning urgently against him. He opened her mouth wide with his and Paula moaned.

At the involuntary parting of her knees, he moved nearer to her body and she slid her fingers down to his tensed ribs, smoothed the hard muscle at his sides, reached to surround his waist. His subtle, clean scent made her throat constrict.

"Paula," he muttered, "Paula." His swift, hard little kisses covered her face, nuzzled her jaw high to make way for his lips to explore her neck.

His hands tangled in the hair at her temples. The sudden moisture of his tongue on her ear sent a thrill into her coiled nerves, brought aching heat to her breasts.

He shifted slightly. For a moment, he continued to kiss her while he unfastened her blouse, then he raised his head to watch his own hands at work, the gradual parting of the silk as far as her waist. Paula saw him swallow convulsively when he dropped the garment behind her on the table, never taking his eyes from the peach satin camisole, held in place only by tiny rolled straps and a wide band of lace clinging to the top of her breasts.

She didn't move. Every cell in her body gave him her unmistakable message and he must have felt it, known it.

"Paula." His voice broke. "I'm only a man. I don't think I can stop this now."

"We aren't going to stop." She shook her hair back, tilting her chin and lifting her breasts. Wanton? Perhaps, but it couldn't be wrong—not with Christophe, not feeling as she did with him.

His teeth, carefully closing on first one, then the other nipple, through dampened satin, were an erotic stimulant. Paula heard a small noise from her own throat—the answering intake of Christophe's breath. The camisole straps slid away. Each throbbing breast was surrounded and lifted in his warm hands. He pushed together fractionally, trailing his tongue over soft flesh, before his mouth opened wider. Paula buried her fingers in his hair, pressing him close.

After a moment, Christophe stood, his breathing labored, chords raised in his strong throat. He pulled the camisole over her head. "Lady," he said. "I can't think straight anymore."

She spread her hands wide on his chest. "I don't want to think at all," she said in a husky voice she didn't recognize. His skin was heated. Slowly, holding back, savoring each moment, each sensation, she massaged him, punctuated every touch with a tiny kiss until his grip on her shoulders hurt.

Her nails fumbled at his belt. Christophe's features darkened. She dropped her lashes, cupped his straining zipper, closed her eyes at the immediate stricture in her belly. He was aroused beyond endurance.

"Wait, Paula." His words were barely audible. "Wait a minute, my love."

Love. Her mind was already darkening as he moved away. He lifted first one, then her other foot, letting her sandals fall to the floor before he knelt. So slowly that Paula had to make fists to stop herself reaching for him, Christophe kissed a trail from one instep to her knee, then inched up her skirt until he found her groin.

"Please..." She couldn't finish the thought. "Please—no. No—" And the fire he breathed into her center cut off anything else she might have said.

Paula's elbows locked, her weight supported on the table with the heels of her hand, while Christophe undid her waistband. He slipped the linen beneath her, taking skimpy satin bikinis with it, before he gazed up at her once more. "You're beautiful," he said hoarsely. "Perfect. Beautiful breasts." He covered them, making small circles over her nipples with his palms. "Smooth skin." The caresses moved across her shoulders, down her spine to her ribs, waist, the flare of her hips.

He put both hands behind her bottom while he pressed his mouth into her navel, and below—down, until she cried out. But she'd never remember her words. Her mind became a white-hot blur, joined to every seared nerve ending by a voluptuous chord of ecstasy.

When her brain cleared and she gripped his biceps, urging him to his feet, Christophe stood over Paula instantly, and she saw the jagged rise and fall of his chest. Her kisses covered every unclothed inch of him until she sucked at taut flesh over his belly and eased low, beneath the waist of his pants. She undid the belt, and the zipper, but he stilled her hands and swiftly removed the rest of his clothes.

Paula gazed into his dark eyes for one endless moment of total understanding, before clamping her legs around his waist, unleashed desire making her strong.

"Sweet, sweet lady." He entered her with a single thrust, jarring a moan from her throat.

His thighs were iron on the backs of her calves, his need fiery steel within her. Their passion mounted, became one, faster—reaching. Nerves, open and raw, surged along the path to Paula's womb. She gritted her teeth and could only hold on, riding the tide of sensation.

With their climax, Christophe lifted Paula, wrapped her tightly against his final, explosive drive. A force burst deep inside her, and she clenched her jaw to stifle a cry.

She felt him sway slightly, grab the edge of the table. The rustle of their clothing, tossed to the floor, came a second before he knelt, still holding her close. Gently he unwrapped her legs from his waist without breaking contact and lay down, stretching Paula on top of him and nestling her face into her neck.

"You are... I want you to marry me," he said. "Don't say anything until you think, *chérie.*"

The pulse in Christophe's throat beat fiercely and Paula pressed her lips against its rapid rhythm. Moisture she tasted there was salty—her own hot tears? "I don't have to think, darling. Can you be happy with someone like me?" She squeezed her eyelids together. Falling in love with this man had been inevitable. A minuscule shred of caution made her rest her mouth on his sweat-slick shoulder and wait for his answer.

"Like you, Paula? I couldn't be happy with anyone *but* you. That's why I persuaded my family we must open a branch here—where you can carry on your apprenticeship. That's why I bought this house—for you. When we got here I felt like a fool knowing you might not...you might not..." His teeth came together.

"I want to marry you," she said simply. "Thank you."

He held the back of her head, and his laugh rumbled against her face. "How like you to say it that way. Rest, my love. For a little while. The closest thing I have to a bed is a futon upstairs. But I'll need more energy that I have now to get us there."

Paula arched away from him, resting her elbows on his chest. "We can wait...a little while." She reveled in being joined with him.

He stroked her back, made long sweeps from her neck to her bottom and pulled her down on his chest again. "A very little while," he murmured against her ear, and she felt his renewed quickening within her. "I love you, Paula."

Chapter Seventeen

Paula stirred when a current of cool air slithered beneath the bedroom door and across the futon. She pulled the down quilt over their naked bodies and snuggled back against Christophe. He muttered in his sleep and wrapped an arm tightly around her.

She should be able to sleep, too, Paula thought. She should be too blissfully exhausted to do anything but drowse in this wonderful man's embrace.

Her eyes refused to close.

Beyond the high window, the sky had darkened and a few stars spar kled like distant pinpricks in a black velvet cradle. This night was peace and security, a magical dream time. Why couldn't she turn off her brain?

Sandi. Paula wriggled until she sat up. "Sandi!" she exclaimed. "Christophe, wake up. I know what it is. I know!"

She was out of bed, scrambling into her clothes, before Christophe reacted. He switched on a lamp standing on the bare floor beside the futon. "What are you doing, Paula?" he asked, rubbing both hands over his face. "It isn't morning, sweet, come back to bed."

"Get up," she urged. "We have to go to Lukas's and Sandi's. Sandi knew, Christophe. Please hurry."

"Sandi knew what?" Christophe asked, slowly pushing aside the quilt. He got to his feet and stood with his arms crossed, shivering

Paula grabbed his clothes and tossed them to him. "She knew about me being locked in the elevator at Kohl's and Lukas didn't. He'd obviously heard about the other things that man did to me—why not the elevator? And someone told her you were buying a barge on Brou wersgracht. Who would do that and why? I think Sandi's got our miss. ing link. She was told that about the barge to lay the groundwork for what would be said after we were found dead." Paula shivered now "You'd have been showing me the barge you intended to buy when we accidentally got locked in The hole in the side would have been slowly letting in water and sinking the thing for days, and by the time they pulled us out, any other damage to the barge would be put down to the beating it took under water."

"Okay, okay." Christophe's eyes were finally wide open. He hopped from foot to foot, pulling on his pants. "That all sounds logical—except I don't see why she didn't tell Lukas about the elevator. You didn't tell me, by the way." His shirt buttoned, he shoved the tails into his pants before buckling his belt.

"At first I was afraid to tell you. I wasn't sure what you believed about me. Then so much happened, I forgot."

"Why do we have to rush to Lukas and Sandi's right now?" Christophe had put on his socks and shoes and began raking his fingers through his hair. A day's growth of beard shaded his jaw.

Paula found a comb in her purse. "You missed it. So did I until a few minutes ago." She combed her hair rapidly "Lukas started to say something about a pear-shaped diamond. He was going to tell us they still had it, but Sandi stopped him. She intends to get rid of that stone and quickly I feel it in my bones. It'll be tonight We have to stop her and make her tell us the truth '

"My God," Christophe said. "There was a pear-shape among the stolen diamonds. It was the most valuable stone. I thought that presale must be all they had, but they held out on the big one. I hope we're not too late "

The clock in the Saab read eleven-thirty when Christophe parked in front of Lukas and Sandi's house. Paula, Christophe close at her heels, leaped out and ran to buzz the intercom. Instantly, without inquiry through the speaker, the door swung open.

Paula clutched Christophe's sleeve. "They always ask who's here," she whispered.

"Maybe—" Christophe stopped. Light from the hall flooded a pale yellow pool over the steps, and Lukas stood in the doorway, his hair wild, a faint sheen of sweat coating his tense face.

"Are you all right, man?" Christophe grasped Lukas's shoulders and backed him inside. "You look ill."

Paula followed, closing the door behind her. Lukas only stared, his gray eyes oddly hollow.

"Lukas." Christophe shook him. "Say something. Where's Sandi?"

"Gone," Lukas muttered and twisted away. He stumbled into his apartment and dropped onto a leather ottoman "She's gone out " Paula saw him rally felt his struggle to regroup

"Where did she go?" Christophe glanced at Paula and she nodded encouragement. "Lukas," he continued. "We *have* to know where Sandi is."

"I don't know. Give me time. Let me think."

The room's angular contemporary furnishings seemed cold to Paula. While she watched Lukas wrestle with his own turmoil, the expensively converted apartment with its ivory walls, its careful arrangement of leather and chrome pieces, took on a brittle quality. The man on the ottoman seemed to shrink and his sterile surroundings to expand.

"There is no more time," Christophe said quietly. "There was another diamond, wasn't there? The pear-shape. And she's taken it to someone."

Misery contorted Lukas's features. "He called. She knew he would. She had to go. It was for her brother, not for her, not for us. Sandi wanted to get her brother back."

"Sandi's been giving the diamonds to her brother?" Christophe said slowly, his expression blank.

"No, no." Lukas jumped to his feet He shook his head, beating closed fists together. "This other man—the one we don't know—picks up the stones. He contacted us and said he could get Hans back if we gave him enough diamonds."

"Wait," Christophe said. "Tell us everything, but calm down. We have to work together, my friend. Start at the beginning. Hans is Sandi's brother, yes?"

"Hans, yes—Sandi's older brother." Lukas took two cigarettes from a silver box. Distractedly he gave one to Christophe and pulled a lighter from his pocket. "She had two brothers. The three of them were in foster homes while they grew up. She never speaks of her parents. The oldest brother left care as soon as he could and went his own way. Sandi doesn't know what happened to him. She and Hans were very close. When he was old enough he made a home for them here in Amsterdam. He worked his way through college and ended up teaching physics in some Berlin university."

"Sit down, Lukas," Paula said, touching his arm lightly "We'll all sit—"

"We can't waste time," Christophe interrupted. He drew deeply on his cigarette.

Paula stared hard at him. "Lukas is worn out. Can't you see that? This will go faster if we don't panic "

"Right, as usual." Christophe inclined his head to her, smiling faintly. "Go on, Lukas."

They all sat. Paula's heart beat rapidly. Her own sense of urgency clawed at her nerves, but she knew rushing Lukas would achieve nothing.

"Six years ago, Hans disappeared. He'd been involved in some underground work, helping people escape from East to West Berlin. The night it happened, he was driving a vehicle into the East. His objective was to create a diversion while two men got out. He never returned. Sandi waited in Berlin, alone, for almost a year. She made inquiries among Hans's friends. They were as much in the dark as she was. Eventually she had to give up and come back here. She'd been a model in a small way, and by then she needed money badly. She...she's lovely..." He covered his face and Paula heard the faint choking noise he made. She looked at Christophe. He'd involuntarily reached a hand toward Lukas. He closed his fingers and returned them to his lap.

"She is lovely," Paula said softly. "And she became very successful. What happened next, Lukas?"

He kept a flattened hand against his brow, shielding his eyes. "She started to live again—emotionally, I mean. We met and married and were very happy—we are happy, or could be. Then this man contacted her, always by phone or note. He said Hans was alive and being kept prisoner by the Soviets. He told her about a network of people who, much like Hans had done, were finding ways to get people out. But their operation was expensive, he said, and some—like us—could afford to help more than others. He wanted diamonds because they're easily transported and highly negotiable. We were helping to pay for those who could not pay and eventually Hans would be returned."

"Only he never has been, and the demands for diamonds have gone on." Christophe bowed his head. "This was extortion, Lukas. I don't know if Sandi's brother is alive or not, but whoever's been doing this had no intention of returning him as long as he kept making you pay. Now I understand where the money is—nowhere I'm likely to find it. Why didn't you tell me? I would have helped. We could have avoided coming to this."

"Sandi was afraid," Lukas said. "She wouldn't hear of risking the chance to get Hans back. She became almost possessed. When you showed up she came close to breaking. We'd already stopped collecting stones, but she was afraid we might need more and knew we probably couldn't get any while you were all over us."

"Why did she believe this man's claims?"

Lukas got shakily to his feet. "Because he knew all the facts. He repeated every detail about Hans on that last night, including the names of some others involved. I believed him, too—then."

"You don't now?" Paula said.

"I don't know what to believe anymore. Sandi's taken that stone and gone to meet him. She thinks the value of the diamond, and her revelation that there can be no more, will convince the man to bring Hans to her. She even hopes it will be tonight. My God, Christophe, she wouldn't let me go with her, and I'm scared to death."

Christophe rose and hugged Lukas quickly. "So would I be if it was Paula."

Lukas didn't notice the comment but Paula glowed. They had to sort out Lukas and Sandi's terrible trouble, then it would be time to get on with their own future—together.

"Now." Christophe clamped a hand on Lukas's shoulder as if to transmit his own strength into his friend's sagging body. "She took the diamond where?"

"I don't know." Lukas's voice cracked.

"Oh, hell...wait..." Christophe said, stubbing out his cigarette. "She thought Hans might be brought to her this evening. Was a place for making the transfer of her brother ever discussed?"

Lukas squeezed his eyes shut. "The Blue Angel—the new World Trade Center."

Paula started for the door. "We can try it. How long ago did Sandi leave?"

"Just before you arrived." A limp shrug raised Lukas's stooped shoulders. "I thought you might be her—that she'd changed her mind about going." Desperation darkened his eyes. "Would he kill her, Christophe? I couldn't live without—"

Christophe took Lukas's arm and shoved him ahead. "She's not going to die. Let's get there and hope it's the right place. I'd roust Peter for reinforcements, but we can't afford the delay. It'll take us half an hour to make it. I'll drive—you direct."

The powerful little car sped south through Amsterdam's central district until buildings became sparser and more industrial in appearance. At Lukas's instruction, Christophe turned onto Beethoven Straat, and minutes later the glass towers of the Trade Center loomed against the sky. Blue by day, its mirrored panels were black at night, festooned with glittering reflections of nearby lights.

"Leave the car in the loading dock," Lukas said. He opened the door before the Saab had completely stopped.

A guard slouched at a revolving door. Christophe threaded a hand through Paula's elbow and sauntered past. "Evening," he said pleasantly. "We want to see the city from my office. Multicorp—fifth floor."

The guard grunted, straightened a fraction, then resumed his original position. Paula felt Lukas at her shoulder and prayed he would do nothing to give them away. "Multicorp?" she muttered to Christophe once they were inside.

"Why not?" He gave a short laugh. "Every building should have one."

Their footsteps echoed through the huge, office-lined lobby. Paula smelled lilacs, too sweet, too heavy, as she passed an alcove. Christophe pulled the three of them to a stop and silence seemed to swell and suffocate.

"She's not here," Lukas said loudly.

"Please, Lukas," Christophe said gently. "She could be anywhere. Be patient."

"There she is." Paula urged Christophe to a railing where they looked down into a lower level scattered with round tables and wrought-iron chairs. "There," Paula whispered, pointing to a table half-hidden by a potted tree.

"Oh, thank God." Lukas ran past them to a still escalator and started down. "Sandi!" he called.

"Damn," Christophe said, dashing for the steps. "The fool couldn't wait."

Sandi had jerked around and looked up. By the time Lukas, then Christophe, leaped from the bottom of the escalator, she was wrenching open a door beside a closed coffee bar. She glanced over her shoulder once before slamming the door. Christophe and Lukas followed, bumping each other in their haste.

Sharp clattering of heels, echoing shouts ricocheting along concrete walls met Paula when she wrestled the heavy door open. Dim lights illuminated an underground garage. She saw one running figure—Lukas—then Christophe heading in the opposite direction. They called Sandi's name repeatedly and darted from pillar to pillar. Only two cars were in sight.

Paula edged along the wall, her palms flattened behind her. Carefully she watched for any move, any glimpse of the magenta sweater Sandi wore. At a corner, Paula peered around and drew back. There was no sign of Sandi. "Christophe!" she shouted, "Lukas! Check the cars!"

She heard a door open, saw the bright flash of Sandi's sweater and swore under her breath. Why had she shouted instead of going quietly to each car herself?

Sandi headed back into the building. Her long hair had come loose and flapped about her shoulders.

Paula was first through the door after Sandi. Inside she stopped, breathing heavily. Christophe and Lukas skidded to a halt beside her. "I can't see her," she gasped. "She must... Oh, no, look. Up there."

Two figures faced each other at the top of the escalator. Sandi's auburn hair glimmered as she pushed it back. The tall man facing her gestured, leaning close, then grabbed and shook her. Lukas and Christophe ran, but Paula was quicker. She took the steps of the other paralyzed escalator two at a time and reached the top in time to see Sandi being shoved through the revolving door. Paula opened her mouth but no sound came. The man wore a ski mask. They should have had Leo Erkel arrested.

"Where's the hell's the guard?" Christophe yelled, heading for the exit. They almost fell over the man's body on the top step.

Paula had started to bend over him when he moaned and sat up, rubbing his head. She rushed on, scouring the darkness, trying to listen for noises other than the ones she made. She heard Christophe ask the guard if he was all right and tell the man to call the police.

"Wait, Paula," he called. "Stay here." Christophe caught up with her and gripped her arm.

A scream sounded, somewhere to her left.

"Sandi," Lukas groaned, breaking into a run but in the wrong direction.

The distant rumble of a train grew slightly, blurring Paula's concentration, before it faded.

Christophe's fingers dug into her elbow. He looked in every direction, his face tense and watchful. "You go back to the building," he said.

Another scream severed the silence. Paula jumped and spun away from Christophe. "Split up!" she yelled, wrenching free. "I'll take the left."

"Paula, no!"

She ignored the plea in Christophe's voice and ran out of the forecourt to a sidewalk. Across a wide street she saw light bouncing off a glass-enclosed bus stop and headed for it. When she was almost there, scuffling, to the right now, stopped her and she advanced more slowly. All that mattered was saving Sandi from that creep. When he'd followed Paula he still hoped to save himself. That would have been enough to stop him from killing her. Tonight was different. Tonight he knew they'd found out about him. He would do whatever was necessary to escape with the diamond.

Paula wanted to call out. Instead she pressed her lips together and tried to make no noise. She crept forward, crouching low, past the bus stop, away from the street—away from help. Sandi mustn't panic. Between them, they could do something as long as they kept their heads.

She didn't notice the drop-off until she fell, slipping and banging, several feet down a bank.

"Stay where you are," a man's voice hissed. "Don't move or you'll both die."

From the ground, Paula stared up at the man and clapped a hand over her own mouth to stifle a scream. His left arm and hand were clamped around Sandi. In his right hand he held a gun pointed at Sandi's temple.

"What do you want us to do?" Paula heard her own small voice. It was steady but seemed far away.

"Over there. Move."

He waved the gun, and in that instant, Paula lunged with both feet, smashing into his ankles.

"You bitch!"

He stumbled back a step, flailing and losing his hold on Sandi.

"Sandi, run!" Paula yelled and flung herself at the man's legs. Bone cracked. She yanked harder and he cursed as he fell, Paula's arms still wrapped around his knees.

Something sharp came down repeatedly on her shoulder and Paula ducked her head, praying for help. He was hitting her with the gun. How long before he pulled the trigger?

His next words were Dutch. He wrestled Paula to her back and worked to capture both her hands on one of his. The gun's dark barrel glistened.

He was going to shoot her.

Paula writhed violently. The gun was slowly lowered to her eye level.

"No, no." Sandi's moan surprised them both. Paula had thought the other woman gone. The man above her started and lost his grip on her wrists.

"Get off me," Paula cried and kneed him in the crotch. Grunting, he doubled up on top of her and Paula grabbed for the gun.

The single shot, close to her ear, echoed on and on. She smelled acrid powder, felt the body above her jerk, then slump over her, heavy and flaccid.

Paula closed her eyes and turned her head away. Something moist and warm splattered her neck. Blood. She was going to be sick.

"Sandi, Sandi." Lukas's voice murmured close by.

Paula felt consciousness slip before the weight rolled away from her and strong arms gathered her up. "Where are you hurt, Paula?" Christophe whispered against her lips. "Say something, *chérie*. You're bleeding."

She shook her head, gulping air, her mind clearing. "Not my blood," she croaked. "His."

Christophe helped her up but kept an arm around her. "Lukas," he said. "We'd better take a look at this bastard. The police should find us pretty quickly but he needs help now."

"He's dead," Paula announced flatly. She'd killed a man.

"Not necessarily," Christophe said, dropping to his knees. "But maybe we'd all be better off if he was."

Lukas joined Christophe and Paula knelt on the other side of the man. "I killed him," she said. Sweat had turned cold on her skin.

"Stop it," Christophe barked abruptly. "The gun's in his hand."

"I made him fire it," she commented dully. "I shot him."

Christophe sighed, reaching beneath the ski mask to feel for a pulse in the man's neck. "Wrong. He shot himself. He would have killed you if he could. And he's still alive."

"Thank God." Tears sprang into Paula's eyes.

Sandi sank down beside Paula and took her hand. "He was going to shoot us both, Paula. He said so. This is all my fault."

A siren wailed closer and closer, and whirling light revolved above them. Men's voices calling to one another jarred Paula as much as the slamming of vehicle doors.

"He needs air," Christophe said, carefully peeling off the mask.

A policemen arrived, his flashlight homing in on the man's face.

Bright frothy blood oozed from the corners of the wide mouth. Blue eyes found Paula's and he tried to smile. Immediately a cough racked him and he lifted his clenched left fist to his lips.

Paula caught Sandi as she fell sideways.

"Do you know this man?" The policeman asked. Other uniformed men scrambled down.

"Yes," Christophe said and buried both hands in his hair.

Lukas found a kleenex and dabbed ineffectually at the man's blood. "This is Peter Van Wersch," he said and began to cry.

Friday of the Fourth Week:

"There's nothing we can do," the doctor said. Tired eyes, too old for his years, swept over each of them. "He wants to see you all. It won't be easy."

Peter lay on a bed in a small observation room, tubes and wires linking him to a battery of monitors above his head. His skin blended with white sheets and walls. Only his eyes, flickering open as Paula and the others entered, showed a trace of lingering life.

"Hello, Peter," Christophe said, going directly to his side. "This is tough, old friend."

A nurse sat watching the monitors. "He must be quiet," she said without turning. "Perhaps you can persuade him to open his left hand. We'd like to clean it."

The dead must be clean, Paula thought bitterly. She stayed a little apart from the others.

Lukas and Sandi stood at the bottom of the bed. "May we have some time alone?" Lukas asked.

The nurse began to protest until she caught the expression in Lukas's eyes and nodded, understanding, silently admitting what she'd been taught never to admit: a hundred nurses, watching a hundred monitors, couldn't save Peter Van Wersch's life. She slipped from the room.

Peter motioned to Lukas and, when he moved close, slowly opened his left hand. In the palm, smeared red with his blood, lay the huge pear-shaped diamond. "Take it," he whispered. "The rest are in my apartment—the freezer—ice cubes. I didn't want them." He coughed, and a trace of blood appeared.

"Don't talk." Lukas wiped the blood away. "You need to save your strength."

"I'm going to die," Peter said and tried to smile.

Sandi held his hand. "Why, Peter? I thought you were our friend. That's why I confided everything to you after Paula told us what had happened to her. You used the information I gave you, just like you used the story I told you about Hans. I never guessed, but you were the only one Lukas and I ever told and you used it against us."

"You had everything." Peter looked at Lukas. "You and Christophe. Golden boys who had it all. Christophe left. If he'd stayed away, we might not be here. But for him it was the same—everything he wanted, he got. But he didn't matter, Lukas. It was you who mattered."

Paula glanced around the stricken faces circling the bed. Peter had raised his hand to Lukas who slowly took the diamond.

"You told me about the man trapping Paula in the alley with the knife." Sandi's voice cracked and she cleared her throat. "We loved you, Peter, but you pulled our strings as if we were your puppets. Because of you, the way you suggested that man's threats to Paula might not be so bad for Kohl's if they made her leave Amsterdam, I trapped her in the elevator to try to make sure she was frightened away. Then I didn't dare tell Lukas. I wanted her to leave and take the suspicion with her like her father had." She began to cry. "It was me telling you about Christophe walking through a gem sale that made you try to kill him and Paula, wasn't it? You said Christophe was trying to buy a barge on Brouwersgracht so I'd help out with the appropriate excuse for them being there when they were discovered. I did all this. It's my fault."

Paula's hand closed around the remnants of the tulip in her pocket. She pulled them out and stared, her vision blurring. "I figured someone had used the old door from the alley to slip me the note yesterday morning. Christophe had mentioned Lukas and Peter lived in the backhouse once, and that they came and went by that door. One of my pots of tulips is in front of it now. Yesterday afternoon I noticed it was pushed away and the tulips smashed. I thought Lukas must still have a key and that he'd left the note, but it was you, Peter. You used your old key to get in and leave the note. You tried to kill us. Why? You could just have stopped what you were doing before it was too late."

"I only wanted him to stay my friend," Peter whispered, indicating Lukas. "I started this to show him his wife didn't care as much for him as I did, that she'd put him, and his family, in jeopardy for her brother's sake. But he still preferred her. She'd betrayed him for a man who's probably dead, but he still wanted her most. I gave him his chances. Why didn't you come to me, Lukas, like you would have done before? You never confided in me. I would have stopped if you had. I wanted you to give her up and be my friend again. But it was only her. You forgot me."

Lukas bowed his head. "I never forgot you, Peter. I trusted you."

"I tried to kill them for us," Peter said, his voice growing fainter. "If...if they had died, it would have been only you and me... Don't you understand yet? Lukas, I love you. I've always loved you." His eyes closed, and a steady buzzing came from one of the monitors. Paula looked up and felt the others do the same. The lead on the cardiogram monitor had gone flat. Peter's lips parted and a breath slipped softly out.

"He's dead," Paula said.

A doctor and two nurses arrived simultaneously, one pushing a cart. The doctor was already reaching for paddles.

In the waiting area, Lukas turned to the others. "They never give up—even when it's all over." He ran a hand over his face and bolted from the building.

Christophe hesitated before following him.

"I called Benno just after we got here," Sandi said without inflection. "I didn't know we'd be getting the diamonds back. He'll be relieved, though I can't expect him to forgive me."

"He will," Paula consoled, peering through the glass doors Lukas and Christophe had used. "So will Anna. They love you."

"Erkel's skipped Holland," Sandi said. "Philip Metter contacted Benno about it." She laughed mirthlessly. "Something good may come out of this, after all. Kohl's and Metter's could be on speaking terms again."

Paula blinked rapidly, feeling the other woman's misery. "I'm sorry about your brother, Sandi. You must have adored him."

"I did. But we all have to learn to let go. I almost had and I will again, as long as I still have Lukas."

"You do, and you always will," Paula reassured. "I think it's time we went home."

"Paula," Sandi said, looking away. "Peter used you. He used me, too, but that was different. He had a reason to punish me. He meant what he said about being in love with Lukas, and I should have guessed that somehow."

"Sandi," Paula began, "please—"

"No. I have to get this out. The things Leo Erkel did to you, then what I did, only helped Peter. They were an unexpected bonus to his plan to get back at Lukas for not being... I hate this... Peter must have longed for Lukas to become his lover and when he married me the love turned to hate."

Paula reached for Sandi's hand. "You couldn't know all this would happen. You were only trying to get Hans back, and no one will blame you for that."

"I blame myself for being selfish. Can you forgive what I've done? I'm not sure I could."

"I can forgive, Sandi. And I know Christophe will, too. Please, let's get out of here."

Outside the swinging doors, Paula and Sandi stopped, silently reaching for each other's hands.

Lukas, crying quietly, rested his face on Christophe's shoulder. Christophe held him. As the doors swished shut he glanced up. Tears glistened in his eyes.

"WILL LUKAS AND SANDI BE OKAY?" Paula asked Christophe.

He stood behind her at the edge of the canal. "I think so," he said. "I pray so."

A tourist barge slid past, cutting the water's surface, leaving a fanning V of ripples in its wake.

Paula turned toward Christophe and stood on tiptoe to kiss his jaw. He immediately found her mouth with his own. Seconds later he raised his head. "We both need sleep," he said. "Our futon awaits."

They had spent the morning with the Kohls, and going to Prinsengracht and the sandstone house had seemed natural afterward. Together, they crossed to the steps and Christophe unlocked the door.

In the bedroom they began shedding their clothes, watching each other, tired, Paula knew, but not too tired to be aroused.

When Christophe lay, his arm beckoning her to his side, Paula knelt on the edge of the futon, savoring the sight of him. "You're going to let everything drop, aren't you?" she said.

"Yes. As Benno says, not only were the stones Lukas's to take— stretching it a bit since they'd been sold—but the losses were covered, and now the diamonds are all back in the vault. I think Benno and Lukas will draw closer together, and I want that. Did you realize Peter was left-handed?"

"No."

"If he'd held the gun in his left hand instead of protecting the diamond, you might be—"

"Don't," Paula said. "We're both alive and well. I can't help being sad about Victor having to take early retirement, though. Poor Victor."

Christophe lunged unexpectedly and pulled her over him. He gazed up into her eyes. "You wonderful softie. I love you. Tomorrow morning we buy rings—Benno insists on helping there. On Monday we'll attend to formalities. I want you to be Paula Renfrew St-Giles by the end of next week."

She grimaced. "That's quite a name... Oh, Christophe, I can't stop worrying about Lukas and Sandi."

"They'll be fine. I'm sure they will."

"Why didn't I guess about Peter? Something should have clicked before it did." Paula sank her teeth into her bottom lip. Christophe's hand on her breast made concentration difficult.

"You didn't guess because Peter was too clever. As a man, I can't believe I never suspected what he was. He fooled me for years. But we all tend to believe the obvious. Seems to me a lot of things around here have turned out to be other than they appeared. Except you, *cherie*."

"Christophe..."

"Shh," he whispered, rolling her to the futon. "We need to catch up on our...*sleep*."

They laughed.

An Independent Wife

by Linda Howard

**Marmie Charndoff—
this one's for you**

Chapter One

The phone on her desk rang but Sallie didn't look up from her typewriter or otherwise indicate that she'd even noticed the noise. With a sigh Brom got to his feet and leaned across his desk to reach the phone and put the receiver to his ear. Sallie typed on, her brow puckered with concentration.

"Sal! It's for you," said Brom dryly, and Sallie looked up with a start to see Brom lying stretched across his desk holding her telephone out to her.

"Oh! I'm sorry, Brom, I didn't hear it ring," she apologized, grinning at him as she took the receiver from his hand. He often ribbed her about being in another world, and it was nothing less than the truth; he often answered her calls as well as his own because usually she was concentrating so hard she didn't hear the phone ring.

He grinned back at her as he regained his seat and said, "It's Greg."

"Sallie," said Sallie into the mouthpiece by way of greeting.

And Greg Downey, the news editor, drawled, "Come see me, kid."

"I'm on my way," she said enthusiastically and hung up the phone.

As she switched off her electric typewriter and reached for the cover, Brom questioned, "Off again, birdie?"

"I hope so," replied Sallie, flipping her long braid back over her shoulder. She loved foreign assignments; they were like bread and butter to her. She thrived on them. Other reporters got jet lag—Sallie got her second wind. Her energy and good humor seemed inexhaustible, and as she rushed off to Greg's office she could already feel the adrenalin flowing through her system, making her heart pump faster and her whole body tingle with anticipation.

Greg looked up as she knocked on his open door and a smile softened his hard face when he saw her. "Did you run?" he asked dryly as he got up and crossed to her, closing the door behind her. "I just hung up the phone."

"Normal speed," said Sallie, laughing at herself with him. Her dark blue eyes sparkled with laughter and dimples peeped out of her cheeks. Greg looked down at her glowing little face and passed a hard arm about her to hug her briefly to him before releasing her.

"Do you have anything for me?" she asked eagerly.

"Nothing for right now," he replied, returning to his chair, and he laughed at the way her face fell.

"Cheer up, I've got good news for you anyway. Have you ever heard of the Olivetti Foundation?"

"No," said Sallie bluntly, then frowned. "Or have I? *Who* Olivetti?"

"It's a European charity organization," Greg began, and Sallie pounced in triumph.

"Oh-ho! I place it now. The world's blue bloods sponsor an enormous charity ball every summer, right?"

"Right," concurred Greg.

"Am I interested?" asked Sallie. "America doesn't have any blue blood, you know, only hot red blood."

"You're interested," Greg drawled. "The shindig is being held this year in Sakarya."

Sallie's face lit up. "Greg! Marina Delchamp?"

"Yeah," he grinned. "How about that, eh? I'm practically giving you a vacation. Interview the dashing wife of the finance minister, attend the ritziest party you've ever imagined, and all on the payroll. What more could you want?"

"Great!" she said enthusiastically. "When is it?"

"End of next month," he grunted, lighting a slim cigar. "That leaves plenty of time for you to buy any new gear if you don't have anything suitable for attending a charity ball."

"Smarty," she teased, wrinkling her pert little nose at him. "I'll bet you think I don't have anything in my closet except pants. For your information, I own quite a few dresses."

"Then why don't you ever wear them around here?" he demanded.

"Because, boss dear, you have a habit of sending me out to the wilds without a minute's notice, so I've learned to be prepared."

"And you're so afraid that you'll miss an assignment that you keep a packed bag under your desk," he returned, not at all fooled by her retort. "But I really do want you to dress up, Sallie. Sakarya could be an important ally, especially since the oil fields on the northern border are producing so heavily now. It helps that Marina Delchamp is an American and her husband is so influential with the King, but it never hurts to look your best."

"Umm, yes, the State Department will be relieved to know that I'm on their side," she said with perfect sincerity, keeping her face straight with an effort, and Greg shook his fist at her.

"Don't laugh," he warned her. "The boys in Washington are going all out with Sakarya. The King knows the power he has with those oil fields. Through Marina's influence with her husband Sakarya has become more pro-Western, but it's still an iffy thing. This charity ball will be the first time such an event has been held in an Arab country and it's going to be covered by all the news agencies. Television will be there, too, of course. I've even heard that Rhydon Baines will interview the King, but it hasn't been confirmed yet." Greg leaned back in his chair and clasped his hands behind his head. "There's a rumor going around that Baines is quitting television anyway."

Sallie's bright eyes dimmed a fraction. "Really?" she asked. "I never thought Rhy Baines would quit reporting."

Greg narrowed his gaze on her, his attention caught by her tone. "Do you *know* Rhydon Baines?" he asked incredulously. It didn't seem likely. Rhydon Baines was in a class by himself with his hard-hitting documentaries and interviews, and Sallie hadn't been a top-flight reporter for that long, but the girl did get around and she knew a lot of people.

"We grew up together," Sallie said casually. "Well, not really together, he's older than I am, but we come from the same town."

"Then I've got more good news for you," Greg said, leaning back in his chair and eyeing her sharply. "But keep it close. It's not supposed to be general knowledge yet. The magazine has been sold. We've got a new publisher."

Sallie's heart jolted. She wasn't sure if that was good news or not. A turnover at the top could mean a turnover at the lower levels, too, and she loved her job. *World in Review* was a first class publication; she would hate to see it ruined.

"Who's the new head knocker?" she questioned warily.

"Didn't you guess?" He looked surprised. "Rhydon Baines, of

course. That's why it's not definite about the interview with the King of Sakarya. I heard that the network offered him anchor man to get him to stay, but he turned them down."

Sallie's eyes became huge. "Rhy!" she repeated in a dazed tone. "My God, I never thought he'd come out of the field. Are you certain? Rhy loved reporting more than—more than anything else," she finished, her heart almost stopping in alarm as she realized what she'd nearly said: Rhy loved reporting more than he loved me! What would Greg have said if she'd blurted that out? She could see her job going down the drain anyway, without anticipating the event.

"The way I understand it," Greg expanded, puffing on his cigar and not noticing the slight hesitation in her speech, "he's signed with the network to do a certain number of documentaries over the next five years, but other than that he's coming out of the field. Maybe he's bored."

"Bored?" Sallie muttered, as if the idea was incomprehensible. "With reporting?"

"He's been on top of the heap for a long time," Greg replied. "And maybe he wants to get married, settle down. God knows he's old enough to have all of his wild oats sowed."

"He's thirty-six," Sallie said, struggling for control. "But the idea of Rhy settling down is ridiculous."

"Frankly, I'm glad he's coming in with us. I look forward to working with him. The man's a genius in his field. I thought you'd be happy with the news, but you look like someone's spoiled your Christmas."

"I—I'm stunned," she admitted. "I never thought I'd see the day. When will the news be made public?"

"Next week. I'll try to see that you're here when he comes in, if you like."

"No, thanks anyway," she refused, smiling ruefully at him. "I'll see him soon enough."

Returning to her desk several minutes later Sallie felt as if she'd been kicked in the gut and, rather than face Brom's questions, she detoured to the ladies' room and collapsed on the sofa. Rhy! Of all the news magazines, why did he have to choose *World in Review?* It would be almost impossible for her to find another job she liked nearly as well. It wasn't that Rhy would fire her, but she knew that she didn't want to work with him. Rhy was out of her life now and she had no room for him; she didn't want to be around him even on a professional basis.

What had Greg said? That perhaps Rhy wanted to marry and settle down? She almost laughed aloud. Rhy was already married—to her, and they'd been separated for seven years, during which time she had seen him only on television. Their marriage had broken up precisely because Rhy *couldn't* settle down.

Breathing deeply, Sallie stood up and smoothed her expression. Worrying about it now would interfere with her work and she was too much of a professional to allow that. Tonight would be plenty of time to plan what she'd do.

That night as she dawdled over the grapefruit half that constituted her supper, her face brightened. The possibility was strong that Rhy wouldn't even recognize her; she'd changed a lot in seven years, lost weight, let her hair grow, even her name was different. And the publisher wouldn't exactly be rubbing shoulders with the reporters; she might go for weeks at a time without even glimpsing him. She was out of the country for long stretches, too.

Besides, would Rhy even care if he discovered that one of his reporters was his estranged wife? Seven years was a long time, and there had been no contact at all between them. The break had been final, absolute. Somehow neither one of them had gotten around to filing for a divorce, but there really hadn't been a need for one. They had gone their separate ways, built separate lives, and it was as if the year they'd been married never existed. The only result of that year was the drastic change in Sallie. Why couldn't she carry on with her job like always, even if Rhy did recognize her?

The more she thought about it, the more it seemed possible. She was good at her job and Rhy wasn't a man to let his private life interfere with work, as she knew better than anyone else. If she did her job and kept out of his way he would never let out any hint of their personal connection. After all, it was all over for Rhy, just as it was for her.

Usually Rhy never entered her thoughts unless she saw him on television, but now that his presence loomed so large in her life again she found the past crowding in on her. She tried to concentrate on other things and managed fairly well until she went to bed that night, when memories of that year swamped her.

Rhy. Sallie stared upward through the darkness at the ceiling, recalling his features and forming them into his face. She could do that easily, for she'd seen him on television any number of times these past seven years. At first she'd been left sick and shaking whenever she glimpsed his face and she would rush to turn the set off, but gradually that reaction had left her, turned into numbness. Her system had protected itself against such intense grief, allowing her to pick up the pieces of her shattered life and try to build again. The numbness had turned into determination and the determination into indifference as she learned to live without Rhy.

Looking back at the timid, insecure girl she had been, Sallie felt as if that girl had been a stranger, someone to be pitied but not really worth wasting any grief over. The wonder wasn't that Rhy had left her, but rather that he'd ever been attracted to her in the first place. No matter how she considered it she just couldn't find any reason why a dynamic man like Rhy Baines would have wanted to marry a mousy little nonentity like Sarah Jerome. She hadn't been the gay, daredevil Sallie then, but Sarah. Quiet, plump, malleable Sarah.

Unless Rhy had married her just because she was malleable, someone he could control, push into the background when he wanted her out of the way, yet someone who would provide home and hearth when he did wander back home? If so, he'd been sadly disappointed, for she'd been malleable on every point except his job. Sarah wanted her husband at home every night, not flying off to report on wars and revolutions and drug smuggling, the very stuff that was the wine of life to Rhy Baines. She had sulked and nagged and wept, terrified that each time he left her would be the last, that he'd come home in a coffin. She wanted only to hold that strong man to her because she lived only through him.

In the end it had been too much for Rhy and he had walked out after only a year of marriage, and she hadn't heard from him since. She'd known that he wouldn't call her because his last words to her had been, "When you think you're woman enough for me, give me a call!"

Cynical, hurting words. Words that had clearly revealed his contempt of her. Yet those words had changed her life.

Sighing at the sleep that evaded her, Sallie rolled onto her stomach and clutched the pillow into a ball against her chest. Perhaps tonight was a good time to dredge up all the memories and give them an airing. After all, she might shortly be seeing her long-absent husband.

They had been acquainted for years, as far back as Sallie could remember. Rhy's aunt had lived next door to the Jeromes, and as Rhy had been her favorite nephew it was nothing unusual for him to stop by at least once a week when he was growing up. The visits became fewer when he left town, but he never let too long go by without calling in on his aunt. By then he was beginning to make a name for himself as a reporter, and he had been hired by a television station in New York City. Occasionally he would walk across to the white picket fence that separated the two houses and talk to Sallie's father, and if Sallie or her mother were about he would speak to them, sometimes lightly teasing Sallie about growing up so fast.

Shortly after she turned eighteen Sallie's parents were killed in a car crash and she lived alone in the small, tidy house she had inherited. It was paid for and the insurance money was enough to keep her going until she had recovered from her grief enough to begin looking for a job, so she let the days drift by, dreading the time when she would have to go out on her own. She became closer to Aunt Tessie, Rhy's aunt, for each lived alone. Aunt Tessie died in her sleep just two months after the death of Sallie's parents and Rhy returned home for the funeral.

He was twenty-eight, devilishly good-looking, with a dangerous quality about him that took her breath away. He was a man who lived on his nerve and his wits and thoroughly enjoyed it, and he'd just been snapped up by one of the major television networks, working as a foreign correspondent. He saw Sallie at his aunt's funeral and called the next day to ask her out. She had thought then that he must be bored, used to as he was to so much glamour and excitement, but she had known when she looked in the mirror that he wouldn't find any glamour or excitement with her. She was short, pretty enough in a quiet way, but a bit on the plump side. Her short mop of rich, dark hair was a good color, dark sable, but it lacked style and did nothing for her small face with its round cheeks. But Rhy Baines had asked her out and she went, her heart thumping half in fear and half in exhilaration at actually being alone with such a gorgeous, sexy man.

Rhy was a sophisticated adult; he probably meant nothing by the kiss he pressed lightly on her lips when he said good-night after that first date. He didn't even put his arms around her but merely tilted her face up with a finger under her chin. To Sallie, however, it was an explosion of her senses and she had no idea how to control it or mask her response to him. Simply, openly, she had melted against him, her soft mouth fused to his. Long minutes later, when he dragged his head back, he was breathing raggedly and, to her surprise, he asked her out again.

On their third date only his self-control preserved her innocence. Sallie was helpless against her attraction to him, having fallen head over heels in love, yet she was taken by surprise when he abruptly asked her to marry him. She had expected him to take her to bed, not to propose, and she humbly accepted. They were married the next week.

For six glorious days she was in ecstasy. He was a marvelous lover, patient with her inexperience, tender in his passion. He seemed amazed at the fiery passion he could arouse in his quiet little wife and for the first few days of their married life they devoted themselves to lovemaking. Then came that phone call, and before she knew it Rhy was throwing some clothing in his suitcase and rushing out the door with only a hasty kiss for her and a terse "I'll call you, baby," thrown at her over his shoulder.

He was gone for just over two weeks and she discovered by watching the evening news that he was in South America, where a particularly bloody revolution had slaughtered just about everyone in the previous government. Sallie spent the entire time he was gone crying herself to sleep at night and vomiting up her meals whenever she tried to eat. Just the thought of Rhy in danger made her cringe. She had just found him after the nightmare of losing her parents and she adored him. She wouldn't be able to bear it if anything happened to him.

He returned looking brown and fit and Sallie screamed her rage and fear at him. He retaliated and the quarrel that followed kept them from speaking for two days. It was sex that brought them together again, his surging appetite for her wildly responsive little body and her helpless yielding to him. That became the pattern of their marriage, with him gone for longer and longer periods even though she promptly became pregnant.

They had even quarreled over her pregnancy, with Rhy bitterly accusing her of becoming pregnant deliberately in an attempt to make him stay at home. She knew he didn't want children just now and that he had no intention of changing his job. Sallie hadn't even attempted to defend herself, for even worse than being accused of becoming pregnant as part of some scheme was the shameful knowledge that she had been too ignorant to take precautions. She had simply never thought of it and she knew that Rhy would be disgusted with her if he knew the truth.

When she was six months pregnant Rhy was wounded in a border skirmish between two developing African nations and he came home on a stretcher. She had thought that his close brush with death would bring him to his senses and for once she hadn't raged and nagged at him when he returned; she was too elated at the thought of having him with her permanently. Within a month, however, he was gone on another assignment even though he hadn't fully recovered from his wound, and he was still gone when she went into premature labor. The network brought him home, but by the time he arrived she was already out of the hospital and their stillborn son had been buried.

He stayed with her until she was recovered physically from giving birth, but she was grief stricken at losing her baby and bitter with him because he had been absent during the crisis. When he left again the atmosphere between them was still cold and silent. Perhaps she should have realized then how indifferent Rhy had become to her, but it still came as a shock that he could so easily leave her forever, as he did on his next trip home. She had returned from buying groceries and found him sprawled on the sofa in the living room, his suitcase by the door where he had dropped it. His face was drawn with weariness, but his charcoal gray eyes had still held that characteristic bite as he looked her up and down, his manner one of waiting.

Unable to stem the words that jumped to her lips, Sallie began berating him for his inconsiderate behavior, his total lack of feeling for her after the trial she had undergone, the pain she had suffered. If he truly loved her he would get another job, one that would let him stay with her when she needed him so badly. In the middle of this, Rhy got to his feet and picked up his suitcase. As he walked out the door he had said sarcastically, ''When you think you're woman enough for me, give me a call.''

She hadn't seen him since.

At first she had been devastated. She had cried for days and leapt for the telephone every time it rang. Checks arrived from him every week for her support, but there were never any notes included. It was as if he would do his duty and support her, but had no interest in seeing her or talking to her. She wasn't woman enough for him.

At last, desperately, knowing only that her life wasn't worth living without Rhy, Sallie decided to *make* herself into a woman who was woman enough for Rhy Baines. With feverish determination she enrolled in the local college and set about gaining the knowledge that would transform her into a more sophisticated person. She signed up for language classes and crash courses in every craft she could think of, forcing herself out of her shyness. She got a job, a low-paying job as a clerk at the local newspaper office, but it was her first job and it was a start. With that paycheck every week, her very own paycheck, came something she could hardly recognize at first, but which became larger with each succeeding check: a sense of self-reliance.

She found that she was doing well in her language classes, was, in fact, at the top of her class. She had a natural aptitude for words and languages and she enrolled in a creative writing class. The time that this consumed forced her to give up her courses in crafts, but her interest in writing grew by leaps and bounds and she didn't miss puttering about with paints and straw.

Like a snowball, her forced activities grew in size and scope until she didn't have an idle hour in her day. Once she began making friends she discovered that it was easy, that she liked being with people. Slowly she began to emerge from the shell that had encased her for all of her life.

With all of her activities, Sallie was seldom still and often forgot meals. Pounds melted from her petite frame and she had to replace her entire wardrobe. She went from slightly plump to almost too thin, and as her face slimmed the exotic bone work of her skull was revealed. Without the roundness of her cheeks to balance them her dark blue eyes became huge in her face and underneath them her high, chiseled cheekbones gave her an almost Eastern quality. She had been attractive before, but now she became something more, a young woman who was striking and unusual. Never classically lovely, not Sallie, but now she stood out in a crowd. As her hair grew she simply pulled it back out of her way, not bothering to keep it cut, and the sable-colored mass began to stream down her back in a thick mane.

As she changed physically her entire manner changed. Her self-confidence soared; she became outgoing and found that she had a keen mind and an appreciation of the absurdities of life that made people seek her out. She was enjoying herself, and thoughts of Rhy became fewer and fewer.

They had been separated for almost a year when she realized that as she had grown up, she had also grown away. The weekly check from Rhy was like a revelation, for as she stared at his bold, sprawling signature on the check she was stunned to find that the crippling pain was gone. Not only that, if Rhy came back to her now it would curtail the exciting new life she'd built for herself and she didn't want that. She had made herself over, made herself into a woman who was woman enough for Rhy Baines—and now she found that she didn't need him. She no longer needed to live through him; she had herself.

It was like being released from prison. The knowledge that she was self-sufficient and independent was like a heady wine, making her giddy. Now she understood why Rhy had put his job over her; like him, she had become hooked on excitement, and she wondered how he had lived with her as long as he had.

With a great sense of relief she mailed Rhy's check back to his address at the network, enclosing a note explaining that she had a job and was trying to support herself, therefore his support was no longer needed, though she did appreciate the thought. That was the last communication between them and that had been rather one-sided as Rhy had never replied to her note. The checks had simply ceased to arrive.

Then fate stepped into Sallie's life. A bridge she was driving across collapsed, and though she was far enough across that her car didn't slide into the river below, several behind her weren't so lucky. Without really thinking about what she was doing she helped in the rescue of the people who had survived the plunge into the river and obtained interviews with everyone involved. Afterwards she went to the newspaper office where she worked, typed up a report of the accident, including her own colorful eyewitness description, and gave it to the editor. It was printed, and she was given a new job as a reporter.

Now, at the age of twenty-six, she had completed her degree and was a reporter for one of the better weekly news magazines and her zest for new experiences had not waned. Now she fully understood why danger hadn't kept Rhy from his job, for she enjoyed the danger, the heart-pounding excitement of taking off in a helicopter while ground troops sprayed automatic fire at the aircraft, the exhilaration of coming down in a plane with only one good engine, the satisfaction of a difficult job well-done. She had rented out her house and now lived in a neat two-room apartment in New York, a mere stopping place between assignments. She had no plants and no pets, for who would take care of them while she was halfway around the world? She had no romantic interests, for she was never in one place for long, but she had scores of friends and acquaintances.

No, she reflected sleepily as she finally began to doze off, she didn't want Rhy back in her life now. He would only interfere with the things she enjoyed. But, thinking about it, she didn't think that he would care what she did if by some chance he did recognize her, and that wasn't likely. After all, he hadn't thought about her in seven years. Why should he start now?

Chapter Two

Sallie stood before her mirror and studied the photograph she held in her hand of herself at the age of eighteen. Then she looked back at her reflection and studied the differences. The most obvious change was that now she had cheekbones instead of cheeks. The hair, too, of course, grown from a short mop that barely covered her ears into the thick braid that hung to her waist. The only thing that hadn't changed was her eyes, large, dark blue eyes. However, if she wore dark glasses whenever she thought she might run into Rhy she could continue indefinitely to keep her identity from him.

She had thought about it from all angles and decided not to rely on Rhy's good nature, which was a chancy thing at best. Rhy was hair-triggered, volatile, never predictable. The best thing to do was to avoid him whenever possible and try to keep Greg from introducing her to her own husband as an old friend from his hometown!

Rhy was supposed to arrive that morning; the news had been broken yesterday that the magazine had been sold to Rhydon Baines, who had resigned as a network foreign correspondent and would hereafter devote his time and talents to the publishing of news, except for occasional documentary specials. The entire building had hummed with the news. Veteran reporters had suddenly become uneasy, checking their credits, reviewing their work and comparing it to Rhy's direct, slashing style of reporting. And if Sallie had heard one comment from an excited woman about how handsome Rhydon Baines was she had heard a hundred. Even women who were happily married were thrilled to be working with Rhy. He was more than a top reporter—he was a celebrity.

Sallie was already bored with the entire business. First thing this morning she was going to ask Greg for an assignment, anything to get away until things calmed down. She'd already been three weeks between assignments so no one would think it odd that she was becoming restless. It was more than a month until the charity ball in Sakarya and she didn't think she'd be able to sit still that long.

Suddenly noticing the time, she cast a last quick glance over her slender form, neat and capable in dark blue slacks and a blue silk shirt. Her hair was pulled back and braided into one long fat rope and, as the final touch, she had added a pair of dark glasses. She could tell anyone who asked that she had a headache and the light hurt her eyes; the glasses weren't so dark that she couldn't work with them on if necessary.

Then she had to rush, and as the elevator in her apartment building was notoriously slow in arriving she used the stairs, running down them two at a time and reaching her bus stop just as the bus was closing its doors. She yelled and pounded on the doors and they slid open and the driver grinned at her. "Wondered where you were," he said jokingly. In actual fact, she was a regular bus door pounder.

She made it to the office with a minute to spare and collapsed into her chair, wondering how she had made it across the street without being hit at least six times. The blood was racing through her veins and she grinned. It was time for some action when her usual method of getting to work was beginning to seem exciting!

"Hi," Brom greeted her. "Ready to meet the man?"

"I'm ready to do some traveling," she retorted. "I've been here too long. I'm growing cobwebs. I think I'll beard Greg in his den and see if I can't get some action."

"You're nuts," Brom informed her bluntly. "Greg's quick today. You'd be better off to wait until tomorrow."

"I'll take my chances," Sallie said blithely.

"Don't you always? Hey, why the glasses? Are you trying to hide a black eye?" Brom pounced, his eyes lighting up at the possibility that Sallie had gotten involved in a brawl somewhere.

"Nope." To convince him she raised the glasses to let him see for himself that her eyes were normal, then set them back in place on her nose. "I've got a headache and the light is bothering me."

"Do you have migraines?" Brom asked in concern. "My sister has 'em and the light always bothers her."

"I don't think it's a migraine," she hedged. "It's probably just a nervous reaction to sitting still for so long."

Brom laughed, as she had meant him to, and she made her escape to talk to Greg before Rhy arrived and all chance was lost.

As she neared Greg's open door she heard him on the phone, his voice curt and impatient, and Sallie's eyebrows rose as she listened. Greg was by nature an impatient man, one of the doers of the world, but he wasn't usually unreasonable but his attitude now didn't strike her as being reasonable. Brom was right, Greg was "quicker" than usual, edgy and irascible, and she had no doubt that it was all due to Rhy's impending arrival.

When she heard the phone crash down into the cradle she poked her head around the door and inquired, "Would a cup of coffee help?"

Greg's dark head jerked up at the sound of her voice and his mouth moved into a wry grimace. "I'm swimming in coffee now," he grunted in reply. "Hell's bells, I didn't know there were so many idiots working in this building. I swear if one more fool calls me—"

"Everyone's nervous," she soothed.

"You're not," he pointed out. "Why the glasses? Are you so famous now that you've got to travel incognito?"

"There's a reason for the glasses," Sallie retaliated. "But because you're being nasty I won't tell you."

"Suit yourself," he growled. "Get out of my office."

"I need an assignment," she pointed out. "I'm at the snapping stage myself."

"I thought you wanted to be here to meet your old hometown pal," Greg shot back. "Anyway, I don't have anything to give you right now."

"Come on," she pleaded. "You've got to have a little something. No riots, no natural disasters, no political kidnappings? There's bound to be a story for me somewhere in the world!"

"Maybe tomorrow," he replied. "Don't be in such a hurry. For God's sake, Sal, I may need you around in case the Man gets testy. An old friend is nice to have around—"

"To throw to the lion?" she interrupted dryly.

Abruptly Greg grinned. "Don't worry, doll, he won't tear you to pieces, only maul you around a bit."

"Greg, you're not listening to me," she groaned. "I've been stagnating here for three weeks. I need to earn my keep."

"You don't have any sense," he observed.

"You don't have any sense of mercy," she retorted. "Greg, *please*."

"What's the damned hurry?" he suddenly yelled. "Dammit, Sal, I've got a new publisher coming in and he's not exactly a babe in the woods. I don't expect to have any fun today, so get off my back, will you? Besides, he may *ask* to see you, and I sure as hell want you here if he does."

Sallie collapsed into a chair, groaning aloud as she realized that she would have to tell Greg the truth. That was the only way he would give her an assignment, and perhaps it wouldn't be such a bad thing if Greg knew. At least then he wouldn't keep trying to throw her at Rhy. And realistically Greg had a right to know the circumstances and be aware of the complications that could arise from her very presence.

Gently she said, "Greg, I think you should know that Rhy might not be so glad to see me."

He was instantly alert. "Why not? I thought you were friends."

She sighed. "I can't say if we're friends or not. I haven't seen him in seven years, except on television. And there's something else. I wasn't going to tell you, but you'll need to know. Do you know that I'm married, but that I've been separated from my husband for years?"

Greg nodded, a sudden stillness coming over his features. "Yes, I know, but you've never said who your husband is. You go by your maiden name, don't you?"

"Yes, I wanted to do everything completely on my own, not capitalize on his name. He's very well-known. As a matter of fact, my husband is... umm...Rhydon Baines."

Greg swallowed audibly, his eyes growing round. He gulped again. Sallie didn't lie, he knew, she was brutally honest, but—Rhydon Baines? That tough, hard-as-nails man and this fragile little fairy with her laughing eyes? He said roughly, "My God, Sallie, the man's old enough to be your father!"

Sallie burst into a peal of laughter. "He is not! He's only ten years older than I am. I'm twenty-six, not eighteen. But I wanted you to know why I want an assignment. The further away I am from Rhy, the better it is. We've been separated for seven years but the fact remains that Rhy is still my husband and personal relationships can get sticky, can't they?"

Greg stared at her in disbelief, yet he believed her. He just couldn't take it in. Sallie? Little Sallie Jerome and that big, hard man? She looked like a kid, dressed all in blue and with that fat braid hanging to her waist. He said softly, "I'll be damned. What happened?"

She shrugged. "He got bored with me."

"Bored with you?" chided Greg. "C'mon, doll!"

She laughed again. "I'm nothing like I was then. I was such a cowardly little snit, no wonder Rhy walked out on me. I couldn't stand the separations caused by his job. I made myself sick with worry and nagged him to death, and in the end he walked out. I can't say I blame him. The wonder is that he lasted as long as he did."

Greg shook his head. It was impossible to imagine Sallie as a timid person; he sometimes thought that she hadn't a nerve in her body. She was willing to take on anything, and the more dangerous it was the more she enjoyed it. It wasn't an act, either. Her eyes would sparkle and the color glow in her cheeks whenever the going got difficult.

"Let me get this straight," he muttered. "He doesn't know that you work here?"

"I wouldn't think so," she replied cheerfully. "We haven't been in touch in six years."

"But you're still married. Surely he sends you support checks—" He stopped at the outraged look on her face, and sighed. "Sorry. You refused support, right?"

"After I could support myself, yes. When Rhy left I had to fend for myself and somewhere along the way I acquired a backbone. I like doing for myself."

"You've never asked for a divorce?"

"Well...no," she admitted, her nose wrinkling in puzzlement. "I've never wanted to remarry and I don't suppose he's ever wanted to, either, so we just never got around to a divorce. He probably finds it convenient, having a legal wife who's never around. No ties, but it keeps him safe from other women."

"Would it bother you? Seeing him again?" Greg asked roughly, more disturbed than he cared to admit by the idea of Sallie being married to Rhydon Baines.

"Seeing Rhy? No," she said honestly. "I got over him a long time ago. I had to, to survive. Sometimes it doesn't even seem real, that I was—that I *am*—married to him."

"Will it bother him, seeing you again?" persisted Greg.

"Certainly not emotionally. It has to be over for him, too. After all, he was the one who walked. But Rhy *does* have a temper, you know, and he might not like the idea of his wife working for him, even under a different name. And he might not want me around to cramp his style. I have no intention of interfering in his private life, but he doesn't know that. So you see, it would be a good idea to send me on assignment and keep me away from him, at least at first. I don't want to lose my job." She topped all of this off with a sunny smile and Greg shook his head.

"All right," he muttered. "I'll find something for you. But if he ever notices that you're his wife I know nothing about it."

"About what?" she asked, playing dumb, and he wasn't able to stifle a chuckle.

Sallie knew better than to push her luck with Greg, so she left him with a quick, heartfelt "Thanks!" and went back to her desk. Brom was gone and she was relatively alone, though only a partition separated their little cubicle from the others, and the clatter of typewriters and hum of voices were as plain as if there was nothing between her and the rest of the office.

By the time Brom returned with a steaming cup of coffee she felt more relaxed, her anxiety eased by Greg's promise to help keep her out of Rhy's sight. She finished the article she was writing and felt pleased with the end product; she liked putting words together to form ideas and felt an almost sensuous satisfaction when a sentence turned out as she had planned.

At ten o'clock the buzz of the office ceased momentarily, then resumed at a lower hum and without raising her eyes Sallie knew that Rhy had entered. Cautiously she turned her head away and pretended to search for something in the drawer of her desk. After a moment the buzz resumed its high pitch, which meant that Rhy had left after taking a quick look over the office.

"Oh, God!" a female voice cried over the others. "Just think, a hunk like that is *single!*"

Sallie grinned a little, recognizing the voice as that of Lindsey Wallis, an exuberant office sexpot with more mouth than brains. Still, there was no doubting that Lindsey was serious in her appreciation of Rhy's dynamic good looks. Sallie knew as well as anyone the effect her husband could have on a woman.

Fifteen minutes later her phone rang and she jumped on it, an action that raised Brom's eyebrows. "Get the hell out of the building," Greg muttered in her ear. "He's on his way to meet everyone. Go home. I'll try to get you out of town tonight."

"Thanks," she said and hung up. Standing, she collected her purse and said, "See ya," to Brom.

"Flying off, little birdie?" he asked, as he always did.

"It looks that way. Greg said to pack." With a wave she left, not wanting to linger, since Rhy was on his way down.

She stepped into the corridor and her heart nearly failed her when the elevator doors slid open and Rhy stepped out, flanked by three men she didn't know and the previous publisher, Mr. Owen. Rather than walk straight toward them she turned and went to the stairs, being careful to keep her eyes lowered and her head slightly averted, but she was still aware that Rhy had stopped and was looking after her. Her pulse thudded in her veins as she darted down the stairs. What a close call!

Waiting at the apartment for Greg to call nearly drove her mad with impatience. She paced the floor for a while; then excess energy drove her to clean the refrigerator out and rearrange her cabinets. That didn't take much time as she hadn't accumulated a lot of either food or utensils. At last she hit on the perfect way to pass the time: she packed her bags. She loved packing, going through her essentials and putting them in their proper place; she had her notebooks and assorted pens and pencils, a tape recorder, a dog-eared dictionary, several paperbacks, a pencil sharpener, a pocket calculator, replacement batteries and a battered flashlight, all of which traveled with her wherever she went.

She had just finished arranging them neatly when the phone rang and she answered it to hear Greg's terse voice giving her the welcome news that he had an assignment for her.

"It's the best I could do, and at least it'll get you out of town," he grunted. "You're on a flight to D.C., in the morning. A senator's wife is making big noises about a general leaking classified information at a drunken party."

"Sounds pretty," Sallie commented.

"I'm sending Chris Meaker with you," Greg continued. "Talk with the senator's wife. You won't be able to even get close to the general. Chris will have a brief on it for you. Meet him at JFK at five-thirty."

Now that she knew her destination Sallie was able to complete her packing. She chose conservative dresses and a tailored pants suit, not her favorite clothes, but she felt that the restrained clothing would help her with the interview, making the senator's wife more trusting.

As usual, she could hardly sleep that night. She was always restless the night before she left on assignment if Greg gave her any warning of it. She preferred having to rush straight from the office to the airport, without having time to think, without wondering if everything would work out, without wondering what would happen if Rhy ever recognized her....

Chris Meaker, the photographer, was waiting for her at the airport the next morning and as she approached him with a grin and a wave he got to his feet, his tall, lanky body unfolding slowly. He gave her a sleepy smile in return and bent down to kiss her on the forehead. "Hi, doll," he said, his quiet, lazily deep voice making her grin grow wider. She liked Chris. Nothing ever upset him; nothing ever hurried him. He was as calm and deep as a sheltered lagoon. He was even peaceful to look at, with his thick sandy hair and dark brown eyes, his brow broad and serene, his mouth firm without being stubborn. And most important of all, he never made a pass at her. He treated her affectionately, like a little sister, and he was protective in his quiet way, but he never made any suggestive statements to her or in any way acted as if he was attracted to her. That was a relief, because Sallie just didn't have the time for romantic ties.

Now he looked her up and down and his level brows rose. "Ye gods, a dress," he said, mild surprise evident in his voice, which meant he was astonished. "What's the occasion?"

Sallie had to grin again. "No occasion, just politics," she assured him. "Did Greg send that envelope he promised me?"

"Got it," he replied. "Have you already checked your luggage?"

"Yes," she nodded. Just then their flight was called over the loudspeaker and they walked over to the boarding area and through the metal detector, then on to the waiting jet.

On the flight to the capital Sallie carefully read the brief Greg had prepared. Considering how little time he'd had, he had included a lot of detail and she became absorbed in the possibilities. This wasn't the type of reporting she usually did but Greg had given her what he had, and she'd return the favor by doing her best.

When they reached Washington and checked into their hotel it looked as if doing her best wouldn't be good enough. While Chris lounged in a chair and leafed through a magazine Sallie called the senator's wife to confirm the appointment Greg had made for an interview that afternoon. She was told that Mrs. Bailey was sorry but she was unable to see any reporters that day. It was a polite, final brush-off, and it made her angry. She had no intention of failing to get the story Greg had sent her after.

It took an hour of phone calls to a chain of contacts but when the hour was up she had interviewed, over the phone, the hostess of the "drunken party" where the general had supposedly revealed the classified material. Everything was vehemently denied, except for the presence of both the general and Mrs. Bailey on the night in question, but when the indignant hostess muttered in passing that "Hell hath no fury" Sallie began to get the idea that Mrs. Bailey was a woman scorned.

It was a possibility. The general was a trim, distinguished man with metallic gray hair and a good-humored twinkle in his eyes. After talking it over with Chris, who agreed with her theory, they decided to pursue that angle.

Forty-eight hours later, tired but satisfied, they caught a plane back to New York. Though her theory hadn't been verified by either of the two principals, the general or Mrs. Bailey, she was content that she knew the reason behind Mrs. Bailey's denouncement of the general. Once they had been checking they had found several restaurants in the capital area where the general had been seen dining with an attractive woman of Mrs. Bailey's general description. Senator Bailey had suddenly canceled a trip overseas to stay with his wife. The general's wife, who had shed twenty pounds and turned her graying hair into a flattering soft blond, was suddenly more in evidence at her husband's side. There was also only Mrs. Bailey's accusation against the general; no one else had added their word to hers and, moreover, the general had not been relieved of his post despite the furor in the press.

Sallie had telephoned all of that in to Greg the night before and he had agreed with her. The article would be placed in that week's issue, and she had barely gotten it in under the deadline.

He was cryptic on the subject of Rhy, commenting only that the man was a mover, and by that she deduced that changes were being made. She would have preferred going on another assignment immediately, but Greg had nothing available and there were always expense sheets to complete and a report to type out. Thankfully, the weekend had arrived and she had a bit more time before she had to go in to the office.

On Monday morning, she reported to work with butterflies in her stomach, but to her relief and surprise the entire day went by without so much as a glimpse of her husband, though the floor buzzed with speculation on the changes he was making in the format of the magazine. She avoided the upper floors, no longer going up to see Greg when an idea came to her; she called him instead, and Brom commented that he'd never seen her stay in one place for so long before.

Tuesday was the same, except that that was the day the magazine hit the newsstands and Greg called to offer his congratulations. "I've just received a call from Rhy," he said gruffly, having picked up the shortened version of Rhy's name from her. "Senator Bailey called him at home this morning."

"Am I being sued?" Sallie questioned.

"No. The senator explained the entire situation and his wife is giving us a retraction of her previous statement concerning the general. You were right on target, doll."

"I thought I was," she agreed cheerily. "Do you have anything else I can do?"

"Just watch your back, doll. Several editors I know are mad as the devil that you're the only one who caught on to what was under everyone's noses."

She laughed and hung up, but the knowledge that her instincts had been right gave her a lift for the rest of the day. Chris came by at lunch and asked if she wanted to share a sandwich with him and she accepted. There was a small cafeteria in the building offering nothing more sophisticated than soup, sandwiches, coffee and cold drinks for those who couldn't get out for lunch, but the meager fare was more than enough for her. She and Chris shared a postage-stamp table and talked shop over cups of strong black coffee.

Just as they were finishing there was a stir among the other people eating lunch and the back of Sallie's neck prickled in warning. "It's the boss," Chris informed her casually. "With his girlfriend."

Sallie sternly resisted the urge to turn around, but out of the corner of her eye she watched the two figures move down the cafeteria line selecting their lunch. "I wonder what they're doing here," she murmured.

"Testing the food, at a guess," Chris replied, turning his head to stare openly at the woman by Rhy's side. "He's checked into everything else. I don't see why he should overlook the food. She looks familiar, Sal. Do you know her?"

Sallie narrowed her eyes in concentration, examining the woman with relief, because that kept her from staring at Rhy. "You're right, she is familiar. Isn't she Coral Williams, the model?" She was almost certain of the woman's identity, that classic golden perfection could belong to no one else.

"So it is," Chris grunted.

Rhy turned then, balancing his tray as he moved to a table, and Sallie hastily lowered her eyes, but not before her heart gave a breath-stopping lunge at his appearance. He hadn't changed. He was still lithe and muscular, and his hair was still the same midnight black, his strong-boned face still hard and sardonic, tanned from long exposure to the sun. By contrast the woman at his side was a graceful butterfly, his exact opposite in coloring.

"Let's go," she said in a low tone to Chris, sliding out of her chair. She sensed Rhy's head turning in her direction and she carefully turned her back to him without any show of hurry. Chris followed her out of the cafeteria, but she was burningly conscious of Rhy's gaze on her as she left. That was twice he had stared at her. Did he recognize her? Was her walk familiar to him? Was it her hair? That long braid was distinctive enough in itself, but she didn't want to have her hair cut because he would certainly recognize her then.

She was still shaken when she returned to her desk, due in large part to her reaction to Rhy's appearance. No other man had ever attracted her the way he did and she found to her dismay that the situation was still the same. Rhy had a raw virility, an aura of barely leashed power that set her heart to pounding and forcibly reminded her of the nights she had once spent in his arms. She might be free of him emotionally, but the old physical ties seemed to be as strong as ever and she felt vulnerable.

Out of habit she picked up the phone and called Greg, but he was out to lunch and she dropped the receiver back into the cradle with a ragged sigh. She couldn't just sit there; her nature demanded that she take some sort of action. At last she scribbled a note to Brom asking him to notify Greg that she'd taken ill with a headache and was going home for the rest of the day. Greg would see through the excuse, but Brom wouldn't.

She hated to run away from anything, but she knew that she needed to think about her reaction to Rhy, and once she was home she did exactly that. Was it only because he was her husband, because she knew him as she knew no other man? He was her only lover; she'd never even been attracted to another man as she had been to Rhy. Old habits? She hoped that was it, and when she realized that she hadn't felt the least flicker of jealousy over Coral Williams she was relieved, because that proved she was over Rhy. All she felt for him was the basic urge between a man and a woman who found each other sexually alluring, nothing more. Certainly she was old enough to control those feelings, as the past seven years had proved to her.

The phone rang late that afternoon and when she answered it Greg said curtly, "What happened?"

"Rhy and Coral Williams came into the cafeteria at lunch while Chris and I were there," she explained without hesitation. "I don't think Rhy recognized me, but he kept staring. That's the second time he's stared at me like that, so I thought I'd better clear out." That wasn't exactly the reason, but it was a good excuse and she used it. Why tell Greg that seeing Rhy had upset her?

"You thought right," Greg said, sighing. "He was in my office not long after Brom brought your note up. He wanted to meet you, since you're the only reporter he hasn't met personally. Then he asked me to describe you, and he got a funny look on his face when I did."

"Oh, no," she groaned. "He's latched on to something—he *would!*" she said in swift disgust. "He's as fast as a snake. Did he ask where I'm from?"

"Be prepared, doll. He didn't ask that, but he got your phone number."

"Holy cow," she groaned again. "Thanks for doing what you could, Greg. If Rhy does find out I'll cover our tracks."

Greg hung up and she began pacing the floor, waiting for the phone to ring again. What should she say? Should she try to disguise her voice? But afternoon faded into evening and still the expected call didn't come, so at last she bathed and went to bed. But she slept restlessly, falling into a deep sleep only in the early hours of the morning.

It was the phone that woke her in the morning, the insistent ringing intruding slowly into her consciousness. At first she thought it was the alarm clock and she tried to shut it off but the ringing continued. When she realized it was the phone she grabbed it and in her haste dropped it to the floor. She hauled it up by the cord and at last got the receiver to her ear. "Hello," she muttered sleepily, her voice sounding thick.

"Is this Miss Jerome?" a deep, husky voice asked. There was a husky quality to that voice that tingled her nerves, but she was too sleepy to pick it up.

"Yes, this is she," she acknowledged, stifling a yawn. "Who is this?"

"I'm Rhydon Baines," the voice said and Sallie's eyes popped open. "Did I wake you?"

"Yes, you did," she said baldly, unable to think of any polite assurance to give him, and a deep chuckle made her shiver with reaction. "Is anything wrong, Mr. Baines?"

"No, I just wanted to congratulate you on the job you did in Washington. That was a good piece of reporting. Sometime when you're free come up to my office for a talk. I think you're the only reporter on my staff I haven't met personally and you're one of my best."

"I—I will," she stammered. "Thank you, Mr. Baines."

"Rhy," he corrected. "I prefer to be on first-name basis with the staff. And by the way, I apologize for waking you up, but it's time you were up anyway if you're going to be at work on time." With another chuckle he said goodbye and hung up and Sallie gasped as she looked at the clock. She *was* going to be late if she didn't hurry, but Rhy would wait a long time if he was waiting for her to put in an appearance in his office!

Chapter Three

The morning went by without anything happening, though she kept a weather eye out for any sign of Rhy. She had to trust Greg to warn her if she should disappear into the ladies' room, but her phone remained silent. Brom was sent out on an assignment to L.A. and their little cubicle was silent after he left; her nerves began to fray under the strain. She ate an apple at her desk for lunch, not daring to risk going to the cafeteria or even venturing outside the building on the chance she might run into Rhy. She was beginning to feel like a prisoner!

Shortly after lunch Greg called and said, "Come up here, Sal. I don't want to talk over the phone."

Her heart leapt into her throat and she rushed up the stairs to the next floor. Greg's door was open, as usual, and she went in. Greg looked up from the papers he was reading and his expression was grim. "Rhy's secretary just called. He wants your file. I had to send it up. I had no choice. He hasn't returned from lunch yet, so you've got a few minutes of grace. I just thought I'd warn you."

She swallowed the lump in her throat. "Thanks for trying," she said, and managed a whimsical little smile. "It was a dumb idea, anyway, trying to hide from him. He probably won't care one way or the other."

Greg smiled in return, but his eyes were narrowed with worry as she left his office.

Deep in thought and facing the fact that Rhy would know her identity very shortly, she punched the elevator button instead of taking the stairs. She took a deep breath and braced herself.

Abruptly she realized that she was waiting for the elevator and the lights showed that it was coming up. Muttering to herself for her stupidity she turned on her heel and headed for the stairs, but just as she reached them the elevator doors slid open and a voice called, "Sallie Jerome! Wait a minute!"

Her head jerked around and she stared at Rhy for several seconds, frozen in her tracks with horror, then she pulled the heavy door open and took a step, intending to run before she realized the futility of it. Rhy had taken a good look at her and the arrested expression on his face told her that she'd been recognized. She couldn't avoid it any longer; he now knew who she was and he wasn't a man to let the matter drop. She released the door and swung back to face him, her delicate jaw tilting upward pugnaciously. "You wanted to see me?" she challenged.

He moved from his stance in front of the elevator and strode the few short yards that separated them. He looked taut, his skin pulled over his cheekbones, his mouth compressed into a thin line. "Sarah," he whispered savagely, his gray eyes leaping furiously.

"Sallie," she corrected, flipping her braid over her shoulder. "I'm called Sallie now."

His hand shot out and he gripped her wrist, his long fingers wrapping about the fragile bones as if to measure them. "You're not only called Sallie instead of Sarah, you're Jerome again instead of Baines," he hissed, and she shivered with alarm. She knew Rhy's voice in all of his moods, the well-remembered husky quality made it distinctive. It was a voice that could sound whispery and menacing when he was angry, rasping when he was hammering out a point on television, or low and incredibly seductive when he was making love. A wild little frisson ran along her nerves at the tone she could detect in his voice now. Rhy was in a dangerous temper and it paid to be wary of him when he was angry.

"I think you'd better come with me," he murmured, sliding his fingers from her wrist to her elbow and moving her to the elevator. "We've got a lot to say and I don't want to say it in the hallway."

He retained his light but firm hold on her as they waited for the elevator to return to the floor and a copyboy stared at them as he walked down the hall to disappear into one of the offices. "Let go of me," she whispered.

"No way, Mrs. Baines," he refused in a soft tone. The bell sounded as the elevator reached their floor and the doors slid open. He moved forward with her into the box and the doors slid closed, leaving her totally alone with him in that small space. His forefinger jabbed the number for the administrative floor and the elevator lurched into movement.

Sallie summoned all of her poise and gave him a polite little smile, determined to hide the sudden coiling of fear in her stomach. "What do we have to talk about? It's been seven years, after all."

He smiled, too, but his smile wasn't polite; the savagery of it sent shivers down her spine. "Then let's talk about old times," he said between his teeth.

"Can't it wait?"

"No," he said softly. "Now. I've got a lot of questions and I want answers to them."

"I've got work to do—"

"Just shut up," he warned, and she did.

The elevator lurched to a halt and her stomach lurched with it. Rhy's manner made her uneasy and she didn't want to be alone with him, much less go through the inquisition she knew she was in for.

He ushered her out of the elevator and down the corridor to his private office. His secretary looked up and smiled when she saw them, but the words she started to say were halted when Rhy hurled "No interruptions" over his shoulder as he followed Sallie into his office and closed the door firmly behind them.

Sallie stood only a few feet away from him and blinked, trying to adjust herself to the reality of his presence. She had been forced to accept his absence and now she just could not accept his presence. He was a mirage, a figment of her imagination, far too virile and forceful to be real.

But he stood by the door, watching her with those unnerving gray eyes, and he was very real and solid. Rather than meet those eyes she let her gaze drift over his body and she noted automatically the way his dark brown suit fit him impeccably, the trousers molding themselves to the muscled length of his legs. Her pulse began to beat a bit faster and she caught her lower lip with her teeth.

"Rhy..." Her voice quavered and she cleared her throat, then began again. "Rhy, why are you acting like this?"

"What do you mean?" he asked, his eyes glinting dangerously. "You're my wife and I want to know what's going on here. You've obviously been avoiding me. Should I have ignored your presence, as you seem prepared to do with mine? Forgive me if I was slow on the uptake, baby, but I was surprised to see you and you caught me off-balance. I didn't think to pretend that I didn't know you.''

She caught her breath in relief. "Oh, that," she said, sighing, weak now that she knew what he wanted. "Yes, I was avoiding you. I didn't know how you'd take the idea of my working for you and I didn't want to risk losing my job.''

"Have you told anyone that we're married?" he barked.

She shook her head. "Everyone knows me as Sallie Jerome. I went back to my maiden name because I didn't want to use the influence of your name.''

"That's big of you, Mrs. Baines," he murmured sarcastically, moving to his desk. "Sit down, I won't bite.''

She took a chair, more than ready now to answer his questions. If he had been going to fire her he would already have done so; her job was safe and she relaxed visibly.

Rhy didn't sit down but instead leaned against his desk, crossed his long legs at the ankle and folded his arms across his chest. He was silent while his glittering gray eyes looked her over thoroughly from head to foot and Sallie began to tense again. She didn't know why, but he made her feel threatened even when he wasn't moving. Then his silence irritated her and she said tartly, "What did you want to talk about?"

"You've changed, Sarah—Sallie," he corrected himself. "It's a drastic change, and I don't mean just your name. You've grown a mane of hair and you've lost so much weight a good wind would blow you away. And most of all, you're doing a damned good job at something I would've sworn you'd never touch. How did you get to be a reporter?"

"Oh, that was just luck," she said cheerfully. "I was driving on a bridge when it collapsed and I wrote it up and turned it in to the editor of the newspaper and he changed my job from clerk to reporter.''

"You make it sound almost logical for you to be one of the top correspondents for a first-class news magazine," he said dryly. "I gather you like your job?"

"Oh, yes!" she said, leaning forward eagerly. Her big eyes sparkled and she tripped over her words in her enthusiasm. "I love it! I never could understand why you were always so anxious to get back to work, but then I was bitten by the same bug. It gets in your blood, hooks you, doesn't it? I suppose I've become an excitement junkie, I only feel half-alive when I'm stuck here in the office.''

"Your eyes haven't changed," he muttered almost to himself, his gaze locked on her face. "They're still as dark blue as the sea and so big and deep a man could drown in them. Why did you change your name?'' he demanded abruptly.

"I told you, I didn't want to trade on your name,'' she explained patiently. "I wanted to stand on my own feet for a change and I found that I liked it. As for Sallie, somehow Sarah was changed to Sallie at college and I've been Sallie ever since then.''

"College?'' he asked, his eyes sharpening.

"Yes, I *finally* got my degree,'' she said, laughing a little. "After you left I took a lot of courses—languages and creative writing—but when I began reporting it took up so much time that I had to get my degree in fits and spurts.''

"Did you go on a diet, too? You've changed everything else in your life, why not get a new figure?'' He sounded almost resentful and she stared at him in bewilderment. Surely he didn't mind that she'd lost a little weight? It hadn't even been that much.

"No, I didn't go on a diet, losing weight just happened,'' she said, her tone reflecting her lack of understanding of the question. "I became so busy that I didn't have time to eat and that still holds true.''

"Why? Why did you change yourself so drastically?''

A sudden tingle told her that this was not a casual conversation, a catching-up on old times, but that Rhy had deliberately brought her around to this question. For what reason she didn't know, but she didn't mind telling him the truth. After all, the laugh was on her. She raised her eyes to his. "When you left, Rhy, you told me to call you when I thought I was woman enough for you. I nearly died. I wanted to die. Then I decided to fight for you, to make myself into a woman you'd want, so I took a lot of courses and learned how to do a lot of things, and along the way I also learned how to do without you. End of story.''

"Not quite,'' he said sardonically. "Your rascally husband has reentered and another chapter has started, and to make the plot really interesting he's now your boss. Let's see,'' he mused, "is there a company policy against employing relatives?''

"If there is,'' she returned clearly, "I was here first.''

"But I'm the boss,'' he reminded her, a wolfish grin moving across his face. "Don't worry about it, baby. I don't intend to fire you. You're too good a reporter for me to let you go to someone else.'' He got to his feet and so did she, but he said, "Sit down, I'm not finished.'' Obediently she resumed her seat and he walked around to take his own chair, leaning back in it as he picked up a file.

Sallie recognized the file as belonging to personnel and she realized that it held her own records. But she had no reason to keep Rhy from reading it, so she watched as he leafed through it.

"I'm curious about your application," he said. "You said no one knows we're married, but what did you put down as your marital status?" he questioned. "Ah, here it is. You've been very honest. You admitted to being married. But your husband's name is, SEPARATED—CONFIDENTIAL INFORMATION."

"I told you no one knew," she replied.

He looked over the application and his brows abruptly snapped together. "Next of kin—none?" he demanded harshly. "What if you'd been hurt, even killed? That does happen, you know! How could I have been notified?"

"I didn't think you'd care," she defended herself. "Actually, I didn't think about it at all, but I can see where you'd want to know. You might want to get married again someday. I'm sorry, that was thoughtless of me."

A vein began throbbing in his temple and she watched it in fascination. It meant that he was furious, as she remembered all too well, but she couldn't think why he should be so angry. After all, she hadn't been killed, so she didn't see anything to worry about.

He closed the file and tossed it back onto his desk, his lips pressed into a grim line. "Get married again!" he suddenly shouted. "Why would I be fool enough to do that? Once was enough!"

"It certainly was," she agreed with heartfelt sincerity.

His eyes narrowed and he seemed to force his temper down. "You don't think you'd like to remarry?" he asked silkily.

"A husband would interfere with my job," she said, and shook her head. "No, I'd rather live by myself."

"You don't have any...er...close friends who object when you take off for days, even weeks, at a time?" he probed.

"I have a lot of friends, yes, but they're mostly in the business themselves so they understand if I go on assignment," she answered calmly and ignored the inference he made. It was none of his business if she had any lovers or not, and suddenly she felt it was important for her pride that he not know he was the only man who had ever made love to her. After all, he certainly hadn't lived the life of a monk, as witness the gorgeous Coral Williams!

"I've read a lot of your articles," he commented, switching to a different tack. "You've been in some tight places—Lebanon, Africa, South America. Don't your *friends* mind that you could get hurt?"

"Like I said, they're in the business themselves. Any of us could come back dead," she returned dryly. "It was the same with you, but you kept going. Why *have* you grounded yourself? You could pick your own assignments, and we heard you were offered the anchor job?"

"Maybe it's a sign of old age, but I got tired of being shot at," he said abruptly. "And I was getting bored, I wanted a change. I'd made some good investments through the years and when *Review* came up for sale I decided to make the change, so I bought it. I'm still signed with the network to do four documentaries for next year and that's always interesting. I have time to do more research, to build a background on my subject."

Sallie looked doubtful. "I think I'd prefer foreign assignments."

He started to say something when the phone on his desk buzzed. In swift irritation he punched the intercom line and snapped, "I said no interruptions!"

Simultaneously the door opened and a soft voice said, "But I knew you wouldn't consider me an interruption, darling. If you have some poor reporter on the carpet I'm sure you've already said all that needs to be said."

Sallie turned her head to stare in amazement at Coral Williams, who was breathtaking in a severe black dress that merely served to flatter her blond perfection. The model was a picture of self-confidence as she smiled at Rhy, fully expecting him to welcome her with open arms.

Rhy said evenly, "I see your problem, Miss Meade," and replaced the receiver. To Coral he said in the same even tone, "It had better be important, Coral, because I've got a lot on my mind."

Such as stumbling over his long-lost wife, Sallie thought to herself, involuntarily smiling as she got to her feet. "If that's all, Mr. Baines...?"

He looked frustrated and ill-tempered. "We'll talk about it later," he snapped, and she took it that she was dismissed. She made her exit with a triumphant grin at a visibly puzzled Coral and gave Rhy's secretary the same grin on her way out.

The first thing she had to do was relieve Greg's mind, so she stopped by his office on her way down. "He knows," she told him matter-of-factly, sticking her head through the door. "It's okay, he didn't fire me."

Greg shoved his fingers roughly through his hair, rumpling the prematurely gray strands into untidy peaks. "You've aged me ten years, doll.'' He sighed. ''I'm glad he knows, that's a weight off me. Is it going to be common knowledge?''

''I wouldn't think so,'' she hedged. ''He didn't mention that. Coral is in his office now, and I don't think he'd want anyone fouling up *that* relationship.''

''What a wonderfully understanding wife you are,'' he mocked, and she stuck her tongue out at him.

With all of the tension behind her she attacked the article she was writing with renewed vigor and finished it that afternoon. Again Chris stopped by her desk, this time to tell her that he was leaving that night for Miami. ''Want to see me off?'' he invited, and she readily accepted.

Sometimes it was nice to see a familiar face in the crowd when you got on a flight in the middle of the night, so she saw nothing unusual about Chris wanting her company. It wasn't until they were on their way to the airport that Sallie realized that Chris had sought out her company several times lately. She liked Chris, he was a good, steady friend, but she knew that it would never develop into anything more serious on her part. Rather than let the situation stew, she asked him frankly, ''Just for the record, why are you asking me to lunch, to see you off, et cetera? Is it for a reason I should know?''

''I'm using you,'' he admitted just as frankly. ''You're good company and you don't expect anything more than friendship. You keep my ego built up, too, because you're a great-looking woman.''

She had to chuckle; in her opinion great-looking women were not petite dynamos with more energy than fashion sense. But it was still nice to have a man voice that opinion. ''Thanks,'' she told him cheerfully, ''but that still doesn't tell me why.''

He raised his sandy eyebrows. ''Because of another woman, of course. What else could it be?''

''Anyone I know?'' she asked.

''No, she's not in this business. She lives in my apartment building and she's the nesting type. She wants a nine-to-five husband, and I can't see myself settling down into that routine. It's a standoff. She won't back down and neither will I.''

''So what will you do?''

''Wait. I'm a patient man. She'll either come around or we won't get together, it's that simple.''

''Why should she do all the giving?'' Sallie asked indignantly, amazed that even reasonable Chris should expect the woman to make all of the adjustments.

"Because I know I can't," he mocked, smiling a little. "I know my limitations, Sal. I only hope she's stronger than I am and can make some changes."

Then he deftly changed the subject and Sallie realized that he had revealed as much as he was going to. They talked shop for the rest of the time, and she waited with him for his flight to be called, sensing that he felt vulnerable. Leaving for a long trip in the middle of the night with no one to see you off was a lonely experience, and she was willing to give him at least one familiar face to wave goodbye to.

It was after ten when she finally got back to her apartment and she quickly showered and got ready for bed. Just as she turned out the lamp the phone rang and she switched the light back on to answer it.

"Sallie? Where in hell have you been?" Rhy demanded impatiently, and as always his husky voice made her spine tingle.

"At the airport," she found herself answering automatically.

"Meeting someone?" he asked, and his voice became sharper.

"No, seeing someone off." She had recovered her poise, and she quickly asked, "Why are you calling?"

"You left this afternoon before we got anything settled," he snapped.

Mystified, she echoed, "Settled? What's there to settle?"

"Our marriage, for one thing," he retorted sarcastically.

Abruptly she understood and tried to reassure him that she wouldn't cause any trouble in the termination of their marriage. "We shouldn't have any trouble getting a divorce, considering how long we've been separated. And getting a divorce is a good idea. We should have done it sooner. Seven years is a long time. It's obvious that our marriage is over in every respect except legally. I see no reason why it shouldn't be terminated on paper, too."

"You talk too much," he observed, the rasp coming into his voice that warned of his rising temper.

Confused, Sallie fell silent. What had she said to make him angry? Why had he brought up the subject if he didn't want to talk about it?

"I don't want a divorce," he said a moment later. "I've found it very convenient, having a little wife tucked away somewhere."

She laughed and sat up in bed, pushing a pillow behind her back for support. "Yes, I can see where it would come in handy," she dared to tease him. "It keeps the husband-hungry women effectively at bay, doesn't it? Still, we've reached the point where to remain married is foolish. Shall I file or would you rather?"

"Are you being deliberately stupid?" he barked. "I said I don't want a divorce!"

Sallie fell silent again, stunned by his insistence. "But, Rhy!" she finally protested incredulously. "Whyever not?"

"I told you," he said with the manner of one explaining the obvious. "I find it convenient to have a wife."

"You could always lie!"

"Why should I bother? And there's always the chance of a lie being found out. No, thank you for the offer, but I think I'll keep you, regardless of who you have waiting in the wings to take my place."

Abruptly Sallie was angry. Why had he called her at all if he didn't want a divorce, and who was he to make snide remarks about anyone waiting in the wings? "You're just being obnoxious!" she charged furiously. "What's wrong, Rhy? Is Coral crowding you a bit? Do you need your convenient wife for protection? Well, you can hide behind someone else, because I don't need your cooperation for a divorce! You deserted me, and you've been gone for seven years, and any judge in the state will give me a divorce!"

"You think so?" he challenged, laughing aloud. "Try it. I've made a lot of friends and divorcing me could be harder than you think. You'd better have a lot of money and a lot of time before you start, and you'd better have a more reliable job. You're in a rather vulnerable position, aren't you? You can't afford to make your boss angry."

"My boss can go straight to—to hell!" she shouted furiously and slammed the receiver down. The phone began ringing again immediately and she glared at it for a moment, then when it continued its irritating noise she reached over and unplugged it, something she rarely did in case Greg needed to reach her.

Then she turned out the lamp and pounded her pillow into shape, but any chance for sleep was now remote. She lay in the darkness and fumed, wishing she could take her temper out on Rhy's head. Why had he called at all if he didn't want to talk about a divorce? If he wanted to use her to keep Coral at a distance he could just find someone else to do his dirty work for him! Personally, she thought Coral was just his type, someone poised and sophisticated who wouldn't care if her husband was more interested in his job than in his wife.

Then, as if someone had turned on a light in a dark room, she knew why Rhy was so stubborn about not getting a divorce, why he had asked all of those prying, suggestive questions about her friends. If she had learned anything at all about Rhy during the year they had been together it was that he was a possessive man. He didn't want to give up anything that belonged to him, and that included his wife. It obviously didn't bother him that thousands of miles might separate them, that they hadn't seen each other in years, his attitude was that once his wife, always his wife. *He* might not want her anymore, but he was too stubborn to give her up if he thought anyone else might want to marry her. What he didn't realize was that her attitude was much the same as his: once was enough.

She admitted honestly to herself that she would never love another man as she had loved Rhy, and even though she had now recovered from the emotional damage he'd inflicted she didn't think she'd ever be able to love so passionately, so demandingly again. Neither was she willing to settle for a lukewarm, comfortable relationship after having known such a love.

Of course, there'd be no convincing him that she didn't want a divorce in order to marry another man. He'd never understand the need she felt to be free of him. While he'd been only a distant figure it hadn't bothered her, but now that he was going to be around permanently she felt stifled. Rhy's character was too forceful, too possessive, and if he thought he had any legal authority over her he wouldn't hesitate to use it in any way he wanted.

For the first time Sallie seriously faced the possibility that she might have to hunt for another job. She loved her job, she liked working for *World in Review,* but there were other publications. And with Rhy threatening to fire her if she tried to divorce him the best thing she could do was spike that weapon before he had a chance to use it.

Chapter Four

Sallie stared morosely at the keys of her typewriter, trying to force words into a reasonable sentence, but her mind stayed stubbornly blank and so did the white paper rolled into the machine. She had always been so enthusiastic about her work, the words pouring from her in swift, flowing sentences, that this block she was experiencing was tying her nerves into king-size knots. She'd never had this trouble before and she was at a loss. How could she write about something that bored her to tears? And this article *was* boring!

Brom had been summoned to Greg's office and now he returned. "I'm off," he announced, clearing the top of his desk. "Munich."

Sallie swiveled in her chair to face him. "Anything interesting?"

"A Common Market meeting. There's some trouble that could break it up. I'll see you when I get back."

"Yeah, okay," Sallie said, and tried to smile.

Brom paused by her desk and his hand touched her shoulder. "Is anything wrong, Sal? You've been acting under the weather for a couple of weeks now. Have you seen a doctor?"

"It's nothing," she assured him, and he left. When she was alone again she turned back to the typewriter and scowled at it. She hadn't seen a doctor; there was nothing to cure boredom. Why was she being kept in the office? Greg knew that she did her best work in the field, but it had been three weeks since she'd returned from Washington and she hadn't been on a single assignment since then, not even a small one. Instead she'd been flooded with "suggestions" for articles that anyone could have written. She'd done her best, but she'd come up against a stone wall now and suddenly she was angry. If Greg wasn't going to use her she wanted to know why!

In determination she switched off her typewriter and made her way to Greg's office. He wasn't there, so she sat down to wait, and as she waited her temper faded, but her resolve didn't. The natural tenacity that kept her on a lead when she wanted a story also kept her firm in her decision to get to the bottom of why suddenly Greg was ignoring her. They'd always had the best of working relationships, respect mixed with affection, and now it was as if Greg no longer trusted her to do her job.

She had to wait almost forty minutes before Greg returned, and when he opened the door and saw her sitting there, a wary, concerned expression crossed his face before he quickly smoothed it away. "Hi, doll, how's the article going?" he greeted her.

"It isn't. I can't do it."

He sighed at the blunt announcement and sat down behind his desk. After toying with a pencil for a minute he said easily, "We all have problems occasionally. What's wrong with the article? Anything you can put your finger on?"

"It's boring," she said baldly and Greg flinched. "I don't know why you've been throwing all the garbage at me, so I'm asking you, why? I'm good at my job, but you aren't letting me do it. Are you trying to force me to resign? Has Rhy decided that he doesn't want his wife working for him, but he doesn't want to make things look bad by firing me?"

Greg ran his fingers through his gray-brown hair and sighed, his hard, firm-jawed face tense. "You're putting me on the spot," he muttered. "Can't you just let things rest for a while?"

"No!" she exploded, then calmed herself. "I'm sorry. I think I know that it isn't your fault, you've always given me the assignments you thought I could handle. It's Rhy, isn't it?"

"He's taken you off foreign assignments," Greg affirmed.

Though Sallie had braced herself for something like that, to hear the words actually spoken and her suspicions confirmed was a worse blow than she had anticipated. She paled and visibly shrank in her seat. Taken off assignment! It was a deadly blow. All of the passion she'd offered to Rhy had been transferred to her job when he walked out and through the years she'd learned that a satisfying job had enriched her life. She didn't doubt that a psychologist would tell her that her job was merely a substitute for what she really wanted, a man, and perhaps it had been at first. But she was no longer the same person she'd been seven years before; she was a mature, independent adult, and she felt as a musician might if his hands were crippled, as if her life had been blighted.

Through a throat thick with horror she murmured, "Why?"

"I don't know why," Greg replied. "Look, honey, all I know is he took you off foreign assignment. You can still cover anything in the States and several things have come up but I kept you here because anyone could have covered the others and I wanted you available in case something more important developed. Maybe I was wrong. I was trying to do what was best for the magazine, but I know how you are about being in one place for too long. If anything comes up, regardless of what it is, do you want it? Just say the word and it's yours."

"It doesn't matter," she said wearily, and he frowned. Defeat wasn't something he expected from Sallie. Then she looked up and her dark blue eyes were beginning to spark with anger. "On second thought, yes, I do want it. Anything! If you can keep me gone for six months straight, that will be fine, too. The only way I'm going to keep from killing Rhy is if I'm kept away from him. Was this supposed to be kept secret, that I'm off foreign assignment?"

"I wouldn't think so," Greg denied. "I just didn't tell you because I kept hoping I could keep you satisfied on other jobs, but nothing came up. Why?"

"Because I'm going to ask Rhy that same question," she said, and a feline smile curved her mouth at the thought of engaging in battle with her arrogant husband.

Greg leaned back in his chair and studied the suddenly glowing little face, alight with the anticipation of a struggle. For a minute he'd been worried about her, afraid that vibrant energy had been snuffed, but now he grinned in appreciation. Sallie came alive when the going was roughest and that was one of the characteristics that made her one of his best reporters. "Give it all you've got," he said gruffly. "I need you back in the field."

Amanda Meade, Rhy's secretary, smiled at Sallie when she entered. Amanda had also been the secretary of the former publisher and she knew all of the staff; proof of her discretion was that no talk had circulated about Sallie's private interview with Rhy, for which Sallie was grateful. She didn't want any gossip starting about them or Rhy might take it into his head to jettison her entirely in order to halt the talk.

"Hi, Sallie," Amanda greeted her. "Is there anything I can help you with, or do you need to see the boss?"

"The boss, if he's available," Sallie replied.

"He's available for the minute," Amanda confirmed, "but he's got a lunch date with Miss Williams at twelve, so he'll be leaving shortly."

"I won't be long," Sallie promised. "Ask if he'll see me."

Amanda buzzed the inner office on the private line and Sallie listened as she explained the reason for the interruption. After only a few seconds she hung up and smiled again. "Go on in, he's free—and he's been in a very good mood lately, too!"

Sallie had to laugh. "Thanks for the information, but I don't think I'll ask for a raise, anyway!"

Crossing to Rhy's office she entered and firmly closed the door behind her, wanting to make certain that none of their conversation was over-heard. Rhy was standing by the huge plate-glass window, staring down at the hordes of people below as they surged up and down the street. He was in his shirt sleeves, with the cuff links removed and lying on his desk and the cuffs rolled back to reveal muscular forearms. When he turned she saw that he'd also removed his tie; he looked more like a reporter than a publisher and he exuded an air of virility that no other man could quite match.

"Hello, baby," he drawled, his rough-velvet voice containing an intimate note that made her pulses leap. "It took you long enough to get here. I was beginning to think you were playing it safe."

What did he mean? Had Greg called to warn Rhy that she was coming? No, she'd just left Greg's office, and in any case he wanted her free to go on assignment. Printer's ink ran in Greg's veins, not blood.

"I don't understand," she said curtly. "What do you mean, it took me long enough?"

"For you to realize you'd been grounded," he replied, smiling as he approached her. Before she had a chance to avoid him he was standing before her, his hard, warm hands clasping her elbows and she quivered at his touch. She tried to move away and his grip tightened, but only enough to hold her. "I was going to tell you the night I called, but you hung up on me," he continued, still smiling. "So I waited for you to come to me."

Sallie was blessed with acute senses and now she wished that they weren't so acute, because she could smell the warm male scent of his body under the quiet after-shave he wore. He was close enough for her to notice that he still, after all these years, didn't wear an undershirt, because she could see the dark curling hairs on his chest through the thin fabric of his shirt. She tore her gaze away from his chest and lifted it higher to his cleanly shaven jaw, to his lips, relaxed and smiling, then higher still, to the direct gaze of those dark gray eyes under level black brows.

With supreme willpower she forced her attention away from his physical attractions and said in a half whisper, "Why? You know how much I love foreign assignments. Why did you take me off?"

"Because I'm not that much of a newsman," he answered dryly, and she stared at him in bewilderment. He released her elbows and slid his hands warmly up her arms, drawing her with him to the desk, where he leaned against its edge and pulled her forward until she stood between his legs. He was more on her level in that position, and the mesmerizing gray eyes looking directly into hers prevented her from protesting at his closeness.

"What do you mean?" she managed, her voice no stronger this time than it had been before. His fingers were massaging the bare skin of her upper arms and involuntarily she began to tremble.

"I mean that I couldn't stand the thought of sending you into potentially dangerous situations," he explained softly. "South America, Africa, the Middle East are all political time bombs and I didn't want to take the chance that you might be caught in one of them if they explode. Europe—even in Europe there are kidnappings, terrorist groups, bombings in air terminals and on the streets. For my own peace of mind I took you off foreign assignment, though Downey nearly had a stroke when I told him. He thinks you're one of the best, baby. I could wring his neck when I think of the situations he's sent you into!"

"Greg's a professional," Sallie defended huskily. "And so am I. I'm not helpless, Rhy. I've taken weapons training and self-defense courses. I can take care of myself. Staying here is driving me crazy! I feel as if I've been put out to pasture!"

He laughed and reached behind her for her braid, pulling it over her shoulder and settling the thick rope over her breast. He began playing with the braid, running his fingers over the smooth twists of hair and the corners of his mouth moved into another smile. "This is quite a mane," he murmured. "I'd like to see it out of this braid and spread across my pillow while I make love to you."

Sallie was rocked on her heels by his words and her cheeks paled. Of all the things he might have said she certainly hadn't expected that! She raised stunned eyes to him and saw his pupils dilated with desire;

then he jerked her forward and she lay against him, trapped by the pressure of his powerful legs clasping hers and his arms as they slid around her.

She gasped at the contact of his hard, warm body and, as they always had, her senses began swimming when he touched her. Fighting for control, she turned her head to him to demand that he turn her loose and he took advantage of the opportunity, fitting her more tightly into the curve of his body with the pressure of his arms, and bending his head down. His mouth was hot and forceful and drugging, and she began wriggling in his grasp, trying to escape from her inevitable response to him as much as she was trying to escape from the man himself. By stretching her willpower to its limits she managed to resist the probing of his tongue between her lips, keeping her teeth tightly clenched. After a moment he lifted his head and his breathing was faster, his eyes still eager.

"Open your mouth," he commanded huskily. "You know how I want to kiss you. Let me feel your sweet little tongue against mine again."

He lowered his head again, and this time her willpower wasn't up to the demands she made on it. Her senses exploded with pleasure at the touch of his lips on hers and when his tongue moved demandingly she let her lips and teeth part and he gained possession of the sweet interior of her mouth. With a groan he tightened his arms and in response her hands slid up his arms and shoulders to climb about his neck. Her slim body quivered at the wild storm his kiss was causing, and helplessly she arched against him, gasping her need into his mouth as she realized just how strongly he was aroused.

It had always been like that. From the first kiss they had shared to the last time he'd made love to her, their physical responses to each other had been strong and immediate. She'd never wanted another lover because she'd known instinctively that no other man could arouse her as Rhy did, even now, despite all of the perfectly good reasons she had for not wanting to respond to him. Her body simply did not listen to her mind, and after a few moments she stopped wanting to protest. She felt wildly alive and drowning at the same time, straining against him even as her senses were overwhelmed by the countless pleasure signals her nerves were giving out.

When he lifted his mouth from hers she was so weak and trembly that she had to cling to him for support. Triumph gleamed hotly in his eyes as he held her up with one arm about her waist and with his free hand he cupped her chin and held it still while he pressed swift light kisses across her face and lips.

"Mmm," he groaned deep in his throat, "that still hasn't changed. It's still dynamite."

His words brought a measure of sanity to her fevered brain, and she struggled to put a little space between them. Yes, it *was* still dynamite, and it had nearly blown up in her face! She was a fool if she allowed Rhy to use his physical attractions to make her forget the reason she'd come up here.

"Rhy—don't!" she protested, turning her face away as his lips continued to nibble at her skin. "Let me go. I came up here to talk to you—"

"We've talked," he interrupted huskily, his voice going even lower and rougher, a signal which told her he didn't want to stop. "I'd rather make love now. It's been a long time, but not long enough for me to forget what it was like between us."

"Well, *I've* forgotten," she lied, once again avoiding his kiss. "Stop fooling around! I'm serious about my job and I don't like being grounded because you think that a woman can't take care of herself in a crisis."

He ceased trying to kiss her, but his eyes were impatient as he stared down at her. "All right, we'll talk about the job, then I want the subject dropped. I didn't say that I don't think a woman can take care of herself. I said that I didn't want *you* in a dangerous situation because I didn't think *I* could stand it."

"Why should you care?" Sallie demanded in surprise. "You certainly haven't exhibited much concern for my welfare since you walked out, so don't ruin my job by acting concerned now."

Abruptly he released her and she moved several feet away from him. She was glad of the distance; she needed all of her wits about her in order to handle Rhy, and his closeness clouded her brain with erotic fever. "My decision is final," he informed her curtly. "You're off foreign assignment, permanently."

She stared at him and her stomach lurched sickeningly at his words. Permanently? She could more easily stop eating than she could give up the dangerous excitement of the job she loved! He couldn't have thought of anything that would hurt her more if he'd planned this for years. "Do you hate me so much?" she murmured, her dark blue eyes turning almost to black with pain. "What have I ever done to you to make you treat me like this?"

"Of course I don't hate you," he denied impatiently, thrusting a long-fingered hand through his black hair. "I'm trying to protect you. You're my wife and I don't want you hurt."

"Drivel!" she cried, her small fists clenching at her side. "Being tied down is worse than anything that's likely to happen to me on assignment! I'm only half-alive here. I'm going crazy staring at that blasted typewriter hour after hour with nothing coming in my head to put down on paper! And don't say I'm your wife! The extent of our relationship was that we slept together off and on for about a year, then you went your way and I went mine, and I'm a lot happier now than I ever was with you. You were an even bigger flop as a husband than I was as a wife!" She stopped and drew a trembling breath, trying to control the urge to break something, to hit out at him with her fists. Though she had a temper she wasn't usually so uncontrolled and she knew that frustration had strained her nerves.

"Flop or not, you're my wife and you'll stay my wife," he stated coldly, dropping the words like stones on her head. "And my wife will not go on foreign assignments!"

"Why don't you just shoot me?" she demanded furiously, her voice rising. "That would be more merciful than driving me mad with boredom! Blast you, Rhy, I don't know why you married me anyway!" she concluded in acute frustration.

"I married you because I felt sorry for you," he informed her bluntly, and the simple statement left her gaping at him in outrage.

"You—you felt *sorry* for me?" she cried, and she thought she'd explode with rage. Of all the humiliating things to say to her!

"You were such a lonely little thing," he explained calmly, as if every word didn't lash at her raw nerves. "And so starved for affection, for a human touch. I thought, Why the hell not? I was twenty-eight years old. It was time I got married. And here was an added bonus."

"Yes," she snapped, stalking to the window to stare down at the street below, anything to keep from looking at the mocking dark face, the sardonic eyes. "You got protection from all of your pursuing girlfriends!" With relish she contemplated planting a fist right in his mouth, except that Rhy wouldn't let her get away with that. She knew that he'd retaliate.

He grinned at her temper and walked up behind her, so close that his breath stirred the hair at her temple. "No, baby, the added bonus was the way you went wild whenever I touched you. You looked so quiet and tame, a plump little dove, but in bed you turned into a wildcat. The contrast was fascinating.''

"I can see you've had a lot of laughs over it!'' she blurted, her face going crimson with humiliation.

"Oh, no, I never laughed,'' he replied, his voice suddenly becoming soft and whispery. "The loving between us was too good. No other woman ever quite matched you. Everything else about you has changed, but not the way you respond.''

Her pride stung, she retorted sharply, "Forget about that. It didn't mean anything.''

"I think it did. It means I've found my wife again. I want you back, Sallie,'' he informed her silkily.

Astonishment spun her around to face him, and she stared up at him with eyes grown huge in her small face. "You're joking!'' she accused, her voice shaking. "It's impossible!''

"I don't think it's so impossible,'' he murmured, catching her close to him and pressing his face into her hair. "I never meant to let you go, anyway,'' he continued, his voice growing low and seductive. She knew that he was consciously using the erotic power of his voice to disarm and attract her, but recognizing his weapons didn't necessarily give her the strength to fight them. She shivered and tried to pull away, but his grip tightened.

"I thought you'd back down and call me. I was fed up with your nagging and determined to teach you a lesson,'' he said, raising his head and looking down into her astounded face. "But you didn't call, and I had my career to see to and time got away from me. Seven years is a long time to be separated, but we've both matured in that length of time, and I intend to pull on that leash you still have around your neck, sweetheart!''

"Don't be silly!'' she said, shaking her head to deny his casual assumption that she had no choice in the matter, that she would tamely let him lead her about. He had a lot to learn about her! "It wouldn't work out, Rhy. We're two different people now. I'm no longer content to putter around a house. There are so many things I want to do that I may never get around to them all. I have to be on the move.''

"I'll be traveling quite a bit with the documentaries I've signed to do. You could always quit your job and travel with me,'' he pointed out, and she recoiled from that suggestion as if he had thrown a snake at her

"Give up my job?'' she echoed, aghast. "Rhy, are you crazy? I don't want to spend my life tagging after you! This isn't just a job to me, it's *my* career, too. If you want us to be together so badly you quit *your* job." She drew her mouth into a hard line and glared her challenge at him.

"I make more than you do," he drawled. "It would be stupid for me to quit. Besides, I own this magazine."

"The entire idea of us trying to live together is stupid," she blasted him. "Why not just obtain a quiet divorce? You won't have to worry that I'll ask for alimony, I like supporting myself—"

"No," he interrupted, his jaw hardening as temper began to flicker in his eyes. "No divorce, under any circumstances."

"All right, maybe you can make it difficult for me to get a divorce," she acknowledged. "But I don't have to live with you and I don't have to work for you. There are other magazines, newspapers and wire services, and I'm good at my job. I don't need you or your magazine."

"Don't you? Like I've told you before, I have a lot of friends and if I put the word out that I don't want you working, believe me, you won't be reporting. Maybe you could get a job in a restaurant or driving a cab, but that'll be it, and I can stop that too if I want." His eyes narrowed on her and a grin split his dark face. "And in the meantime, you're still my wife, and I intend to treat you as such."

The threat was implicit in his words and she sucked in her breath. Alarm rioted along her nerves as she realized that he intended to resume his marital rights. "I'll get a court order forcing you to stay away from me!" she ground out, too angry now to back down even though she knew that, if dared, Rhy would go to any lengths to get what he wanted.

"A court order might be difficult to obtain if the right pressure is brought to bear," he mocked, enjoying his power over her. "And after a little while you just might decide that you like having me around, you did before. If I remember correctly, and I do, that was the basis of all your complaints, that I was never there. Let's try the whole bit again, hmm?" he murmured cajolingly. "And you wanted kids. We'll have kids, all you want. As a matter of fact, I'm willing to start on that project right now."

Sallie ground her teeth in rage, more upset than he could know by his reference to having children. The beast! "I've had a baby, thank you!" she choked, lashing out in her raging need to hurt him as she'd been hurt, as she still hurt. "And if *I* remember correctly, Mr. Baines, you didn't want him! I carried him alone, and I had him alone and I buried him alone! I don't need you or anything about you!"

"I don't care whether or not you need me," he said, his mouth tightening into a grim line at her reckless words. "I can make you want me, and that's all that matters. You can spit fire at me all you want, but you and I both know that if I want you I can have you. Make up your mind to it, you're mine and I'm not about to let you go. I'm ready to settle down now, for real this time. You're my wife, and I wouldn't mind a couple of kids before we're too old."

She strangled on the hot words that bubbled in her throat and jerked away from him. "No," she refused savagely. "No to everything. No to you and no to your kids. Let someone else have the honor! I'm sure Coral would be more than eager to take on the job. And since she's waiting for you now I won't keep you any longer!"

His roar of laughter followed her as she stormed out of his office and Amanda Meade stared at her with round eyes. Without a word Sallie slammed the door and stood in the hallway, shaking with temper. The most galling thing of all was that she was helpless. Rhy had the power to destroy the career she'd so carefully, lovingly created for herself and he'd do it without a moment's thought if he wanted her.

She returned to her desk and sank into her chair, trembling inside. Why was he doing this to her? He couldn't be serious—could he? The memory of his hot kisses returned vividly and blood surged into her cheeks. *That* hadn't changed! Was it just sex that he wanted from her, that and the challenge she now represented to his male ego? She had been his once and she might have guessed that he'd be unable to endure the thought that now she didn't want him.

The only thing was, she wasn't so certain now that she didn't want him. Making love with him was fantastic, and she'd never forgotten the heated magic of his caresses. For just a minute she sank into a delicious daydream of what it would be like to be his wife again, to live with him and sleep beside him and make love with him; then cold reality intruded. If she went back to him, then what? He'd already grounded her. He'd take her away from her job entirely, perhaps even get her pregnant again. Sallie thought longingly of a baby, but she knew Rhy well enough to think beyond that. She could see herself with a child and Rhy growing bored and restless as he had before, resentful that she'd become pregnant. He wouldn't be faithful; he wasn't now, so why should he be later?

He'd tire of her and she'd be both without a job and hampered by a baby. Top jobs in the reporting field were hard to come by and required more than dedication; they required a reporter's whole life. If she left the field she'd have a difficult time returning, carving another niche for herself, and if there was a baby, what would she do then?

The thought of what could happen if she returned to Rhy frightened her and she knew that if she had a choice she would take her job. It had never let her down as Rhy had. And she loved what she was doing. She knew just how precious her independence was, and she wasn't about to sacrifice it for physical gratification.

She couldn't think what to do. Her nature was to act, but in this situation there was nothing she *could* do. Rhy would block any effort she made to get another job unless she disappeared and took another name, moved to another section of the country. The thought shook her; it seemed so drastic, but even before her nerves had settled she was making plans. Why should a little thing like creating another identity stop her? Hadn't she learned that she could handle almost anything? She would hate to give up her job, this particular job, but she could find another if she had to. The important thing was to stay away from Rhy.

It was still a few minutes before lunchtime, but she jerked the cover over her typewriter and slung her purse over her shoulder. If she knew Rhy he would start maneuvering immediately to hem her in, and she had a lot of things to do to protect herself.

She caught a taxi to the bank where she kept her checking and savings accounts and closed both of them out. She didn't know if Rhy could block any withdrawals if she needed money in a hurry, but it seemed wise not to take the chance. Over the years she had managed to save several thousand dollars, enough that she would be able to support herself while she looked for another job, and she felt more secure with the cashier's check in her purse. Rhy would find that she was no longer a helpless little ninny for him to intimidate!

She was rarely hungry, but she'd burned a lot of calories that morning and her stomach was beginning to protest. On impulse she stopped at the bar and grill just around the corner from the *World in Review* building and found an empty booth in a dark corner. It was like going into a cave until her eyes adjusted to the dimness, then she recognized several of the staff either sitting at the bar or tucking into lunch in one of the dark booths. She ordered a grilled cheese sandwich and coffee and was waiting for her food when Chris dropped his lanky form into the seat opposite her. It was the first time she'd seen him since he'd returned from Florida, and she noticed how tanned he looked, even in the dimness of the bar.

"Florida suits you," she commented. "How have you been?"

He shrugged, his quiet face wry. "I'm still at a standoff, if that's what you're asking. What about you, doll? I've heard a rumor that you've been grounded."

"It's true," Sallie admitted, frowning. "Orders from the top."

"Baines himself? What'd you do?"

"It's not what I did, it's what I am. He thinks foreign assignment is too dangerous for me."

Chris snorted in disbelief. "C'mon, Baines is too good a newsman to ground you for a stupid reason like that. Level with me, Sal. What's going on? I saw him staring at you that day in the cafeteria."

"Oh, it's true that he thinks foreign assignment is too dangerous for me," she insisted. "But that's only part of the reason. He thinks I'd be a nice addition to his personal scalp collection, if you get my meaning. Unfortunately, I don't agree."

Chris whistled soundlessly through his teeth. "Big boss is after you, eh? Well, I agree with him that you're a fetching little witch. The only difference is, I never had the guts to tackle you."

Sallie exploded into laughter, knowing that while Chris might like her well enough he'd never been attracted to her romantically. Though he was the footloose type he was attracted to nesting women; he wanted someone who could provide a stable base for him when he returned from his wanderings. Sallie was too much of a wanderer herself for Chris to be interested. He kept a straight face while she rocked with laughter, holding her sides, but his brown eyes danced with amusement.

Afterward they returned to work together, and as they entered the lobby Chris had his arm affectionately around her waist. The first person Sallie saw was Rhy, waiting for the elevator, and as he looked at them and saw Chris with his arm about her his eyes flared, then narrowed to furious slits.

"Uh-oh, trouble," Chris muttered to her, then gave her a grin. As the elevator opened and Rhy stepped in Chris compounded his sins by hugging her close and kissing the top of her head. In the last glimpse Sallie had of Rhy before the doors closed and hid him from view he looked murderous.

Chapter Five

"You fool," Sallie whispered to Chris, torn between laughter and genuine concern. Rhy was a dangerous man when he was angry. He was strong enough and wild enough and mean enough to handle just about anyone he wanted to handle, and he'd taken a lot of specialized training. Underneath his perfectly tailored three-piece suits Rhy was a half-civilized commando and he could hurt Chris badly. "Are you trying to get yourself killed? Rhy has a hair-trigger temper!"

"I didn't want him to take you for granted," Chris explained lazily. He gave her a crooked grin. "Feel free to use me any time you need the safety of numbers, the least I can do is return the favors you've done me. I use you, you use me in return."

Sallie drew in her breath. The idea was tempting, to pretend to Rhy that she was wildly in love with Chris, except that she didn't think she could act well enough to make it convincing and she would hate to push Rhy far enough that he lost his temper and hurt Chris.

"Thanks for the offer, but I don't think it'd be very smart to act out our charades in front of him," she declined. "I like your face as it is. But if you don't mind I'll throw up your name as a smoke screen to hide behind."

"Okay by me." He regarded her seriously. "Why are you trying to get away from him? He's got everything a man—or a woman—could want."

"I knew Rhy before he bought the magazine," Sallie explained with caution, not wanting to tell him too much. "He wants to renew the relationship and I don't. It's that simple."

"Except for the feeling that you're leaving a lot untold, I believe you," Chris mused almost to himself and left her with a smile.

After returning to her desk Sallie waited all afternoon for a call summoning her to Rhy's office, but the call didn't materialize and she finally realized that he was more subtle than that. He'd let her worry about it, become anxious and vulnerable. She'd show him!

With a flourish she pushed aside the article she'd been working on and rolled a clean sheet of paper into the typewriter. If Rhy wanted to play dirty, then she had no scruples about not doing her work. Instead of concentrating on that stupid article she'd begin her memoirs! If she wrote her life story down as it happened, when she got old it would be finished and she wouldn't have to try to remember all of the details!

Adrenalin flowed through her veins and her fingers flew over the typewriter keys. For the first time in weeks words spilled out of her brain and she scarcely paused to get them in order. She felt elated, alive again. Enthusiasm pulsed through her body.

Suddenly she dropped her hands, staring at what she'd written. Why play around with her memoirs? Why not take her own experiences and weave them into a novel? She'd always wanted to write a book but she'd never had the time. Now she had the time, and she wanted to laugh aloud at the thought of using Rhy's time and money to begin a new career for herself.

Feverishly she put a fresh page in the typewriter, then sat for several minutes, stumped by her first problem—what name should she use for her heroine? Could she just leave a blank space and insert the name later? Then she realized that she had to have a name before she could visualize her character, and that thought led her to ponder the physical attributes of her creation. Writing a book was different from writing an article of an eyewitness report. Then she had facts to deal with, but with fiction she had to create the details herself. Except for that first creative writing course she was trained in facts and this was harder than she'd imagined.

But before the day was over she had sweated eight pages out of her imagination and she glared impatiently at the clock, which insisted that it was time she left. She slid her precious eight pages into a folder and tucked it under her arm. She would work on them at home, on her own typewriter.

Seldom had anything held her concentration in such a tight grip and when she finally went to bed that night the plot and scenes kept darting around in her mind. This was a challenge that equaled the most dangerous of assignments, and she felt the same enthusiasm, the same drive to get it accomplished. She almost resented the hours she was forced to waste sleeping, but at last she drifted off into a deep, dreamless sleep, the most restful she'd had in weeks.

For a week she worked on the manuscript during every spare moment, taking it to work with her, sitting up late at night and typing until she was so tired that she had to sleep. Rhy didn't call her and she was so caught up in her project that she ceased waiting for him to make a move. She was aware of his silence only with the outer edge of her consciousness, and she didn't worry about it. So long as he didn't try to resume their relationship she was content to let time slide by and, judging by the number of times she saw Coral Williams either entering or leaving the building, Rhy felt no sense of urgency either.

She was ready to leave one afternoon when her phone rang, which startled her, as that had become a rarity. Since Brom was still away she snatched it up and heard Rhy's gravelly voice say tersely, "Get up here, Sallie. We have a problem."

Staring at the phone after he'd hung up, Sallie wondered about the nature of the "problem." Did he mean that they personally had a problem—if so, she had to agree—or did he mean that the magazine had a problem? Had something come up that required her personal qualifications? Was Rhy backed into a corner where he would have to use her or lose a story? She relished that thought as she made her way up to Rhy's office, wondering just how he would handle that situation.

Amanda waved her into Rhy's office with an urgent "They're waiting for you!" and when she entered she saw that Greg was also present, prowling restlessly about the office while Rhy was sprawled back in his big chair with his feet propped on his desk; he looked physically relaxed, but the glitter of his eyes revealed his mental alertness.

Greg turned as she entered and glared at her, his jaw belligerent. He always looked like that when he was upset and Sallie caught her breath in alarm.

Without greeting Rhy she said huskily to Greg, "What's wrong? Has anyone been hurt?" Two years ago one of her closest friends had been killed in South America while covering a revolution, and the tragedy had made her highly sensitive to the risks they all took. She never worried about herself, but now she braced herself to receive the news that another reporter had been wounded, perhaps killed. Her tension was evident in her low-toned voice and Greg picked it up immediately.

"No, no one's been hurt," he assured her gently, remembering the only time he'd ever seen her break down, when he had told her that Artie Hendricks had been killed.

She sighed in relief and sank into a chair, glancing at Rhy to find his face still, his eyes furious.

Puzzled, she looked back at Greg. "Then what's wrong?"

"The Sakaryan charity ball is next week," Greg informed her, crossing the office to sit down beside her.

"Yes, I know. I was supposed to cover it," she said dryly and shot a scathing look at Rhy. "Who're you sending in my place?"

"I *was* sending Andy Wallace and Patricia King," Greg snapped. "But Marina Delchamp has refused to grant a personal interview. Dammit!" he exploded in frustration, pounding his fist on the arm of the chair. "It was all set up and now she refuses!"

"That doesn't sound like Marina," Sallie protested. "She's not at all snobbish. There must be a reason."

"There is," Rhy drawled the answer from his relaxed position. "She won't talk to anyone but you, or so she says. Why does it have to be you? Do you know her personally?"

Sallie grinned as she realized that her wishful thinking had come true—Marina had placed Rhy between a rock and a hard place, and he wasn't enjoying the situation.

"Yes, she's a friend of mine," she admitted, and if Rhy thought it strange that she knew the gorgeous ex-model he said nothing. Now Marina was the wife of one of the most powerful men in Sakarya and in charge of the charity ball, and she could choose any reporter she wanted.

"Talk to her, convince her to talk to Patricia King instead of you," Rhy ordered. "Or get the interview over the phone." The satisfaction in his tone revealed that he thought he'd just solved the entire problem and she bristled, but struggled to hide her temper.

"I suppose when you're the wife of the finance minister you can give interviews or not, whichever you want," she said casually.

"Sallie," Rhy informed her with deadly calm, "I'm ordering you to get that interview over the phone."

"But it won't work!" she said, widening her eyes in innocence. "Marina can talk to me whenever she'd like if that's all she wants. She wants to *see* me. And I have an invitation to the ball anyway," she finished smugly. She had been intending to take on part of her vacation next week and fly to Sakarya at her own expense, but now she saw a way of defeating Rhy and it was all she could do to stop herself from laughing aloud.

"It won't work," Rhy warned softly. "I said no foreign assignments and I meant it. You can't go."

Beside her, Greg cursed beneath his breath in frustration and got to his feet, shoving his fists into his pockets. "She's the best reporter I've got!" he said in restrained violence. "You're wasting her!"

"I'm not wasting her," Rhy snarled, coming out of his chair with a lithe twist of his body that had him instantly poised, ready to react. In that instant Sallie read danger in his narrowed eyes. "I've told you before, Downey, she's off anything that even smells like it might be dangerous, and that includes any damned party in an oil-rich desert where every power in the world is jockeying around trying to figure out how to get control of that oil!"

"Are you blind?" Greg bellowed. "She thrives on danger. She carries it around with her! Dammit, man, she can't even catch a bus in a normal manner! Her everyday life would turn a sane person's hair gray!"

Deftly Sallie put herself between the two big, angry men and tilted her delicate jaw at Rhy. "If Marina refuses to see Patricia I suppose you just won't get an interview," she said, bringing the conversation back to its original subject. Triumph gleamed in her dark blue eyes. "It's me or no one. How much of a newsman are you?"

His jaw clenched in anger, but he shot a look at Greg. "Get out of here," he ordered harshly, jerking his eyes back to her. "My answer is still no."

"Suit yourself." She left the office with more poise than she would have thought possible, but chuckled to herself as she collected her belongings and left the building.

She wasn't surprised the next morning when she was directed to Rhy's office as soon as she entered the building. She stalled for a few moments, enjoying making him wait while she put up her shoulder bag and locked the manuscript in her desk, then she carefully wiped all traces of amusement from her expression as she went to meet him.

Instead of the frustrated anger she'd expected to see on his face he wore a look of intense satisfaction, and she felt a twinge of uneasiness. "I've solved our problem," he almost purred, moving close to her and reaching out to stroke her hair.

Diverted, she slapped his hand away in irritation. "I'm going to cut my hair!'' she said curtly. "Maybe then you'll keep your hands to yourself.''

"Don't cut it,'' he advised. "You wouldn't like the consequences.''

"I'll cut my hair if I feel like it. It's nothing to you!''

"We won't argue that now, but I'm warning you, don't cut your hair or I'll turn you over my knee.'' With that threat he left the subject and quirked an inquiring eyebrow at her. "Don't you want to hear about my solution?''

"No. If you like it that well I know I'll hate it,'' she said, admitting fantastically that he'd obviously thought of some way to get around Marina.

"I wouldn't say that,'' he murmured. "You used to like it quite well. You can go to Sakarya, darling.'' He paused and watched her eyes light up with delight, then he delivered the bomb. "And I'm going with you.''

Aghast, Sallie stared up at him. Her thoughts whirled madly as she tried to think of some way out of this situation, but all she could say was, "You can't do that,'' in weak protest.

"Of course I can,'' he said, smiling in a predatory manner that gave her chills. "I own this magazine and I'm a newsman. Other than that, I'm your husband—all excellent reasons why I can go to Sakarya with you.''

"But I don't want you along! I don't need you.''

"Poor baby,'' he said in mock sympathy, then reverted to his normal tone. "There's no way out of it. If you go, I go. I want to make certain that silky skin of yours stays whole.''

"I'm not a child or an idiot. I can take care of myself.''

"So you say, but you still aren't changing my mind. Sorry if I've messed up your plans. Did you have it set for your boyfriend to go along with you? What's his name—the photographer?''

The skin on the back of her neck prickled as she caught the threat in his tone and she knew that he hadn't forgotten that day when he had seen Chris hug her. "Leave Chris alone!'' she flared. "He's a good friend.''

"I can imagine. He went with you to Washington, didn't he?'' Rhy gritted savagely, abruptly catching her wrist and pulling her against him. "And he's the one you went to the airport to see off, isn't he?''

"Yes, he is,'' she admitted, surprised that he should remember that. She tried to release her wrist, and he anchored her to him with his other arm, sliding it about her waist.

"Here's another warning for you,'' he ground out. "You're still my wife and I won't tolerate another man in your bed. I don't care how long we've been separated. If I catch him with you I'm going to push his teeth through the back of his head and then I'm going to take it up with you. Is that what you want? Are you trying to push me into proving how much I want you?'' Without waiting for an answer he bent his head and ground his mouth against hers, forcing a response from her and parting her lips to allow his deeper kiss.

The familiar taste of his mouth tore away the years that had separated them, and she gasped at the lash of desire that sent her hands up to cling to his heavy shoulders as she pressed herself to him. It was their first kiss all over again. She melted, and her awareness of the world around her faded. Even as she responded to him she writhed inside with shame that she didn't have more self-respect than to be so vulnerable to him. He'd never really cared about her, he'd admitted it, but he liked going to bed with her, and she was too weak to resist him. It was odd that no other man had ever tempted her as Rhy did, but then, she'd never known another man like him. He was hard and brutal, but he was strong, and the force of his personality swept lesser people to the side.

But their attraction wasn't all one-sided, she realized dazedly a moment later when his hard hands slid down to her waist and clenched almost painfully on her soft flesh as he pulled her even closer to his taut frame. He groaned against her lips and a tremor rocked through him. ''Sallie,'' he muttered, lifting his mouth a scant inch from hers. ''Let's go to my apartment. We can't make love here, there are too many interruptions.'' His voice was a low growl, rough with his passion, and she shivered in sensual reaction.

''Let me go,'' she protested, her hands suddenly finding the strength to push against him as panic flared with the realization that it might be impossible to control him now. Their brief marriage had given her an intimate knowledge of his nature and now she admitted to herself that she'd forgotten none of it. She knew by the dark flush on his cheekbones, the timbre of his voice, the dilated glitter of his eyes, that he was half-wild with desire, near the point where he would take her regardless of where they were.

''No,'' he denied, his mouth twisting savagely. ''I told you I'll never let you go.''

She fought her way out of his embrace, but she had the uneasy feeling that he'd allowed her to gain her freedom, and spots of color also stained her face as she stared at him. ''You'll have to,'' she told him fiercely. ''I don't want you anymore!''

"I just proved you wrong in that!" he said on a short bark of laughter.

"I'm not talking about sex! I don't want to live with you. I don't want to be your wife. I can't stop you from traveling with me, you're the boss, but I won't sleep with you."

"Won't you?" he murmured. "You're my wife, and I want you back. Legally you can't refuse me my marital rights."

His determination, the steel in his gray eyes, alarmed her and she stepped back from him. Desperately she seized on Chris, throwing his name up like a shield to hide behind. "Look, Rhy, you're an adult, surely you can understand that my affections are elsewhere. Chris is special to me—"

A little muscle in his jaw began to twitch and she stared at it in fascination, forgetting what she'd been about to say. Rhy's hands closed painfully on her waist again and he ground out, "I told you what I'd do if I caught him with you and I meant it."

"Be reasonable," she implored, pulling vainly at his hands in an effort to ease the painful pressure. "For heaven's sake, I'm not demanding that you terminate your relationship with Coral!"

An odd expression crossed his face. "No, you're not, are you?" he said slowly.

He looked down at her with growing menace and to escape the impression she had of a time bomb ticking its way to the moment of explosion she managed a casual laugh. "I never thought that you'd live the life of a monk all these years." She tried to soothe the temper in him. "I've no right to object in any event."

Instead of soothing him her words seemed to inflame him more, and the tension in his arms lifted her on her toes. "I'm not that modern and openminded," he said almost soundlessly, his taut lips barely moving. "I don't want another man touching you!"

"Isn't that a dog-in-the-manger attitude?" she hurled at him and winced in pain as his fingers clenched. "Rhy, please! You're hurting me!"

He cursed vividly, then moved his hands from her waist in the manner of one freeing a bird and she swiftly moved a couple of steps from him, her hands automatically massaging her aching flesh. As he merely stood there watching her and made no move to break the silence that fell between them she decided that the best thing she could do was to get out of there. She couldn't handle Rhy when he was angry, he could reduce her to putty if he really lost his temper and she knew him well enough to know that he was on the verge of violence.

She edged toward the door and he moved suddenly, placing himself between her and her escape. "Don't fight me," he warned, still in that soft, nearly soundless voice. "You can't win and I don't want to hurt you. You're mine, Sallie."

Fear edged along her nerves. She'd seen Rhy in a lot of moods, in a lot of tempers, but she'd never before seen him with this wild savagery in his eyes. "I need to go to work," she muttered warily, watching him for any movement.

"You work for me. You go when I say you can go." He bit out the words, his eyes locked on hers, and she was helpless to look away. Was this how a snake paralyzed a bird?

Desperately she searched her mind for something to say that would break his concentration on her, but nothing surfaced and she squared her shoulders, ready to make a flight of it if necessary. She wouldn't be molested, not even by her own husband! All of the pride and dignity that she'd so painstakingly amassed for herself was in the tilt of her chin as she raised it at him. "Don't push me," she warned him evenly. "If you're even half the man you used to be you know that I'm not willing."

"You would be, after a minute," he retorted with brutal truth, but not by a flicker of her lashes did she betray the jolt he gave her with that statement.

"Don't confuse the past with the future. The days are long gone when I thought the sun rose and set on you."

"Good," he said, his mouth twisting. "I never wanted to be an idol. But don't make me out to be a villain, either."

With inner relief Sallie sensed that the danger was past, at least for the moment. She was tempted to try arguing with him about the trip to Sakarya, but she knew better than to provoke his temper again. "I really do need to get to work," she insisted.

After a moment he stepped to one side. "All right," he permitted, his tone at once tender and warning. "But we're not finished, baby, and when you go to Sakarya I'll be with you every inch of the way."

With that warning ringing in her head Sallie slipped past him and returned to her desk. She began trembling with delayed reaction and with difficulty she tried to concentrate on her writing. But she'd reached a slow spot. She couldn't decide just how the action should go and eventually her thoughts wandered back to Rhy.

Once she would have been delirious with joy if he'd announced that he wanted her with him, wanted her to have his children, but that was a long time ago, and she'd been a different person then. Why couldn't he accept that? Why was he so insistent on resuming their marriage?

She couldn't believe that he was motivated by jealousy. It had to be that possessiveness of his, because jealousy indicated caring, and she knew that Rhy had never loved her, not even in the early days. Their only bond had been a sexual one and he wanted to renew that bond now, but she was determined to break the weakness that made her respond to him.

Then the thought occurred to her that it was one thing to be an ordinary, quiet, stay-at-home little housewife and quite another for her to be a globe-trotting, successful reporter. She was more of a feather in his cap now, wasn't she? She hadn't been glamorous enough for him before! Was that why he was suddenly so interested after years of neglect? Rage burned in her for a moment; then she had the disquieting thought that if that was the case he wouldn't have grounded her, he'd have kept her in the limelight.

She didn't understand him; she'd never understand him. Why didn't he leave her alone?

It had to be the tension caused by her scene with Rhy that produced the pounding headache she had that afternoon when she went home. She wanted nothing more than peace and quiet, so she indulged herself with a hot bath and, rather than get dressed afterward, she merely pulled on her comfortable pink robe which zipped up to her throat and sat down at her typewriter to work her way out of the doldrums.

It was still early, not yet seven, when her doorbell rang and she frowned irritably as she switched the typewriter off. Just as she reached the door she thought better of opening it in case Rhy had decided to press his attentions. "Who is it?" she asked warily.

"Coral Williams" was the cool reply and Sallie's eyebrows rose in silent astonishment as she unlocked the door and opened it.

"Come in," she invited the striking blonde, then indicated her robe with a movement of her hand. "I'm sorry about the way I'm dressed, but I wasn't expecting visitors."

"No, that's true enough," Coral admitted, walking into the apartment with the prowling slink of a model. She was both cool and dramatic, dressed in a lemon yellow evening gown that should have made her hair look brassy but didn't. "Rhy is taking me to a Broadway opening, so I knew he wouldn't be here tonight."

Aha! Sallie thought to herself. It looked as if Coral was checking out the competition, but who had told her? "He isn't likely to be here any other night either," she denied, and the amusement in her eyes and voice must have gotten through to Coral because the woman bit her lip and flushed.

"Don't try to hide it from me," she said huskily, her voice growing thick as if she was near tears. "Rhy told me himself."

"What?" Sallie's voice rose in astonishment. Was Rhy going to start advertising their marriage? Did he think that public knowledge might weaken her stand?

"I know how hard it is to resist Rhy when he decides that he wants a woman," Coral was saying. "Believe me, I know! But you're not in his league and he'll only hurt you. He's had other women, but he's always come back to me and this time won't be any different. I just thought I'd let you know before you get in too deeply with him."

"Thanks for the warning," Sallie said, her inner amusement breaking out in a smile that made Coral look at her in disbelief. She couldn't help it; she thought it was funny that her husband's mistress should warn her about becoming too serious about him! "But I don't think you have anything to worry about. I'm not interested in having an affair with anyone, and you'll be doing me a favor if you can keep Rhy's attention away from me."

"How I'd like to!" Coral admitted wryly, glancing at Sallie with disturbing honesty. "But I knew when I first saw you that Rhy was interested, and he won't give up easily. Why do you think he's going on this Sakarya trip with you? If I were you, and if you're on the level about not wanting an affair with him, I'd check into the hotel bookings, because if I know Rhy there'll only be one room available!"

"I know that," Sallie chuckled, "and I'm ahead of him. I've already thought of another place to stay. With a friend." She didn't add that the friend was Marina Delchamp and that she hoped to stay in the palace. She was fairly certain that Marina would offer her sanctuary and would, in fact, greatly enjoy helping her to thwart Rhy.

Suddenly Coral laughed. "Maybe I was worried about nothing. You seem more than capable of looking after yourself. It must be that braid that makes you look so young."

"Probably," Sallie agreed blandly, thinking that in all probability she was Coral's age.

"You've set my mind at ease, so I'll leave now. Rhy is supposed to meet me in half an hour and I'll probably be late." Coral glided to the door and Sallie opened it for her, feeling rather like a servant opening a door for a queen, but laughter still lurked in her eyes as she returned to her writing. Coral acting concerned for another woman was a performance worth watching! Not for a second did she believe that the beautiful model cared a snap of her fingers about another woman's feelings. What Coral so carefully guarded was Rhy's attention, his time, and with a shake of her head Sallie wondered what made Rhy so sinfully attractive.

Perhaps if she knew what made her so vulnerable to Rhy she'd be able to fight him, but she could pinpoint no concrete reason. It was everything about him, even the qualities that made her so angry. He was all man, the only man she'd ever wanted.

Realization struck and the force of it made her break out in a cold sweat, but she forced herself to admit the truth. She still loved him; she always had. She had tried to push her love away in self-defense against the crippling pain she'd felt when Rhy had left her, but she hadn't been able to kill it. It had flourished in the darkness of her subconscious and now she could no longer deny that it existed. She sat at the typewriter, staring blankly at the keys, and let the knowledge creep into her consciousness. She couldn't stop the tears that welled in her eyes, though she stubbornly refused to let them fall. Love was one thing, but compatibility was quite another, and she was no longer a starry-eyed young girl who believed that love could conquer all. She and Rhy were the mismatch of the century, even more so now than in the beginning. At least then she'd thought him the center of the universe and would gladly have followed him into the jaws of death if he'd only asked her.

But he hadn't asked her; he'd gone alone, disregarding her fears and clinging timidity. When had he ever cared how she felt? He was too forceful, too self-confident, to put her opinion, her feelings, above his own. It had been that way then and it was still the same. Wasn't that how he was acting now? What she wanted just didn't count! Look at the high-handed manner in which he'd stopped her career in its tracks and demanded that she resume their married life. What about her plans, what she wanted out of life?

Drawing several deep breaths, Sallie tried to force her thoughts into order. If she went back to Rhy what would she have? The answer was simple, she would have Rhy—for as long as he remained interested. Or perhaps she wouldn't even have his undivided attention at all. She couldn't discount Coral Williams, and Rhy had never promised fidelity. He'd made no promises at all, other than ones of physical pleasure. So, if she went back to him, she'd have sensual satisfaction and what joy she could find in his company.

On the other side of the coin, what would he gain from a reconciliation? Once again, the first thing that came to mind was sex. That fierce attraction was mutual, unfortunately, for it made him unreasonable. If Coral was pushing him for a commitment Sallie's return would put a stop to that particular demand, and from what Coral had just told her Rhy wouldn't have any worries that Coral might leave him. No, Coral would stay for as long as Rhy wanted her, and if he could have both women at once he probably would.

Sallie winced from that thought. No, Rhy wasn't like that. She didn't think him capable of fidelity to any one woman, but he didn't play games. A woman had to accept him as he was. That had been their trouble. She'd wanted him to be something he wasn't: an ordinary husband. Rhy had refused to change, or even compromise.

So she'd changed, slipped out from under his thumb, and he resented that even while she challenged him. She'd belonged to him once and he couldn't tolerate the idea that she no longer wanted to. That possessive streak of his had to be a mile wide. She'd been his once, and he wanted her back, and he'd move heaven and earth to get her, even if he had to destroy her career to do so.

She *couldn't* go back to him, though deep down she craved to do just that. Her own identity was at stake. Rhy would swamp her, smother her. Then, when he was no longer interested, he'd walk out, and she didn't think she could survive that again.

No, she had to follow her own path, and if it led her away from Rhy she had to accept that. Odd how she could love him and yet be willing to spend her life separated from him, yet that was the way of it. She knew instinctively that Rhy would destroy her sense of self, her confidence, if she allowed him control over her emotions again.

There was no hesitation; she had to choose the path that was right for her, and that path didn't include Rhy. Perhaps no other man would ever make her heart pound madly as the lightest touch from Rhy could do, but if that was the price, she'd pay it. She had to.

When this trip to Sakarya was over she would turn in her notice and leave town. She couldn't wait any longer. Rhy was closing in, and she'd have to keep her guard up every minute.

Chapter Six

The night before they were due to leave for Sakarya Sallie went to bed early, hoping that she'd be able to get to sleep since the flight would be long and she'd never been able to rest on a trip. She was always too keyed up, too restless, and to her dismay she felt the same way now. The thought of traveling with Rhy, when every self-preserving instinct in her screamed to keep as far away from him as she could, had all her nerves tingling in mingled fear and expectation. It was rather like petting a beautiful tiger, wanting so desperately to touch something so lovely but knowing at the same time that the tiger could kill you.

She turned restlessly in the bed, tangling the sheets, and when the doorbell rang she jumped out of bed with a sense of relief and grabbed her robe, shrugging into it as she ran to the door. Just as she reached it she skidded to a stop and called, "Who is it?"

"Chris," came a muffled voice and Sallie's brow knit in puzzlement. What was he doing here? He'd been on the road a lot lately, due to Rhy's influence, no doubt, but he'd arrived back in town the day before, and he'd been fine earlier when she'd seen him long enough to say a quick hello. Now he sounded as if he was sick, or in pain.

Quickly she unlocked the various locks on the door and opened it. Chris had been slumped against the doorframe, and he straightened, giving her a glimpse of his drawn face. "What's wrong?" she asked swiftly, catching his sleeve and pulling him in so she could close the door. She fumbled with the locks again, then turned to him. He'd jammed his hands deep into his pockets and stood regarding her with deep, silent misery evident in his brown eyes.

Sallie caught her breath. Had someone been killed? That was always her first thought, her deepest fear. She held out her hand to him and he took it, squeezing her slender fingers in a painful grip. "What is it?" she asked softly. "Chris?"

"I didn't know it would hurt so bad," he groaned, his voice so low that she could barely hear him. "Oh, God, Sallie, I didn't know."

"Who is it?" she demanded, grasping his arm urgently with her free hand. "Chris Meaker, if you don't tell me—"

He shook his head as if to clear it, as if he'd abruptly realized what she thought. "No," he said thinly. "No one's dead, unless you want to count me. She's left me, Sallie."

Sallie gaped at him, remembering that he was in love with a woman who wanted the same things she'd once wanted, a nice, normal husband who came home every night, who fathered children and loved them and was around to see them grow up. Evidently the woman had decided that she couldn't live with Chris's job, with knowing that every trip could be his last one. Granted, some of the assignments weren't that dangerous, but it was a high-risk job at best. She hadn't been able to take it, either, the constant worry about someone she loved desperately. Only by cutting Rhy out of her life had she been able to function again.

"What can I do?" she asked in quiet sympathy. "Tell me how to help."

"Tell me it'll get better," he begged, and his voice cracked. "Sallie, hold me. Please, hold me!" To her horror his face twisted and he began to sob, jerking her to him with desperate arms and holding her so tightly that she couldn't breathe. His entire body was shaking and he buried his face in her neck, wetting her skin and hair and collar with his salty tears. Great tearing sobs tore from him and she put her arms around him, giving him what he'd asked for, someone to hold him. She knew what he was feeling; dear God, she knew exactly what he was going through. She'd cried that way for Rhy, feeling as if he'd torn her insides out and she'd die from the pain of it.

"It'll get better," she promised thickly, tears blurring her own voice. "I know, Chris. I've been there."

He didn't answer, but his arms lifted her, taking her from the floor. He drew a deep, shuddering breath and swallowed, trying to control himself. "God knows it can't get any worse," he whispered, and lifted his head. For a moment his brown eyes, wet and miserable, stared into her wet blue ones, and then he dipped his head and fastened his mouth to hers, kissing her with silent desperation. Sallie understood and she kissed him back. He wasn't kissing her for any sexual reason; it was merely a reaching out for human contact, a plea for comforting. She'd always liked Chris; at that moment she came to love him. Not the deep, ravenous love she had for Rhy, not even a man-woman type of love. She simply loved him as a human being, a fellow creature who was vulnerable and who needed her. She'd never been needed in her life before; she'd been dependent on her parents, then dependent on Rhy. Certainly Rhy had never needed her!

Chris pulled his head back and sighed; then he rested his forehead against hers. "What can I do?" he asked, but she knew that he didn't expect an answer. "How long does it take?"

Now that she *could* answer. "It took me a couple of months before I could even begin to function again," she told him truthfully, and he winced. "But I worked at getting over it harder than I've ever worked at anything in my life, either before or since."

"I can't believe she did it," he groaned.

"Did you have a fight?" Sallie asked, leading him to the sofa and pushing until he sat down heavily.

His head moved wearily back and forth. "No fight. Not even an ultimatum. My God, you'd think she'd at least give me a warning! If she wanted to tear my guts out she bull's-eyed first shot!"

Sitting down beside him, Sallie took his hand and held it. With the insight of someone who had been there, she felt that she understood very well the motives of Chris's unnamed lady. He thought it was perfectly all right for him to risk life and limb while she waited patiently at home for him—how much warning did he think she'd have of his death? Did he think the pain would be any less for her if she was suddenly told that he hadn't made it back? Men were so arrogant and selfish, even Chris, and he was one of the most likeable people she'd ever met. Aloud she said, "Don't expect someone to give in just because you can't. You'd have made each other miserable. Face it, you're better off apart."

"I've never loved anyone before," he protested hopelessly. "It's not so easy to give up someone you really love!"

"I did, and I didn't have a choice either. He left me flat on my face."

Chris sighed and stared at the pattern of the carpet, and Sallie could read his anguish in the lines of his face. Chris had always seemed younger than his years, as if life had passed within touching distance of him but had never actually touched him, glancing off his inner calm like light off of a mirror. Now he'd aged and the boyishness was gone from his face.

"Her name is Amy," he said abruptly. "She's quiet, a little shy. I guess it took me a year of chance meetings in the hallways before she'd do more than smile at me when I spoke. Then it took me another year to get her into bed—" He stopped and glanced at her, his mouth going grim. "Forget I said that. I don't usually kiss and tell."

"It's forgotten," Sallie assured him. "Did you ask her to marry you?"

"Not at first. I've never wanted to be married, Sal, I'm a lone wolf, like you." He shook his head as if he didn't understand himself. "It kind of sneaked up on me, the idea of getting married. So finally I asked her and she cried. She said she loved me but that she couldn't take my job, and she'd marry me if I changed jobs. Hell, I love my job! Mexican standoff."

"And she cut her losses," Sallie murmured.

"She also hedged her bets." He gave her a wry, self-mocking smile. "She had another game going with a nine-to-five guy. She told me tonight that they're getting married later this year."

"Is she bluffing?"

Chris shook his head. "I don't think so. She's wearing a diamond."

After sitting quietly for a moment Sallie said frankly, "You've got a choice, you know. You can have Amy or you can have your job, but you can't have both. Decide which one's the most important to you and forget about the other."

"Did you forget about your guy when you chose your job over him?" challenged Chris.

"You've got it wrong. I was in Amy's shoes, not yours. He chose *his* job over *me*," said Sallie. "I've never forgotten him, but I've done very well without him, thank you."

It wasn't until Chris spoke that she realized how much information she'd given him with her stray comments; or perhaps it was just that Chris was intuitive, sensing her moods and thoughts without any concrete evidence. After looking at her thoughtfully for a moment he murmured, "It's Baines, isn't it? He's the one who walked out on you."

Her stunned expression had to tell him the answer, but after a minute she gathered herself enough to admit, "He's the one. And let me tell you, when Rhy Baines walks, he walks *hard!*"

"He's a fool," Chris said mildly. "But he wants you back, doesn't he?"

"Not permanently," Sallie replied with a touch of bitterness. "He just wants to play for a while."

Chris looked at her for a long time, his brown eyes moving over her small face, shuttered now to keep from revealing any more of her inner pain. When it became evident that she had nothing more to say he leaned forward and gently kissed her, but this time he was offering comfort instead of taking it. Sallie closed her eyes and let the kiss linger, neither responding nor rejecting but letting time expand as his mouth moved lightly over hers. She'd never been kissed like that before, without passion, as a friend.

The strident demand of the telephone caused Chris to remove his mouth and with a murmured "Excuse me" Sallie stretched to reach the yellow receiver. When she answered she felt a tingle of alarm when a husky voice demanded, "Have you finished packing?"

"Of course," she said crisply, feeling insulted that he felt he had to check up on her. What did he think she'd do, wait until the last minute to throw everything together? Because of that, and also because of a certain streak of feminine perversity, she added, "I was just talking to Chris."

She could feel the thickness of the silence on the line; then the growing crackle of Rhy's anger leapt out at her. "Is he there?" he finally bit out, the words almost exploding from his lips. Sallie had a mental picture of him, his teeth bared in a snarl, his cheekbones taut and savage with his rage. The gray eyes would be flinty, with red sparks snapping in them. The tingle of alarm inside her changed to one almost of pleasure.

"Of course he's here," she responded, knowing that she was flirting with danger. What would she do if Rhy's temper roared out of control? The last thing she wanted to do was cause any trouble for Chris, but somehow Rhy goaded her past responsible actions. "I don't give up my friends just because you snap your fingers," she heard herself adding.

His voice was a low growl, almost too low to hear. "When I snap my something it won't be my fingers. Get rid of him, Sallie, and do it now."

Immediately she bristled. "I will not—"

"Now," he whispered. "Or I'm coming over. I'm not playing, baby. Get rid of him. Then come back and tell me you've done it."

Furiously she tossed the receiver onto the table and got to her feet.

Without a word, not wanting Rhy to hear anything she said to Chris, she held out her hand to him, and with a puzzled look he took it, rising lightly to his feet. Sallie led him to the door, then stretched on tiptoe and kissed him gently. "I'm sorry," she murmured. "He's ordered me to get rid of you or he's going to come over here and get violent."

For a moment Chris looked like his old self, one eyebrow rising in mild mockery. "This sounds serious. Sallie, old girl, I think you've left a lot out of your story."

"I have, but there's no use in raking over old ashes. Will you be all right?" she asked, concern evident in her voice and eyes, and he quickly hugged her.

"Of course I will. Just telling you helped. Kissing you helped even more." He gave a crooked grin. "She knocked me for a loop, but I'm not giving up. She cried when she told me she's marrying this other guy, so it's not hopeless, is it?"

Sallie grinned back. "Doesn't sound hopeless to me."

He flicked her cheek with one finger. "Have a good time in Sakarya," he teased, and she stuck her tongue out at him. After he'd gone she carefully locked the door and returned to glare balefully at the telephone receiver lying there waiting for her. She was tempted to let him wait a few more minutes, but it was like a dose of bitter medicine: soonest done, soonest over with.

With that thought she snatched it up and nearly snarled, "Well, he's gone!"

"What took you so long?" he barked in demand.

"I was kissing him goodbye!" she retorted furiously. "And now I'm *telling you* goodbye!"

"Don't hang up," came the soft warning. "I'm going to give Meaker just enough time to get home, then I'm going to call and make sure he's there. For your sake, you'd better pray that he goes straight home."

"Your bully act is getting boring," she snapped, and slammed the phone down, then unplugged it. Marching into her bedroom she unplugged that phone too, but not before it began ringing. Muttering furiously to herself about what she'd like to do to Rhy Baines, she stomped around the apartment turning off lights, then flung herself on the bed and once again tried to go to sleep. If it had been difficult before it was impossible now. She was burning with righteous indignation, and she wondered how anyone could be such a hypocrite. It was perfectly all right for him to blatantly carry on his affair with Coral right in front of her, but he had no intention of allowing her the same freedom. Not that she wanted to have an affair with Chris any more than he wanted one with her, but that was beside the point.

Then her thoughts turned to the trip to Sakarya. After tonight Rhy would be his most demanding, his most seductive, and to her dismay she recalled that in the past he'd had no difficulty at all in getting her to bed. She'd been lucky that, since he'd discovered her identity, the only times he'd kissed her they had been in his office where there had been scant opportunity for a seduction scene; she had her doubts that she'd have been so successful in stopping him otherwise. She was too honest to delude herself even when the truth was painful. She loved Rhy, but even if she didn't she'd still want him physically. Only her pride and her deep-rooted fear of being hurt again kept her from giving in to him.

It was after midnight before she finally drifted into sleep and the flight to Paris, the first leg of the trip to Sakarya, was an early one. She was pale with weariness before she even left her apartment to meet Rhy at the air terminal. She was determined to be as businesslike as possible, both to keep him at a distance and to show him that he hadn't upset her with his jealous rage of the night before, but right from the start her attitude was difficult to maintain. When he saw her walking toward him Rhy got to his feet and came to meet her, taking her larger tote bag from her arm and bending down to press a brief warm kiss on her lips. "Good morning," he murmured, letting his dark gray eyes drift down over her body. "I like you in a dress. You should wear one more often."

So he was going to ignore last night, was he? Though she'd intended to do the same thing she felt a flare of irritation that he'd beaten her to the punch. Then she shrugged mentally and gave him a cool glance. "I thought the Sakaryans would prefer dresses over pants." She usually wore pants while traveling both for comfort and convenience, but considering the nature of the assignment she'd packed only dresses. For the flight she'd chosen a lightweight beige dress, sleeveless, with a low-scooped neckline, but the dress also had a matching long-sleeved jacket, and she was wearing it now, for despite the heat of summer in New York City she often felt cool in the early mornings, and she'd learned from experience that the temperature-controlled jetliners were too cool for her. She had also changed her hair from the informal braid to a neat coil on the back of her head. There wasn't a lot she could do with her hair, because of its length, but for more formal gatherings she always put it up.

"I also prefer dresses," he commented, taking her arm. "You have great legs, and I like to see them. You used to wear dresses a lot, as I remember.''

That's right, remind me, she thought savagely, but she managed to give him an impersonal answer. ''When I started working I found that pants are more suitable for the type of work I do.'' To change the subject she questioned, ''Do you have the tickets?''

''Everything's taken care of,'' he assured her. ''Do you want a cup of coffee before the flight's called?''

''No, thanks. I don't drink coffee while I'm traveling,'' she felt compelled to explain, and took a seat in an armchair. The glint in his gray eyes as he seated himself opposite her told her that Rhy was well aware why she hadn't chosen the sofa, but she ignored him and amused herself by watching the parade of early-morning travelers.

Their flight was five minutes late, and Rhy was already restless when the loudspeaker called their flight number. He got to his feet and took her arm, and suddenly he gave her a whimsical smile. ''Those are some spikes you're wearing,'' he commented. ''You come up to my chin...almost.''

''They're also dangerous weapons,'' she said, her mouth curving.

''Are they? Are you planning to use them on me?'' he asked, and before she could turn her mouth away he swooped his head down and captured her lips in a hard, hungry kiss that took her breath away.

''Rhy, please!'' she protested, determined to hide the curling response she felt whenever he touched her. ''We're in public!''

''I get more chances to touch you in public than I do in private, so I'm going to take advantage of them,'' he muttered in warning.

''This is business!'' she hissed. ''Try to remember that. It won't do the magazine any good if a reporter acts badly in public.''

''No one here knows you're a reporter,'' he retorted with a grin. ''Besides, I'm your boss and I say it's okay.''

''I have standards, even if you don't, and I don't like being pawed! Are you going to catch this flight or not?''

''I wouldn't miss it for the world,'' he drawled, and she caught his hidden meaning and flushed. Beyond any doubt Rhy was planning on a reconciliation during this trip, and she was equally determined to prevent such a thing from happening. Marina would never turn her away, she was certain, and she relished the thought of Rhy's fury when he found she'd evaded him.

But for now she faced a long flight in his company and she didn't relish *that*. Not only did his presence make her nervous, she was a restless traveler under the best of circumstances. Before they'd been in the air an hour she'd flipped through several magazines and made a stab at reading a paperback she'd brought with her, then abandoned that for a book of crossword puzzles. When she discarded that and tried reading her book again Rhy reached out and took her hand.

"Relax," he advised, rubbing his thumb across the back of her hand, a gesture guaranteed to keep her from relaxing. "It's a long flight, and you're as jumpy as a flea. You'll be worn-out before we get to Paris, let alone Sakarya."

"I'm not a good traveler," she admitted. "I'm not good at sitting still with nothing to do." Already she was bored, and she yearned for her manuscript, but she'd been afraid to risk losing it, so she had left it behind.

"Try to take a nap," he advised. "You'll need it."

"I can't do that, either," she said with a rueful grin. "I'm just nervous enough of heights that I don't trust the pilot enough to go to sleep and let him handle it all."

"I didn't know you were afraid of heights," he said, and she bristled.

"I'm not afraid, I'm nervous. There's a difference. I fly all the time— or *used* to—and I've been in plenty of tight spots without going to pieces. I've even enjoyed some of them. In fact, I once took a few flying lessons, but that's another thing I didn't have the time to keep up."

"You've been busy," he said on an odd note. "What other accomplishments have you added since we parted company?"

He seemed to resent that and she suddenly felt proud that she had accomplished so much. At least he'd know that she hadn't been pining for him. "I speak six foreign languages, three fluently," she enumerated coolly. "I'm a fair shot, and I've learned how to stay on a horse. I've had to give up a lot of things I've tried—and that includes cooking and sewing, because I realized how boring they were. Anything else?"

"I hope not," he retorted, his mouth quivering with amusement. "No wonder Downey sent you into so many hot spots, you probably bullied him into it!"

"Greg can't be bullied, he's tough as nails," Sallie defended her editor. "And he'd be in the field himself if he could."

"Why can't he? I remember him as one of the best, but he suddenly grounded himself, and I've never heard why."

"He was shot up pretty badly in Vietnam," Sallie explained. "And while he was recovering his wife died of a stroke. It was quite a shock, there'd been no warning at all, but all of a sudden she was dead. They had two children, a boy and a girl, and the little girl had a hard time adjusting to her mother's death, so Greg decided to stay home with the kids.''

"That's rough," Rhy commented.

"He doesn't talk about it much."

"But he told you?" he asked sharply.

"In bits and pieces. Like I said, he doesn't talk about it much."

"A field reporter doesn't need a family. The old Pony Express advertised for riders who were orphans and had no family ties, and I sometimes think that should hold true for reporters, too."

"I agree," she said sharply, not looking at him. "That's why I don't want any ties."

"But you're not a reporter any longer," he murmured, his long fingers tightening around her hand. "Consider this your swan song, because after this your position will be that of Mrs. Rhydon Baines."

Swiftly Sallie jerked her hand away from him and stared out at the cloud cover below them. "Are you firing me?" she bit out angrily.

"I will if you force me to. I don't mind if you work so long as you're home every night with me. Of course, when we have children I'll want you to be home with them while they're small."

She turned furious blue eyes on him. "I won't live with you," she said bitterly. "I *can't* live with you and be more than half-alive myself. The thought of being a housewife again is nauseating."

His mouth turned grim. "You're lying to yourself if you believe that. You've changed a lot of things, but you can't change the way you feel about children. I remember how you were when you were pregnant with our son—"

"Shut up!" she flared, her fingers curving into her palms as she strove to control her pain at the memory of her dead child. "Don't talk about my baby." Even after seven years the pain of losing him was raw and unhealed, and for the rest of her life she would mourn that small, lost life.

"My son, too," Rhy said tightly.

"Really?" she challenged, lowering her voice to keep others from hearing her. "You weren't there when I gave birth, and you were seldom home during my pregnancy. The only role you played was to physically father the baby. After that, I was on my own." She turned away, swallowing in an effort to control the tears that threatened as she remembered her son. She'd never heard him cry, never watched him look about at the strange new world he'd entered, but for several magic months she'd felt his movements as he kicked and turned inside her and he'd been real to her, a person, and he'd had a name. She had somehow known she would have a boy, and he had been David Rhydon Baines, her son.

Rhy's fingers closed over her wrist so tightly that the fragile bones ground together and she winced with pain. "I wanted him, too," Rhy ground out, then almost flung her wrist aside. The next several hours passed in silence.

There was no layover in Paris and Sallie guessed that Greg had made the arrangements, because he always arranged things as tightly as he could, sometimes resulting in a missed flight when the first flight was only a little late. She and Rhy had barely checked through customs when their connecting flight was called, and they had to run to make the plane. From Paris it was another seven hours before they landed at the new, ultramodern jetport in Khalidia, the capital of Sakarya, and because of the time change, instead of the night their bodies were ready for, they were thrown into the middle of the Sakaryan day.

Their weariness and the long hours had largely erased the constraint between them, and Sallie didn't protest when he took her arm as they walked across the tarmac to the low, sprawling air terminal. The heat was incredible, and she was actually grateful for Rhy's support.

"I hope the hotel's decent," Rhy muttered beneath his breath, "but the way I feel right now I don't care what it's like as long as I can catch some sleep."

She knew the feeling. Jet lag was worse than simply missing sleep, it was total drain. She certainly wasn't up to battling with Rhy over where she would sleep!

They couldn't find anyone who spoke English, but several of the Sakaryans spoke French and both she and Rhy knew that language well. The taxi driver who took them to the hotel in a remarkably battered Renault spoke a rough French, and from what he said they gathered that Khalidia was being overrun by Westerners. Many Europeans had already arrived, and many Americans, including a man with a big camera, and it was said that the King would be on American television. He did not have a television himself, but he had seen one, and he thought that the big camera was one used for making the pictures for the television.

He was talkative, as taxi drivers the world over seemed to be, and he pointed with pride to the gleaming new buildings existing alongside ancient structures baked white by the merciless sun. Sakarya had the intriguing blend of old and new that so many developing nations displayed, with gleaming Mercedes limousines purring up and down the same streets used by donkeys. Camels were still used for travel in the Sakaryan desert, but overhead contrails were left by the sleek, screaming jets of the Sakaryan Royal Air Command.

The King had been educated at Oxford but, despite his absorption of European culture, he was by nature a cautious man, rather resistant to change. The Sakaryan nation was not a new one; it dated back to the day of Muhammad, and the family of Al Mahdi had held the monarchy for over five hundred years. There were deeply ingrained traditions to consider whenever modernization was discussed and for the most part life in Sakarya went on as before. Motorized vehicles were nice, but the Sakaryans had gotten along without them before and would not mind if suddenly there were no more automobiles. The jetport was too noisy and the people who arrived on the big jets had strange customs. However, the big new hospital was a source of pride and the children were eager to attend the new schools.

The man who had accomplished this modernization was the man Marina Delchamp had married, Zain Abdul ibn Rashid, the finance minister of Sakarya and a man of considerable influence with the King. He was a dark, hawklike man with the coal black eyes of his race, and he'd been an international playboy since his college days in Europe. Sallie wondered if he loved Marina or was attracted only to her shining blond beauty. Did Zain Abdul ibn Rashid cherish Marina's gallant spirit, her natural dignity?

She worried over her thoughts like a terrier, for it wasn't easy for East to meet West. The cultural differences were so vast. Despite their spasmodic correspondence and the long intervals between their meetings Sallie considered Marina a true friend and she wanted her to be happy. She became so engrossed with her worries that she forgot to watch the scenery and was startled when the driver said in French, "The Hotel Khalidia. It is new and rich. You like it, yes?"

Peering around Rhy's shoulder Sallie admitted that she liked it, yes. The hotel was shielded on three sides by a row of carefully nurtured trees and beyond the trees was a high rock wall. The architecture wasn't ultramodern; instead, every effort had been made to insure that the hotel blended with its surroundings. The inside might offer every modern convenience, and she sincerely hoped it did, but the outer facade could have been ageless; it was clean and uncluttered in line, built of gleaming white stone, with deeply recessed windows.

Trying to keep up with Rhy, Sallie found that she was ignored when she tried to explain which cases were hers and which belonged to Rhy. A black-eyed young man in Western dress gave his attention solely to Rhy, not even glancing at her, and she received the same treatment from the desk clerk. The young man disappeared with their luggage and Rhy pocketed the room key.

When they were a few steps away from the desk clerk Sallie caught Rhy's arm. "I want a room of my own," she insisted, looking him in the eye.

"Sorry. I've registered us as man and wife and you'll have a hard time persuading an Islamic man to give you another room," he informed her with evident satisfaction. "You knew what to expect when you came on this trip."

"What do I have to say to get it through you head—" she began in frustration, and he cut her short.

"Later. This isn't the place for a public argument. Stop being difficult, all I want is a shower and a few hours' sleep. Believe me, you're perfectly safe right now."

She didn't believe him, but she had to retrieve her luggage, so she followed him into the elevator, and he punched the button for the fourth floor.

Even as tired as she was the charm of the room made her catch her breath and she barely noticed as Rhy tipped the young man who'd brought up their bags. Though actually only one large room, it was separated by intricate wrought-iron screens in two areas, a sitting room to the front and the bedroom to the rear. A balcony ran the length of the room and it was furnished with two white wicker chairs with thickly padded cushions and a wicker lounger. A small tea table stood between the two chairs. Stepping onto the balcony, she could see the huge swimming pool below, set among palm trees, and she wondered if women were allowed to use the pool.

Returning to the room, she inspected the divan-style bed and smiled at the number of vari-colored cushions that adorned it. The parquet floor was covered in this area by a rug that looked Turkish but was probably a mass-produced copy. That made no difference, the effect was still stunning. Of all the hotels she'd stayed in she already liked this one the best. The food might be terrible, the service nonexistent for all she knew, but she adored the room!

Then she looked up and met Rhy's penetrating gaze and she paled. He'd removed his jacket and his shoulders strained at the material of his white shirt, and something in his stance told her that he was alert to her every movement. "Why don't you take a shower?" he suggested. "I'll make some phone calls and make certain everything's set up for the interview, which could take a while."

She wanted more than anything to grab her suitcases and run, but she knew that Rhy was waiting for just such a move. She would have to trick him and she wasn't certain just yet how to manage it. And a bath sounded like heaven....

"All right," she agreed wearily, picking up her suitcase and taking it into the bathroom that opened off to the right of the sleeping area, carefully locking the door behind her.

Despite her weariness, the bathroom delighted her. It could have come straight out of a Turkish harem with the black-tiled sunken bath, the mosaics, the rich jewel-like colors. She flung her dress off and peeled off her damp underclothing, sighing with relief at the sensation of cool air on her sweaty skin. She turned on the crystal taps that let the water pour into the huge tub and slid with a sigh into the cool water, then splashed about with a fantasy of having servants waiting to help her from the bath and prepare her body with perfumed oils for the coming night with the dark, exciting sultan....

Then reality intruded with the thought that she'd go mad under such circumstances, and she had enough to worry about now without bringing a sultan into it. She got out of the bath and toweled herself dry; then she debated what to wear. If she changed into street clothes Rhy would watch her like a hawk, but she had no intentions of parading around before him in a nightgown. She finally settled on a sapphire blue caftan and zipped herself into it, then took down her hair and brushed it vigorously.

She was too tired to braid it so she left it loose. After picking up her scattered clothing and tidying the bath she unlocked the door and carried her suitcase out.

Rhy was on the phone and he barely looked in her direction as she put belongings away, trying to behave as if she meant to stay. She wandered around the room, fighting to hold off the sleepiness that was growing stronger and listened as Rhy talked to several people.

After some time he covered the mouthpiece with his hand and said to her, "Why don't you go ahead and get some sleep? I don't know how long I'll be."

She didn't want to go to sleep, every instinct screamed against it, but she couldn't leave with him watching her. Besides, she was so tired; every bone and muscle in her ached from the long hours sitting in the plane. She could rest for just a few minutes until Rhy got off the telephone. She was a light sleeper; she'd hear him when he went into the bathroom.

She pulled the shades over the doors to the balcony and dimmed the room into semidarkness, then crawled among the pillows on the divan with a sigh of ecstasy. She stretched out her aching legs, turned her face against a pillow and was instantly asleep.

She was aroused some time later when someone muttered, "Move over," and she rolled over to make room for the warm body that slid next to her. Dimly she was aware that she should wake up, but she was so comfortable and the quiet hum of the central air conditioner lulled her back to sleep.

The time difference was confusing; when she woke it was dark, but she'd slept for hours. Still groggy, she peered at the dim figure coming out of the bathroom. "Who is it?" she called thickly, unable to clear the cobwebs from her mind. She wasn't certain just where she was, either.

"Rhy," the rough-velvet voice answered. "I'm sorry I woke you, I was just getting a drink. Would you like a glass of water, too?"

That sounded heavenly and she sighed a yes, then began struggling into a sitting position. In only a moment a cool glass was being put into her hand and she drained it thirstily, then gave it back to him. He returned the glass to the bathroom as she fell back among the pillows and thought drowsily that he must have eyes like a cat because he hadn't turned on any lights.

Just when the bed dipped beneath his weight again she remembered that she'd been planning on slipping out and her heart lurched with fear. "Wait—" she gasped in panic, reaching out to thrust him away, and her hand encountered smooth warm flesh. Shocked, forgetting what she'd been about to say, instead she blurted out, "You don't have anything on!"

In the darkness he gave a rough chuckle and turned on his side to face her, his heavy arm sliding around her waist and overcoming her futile resistance to pull her snugly against him. "I've always slept in the raw...remember?" he teased, his lips brushing her temple.

Her breath halted in her chest, and she began to tremble at the pressure of his strong, warm body against her. His male scent filled her nostrils and made her senses begin to swim. Desperately fighting her growing need to press herself to him and let him do as he wanted, she put her hands against his chest to push him away and instead found her slim fingers twining in the hair that covered his chest.

"Sallie," he muttered hoarsely, searching for and finding her lips in the darkness, and with a moan she lifted her arms to cling around his neck. She knew she should resist him but that had never been possible and even now, when she had such good reasons for fighting him, the temptation of knowing again such wild satisfaction kept her from shoving him away.

Nor was he unaffected; his big body was trembling against her when he lifted his mouth from hers, scattering kisses across her face and eyes. She felt him slide down the zip of the caftan and pull it from her shoulders, bunching it about her waist, then his shaking hands were exploring the delicately swelling breasts he had bared. Helplessly she buried her face in his shoulder, shuddering with the force of the desire he'd awakened, not wanting him to stop, knowing she'd go mad with frustration if he stopped.

Fiercely he stripped the caftan away from her and threw it aside, and she had a brief moment of sanity as he turned back to her. Her hands clutched at his powerful shoulders and she moaned weakly, "Rhy...don't. We shouldn't."

"You're my wife," he muttered in reply, taking her in his arms again and pressing his weight over her. She gasped at the wild, sweet contact of his bare flesh against hers, then the passion-tart possession of his mouth over hers sucked away her protests, and again her arms lifted and clung about him.

It was as if the years of separation had never been; their bodies were as familiar with each other as they had been long ago. Caught up in the whirlpool of his passion she could only respond, only return the passion he so freely gave. He wasn't gentle; except for the first time, Rhy had never been a gentle lover. He was fierce, tender, erotic, wildly exciting, and she was unable to stem her passionate reception of his lovemaking. It was just as it had been before—no, it was better; he drove her beyond sanity, beyond caring, beyond knowledge of anything except him.

Chapter Seven

Sallie came awake slowly, too comfortable and content to easily relinquish her hold on slumber. She felt utterly boneless, weightless, as if she were afloat. Her body was moving up and down in a gentle rhythm and beneath her head a steady, soothing drum kept time with her heart. She felt so marvelous, so safe....

The shrill ringing of the telephone was a rude interruption into her euphoric state and she muttered a protest. Then her bed moved beneath her and she clutched at it, only to find that instead of sheets her fingers were clinging to hard, warm skin. Her eyes popped open and she raised her head as Rhy stretched out a long, muscular arm and lifted the receiver from the bedside extension. "Hello," he muttered sleepily, his voice even huskier than usual as he wasn't completely awake. He listened a moment, said "Thank you" and hung up, then, with a sigh, closed his eyes again.

Hot color ran into Sallie's cheeks and hastily she tried to scramble away from him and pull up the sheet to cover her nude body. She was prevented from moving by his arms, which tightened about her, holding her in place on his chest. His eyelids, with their thick black lashes, lifted and he surveyed her flushed, tousled, early-morning beauty with a satisfied gleam in his gray eyes.

"Stay here," he commanded huskily. His hand quested down her side, smoothing her silky skin, and he murmured against her ear, "I feel as if I have a kitten curled up on my chest. You hardly weigh anything."

Involuntarily she shivered in delight at his warm breath in her ear, but she made an effort to free herself, saying, "Let me up, Rhy, I want to dress—"

"Not yet, baby," he crooned, brushing her long hair back to press his lips into the small hollow below her ear. "It's still early, and we don't have anything more important to do than getting used to each other again. You're my wife and I like the feel of you in my arms."

"*Estranged* wife," she insisted, trying to arch her head away from his insistent lips, but instead she found herself merely tilting her head back to allow him greater access to her throat. Her heart began pounding when he found the pulse beating at the back of her neck and sucked at it hungrily, as if he wanted to draw her life's blood out of her body.

"We weren't estranged last night," he murmured.

"Last night..." Her voice failed her and after a moment she managed to continue. "Last night was the result of memories, an old attraction, nothing more. Let's just mark it down to auld lang syne and forget about it, shall we?"

He relaxed back against the pillows but kept her cuddled close against him. Surprisingly her statement didn't seem to anger him, for he smiled lazily at her. "It's okay to surrender now," he informed her gently. "I won the war last night."

She almost winced with pain at the thought of giving him up again, yet she knew she couldn't be happy with him now. She let her head fall onto his shoulder and for a moment she allowed herself to relish his closeness. He stroked her back and shoulders, playing with her hair, pulling it all to one side to drift over his chest and shoulder. His touch was sapping her strength, as always, and while she still had the presence of mind she raised her head from the haven of his wide shoulder and gazed at him seriously.

"It still won't work," she whispered. "We've both changed, and there are other considerations now. Coral's in love with you, Rhy. You can't just turn your back on her and hurt her like that—or were you planning on keeping her on the side?"

"You're a little cat," he observed lazily as his hand began questing more intimately, "always scratching and spitting, but I've got a tough hide and I don't mind if you're a little temperamental. Don't worry about Coral. What do you know about her, anyway?"

"She came to my apartment," Sallie confessed, "to warn me that you weren't serious, that you always came back to her." She tried to squirm away from his boldly exploring fingers and found instead that the friction of her skin against his made her catch her breath in longing.

He swore beneath his breath. "Women," he growled, "are the most vicious creatures on earth. Don't believe her, baby, Coral doesn't have any hold on me. I do what I want to do with whomever I choose—and right now I choose my wife."

"It isn't that easy," she insisted. "Please, Rhy, let me go. I can't make you understand when you're holding me like this—"

"Then I'll keep holding you," he interrupted. "The bottom line is this, you're mine and you'll stay mine. I can't let you go and I hope you're not in love with that photographer of yours because if you are I think I'll kill him!"

White faced, Sallie stared at him, at his suddenly narrowed eyes and clenched jaw. He reacted on a purely primitive basis to the thought of another man touching her, and abruptly she knew that it had been stupid to let him think she was involved with Chris. Not only was that a challenge to Rhy's virile domination, it wasn't fair to Chris to use him as a shield. Rhy was dangerous, he could hurt Chris and it would be her fault.

On the other hand, it went completely against her grain to let Rhy have everything his way, especially after last night. He'd certainly had everything his way then; except for that one feeble protest she'd made she hadn't attempted to ward him off at all. Even that lone effort hardly counted, because she hadn't tried to fight him off; she'd only said "no" and of course it had been a waste of breath for all the attention Rhy had paid to it.

Nor did she feel free to tell him anything about Chris. Chris's calm, lazy manner went hand in glove with such a strong sense of inner privacy that she was still surprised that he'd confided in her, and she refused to betray that confidence just to pander to Rhy's ego.

She still hadn't said anything, and suddenly Rhy's patience snapped. His hands tightened on her and he rolled, taking her with him and pinning her firmly beneath him. "Maybe you need to be shown again just who you belong to," he said violently, his mouth hard, his eyes glittering with an anger that wasn't quite anger.

Sallie's heart jolted as she felt his muscular legs parting hers, and she knew that he was going to make love to her again. Already she was drowning in the warmth that flooded her, and her heartbeat settled into a rapid pounding. But even as she slid her arms around his neck she heard herself insisting steadily, stubbornly, "I belong to myself. No one else."

"You're *mine,* Sallie! Damn you, you're *mine!*"

With his violently muttered words echoing in her ears she gave herself up to this overwhelming possession and even though her mind protested her senses were too enthralled by the delights he offered to let her argue with his blindly possessive instinct. She loved him, loved him so much that after those seven long, lonely years without his touch, now that he'd overcome her resistance and made love to her again, she wanted nothing more than to revel in the intimacy of their closeness. He couldn't give her love, but he could give her this, and it was as much of himself as he would ever give any woman. She clung to his broad shoulders and matched his fiery demands with her own, and when he finally moved from her to collapse on his back they were both satisfied and trembling with exhaustion. Unable to stand the space in the bed that separated them Sallie slid across to him and curled up against his chest, her lips pressing against his throat. As suddenly as cutting off a light she was asleep, her hands clinging to him even in sleep, as if she couldn't bear to let him go.

Awakening from her doze, Sallie stirred, opened her eyes and raised her head to find Rhy just awakening, too, his eyes still sleepy. Memories of the many mornings years ago when they'd made love and gone back to sleep made her feel eerily as if those intervening years had never been. His hand smoothed her hair back from her face, then slid around to clasp her slender neck with those strong lean fingers. "You never did tell me," he whispered. "Are you in love with him?"

She closed her eyes in resignation. He had the determination of a bulldog. But what could she tell him? Would he believe her or even understand if she told him that the way she loved Chris wasn't romantic or even sexual? The fingers clasping her neck tightened warningly and she opened her eyes. "Chris is none of your business," she said finally, tilting her chin at the grim temper that hardened his mouth. "But I haven't slept with him, so make of that what you like."

Silence followed that challenge and confession for several minutes, and when she summoned the nerve to look directly at him again she was jolted by the look of raw desire on his face. "Don't...don't look at me like that," she whispered, lowering her eyes again.

"I want you," he said hoarsely. "I'm going to have you. I'm glad that you don't have a lover now because I don't want any complications to stand in my way."

Wearily she shook her head. "No, you still don't understand. Just because I'm not sleeping with anyone doesn't mean that I want to take up our marriage again. For the record, I've never slept with anyone but you, but I just don't want to live with you. I don't think it'll work. Don't you see?'' she pleaded. ''I need my job the way you needed yours when we were first married. I can't be happy staying at home and cleaning house now, I need more, more than you're willing to give. I need my freedom.''

His face was taut as he stared at her, his eyes restless. ''Don't ask me to send you on a dangerous assignment,'' he muttered. ''I can't. If anything happened to you and I was the one responsible for your being there I couldn't live with myself. But as for the job—maybe we can work out a compromise. Let's give it a try, see how we get along together. All we ever did before was make love. We didn't get to know each other as people. We'll be here for three more days. While we're here let's just enjoy each other and worry about the future when we get back to the States. Can we manage three days together without fighting?''

''I don't know,'' she said cautiously. The temptation to enjoy those three days stole away her strength. She knew Rhy, knew that his idea of a compromise was to hem her in so that she had to do things his way, but there was nothing he could do while they were here. She had already taken the precaution of drawing out her savings, and once they returned to New York she knew she'd have to leave, but for now...for now why couldn't she simply enjoy being with her husband and loving him? Three days was so short a space in which to store up enough memories to last a lifetime! Why couldn't he see that they were hopelessly incompatible?

''All right,'' she finally agreed. ''But when we get back don't expect me automatically to move in with you. I'll hold you to that compromise.''

His strong mouth curved with amusement. ''I never thought any differently,'' he said wryly, thrusting his fingers through her hair at the back of her head and pulling her down for his kiss. The kiss began casually, then gradually deepened until they were clinging together in mutual need that could only be satisfied one way.

As they dressed to attend the half-party, half-press conference that Marina was giving prior to the charity ball, Sallie was struck by how familiar it seemed, the same routine of so many years ago emerging without them having to talk about it. She used the bath first, then, while she was putting on her makeup and arranging her hair, Rhy showered and shaved. He waited until she'd put on her lipstick, then grabbed her and kissed her, smearing the color outside her lip line, chuckling to himself as she flounced back to the mirror to repair the job. How many times had he done that in the past? She couldn't remember. It was part of their marriage, and when she met his eyes in the mirror she knew that he was remembering, too, and they smiled at each other.

The gown she'd chosen was a pale rose silk, simply cut, as her lack of stature wouldn't permit anything frivolous or she looked like a doll. The color was extremely flattering to her dark blue eyes and glossy sable hair and Rhy eyed her with male appreciation as he zipped her up.

"I don't think it's safe for you to leave this room." He bent down to murmur in her ear. "Some wild sheik will steal you and take you into the desert and I'll have to start a war to get you back again."

"What? And ruin a good story?" she mocked, meeting his eyes in the mirror. "I'm certain I could escape, and just think what good reading that would make!"

"I would laugh," he said wryly, "but I know firsthand the kind of dangers you've faced, and it damned near curdles my blood. It's one thing for me to risk my hide and quite another for yours to be endangered."

"Not really," she argued, leaning forward to brush her finger under her eye and remove a tiny smudge she'd just noticed. "When we were together before, I was terrified that you'd be hurt and I nearly died when you were shot. Now I understand what sent you back to the field as soon as possible, because I became hooked on excitement, too."

"It wears off," he said, an almost weary look passing over his hard features. "The danger became almost a bore, and the thought of sleeping in the same bed for more than a few days in a row grew in attractiveness. Roots don't necessarily tie you down, baby, they can help you to grow bigger."

"That's true, if the pot's large enough so that you don't become root-bound," she pointed out and turned to face him. She was smiling but the expression in her eyes was serious and he tilted her face up to him with one long finger under her chin.

"But holding on to you is so much fun," he teased.

"Don't you ever think of anything else?" She shook her head in amusement.

"When I'm with you? Rarely." His gray eyes took on a glint of passion as he looked down at her. "Even before I knew who you were all I had to do was catch a glimpse of that sassy braid switching back and forth across your trim little rear and I wanted to chase you down in the hallways.''

Sallie smiled, but inwardly she recognized that all of his words, his actions, were based on physical attraction and not on an emotional need. Rhy wanted her, there was no doubt about that, but the realization was growing in her that he was incapable of love. Perhaps it was just as well. If he loved as intensely as he desired, his love could be soul destroying.

The party was being held in another hotel as the Al Mahdi palace was being readied for the ball and Marina's husband did not want their own home opened to the public for security reasons. The circular drive in front of the hotel was choked with limousines and there was a confusing mixture of accents as Europeans and Americans mingled with the native Sakaryans. Security was tight; the doors and lower windows were posted with guards, fierce-looking Sakaryans in boots and military uniforms, with cocky little berets on their heads, watching the crowd of foreign visitors with their fierce black desert eyes. Their credentials and invitation were checked and rechecked as Sallie and Rhy moved slowly forward in the swarm of people.

But once inside they were guided smoothly into the suite being used and all outward signs of security vanished. There was soft, soothing music playing and the light tinkle of ice cubes against glass testified that many people were relaxing.

The suite was simply furnished in the Arabic way, but there were enough seats for anyone who preferred to sit instead of stand. The colors blended simply, golds and browns and whites, and Sallie discerned Marina's touch in the many plants and flowers that dotted the rooms and both cheered and soothed. She looked about for her friend but was unable to catch sight of her in the constantly moving flow of humanity.

"Why is the security so stiff outside?" she asked, leaning close to Rhy so no one else could hear her.

"Because Zain isn't a fool," Rhy growled. "A lot of people would like to see him dead. Relatives of the King who are jealous of Zain's influence, religious purists who don't like his progressive politics, terrorist left-wingers who don't need a reason, even Communists. Sakarya is an important hunk of real estate these days."

"I heard about the oil reserves," she whispered. "Are they that large?"

"Massive. If the surveys prove correct Sakarya will have reserves second only to the Saudis."

"I see," she mused. "And since the finance minister is married to an American woman his sympathies will naturally lean to the West. That makes his influence with the King doubly important. Good heavens, is it safe for Marina to live here?"

"As safe as Zain can make it, and he's a cunning man. He intends to die of old age."

She intended to ask more but a flash of bright hair caught her eye, and she turned her head to see Marina bearing down on her. Her friend was gorgeous, glowing, her lovely spring green eyes sparkling with gaiety. "Sallie!" she exclaimed, laughing, and the two hugged each other enthusiastically. "I wasn't sure you were going to make it! I couldn't believe it. Someone kept wanting to send another reporter in your place. I refused to see her, of course," she said with laughing triumph.

"Of course," agreed Sallie. "By the way, Marina, let me introduce my publisher, Rhydon Baines. He's the one who tried to foul things up for us."

"You're kidding!" Marina smiled up at Rhy and gave him her hand. "Didn't you know Sallie and I are old friends?"

"Not until after the fireworks," he said wryly. "I soon found out. Is Zain here? It's been a long time since I've seen him."

Recognition lit Marina's eyes. "You're *that* Rhy Baines? Yes, he's here somewhere." She turned her head to locate her husband, peering around groups of people. "Here he comes now."

Zain ibn Rashid was a lean, pantherish man with a darkly aquiline face and a rather cruel smile, but he wore his exquisitely tailored suit as casually as an American teenager would wear jeans. Sensuality curled his upper lip and hooded his piercing black eyes, and with a shock Sallie realized that she'd only met one other man who exuded that aura of raw sexuality, Rhy. It was ironic but rather inevitable that she and Marina had married the same type of man, both untamed and unlikely ever to be tamed.

"Rhy!" Zain had transferred his gaze from his wife to glance casually at the couple with her and now his black eyes opened with recognition and he extended his hand. "I'd heard you were going to interview the King, then that the plans were changed. Are you going to do the interview after all?"

"No, someone else will do that. I'm here on a different matter entirely,'' Rhy said in a wry tone, nodding his head to indicate Sallie. "I'm here as a bodyguard for the reporter from *World in Review*. Sallie, let me introduce Zain Abdul ibn Rashid, the minister of finance—''

"And my husband,'' Marina broke in impishly. "Zain, Sallie is my friend I've been telling you about.'' Then she looked at Rhy. "What do you mean, bodyguard? I thought you were the publisher of the magazine?''

"I am,'' he admitted, unperturbed. "I'm also her husband.''

Irrepressible Marina squealed and hugged Sallie again. "You're married! When did this happen? Why didn't you write me?''

"I haven't had time,'' Sallie blurted without thinking while she shot Rhy a glance that promised revenge. He merely smiled at her, well satisfied with his announcement.

Zain was grinning openly. "So you finally got caught. We'll have to celebrate, but when I don't know. Marina has thrown the country into an uproar. I'll be glad when this is over.'' He gave his wife a look that held for several seconds before he jerked his eyes away, but Sallie had seen his expression and she heaved an inward sigh of relief. He'd looked at Marina with absorbing tenderness before pulling his sardonic mask back in place. He really loved Marina; he hadn't chosen her simply for her golden beauty.

"I can't stay any longer, I have to circulate.'' Marina sighed, putting her hand on Zain's arm. "Sallie, I promise that after the ball we'll curl up and talk our heads off.''

Sallie nodded. "I'll see you then,'' she said as Marina left to attend to the other guests, with Zain a watchful escort.

"She's beautiful,'' Rhy commented.

"Yes.'' She glanced at him from under her lashes. "Even more beautiful than Coral.''

"Am I supposed to argue with that?'' he drawled.

She shrugged and didn't answer. Instead she questioned, "How long have you known Zain?''

"Several years,'' he said noncommittally.

"How did you meet him?''

"What is this, an interview?'' he parried, taking her arm and steering her to the side. He signaled a waiter who came over with a tray of glasses. Rhy took two glasses of champagne and gave one to Sallie.

"Why aren't you answering me?'' she persisted, and at last he gave her an exasperated look.

"Because, baby, I wouldn't like my answers to be overheard, and neither would Zain. Now be a good girl, and stop being so nosy."

She glared at him and turned her back, walking slowly among the ebb and flow of people as she sipped from her glass. Nosy! Asking questions was her job and he knew it. But he was the most contrary man she'd ever met, she thought idly, tracing her finger along the rim of a jade vase. Contrary and arrogant, he didn't know what it meant to be thwarted in anything he wanted.

"Stop sulking and start taking notes," he whispered in her ear. "Notice who's here and who isn't."

"I don't need you to tell me how to do my job," she flared, walking away from him again.

"No, what you need is a good spanking," he murmured, his long legs and greater strength making it easy for him to stay even with her in the press of people.

Perhaps he had hoped to get a rise out of her with that ridiculous statement, but she ignored him and continued her wandering progress through the suite. She rarely took notes at a function like this, having learned that it made people self-conscious. One of her assets was that she had an excellent memory and she used it, identifying the European blue bloods and financial giants. Social events weren't really her field, but she was able to put a name and a country to the important people and most of the not-so-important ones, as well.

Rhy caught her arm and leaned down to whisper, "There's the Deputy Secretary of State to your right. And the French foreign minister beside him."

"I know," Sallie said smugly, having already spotted the two men. "But I haven't seen a representative of a Communist nation, so I suppose Zain's influence is making itself felt."

Just then a tall, thin, distinguished gentleman with gray hair and kindly blue eyes approached them and extended his hand. "Mr. Baines," he greeted Rhy cordially in a clipped British public school accent. "Nice to see you again."

"It's a pleasure to meet you again, Mr. Ambassador," Rhy replied, taking the other man's hand. "Sallie, I'd like to introduce you to Sir Alexander Wilson-Hume, Great Britain's ambassador to Sakarya. Mr. Ambassador, my wife, Sallie."

The pale blue eyes lit as the ambassador took Sallie's hand and gently lifted it to his lips with old-world courtesy. "My pleasure entirely." He smiled as Sallie murmured a conventional greeting. "Have you been married long, Mrs. Baines?"

An impish smile curved her lips. "Eight years, Mr. Ambassador."

"My word! Eight years!" He gave her a startled glance and abruptly she wondered if he'd had reason to assume that Rhy wasn't married when he'd known him before. But if that was the case the ambassador covered his confusion with perfect poise and carried on without a hitch. "You hardly look old enough to have been married a year."

"That's true," Rhy agreed smoothly. "She's aged well."

The ambassador gave him a rather startled glance, but Sallie merely smiled at Rhy's impudence despite the hollow ache that had bloomed inside her at the thought of Rhy's blatant infidelities. She'd just have to get over that, she told herself firmly. Only a naive fool would expect a man like Rhy to be faithful; he was far too physical, and far too attractive!

It was several hours later, when they were at last in a taxi returning to their own hotel, that Sallie commented evenly, "Poor man, the ambassador covered up for you well, didn't he? But now he considers you a philanderer."

"I'd hoped you wouldn't notice," Rhy replied wryly, "but you don't miss much, do you? But don't paint me blacker than I am, Sallie. You said you never thought I'd live like a monk, but I very nearly did. I've had a lot of social dates that ended when I took the lady home, nothing more."

"You're lying," she stated without expression. "I suppose you expect me to believe that Coral Williams is just a friend?"

"She's not my enemy," he said, his mouth twitching in amusement. She didn't believe him when he continued. "I wanted to make you think she was my mistress to make you jealous, but I guess it didn't work."

She began to laugh in disbelief. She'd never heard such a ridiculous tale before in her life. Rhy was a sensual animal, his passions never far from the surface, and easily aroused. She'd have to be a fool to believe he'd been faithful to her during the seven years they'd been separated. She didn't even believe he'd been faithful to her while they'd been together! "Sorry." She laughed. "Try a tale that's more plausible. Besides, it doesn't matter."

He drew in his breath in a hiss, and glancing at him she saw the flare of anger in his eyes. "I'll make it matter," he promised her grimly. Or was it a threat?

She knew that he intended to make love to her as soon as they were in their hotel room in an attempt to tear down her convictions, and she eyed him warily. She'd agreed to spend the three days with him and she'd known that they would be sleeping together, but she intended to limit their lovemaking to the nights. After all, his desire was familiar to her, even after all these years. What she wanted to do was talk to him, learn about him, get to know him in the way she'd never known him before. He was her husband, but he was still a stranger to her. Sadly she realized that even though she planned on leaving when they returned to New York she was still searching for some way to believe that they could be happy together even when she knew the search was futile.

They had just entered the hotel room, and Rhy was shrugging out of his formal jacket when the phone rang. With an impatient curse he snatched it up and barked, "Yes?"

Sallie watched him as he listened, saw the frown that darkened his brow. "I'll be right down," he said, and hung up, then pulled his jacket back on.

"Who was that?" she asked.

"The desk. There's a message for me. I'll be right back."

After he'd gone she undressed and hung away her gown, then put on a lightweight white blouson dress, all the while mulling over what he'd said. A message for him? Why hadn't they given it to him over the phone or, better yet, when they'd walked through the lobby not five minutes before? It didn't sound plausible, and without hesitation she left the room and made for the elevators. She made her living by being curious, after all.

But she was more than curious, she was cautious. She left the elevator at the second floor and walked down the stairs the rest of the way. Her cautiousness was rewarded. She opened the door at the bottom of the stairs and looked out to see her husband standing with his arm around Coral Williams, who was staring up at him with tearstained eyes. Sallie couldn't hear what they were saying, but Rhy went with Coral to the elevators and the doors slid shut behind them.

Her lips pressed firmly together, Sallie returned to their hotel room and swiftly gathered her clothing. So much for his tale of being faithful! It had to be more than a casual relationship for Coral to follow him to Sakarya. And she wasn't going to wait for him to listen to any more of his lies!

She had to act swiftly; she had no way of knowing how long he would stay with Coral. She scribbled a note, not paying attention to what she was writing, but it was something to the effect of sorry, she just wasn't interested. Then she picked up her suitcase and purse and left, once again taking the stairs.

Finding a taxi was easy, a fleet of them was waiting outside the hotel; her problem now was finding a place to stay. She was aware that hotels were few and far between in Khalidia. In French she explained to the driver that she wished to go to another hotel but not one that was well-known. He obliged, and when Sallie saw it she understood why it wasn't well-known; it looked as if the French Foreign Legion should come swarming over the walls. It was small and old and simple, and the fiercely mustachioed man who seemed to be in charge looked her over thoroughly before saying something in his own language to the taxi driver.

"He says there is a room, if you wish it, but it is not of the finest," the driver translated. "Also you must pay in advance and you must stay in your room as you are not veiled and your man is not with you."

"That seems fair," Sallie replied. To stay in the room was just what the doctor ordered; it would insure that Rhy couldn't find her. "But what shall I do for food?"

The Sakaryan's dark eyes slid over her, and then he revealed that he spoke some French by informing her rustily that his wife would bring food to her.

Delighted that she'd be able to communicate Sallie thanked him and beamed at him, her big eyes sparkling. When the driver had left Sallie lifted her suitcase and waited expectantly for her host to lead her way to her room. Instead he glared down at her fiercely for a moment, then leaned down and took the suitcase from her hand. "You are too small," he growled. "My wife will feed you."

Then he took her up the narrow stairs to her room and left her there, and Sallie examined what was to be her sleeping quarters for the next two nights. The room was spotless but contained only a single bed and a washstand on which stood a blue urn of water and a washbasin. But the bed was covered with an exotic spread and was strewn with cushions, and the mattress was comfortable, so she was satisfied.

The proprietor's wife brought up a tray loaded with cheese, bread, orange juice and coffee. She looked Sallie over from head to toe, her expression shocked at the sight of Sallie's slim legs, but she gave a timid smile in response to Sallie's grin.

After eating, Sallie took off her dress and shoes; if she was to be confined in this small room for forty-eight hours she might as well be comfortable. Digging in her suitcase she produced the long T-shirt that she had packed and pulled it on; wearing only that and her panties she was as cool as she could get and still have any clothes on. Then she unpacked her clothing and hung everything up to air.

With nothing else to do she lay down on the bed and tried to lose herself in one of the paperback books she'd brought, but the heat was becoming oppressive and she thought with longing of the air-conditioned comfort of the Hotel Khalidia. Flopping onto her back she raised the book to fan herself, and only then did she notice the old-fashioned paddle fan on the ceiling. "Shades of *Casablanca!*" she cried in delight, jumping up and looking about for the switch. She wouldn't even have sworn that the hotel was wired for electricity, but there was a switch on the wall, and when she flipped it the fan creaked into motion. The gentle movement of air against her skin relieved the sensation of smothering, and she fell back on the bed.

She tried again to read her book, but thoughts of Rhy kept breaking into her concentration, and suddenly a raw sob burst from her throat. Amazed at her tears and yet helpless to stop them, she bowed her head onto the bed and wept until her chest hurt and her eyes were swollen. Crying for Rhy? She'd sworn seven years ago that he'd never make her cry again, and she had thought she was over all her illusions about him, but seeing him with his arm around Coral had hit her like a sledgehammer. Was she always going to be a fool over the man? What was the old saying? "I have cried for these things once already," or something to that effect, yet here she was crying for them again. And it was a waste of time.

She should be glad that she'd seen Coral before she'd allowed Rhy to make a complete fool of her. It was her stupid weakness for him that allowed her, even knowing that she was stupid, still to respond to his lovemaking—crave his lovemaking, if she was honest with herself. And subconsciously she'd been hoping that somehow things would work out between them. She might as well face the truth once and for all: the reasons Rhy wanted her back were not emotional ones; they were all physical. Sex between them was good. It was more than good. They were a matched pair with their needs, their instincts and responses, each knowing just how to drive the other wild. And it wasn't anything they thought about; it was inborn in both of them, whatever it was that made each of them so physically attractive to the other.

Having known his lovemaking, hadn't she refused all other men because she'd known that they couldn't compare with what she'd had with Rhy? She couldn't see Rhy refusing women like that; his sexual appetites were too urgent and strong, but there was no doubt that he had a weakness for her. But sex just wasn't enough for her! She loved him and she wanted that love to be returned. They couldn't spend their lives together in bed; there had to be something else.

With fierce determination she dried her tears and looked about for something to do. Reading couldn't help and she wished that she had brought her manuscript with her. But even if it wasn't here she could write in longhand, couldn't she, and type it up when she returned home? She knew that she could lose herself in writing, push the pain inside her away.

She never went anywhere without several pads tucked into her bag so she dug one out and sat down on the bed with it balanced on her knee, as there was nothing to use for a desk. Grimly she made herself recall where she'd left off, and after a few minutes the writing became easier. So what if Rhy had let her down again? She still had herself, her newly discovered talent and her integrity. She had learned how to live without Rhy, and she'd been a fool to have stayed with the magazine once she had learned he'd bought it. She was vulnerable to him, she always had been, but she knew that she didn't dare let him resume the prominent position that he'd once held in her life. It had nearly destroyed her, that mad need for his touch, his smile, his presence.

But what if she had a baby? The thought came out of nowhere and she dropped her pen, her hand straying over her flat stomach, and she wondered. Thinking back, counting, she realized that it was possible, even likely. But there was a difference now: she wouldn't be terrified at being on her own. She would gladly welcome a chance to have her child all to herself. Part of her longed for a baby, ached to hold a small wriggling body in her arms. She'd never been able to hold her son; they had taken him away immediately and she'd had only a glimpse of his blue little face. Another baby...another son. Suddenly she hoped it was so with a fierce, wild yearning. Perhaps she couldn't have Rhy, but she could have his baby, and she could give to her child the love that Rhy didn't want.

Chapter Eight

On the morning of the charity ball Sallie was a mass of nerves, partly a result of being shut up in that tiny room for two days and partly because she so dreaded facing Rhy again. She knew as well as she knew the color of her eyes that he hadn't left the city; he was waiting for her to surface at the ball. He would be furious, and that was an understatement.

But she dressed in the lavender silk dress that she'd chosen for the ball and noticed that it darkened her eyes to violet. A touch of mauve eyeshadow made her eyes pools of mystery and she underlined the air of sophistication by pulling her hair back from her face in a severe coil that was secured by three tiny amethyst butterflies.

It was almost time for her taxi, so she picked up her suitcase, since she would not be coming back there after the ball, and carefully made her way down the narrow stairs, not wanting to turn her ankles in her high heels. The Sakaryan proprietor was seated just to the right of the stairs, and he got to his feet as she descended. His gaze went over her thoroughly, and she sensed the tension of his powerful muscles. She had the uncomfortable feeling that this Sakaryan would like to start a harem, with her as his first concubine!

But he said, in his rough French, "It is dangerous for you to be in this part of the city alone. I will walk with you to the taxi, yes?"

"Yes, thank you," she said gravely, and noticed that he didn't offer to carry the suitcase for her this time, but she was grateful for his escort even for the short distance to the taxi waiting outside. Her driver grinned and got out to open the door as they approached.

At the palace gates she had to leave the taxi as the driver wasn't cleared to enter the palace grounds. Her name was checked off on the list of guests and a hawk-faced guard escorted her to the palace and even stored her suitcase in a small cupboard before taking her to the enormous chamber that had been decorated for the ball.

Though she was early there were already a fair number of people standing about, the women dressed like so many butterflies, and the abundance of jewels made her eyebrows arch. To her delight there were also a number of Muslim guests, and she was certain that not all of the dark men, some wearing their native headdress and some in European clothing, were Sakaryan; probably Rhy could put a name to most of them. And there were a few Muslim women, too, well dressed, quiet, looking about with their huge, liquid dark eyes. She would have loved to talk to them, ask about their lives, but she had the feeling that her nosiness wouldn't be very well received.

Suddenly Sallie felt a tingle along the left side of her face, and she lifted a hand to touch her cheek. Then she knew, and she turned her head slightly to look straight into Rhy's furious gaze. His eyes were like flint, his jaw carved out of granite. Sallie tilted her chin and gave him back as good as she got as he strode toward her with suppressed savagery in every line of his muscular body.

She stood her ground, and when he reached her he encircled her slim waist with his hard fingers, a grip that didn't hurt but which she knew she couldn't break. A voice gravelly with temper growled, "You need to be shown who's boss, baby, and I'm just the man to do it. Where the *hell* have you been?"

"At another hotel," she informed him casually. "I told you from the beginning that I didn't want to resume our marriage, and I meant it."

"You agreed to give it a three-day trial," he reminded her grimly.

"So I did. I'd have agreed to rob a bank if it would have kept you from watching me. So what?" She raised her head and looked him straight in the eye. "I lied to you and you lied to me. We're even."

"How did I lie to you?" he snapped, his nostrils flaring in rage that he had to control because they were in public.

"About Coral." She gave him a wintry smile. "You don't seem to realize that I don't mind if you had other women—I really don't *care*—" that was a lie if she'd ever told one "—but I do object to people lying to me. So you've been a virtual monk, have you? Am I to believe that Coral followed you all the way to Sakarya with tears in her beautiful eyes on the basis of a platonic relationship?''

"I don't know how you found out about Coral—" he began impatiently, but she interrupted.

"I followed you. I have a nosy nature. It's part of being a reporter. So, my dear husband, I saw you comfort your mistress and take her to her room, and you didn't leave immediately or you would have caught *me* leaving!''

"It's your fault that I took her to her room," he snarled, his fingers tightening on her wrist. "I didn't ask her to follow me and I didn't lie to you. She isn't and never has been my mistress. But there she was, and she was crying, and I wondered if you'd been right when you said she was in love with me. I've never thought she was, she went out with other men, and I dated other women, but there was the possibility that you'd seen something I'd missed. I thought I owed her an explanation, so I took her to her room and told her the truth about us. Fifteen minutes later I went back to our room and found only that damned note of yours! I could break your neck, Sallie. I've been half out of my mind worrying about you!''

"I've told you I can take care of myself," she muttered, wondering if she could believe this or not. But she didn't dare believe him! How could she? She knew him too well, knew the strength of his sexual appetite.

Further conversation was prevented at that point by the entrance of the King of Sakarya, His Royal Highness Abu Haroun al Mahdi. Everyone bowed and the women curtsied, including the Americans in the group, and the King looked pleased. He lacked the stature of many Sakaryans, but five hundred years of rule were evident in his proud carriage and straightforward gaze. He greeted his guests first in perfect English, then in French, and finally in the Arabic tongue.

Sallie strained up on her toes for a better look at him, and for a moment her eyes were solidly locked with those of the monarch. After a second's hesitation he gave her a nod and a slow, faintly shy smile which she returned with her own warm, friendly smile; then they were blocked from view by a group of people moving closer to him.

"You've made a hit," Rhy observed with narrowed eyes.

"All I did was smile at him," she defended crossly, for it seemed as if he was accusing her of something.

"Your smile is an open invitation, baby," he drawled.

He was going to be impossible; he would make the day as difficult for her as he could. "Isn't it time for the fashion show to begin?" she said, grateful for anything that would relieve her of his undivided attention.

"In half an hour," he replied, drawing her with him to the room where the fashion show would take place. Some of the top designers of the world had put together the show for Marina and already the chairs that had been placed about the runway were half filled. Exquisitely gowned women laughed and chattered while their suave escorts looked on with veiled interest.

A thought struck Sallie and she muttered to Rhy, "I suppose Coral is modeling?"

"Of course," he affirmed, his voice hard.

"Then we might as well find seats," she sniped. "I don't suppose wild horses could drag you away."

His fingers bit painfully into her arm. "Shut up," he snarled. "My God, can't you just shut up?" His head snapped around and before she could protest he was marching her firmly out of the room. He barked a question at a guard who saluted smartly, for some reason, and led them down a passageway to a small room. Rhy bodily pushed her into the room and closed the door behind them.

Hoping to divert him from the black rage she could see in his face Sallie said hastily, "What room is this?" while she looked around the small chamber as if she was vastly interested.

"I don't care," Rhy replied, his voice so rough that the words were barely intelligible, and then he advanced on her with dark purpose evident in his face. Sallie backed away in alarm but had taken only a few steps when he caught her.

He didn't say anything else; he simply pulled her to him and covered her mouth with his and kissed her with such devouring hunger that she forgot to struggle. It would have been useless in any case; she was no match for his strength and he held her so closely that their bodies were pressed together from shoulder to knee. Blood began to drum in her ears and she sank against him, held up only by his arms.

Long minutes later he lifted his mouth and surveyed her flushed, love-drugged face. "Don't talk to me about other women," he ordered in a low tone, his uneven breath caressing her lips. "No other woman can excite me like you do, even when you're not trying to, you little witch. I want you now," he finished on a groan, bending his head to brush her lips with his.

"That—that's impossible," she whispered, but her protest was only a token one. The sensual fire that burned in him burned in her, also, and if he had persisted she wouldn't have been capable of resisting. As it was he retained some sense of their location and put her away from him with shaking hands.

"I know, dammit." He sighed. "I suppose we'd better go back if you want to see the fashion show—and not another word about Coral," he warned darkly.

Her fingers trembling, she repaired the damage he'd done to her lipstick and offered him a tissue to wipe the color from his mouth. He did so, smiling a little at the smear of color that came off on the tissue.

"What did you say to the guard?" she finally asked, obeying a need to make nonvital conversation.

"I told him you were feeling faint," he replied. "And you did look pale."

"Do I now?" she wondered aloud, touching her cheeks.

"No. You look kissed," he drawled.

The blood was still rushing through her body in yearning when they took their seats for the fashion show, and the parade of models barely registered on her consciousness. She was too aware of Rhy's tall body beside her, so close that she could feel the warmth of him, smell the unique muskiness of his body. Her heart pounded heavily in her chest. Only Coral made any impression on her, her eyes fastened on Rhy as if drawn to him, the pouty, sensuous smile on her perfect mouth meant for him alone. Glancing sideways at Rhy, Sallie saw that his expression remained closed except for a slight tightening of his jaw that spoke volumes to her, and she looked back at Coral with nausea boiling in her stomach.

The program was full, every minute ordered. After the fashion show there was a thousand-dollar-a-plate dinner, with all of the proceeds going to charity. Then dancing, then entertainment by a top American singer. Sallie lived through the hours feeling as if she was walking underwater. Rhy was with her every minute, but she couldn't forget the fleeting expression on his face when he'd seen Coral.

Why was she allowing him to torment her like this? She had no illusions about him, and she had already determined her own course of action. When they returned to New York she would leave, it was as simple as that. But for some reason she couldn't shake her deep sense of misery, and as a result she drank more champagne than she meant to, realizing that fact only when the room swirled mistily around her and she clutched at Rhy's arm.

"That's enough," he said gently, taking the glass from her fingers and setting it down. "I think you could stand something to eat, a slice of cake maybe. Come on."

With tender concern he made certain she ate, watching her closely all the while. When she felt better she smiled thankfully at him. "How much longer before the interview?" she murmured.

"Not much longer, honey," he comforted, as if sensing her unhappiness.

But at last it was over with and Sallie and Marina were alone in a private chamber the King had donated for their use. "He's really a dear," Marina explained. "I think he's shy, but he tries so hard to disguise it. And of course he was brought up to disregard women in every way but the physical, and he can't quite become used to meeting them socially despite his English education."

"Did your husband go to the same school?" Sallie asked, thinking that Zain didn't seem to have any problem with women.

"No, and his attitude could bear some improvement, too," Marina said with wry amusement. "Listen, he kept a harem until we were engaged. I made him give them all up before I would agree to marry him!" she explained smugly.

Sallie choked on her laughter and gasped. "A harem? You're kidding! Do they still have those things?"

"Of course, why do you think the royal families have so many princes? Muslim religion permits three wives and as many concubines as a man can support, and Zain most definitely had his selection of concubines to occupy his nights!"

"What did you say to him to make him give them up?"

"I gave him a choice, he could have me or he could have other women, but I made it plain that I had no intention of sharing him. He didn't like the idea of giving up his harem, but he finally realized that my ignorant American mind just couldn't accept it."

Their eyes met and they went off into gales of laughter, and of course that was the moment when they were interrupted by Rhy and Zain. "I thought this was a serious interview," Rhy commented, strolling forward to drop his long length beside Sallie.

"And I thought it was a private one," she retorted.

Zain's strong mouth quirked as he stretched his long frame out close to Marina. "We couldn't resist," he explained. "I introduced Rhy to

His Majesty,'' he said, flexing his broad shoulders as if he was weary, and he chuckled at the memory. "I think I made some diplomats jealous, especially when they had a long chat in voices too low to carry!''

"The State Department will probably try to debrief me,'' Rhy added.

A memory clicked in Sallie's mind, and she said casually to Zain, "How did you meet Rhy?''

"He saved my life,'' Zain replied promptly, but no explanation followed and Sallie's eyebrows arched.

"You don't need to know,'' Rhy teased. "We were both where we weren't supposed to be and we barely got out alive. Let it rest, baby. Tell us how you and Marina met, instead.''

"Oh, that's simple enough.'' Marina shrugged. "We met in college. There's nothing unusual in that. Now, why don't you two run along? How can Sallie and I talk with witnesses present?''

Both men laughed, but neither made a move to leave, so they had to be included in the conversation. To be truthful, it was impossible to exclude them. Rhy wasn't there for an interview, but he was still a reporter and gradually he got one anyway. Despite her exasperation Sallie could only admire the way he posed his questions to Zain. Some were blunt, posed point-blank; others he merely hinted at, letting Zain evade the question or answer it as he wished. In response to that consideration Zain was open with his answers, and Sallie knew that she was listening to potential dynamite. He told Rhy things that perhaps even foreign heads of state hadn't been told, and he seemed to have perfect confidence that Rhy would know what he could report and what he should forget.

Slowly Sallie began to understand the razor-sharp brain of the man who handled the finances of a booming economy and was slowly easing his country into the twentieth century. He was an adventurer, but he was also a patriot. Perhaps that was why the King had such great confidence in his young minister of finance, why he was allowing Sakaryan policies to be shaped along Western lines.

The role that Marina played in those policies wasn't small, she realized. As Zain had vast influence with the King, so Marina had vast influence with Zain. She didn't know if he would admit it; a man who had kept a harem until fairly recently wasn't likely to admit even to himself that his wife was a major factor in the direction his politics had taken. Nor would the King be likely to be happy if told that Marina was the indirect influence behind his throne. Yet the smiling, beautiful young woman, so obviously in love with her husband, was playing a powerful role in a scenario that could affect the entire world through its effect of Sakaryan oil.

At last the conversation became more general and Marina asked if perhaps Sallie would be free to visit later on in the year. Sallie had opened her mouth to accept when Rhy broke in before she could say a word. "I'm set to be filming a documentary in Europe late this fall and early winter," he said, "and Sallie will be with me. I don't know yet how the schedule will be, but I'll let you know."

"Do," urged Marina. "We see each other so little now. At least when I lived in New York we managed to catch each other in town once every month or so."

Sallie didn't comment, but privately she thought that Rhy was taking a lot for granted. Was he in for a surprise when she walked out of his life and disappeared forever!

It was late when they left the palace, and as they just had time to catch their flight Zain had arranged for an escort to the airport. Sallie and Rhy rode in Zain's personal limousine, and their luggage was checked and they were waved on board without pause.

Rhy had been ominously silent during the entire ride, and he was still not speaking when they buckled themselves into their seats. That suited her fine; she was tired and she didn't feel like arguing with him. Somehow she always came off second best when they fought. She was too impulsive, too reckless, unable to control her temper, whereas Rhy coolly plotted each move in advance.

When they were airborne the stewardesses began distributing the small airline pillows and blankets to those passengers who desired them, and because it was so late Sallie decided she would try to sleep and accepted them, then tilted her seat back. "I'm tired," she told Rhy's grim profile. "Good night."

He turned his head and his hard eyes burned her. Then he let his seat back, too, and slid his arm under her head, pulling her over to rest on his shoulder. "I've spent two hellish nights wondering where you were," he growled against her temple while he spread the blanket over her. "You'll sleep where you belong." Then he tilted her head back and his hard mouth closed on hers, claiming her lips in a possessive kiss that lasted long enough for him to be aware of her response. Then he drew back and resettled her head against his shoulder, and she was glad of the chance to hide her burning face. Why did she have to be so weak and foolish? Why couldn't she control her response to him?

After that kiss she was sure she wouldn't be able to sleep, but somehow she fell asleep immediately and woke only once during the long flight when she shifted and Rhy pulled the blanket up over her again. Opening her eyes in the dim cabin she looked up at him and whispered, "Can't you sleep?"

"I've been asleep," he murmured. "I was just wishing that we were alone." He pulled her close and kissed her again, leaving her in no doubt as to just why he wished they were alone. His kisses lingered and became hungry, pressing again and again to her mouth, until at last he muttered a frustrated curse and leaned his head back. "I can wait," he growled. "Barely."

Sallie lay against his shoulder and bit her lips to keep from whispering the words of love that sprang to her tongue. Tears burned her eyes. She loved him! It was so painful that she thought she'd scream. She loved him, but she couldn't trust him with her love.

They changed flights in Paris again and because the days they had spent in Sakarya hadn't been exactly restful jet lag hit both of them hard. Sallie had a splitting headache when they finally landed at JFK and from the taut, weary look on Rhy's face he didn't feel much better. If he had started an argument then she would have become hysterical, but instead he dropped her at her apartment and left without even kissing her.

Contrarily, that made her want to cry, and she lugged her suitcase up to her apartment and savagely emptied it. After taking a swift shower she fell on the bed and found to her fury that sleep eluded her. She remembered the sleepy sensuousness of his kisses during the flight, how comfortable she had been cuddled against his shoulder, the security of his arms. She burst into angry, aching tears and eventually cried herself to sleep.

But when she awoke the next morning her mind was clear. Rhy was driving her crazy, and if she didn't leave now, as she had planned, he would eventually wear her down. She would go to work today, type up the interview she had gotten with Marina and quietly turn in her notice to Greg. Then she would come back home, close up the apartment, pack her clothing and get on a bus going anywhere.

She dressed and took the bus to work, arriving a little late due to an accident that caused a traffic jam. When she entered the noisy newsroom the clatter dropped to almost silence, and it seemed to her that everyone turned to stare at her. A blush rose to her cheeks without her knowing why, and she hurried to her little cubicle. Brom was there, busy at his typewriter, but when she sat down and pulled the cover off of her own typewriter he stopped what he was doing and swiveled in his chair to look at her.

"What's wrong?" Sallie demanded, half laughing. "Do I have something on my face?"

In answer Brom leaned over and turned her wooden nameplate to face her. Aghast, Sallie stared at it. It was a new nameplate. And instead of SALLIE JEROME it blatantly declared for all the world to see, SAL-LIE BAINES. She collapsed in her chair and stared at it as if it would bite her.

"Congratulations," Brom offered. "That must've been some trip."

She couldn't think of anything to say; she just continued to stare at the nameplate. Evidently it had only appeared that morning, and she wondered at Rhy's motive. Uneasily she sensed that he was drawing the net tighter about her and that perhaps she had waited too long to make her break. But there was no help for it now, and her professional integrity wouldn't permit her to leave without finishing the interview with Marina.

"Well?" Brom prompted. "Is it true?"

"That we're married?" she replied crisply. "It's true enough, for what you want to make of it."

"And just what does that mean, Madam Sphinx?"

"It means that a wedding does not a marriage make," she mocked. "Don't take this too seriously."

"Listen, you can't be half-married, or casually married. Either you are or you aren't," he said in exasperation.

"It's a long story," she evaded, and was saved from further questioning when the phone rang. With a smothered sigh of relief she snatched it up. "Sallie Jerome."

"Wrong," Greg growled in her ear. "Sallie *Baines.* Your closet husband has gone public and it's a load off my mind. You had me in a tough spot if he'd found out I knew about you. But it's all over now and it's all between the two of you."

"What do you mean?" she asked warily, wondering if Rhy had done something else to hem her in that she hadn't yet heard of.

"Just that, doll. As far as I'm concerned you're not one of my best reporters now, you're his wife."

In blind anger Sallie forgot that she'd been planning on turning in her notice anyway and she hissed between her teeth, "Do you mean you won't give me any more assignments?"

"That's exactly what I mean. Take it up directly with him. For crying out loud, he's your husband and from what I can see he's more than willing to try a reconciliation."

"I don't want a reconciliation," she said, reining in her temper and keeping her tone low so Brom couldn't overhear. "But a reference will do just fine. Will you give me one?"

"I can't, not now that he's made it common knowledge that you're his wife. He's my boss, too," Greg explained dryly. "And he's made it clear that anything concerning you is to be okayed by him personally."

"Has he?" she demanded furiously as her anger broke out of control. "I'll have to see about that, won't I?" She slammed the phone down and glared at it, then turned her burning gaze on Brom, who threw his hands up in mock surrender and ostentatiously turned back to his typewriter.

She expected to be summoned to Rhy's office at any moment, and she couldn't decide if she wanted to see him or not. It would be an exquisite relief to unleash her temper and scream at him, but she knew that Rhy would also take advantage of her lack of control and would probably provoke her into revealing all her plans. The best thing she could do was to complete her report and leave. She knew her weaknesses, and the two worst ones were her temper and Rhy. The sensible thing to do was not to allow either of them to gain the upper hand.

She tried, but concentrating had seldom been more difficult. Her mind raced, going over her packing, the steps she had to take to close up her apartment, where she might go, and in the middle of all her plans would flash a picture of Rhy, naked, his eyes hungry as he reached for her, and her body would remember his touch and she'd tremble in reaction. She ached for him; why hadn't he come up to the apartment with her last night? Of course they'd both been tired, exhausted and irritable, but still... What a fool she was! The last thing she needed was more of his addictive lovemaking! It would be hard enough now to get over him, to forget again the wild sweetness that had consumed her.

The morning slipped past, and she grimly determined to work through lunch, but her plans were derailed when Chris stopped by her desk, his brown eyes shuttered as he silently lifted her nameplate and studied it, then returned it to her desk without comment. "Can you get away for a little while?" he asked quietly, but even so Sallie caught the undertone in his voice, perhaps because she was so miserable herself that she was sensitive to the suffering of others.

"It's lunchtime, anyway," she said without hesitation, turning off the typewriter and covering it. "Where do you want to go?"

"Will he mind?" Chris asked, and she knew who he meant.

"No," she lied, and gave him a cheeky little grin. "Besides, I'm not asking him."

He didn't speak again until they were out of the building and weaving their way through the hurrying, dodging, sidestepping lunch crowd that filled the sidewalks. He lifted his head and peered at the heat ball of the sun with slitted eyes as he commented, "Are you really married to him? It's not easy to get married that fast unless you detour through Vegas."

"I've been married to him for eight years," she admitted, not meeting the questioning glance that she felt him shoot at her. "And we've been separated for seven of those years."

They walked in silence for a while, then Chris caught her hand and indicated a coffee shop. That was as good as anything and they went inside, where they were shown to a small table along the wall. Sallie wasn't hungry and she chose only fruit juice to drink and a small salad, knowing that the salad wouldn't be eaten. Chris didn't seem very hungry either, for when their food came he merely drank his coffee and stared broodingly at the tuna sandwich on his plate.

"It looks as if you're back together now," he finally said.

Sallie shook her head. "It's what he wants."

"And you don't?"

"He doesn't love me," she said sadly. "I'm just a challenge to him. Like I told you, he just wants to play for a while. It doesn't matter to him that he's destroying my life in the process. He's already wrecked my career, and he swears that he'll blacklist me, keep me from getting another job as a reporter."

Chris swore, something he rarely did, and met Sallie's surprised gaze with gold lights of anger leaping in his dark eyes. "How could he do that to you?" he muttered.

She managed a careless shrug. "He says he's afraid I'll get killed. That he can't stand the thought of me in the middle of a revolution." But how many times had Rhy left her to do just that, leaving her behind in a frenzy of worry?

"Now *that* I can understand," said Chris, giving her a wry smile. "I'll admit to having a few worries about your pretty little carcass myself, and I'm not even married to you."

"But you won't quit for Amy," she reminded him bluntly. "And I won't quit for Rhy—if I have any choice. He's hemming me in, Chris. He's tying me down and smothering me.''

"You love him."

"I try not to. I just haven't succeeded very well so far." Then she shook her head. "Forget about me. Is the situation still the same with Amy?"

He tilted his head a little to one side. "I still love her. I still want to marry her. But she still won't marry me unless I quit reporting, and the thought of stifling myself in a nine-to-five job makes me break out in a cold sweat."

"Can you give in? Greg did, for his kids."

"But he didn't for his wife," Chris pointed out. "He had to lose her before he left the field. If she were still alive he'd probably still be out there chasing down a story."

That was true and she sighed, looking away from him. The demands made by children were so much harder to deny than those made by adults because children saw things only in relation to themselves and couldn't comprehend that their parents' needs should be as important as their own. They had no compunction about making their needs clear, demanding that they be taken care of, while adults for some reason drew back, refrained from pushing too hard, knowing that no one owed them anything and therefore they didn't ask. Except she had asked—she had demanded—that Rhy change his job and stay with her, and it had gained her exactly nothing. Rhy had made it plain that her happiness wasn't his responsibility. He had his own life to live. Nor could she offer Chris any hope, any solution, for she could see none for herself. No matter what they did, misery would be the result.

"I'm going to leave," she said aloud, then looked at him in horror, not having meant to announce her intentions.

He caught the look and waved his hand. "Forget it. It won't go any further," he assured her. "I kind of thought you might do that, anyway. You've got the guts to do what you have to do, no matter how it hurts. You're cutting your losses. I just wish I could."

"When you're ready you will. Don't forget, I've had seven years to get used to being without him." She gave him a tiny smile. "I'd even convinced myself that it was all over between us. It didn't take Rhy long to shatter that little fairy tale."

He looked at her as if he wasn't really seeing her, his dark eyes taking on the introspective blankness of someone walling himself up inside. He'd been hurt, just as she had. There was nothing so calculated to batter the self-esteem as to hear a loved one saying, "You have to change," the insidious little phrase that really meant, "I don't love you as you are. You're not good enough." There were deeper hurts, more violent hurts, yet somehow that particular hurt had such a nasty sting. She knew it well now, and she swore that she'd never ask anyone to change ever again. Had Rhy been hurt by her insistence that he change? She tried to picture a confused, hurt Rhy and failed utterly. He had a stainless-steel character that never faltered, never let itself be vulnerable. He'd brushed her clinging arms off like so many cobwebs and went on his way.

"I'll get over her," said Chris quietly, and on his face was the smooth blank look of acceptance. "I guess I'll have to, won't I?"

They walked back to the office in silence, and as they entered the empty elevator Chris punched the button to close the door and held his finger on it, staring fixedly at her.

"Keep in touch," he said softly. "I wish it could've been you, Sal." He curved his hand around her neck and bent to lightly touch his lips to hers and she felt tears sting her eyelids. Yes, why couldn't it have been Chris for her, instead of Rhy?

She couldn't promise that she'd be in touch, though she wanted to. Once she left she couldn't risk doing anything that might give Rhy a clue to where to find her, and anything Chris didn't know he couldn't divulge. She left the elevator with only a long look into his face that said goodbye; then she went back to her desk and tackled the report again with grim determination.

The sense of now or never gave her the concentration she needed and in less than an hour she sent the finished report on to Greg's office. She stood and stretched her tired, cramped muscles and casually got her purse and left the building without speaking to anyone, as if she was merely leaving for an appointment, when in reality she intended never to return. She regretted that she had to leave without telling Greg, but he'd made it painfully clear that his first loyalty was to Rhy, and she knew that he would immediately report her resignation.

Caution made her cash the cashier's check she'd been carrying in her purse and convert most of the money into traveler's checks. Who knew what means Rhy might use to hold her? She had to get out and do it now.

It was almost three-thirty by the time she reached her apartment and it was only instinct, but when she opened the door the hair on the back of her neck lifted. She stared around at the familiar furniture and she knew that something was different. Looking about she saw that several things were missing: her personal awards were gone, her books were gone, her antique clock was missing. Thieves!

Rushing into the bedroom she stared aghast at the emptiness. The closet doors stood open, revealing the lack of contents. Her cosmetic and toiletry items were gone from the bathroom, even her toothbrush. All of her personal items had disappeared! Then she went utterly pale and raced back into the bedroom to stare in horror at the uncluttered surface where her manuscript and typewriter had rested. Even her manuscript had been stolen!

A noise in the doorway made her whirl, ready for battle if the thieves had returned, but it was the landlady who stood there. "I thought I saw you," Mrs. Landis said cheerfully. "I'm so happy for you. You're such a nice girl, and I always wondered when you were going to get married. I'll hate losing you, but I know you're anxious to settle in with that handsome husband of yours."

A cold feeling settled in Sallie's stomach. "Husband?" she echoed weakly.

"He's the first celebrity I've ever met," Mrs. Landis rattled on. "But he was so nice, and he said he'd made arrangements for your furniture to be put in storage by this weekend so I can rent the apartment out again. I thought it was so thoughtful of him to handle it all for you while you were working."

By now Sallie had gotten control of herself, and she managed a smile for Mrs. Landis. "It certainly was," she agreed, her hands clenching into fists by her sides. "Rhy thinks of everything!"

But he hadn't won yet!

Chapter Nine

She was so angry that she was shaking helplessly, unable to decide what to do. She got on a bus and rode aimlessly, wishing violently that she could get her hands around Rhy's throat. He'd literally stolen her clothing, all of her personal possessions. That was bad enough, but she could get along without all that if she had to. The one thing she couldn't leave behind was her manuscript, and she couldn't think of any way to get it back, either. She didn't even know where Rhy lived, and his telephone number wasn't listed.

But she had to find somewhere to spend the night, and at last she left the bus and walked the teeming sidewalks in the steamy hot afternoon sun until weariness prompted her to choose a hotel at random. She checked in and sat for a long time in a daze, unable to think of any action she could take. Her mind darted about erratically, trying to devise a way of retrieving the manuscript without having to see Rhy again But to find the book she had to find out where Rhy lived, and to do that she had to talk to him, something that she wanted to avoid.

The theft of her book seemed to have paralyzed her, robbed her of her ability to act. She thought bleakly of simply beginning again, but she knew that it wouldn't be the same; she couldn't remember all of the details of her exact phrasing. She cried for a while, out of anger and despair, and when she finally decided to call Rhy at the office she realized that she'd waited too long; everyone would have gone home.

So there was nothing to do but wait. She showered, lay on the bed and watched television, then drifted to sleep with the set still on, only to waken in the early hours of the morning to the crackle of static.

She was starving because not only hadn't she eaten the lunch she'd chosen, she hadn't had dinner the night before, either, and her empty stomach was the last straw; curling up like a child she wept brokenly. How *dare* he!

But Rhy would dare anything, as she knew to her cost. She drifted back to sleep and when she woke again she had a pounding headache and it was nearly ten a.m. She took another shower and dressed, then breathed deeply several times and sat down by the phone. There was no way out of it. She had to talk to him.

Before her courage deserted her she dialed the office number and asked for Mr. Baines. Of course Amanda answered and Sallie managed a calm good morning before she asked to speak to Rhy.

"Of course, he said to put you through immediately," Amanda replied cheerfully, and Sallie's nerves screamed with tension as she waited for Rhy to come on the line.

"Sallie." His dark, rough-velvet voice in her ear made her jump and bang the receiver against her already aching temple. "Where are you, darling?"

She swallowed and said hoarsely, "I want my book back, Rhy!"

"I said, where are you?"

"The book—" she began again.

"Forget the damned book!" he rasped, and it was all her nerves could stand. She gulped, trying to swallow the sob that tore out of her throat, but it was swiftly followed by another and abruptly she was crying helplessly, clinging to the receiver as if it was a lifeline.

"You—you stole it!" she accused between sobs, her words almost unintelligible. "You knew it was the one thing I couldn't leave without and you stole it! I hate you, do you hear? I hate you! I never want to see you again—"

"Don't cry," he said roughly. "Baby, please don't cry. Tell me where you are and I'll be there as soon as I can. You can have your book back again, I promise."

"Written on water!" she jeered, wiping her wet cheeks with the back of her hand.

He drew an impatient breath. "Look, you'll have to see me if you want the book back. And since that seems to be the only hold I have on you, I'll use it. Meet me for lunch—"

"No," she broke in, looking down at her wrinkled slacks and top. "I—I'm not dressed."

"Then we'll have lunch at my apartment," he decided briskly. "I'll phone the housekeeper and have a meal prepared, so meet me there at twelve-thirty. We can talk privately there."

"I don't know where you live," she confessed, surrendering to the inevitable. She knew it was an error to see him again; she should just leave the manuscript and forget about it, try to start again, but she couldn't. Whatever the risk, she couldn't leave without it.

He gave her the address and instructions on how to get there, and just before he hung up he asked gently, "Are you all right?"

"I'm fine," she said bleakly, and dropped the receiver onto its cradle.

She got up to brush her hair and stared aghast at her reflection in the mirror. She was pale, hollow eyed, her clothing wrinkled. She couldn't let Rhy see her like this! And she didn't have so much as a tube of lipstick in her purse!

But she did have money, and there were shops on the ground floor of the hotel. Making up her mind, she took the elevator down and hurriedly purchased an attractive white summer dress with a tiny floral design on it and a pair of white high-heeled sandals.

In another shop she bought makeup and perfume; then she dashed back up to her room. Carefully she made up her face and repaired the ravages of tears and worry, then dressed in the dainty cotton dress and brushed her hair out; she didn't have the time to do anything with it so she left it streaming down her back in a rich sable mane.

She took a taxi to Rhy's apartment, too nervous to face the crush of a bus at lunchtime. When she got out at his apartment building she glanced at her watch and saw that she was a few minutes late. She paid the taxi driver and hurried to the elevator and punched the button.

As soon as she rang the doorbell the door swung open and Rhy loomed before her, his dark face expressionless.

"I'm sorry I'm late—" she began, rushing into speech in an effort to disguise her nervousness.

"It doesn't matter," he interrupted, standing aside to let her enter. He'd discarded his jacket and tie and unbuttoned his shirt halfway, revealing the curls of hair on his chest. Her eyes riveted on his virile, masculine flesh and unconsciously she wet her lips with her tongue. Just the sight of him weakened her!

His eyes darkened to charcoal. "You teasing little witch," he muttered, and his long fingers moved to his shirt. He unbuttoned the remaining buttons and pulled the shirt free of his pants and peeled out of it, dropping it to the floor. The sunlight streaming through the wide windows gleamed on his chest and shoulders where a light dew of perspiration moistened his skin and revealed all his rippling muscles.

Sallie stepped back, wanting to escape from the need she felt to touch his warm skin and feel the steelness of muscle underneath, but she made the mistake of raising her eyes to his. The hungry, blatant desire she saw there froze her in her tracks.

"I want you," he whispered, advancing on her. "Now."

"I didn't come here for this," she protested weakly, and made a futile attempt to evade him. His long arms encircled her and pulled her against his half-naked body, and she began to tremble at the erotic power he had over her. The scent of his skin, the warmth, the living vibrancy of him, went to her head and intoxicated her so that she forgot about pushing him away.

He attacked with his mouth, overpowering her with kisses that demanded and devoured, sucking all of her strength away so she couldn't resist when his shaking hands moved over her curves and renewed his intimate knowledge of her. She raised her arms and locked them around his neck and kissed him back, her response burning out of control and fanning his own fires.

She rested plaintively against him when he raised his head to gulp in deep, shaking breaths and the half smile that formed on his mouth before being quickly banished revealed that he was aware of his triumph, of her capitulation. With slow, easy moves, as if he didn't want to startle her, he unzipped her dress and slid it down to puddle around her feet. Sallie simply watched him in silence, her big eyes nearly black with desire. She couldn't resist; she couldn't make any plans. All she could do was feel, feel and respond. She loved him and she was helpless against his love.

But at least her desire was returned. She was dimly aware that he was shaking, trembling in every muscle of his big frame as he lifted her gently into his arms and carried her into his bedroom. He placed her on the bed and lay down beside her, his hands pulling at the bits of clothes that remained to separate skin from skin. He couldn't disguise his need for her, just as she had no defenses against him. Hoarsely he whispered to her, disjointed words and phrases that made her quiver in response and cling to him as she drowned in the tidal wave of sensation he evoked.

When the world had righted itself again she was lying in his arms while he slowly stroked her hair, her back, her arms. "I didn't intend for that to happen," he murmured against her temple. "I'd planned to talk first, eat our lunch together and try to act like two civilized people, but the moment I saw you nothing was important any longer except making love to you."

"That's all you ever wanted from me anyway," she said with simple, weary bitterness.

He gave her a brooding glance. "You think so? That's part of what I wanted to talk about, but first, let's see about lunch."

"Won't it be cold?" she asked, pushing her hair back from her face and sitting up and away from his arms.

"Steaks and salad. The salad is in the fridge, the steaks are ready to grill. And I gave Mrs. Hermann the rest of the day off so we won't be disturbed."

"You have everything planned, don't you?" she commented without any real interest as she began dressing, and he swung his long legs over the side of the bed to stand and watch her lethargic movements.

"What's wrong?" he asked sharply, coming to her and cupping her chin in his hand to look into her pale face. "Are you ill?"

She felt ill, achy and depressed after the soaring passion of his lovemaking, and she was stupidly weak. But she knew that her only ailments were an inability to cope with Rhy and the fact that she hadn't eaten in over twenty-four hours.

"I'm well enough," she dismissed his concern. "Just hungry, I suppose. I haven't eaten since yesterday morning."

"Great," he half snarled. "You need to lose some more weight. You must weigh at least ninety pounds. You need someone to watch you and make certain you eat, you little fool!"

He probably had himself in mind, but she didn't argue with him. In silence she completed dressing and waited until he had dressed also. Then she followed him into the neatly organized kitchen. He refused to let her do anything and made her sit on a stool while he grilled the steaks and set the places on the table in the small dining room.

He opened a bottle of California red wine to drink with the meal and for several minutes they ate in silence. Then Sallie asked without looking up from her salad, "Where is my manuscript?"

"In the study," he replied. "You've got a way with words. It's good reading."

She flung her head back as anger struck her. "You had no right to read it!"

"Didn't I?" he asked dryly. "I thought I had a perfect right to read what you'd been writing all those days when you were supposed to have been working for my magazine. You've been drawing a check every week and not writing a word of the articles assigned to you. If it hadn't suited me to keep you quietly at your desk I'd have fired you weeks ago."

"I'll repay every penny I've drawn since you bought the magazine," she flared. "You still had no right to read it!"

"Stop spitting and scratching at me, you little cat," he said in amusement. "I did read it, and there's nothing you can do about it now. Instead, think constructively. You've got a manuscript with strong possibilities, but it's also got some rough edges, and there's a lot of work that needs to be done on it. You need a place to work on it where you won't be disturbed, and you certainly don't need to worry about paying the rent or buying groceries."

"Why not?" she muttered. "Thousands of writers worry about those things."

"But you've never had to," he pointed out. "For your entire life you've had financial security, and it's something you're used to. You won't have a paycheck coming in now, because you're off the payroll as of yesterday, and it'll worry you when your savings begin shrinking. It takes time to write a book and get it on the market. You'll run out of money before then."

"I'm not a helpless baby and I'm not afraid of work," she replied.

"I know that, but why worry about any of that when you can live here, work on your book without interruptions and keep your savings?"

She sighed, feeling trapped. On the surface it was a logical suggestion, but she knew that the proposal was only a way of getting her back under his thumb where he thought she belonged. If she had any sense she would leave at the first opportunity, even if she had to sacrifice the manuscript, but she'd already passed up one such opportunity and she painfully admitted to herself that it was too late for her to gain her freedom. She was caught again in her own stupid, helpless love for Rhy, knowing that her love wasn't returned except in the lowest form—physical desire. He desired her, and for that reason he wanted her around now, but what would happen when he tired of her again? Would he simply walk out as he had before? Knowing that she was leaving herself wide open for another broken heart she stared into her salad and said expressionlessly, "All right."

He drew in a quick breath. "Just like that? No arguments, no conditions? Not even any questions?"

"I'm not interested in the answers," she replied, shrugging. "I'm tired of fighting you, and I want to finish my book. Other than that, I don't care."

"You're great for a man's ego," he muttered under his breath.

"You trampled all over mine," she snapped in reply. "Don't expect kid gloves from me. You've got what you wanted, me out of a job and living with you, but don't ask for blind adoration because I'm fresh out."

"I never asked for it anyway," he rasped. "And for the record, I'm not trying to chain you down. It was that particular job that I objected to, for reasons you know. All I'm asking from you is time for us to be together, to try to work things out. If we can't stand to live together for six months I'll consider a divorce, but the least we can do is give it a try."

"And if it doesn't work out we'll get a divorce?" she asked cautiously, wanting to be certain.

"Then we'll talk about it."

Glancing at his implacable face she saw that he wasn't going to give her a promise of a divorce so she gave in once more. "All right, six months. But I'm going to be working on my book, not cooking for you and washing your clothes and cleaning this place. If you're looking for a little homemaker you're going to be disappointed."

"In case you haven't noticed, I'm a wealthy man," he said sarcastically. "I don't expect my wife to do laundry."

She lifted her head and stared at him. "What are you getting out of this, Rhy? Other than a sleeping companion, I mean, and you can have that anytime you please without going to all this trouble."

His lids shadowed his gray eyes and he murmured huskily, "Isn't that enough? I want you. Let's just leave it at that."

To Sallie's surprise the arrangement worked rather well and they quickly fell into a routine. Rhy would get up every morning and prepare his own breakfast, then wake her with a kiss when he was ready to leave. She would linger over her own breakfast, then spend the rest of the morning in the study, working. Mrs. Hermann turned out to be a plump, gray-haired model of efficiency, and she took care of the apartment just as she had before, making Sallie lunch, cooking the evening meal and leaving just before Rhy arrived home.

Sallie would serve dinner herself, and while they were eating Rhy would tell her about how things were going with the magazine, what had happened that day, ask questions about how her book was progressing. She found herself remarkably at ease with him now, though their relationship never quite achieved true companionship. She sensed that they were both holding something of themselves back, but perhaps that was to be expected when two people with such strong wills tried to live together. There was always the thought that good manners should prevail or the frail fabric of their marriage would be torn beyond repair.

As the days turned into weeks and the stack of pages in the study kept growing she welcomed Rhy's advice and experience. Her own writing style was direct and uncomplicated, but Rhy had the knack of stripping an idea down to the bare bones. It became their custom after dinner for him to read what she'd written that day and give her his opinion. If he didn't like something he said so, but he always made it plain that he thought her overall effort was good. Sometimes she threw out entire sections and began anew, all on the basis of Rhy's criticisms, but at other times she stubbornly clung to her own words as she felt that they better conveyed her own meaning.

Her best work seemed to be done in the evenings when Rhy sat in the study with her, reading articles and paperwork he'd brought home with him or doing his preliminary research on the documentary he was scheduled to film within three months. He seemed content, all traces of the restlessness she remembered gone, as if he had indeed burned out his need for adventure. In an odd way she was also content; the mental stimulation she received from creating a book was more than enough to occupy her imagination. They worked together in harmony and relative silence, broken only by the ringing of the telephone when Greg called, as he often did, and their own occasional comments to each other.

Then, when it was growing late, Sallie would cover the typewriter and leave Rhy still working while she bathed and prepared for bed. Sometimes he would work for an hour or more after she was in bed, sometimes he followed her closely to the shower, but always—always—he would get in bed with her and take her in his arms and the restrained civility of their manner would explode in hungry, almost savage lovemaking. She had thought his passion would wane as he grew used to having her around again, but his desire remained at a high pitch. Occasionally when they worked together she would watch his absorbed face, fascinated that he could look so calm now yet turn into a wild sensualist if she were to put her arms around him and kiss him. The thought teased at her brain until she would ache to do just that, to see if she could divert his thoughts from his work, but over the years she had developed a deep respect for a person's work and she didn't disturb him.

Only two incidents broke the surface harmony of those first weeks. The first occurred early one evening as she was clearing away the dinner dishes and putting them in the dishwasher. Rhy was already in the study, reading what she'd written that day, so when the phone rang she answered it on the kitchen extension.

"Is Rhy there? Could I speak to him, please?" asked a cool feminine voice and Sallie recognized it instantly.

"Certainly, Coral, I'll get him to the phone," she replied, and placed the receiver on the cabinet top while she went to the study.

He looked up as she entered. "Who was that?" he asked absently, looking down at the pages in his hand.

"It's Coral. She wants to speak with you," Sallie replied in amazingly level tones, and returned to the kitchen to finish her chores. The temptation to listen in on the kitchen extension made her pause for a second, but only a second, then she firmly replaced the extension.

She tried to tell herself that it was nothing but jealousy eating at her insides. Coral had enough self-possession that if she wanted to see Rhy she would have no scruples about calling him at home. Were they still seeing each other? Rhy never mentioned where he went for lunch—or with whom—and about once a week he was late getting home in the evening. As engrossed as she was in the progress of her book she hadn't really noticed or thought anything of it, and she also knew that deadlines had to be met and things could happen that would make a long day necessary.

But Coral was so breathtakingly beautiful! How could any man not be flattered that such a lovely woman obviously adored him?

She couldn't stand it if Rhy was still seeing her, Sallie knew. For a while she had convinced herself that it didn't matter to her if Rhy had other women because she was over him, but now she knew differently. She loved him, and all her defenses had been shattered. He had won a complete victory, if he only knew it, but somehow she had kept herself from admitting aloud that she loved him. He never mentioned love, so neither did she.

When she didn't return to the study Rhy came in search of her and found her standing in the kitchen with her hands clenched.

"Aren't you coming—" he began, then cut his words off when he saw her taut face.

"I can't stop you from seeing her," Sallie said harshly, her eyes black with pain and fury. "But don't you dare let her call you here! I won't put up with that!"

His face darkened and his jaw tightened with temper. It was as if the weeks of politeness had never been. At the first sign of hostility their tempers broke free like wild horses too long held under control. "Hadn't you better get your facts straight before you make wild accusations?" Rhy snarled, coming forward to glower down at her. "You should've listened on the extension if you're so interested in my activities! As it happens, Coral asked me to have lunch with her tomorrow, and I refused."

"Don't deny yourself on my account!" she hurled rashly.

His lips twisted in a travesty of a smile. "Oddly enough, I've been doing just that," he ground out between his teeth. "But now, with your permission, I'll show you just what I *have* been denying myself!"

Too late she moved, trying to avoid his hands as they darted out to catch her, but he swung her up in his arms and strode rapidly to the bedroom. Furiously Sallie twisted and kicked but the difference in their sizes and strength left her helpless against his powerful body. He dropped her on the bed and followed her down, capturing her mouth with his and kissing her with such angry demand that her struggles turned abruptly into compliance. They made love wildly, their pent-up frustrations erupting in the force of their loving.

Afterward he held her clamped to his side while, with his free hand, he stroked over her nude body. "I'm not seeing Coral," he muttered into her hair. "Or any other woman. The way I make love to you at night should assure you of that," he concluded wryly.

"It made me see red when she called," Sallie admitted, turning her head to brush her lips across his sweaty shoulder.

She could feel the tremor that ran through his body as her lips touched him and his arm tightened about her. "You were jealous," he accused, self-satisfaction evident in his tone. She gasped in a return of anger and tried to wiggle away from him, only to be hauled back against him for another whirlwind possession.

The second incident was her fault. One morning she decided to go shopping, the first time she'd done so since Rhy had moved her in with him. She needed several little things, and she passed the morning pleasantly, then decided to stop by and see her old friends at the magazine, maybe eat lunch with Rhy if he wasn't busy.

First she poked her nose into the large room where she'd worked and was greeted loudly and cheerfully. Brom was off on assignment, and for a moment she felt a twinge of envy, then the exuberant welcome of the others made her forget that she was no longer a free-flying bird. After several minutes she excused herself and went up for a few minutes with Greg. She wasn't certain that she'd ever forgive him completely for switching over to Rhy's side, even though she was now living with her husband in relative harmony, but Greg was an old friend and he was dedicated to his job. She didn't want any coolness between them.

After a restrained greeting she and Greg rapidly regained their former easy mood. They parted with Greg's grinning comment that having a full-time husband must be good for her, she looked contented.

Like a cow, Sallie thought to herself in amusement as she went up to Rhy's office. She was still smiling when she stepped off the elevator and literally ran into Chris.

"You're back!" he exclaimed in instant delight, holding her at arm's length and looking her over. "You're blooming, darling!"

Sallie's eyes widened in dismay as she realized that she hadn't let Chris know that she was still in town. Greg knew, of course, but Greg wasn't exactly talkative about personal details. "I've never been gone," she admitted ruefully, smiling up into his dark eyes. "Rhy caught me."

Chris's eyebrows rose. "You don't look as if you're wasting away," he drawled mildly. "Maybe the situation isn't as bad as you thought it'd be?"

"Maybe," she said laughing. "Greg just told me that I look *contented!* I can't decide if I'm insulted or not."

"Are you really happy, honey?" he asked in a gentle tone, and all of his joking was gone.

"I'm happy in a realistic way," she replied thoughtfully. "I don't expect heaven anymore, and I won't be destroyed when what I have ends."

"Are you so sure that it will?"

"I don't know. We just take every day as it comes. We manage to get along now, but who can say that it'll always be like that? What about you? Did you and Amy...?" She stopped, looking into the level, accepting brown eyes, and she knew that he was alone.

"It didn't work." He shrugged, taking her hand and leading her to the window at the end of the hallway, away from the elevator doors.

"She's married to that other guy now, she won't even talk to me on the phone."

"I'm sorry," she murmured. "She got married so soon. I thought she wasn't supposed to marry him until later this year?"

"She's pregnant," Chris said rawly, and for a moment his face twisted with his inner pain, then he drew a deep breath and stared at Sallie with wry self-mockery. "I think it's my baby. Well, maybe it's the other guy's, I don't know, but I know that it could be mine, too. I'm not even sure Amy knows. I don't care. I'd marry her in a minute if she'd have me, but she said I'm too 'unstable' to be a good father."

"You'd marry her even knowing that she'd slept with another man while she was going out with you?" Sallie asked in amazement. That was love, love that accepted anything.

He shrugged. "I don't know what she did, but it wouldn't make any difference to me. I love her and I'd take her any way I could get her. If she called me now I'd go to her, and to hell with her husband." He said it in a calm, flat tone, then he shook his head. "Don't look so worried," he advised, a smile coming to his face. "I'm all right, honey, I'm not falling apart."

"But I care about you," she protested weakly.

"And I care about you." He grinned down at her and suddenly lifted her in his arms, swinging her around giddily, laughing as she protested. "I've missed you like mad," he told her, his brown eyes turning impish. "I don't trust anyone else to give me advice on my love life—"

"Take your damned hands off my wife."

The toneless words were dropped like stones and Sallie struggled out of Chris's grip to whirl and find Rhy standing just outside his office door, his eyes narrowed to slits. Automatically she looked at his hands. They weren't curled into fists but were slightly cupped, his long fingers tense through his arms, his stance, relaxed and loose. Those hands could strike without warning, and Rhy looked murderous. She moved forward, casually putting herself between Rhy and Chris, but Rhy moved to the side and another clear path to Chris. As he moved Amanda came out of the office and stopped in her tracks at the sight of Rhy's bloodless face.

Chris didn't seem disturbed; he remained relaxed, his mouth curling into a wry smile. "Easy there," he drawled in his slow, humorous tone. "I'm not after your woman. I've got enough woman trouble of my own without taking on someone else's."

By then Sallie had reached Rhy, and she put her hand on his arm, feeling the rigid muscles there. "It's true," she told him, smiling like mad in an effort to hide the fear that had her heart thudding. "He's madly in love with a woman who wants him to settle down and stop dashing off to other countries at the drop of a hat, and he likes to tell me all about it. Does the plot sound familiar?"

"All right," Rhy uttered, his lips barely moving. His face was still frozen in white rage, but he growled at Amanda, "Go on to lunch. Everything's okay."

After Amanda and Chris had left she and Rhy stood in the hallway staring silently at each other. Gradually he relaxed and said tiredly, "Let's get out of this hallway. The office is private."

She nodded and preceded him into his office, and no sooner was the door closed behind them than he caught her in his arms, holding her to him so tightly that her ribs protested in pain.

"I've never been out with him," she managed to reassure him as she gasped for breath.

"I believe you," he whispered raggedly, his lips brushing across her temple, her cheek, the corner of her eye. "I just couldn't bear to see you in his arms. You're mine, and I don't want any other man touching you."

Her heart pounding, Sallie lifted her arms about his neck and clung to him. She was giddy with hope. The violence of his reaction couldn't be simple possessiveness; his emotions had to be involved to some extent for him to be shaking like this, his hands almost punishing as he touched her. But she couldn't be certain, and she held back the most reassuring phrase of all that trembled on her tongue: I love you. She couldn't say it to him yet, but she had begun to hope.

"Hey, I came to see if you want to have lunch with me," she finally said gaily, lifting her head from its resting place on his shoulder.

"That's not what I want," he growled, his eyes straying suggestively to the sofa, "but I'll settle for lunch."

"I'm afraid we caused a scandal," she teased as she walked beside him to the elevator. "It'll be all over the building before the end of the day."

He shrugged negligently. "I don't care. Let it be a warning to any of your other pals who might want to hug you. I'm a throwback, a territorial animal, and I don't allow any encroachment into that territory."

At once she felt an icy shaft of pain in her heart. Was that all she was to him, a part of his territory? Thank heavens she'd kept silent a moment ago instead of blurting out her feelings for him! She was a fool to look for any deeper feelings from him; he didn't have any, and she'd always known that. He *was* a throwback, his instincts swift and primitive. He saw to the satisfaction of his needs and didn't waste time on anything as foolish as love.

Chapter Ten

The sense of accomplishment she felt as she stared at the last page of the manuscript surpassed anything she'd experienced as a reporter. It was finished! No longer was it a figment of her imagination. It existed; it had an identity. She knew there was still a lot of work to be done on it, rereading, correcting, rewriting, but now it was, for all intents and purposes, complete. Her hand reached for the telephone; she wanted to call Rhy and share this moment with him, but a wave of dizziness made her fall back weakly in the chair.

The dizziness was only momentary, but when it had passed she remained as she was, the impulse to call Rhy having faded. That was the fourth spell this week.... Of course. Why hadn't she realized? But perhaps she'd known all along and hadn't allowed the thought to surface until now. The book had claimed all of her attention, all of her energy, and she had pushed herself to complete it. But as soon as it was finished her subconscious had released the knowledge of her pregnancy.

Glancing at the desk calendar she decided that it had been the first night in Sakarya. "When else would it have been?" she murmured to herself. That was the first time in seven years Rhy had touched her, and she had immediately become pregnant. She gave a smile of self-mockery, then the smile became softer and she drew the calendar to her to count the weeks. Her baby would be due around the beginning of spring, and she thought that was a wonderful sign, a new beginning.

This baby would live, she knew. It was more than a new life, it was a strengthening of the fabric of her marriage, another bond between her and Rhy. He would make a wonderful father now, much better than he would have been years before. He would be delighted with his baby.

Then she frowned slightly. Filming on the documentary was scheduled to begin next month, and Rhy had planned on taking her with him. He might change his mind if he knew she was pregnant. So she wouldn't tell him until after they returned! She wasn't about to let him leave without her; it would be a rerun of their early days, and she wasn't sure enough of either him or herself yet to endure a long separation.

She realized that she had a lot to do before then; first and foremost she needed to see a doctor and make certain everything was normal and that traveling wouldn't hurt the baby, and begin taking the recommended vitamins. She should also buy new clothing, because by the time the filming was done she would probably have outgrown her present wardrobe. She pictured herself round and waddling and grinned. Rhy had missed most of her first pregnancy, but this time she would insist that he help her to do all of the little things she'd had to manage by herself before, like getting out of bed.

Of all the nights for Rhy to be late, she thought, he had to pick this one. He called at five and told her wearily that it would probably be eight or later when he made it home. "Eat without me, baby," he instructed. "But keep something hot for me. I don't think I can face a sandwich."

Swallowing her disappointment, she agreed, then suggested jokingly, "Do you need any help? I'm an old hand at meeting deadlines."

"You don't know how tempting that offer is." He sighed. "But work on the book instead, and I'll be home as soon as I can."

"I finished the book today," she informed him, her fingers tightening around the receiver. "So I'm taking a break." She had wanted to tell him when he first walked in the door, but she couldn't wait that long.

"You did what? Oh, hell," he said in disgust and Sallie's mouth trembled in hurt surprise. Then he continued, and she brightened again. "I should be taking you out to celebrate instead of working late. But I'll be home as soon as possible, then we'll do some private celebrating, if you understand my meaning."

"I thought you were tired." She laughed and his low chuckle sounded in her ear.

"I am tired, but I'm not dead," he replied huskily. "See you in a few hours."

Smiling, she replaced the receiver. After eating her solitary dinner she took a shower and settled down in the study to begin rereading the book, scribbling changes and corrections in the margins as she went. The work was absorbing, so much so that when she heard Rhy's key she was surprised at how swiftly the time had passed. She shoved the manuscript aside and jumped to her feet, then had to cling to the back of a chair for a moment when dizziness assailed her. Slowly. She must remember to move slowly.

Rhy entered the study, his tired face breaking into a grin as he surveyed her attire, a transparent dark blue nightgown and matching wrap. He tossed his jacket aside and tugged his loosened tie completely off, throwing it on top of his jacket. He began unbuttoning his shirt as he came to her. "Now I understand the charm of coming home to a negligee-clad wife," he commented as he slid his arms around her and pulled her up on tiptoe for his kiss. "It's like a shot of adrenalin."

"Don't become too fond of the practice," she warned. "I just took my bath early because I had nothing else to do. Are you very hungry?"

"Yes," he growled. "Are you going to make me wait?"

"You know I meant for food!" Laughing at him, she crossed to the door. "Wash up while I set the table. I've kept things warm."

"Don't bother with the dining room," he called. "The kitchen is fine with me, and a lot handier."

She did as he instructed and set his plate in the kitchen. He joined her there and while he ate they discussed the book. Rhy had already talked to an agent that he knew, and he wanted to hand the book over before they left for Europe.

"But it isn't ready," Sallie protested. "I've already begun making corrections for retyping."

"I want her to read it now," Rhy insisted. "It's a rough draft. She won't expect it to be word perfect right now."

"She?" Sallie asked, her ears pricking up.

"Yes, she," he mocked, his gray eyes glinting. "She's a bone-thin bulldozer by the name of Barbara Hopewell, and she's twenty years older than I am, so you can draw in your claws."

Sallie glared at him. She had the feeling that he'd purposely tricked her into revealing her jealousy and she didn't want him to gain too much of an advantage on her.

"Why are you in such a hurry?" she demanded.

"I don't want you worrying about the book while we're in Europe. Hire a typist, do whatever you have to, but I want the book out of the way before we leave."

Because she was feeling resentful over his gibe about jealousy she propped her elbows on the table and gibed back at him. "Has the thought occurred to you that now that the book's finished I'll be bored sitting around here all day? I need to be looking for a job, not jaunting around Europe."

If she'd wanted to rile him she succeeded beyond her wildest expectations. He turned pale; then two hectic spots of temper appeared on his high cheekbones. Slamming his fork down on the table he reached across and grasped her wrist, hauling her to her feet as he stood up himself. "You never miss a chance to twist the knife, do you?" he muttered hoarsely. "Sometimes I want to break your neck!" Then he jerked her against him and brutally took her lips, not allowing her a chance to speak even if she could have thought of anything to say, and with their mouths still fused he slipped one arm behind her knees and lifted her easily, her slight weight nothing to his powerful arms.

Sallie had to cling to him; the swift movement as he jerked her to her feet had made her head swim alarmingly and she felt as if she might faint. Neither could she understand why he had reacted so violently, or what he meant about twisting the knife. Confused, all she knew was that she'd made him angry when she hadn't really meant to, and she offered him the only comfort she could, the response of her lips and body. He accepted the offer hungrily; the pressure of his mouth changing from hurtful to persuasive, and he carried her to the bedroom.

Afterward she lay curled drowsily against him, wrapped in the security of his own special male scent and the warmth of his nearness while he lazily stroked her abdomen and pressed kisses along the curve of her shoulder.

"Did I hurt you?" he murmured, referring to his urgent lovemaking, and Sallie whispered a denial. "That's good," he replied huskily. "I wouldn't want to..." He paused, then after a moment continued. "Don't you think it's time you told me about the baby?"

Sallie sat bolt upright in the bed and turned to stare at him with huge eyes. "How did you know?" she demanded in astonishment, her voice rising. "I only realized it myself today!"

He blinked as if she'd jolted him in return; then he tipped his dark head back against the pillow and roared with laughter, tugging her down to lie against his chest. "I should've guessed," he chuckled, his hand smoothing her long hair away from her face. "You were so wrapped up in that book you didn't even know what day it was. I knew, darling, because I'm not a complete ignoramus and I can count. I thought you

were deliberately keeping me in the dark because you didn't want me
to have the satisfaction of knowing you're pregnant.''

"Gee, you must think I'm a lovely character," she muttered crossly
and, turning her head, she sank her teeth playfully, but firmly, into his
shoulder. He yelped in pain and instantly she kissed the wound, but she
told him defiantly, ''You deserved that.''

"Out of consideration for your delicate condition I'll let you get away
with that," he mocked, tilting her face up for a kiss that lingered.

"Actually," Sallie confessed a moment later, "I wasn't going to tell
you just yet."

His head snapped around, and he cupped her chin in his palm, forcing
her to look at him. "Why?" he growled.

"Because I want to go to Europe with you," she stated simply. "I
was afraid you'd make me stay here if you knew I'm pregnant."

"Not a chance. I wasn't with you before, but I'm planning on being
with you every day of this pregnancy—with your permission, Mrs.
Baines, I'll even be with you when our baby is born."

Her heart stopped, then lurched into overtime. Too overcome to
speak, Sallie turned her face into his shoulder and held him with desperate hands. Despite everything he had ever said—and all the things
he had never said—she began to hope that Rhy really did care for her.
"Rhy—oh, Rhy!" she whispered in a choked voice.

Misunderstanding the cause of her emotion he gathered her close to
him and stroked her head. "Don't worry," he murmured into her hair.
"This baby will be all right, I promise you. We'll get the best obstetri-
cian in the state. We'll have a houseful of kids, you wait and see."

Clutching him to her Sallie thought that she'd be satisfied with only
this one, if it lived. That, and Rhy's love, would make her life complete.

Caught up in a whirlwind of activity preparing for the trip to Europe,
which included readying not only her own clothing but Rhy's as well,
as he was working late more and more often in an effort to tie up all
loose ends before they left, and hammering the book into its final shape,
Sallie hardly had a moment to think during the next few weeks. The
doctor had assured her that she was in perfect shape, though she could
stand to gain a few pounds, and the baby was developing normally. He
was also in favor of the trip to Europe so long as she remembered to
eat properly.

She had never been happier. Four months ago she had thought that
Rhy meant nothing to her, and all she wanted was to be free of his

restricting influence. She still fumed sometimes at the high-handed methods he'd used to restore her to her position as his wife, but for the most part she was glad that he didn't know how to take no for an answer. She was more deeply in love with him now than she'd ever been as an insecure teenager, for she'd grown in character in those years away from him. Her feelings were stronger, her thoughts and emotions more mature. Now he acted as if he never wanted her out of his sight, and he seemed so proud of the child she carried that she sometimes thought he was going to hang a sign around her neck announcing her expectant state.

Disaster struck without warning a week before they were due to leave for Europe. It was one of those picture-perfect autumn days when the sunshine was warm and the sky was deep blue, yet the air carried the unmistakable fragrance of approaching winter. Sallie made one last shopping trip, determined that this would be *it,* and took her purchases home. She felt marvelous, and her eyes sparkled and her skin glowed; she was smiling as she put away the articles of clothing she had bought.

Her senses had always been acute, but she still had no warning of what was to come when the doorbell rang and she called out to Mrs. Hermann, ''I'll get it. I'm right here!''

She pulled the door open, smiling warmly, but the smile faltered as she recognized Coral Williams. The model looked beautiful, as always, but there was a haunted expression on the exquisite face that made Sallie wonder uneasily if Rhy had been wrong, if Coral was suffering because he'd stopped seeing her.

''Hello,'' she greeted the other woman. ''Will you come in? Is there anything I can do for you?''

''Thank you,'' Coral replied almost inaudibly, walking past Sallie and standing uncertainly in the foyer. ''I...is Rhy here? I tried to phone him, but his secretary said he's out of the office and I thought he might perhaps...'' Her voice trailed off and pity welled up in Sallie's throat. She knew all too well how it felt to suffer from the lack of Rhy's love, and she was at a loss as to what to do. She sympathized with Coral, but she wasn't about to hand over Rhy to the other woman, even if Rhy was willing.

''No, he's not here,'' Sallie replied. ''He's often out of his office now. He's very busy preparing for our trip to Europe.''

''Europe!'' Coral turned very white, only her expertly applied makeup supplying any color to her cheeks. She was unnaturally pale anyway and the severely tailored black dress she wore only pointed up the hollows of her cheeks and her generally fragile appearance.

"He's filming a documentary," explained Sallie. "We expect to be gone about three months."

"He—he can't!" Coral burst out, clenching her fists.

A sudden chill ran up Sallie's spine and unconsciously she squared her shoulders as if in anticipation of a blow. "What is it you want with Rhy?" she challenged directly.

Coral stiffened too, staring down at Sallie from her superior height. "I'm sorry, but it's private."

"I don't accept that. If it concerns Rhy it concerns me. He *is* my husband, you know," she ended sarcastically.

Coral winced as if Salllie'd scored a hit, then recovered herself to say scornfully, "Some husband! Do you really think he spared a thought for you when you were separated? The old adage of 'out of sight, out of mind' was never more true than with Rhy! He was out with a different woman every night, until he met me."

Sallie shuddered with the sudden violent desire to punch Coral right in that perfect mouth. The woman was only saying what she'd always thought herself, though privately she wanted very much to believe Rhy's assertions that his relationships with other women had been platonic. Certainly she couldn't fault his behavior since she'd been living with him again. A woman couldn't ask for a more attentive husband.

"I know all about your relationship with Rhy," she declared solidly. "He told me everything when he asked me to come back to him."

"Oh, did he?" Coral asked wildly, her voice rising in shrill laughter. "I doubt that. Surely some details are still private!"

Abruptly Sallie had had enough and she moved to open the door again so Coral could leave. "I'm sorry," she said firmly. "I'm asking you to leave. Rhy's my husband and I love him and I don't care what his past is. I'm sorry for you because you lost him, but facts are facts and you might as well face up to them. He won't come back to you."

"What makes you so certain of that?" Coral yelled, losing all control, her face twisting with fury. "When he hears what I've got to tell him he'll come back to me, all right! He'll leave you without even a consoling pat on the head!"

For a moment the woman's certainty caused Sallie to waver; then she thought of the child in her womb, and she knew that Rhy would never leave her now. "I don't think so," she said softly, playing her ace. "I'm pregnant. Our baby will be born in March. I don't think any of your charms can equal that in Rhy's view."

Coral reeled backward as if she might faint, and Sallie watched her in alarm, but the woman recovered herself and burst into peal after peal of mocking, hysterical laughter, holding her arms across her middle as if she found Sallie's announcement hilarious. "Priceless!" she gasped when she had enough breath for words. "I wish Rhy could be here. This lacks only his presence to be the hit comedy of the year!"

"I don't know what you're talking about," Sallie broke in stiffly, "but I think you'd better go." The amused, malicious glitter in Coral's eyes made her uncomfortable, and she wanted only for the woman to leave so she could be alone again and recapture her mood of confident serenity.

"Don't be so sure of yourself!" Coral flared, her hatred plain on her face. "You managed to pique his interest by acting as if you wanted nothing to do with him, but surely you know by now that he's incapable of staying faithful to any one woman! I understand him. Some men are just like that, and I love him despite his weakness for other women. I'm willing to allow him his little affairs so long as he comes back to me, whereas you'll drive him mad with boredom within a year. And don't think a baby will make any difference to him!"

Beyond Coral, Sallie saw Mrs. Hermann hovering in the doorway, her round face frowning with worry as she listened to Coral's abusive tirade. Instinctively disliking having a witness to the nasty scene Coral was creating Sallie jerked the door open and snapped, "Get out!"

"Oh, I'm glad to go!" Coral smirked. "But don't think you've got everything your way! Women like you make me sick, always acting so sure of yourselves and sticking your noses in where they don't belong, thinking some man will admire you! That's why Rhy pulled you off of foreign assignments, he said you were making a fool of yourself trying to act as tough as any man. And now you think you're something special just because you're pregnant! That's nothing so special. Rhy's good at getting women pregnant!"

Despite herself Sallie reeled in shock, not quite certain she understood what Coral was saying. The sight of her suddenly pale face seemed to give Coral some satisfaction because she smiled again and spat out, "That's right! The baby you're carrying isn't the only child Rhy has fathered! I'm pregnant, too, and it's Rhy's baby. Two months pregnant, honey, so tell me what that means about your perfect marriage! I told you, he always comes back to me!"

Having delivered her blow Coral stalked out with her head held at a queenly altitude. Unable to completely take in what the woman had said Sallie closed the door with quiet composure and stared across the room at Mrs. Hermann, who had pressed a hand over her mouth in shock.

"Mrs. Baines," Mrs Hermann gasped, her voice rich with sympathy. "Oh, Mrs. Baines!"

It was then that Sallie understood just exactly what Coral's words had meant. She was pregnant, and it was Rhy's baby. Two months pregnant, she had said. So Rhy had not only lied about his relationship with Coral, he'd continued it after his reconciliation with Sallie. In dazed horror she thought again of all the nights when Rhy had supposedly been working late. She'd never thought to call him at the office to check up on him. She would have been insulted if Rhy had checked up on her, so she'd accorded him the same respect and he'd abused it.

Numbly she went past Mrs. Hermann into the bedroom, Rhy's bedroom, where she'd spent so many happy nights in his arms. She stared at the bed and knew she couldn't bear to sleep there again.

Without thinking about it she jerked down the suitcases from the top of the closet and began filling them helter-skelter with the clothing she'd bought to take to Europe. She had money and she had a place to go; there was no reason for her to stay here another minute.

She paused briefly when she thought of the manuscript, but it was safely in the hands of Barbara Hopewell, and she would get in touch with her later. Later...when she could bear to think again, when the pain had subsided from the screaming agony that was tearing her apart now.

When she carried the suitcases out into the hallway she found Mrs. Hermann there, hovering, wringing her hands in agitation. "Mrs. Baines, please don't leave like this! Try to talk things out—men will be men, you know. I'm sure there's an explanation."

"There probably is," Sallie agreed tiredly. "Rhy's very good with explanations. But I just don't want to hear it right now. I'm leaving. I'm going somewhere quiet and peaceful where I can have my baby, and I don't want to think about my husband and his mistresses."

"But where will you be? What shall I tell Mr. Baines?" the housekeeper wailed.

"Tell him?" Sallie stopped and thought a minute, unable to think of any message that could adequately express her state of mind. "Tell him...tell him what happened. I don't know where I'm going, but I know that I don't think I ever want to see him again." Then she walked out the door.

Chapter Eleven

The days passed slowly, dripping out of existence. Like a salmon returning to the place of its birth to spawn and die she had returned to her own origins, the little upstate town where she'd grown up, where she'd met Rhy and married him. Her parents' house was empty and neglected and many of the old neighbors had died or moved on and she didn't know any of the children who played now in the quiet streets. But it was still home, and she moved back into the small house and tidied it up, refurnished it with the minimum of furniture for her needs. Then she waited for time to work its magic healing process.

At first she was unnaturally calm, numbed by her sense of loss and betrayal. She'd just gotten used to living with him, and now she was alone again with the solitary nights pressing down on her like an invisible weight. She didn't try to think about it or straighten it out in her mind; there was no use in driving herself mad with if onlys and might have beens. She had to accept it, just as she would have to if he'd died.

In a sense that was what had happened. She'd lost her husband as irrevocably as if he had died. She was as alone, as empty. He was in Europe now, half a world away, and he might as well have been on another planet.

Then she realized that she was neither alone nor empty. His baby moved inside her one day and she stood with her hands pressed over the gentle fluttering, overcome by the feeling of awe that a living creature was being nurtured inside her body. Rhy's baby, a part of him. No matter if she never saw his face again she would always have him near. That thought was both painful and comforting, a threat and a promise.

The numbness wore off abruptly. She woke in the dark, silent hours before dawn one morning, and her entire body ached with the pain of her loss. For the first time she cried, weeping with her face pressed into the pillow, and she thought about it endlessly, trying to understand the hows and whys of his behavior. Was it her fault? Was it something about her that challenged Rhy to subdue her, then forced him to lose interest once she was captured? Or was it Rhy's own nature, as Coral had charged, an inability to be faithful to one woman?

Yet that denoted a certain weakness of character, and that didn't describe Rhy. A lot of adjectives could be used to describe him—arrogant, hot-tempered, stubborn—but weakness in any respect wasn't one of them. She would also have sworn on his professional integrity, and she felt that integrity was not an isolated thing in a person, restricted to only one field; integrity spread out, showing itself in every aspect of a person's behavior.

So how could she explain his infidelity? She couldn't, and the question tore at her. She forced herself to eat only because of the baby, but even so she grew pale and thinner. Sometimes she woke up in the middle of the night to find her pillow wet, and she wanted Rhy beside her so badly that it was impossible to get back to sleep. At times like that she wondered why she'd run off, like a fool, and left the field clear for Coral. Why hadn't she stayed? Why hadn't she put up a fight for him? He'd hurt her, he'd been unfaithful, but she still loved him and surely it couldn't hurt any more if she'd stayed with him? At least then she'd have had the comfort of his presence; they could have shared the miracle of the growing child she carried. During those dark predawn hours she sometimes determined to pack her clothes first thing in the morning and fly to Europe to join Rhy, but always, when the morning came, she would remember Coral and the baby that she carried. Rhy might not want her to join him. Coral might be with him. Coral was more glamorous anyway, more suited for a life in the limelight with Rhy.

It wasn't in her nature to be indecisive, but for the second time in her life she'd lost her bearings, and both times had been because of Rhy. The first time she had eventually found her feet and pursued a goal, but now she was unable to plan anything more complicated than the basic needs of living. She ate, she bathed, she slept, she did what had to be done. She had read enough to know that part of her lethargy was due to being pregnant, yet that wasn't excuse enough to explain her total lack of interest in anything beyond the next moment.

As the late fall days passed and winter drew closer she became aware that Christmas was near. Somehow every Christmas since the death of her parents had been spent alone, and this one would be no different. But next year, she promised herself, gazing at a brightly decorated tree as she made her weekly trip to the nearest grocery store, she would have a real Christmas. The baby would be about nine months old, bright eyed and inquisitive about everything in its world. She would decorate a tree and pile gifts beneath it that would fascinate a crawling baby.

It was a vague plan, but it was the first plan she'd made since leaving Rhy. For the baby's sake she had to pull herself out of the doldrums. She had a book in the works; she needed to contact the agent and see about publication and perhaps start work on another book. She had to have some means of taking care of the baby or the first thing she knew Rhy would be demanding custody of his child. Fiercely she determined that she'd never allow that to happen. Rhy had another child; she only had this one and she'd never let it go!

Two weeks before Christmas she finally made a firm decision and dialed Barbara Hopewell's office with her former briskness. When Barbara came on the line Sallie identified herself, and before the other woman could say anything she asked if any progress had been made in locating a publisher.

"Mrs. Baines!" Barbara gasped. "Where are you? Mr. Baines has been going mad, trying to complete filming in Europe and flying back here every free moment he has in an effort to trace you! Are you in town?"

"No," Sallie replied. She didn't want to hear about Rhy or how hard he'd been looking for her. Oddly enough, she'd expected that he would make an effort to find her if only because of the child she carried. "And where I am doesn't matter. I only want to discuss the book, if you don't mind. Has a publisher been found?"

"But..." Then Barbara changed her mind, and she answered in an abrupt tone, "Yes, we have a publisher who is extremely interested. I really need to schedule a meeting with you, Mrs. Baines, to go over the details of the contract. May I make an appointment?"

"I don't want to return to New York," Sallie said, her throat constricting at the thought.

"Then I'll be glad to meet you wherever you want. Just set the time and tell me the location."

Sallie hesitated, unwilling to divulge her hiding place, yet equally unwilling to leave it for a meeting at any other location. Then she quickly added up the dates and realized that Rhy would still be filming in Europe for another month. Barbara had said that he flew back as often as he could, but she knew that schedule, and it was a tightly packed one. The odds were that he would be unable to leave on a moment's notice even if Barbara did happen to be in touch with him and let slip that she'd talked to Sallie.

"All right," she agreed reluctantly and gave Barbara her address. They agreed on a time that Thursday for Barbara to come to the house.

That was only two days away and Sallie felt even more confident that Rhy wouldn't find out her hiding place. When she saw Barbara on Thursday she would get her promise not to tell Rhy; she hadn't wanted to discuss the matter over the phone, knowing that anyone in Barbara's office could listen in on an extension.

She couldn't sleep that night; she was too anxious that she had made a mistake in revealing her bolt hole to relax. Somehow she had the feeling that Rhy was one step ahead of her, as usual. Lying in her bed, tense and unable to close her eyes, she imagined all sorts of what ifs: What if Rhy had been in New York even then? What if Rhy had even been in Barbara's office and was on his way upstate now? What if she got up in the morning to find him on her doorstep? What would she say to him? What was there to say?

Tears seeped from beneath her lids as she squeezed them slightly shut in an effort to banish the picture she suddenly had of Rhy's dark, lean face. Pain pierced her sharply and she turned on her side to weep, hugging the pillow to her face in an effort to stifle the sobs. "I love him," she moaned aloud. That hadn't changed, and every day apart from him was an eternity.

Abruptly, desolate in her loneliness, she admitted to herself that she wanted to go back to him. She wanted his strength, his physical presence, even if she couldn't have his love. She wanted him there to hold her hand while she gave birth to their child and she wanted to have other children. The thought of Coral and that other baby tore at her insides, but gradually she was realizing that her love, her need, for Rhy was stronger than her anger. She had to accept him as he was if she wanted to live with him.

She dozed eventually, toward dawn, and woke only a few hours later to the steady, dreary sound of cold rain pouring down. The sky was gray, the streets stark and cheerless. Snow had not yet arrived and given everything its winter-wonderland effect, but the trees were denuded of leaves and the bare branches rattled against each other like bones of a skeleton. There was nothing to get up for but she did, and managed to occupy herself by trying to work out a sketchy outline for another book. This one would be more difficult, she knew, for the first one had been partially rooted in her own experiences. This one would have to be totally from her imagination.

By midafternoon the rain had stopped but the temperature had dropped, and when she turned on the television she learned that the rain was supposed to begin again later that night, then turn to sleet and snow before morning. Sallie made a wry face at the weatherman on the screen. It was possible that bad road conditions would keep Barbara from making their appointment and she felt horribly disappointed. Her interest in the world around her was returning and she wanted to get on with the business of living.

After an hour of pacing around, boredom overcame her and she felt stifled in the small house. It was cold outside, and damp, but she felt that a brisk walk would clear the cobwebs from her mind and perhaps relax her enough so she could sleep that night. Not only that, she told herself righteously, but the doctor had wanted her to take some form of exercise every day. A walk was just the thing.

She wrapped herself up warmly, pulling on knee-high boots and shoving her hair up under a dark fur hat that covered her ears. After buttoning her heavy coat up and wrapping a muffler about her throat she set off briskly, shivering at first in the cold air, but gradually movement warmed her and she began to enjoy having the streets to herself. It was almost sundown and the dreary sky made it that much darker. The water dripping from the trees onto the sidewalk and street was the only sound except for the clicking of her boots, and she shivered again but not from the cold this time. Why was she walking like an idiot when she could be back safe and snug in her warm house? *And why was she running from Rhy when all she wanted was to be back in his arms?*

Stupid, she mentally berated herself as she headed for home. Stupid, stupid, stupid! And spineless on top of that! She would be the biggest fool alive if she left the field clear for Coral! When this weather cleared up and she could travel safely she'd leave for Europe on the first plane out, and if she found Coral with Rhy she'd tear out all of that gorgeous blond hair. Rhy would not get off completely free, she promised herself, the light of battle sparkling in her eyes. She had a lot to say to him, but she meant to keep him! After all, hadn't these past seven years taught her that he was the only man for her?

Retracing her steps faster now, she turned the corner and came in sight of her house. She was so caught up in her plans that at first she didn't see the taxi in front of her house; it wasn't until a tall man who moved with the litheness of a panther ducked down to pay the driver that her gaze was drawn to the cab. She stopped in her tracks and the breath stopped in her chest as she stared at the proudly held dark head, bare despite the dripping trees. The taxi pulled away with a flash of red taillights and the man set a single flight bag on the wet sidewalk and stared at the house as if mesmerized by the sight of it. No lights were on and it could have been empty, she realized, except for the curtains that covered the windows. Was that what he was thinking? she wondered with sudden pain. That it was empty after all?

"Rhy," she whispered and began walking again. The sound of her boots drew his attention and his head turned swiftly, like that of a wild animal sensing danger. He froze for a moment, then began walking toward her with a purposeful stride. Just like him, she thought, trying not to smile. There was no self-doubt in that man. Even when he was wrong he was confident.

But when he was close, when he stopped with only three feet separating them, she had to bite her lip to keep from crying out with pain. His lean face bore the marks of suffering; there were harsh shadows under his steely eyes and lines that hadn't been there before. He was tired of course, and the grayness of exhaustion enhanced the grimness of his expression. He'd lost weight; the skin was pulled taut over the high, proud cheekbones.

He shoved his hands deep into the pockets of his overcoat and stared at her, his bleak gaze roving over her small, delicate face and her rounded form beneath her coat. Sallie quivered with wanting to throw herself into his arms, but he hadn't opened them to her, and she was suddenly afraid that he didn't want her. But why was he here?

"She lied," he said tonelessly, his voice even harsher than before and almost beyond sound. His lips were barely moving as he seemed to force out his next words. "I'm dying without you, Sallie. Please come back to me."

Incredulous joy rocketed through her veins, and she closed her eyes for a moment in an effort to control herself. When she opened them again he was still staring down at her with a desperate plea in his gray eyes, his lips pressed grimly together as if he expected the worst. "I was planning on it," she told him, her voice tremulous with joy. "I'd just now decided that as soon as the weather cleared I was taking a plane to Europe."

A shudder quaked visibly through his body; then he pulled his hands out of his pockets and reached for her at the same time that she stepped forward. Hard arms enfolded her in a tight, damp embrace, and she put her arms around his neck and clung desperately, tears of happiness running down her face. He caught her mouth with his and held it, kissing her deeply and reassuring both of them that they were together again; then he lifted her completely off the ground, turning round and round on the sidewalk in a slow circle as they kissed.

At some point it began to rain again; they were both soaked by the time Sallie glanced up at the pouring skies and laughed. "What fools we are!'' she exclaimed. ''Why don't we go inside instead of standing out in the rain?''

''And you don't need to catch a chill,'' he growled, putting her on her feet and leaning down to lift his flight bag. ''Let's get dried off, then we can talk.''

He insisted that she take a hot shower while he changed into dry clothing, and when she came out of the bath she found that he'd made coffee; two steaming cups were already on the table.

''Oh, that's good.'' She sighed as she sipped the hot liquid and it completed the warming job that the shower had started.

Rhy sank into a chair at the table and rubbed a hand over the back of his neck. ''I need this to keep me awake,'' he said wearily.

Sallie looked at him, seeing his exhaustion etched into every line of his face, and her heart clenched painfully. ''I'm sorry,'' she said softly.

He made a gesture with his hand, waving aside his weariness, and silence stretched between them. It was as if they were afraid to begin, afraid to say anything personal, and Sallie stared into her coffee cup.

''Chris is gone,'' said Rhy abruptly, not looking at her.

Her head jerked up. ''Gone?'' she echoed.

''He quit. Downey told me—hell, I don't know how long ago it was. Everything's a blur. But he quit, said he was moving on to another city.''

For a moment Sallie had hoped that Chris and his Amy had gotten together, that he'd quit his job to settle down, but she knew that it just hadn't happened for Chris. A shaft of pain pierced her as she thought of how close she'd come to losing Rhy, and she quickly took another sip of coffee. She blurted, ''I suppose Barbara called you?''

''Immediately,'' he acknowledged. ''I owe her a lot to make up for that favor. I completely wrecked the shooting schedule to get on the first flight to New York. Everyone thinks I've gone berserk anyway, flying back and forth cross the Atlantic whenever we had a break. It drove me crazy,'' he admitted grimly. ''Not knowing where you were, if you were all right, knowing that you believed what that vicious little tramp told you.''

''Mrs. Hermann told you what she said?'' Sallie asked, wanting to know if Coral's story had been related correctly. Wild hope was bubbling in her; he'd said that Coral had lied, and he certainly wasn't acting like a man who was guilty of anything.

''Word for word, with tears pouring down her face like a waterfall,'' Rhy growled. He reached out abruptly and took Sallie's free hand, clasping it firmly in his long fingers. ''She lied,'' he told her again, his husky voice taut with strain. ''If you've ever believed anything, believe that.

Coral may be pregnant, but I swear I'm not the father. I've never made love to her, though she tried hard enough to instigate an affair.''

The words jolted Sallie. His voice had an undeniable ring of truth to it, but still she squeaked incredulously, *"Never?"*

A flush darkened his cheekbones. "That's right. I think I was a challenge to her ego. She just couldn't believe that I wasn't interested in sleeping with her even when I told her I was married and that I'd never been as attracted to any other woman as I was to my wife," he said, watching her steadily. Sallie blushed under his regard, and his hand tightened on hers. "I think she hated you because of that," he continued, his eyes never leaving her face. "I turned her down in favor of you, and she tried her best to tear us apart, to hurt you. Maybe she didn't plan on doing what she did, if you want to give her the benefit of the doubt. If she truly is pregnant she probably wanted me to give her the money for an abortion. A pregnancy is poison to a model, and I can't see Coral as a doting mother.''

Sallie sucked in her breath. "Rhy, would you have?"

"No," he growled. "And I could've killed her when Mrs. Hermann told me what she'd done.''

"But...surely Coral has the money herself...?"

"Don't you believe it," he muttered. "She likes the high life too well to save anything and she loses heavily in Atlantic City and Vegas. She's not a good gambler," he finished starkly.

"But why did you go out with her at all if you weren't interested in her?'' Sallie asked. That was the biggest flaw in Rhy's story. He and Coral had been constant companions, and she wasn't fool enough to think things hadn't progressed beyond hand-holding.

"Because I liked her," he replied abruptly. "Don't ask me for proof of my faithfulness, Sallie, because I haven't got any. I can only tell you that Coral wasn't my mistress, even before I found you again.''

"Take it on trust?" she queried, her voice going tight.

"Exactly," he said in a hard voice. "Just as I have to take it on trust that you haven't been involved with any other man. You have no proof, either.''

Sallie scowled down at the tablecloth and traced a pattern on it with the hand he wasn't holding. "I've never been interested in any other men," she admitted with ill-grace, hating having to reveal that secret to him. "I've never even bothered to date.''

"And for eight years you've been the only woman I could see," he replied in a strained voice, releasing her hand and getting up to stride restlessly around the small kitchen. "I felt like a fool. I couldn't understand why a timid little rabbit like you were then had gotten under my skin like that. I wouldn't have put up with one scene over my work from any other woman, but I kept coming back to you, hoping you'd grow up and understand that I *needed* my work. You said you were hooked on excitement, on danger, and that's exactly the way I was. A danger junkie.

"I never meant to leave you permanently," he said jerkily. "I just wanted to teach you a lesson. I wanted you to beg me to come back to you. But you didn't. You picked up and carried on as if you didn't need me at all. You even sent my support checks back to me. I buried myself in work. I swore I'd forget about you, too, and sometimes I almost did. I enjoyed the company of other women, but whenever things began getting involved...I just couldn't. It made me furious, but I'd remember how it had been with us, and I didn't want second best."

Sallie stared at him, thunderstruck, and he glared at her as if she'd done something terrible. "I made a lot of money," he said with constrained violence. "A lot of money. I bought some stocks and they went out of sight and I ended up a rich man. There was no longer any need to put myself on the line to get a story and getting shot at had lost whatever perverted thrill it had held for me, anyway. I wanted to sleep in the same bed every night, and finally I admitted to myself that if there was going to be a woman in that bed it had to be you. I bought the magazine and began trying to trace you, but you'd left here years before, and no one had any idea where you were."

"You tried to find me?" she asked, her eyes going wide with wonder. So Rhy hadn't simply forgotten about her for those years! "And this time? You've been trying to find me this time, too?"

"It seems like trying to find you has become a habit." He tried to make a joke, but his face was too tightly drawn to express any humor. "I didn't even think of hunting for you here. I've been checking with newspapers in all the major cities on the thought that you were likely to get a job as a reporter. You threw it in my face so often that you were bored without a job that I thought you'd go right back to work."

"I thought I'd be bored," she admitted, "but I wasn't. I had the book to work on, but most of all, you were there."

His face lightened curiously. "You sure put up a good fight, lady," he said wryly, and he gave her a wolfish grin that held no humor.

"I didn't have a chance," she denied. "Having me working for your magazine like I did gave you all the aces."

"Don't you believe it," he said roughly. "I caught a glimpse of a long braid swinging against a slim little bottom, and it was like I'd been kicked in the gut. Without even seeing your face I wanted you. I thought it was a vicious joke on me to find a woman I wanted just when I'd begun the search for my wife, but the few glimpses I had of you made me determined to have you. Then I ran into you in the hallway and recognized you. The dainty little elf with that bewitching braid was my own wife, changed almost beyond recognition except for those big eyes, and you made it plain that you weren't interested in anything about me. I'd spent eight years with the feel of you branded on my senses until I couldn't even see another woman, and you didn't care!''

"Of course I cared!'' she interrupted, standing up to face him. She was trembling with strain, but she couldn't let him think that he meant nothing to her. "But I didn't want you to hurt me again, Rhy! It nearly killed me when you left the first time, and I didn't think I could stand it again. I tried to protect myself from you. I even convinced myself that I was completely over you. But it didn't work,'' she finished in a small voice, staring down at the tiled floor.

He drew a deep, shaking breath. "We're two of a kind,'' he said roughly. "We're as wary and independent as wild animals, the both of us. We try to protect ourselves at all costs, and it's going to be hard to change. But I *have* changed, Sallie. I've grown up. I need you more than I need excitement. It's hard to say,'' he muttered. "It's hard to deliberately leave yourself open to hurt. Love makes a person vulnerable, and it takes a lot of trust to admit that you love someone. Why else do people try so hard to hide a love that they know isn't returned? I love you. You can tear me to pieces or you can send me so high I lose myself. Trust has to start somewhere, Sarah, and I'm willing to make the first move. I love you.''

Hearing him call her Sarah swept away all the long years of loneliness and pain, and she raised a face that was pale and streaked with slowly falling tears. "I love you, too,'' she said softly, making the words a litany of devotion. "I've always loved you. I ran away because I was hurt. I was insecure and didn't feel that you loved me, and Coral tore me apart with her vile insinuations. But today I decided that I loved you too much to just let you go, hand you over to her without a fight. I was coming after you, Rhy Baines, and I was going to make a believer out of you!''

"Hey,'' he said just as softly, opening his arms and holding them open for her. "Go ahead. Make me believe it, darling!''

Sallie dived into his arms and felt them enclose her tightly. She couldn't stop the tears that wet his neck, and he tried to comfort her, gently kissing the moisture from her cheeks and eyes.

They had been apart for too long. His kisses became hungry and his hands roamed over her gently swelling body, and Sallie cried out wordlessly as desire flamed through her. He lifted her and carried her to the bedroom, the same bedroom where eight years before he'd carried her as an innocent bride and initiated her into the intoxicating sensuality of his lovemaking. It was the same now as it had been then; he was gentle and passionate, and she responded to him with all her reserve finally gone. When the fire of their desire had been sated she lay drowsily amid the tangled covers of the bed. His dark tousled head was pressed into her soft shoulder and his lips sleepily nuzzled the swell of her breast. His lean fingers stroked the slight swell his child made and he murmured against her flesh. "Was it all right? There's no harm in making love?"

"None," she assured him, lacing her fingers tenderly in the thick hair that curled onto his neck. She couldn't get enough of touching him; she was content to lie there with him resting heavily against her, worn-out from traveling and their loving.

He was already half-asleep but he muttered, "I don't want to tie you down. I just want you to fly back to me every night."

"Loving you doesn't tie me down," she answered, kissing his forehead, which was all she could reach. And it didn't. She was surprised. Where had all her fears for her independence gone? Then she knew that what she'd really feared had been being hurt again. Rhy's love would give her a springboard to soar to heights she'd never reached before. She was free as she'd never been before, free because she was secure. He didn't hold her down; he added his strength to hers.

"You've got talent," he whispered. "Real talent. Use it, darling. I'll help you in any way I can. I don't want to clip your wings. I fell in love with you all over again when I found you, you'd grown up, too, and become a woman who drove me mad with your nearness and wild with frustration when we were apart."

Sallie smiled in the darkness. It looked as if all those crash courses so long ago had finally paid off.

He went to sleep on her shoulder, and she slept, too, content and secure in his love. For the first time she felt that their need for each other was something permanent. She had always felt the tug of the bond that held her to him, but until now she hadn't known that he was equally bound to her. That was why there had been no divorce, why he hadn't even made an effort to obtain one. They belonged to each other and they always would.

* * * * *

ALL THAT GLITTERS

by *New York Times* bestselling author

LINDA HOWARD

Greek billionaire Nikolas Constantinos was used to getting what he wanted—in business and in his personal life. Until he met Jessica Stanton. Love hadn't been part of his plan. But love was the one thing he couldn't control.

From *New York Times* bestselling author Linda Howard comes a sensual tale of business and pleasure—of a man who wants both and a woman who wants more.

Available in May 1998
at your favorite retail outlet.

MLH432-T

MIRA™